Drew James was born and raised in South-East London, and after studying at The BRIT School for Performing Arts and Technology, gained vast experience in the world of luxury fashion before being inspired to write this book. Other written works include the comedy play, 'The Butch(er) Queen Of Soho,' as well as 'The Raven Returns,' coming soon.

For more information and contact, please visit www.drewjamesauthor.com.

Join the conversation on social media @DrewJamesAuthor.

#AFarceOnFifthAvenue #AFOFA #DrewJamesAuthor

BOOKS BY DREW JAMES

A Farce On Fifth Avenue

The Raven Returns

# A Farce on Fifth Avenue

Drew James

**CAPOCCI**
Publishing UK

Print edition, Great Britain 2018

(ISBN: 978-0-9926021-2-3)

Also available as e-book:

Version 3.0, Great Britain 2018

(ISBN: 978-0-9926021-1-6)

First published, Great Britain 2013
By C A P O C C I Publishing UK

Artwork by Aaron Favaloro © 2018
www.aaronfavaloro.com

Cover by Jacopo Maria Cinti © 2018
www.jacopocinti.com

For everyone I have worked in retail with.

# CHAPTER ONE

"I'm very sorry Miss Ravens, but you do not have the experience required to fill this position…"

Sat in the plush offices of Palazzo—one of the finest Italian luxury brands in the world—Chloe stared at Victoria from human resources in total disbelief, and thought to herself: 'Bitch please, the only experience you have, is from 'blowing' your way to the top!'. Instead, she feebly managed to push out:

"But I, I mean Regina said she would give me a good reference… I studied at Parsons… I have a degree, and a masters in fashion…"

The trouble was, what Regina meant and said were two different things entirely, and having a degree meant zero in the world of fashion (especially in retail). It wasn't what you knew, but whom you knew that counted. Regina Hall was the store director, company shareholder, and a general bitch. Divorced but 'married' to Palazzo, there was nothing that she wouldn't do to secure her position within the company; she gave up everything in her life except work.

She was nothing special to look at, although she had a presence that commanded respect. Her dark brown hair was always scraped back into a short ponytail and secured by a clip (boring, yet professional and tidy). Her witch-like nose mirrored her cold demeanour, and her stiff body language similarly matched her icy interior. All those late nights at work followed by early morning wake-up calls had taken its toll; etched on her face over the years for all to see. But it had been worth it; she had turned Palazzo into one of the most iconic brands on Fifth Avenue.

By day, the five storeys of white marble cladding glistened in the bright light of the Sun; by night the extravagant window displays shone with elegance, as passers-by dreamt of the luxury items they contained. Gold italic letters spelt out '*P-A-L-A Z-Z-O*' above the shop front windows, and occasionally a few got stolen as thieves stupidly mistook them for *real* gold. People were so desperate to own anything by the brand; they sometimes went to extreme measures.

At the door, security guards dressed in slim-cut black suits with a crisp white shirt, and a narrow black tie were on standby. Their Italian made shoes compromised comfort for style—could they really run after shoplifters in those? They were so slick; you would expect them to guard the President of the United States, not a store. The grand glass doors featured large handles in the shape of an italic '*P*,' and as they opened for you to enter, the most extravagant foyer you could ever imagine greeted you.

The creamy marble floor challenged you to grace it, without slipping, leading you through the ground floor which was a paradise for accessory hunters. Handbags, wallets, purses, clutch bags, portfolios, and trunks made from the most beautiful leathers and fabrics were all found here. At the back of the floor, a discreet parlour showcased fine jewellery behind glass walls and vitrines, colourful like a hard candy shop. In the centre of the store, a grand gold staircase took you up to the treasures above; or you could take the elevator: a glass cylinder that gave you a tour as you rose up through the most beautiful, yet intimidating store in the world.

The first floor housed the men's collection, which offered masculine and stylish designs. Womenswear draped on hangers like a fashion catalogue on the second floor; while up on the third, was a restaurant and bar: where ladies of leisure lunched, businesspeople met, and fashion victims congregated, all hoping to be seen dining there. The fourth was the most secret of all floors: the VIP clientele lounge; where only the most loyal, rich, and notable clients were looked after.

The fifth floor was the brand's very own office space, including human resources, store management, and the press department. All of which had been relocated from the head office in the Garment District to a prestigious (and more upmarket) location. The staff at Palazzo were immaculately dressed in dark brown suits, like an army styled by Vogue. If you had to work in retail, then this was the place to be, and it was all thanks to Regina. She was considered as fashion royalty from within the company and out; everyone worth knowing in fashion knew of her, and of her importance. The most respected, but feared member of management in Palazzo. There were two types of people that worked under her: 'Lickers' and 'Workers'.

The 'Lickers' were employees that lived and breathed Palazzo; they took their role in retail very seriously; they pounded the marble floor with self-importance, as if going to the stock room for an item was the most important thing, right there and then. Their title came from their ability to 'ass-lick' the management to the highest degree (especially Regina). They greeted her on the shop floor with fake smiles and air kisses and laughed at anything she said (even if it wasn't funny). Yes, they worshipped her, but only because they feared her; she equally adored them, because they posed no threat to her power.

Then there were the 'Workers' who were quite the opposite: they were the ones that had a life outside of work. They were a mixed bag of people who accepted that working in luxury fashion was just that; selling handbags and not saving lives. They treated Regina like an average person, not like the great store director she thought she deserved to be known as. They didn't accept her self-made rules and policies, and because of this, they were the *real* threat. They were secretly against her; the ones that she had no use for, with their own ideas on how they worked and whom they listened to. The ones she couldn't control or brainwash.

Now and then, there would be a member of this group that was an exception to the rule and Regina would take a liking to them; keeping her enemies close. It didn't happen often, but sometimes there would be a clever one, far too much for Regina to convert. So instead of trying to win them over, she would simply keep a close eye by pretending to be nice, raise their pay-checks even, but secretly plotted a way to get rid of them behind their backs.

At the end of the day, it was simple: if she liked you, you were safe; if she didn't, you were *fucked!* If you think about it, it was quite smart of her. Why build a workforce of creative thinking, self-motivated people, with a mixture of personalities and abilities, when you could have robots mindlessly doing your bidding? Retail robots that you didn't have to fear, because robots can be destroyed and ordered to do whatever you wanted them to do.

*

Before starting as a sales assistant in womenswear, Chloe had heard all about Regina from her best friend, Dominic. They met in Mission (a packed out gay bar where they danced all night heavily intoxicated, resembling a scene from some sort of eighties movie). Eventually—after much drinking and debauched dance moves—they were ejected for accidentally setting the cocktail bar alight with a round of flaming hot Sambuca's. Ever since then, the pair had become inseparable and like an 'old married couple'. Although she loved fashion, Chloe's favourite pastime was getting hammered with Dom in New York's gay bars (partly the reason as to why she was still single).

Twenty-eight-year-old Dominic was rather handsome, had a great body, and was always well dressed. His hair was never out of place, and his complexion was perfect with just a hint of designer stubble. He was vain enough to wear a touch of make-up, but not too much. He couldn't stand queens that wore too much slap (and poorly applied too).

"Blend is your friend!" he would yell at guys that had foundation, tiding at their jawlines.

Dom moved to New York from London with his parents when he was just eighteen; his father had relocated them to New York with his investment banking company. Years later, his father had an affair with a much younger American woman (not that much older than Dom in fact), and his mother returned to London. By then, he had adapted to life in New York, having just started working at Palazzo, so he chose to stay in the 'Big Apple'. He wasn't going to throw his green card away! To keep Dom sweet, his father lavished him with an apartment in the trendy Greenwich Village area (and he was cool with that); although, he loved his mother dearly and missed her very much.

Having both parents in two of the most famous cities in the world was a bonus; but for now, it seemed like New York offered a better life and opportunities, too good to give up. When Dominic told Chloe he worked for Palazzo she knew that this wasn't just a chance meeting. Becoming Dom's fag-hag overnight had its benefits; it meant Chloe didn't need to ask for help to secure her a job.

"Hun, why don't I put in a good word for you? We need a blonde bombshell for the client's husbands to look at…"

"Really—you would do that?" she said, wide-eyed.

"Okay, I mean don't get ahead of yourself here… You would only be a shop girl, but it's a start, and you look great! That's all that matters; experience comes secondary to looks at Palazzo babe."

"Well, of course… An assistant at first, but after a year or so, I'll get promoted when they see how great I am with people; I'll be top of sales at Palazzo in no time. Trust me. I've got this…"

Dominic had seen and heard it all before; all of the big talk; all the hopes and dreams of a high flying job in fashion, from girls fresh out of fashion school. He decided to give her a heads up on the reality of life at Palazzo.

"Okay girl… For you to do just that, you need to listen up. Regina Hall is the store director,  you need to suck up to her like never before—but not too much—she'll become suspicious—just with things like offering to do extra shifts. Eat, sleep, and shit Palazzo… Ask her for permission to do absolutely anything, and everything—that sort of stuff… Oh, and we probably shouldn't be friends at work, because that bitch can't *stand* me, darling!"

'Pretend that Palazzo is my whole life? Well, that'll be easy,' Chloe thought.

Dom did stick to his word and got her an interview with the department manager, at which she was successful in getting hired. But after four years of working hard on the shop floor, she was starting to lose hope. At first, sucking up for extra shifts and following Dom's advice was a breeze; she loved being in the glamorous realms of Palazzo. But as if the walls were smoke and mirror, the mirage began to slip, and Chloe became more and more frustrated.

Frustrated from seeing talented, kind people leave their jobs just because Regina didn't like them and stood in their way of a career; from growing them within the company, and only in the way of them being happy at work (she sucked the joy out of everything). Chloe was fed up with seeing all the wrong candidates selected for promotion; just because they ass-licked Regina, like school children bringing apples to their teacher. It was wrong, and Chloe was at her tipping point; she couldn't be that two-faced (no matter how much she thought she could be) and there was no way she could not be friends with Dom—which did her no favours as he had warned.

Chloe didn't feel as positive about it as she had before; Leaving Palazzo and starting from the very bottom in a new company was something that daunted her very much. She had invested years working at Palazzo, hoping it would pay off; going through all that again with another company simply added years on to where she wanted to be in life. Chloe had expected to secure herself in a career she loved by the time she was at least thirty years old; she could now feel her youth slipping away (stuck on the shop floor) with just a year left to achieve her self-imposed target.

Her parents were also badgering her to find a boyfriend and settle down, move back to Boston, be with her family once again. Something she wanted, but not before she achieved her career goals. Relationships, marriage, even the thought of going on holiday was sidelined for the sake of a fabulous career in fashion. In some ways, she was more like Regina that she would care to admit, and as for Boston—well that wasn't going to happen.

New York suited her more; it was where she needed to be if she had any hope of making it happen. The pressure was growing inside of her more and more each day as weeks and months passed. All of that time spent dreaming and working, what was it all for? There had to be something better, surely? The burden of expectation weighed her down; she couldn't help but wonder where she had gone wrong. The fear of failure was starting to overtake the hope of success, but she couldn't give up—not now.

That was until one lunch break when Chloe logged onto the staff portal to look for internal vacancies; desperate to get off the hamster wheel, known as the shop floor. Checking the portal's pages had become a habit, and the same old jobs kept cropping up (the most exciting opportunity was for cleaning the customer toilets).

"Please let there be a job in the offices... I'll be a tea lady at first, anything!" And today, it was as if someone had finally listened to her:

## PALAZZO PRESS OFFICE ASSISTANT

MUST HAVE AT LEAST TWO YEARS EXPERIENCE WORK-ING WITHIN THE COMPANY, APPLICABLE QUALIFICA-TIONS AND A REFERENCE FROM THE STORE DIRECTOR. POSITION TO BE FILLED BY NEXT WEEK.

The press office at Palazzo was notorious for being very difficult; everything had to be a drama, and they never seemed to dress the right people. The press team would continuously miss out on great opportunities because they considered themselves untouchable. They made contacts feel as though they should be lucky to be dealing with the iconic Palazzo in the first place. Chloe, on the other hand, wasn't like that; she thought she knew exactly how to turn it all around and generate great press for the brand across North America.

'This is perfect! I have the experience and the knowledge; I just need the reference from Regina,' she told herself.

That was easier said than done—but Chloe couldn't help herself. The closing date was today, and there was no way she was going to miss out on applying for this job after waiting, and working hard for all these years; surely she could apply now and ask Regina for a reference later? With that in mind, she went ahead and submitted her online application with a click of a mouse; immediately sending it through to HR who intended to recruit from within as quickly as possible.

New York Fashion Week wasn't far away, and the press office had already burnt their way through several out-sourced temps who couldn't hack the toxic environment. They needed an assistant to help with the hectic schedule—fast! Victoria thought she could find a suitable candidate by recruiting from inside Palazzo (someone who knew what they were getting themselves into) and had been loyal thus far.

While Chloe was on lunch job searching, Dom took a trip down to the menswear floor to catch up with Stefano; another queen he knew from the New York club scene. The womenswear floor was boring without his sidekick, and he wanted gossip to make the shift go quicker—but he got much more than that.

The conversation with Stefano didn't get very far before Dom's eyes were alerted to a handsome man entering the department. He was tall, hunky, and chiselled; like a model straight out of GQ. He had a great physique with sun-bleached, blonde tousled hair that was of jaw length. Very 'California-beach' style. Dom made a beeline for him—expertly elbowing Stefano out of his way—to approach him first.

"Hello, welcome to Palazzo. Are you looking for anything in particular, *Sir?*"

The man smiled back at Dom's flirtatious greeting, sweeping a lock of long sun-kissed blonde hair behind his ear.

"I sure am... I am looking for those sneakers. Ya know the ones with the logo on the side? They're in all the magazines right now..."

Dom knew which ones all right—every motherfucker wanted them—and they were hard to come by.

'Typical,' Dom thought, but not wanting to disappoint or make him leave too soon, he looked down at the client's feet to guess his shoe size.

"Well, as you know they are very popular right now—*Everybody* wants them—but let me see if there is anything I can do."

Dom loved to play the tease, and luckily, he had a few pairs on hold; this handsome stranger was worth letting his good client down for, and he would deal with that issue later. Right now, Dom just wanted to spend as long as possible with this sexy stranger. There was an unexpected spark, an air of electricity that fired up Dom's stomach; he hadn't felt this excited about a man in a long time.

Hurrying to the stock room, he picked out the largest size from the few pairs he had on hold, not knowing if they would fit or not—but it was worth a try. Before heading back out onto the shop floor, he popped a breath mint and checked his appearance in the glare of a computer screen. Just as he went to grab the door handle to head back out, the stock room door swung open, narrowly missing his face.

"Oh my God! I saw him first… What's this?… I thought those were on hold for your *special* client?" Stefano said, with his arms crossed as he stood in his way.

"Yes, but this guy will be *more* than a special client if I have my way… Now move!"

Blocking Dom's exit, Stefano grabbed the box of sneakers, starting a playful tug or war.

"Hands off, you jealous bitch!" Dom laughed, playing along with him—secretly loving the attention.

Realising he wasn't going to let go, Stefano went to ruffle his hair instead. He loved to tease Dom; he wouldn't admit it, but there was a hint of sexual tension behind his frolics. Eventually, he let him pass, following him back out onto the shop floor so he could watch him rattle and make a fool of himself. But that wasn't Dom's nature; he was too cool to come across an idiot, no matter who it was.

"Okay, this is the very last pair," Dom lied, escorting the man to a sofa in the shoe area. "Now, I'm not sure if they will fit you, but it's worth a try if you really want them…"

"Ha! I bet that's what you say to all the guys around here," he said, smiling as Dom unboxed the sneakers for him to try.

Getting up to look at them in the mirror, the man pulled up the waistband of his jeans (they had slipped down while he was lacing up the sneakers), giving Dom a cheap thrill with a glimpse of his boxer shorts. As he checked out the sneakers in the mirror, Dom had a chance to check him out too. He had a great ass; high and firm through ripped blue jeans. The sleeves of his white T-shirt were rolled up; showing off his tanned, smooth biceps. He was perfect—and so were the sneakers. "Seems like the shoe fits Cinderella," Dom quipped with his witty tongue.

"I'll take them," the man said, with a cheeky smirk.

On the first impression, Dom wasn't sure about his persuasion; he was just desperate to be in this beautiful creature's company. A quick wink back confirmed that he had indeed caught Dom's joke; a straight guy wouldn't have understood, and just thought he was a bitch. Wrapping up the sale at the till, Dom tried his best to drag out the process for as long as possible; he knew that soon enough, this guy was going to walk out of the store and he may never see him again.

Dom's heart beat fast with anticipation, wondering what he could do to stall him. He wanted to slip this guy his number, but that was highly unprofessional of him—or was it? As the receipt printed, Dom had a '*fuck-it*' moment and scribbled his phone number on the back—taking his chance.

"Your receipt sir…" Dom said, passing over the bill with his number facing upwards, ensuring that he wouldn't discard it. The man quickly scanned his handwritten note and smiled. "Thanks for shopping with us today. I hope to see you again soon…"

"Thanks… You've been very helpful—what's your name?" He said, sweeping a lock of golden hair behind his ear seductively.

"D-D-Dom," he stuttered back—freezing up for the first time—he didn't expect such a direct question, causing him to blush.

Dom could see Stefano, pointing and laughing at him in the distance. The customer smiled, this time showing his perfectly white teeth, taking the gold Palazzo shopping bag from Dom (who was now hypnotised). The bag swung with the heaviness of the shoe box inside it as he made his way to leave, and just before heading down the staircase, he looked back and waved. Dom was glued to the spot by his beauty; watching him, as he disappeared out of sight. It was as though the past thirty minutes was all but a dream.

"So… Did you get his number?" Stefano said, rushing over to Dom by the till to tease him some more.

"Nope… But he got mine…"

**

An email had popped up in Regina's inbox (like any other she received every minute of the day), catching her eye instantly. Victoria was always bothering her with something, but Regina quite liked that. It made her feel important; it confirmed that her staff respected her position of authority. Looking up from her paperwork through her black frame glasses, she reached for the mouse. Opening the email, she could hardly believe her eyes.

---

**From:** Victoria Bell
**To:** Regina Hall
**Subject:** Press Office Reference For Chloe Ravens

Hi Regina,
I am contacting you regarding Miss Chloe Ravens' application for the press office assistant vacancy. However, it is missing your approval as necessary to proceed. Please see her application attached.

Please, can you supply your approval as soon as possible so that we can offer an interview as quickly as possible?

Kind Regards,

Victoria Bell
Human Resources
**Palazzo S.P.A**
**Fifth Avenue, New York.**

---

The fire inside Regina's veins began to heat up her otherwise cold blood. There was nothing more she hated than over-confident, arrogant wannabe's that thought they were capable of being something other than what they were. Everyone at Palazzo had a role that she had given them, and it was their duty to carry on doing it until she agreed otherwise. Chloe was so excited about the vacancy, she had forgotten all about protocol and procedures.

Something that Dominic reminded her of when she returned from her lunch break, eager to share the good news with him. "Erm... Aren't we forgetting something here? You need to go and kneel at her feet this instant!"—it was as though she hadn't listened to a word he had said.

"Okay, calm down... I'll go now. I'm sure she will think I'm efficient, confident, and ready for a new challenge."

"Well, you certainly have a challenge on your hands now. She doesn't like confidence and determination—remember? Go!—*now!*"

But before she could act on his advice, Regina was already marching through the shop floor to confront Chloe herself. The sound of her high heels striking the marble floor was unmistakably hers.

"Miss Ravens—a *word?*" she said through thin tight lips, entering the office used for packing and wrapping.

Chloe nervously gritted her teeth at Dom before following her inside.

"So… I've just received your application for the press office vacancy this afternoon. Congratulations on wanting to go further within the company."

Regina's eyes penetrated her; burning into her almost—like a laser trying to fry Chloe's brain—as if she were some cyborg sent from the future to eliminate fashion dreams from prospering. There was nothing Chloe could do now, except to own her mistake and go with it; now was the time to sell herself and get Regina on her side.

"Oh, thanks… I just want this so much… You know? I'm determined and ready for the next step. I just had to act instantly, in fact, I was about to come and see you about my reference…"

You only had to look at Regina's face to see that this was not going down well with her.

"Yes, well… Determination will certainly get you places."

"I always believed so too… So, will you please support my application?"

Determination got you nowhere in Palazzo, and if it did, it usually wasn't where you wanted to go. Regina stood up straight at Chloe's brave request, even more so than she was already; if such a thing were possible. 'What a nerve this girl has!' she thought. There was an awkward pause while she eyed Chloe up and down. Regina knew she shouldn't have employed her in the first place—what with being Dominic's friend—but their previous department manager loved her so much; she had insisted on her appointment. Chloe also fitted the bill looks-wise, which even she couldn't deny; something else to hate her for.

Regina snapped out of her daze, coming to a decision.

"Oh, you'll get your reference…" And with that said, she turned and stomped out of the packing room, throwing open the heavy door.

Dominic had been trying to listen in on their conversation, nearly coming face-to-face with Regina upon her abrupt departure. He quickly tried to style out the fact he had just been caught ear-wigging by suddenly fixing garments on a nearby rail. Of course, she knew what he was up to, but she didn't care less; she now had Chloe where she wanted her, and that was enough satisfaction. In time she would have him there too, and that thought pleased her more than he could ever know.

"See… That wasn't so bad," Chloe said once Regina was out of earshot.

She had impressed herself; she had just survived a showdown with Regina, and quite successfully too she thought. Dominic's face didn't agree, but he wasn't going to piss on her parade. Instead, he thought it a better idea to go out after work and celebrate new beginnings—which was bound to be a messy affair when it concerned them and alcohol.

Regina left work most nights around ten o'clock, and sometimes even later. She had to email all the figures over to Italy, catch up on emails, and prepare for meetings she had the next day with senior staff. But tonight, there was an extra task to complete before shutting down her computer.

"Oh yes, that little tramp's reference… I almost forgot."

She opened a replying email to Victoria to get this task out of the way so she could go home, but this was worth taking the extra time to do because the thought of squashing Chloe's dreams filled her with joy. Even though Victoria thought Chloe's application had potential, she was very much Regina's ally and would do whatever she was told to do; she was just another puppet, that was as unqualified as everyone else Regina had promoted into a position of responsibility.

Regina knew Chloe would probably do a fantastic job in the press office, but that was even more reason for her not to support her application; it would only highlight the fact that she had been poorly overseeing them for years, and no one was allowed to question her authority. She lived on power, a power that Chloe took away from her when she failed to beg for a reference. Now was the time to show just how powerful she was; to teach her a valuable lesson. It was time Chloe played her game, by her rules.

---

**From:** Regina Hall
**To:** Victoria Bell
**Subject:** RE: Press Office Reference For Chloe Ravens

Victoria,

As previously discussed, I believe we have already found the ideal candidate for this position, but by all means feel free to give Miss Ravens an interview. It should be first thing tomorrow morning as we need to fill this position quickly—given that Fashion Week is upon us. I agree that she does have some relative experience and qualifications needed for this role, but unfortunately, Miss Ravens cannot comply with management on policy and procedures. Thus, she has much to learn from the business before she is ready to take on such a position.

Therefore, it is with deep regret that I cannot fully back the application of Miss Ravens for the title of press office assistant at this present time.

Regards,

Regina Hall
Store Director
**Palazzo S.P.A**
**Fifth Avenue, New York.**

---

Besides, Regina already had someone in mind for the position, and it wasn't Chloe. As usual, she was always one step ahead; the posting on the portal was only uploaded to follow company guidelines, not thinking anyone would dare ask for her permission to apply for it. There was someone else in the frame that had sucked up to her, enough to earn themselves a step up the ladder; someone who wasn't going to rock the boat.

Keeping an eye on Chloe Ravens would be easier if she was suppressed on the shop floor; interviewing her was pointless, but it would be worthwhile, just to put Chloe in her place.. Regina's power-hungry ego feasted on opportunities like this. And now Regina knew just how much Chloe wanted the job she would enjoy it even more.

# CHAPTER TWO

Chloe arrived hungover from the antics of the night before; scraping the clock to make her shift on time. Rushing to get ready, she changed into her uniform—Wonder Woman style. As she passed a mirror on the way out, she caught sight of her hair which was a frizzy mess; on closer inspection, her eyes were puffy and bloodshot.

She ran her fingers through her hair, trying to tame her golden locks as best she could. Taking a lip-gloss out from the breast pocket of her blazer, Chloe glazed her lips in a final attempt to look more presentable for the public. Today was going to be tough if her reflection was anything to go by.

Sprinting to get out onto the shop floor, she could hear the department phone line ringing. She leapt like a gazelle over to the mini desk by the fitting rooms, grabbing the handset from the dock to save the call.

"Good morning, Palazzo Fifth Avenue," she answered in a professional manner that had been perfected over the years and could reel off without even having to think about it (even with a hangover).

"Good morning… Can I speak with Chloe please?"

"Yes, speaking…"

"Oh, hi—it's Victoria from HR here. Please come up to the office at ten-thirty… We will interview you for the press office assistant position you've applied for… We'll be in the boardroom."

"Oh, so quick? Do I need to prepare anything?"

"No, just bring yourself, and please be on time."

"Yes, of course—thanks for calling." Placing the handset back down, Chloe was overcome with a sudden feeling of doom.

Looking up in the fitting room mirrors at the less than perfect sight staring back at her, she started to panic. '*Fuck!* Why today? I knew I shouldn't have gone out last night… Where the Hell is Dominic when I need him?' she fretted. Pulling the department diary out from the mini desk, she flicked to the current week where the team rota was copied. 'Damn—it's his day off... No wonder why he suggested going out—It's his *fucking* day off!'

The day she really needed him, and he was probably still in bed; or in the bed of that incredibly handsome man that he had deserted her for at the bar. Chloe had no time to get nervous now; it was nine-thirty already, and the store had opened for business. Mornings were usually quiet, and today was a good example. She had a whole hour to think about the questions Victoria might ask—and more to the point—who was going to conduct the interview? Was Regina going to be grilling her, and could she survive another impromptu encounter?

All these thoughts made her heart race faster as her head began to tighten and pulse as if it were being cranked in a vice. She only had herself to blame; besides, how was Dom to know they would call her for an interview the very next day? Still, the slow drag of the morning shift meant she had enough time to run through some possible questions in her head. She pulled out some paper from the till printer and started jotting down various lines she could use in the interview, but it was no good. Her mind was mush, and her colleagues were distracting her with loud chatter; holding some kind of morning meeting.

"Hey, guys, what's up?" Chloe said as she approached the gathering of brown suits; accepting that she wasn't going to come up with anything productive in her state.

Kim turned to face her, with a flick of her hair. "I was just saying to the team that after lunch I will have an interview for the press office position, and to just let you guys know that I won't be back on the floor until later this afternoon."

Kim Wei was a small, slim Chinese girl with jet-black hair that was long and dead straight. Her skin was complete perfection and had no need for make-up, she was also the perfect employee; definitely one of the 'Lickers'.

'*Fuck!*' Chloe winced—this wasn't what she wanted to hear right now.

She didn't even think for a minute that there would be competition, especially from a colleague in her own department. The vice (that was her head) cranked another three-sixty, intensifying the throbbing as her mouth dried up, as her heart rate caught up. Today wasn't a good day to be having a hangover (if such a day existed) and there was no way she would tell her colleagues that she too was interviewing for it. She preferred to save herself the embarrassment in case she didn't get it. Learning that Kim was also going for the job was a blow to her confidence; she doubted her chances even more than before because Kim was a Palazzo do-gooder.

The harsh spotlighting of the shop floor, mixed with the alcoholic aftermath, was beginning to make her forehead glisten with sweat. Her hair stuck to her face and she could have sworn she smelt Sambuca perspiring from her skin—timeout! She needed water and painkillers—fast! Making a swift exit from her colleagues and back up to the staff changing room, Chloe sat on the bench by her locker and dialled Dom's number.

"Pick up… *Pick up* you little shit…"

The phone kept on ringing, but she refused to give up. When it went to voicemail, she redialled, insistent on speaking to him; this was an emergency, and there was no way he was getting out of this one. He was responsible for this mess as far as she cared, and she urgently needed his advice; Dom always knew what to do in situations like these. Eventually, he answered.

"Oh God… What time is it, you crazy bitch?"

"Dom, listen… I have my interview—in like half an hour! I'm completely hungover and not prepared for this right now."

"What? Okay—Calm down—this is what you do… You go in there and… You give it your best shot—simple."

Silence… Chloe expected there to be more; was that it?

Was that all he could say?

"And what else?"

Hearing the tone of panic in her voice, Dom tried his best to soothe her; sometimes she was more dramatic than him, and that was quite something. Although, he wasn't in much of a fit state for giving advice.

"Look, just tell them that you have studied fashion and you have good experience working for the company… You will be fine babe; besides, there's not much you can do about it now… At the end of the day, if they want you—they will give it to you. Your fate is already sealed by Regina; we just don't know the outcome yet… So stop stressing and just go through with it. I'll meet you outside after work. We'll go grab a sub at the deli, and you can fill me in okay? Text me as soon as you get out of the interview."

"But what—" she started, before realising he had hung up so he could go back to sleep; there was nothing he could possibly do anyway.

In total despair, she put her face in her hands for a moment before glancing at her watch to check the time. Another pang rang through her: 'It's ten-fifteen!' she freaked. Chloe rushed over to the sink to evaluate the make-up situation. Her sweat-infused foundation needed blotting with a paper towel, resembling a liner from an empty basket of fries afterwards. Popping an aspirin and gulping lashings of water, she left the locker room in a dash to get to the interview on time—expertly applying more lip-gloss on-the-go. Taking the back of house stairwell to the very top of the building was a tiring job, especially in her state.

The fifth floor offered a brilliant view of the avenue from the front facing, open-plan office. Having made it up there just in time, Chloe sat on a small grey sofa waiting nervously outside the boardroom; ready to be called in but growing desperate for the toilet in anticipation. She could see the restroom just down the corridor taunting her, so she decided to get up and go while she still had the chance. Just as she began to make her move, the boardroom door opened swiftly. In a black jacket, blouse, and pencil skirt combo stood Victoria.

"Chloe, come on in."

Ignoring that she was bursting for the toilet, Chloe stepped inside. Sat behind the desk in the boardroom was the head of the press office; another mega bitch. Myra Parks greeted Chloe with a loose handshake that made her feel even more nervous. Her hand was stone cold, probably due to the fact her fashion diet gave her poor circulation; she never ate anything but salad leaves and just a handful of grapes for lunch. Myra's image was just as inviting as her handshake: a short lady with cropped black hair, and big round spectacles that made her look like a fashion nerd.

Victoria slinked back into her chair next to Myra and pulled out Chloe's job application from her employee record. Victoria was known for being a bit lousy; not the best HR representative in the world. Of course, she had studied in this field, but she wouldn't have been top dog for the role, and that was on image alone. She was loyal to Regina, and that was precisely the type of person Chloe was putting herself up against in Kim.

"So, Chloe, why have you applied for this position?" Victoria said, looking up at her as she clasped her hands together above the desk.

Chloe gave it a minute's thought before launching into an answer she only just had the brainpower to muster.

"Well, I have worked here for four years now, and I'm ready for a new challenge. I have learnt so much about the company; I feel that I would fit into this role naturally—having a degree in fashion and being top of the sales chart is evidence that I can style people—as well as having gained so much knowledge about Palazzo. I'm sure I will be a strong asset to the team."

She was rather pleased with her answer; maybe being a little bit drunk still was helping her after all? Victoria digested her response, taking a beat to make some notes while Myra just sat there; looking totally uninterested by what was going on around her. 'They may as well have just used a mannequin to take her place,' Chloe thought.

"That's all very well, but the press office is less about styling people and more about communication… I have a reference here stating that you have difficulty reporting to management," Victoria said, not having the nerve to look up at Chloe as she delivered the blow; continuing to look down at her papers.

"What? I mean… I wasn't aware of that," Chloe said, shocked by what she was hearing.

She thought she was an ideal employee; an ambassador of Palazzo if you will. Maybe not a 'Licker,' but she was the top salesperson in her department, and she represented the brand image-wise (though not today).

"Well, moving on, as you can imagine we have a lot to get through this morning. Myra would like to ask some questions too…" Victoria passed the baton over with awkward relief.

Myra quizzed Chloe for another twenty minutes, to which Chloe was pleasantly surprised. She seemed much more helpful and not like her reputation, but then again, Myra had mastered playing the corporate game for several years and knew how to play people. Besides the reference, Chloe thought that it was all going rather well; she had managed to showcase her friendly personality. An attribute one had to be born with and just couldn't learn—not like being two-faced.

"Okay, well I think that's all for now…" Myra said, looking back to Victoria—who had zoned out completely and was simply going through the motions as Regina had instructed.

"Thank you, Chloe… We have one more candidate to see, but we will be in touch this afternoon."

As Chloe left the boardroom, she couldn't help but feel unsettled by the meeting. Knowing that the 'other candidate' was Kim didn't help. 'I've done everything I can. I think they liked me,' she reassured herself as she made her way back down to her department. She had only just stepped back onto the shop floor to find Kim already on her back.

"Hey, Chloe… Where have you been? It's nearly lunchtime," she scorned.

Kim acted as though she was the department manager, without the pay and the title of course; which was very much appreciated by Regina. Chloe scrambled to find a plausible excuse from her pickled brain without having to tell her the truth. She certainly didn't want Kim to know where she had indeed been; that would only strike up a conversation about what kind of questions they asked had her, and she wasn't willing to give this snake any pointers. Kim was a 'Licker,' she already had an unfair advantage in Chloe's eyes.

"Err, I wasn't feeling too great, so I asked if I could go home, but it's not possible as we are short on staff."

"Well, I could have told you that... Next time there is a problem come and see me... And maybe not go out the night before a shift? Just saying..."

Satisfied with making her importance known, Kim left with a swish of her hair to go serve a client with her over-enthusiastic self. The store now had foot-flow, and that was all Chloe needed right now— customers dragging out her hangover even more. Before a customer could grab her, she escaped to the corner where there was a computer for stock checks (usually used by staff for hiding more than for checking stock) and took out her phone to message Dom right away. Checking cautiously over her shoulder; she typed quickly.

HEY, JUST CAME OUT FROM INTERVIEW... THINK IT WENT WELL—NOT SURE... WILL KNOW LATER THIS AFTERNOON. SEE U OUTSIDE AFTER WORK. XXX

Chloe was too nervous about the outcome of the interview to eat much on her lunch break, and the rest of the afternoon was painful, to say the least. No regular clients came in to drop a small fortune, and most of the walk-in customers were just browsing. As the afternoon continued to drag on, there was only one thing on Chloe's mind: the result of the interview, which caused her customer service to lack sparkle, but she couldn't help it.

By now, Kim had returned from her interview and was buzzing about how well it went to everyone and anyone that would listen.

"Oh my God! It went so well... Myra and I completely hit it off—we talked about Fashion Week, and the tasks I would be in charge of and everything..."

'*Damn!*' Chloe thought, worrying that her interview didn't go that far into detail.

Desperate to know more she plucked up the courage to join the conversation since Kim always knew so much.

"So when will we—*you*—find out if you got the job?"

"Oh, I'm pretty sure I've got it... I just feel it you know? But as a matter of formality, I have to go after work to see them again."

'Great' Chloe thought, she would have to endure the rest of the shift, and possibly longer before she would be put out of her misery. But as the afternoon eventually came to a close, Chloe received that dreaded call from Victoria asking to see her before she left work; this was it, the decision that would dictate her future at Palazzo.

Chloe wrapped up her last and only sale of the day, just in time to end her shift; a painstaking ninety minutes of hard selling to a customer who decided to buy the cheapest belt on offer. The agony of waiting, knowing that soon she would discover her fate, made the last hour stretch more than necessary.

'If only this customer knew what I was going through, maybe then she would hurry the *fuck* up!' Chloe raged inside, but on the outside, she wore a gentle smile—a retail skill she had now mastered to perfection.

"Thank you for shopping with us today Ma'am. We hope to see you in-store again soon..." she said, wrapping up the sale abruptly; prompting the customer to leave.

Turning away from the client, Chloe bowed her head so she wouldn't attract unwanted attention from waiting customers; storming towards the staff stairwell. As she climbed the stairs once again, her legs felt like jelly; her feet were killing her from standing up all day in mass-made, staff uniform high-heels on a marble floor—along with the tiring emotions of the day—and exhausted from being hungover to boot.

She finally landed on the fifth floor and was about to turn the corner when she saw a jubilant Kim further down the corridor; shaking hands with Victoria outside the boardroom. Chloe's heart sank; it was evident from Kim's smile that she had indeed got the job. But before Kim could turn and come face-to-face with her, Chloe expertly dodged into the nearby ladies restroom (that she so desperately needed earlier as much as she did now), bumping into her was the last thing she wanted. Locking herself into a cubicle, she prayed that Kim wouldn't need the toilet otherwise she would be trapped, but luckily she didn't.

After a few minutes, Chloe poked her head around the restroom door, looking out onto a clear hallway. Taking a deep breath, she walked over to the boardroom to face her fate. Even though it was only seconds away, that short distance seemed like a mile; it felt as though she were watching a movie of herself knocking on the boardroom door, not reality. The door handle turned and made a crunching sound as it opened—her visit had been anticipated.

"Chloe, please come in; take a seat," Victoria said, but Chloe already knew what was about to unfold; her stomach lurched.

'You can drop the act bitch… I already know,' she said to herself.

\*

Dominic sensed despair from the minute Chloe had stepped out of the staff entrance to meet him; he opened his arms for a comforting hug.

"Oh, hun… At least you tried."

"Regina said she would support my application—I didn't dream that up—I don't understand why she would set me up to fail like this…"

"*Girl!* Get real… It's Regina we're talking about here; she will stand in your way until it benefits her… All you can do is lick her ass in the meantime and hope for the best—which you didn't do!" he added.

"Yeah, I know… I just really thought that after four years of giving this company all I have, that finally, it would pay off—what else can I do? I really thought she would be happy for me and support me; I guess she just doesn't like me…"

Realising that the penny still hadn't dropped, it was time for her to be told straight, even if it wasn't what she wanted to hear right now. Strolling to their favourite sandwich shop, Dom gave her the truth.

"Okay. Rule. Number. One," he said, clapping his hands in staccato, matching the rhythm of his words. "Regina Hall is not your friend! She is your manager, and not only your manager but a jealous one at that—"

"Yeah I know, but what have I done for her to hate me so much," Chloe fought back. Dom rolled his eyes, he still couldn't believe she was so 'blonde' about it all.

"Do I have to point out everything around here? She will only let you move department if it makes her look good… The secret to getting what you really want is to wait until you are no longer her pawn… It's simple, you're younger, prettier, and much more useful to her as a shop girl babe. Besides, why should she let you go to the press office? Every idiot wants that job in that hole—and you're far too good at selling this shit—you make the company too much money at the end of the day, and they don't want to lose that."

"I have a degree in fashion—"

"Honey, unless you have a degree in the dark arts—nothing will impress Regina…" Dom said, which she couldn't disagree with.

"Yeah well, you haven't heard the whole story yet."

"Oh yeah? Well… Tell me!" Dom hated being left out of the latest Palazzo gossip, but Chloe decided he deserved to be punished a little for having the day off.

"I'll tell you all over a sub at the deli…" she said as they walked arm-in-arm.

In exchange, Chloe listened to Dom's excitable chatter about the night before all the way down Fifth Avenue towards Forty-eighth Street.

"So, that hot guy you left me with last night—"

"Err, excuse me? I left *you* with?" If she remembered correctly, it was *him* that had left *her* to go home with some random stranger he had taken a liking to.

"Well, anyway… His name is Jason Hart."

"Oh, so you didn't sleep with him then?"

"Why do you say that?"

"Well, you know a guy's *name* for once," Chloe said, laughing at her own joke. Her loud outburst had made passers-by look at her as if she were deranged.

Understanding that she was implying he was a total slut, Dom pushed into her playfully—making her swerve to avoid knocking into people and their shopping bags. However, for once—she was right.

"No, it's true. I didn't sleep with him… In fact, I served him at work when I ventured down to menswear to see Stefano yesterday—when *you* decided to leave me to go job-hunting again—and then I bumped into him last night at the bar…"

Chloe raised an eyebrow, she wasn't buying any of it; she couldn't believe he had set up their whole night out so he could meet some random guy. The truth was, that after Dom had suggested to go out for drinks to cheer her up, he had received a message from Jason asking him to see him again. Not wanting to disappoint either of them (and excited to see the sexy stranger as soon as he could) he merely told this Jason guy where they were planning to go.

Three was a crowd, but this wasn't a date; this was just a second look. By having Chloe there, it gave him a get-out-of-jail card in case he turned out to be a complete weirdo. All Dom knew was that he wanted to see him again, and Chloe needed a drink to take her mind off work matters. He was being a Samaritan, but he wasn't stupid—she had him sussed out.

"Yeah-yeah, okay… He's asked me out on a date, this Saturday. He's an artist from Los Angeles; in New York to sell some of his work— as if he couldn't get any more attractive."

"Wow, you bagged a good one… All that sleeping around finally paid off."

"This time it feels different… from the moment I saw him, I was so attracted and intrigued by him. It exceeds sexual tension, it's like something has clicked—unlocked energy."

"Oh my! Is Dominic Fraser falling in *lurve?*"

"I wouldn't go that far… ask me after the date."

Dominic continued to speak about Jason as they reached NY Subz where Chloe ordered her favourite sandwich: turkey salad with low-calorie dressing, while Dom went for a more heartburning spicy pepperoni and cheese to refuel after last night. With freshly made sandwiches in hand, they found seats by the window, perched upon red leatherette stalls. Unwrapping their subs, Dom impatiently pressed Chloe for the rest of the gossip.

"Okay, you're killing me here—enough about Jason—tell me all about happened at work today."

He couldn't stand to wait any longer and had exhausted himself by talking endlessly; now it was his turn to listen, and he needed to focus on eating.

She didn't know where to start and recalling the day's events caused her to lose appetite again; she picked at her sandwich as she began to bring Dom up to speed—beginning with Victoria's phone call—right up to the final outcome.

"Wow, Kim kept that quiet… I can't believe she applied for the job without any of us finding out," Dom said, diving into his sub.

Salad and dressing dripped out the other end as he took large bites. He was surprised at what he had heard, he was usually on the ball; the first to find out what people were up to in that place.

"I mean like *hello!* I didn't see that coming either, and when I went up to the office this evening—I saw her shaking hands with Victoria like they were sealing some kind of secret deal. Obviously, she is the chosen one—I am such a sucker… Ya know, now I'm thinking about it; I'm angry… they knew they were going to give it to her all along!"

'Finally,' Dom thought, she was finally getting it.

"Of course they did babe... Kim's a little backstabbing, two-faced bitch. Brown nosing to earn her stripes, and that Victoria... Nothing but a lanky, saggy-ass Regina Hall drone," Dominic said, trying to make Chloe laugh by doing what he did best; taking a strip or two off people and being a complete bitch.

It usually worked, but not this time. Not knowing what to say wasn't usually one of his traits, but since Chloe was upset about it all, he decided that tonight wasn't the night to perform the 'Dominic Fraser Show'. He could see she was drained from the rather emotional day, so after they finished eating, he called it a night and walked her to the train station.

"Call me when you get in—let me know you got home safe, okay?"

Hugging Chloe goodnight, he left her to catch the train home. The train journey from Williamsburg to Fifth Avenue was usually packed with commuters both ways; however, it was so late in the evening that the train was calm enough for her to think things through. Feeling defeated, Chloe wondered what she could have done differently—but more importantly, what she would do next.

She turned the day's events over in her head, again and again, until she reached her front door. Living in Williamsburg felt like a mission away from Fifth Avenue compared to Dom's place. She always thought he was so lucky for that, but there was no way she could live closer to work on her salary (and neither would he without daddy's help). Chloe liked where she lived, it was cosy, her neighbourhood was trendy and creative; she much preferred the vibe compared to upscale Greenwich Village.

Slamming the door shut, Chloe threw her bag down the second she could—boy did it feel good to be home. All she wanted to do, was to slip into her comfy pyjamas, perfect for lazy days and sofa surfing. As she got changed, Chloe felt a slight pang of hunger; now back in her comfort zone, her appetite had crept back. Instead of whipping up a culinary delight, she chucked a ready meal into the microwave and slammed the door. Setting the minutes on the microwave and hitting the 'start' button, she could hear her phone ringing from the depths of her bag by the doorway. Rooting to the bottom of her well-used, but stylish leather tote bag, Chloe's thumb expertly caught the call—it was Dom.

"Hey, you whore… You didn't call me! I just wanted to make sure you're not drinking yourself into oblivion—without me?"

"Sorry… I've only just got in."

"That's okay, I'm calling because I know how you like to rack things over in your head until you've given yourself the flu or something, but try not to think about it too much—stress weakens the immune system don't ya know?"

"I know… I'm sure I'll be fine… I'm just thinking about what you said; I know you've warned me plenty of times before, and I thought I *was* playing the game—but you're right… I should have begged Regina first. This shouldn't be a surprise to me at all… I guess I just can't lick ass that well—maybe you should give me tips. I haven't heard any of your ex-boyfriends complaining?" she said, taking out a fork from the top drawer of the kitchen, and rested her sorry feet by sitting on a stool in front of the microwave; waiting for the timer to finish, and for Dom's comeback.

"How dare you! But yes, you're completely right on both accounts… You haven't played the game good enough. Regina is always one step ahead, and now she is playing you… It will always be on her terms, and being friends with me hasn't helped you… She can't bear me because I actually have my own mind, not a zombie like the others; she can't brainwash me, and she knows I am educating you on the reality of that place."

The microwave stopped revolving and pinged to a halt. Placing the phone between her ear and shoulder, Chloe opened the door and carefully picked up the softly melted tray of bubbling cheese macaroni with hands like pincers; quickly flinging it onto the kitchen side before it burnt her fingers. Peeling away the film lid, she picked up a fork and started to stir her comforting snack—trying to take some of the heat out of it so she could dig in.

"Do you really think she would punish me for being friends with you?"

"Are you clinically insane? Of course, she would; the woman is poison... Anyway, listen—I'm calling you because I have an idea: tomorrow we will go up to the personal shopping floor and have a little chat with Melinda."

"Melinda Rogers? The store dinosaur? *Why?*" Chloe interrupted.

"Well, you girls have something in common now; you could learn a thing or two from her... Remember I told you about when I first started? I would always help Melinda with her clients—I'd go up and down for her all day—because she was the only person in there with an ounce of personality, and knew what she was doing. That's what did *me* no favours... Her and Regina go *way* back... Melinda once told me that she was in line for Regina's job."

Chloe dropped her fork and almost spat out half-chewed hot macaroni.

"*What?* She would have been a brilliant store director—what happened?"

"Well, I'll let her explain... It sounds so much better coming from her mouth than mine, and I don't really know all of the details... Anyway—see you tomorrow... Oh—and seriously girlfriend? *Two* dinners in one night?"

Chloe hung up, cutting him off deliberately in playful response to his judgement of her dietary decisions; putting the phone down and picking the fork back up to resume eating. Thinking about what he had just said, she started to smile; she didn't understand how exactly Melinda could help, but she was intrigued to find out. Once again, Dom had managed to pick her up and offer some kind of consolation; sitting there eating her pasta, she could feel her mood lift. And just like that, she had a reason to get up and go to work again.

# CHAPTER THREE

S tanding by the scarf table folding silk accessories, Chloe noticed Dominic looking rather shifty from the side of her eyes.
'Hmmm, he is up to something,' she thought, as he approached with
caution.

"Babes lets go now while it's quiet… No one will notice we're gone,
because everyone is pandering after that client who spent $20,000 the
other week."

And he was right, no one would notice—or care.

The womenswear floor had been manager-less for months thanks
to Regina, who had cleverly managed her out of the business (realising
she had potential and likeability that she couldn't compete with), and
the other department managers were too busy with their own floors.
Chloe and Dom took their chance and made a quick escape towards
the elevator, it was the easiest and fastest option for them to take; even
though staff were only permitted to use the back of house stairwell.

The fourth floor had a unique code that only VIP clients could
access via the elevator. The code changed daily and only given out
when an appointment was made with the personal shopping team, to
make sure no one entered uninvited. Dom always knew the code; every
day he would find out what it was from one of the store butlers he
flirted with (who proved to be a beneficial contact to have).

Stepping into the elevator, Dom punched in the four-digits to
quickly close the doors, before any of their colleagues saw. It raised
two floors before its doors parted open onto a long dark corridor that
was instantly calming, and moodily lit. The music was soothing, and
the floorboards were stained a deep brown; a stark contrast from the
lower levels, where electronic beats powered posing clients in brightly
lit changing room mirrors.

Chloe looked at the artwork gracing the walls as they walked along. 'These must have cost thousands,' she estimated. Towards the end of the corridor was an antique desk with a receptionist sitting behind it. Her long legs were crossed underneath, her stilettos were about six inches high and would make her very tall indeed. Her hair was a mass of perfectly blown brunette curls, and her outfit was clearly the latest fashion from the Palazzo spring/summer runway; in fact, she could have just stepped off it—very sexy—very Italian. Behind the reception desk, were two automatic glass doors that slid apart to open, frosted in the signature Palazzo italic '*P*,' monogram.

"Sandra darling… It's been forever!" Dom said as they approached. She got up from her position—revealing her statuesque figure—so they could 'kiss' either side of each other's face (he sure knew how to butter people up). "We're here to see Melinda…"

Sandra glanced at Chloe, smirking sarcastically—taking satisfaction that she considered herself much prettier and sexier than her—looking down at her drab, brown uniform.

"She's in room one… Go straight ahead; she's just finished with a client."

"Thanks, darling—we must catch up over lunch soon," Dom said, as he walked past the desk without giving her a second look.

Chloe's mouth curled up into a smile as she followed him; she knew just as well as Sandra that Dominic had no intention of speaking to her again this week—probably not for the rest of this month—let alone organise a whole entire lunch date together. It was the thing to do at Palazzo, in-store protocol some would say. The doors parted to reveal a beautiful and large lounge area.

'You could rent this place out for a fortune,' Chloe thought.

After the lounge area, another corridor appeared—this time the floor had a lovely patterned carpet leading off to several private rooms—it was almost as if they had been teleported to some luxurious hotel in Manhattan. Dominic rapped his fist on the door of room one, where Melinda usually entertained her clients; her office if you like.

"It's open…" a soft voice said from the other side.

Pushing the door open, they both walked into a room that was complete with a leather sofa, changing room, private bathroom, and a window from which you could see the avenue below. It was furnished like a luxury apartment within the store; you *really* could rent this place out.

"Hello, you two… Come to help me clean up? I've just had an appointment with a Saudi Princess—she spent a fortune—but all of this stuff can go back," Melinda said, heaving a massive bundle of expensive clothes from the changing room, tossing them into a heap on the sofa; like they were worthless rags.

"Oh, we will help you sort that out… Most of it's from our department anyway so we can take it back downstairs for you—that way we have an excuse as to why we're not on the shop floor," Dom cleverly suggested.

"Okay—deal!" Melinda said with relief. She was pleased to have helpers to sort out her mess, which was often the case; it was always the sales assistants that cleaned up after the personal shoppers (it wasn't like they had targets too or anything).

Melinda was in her sixties, you could tell by the way her skin sagged on her neck, and the backs of her hands were aged accordingly. Her hair was a dark golden shade, almost red, and slightly messed up from all the rushing around the store she did for her clients; nevertheless, you could tell that in her day she would have been a total fox. She still had that beauty about her, always well dressed, and had a figure that any twenty-year-old something would *die* for!

She had worked for the company for over thirty years and was now ready to give it all up; she didn't need to work in a shop at her age, but she was their living, breathing client book. She knew every wealthy family in the city and was a valuable asset to Palazzo; her sales alone would rake in millions of dollars a year, and for that reason she was indispensable. They sat on the sofa, buttoning and zipping the clothes back up, before hanging them neatly on a gold roller-rail beside them.

"So kids, what's the latest?" She sensed there was gossip to be had; why else would they be visiting her by surprise?

"Well, Chloe interviewed for the press office job yesterday…"

"Oh, did you, sweetie… And how did that go?"

Melinda and Dom both looked at Chloe, waiting for a response; Chloe's fingers flustered to button up a blouse, feeling her anger and disappointment all over again—thinking about what to say. "Well… I thought it was going well… And then, well—"

"Well, she didn't get it!" Dom said, stepping in to finish her stammered reply—this was not a time for beating around the bush.

Melinda offered Chloe her hand, a hand that felt nice and warm; very comforting and motherly.

"Oh, honey… I'm sorry, but don't let it get to you—trust me—it's not the end of the world when it concerns this place… There's more opportunities out there for you, believe me, they did you a favour!"

Something that Chloe couldn't quite accept right now. She had blown her chances and all because she didn't beg on her knees for it first. Since she was too upset to continue the story, Dom explained why he believed Regina was making an example out of her.

"Well, that sounds about right… That woman is a piece of work," Melinda said.

Dominic looked at Chloe, pulling an 'I told you so' face.

"But why—what is her *freaking* problem? Why doesn't she want her staff to be happy? Surely if everyone were happy, we would all do a better job?" Chloe said, frustrated that she seemed to be the only one that could see it.

Melinda got up from the sofa to hang her final garment and moved gracefully over to the coffee table; her face looked as though she was hiding a very juicy secret. Taking her time, she reached over to the teapot on the coffee table and poured out what the Princess had left behind; it was still warm enough to drink. Chloe and Dom sat there patiently awaiting her pearls of wisdom, sensing she had something rather interesting to say.

"You would think so, wouldn't you? But her house is built of cards my dear," she finally said, breaking the silence and suspense.

'What does that mean?' Chloe wondered, intrigued as to why she would suggest Regina was fragile when she was quite the opposite.

It was a story from long ago, way before they had both started working at Palazzo, but Melinda was happy to have an audience. She reached for an old book in her mental library, and blew the dust off the jacket—it hadn't been read for some time. Sitting comfortably on the couch next to a packed and tidy rail of clothes, Dom and Chloe perked up; almost salivating at the prospect of what she had to tell them. Chloe knew he had brought her here for a reason, and she couldn't wait to find out what it was.

Relaxing back into the soft leather couch, Melinda crossed her legs and sipped on her tea; she was now ready to begin. "Well, I don't know how much Dominic has told you already; I don't think he knows the full story himself... As I'm retiring next year, I don't see the harm in telling you *everything.*"

Wow—she had only spoken a few sentences, and already what revelations: Melinda Rogers, the longest serving employee was retiring, and what was this *everything* she had to tell them?

"Keep this to yourselves! You can't trust everyone in here—a lesson you have now learnt my dear," she said, directing her comment at Chloe.

She dipped her head to escape Melinda's truthful gaze before looking back up to listen further; indeed, she had learnt the hard way.

"Some people say that Regina Hall is all my fault—"

"What do you mean?" Chloe said, surprised at her opening line; forcing Melinda to side-track.

"Well, I was the one who employed her of course... Long before all that you *think* you know of this place, I was in line to be the store director... Palazzo was just a small Italian leather goods company selling bags, purses, and shoes—not like these hooker stilts we sell now. The clothing was very basic and sparse back then: a cashmere jumper here, a leather jacket there, the odd silk scarf. Nothing special, but beautifully made."

Listening to this glamorous woman speak was akin to a Hollywood legend, telling her life story.

"Anyway—Alfredo Palazzo brought the company to New York in the late-fifties. In the seventies, I started working for him as an assistant—a young twenty-year-old back then. I thought I was the business…. Alfredo was a great boss, and very generous; every Christmas we would have a huge party at an Italian restaurant Downtown with everyone from the company, and all of his family would be there too… everyone who worked for him brought their partners and friends, and we all just had such a *fabulous* time!"

"Wow, nothing like it is now—invite friends and partners to a staff party? We're lucky if we get an invite ourselves!" Dom said with a scoff.

"It must be around twenty years ago or so when it all started to go horribly wrong," Melinda continued as Dom and Chloe listened, like two children during story time at play-school.

They were enjoying having tea with Melinda, and to think that they were at work getting paid; they would pay *her* to hear this story.

"Here, have some cake—the Princess didn't eat a thing—so yes, anyway… Alfredo stepped down in the eighties and handed the business over to his son Pascale—he was the one to revitalise the brand with full ready-to-wear collections. He too retired and announced that he would hand the company over to his son—Gianni was only a young man when he took over—but he had worked alongside his father and was groomed to do so from day one. It was clear from a young age that he had an eye for style—it runs in the family. Around the same time, it was also announced that the company was losing money; the avenue was seeing more and more designers from Europe open up great stores, and no one cared about us anymore—we just weren't fashionable enough to keep up—the world had moved on… Times were hard, and at one point we weren't sure whether we would get paid or not, but I still turned up for work because Alfredo and his family had been kind-hearted people, and we were all like one big family... The good news was that Pascale and Gianni had managed to sell a portion of the company to a board of investors, and that big money investment allowed us to move to this very store."

Chloe thought maybe Melinda was mistaken; Palazzo, like one big family? Generous and kind-hearted? How times had changed. Her mind had sidetracked; she shifted herself mentally back to those times but woke herself from her daydream—hoping she hadn't missed anything.

"Just before Pascale retired, he came to me and said: 'Miss. Rogers, you have been the most loyal member of staff; you know everyone and everything that my son needs to know. Before I leave, I wish to appoint you as the new store director to assist my Gianni,' and with that, he told me about their future plans. He hoped it would save Palazzo; giving Gianni a chance to grow and pass the business down to his own children one day... He asked me to come up with a business plan for a new, modern, and fashionable Palazzo—and that's when I employed Regina as my assistant. She was already an employee in the jewellery department, and I trusted her; she was mature, hard-working, and extremely reliable—too reliable it transpired—but I needed an assistant to help me while I carried out the new business plan. The future success of the company was partly up to me, and it was my responsibility to help make it into something amazing—something that would bring us back to Vogue."

And that is precisely what Melinda did; she drew up plans for a huge store to rival all the others on Fifth Avenue. She proposed the company went back to its Italian roots, revamp the ready-to-wear collections, and brand image. Melinda came up with the idea for the italic 'P,' monogram to be re-introduced, as well as the new store concept; she knew the company's heritage inside out and could bring out all the best bits. Meanwhile, Regina would help translate her plans and ideas back to the investors, in Italian.

It was also Melinda's idea that Palazzo needed to be young and sexy, to compete with the new era of Italian designers—something the seventies and eighties had taught her. The night before she was due to reveal her plans, Melinda left her dossier on her office desk—safe and ready for her presentation. Leaving work with a spring in her step (and excited about presenting her plans), Melinda stepped out into the busy streets of New York to meet her husband, who always waited outside for her to walk home together. Full of inspiration and promise for what was about to happen to both her career and Palazzo, she began her journey home without a second thought.

Melinda's husband waved from across the street, happy and excited to tell him all about the latest work developments, she stepped off the sidewalk to cross the avenue. From out of nowhere, a taxi shuttled towards her at full speed—in true New York fashion—knocking her up into the air, at least a foot high; before landing back down on the bonnet, and then back onto the cold tarmac—all in a quick minute. She was hospital bound for six months, her husband never left her side and brought her fresh flowers each day.

After hearing this part of the story, Chloe and Dominic were astonished—looking at each other in pure disbelief. Melinda could see that they were surprised and wondering if it were all true.

"Oh, that's the truth—I swear!"

"But what happened to your plans, and to the company while you were in hospital?" Chloe said, really getting into it; as if it were a soap opera—only she didn't have to wait long for the next episode.

"Well, that's when Regina muscled her way in and took over of course… A colleague visited and told me what was happening at work, and told me I needed to return to see it for myself… And when I did, it was like a car had hit me all over again. Nearly a year had passed, and the plot for the new store had been secured; decisions had been made on the store's design without me… As I clearly wasn't going to come back to work for a while after my near death experience, Gianni was only too happy to let Regina take over… Especially after she had given a glittering presentation with all my ideas and inspirations—in *Italian* might I add—and saved the day. I thought maybe I could step back into my old job and take back control, but Regina made it very clear that she was now in charge."

Returning back to work was a great shock for Melinda; so much had advanced in the building of the new store. Hoarding with the gold Italic '*P*,' monogram masked the new site (where today's store now stood), in a prime location; next to all the other major designer boutiques. Regina had managed to push her way into the role of acting store director, and the investors loved her for saving money and time on the project. They believed in her brand vision and ideas, which unknown to them—was all Melinda's. She had sucked them in like a vampire, and they urged Gianni to keep her on—officially as store director.

"I knew that woman had ambition, but I just didn't realise how much… When I finally saw the Palazzo monogram on the new store, that's when it all fell into place—she had stolen my plans while I was lying in a coma—the *bitch!* Pascale had already left by then, and Gianni became very close to Regina; he put all of his trust in her—of course, he had no clue that the entire project was all my idea—it was like I was invisible. It took two years before the new store was unveiled… Sitting back and watching all the plans and preparations unfold, while she took the credit, was a painful process. I became bitter and resentful, but it did me no favours—I guess I was jealous of her—and I grew distant to the other staff members; I simply didn't care anymore. More and more staff were being employed for the store opening: younger, sexy, model-like assistants… One day, Regina told me that I was no longer needed on the shop floor, but she couldn't fire me; so instead, she told me that I would be the manager of personal shopping… she wanted me out of her sight, and she knew that I wouldn't take any of her crap after the accident; besides, I knew all the old clients, and she needed me to pull in the money for the huge targets the investors projected for the new store. She had created this role especially for me—to move me out of her way—but to keep me making money for the company. Which makes her look good in the end, right?"

Melinda took a breath and a sip of tea; her face appeared to look saddened at recalling the memories.

"But why didn't you sue, or say something?" Chloe added, she couldn't understand why she had let Regina steal her ideas and screw her over so badly.

"Oh, honey—you try coming out of a coma and then have a show-down with Regina! When that car ran me over, my life flashed before my eyes; I thought I was a dead woman—and yes—seeing her steal my future was painful… but seeing all the work that she had to do, all those late nights and early mornings; watching her age in the space of two years, so quickly… I began to be grateful in the end, happy to be run over by a taxi and survive; because that amount of work probably would have finished me off! And that is why she is still here; that is why no one contests her, because no one will take on the amount of work she does. It's impossible—inhuman even. She is devoted to Palazzo; I on the other hand, still look fabulous and have no stress at work—and what proof did I really have? I did make a hint about her stealing my position several years back, and she raised my salary to keep me off her back—a small price to pay for a career. Proof that she will stop at nothing kids," Melinda said, finishing her cup of tea, while Chloe and Dom both sat, stunned into silence.

"So, what you're saying is that she has a plan for everything, right? Even the press office vacancy? It's all a set-up—just like how she set you up?" Chloe said, reading between the lines.

Melinda stood up and began to clear the china cups and saucers from the coffee table. "Of course dear! Nothing is by chance, it's all in her master-plan; her plan to keep her feared and on top."

"Well, that explains a lot… You don't think getting hit by a taxi was planned too, do you?" Chloe said.

"*Ha!* You're not the only one to come up with that theory… I wouldn't put it past her."

"I've checked the portal every day, and there have been no interesting jobs on there lately… Then, out of nowhere this press office role suddenly pops up with an urgent closing date… And to top it all off, there was only one other applicant: Kim!"

"Well, I'm glad you managed to work that all out for yourself sweetie; see what I'm saying now? That Kim from your department is such a sucker too—of course, she was the only applicant. Regina doesn't just hire people for no reason; she handpicks her puppets… If you have come here looking for my advice—stop trying to look for opportunities here—it's not worth it. Look at the type of clients we get, how much they spend, be more inquisitive as to who they are—and how they may help you. Use this time to network for yourself, not just to make money for Palazzo. There are many donkeys here that do that for them already; now is the time to excel yourself outside of work, create opportunities from the people you can meet here. Don't wait around for something to happen—you will only waste precious time—you will both do yourselves a huge favour in the long run. Take it from me; you do not want to work under Regina Hall!"

Such things were never heard from members of management at Palazzo, they were too busy with pleasing Regina and trying to keep their jobs at the same time. It was both refreshing and powerful to hear it coming from a senior member of staff.

"I'm so grateful that you told us… We won't say a word to anyone! They don't deserve to know," Chloe said.

Dominic agreed with her and suggested they better get back to work. They had been gone for nearly an hour, and they didn't want a search party being sent out to look for them. As they got up to leave, they both helped each other roll the rail back down the corridor to the elevator. As they called the lift up from the ground floor, Melinda hugged them both and left with a few more words of wisdom.

"Thanks for helping with the rail kids, and remember—create your own future while you're here."

She whispered the latter in case other personal shoppers were around to overhear; you just never knew who was lurking around for gossip in Palazzo. The elevator bell rang, and the doors parted open, to which Chloe and Dom rolled the rail into; pressing the button for the second floor. In total silence they made their way back down to the womenswear floor, still processing what they had just heard. As they stepped out of the lift onto the floor, Kim came storming towards them—apparently in a bitch fit. "And where have you two been?"

"Err... Eyes... Rail... Clothes, where do you think?" Dom said, waving his hand for her to move out their way.

"Melinda called us up to help tidy after one of her clients," Chloe explained to soften his sass, stifling a fit of the giggles.

"Well... Hurry up and put it back into stock... We've been short staffed because of your lengthy departure!" Kim snapped, annoyed that she had been put in her place by underlings. She turned on her heels and flounced off, flicking her hair as she did, which bounced annoyingly down her back from side to side; like a High School cheerleader.

"Man... I cannot wait for her to *fuck* off up to the press office!" Dom said as they headed to the stock room.

Chloe smiled, feeling confident and lucky; lucky to have such a great friend at work, and confident now Melinda had helped her to understand that promotion didn't necessarily mean you had talent—or a future at Palazzo. In fact, it said quite the opposite.

# CHAPTER FOUR

Some people dreamt of shopping at Palazzo, but would never dare set foot inside. Some saved up so they could buy a particular piece—like a handbag on their birthday. Others could afford to shop at Palazzo as if there were no tomorrow, while many couldn't afford to shop there at all. The store saw many different types of client's day-in-day-out, but Palazzo was no stranger to a big spender—it was a money magnet.

Russian businessmen spoiled their model-like daughters on a new wardrobe of clothes; enough for a lifetime, not just one season. Middle Eastern women carried wads of cash, stashed in their designer handbags; ready to be spent on scarves, shoes, and even more bags. Hard-core, trend-savvy students from the Far East, deliberated over which two identical items were in the best condition, after having spent most of the day choosing what to buy in the first place.

'Can I have a new one?' They would ask, already handling the fourth bag that the sales assistant had fetched for them; unhappy with its pristine condition.

In this instance, Dominic would usually reply with a smart comment such as: "Of course you can—that one *is* brand new! In fact, everything here is new… We don't sell second-hand items, *Ma'am*," serving a fake smile with it, so they knew exactly where they stood with him.

Big spending clients were what Palazzo was all about; the luxurious store was designed with these clients in mind, and they loved to shop there. Palazzo was a place to see and be seen at, not just to buy clothes, but also to dine in the restaurant on the third floor; or to have champagne at the bar. The stylish bar was a solid slab of white marble, with a gleaming gold mirrored top; beautiful white leather seats surrounded it, while ornate gold leaf and glass chandeliers hung above. The bartenders wore a traditional cocktail waistcoat and were extremely handsome—just like catalogue models.

Most of the staff could speak more than one language, catering to the many nationalities that visited, so they could experience the best quality service available. Sometimes, assistants would organise for the client's shopping bags to be sent to their apartment or hotel; in champagne coloured vans emblazoned with the 'P,' logo. Everything was thought of for the client who could afford it. The core value of Palazzo and its staff was to give excellent customer service to everyone in a luxurious environment, and in a manner that left a lasting impression.

The very best clients were called V.I.C's (Very Important Clients) and only Melinda's personal shopping team looked after them in the luxurious upstairs apartment; away from the busy shop floor, where they could shop and drink champagne in private. Personal shoppers didn't wear the usual brown, soldier-like uniform, but in the collections of that season; they exuded the image of Palazzo and would rake in tens-of-thousands of dollars from just one customer at a time. The highest bill they had put through in one single transaction was for $500,00! Imagine being able to spend that kind of money in one go, and that client probably went on to spend more in other stores on the avenue afterwards.

Chloe had developed a good client base over the years, not quite like Melinda's, but she had a few to choose from to start networking with. However, she had no idea where, or how to start. Big spending clients weren't interested in assistants sucking up to them and would treat them like any other shop worker, in any other store. Most of the time, serving high net-worth clients lived up to the glamorous image Palazzo had to the outside world; but every now and then, there would be the one customer who would remind you that at the end of the day, you were still just working in a shop—no matter how glorified it was. Saturday was a busy day for Palazzo, and most of the staff were scheduled to work.

The womenswear team consisted of Sarah: a New Yorker with an annoying voice to match, and big red frizzy hair. Then there was Tristan: a mixed-race, African-American guy who was extremely tall and handsome. He was quite the ladies man; one of the only few straight men in the whole store who had ploughed his way through many of the female staff members. Sarah once spread the rumour that he had in fact 'boned' Regina—a story he hadn't admitted or denied. Working alongside them was Soraya: a petite and quiet Indian girl; who was very much the princess, and totally into her beauty regime—almost too much. She was borderline prissy and rather lazy when it came down to hard work. And then there was Dom, Chloe, and of course Kim—who could forget Kim?

Each morning they would complete the department chores between them (some more than others) and get ready for the store to open. As Chloe cleaned the glass tabletops, her mind wandered as she thought about what Melinda had meant by networking with clients. An exciting prospect at first, but when she thought about it in depth, it was a job easier-said-than-done. She recalled all the clients she had ever served and there didn't seem to be a single one that could possibly help with her career goals.

Mrs Ruthenstock was her one of her top clients, she was in her late fifties, and considered as old money. Chloe quickly realised that she was a good customer, and would always set things aside for her at the beginning of the season—which helped Chloe reach target and commission every month—other than that, she wasn't much use to her as a contact. Then there was Karen Saunders: the founder of a very successful online business selling same-day loans—paid back with high-interest rates of course. She was a fantastic client that you could always count on for at least $20,000 a season.

But yet again, Chloe wasn't exactly sure how she could help her either… Not unless she wanted a loan with extortionate repayments. Saturday's also invited clients that you wouldn't usually get on a week-day (a sort of 'open-day' for crooks and cranks). As the morning got busier, Chloe was growing tired of running around after a group of girls, who were trying on shoes with no intention to buy.

The store had the policy to treat every customer like a V.I.C, and that meant bringing out three items from the stock room for every client to try on (even if they asked for just the one). Palazzo believed this selling ceremony was a sign of their assistants always thinking of the customer first; however, it wasn't such a good idea when serving three teenage girls on a busy Saturday, with tons of shoes. Something that the higher-ups, who made this rule wouldn't know about—having never spent a day on the shop floor in their entire lives—but completely qualified to call the shots.

Sitting there gossiping about which pair looked better; the girls must have tried the whole collection on display. Boxes of shoes were now mounting up as Chloe tried her best to minimise how many they had; returning a pair when they asked to see another. Unfortunately for Chloe's feet (and sanity) they always asked to see the pair she had just put back again. Alas, she gave up trying to tidy as she worked; instead, Chloe just left them all on the shop floor, as she stood there with a forced smile on her face.

"O-M-G! That pair would totally go with that pink sequinned mini-dress you have!"

'Where is she from? The fucking Valleys?' Chloe said to herself, as she gave them a look of the 'evils'.

"Yeah I know, but my dad would freak if I actually left the house in that with those shoes."

A third girl then asked: "Which ones do you think would suit me?"

Chloe's mind drifted off—how long was this going to last? Her patience was waning, and she really just wanted to say: "Who gives a fuck about what pair would go with what dress, and on who? You're not going to buy any of them anyway... And if you're asking me, I think these slippers would look great—slapped around your face, bitch!"

However, Chloe came back down to reality when all three of the girls abruptly stood up and left without apologising for completely wasting her time—something that Palazzo staff were used to and always had to be polite about. Without even a moment to breathe, another customer approached her. A pet hate of Chloe's, was when customers didn't know what shoe size they were.

"Can I try this on in my size," a woman asked, holding out the shoe in question, without even looking at her—never mind a 'please' or 'thank you'.

"Certainly, Ma'am… What size do you wear?" Chloe said, ignoring her rude manner; trying to remain professional.

"I don't know; you're the expert—you tell me…"

"Okay, not a problem… I will bring a few sizes for you to try, and we can start from there," Chloe said estimating her shoe size by eye, managing to rise above it.

Going into the stock room to fetch the shoes, and once locked inside (away from the shop floor), Chloe let her anger rip out of her chest—like a monster unleashing itself. It was a contrast to how she behaved on the shop floor; like an actress who played the sweetheart on stage and the diva-off it.

"How can you not know what size to take, you *fuck-tard?* I mean, is this the first time you're buying shoes? Have you been walking around bare-foot all your life?"

You could say that the job was beginning to get to her. She had the right qualifications in fashion studies, surely she was worth more to Palazzo than just a sales assistant? Unsure whether Melinda's advice had helped, or just fuelled her hatred for Regina, Chloe's patience was at an all-time low; she thought it best to take her lunch break as soon as she was finished with the customer.

The staff room hardly seated a quarter of the staff that worked there, and had no windows or air-con; not exactly the sanctuary that was needed from hectic shop life. Chloe usually packed lunch to bring to work with her, which not only saved money but allowed her to maximise her hour to the fullest. Sitting down to tuck into her salad, she saw Kim heading towards her.

'Please don't sit here,' Chloe muttered to herself, noticing that her table was one of the only few options left.

The canteen was busy and full, as it always was on the weekend with all the extra part-time staff.

"May I sit with you?" Kim said, standing with her tray of food.

"Erm… Sure…" Chloe hesitated; rolling her eyes as she moved her bag off the chair—she couldn't exactly say no.

The pair certainly wouldn't sit down to lunch together for a friend-ly catch up usually, making the situation quite awkward. Sitting mostly in silence, Chloe kept herself busy by texting Dom—hoping that this would deter Kim from starting a conversation. It was Dom's weekend off, which added to her boredom at work even more. He was probably cruising guys at the gym, or at home preparing for his date with Jason, later that evening.

OMG   WORK   IS   SOOO   BORING!   AND   TO   TOP
IT   OFF,   I'M   HAVING   LUNCH   WITH   KIM   :(

Almost instantly, Dom replied, which Chloe read with her head down looking at the screen; encouraging Kim to keep to herself..

FIND OUT WHEN SHE IS GOIN 2 PRESS OFFICE

The thought of speaking to Kim—other than for work-related reasons—didn't thrill her, but Dom was right; she needed to use this opportunity to get the gossip.

"So… Did you ever find out about the press office job? Whether you got it or not?" Chloe started, trying to sound genuine.

Kim paused from taking a bite of her sandwich and looked up at her; they never spoke to each other off the shop floor (there was a mutual understanding of dislike between them), but Kim was bursting with pride at her new position and dying for someone to ask her. Finally, someone had; this was her chance to boast about her success.

"Well, I'm not meant to tell anyone… It will be announced on Monday in the staff meeting… But if you promise not to tell…"

"Oh, I won't tell anyone… I mean, I wouldn't want to ruin things for you," Chloe said, trying to sound genuine once more.

Did Kim really think she wouldn't tell Dom straight away? On the other hand, she probably wanted her to. The prospect of being talked about excited her; she was going to be an essential member of staff after all. The press office team were full of self-importance, and treated the sales staff like their mignons; a quality that Kim didn't need much practice with.

"Well,… I got the job of course!" Kim said, with no effort to act coy.

"Of course you did! I didn't doubt it for a second… So, when do you start?"

"I start straight away; on Monday. I can't wait… I get a uniform budget too!" Pleased to have someone to brag to, Kim confided in more details. "I know we haven't exactly met eye-to-eye, but I just want you to know that you are a valued member of staff."

"Oh… Err… Thanks?" Chloe awkwardly replied. Deep down, she really wanted to tell her to shove her approval up her ass and say: "Screw you! Who do you think you are—you little maggot—my manager? That should have been my job!"

If only she had the guts to actually say it; she would feel a whole lot better, but almost certainly make trouble for herself in the long run. Kim's banal voice continued on in the background as Chloe contained her anger.

"I hope that I can count on you to do things for me… You know like sourcing dresses and stuff… Maybe we can work together?"

'Work together?' Chloe thought, 'I'd rather work at Walmart!'

Instead, Chloe saw this as an opportunity. Maybe if Kim trusted her more, if they were 'friends', then Chloe might seem more appealing to Regina or (at the very least), have access to inside information on the latest Palazzo happenings.

"Sure Kim, you don't even need to ask; you can count on me."

The staff room door flung open, causing a loud crash as it hit the wall on the other side; everyone looked to see who it was that had made such an entrance. Most people resumed with their chatter and carried on eating their lunch once they saw it was just the menswear manager, but Chloe knew he had come for her—his eyes fixed on her as he walked over to their table.

"Excuse me, Ladies, I don't mean to disturb your lunch... Chloe, when you've finished, will you please help us in menswear? We're rushed off our feet; I've made arrangements so that your floor won't be short."

Ben was the only 'cool' manager in the store, besides Melinda of course; he let his staff have secret breaks and bent the rules to benefit his team. He understood that people had lives outside of work; and for that reason, Chloe was glad to help him for the remainder of the afternoon. Serving female customers could sometimes be traumatic; they never knew what they wanted, and on a Saturday they seemed to get even worse. They would come in asking for a simple black pencil skirt, then leave with two pairs of party shoes and a handbag (after you had presented them with all the black skirts in the world, but none of them had been right). What a bore! Some customers were like energy vampires, sucking the life from within you in an instant.

Returning to the shop floor from lunch, Chloe made her way down to the menswear department. Entering the men's floor from the 'staff only' door, she could see that they *were* swamped indeed. The afternoon wasn't going to be a smooth ride it seemed; sometimes it was better to be busy as it made the hours pass quicker to home time. Eager to get stuck in, Chloe noticed a shy looking man browsing the rails of ready-to-wear.

He stopped to look at some leather biker pants: very expensive, and very sexy; the type of pants you would expect a Hollywood actor to wear in a sexy aftershave ad. They were also a key piece from the men's fashion show and featured in the Palazzo spring/summer campaign—splashed across the world. Chloe tried to read the client, she couldn't imagine him wearing them at all; he was balding at the front, of average build and height, and just average in general.

His stomach spilt over his belt, the thought of his 'overhang' in these leather biker pants made her feel bilious. Usually, young and well-built, confident guys went for this style, and you didn't mind eyeing up their bulge when they posed in the changing room mirrors—a perk of the job Dom would say. However, she decided that he would be a good one to start with, and easy to get rid of at the same time.

"Good afternoon Sir," she said as she approached him.

"Err, yes… I'd like to try these on in my size, please," he nervously stammered back.

Chloe felt sorry for him; she knew this wasn't going to be a good look, but ever the professional, she fetched his size anyway and stuck to the three item rule. She brought out the size he had asked for along with a size up (she knew they were a tight fit), and a plain white T-shirt to complement the biker look. With all the garments in hand, she escorted him to the changing room area. It resembled a gentlemen's lounge (like the kind you would find in a private members club) with low lit lamps and velvet panelled walls. There was even a waiter on standby to serve brandy, whisky, and champagne to clients that were in the mood to shop.

"Okay… I'll be outside if you need anything, Sir," she said, closing the door so he could get changed in privacy.

She heard the door lock and waited patiently outside in case he called for her, but after a while, Chloe started to become a little suspicious—something felt strange. She continued to wait, making herself look busy by tidying a table nearby which stored silk ties and pocket squares. Other customers started to look at her, trying to catch her attention; wondering why she wasn't serving anyone when the store was busy. She was aware that they were giving her the 'do you work here or what?' stare; she couldn't stand there all day doing nothing, so she knocked once more.

"Is everything okay Sir?"

"Err… Yes… I will be out in a moment," he said, sounding rushed and panicked—out of breath even.

Feeling sorry for him, she told him to take his time and moved on to another client—estimating that she could probably help someone else and return in good time. She had left the client for what felt like only fifteen minutes, and it was a good job she did; she managed to put through her only sale of the day for a three-thousand dollar leather briefcase.

Finally having made some money, Chloe took a breath of satisfaction and relief; but the feel-good sensation was soon replaced with a pang of worry. Rushing back to the changing room (dodging more waiting clients), she hoped the customer she had deserted wasn't annoyed with her—or even worse—that he hadn't stolen the items she had left him with. Entering the fitting room lounge, she could see the door was ajar.

"Sir, so sorry to leave you," she began, poking her head around the door to peek inside.

Her heart skipped a beat; the customer had left. She pushed the door fully open and thanked the Gods that the leather pants and T-shirt were all still there.

'That was a close one!' she said to herself.

One pair of pants were neatly folded on a chair, along with the T-shirt; it appeared he hadn't even tried them on, but the other pair was left on the floor in a heap. As she bent down to pick the pants up, she paused and straightened up fast—as if she had seen a ghost. It appeared that the customer had taken the time to publicly relieve himself and had left the evidence (in the form of bodily fluid) all down the changing room mirrors. Shocked into disbelief, Chloe ran out of the changing room to tell Ben immediately; trying not to cause a scene.

'All that time, and he was jerking off… And I felt sorry for him—how disgusting!'

Chloe felt like she had been violated; how degrading having to deal with such a thing, at Palazzo of all places. He wasn't the first, and certainly wouldn't be the last client to give such a shock—at least she wasn't the poor cleaner!

\*

The day finally drew to a close and Chloe was grateful she had made it through her shift; going home to have a long soak in the bath was the best thing she could think of right now. Some of her colleagues were going out for an after-work drink, but Chloe couldn't think of anything worse; the last thing she wanted to do was to socialise, as well as work with these people—other than Dom of course. After the experience she had earlier that day, Chloe wondered how on Earth she was going to meet possible contacts to help boost her career—when some of the clientele weren't exactly highbrow themselves.

Deflated, she took out her phone to call Dom but remembered that tonight was his hot date with this Jason guy. She imagined him rushing around in a flap: deciding what shirt to wear, with what pair of jeans. He was such a tart, and the thought of him panicking put a smile on her face. It had been a while since she had gone on a date herself, and she knew how excited Dom was to see Jason once again; so she sent him a good luck message.

HAVE A GREAT TIME TONIGHT… CAN'T WAIT TO HEAR ALL ABOUT IT! P.S. KIM IS STARTING IN PRESS OFFICE ON MONDAY… LET THE GAMES BEGIN! XXX

Heading for the subway and feeling drained of energy, Chloe felt like an old lady going home alone on a Saturday night. The store was closed on Sunday's, and after a week of hell at work, it was more than welcome. She needed time to herself, before what was left of the weekend vanished, and the madness started all over again.

Monday was going to be a big day at work, what with Kim starting in the press office; there was bound to be drama and gossip. Either way,

Chloe now had something to work on: a new mission, a new career goal, and this time things were going to be different. She didn't know exactly how, or when things were going to change—but one thing was for sure—things *were* going to change; starting Monday, with Kim's departure.

**

Chloe had been right; Dom *was* in a flap. His bedroom was a tip, and most of his wardrobe had been thrown on the floor; in search of the perfect outfit. While Chloe was slogging it out at work, Dom's priority was to pump up his chest and arms in the gym. His body had to be in the best shape possible, in case things got psychical later. Although he would have jumped at the chance of sleeping with Jason on their first encounter, Dom resisted spending the rest of the night with him. Instead, Dom walked him back to The Plaza hotel where he was staying, leaving Chloe to catch a cab ride back to Williamsburg.

Walking up to the hotel entrance, Dom said goodnight, fighting the urge to step inside with him; deciding that to leave him wanting more would be the better option. For some reason, something felt different this time, and he didn't want to come across 'easy'. For once, a man had taken an interest in him, made him feel rather special and good about himself; not just like a piece of meat—there was a connection. Jason was definitely his type, and not like all the others he had met before in New York's gay bars.

"So… I'm in town for another week; we should hang out… Maybe you could show me around on Saturday?" Jason had suggested.

"Erm… For sure; I'd like that," Dom said, trying to act cool.

Now that evening had come.

Throwing on a new shirt that he had purchased from work especially with his staff discount; Dom doused himself in his favourite cologne—enough to last all night long just in case the date did. He looked smart but sexy in fitted jeans that showed off his ass perfectly;

his biceps filled the short sleeve shirt well—the last minute pump up at the gym *really* was worthwhile. Rushing out the door, Dom headed straight for the subway to make his way over to The Plaza.

The train was packed with shoppers, commuters, and tourists all going in different directions. Although the trains were running smoothly, his nerves weren't—making him somewhat anxious and on-edge. He didn't want to be late and keep Jason waiting, but he also didn't want to seem too keen at the same time. Riding the train, he suddenly remembered he hadn't replied to Chloe's 'good luck' text. He whipped out his phone to compose a message, ready to send once resurfaced from underground.

HEY HUN, JUST ON WAY TO MEET J… SUPER EXCITED—
WILL KEEP YOU FILLED IN… HOPE WORK WAS OK?

Tapping away on his phone had made Dom forget about his nerves—even if it was for just a minute—before painstakingly watching the stations go by again until he had finally reached his destination. He made sure to be the first one off the train and up the escalators, taking two steps up at a time; working out his thighs one last time—swerving and dodging other passengers on his way up to the top. Back on the streets, he still had zero signal to send the message to Chloe; he continued to walk briskly down Fifth Avenue towards The Plaza.

Scooting past Palazzo, Dom hoped he wouldn't bump into anyone from work; now wasn't the time for polite chit-chat—he couldn't care less about anything regarding Palazzo right now—he was on a mission. His pace grew faster, until he approached the enormous twenty-storey building, with its light grey stone exterior; tastefully illuminated as the Sun began to set. Slowing himself down before he approached the hotel entrance and walking in, Dom soaked up the beautiful lobby; looking around, there was no sign of Jason. Checking his watch for the hundredth time, he felt a sudden wave of worry.

'I'm five minutes late, and he's not here! What if he doesn't come down? What if he isn't even staying here?'

Taking a deep breath, Dom calmed himself down yet again by sending the saved message to Chloe—which sent through successfully this time. Putting the phone back into the back pocket of his jeans, Dom looked up and saw Jason walking towards him; his heart pumped faster at the sight of him. He looked even more amazing than Dom had remembered—which did no favours for his nerves.

His eyes immediately locked onto Jason's open white shirt, which revealed the crease of his hairless tanned chest; his eyes then scanned down to the rest of his outfit: blue jeans that were ripped stylishly at the knee, with well-worn brown cowboy boots, carrying a tan leather bomber jacket. Jason oozed sex appeal that made a few heads turn as he strutted through the hotel lobby; he looked just like a Hollywood star.

"Hey, Mister," Jason said, casually putting his arm around Dom, pulling him in closer for a brief hug; close enough to smell Dom's heady scent. "I thought we'd have a drink here first, then you can show me around this city."

Dom was frozen by Jason's aura as he gave him a doe-eyed look; he was a catch! Onlookers were instantly drawn to him—probably assuming he was a celebrity or something—he just had that look about him, and Dom felt lucky to be in his presence. Dom was quite the catch himself and had his fair share of good lookers in the past, but they always knew it—which was so unattractive. With Jason, it was different; it was as though he was oblivious to the fact that everyone was staring at him—or maybe he was just so used to it that he didn't notice the attention he got?

A group of women—sat at the bar—had started to stare and were obviously talking about him. Dom gave them a cheeky smile back as if to say: "Yeah I know, he's hot… And he's with me bitches!"

The champagne bar had a great view of Central Park, and its interior was beautifully fitted with gold and emerald furnishings that married the old with the modern. Jason had a table reserved that was secluded from the other patrons, but still in view to see the goings on of the room. On the table waiting, was a bottle of champagne which had a '2002' vintage—Dom was instantly impressed.

'*Fuck!* That must be at least $200 or so,' he thought.

"Is champagne okay with you?" Jason said, not that he could say no with it already ordered.

"Of course… It's my favourite."

Jason sensed his nervous disposition and was happy with his choice of drink, soon the bubbles would work their magic and help loosen him up a bit; to be the Dom he first met on the shop floor: confident, handsome, and very sexy. Palazzo was Dom's domain where he could be sure of everything, now he was in an unknown arena. Jason poured the champagne and quizzed him about how his week had been, eventually helping Dom to relax a little ( a few gulps of fizz did the trick). It wasn't that hard for Dom to let go and be himself; Jason's company was an exciting and warm place that made him feel good inside, and Jason loved a guy that made him laugh… And Dom was doing precisely that.

"So… What's it like working at Palazzo?"

"Great! If you can stay out of the politics and keep busy… Don't get me wrong, I like it most of the time—but that place can attract some crazy people," Dom said, taking another large gulp.

"Oh really? Like me?"

"Ha! Are you serious? Literally, the whole store was drooling over you… Didn't you notice?"

"No…. The only person I noticed was you."

Noticing Dom's glass was empty, Jason took the champagne from the ice bucket and poured again. Dom could feel his cheeks redden, was it the champagne or the charm? Either way it made him feel amazing, but he tried his best not to show it; instead, he took another sip of freshly served champagne.

"So you didn't notice my colleague elbow me out of the way to serve you… And then watch the whole time you were at the store?"

Jason gave it a thought before answering, taking a sip of champagne; trying to act cool because the truth was entirely different.

"All I remember was heading to the men's floor, and you were there right away—ready to help me."

Dom couldn't believe what he was hearing. Surely Jason noticed everyone staring at him wherever he went—even in this bar? Or was he just so used to it that he was immune? Jason could see Dom thought he could smell bullshit—his raised eyebrow and cocked chin gave it away.

"Seriously! All I saw was you... And I thought this guy is cute... Then you opened your mouth, and I heard your English accent... And I was like, I need to know this guy; I need him to have my number or something... All the time I was trying to think of how to make a move—but I didn't wanna make it awkward—because you were at work... Then you made some comment about me being a Cinderella or something? And I was like... Okay... He's definitely flirting with me here... Luckily you gave me your number otherwise I would have had to come up with a way to leave you mine."

The bottle was near finishing, and the alcohol was starting to take effect—not to mention that nearly two hours had flown by as if it were seconds.

"I suppose drinking before dinner wasn't such a wise decision," Jason said.

"Do you wanna grab something to eat?"

"Sure, but to be honest, I hate stuffy places like this... I know I'm staying here, but it's not really my style. How about we go grab a burger or something? Do you know a good spot?"

Hearing that Jason was a burger and fries kind of guy made Dom like him even more and knew exactly where to take him.

"Sure... I know this great burger place, not too far from here."

"Do you mind if we walk there?"

"No, not at all... I like walking, and it's a great evening for it."

"Well, that's another thing we have in common then... I pretty much walk everywhere. In L.A nobody walks, so when I visit a city, I try to see as much as I can by foot… Especially if I have a native to show me around," he said with a wink.

"Oh, well I'm from London originally remember?" Dom said, now knowing that Jason loved to hear his accent.

"Well, if I'm ever in London…" Jason began, as he picked up the bar tab for the champagne, tipping the waiter.

Dom reached for his wallet, knowing he couldn't really afford it, but Jason had paid in a flash and motioned Dom to put his money away—making Dom blush a little for the second time, and feeling slightly out of his league. 'I could never just throw down $200 for a bottle of champagne,' he told himself. They left the hotel and walked to the burger place, talking the entire distance and making time fly past once again.

"So tell me, are you interested in art?" Jason said, starting the conversation so there wasn't an awkward silence—not that there had been so far—Dom had been a motor-mouth thanks too the champagne.

"Yeah, of course, I am."

"Oh yeah… Who's your favourite artist then?"

"I know it's passé, but I love pop art… Warhol is my favourite."

"Oh, really? Well, that's funny… That's why I'm here in New York… I'm selling a piece that is inspired by his portraits. My style is based on photography and screen-printing too. What is it that you like about Warhol?"

This was quite revealing for Jason; he could always tell what kind of person they were from the type of artwork they liked. Dom, however, was a bit embarrassed about calling it passé (after Jason revealed it was similar in style to his own work).

"I suppose, it's those iconic images of celebrities… I remember as a kid, seeing the portrait of Marilyn Monroe, and I remember just being completely obsessed with her ever since… I knew from the moment I saw it that she was a legend… Without knowing anything about her."

Smiling at Dominic, Jason felt that he had him summed up perfectly. He was attracted to his warm, kind personality—as well as his good looks and accent—but now with his taste in art too. They soon arrived at the busy burger joint, which was definitely more relaxed than the dining room at The Plaza. It was a trendy new establishment with hanging light bulbs and copper tone tabletops, and a warm, inviting atmosphere. You could watch the chefs cooking burgers behind an open grill, which filled the place with the delicious smell of succulent beef burgers; you could hear them sizzle in the background and it made diners salivate the minute they walked through the door.

By now they had walked off their tipsy state and were starving—the smell added to their hunger pangs—Dom had picked the right place. The burgers arrived, cooked medium with cheese, red onion chutney, ketchup, mustard, a thickly sliced pickle, and a generous basket of fries. Rather than beer, they opted to go for sparkling water—which was very refreshing; they had talked themselves dry after the champagne. After completing a whole burger to himself, Jason made no hesitation in ordering another—Dom was impressed with his appetite. It was sexy, especially as his rock hard body probably needed the calories. Dom hoped Jason would have the same enthusiasm when it eventually came down to eating him too. Jason tucked in and kept Dom occupied with more questions so he could focus on chomping down burger number two.

"So… If you're from London… How did you end up in New York?"

"My dad moved my mum and me here with his job… She's back in London now… They split up years ago, and my dad remarried… Sheena's like, eight years older than me—a total gold digger—but I don't see them much to care enough about her."

"You don't live with them?"

"Hell no! I'm not that much of a sadist… You think I can put up with Palazzo and living with them? How about you?"

"I was born and raised in California baby… Come on, let's get out of here."

Jason asked for the bill and threw down his Amex on the table.

"Wait... You paid for the champagne... Let me pay for the food at least," Dom said, insisting on paying—still feeling slightly uneasy by the whole champagne situation; this was something he could at least afford to cover.

"No way... You're my guest for the evening, and I'm taking you out..."

"Well, actually... You're my guest, in my town Mr *Hollywood!*"

Jason's mouth lifted into a cheeky grin, lapping up Dom's playfulness. "Well, actually... London is your town, but okay... We'll split... And I won't take no for an answer!"

Walking the short distance back to The Plaza, Jason stripped off his leather jacket—suffering from a case of 'the meat sweats'. The breeze blew open his shirt, giving Dom a glimpse of his tanned chest every-now-and-then—which provoked Dom's imagination. 'I bet he's great in bed!' He wanted to lunge on him so badly but wondered why Jason hadn't made a move already. The truth was that Jason wasn't big on public displays of affection, and the busy streets of New York weren't the time or the place. The most he could manage was to play footsie under the table at the restaurant.

"So, how about we order some drinks to my room? We can chill out there and watch a movie? That's if you want to of course?" Jason suggested.

"Great... Sounds perfect to me," Dom said, desperate to finally be alone with him.

Back at the hotel, Jason called the elevator to the ground floor; Dom was excitable, knowing that he would probably get to kiss him very soon. Dom's fear that he was out of Jason's league started to return, but he needn't have worried; Jason had already fallen in love with his warm, kind nature, and his accent turned him on big time! Jason's suite was on the seventh floor; it had a king-size bed and was spacious with a walk-in wardrobe. The bathroom was fitted with a free-standing bathtub and a large wet-room—as well as a living area with a huge TV—the view from the window wasn't too shabby either.

"This isn't really my style… I prefer something more masculine and contemporary," Jason said, as he opened the door; trying to excuse the taste in decor.

The room was, of course, luxurious; decorated with luxurious fabrics and furnishings, which gave it a grand feeling. Dom didn't like the classic style either; he was more of a modern and minimalist when it came to interior design.

"The gallery who invited me to New York insisted I stayed here, and since they are paying for the trip… I just went along with it," Jason said, feeling his levels of coolness depleting as Dom looked around the room.

"Well, this place is a New York landmark; an icon… Just like Warhol and Monroe."

Jason smiled back at him as he flung his leather jacket over a chair and started to take off his cowboy boots—groaning at the relief of removing them after all the walking they had done. Dom followed by taking off his sneakers, neatly placing them by the door which made Jason laugh—he knew Dom was a 'good boy'.

Walking over to him, Jason opened his arms to initiate contact. Dom followed by putting his arms around Jason's waist—on finally making contact, it felt like an electric spark had fired off. Taking Dom's face into his hands, Jason kissed him gently—teasingly at first—building up to passionately unleashing the tension and desire that had been brewing all evening. Dom melted into Jason's kiss like a marshmallow in a mug of hot chocolate.

Pulling away, Jason rested his forehead onto Dominic's to look at his face. "You're so sweet," he said with a satisfying smirk; biting his lip. Dominic started to blush, he couldn't believe that this super hot guy from L.A was actually into him. "What are you doing tomorrow?"

Dom was confused—was he chucking him out already?

"Nothing planned… Why?"

"Great, you can stay here with me then… We can hang out some more… I mean, your workplace is just five minutes away."

"Oh, no worries… I don't have to work until Monday…"

"Sure, but I'm here until Friday… Can't you stay here with me until then? I want to be with you as much as possible before I go back to L.A," Jason said, pulling him in for a kiss once more—as if it would sway the decision in his favour.

Guiding Dom to the bed as they kissed, he pushed him onto it. Kissing each other felt like the pull of a magnet; like a buzz of electricity was being conducted through their lips; feeling so natural and as if this was supposed to be happening right now, at this moment. Jason took the fact that Dom hadn't resisted as confirmation he was indeed going to stay with him. Dom couldn't believe what was happening—it was like a scene from a film—the gay man's answer to Pretty Woman. Melting there on the bed, staring into Jason's eyes, Dom felt like his time had finally come to fall in love with someone special.

"I knew kissing you would feel good, but I didn't think it would be this good," Jason said.

Dom laid on the bed with Jason's weight on top of him; staring into his eyes. "I'm just gonna go to the bathroom," he said, prompting Jason to get up.

Dom got up and off the bed (not wanting to escape) for the chance to freshen up and message Chloe with the latest—he had to share his news with someone before the evening got even more intense. Looking into the bathroom mirror, Dom told himself: 'This is it… This time it's going to be so different.'

Pulling his phone out from his jeans pocket, a message from Chloe already awaited him.

OMG, I'M SUCH AN OLD WOMAN! IN BED WATCHING MOVIES… HOPE DATE IS GOING WELL… TXT ME WHEN YOU CAN—I'M DYING TO KNOW DETAILS!!! XXX

Dom quickly tapped a reply, not wanting to waste too much time away from Jason.

HEY! DATE IS GOING VERY WELL… I HAVE MAJOR NEWS…
CAN'T WAIT TO SEE YOU ON MONDAY! ARRIVE EARLY
FOR COFFEE… ENJOY THE REST OF THE WEEKEND… I
                    KNOW I WILL! X

Putting his phone down by the sink, he looked at his reflection in the lit mirror and ran the water. He splashed water on his face, and as he looked up again, the bathroom door opened—Jason walked in completely naked. His tanned, toned body looked perfect in the artificial light of the bathroom—Dom couldn't believe just how lucky he was. Without hesitation, Jason stepped into the shower and ran the faucet—wetting his hair and smoothing it over his head—as if to put on a show for Dom.

Watching him was like watching a porno; he knew exactly what he was doing, and it was working. The water poured off his body, making his skin glisten; now starting to turn slightly red from the hot water beating down on him. The bathroom was now beginning to steam up, and so was Dom's evening—his eyes panned down from head to—

"Hey… You gonna stand there and watch? Or you gonna join me?"

Dom didn't waste a moment more and got undressed in an instant. Dropping his clothes onto the bathroom floor in a heap, he slowly removed his Calvin Klein briefs in a teasing manner. Jason stood there under the steamy water, waiting and watching; it was apparent from the view that he was having an effect on Jason too. Joining him in the shower (which could have accommodated at least four people), the feeling that something extraordinary was happening washed over him, as did the water from the hot shower he was now sharing with the equally hot, Jason Hart.

# CHAPTER FIVE

**M**onday morning had arrived; the weekend had frustratingly whizzed by, and Chloe was grateful to have had Sunday off at least. Today was to be a very eventful start to the week and Chloe had arrived earlier than usual, to catch up with Dom over a coffee. She hadn't heard from him since Saturday night and assumed he had lots to tell. Getting changed in the locker room, Chloe was mixed with emotions; excited to see Dom, but dreading the morning meeting at the same time.

Kim was to be announced as the new press office assistant—making her appointment official. For Chloe, it was just another way to be told that she wasn't good enough; she wasn't ready for another emotional battering. Rather than worry about what was coming, she decided that dealing with things as they come would be the best way to get through the day, and got dressed in her uniform. She folded away her clothes neatly into her locker and checked her make-up in the mirror, one last time.

After a lazy Sunday, she looked fresh, unlike some of her colleagues who were apparently out partying all weekend by the look of their faces. This gave her a small lift; knowing she had scored an advantage in the looks department and left the changing room for the staff kitchen. Dom had already made Chloe a cup of coffee (he knew exactly how she liked it): not too strong, and with plenty of milk—more of a latte.

Dom, on the other hand, was a triple shot, cappuccino kind-of-guy. Standing at the kitchen side, stirring sugar into his coffee, Dom looked just as refreshed as Chloe—even more so in fact; he looked like he had rested well, and there was something else about him that seemed to shine from within. He knocked Chloe off the leaderboard for radiance by miles.

'What is his secret?' she wondered; although, she probably could have guessed exactly *what* it was.

"Wow! Dominic Fraser, you look amazing! Someone has had a good weekend I see—you're glowing," she said, kissing his cheek as he handed her the coffee, with a huge grin. "So? Tell me everything... I want to know everything from the start."

Chloe couldn't wait to hear his stories; for a moment she had forgotten all about the morning meeting. They sat at a table out of earshot from nosey colleagues (who loved to involve themselves in other people's business).

"Well, Saturday I went shopping, and the gym... Of course, I couldn't really relax as I was so excited—but nervously excited—you know what I mean?"

Chloe blew into her hot coffee, forcing it to cool; taking cautious sips, she listened to Dom's story unfold—she was gripped already.

"Anyway—I got ready... I totally did not know what to wear, and I didn't wanna be late... But I managed to look *hot*—naturally... We arranged to meet at The Plaza... That's where he's staying..."

"Ooh, Nice!" she chipped in, not wanting to disturb his train of thought but to encourage it along.

"Yeah, I know! So, I went to his hotel, and I didn't think he was gonna show up... I was really nervous by this point... Then I saw him coming towards me, and my God—he looked hot as *fuck!*"

"Yeah, I remember... He was really hot—but go on..." Chloe pressed, annoyed that she had to drag it out of him.

"We stayed there in the bar and drank champagne... Like a $200 bottle of champagne! He paid thankfully—we got a bit tipsy, so we decided to grab a bite... I took him to that new burger place down on Ninth—easy and laid back. I didn't wanna eat in front of him at first—especially not a massive burger—no matter how starving I was... But then he pigged out on two burgers, so it was fine in the end."

"Okay, but did you guys make out or what?" Chloe blurted impatiently.

"You said, you wanted to know everything from the start!" Dom said, taking pleasure in stretching out his story—building up the drama.

"Yeah-yeah-yeah… Get on with it! So did he kiss you?"

Dom couldn't help but smile; he didn't want to say too much, too soon. He felt terrible that he had good news to spill, knowing Chloe was going through a bad patch at the moment, but he knew she would be happy for him—so continued on with the juicy part—she did ask after all.

"Well, I was thinking… Maybe he's not attracted to me, and just wanted to make new friends in the city or something? I was dying for him to jump me, but he never did… A few times he touched me or was playful, but it wasn't until after dinner that things really started to heat up."

"Really? So what happened? Come on *bitch*…" Chloe urged.

Dom laughed at her desperation to know the full story. "We left the burger place, and he suggested we go back to his hotel… For some 'drinks' in his room."

"Uh-huh… Drinks—yeah… Right!"

"Well, to cut a long story short—we went to his room, and we didn't even order the drinks… He grabbed me, and we started making out. Then… Wait for it… He asked me to stay with him!"

"I knew it! You little *fucker!*" Chloe couldn't help shouting out with excitement.

By now their colleagues were trying to listen in; what spicy information could they possibly be sharing on a Monday morning? Did they know something that they didn't about the meeting?

"Wait, there's more… Not only did he ask me to stay, but he wants me to stay there for the rest of the week!"

Chloe's face was a picture of disbelief, excitement, and jealousy—all at the same time—but she was, of course, pleased for Dom.

"Oh. My. God! You're staying with him at The Plaza hotel? No wonder why you look so good this morning… I take it you just rolled out of bed and strolled over here then?"

"You could say that…"

"I can't believe it… You're so lucky; you're literally staying just down the street… So I take it you have had—"

"Of course! We couldn't keep our hands off each other all week-end… We had a massage in the hotel spa yesterday and just relaxed in his room all afternoon ordering room service… Tonight, after work we are going for dinner, and then back to the hotel again." Dom couldn't stop smiling at finally being able to share his saucy secrets.

"So, he must really be into you then? Or is he paying you a service charge for the week? Does this mean you're a rent boy now?"

"Ha-ha—funny as ever! But seriously… He is the best. I have never felt like this before… I think this could be it for me; no other guy could compare to Jason."

"Someone's going to *Hollywood* bitches!" Chloe said, in a ghet-to-fabulous accent as she snapped her fingers in the air.

He was happy that she too had picked up on the idea, and that it wasn't just all in his head. Moving to L.A for a hot husband would be the best '*Fuck You*' he could leave Palazzo with.

"Anyway, drink up… Looks like it's time for the big reveal," Dom said, checking the wall clock; noticing their colleagues slowly disappearing from the kitchen.

*

A new week usually started with a store meeting and a recap of the figures and targets—this made everyone aware of where they were at for the month—but today there was something extra. The entire team stood in a semi-circle on the ground floor, waiting for the meeting to start—except for Soraya who had just scraped the clock and made it on time. Tardiness wasn't her strongest point, usually spending way too much time on her make-up in the mornings—turning up for work in a full-face contour.

Kim also looked extra groomed, she was ready for everyone's eyes to fall on her; it was her big day. She stood there with a few other girls who all stuck together; all 'Lickers' of course. The department managers stood at the front while Ben read out the weekly results. Just as he was finishing reading out the figures, awkwardness started to infiltrate the air. The click-clack of Regina's high heels rang through the marbled foyer; staff members began to look around to confirm who it was (not that they needed to). Some even said good morning to her and gave fake beaming smiles—more 'Lickers'.

"Okay, guys… I wish you all a great week ahead, but now I will pass you over to Regina for some exciting news…" Acknowledging Regina, Ben edged out of the way, handing over her audience.

Chloe and Dom rolled their eyes at each other, stifling giggles—this was such a performance for such trivial news; Regina loved to make a 'hoo-ha' out of the mundane. She leant on a glass cabinet with her legs stretched out in front of her, as if to show off her new Palazzo black high-heels (despite not having the best legs in town). She now had the full attention of everyone—even the store cleaners stopped working to listen to her.

"Thank you," she said coolly; enjoying her moment. "As Ben said, I have some very exciting news…" She took a beat to look around, trying to build up suspense—not knowing this was 'old news' to some already. "It's not often that people show the skills and potential to grow within this company, but Palazzo has found a new team member for the press office. This role requires excellent knowledge of the brand, its image, its future, and especially its place in the global fashion market. Not something everyone has the vision for… So it is with great pleasure, I can reveal Kim Wei from womenswear, will be the new assistant to Myra Parks and her team in the press office… I'm sure you will all join me in congratulating her and will offer your support in her new role… She will still be working closely with the retail team—especially her team from womenswear…"

Regina looked at Chloe as if to say: 'I mean *you!*' Causing her to gulp a dry swallow that was almost audible. Even though her speech wasn't exactly groundbreaking, people automatically clapped and cheered—like seals at feeding time. Kim bowed her head to feign embarrassment, but Chloe and Dom knew she just loved the attention. The girls she stood with were elated and took it in turns to hug her (probably thinking they were one step closer to promotion themselves by association).

"So, from today Kim is now a level-two member of staff—so please co-operate… I don't want to hear of any bad feedback; there will be action taken against anyone who fails to adhere to these instructions… Have a great day, and remember the core value of Palazzo: to give world-class customer service in a luxurious environment, and in a luxurious way."

Regina gave one final icy glance over the whole team before leaving the shop floor—taking the lousy atmosphere away with her. Staff started to trawl off into their own departments to start work, exchanging greetings with friends from other floors; planning lunch breaks with one other. Dom and Chloe slowly wandered up to the second floor, hanging back from the others.

"How lame was that speech?" Dom said.

"I know, I thought I was gonna puke into my hands… How patronising was that? '*It's not every day someone shows potential.*' What the *fuck* does she mean by that? Are the rest of us working here invisible or something? I'm starting to get pissed with this place now… It's a joke!"

**

Kim's morning was spent getting acquainted with her new team, which consisted of Myra Parks: the head of the department, and one other assistant: Sylvia Stuttgart. The team was small, but they had influence; sales assistants saw them as the most glamorous staff in the company (next to personal shopping). They were always invited to red carpet events, Fashion Week, award ceremonies, and of course—the Palazzo runway show at Milan Fashion Week. Kim couldn't wait to get stuck into her new job and enjoy all the frills that came with it.

"Okay, so now you have met the people; seen the office—it's now time to get you looking the part," Myra said rather patronisingly, desperate to get rid of the brown uniform she was wearing out of her office. "Go down to the floor and pick your uniform... You'll need one business outfit—including shoes—and one event dress that can be accessorised or dressed-up, or something... *Go!*"

"Will I have enough budget for all that?"

"Honey, you have $3,000... With staff discount on top; what more do you want? Oh, and you get that every season... Go now—and hurry up! We have a lot of work to do here," she said, waving her hands to dismiss her from her presence.

Staff discount was a generous fifty percent, so Kim's allowance had just doubled. Every woman dreamt about spending thousands of dollars at Palazzo, and for Kim, this was now a reality. As if being overjoyed with the newfound power wasn't enough, she couldn't wait to show off her new staff benefits to her old colleagues back on the shop floor. She raced down to the womenswear floor with a sense of authority; today was the start of her new life, the way she had always intended it to be.

Dom and Chloe were enjoying the slow start to the week by standing at a glass table folding knitwear and gossiping about his plans for the rest of the week with Jason. Sarah, Tristan, and Soraya were all surprised at this morning's big announcement; discussing why Kim had been chosen for the job—speculating on many possibilities. Little did they know that Kim was employed merely for her good looks, work ethic, and the ability to do exactly what she was told; she was nothing more than a pawn in a game that would keep Regina winning every time.

Kim knew from the very start that she would have to make sacrifices, to get to where she wanted to go in her career. She had read every positive thinking, 'How To Succeed In Business' book there was—which had made her very determined. She soon discovered that fashion was an easy game to play (if you knew how to play it), and with this knowledge, she joined Palazzo; one of the best-paid companies on Fifth Avenue—which also helped with her expensive taste.

With her first pay packet, she treated herself to a classic black leather Palazzo shoulder bag (she had also learned that looking the part was as essential, as acting it was). She had something to prove (not just to herself), which meant strictly hard work and strategic choices; no making friends, and plenty of egos massaging members of management—especially the highest in the line of duty; Regina.

There were times when she would catch Chloe and Dom laughing to themselves on the shop floor; she longed to be a part of that. Enjoying work and liking the people you worked with (with all the excitement of mini-dramas and gossip) was something Kim missed, but she also understood that it got you nowhere. If only Chloe and Dom knew the girl behind the facade she had built; the mask she wore to get a promotion; maybe then, they too would understand that she was just like them: smart, determined, friendly, funny, and talented—not just another Palazzo puppet.

Kim actually liked Chloe (in some ways they were quite similar); not being friends with her made it easier to get ahead at work, but it also disheartened her—the same way she could see the job was disheartening Chloe. At the same time, she didn't have time to feel sorry for her; she had a mission to complete. Why should she apologise for being intelligent enough to have a game plan?

A concept Chloe was only just getting to grips with (despite being forewarned). Kim couldn't deny that Chloe was the best salesperson in the team and had a great eye for style; enlisting her to help pick out uniform was a chance to bridge the gap between them while getting the 'Chloe Ravens makeover' treatment. Entering the womenswear department, Kim walked up to the glass table; Dom and Chloe were still folding knitwear and chatting.

"Hey guys…" she said, weary of being snubbed by Dom like usual.

"Oh… Kim… Hi… Congrats on your new job," Chloe said, trying her best to feign surprise; as though she hadn't told Dom before the news officially broke. Dom rolled his eyes (it was a habit whenever Kim spoke), and flashed her a sarcastic smirk; he didn't have the energy to be a 'frenemy' and carried on folding.

"Myra's sent me on my first assignment… To blow my uniform budget! I was hoping you guys could help?"

"Sure," Dom said, quickly stepping up to the challenge, which pleasantly surprised her.

This was probably the first time he had been kind to her—ever!

"Okay, great! Well, what do you think I should get? Myra said I definitely have to get a cocktail dress for events, a day suit, and some accessories…"

Dom flicked through the rails and stopped at the ugliest dress on the shop floor he could find at that moment: a salmon tone shift dress—bland enough to wash out her complexion.

"Oh, you should get this… It would totally make your eyes pop."

"*Pop out* you mean!" Chloe interrupted, grabbing the dress out of his hand; putting it back on the rail where it belonged.

She shot him a look, telling him to '*be nice*'. He knew it would be evil to put her in ugly outfits (to get back at her for being such a bitch to work with over the years), even though it would have been entirely worth it.

"Actually… I think for your first uniform, just cover the basics."

Chloe's stylist instincts began to kick in; she started selecting a few things off the rails, laying them out on the glass table top.

"Cover the wardrobe essentials… A simple black cocktail dress made from light wool: perfect for business meetings, and easily dressed up with accessories for the evening… A gold leather clutch bag: again, easy to wear with many different outfits—both night and day… Gold will make your skin glow even more, and it always compliments black."

"I love it, but what about shoes?" Kim said, enjoying the attention from Chloe; feeling just like one of her clients. She knew how to sell an image, a lifestyle, and was naturally gifted in making people feel great in a believable manner; not forced.

"Again, go basic... But no flats! You're corporate now... Simple, black six-inch court shoes for the day... For the evening, go for the gold platforms to match the bag..."

Chloe went on to pick clothes that covered the whole uniform allowance: mainly separates that she could mix-and-match for multiple looks; making her budget stretch as far as possible. Moving over to the accessories counter, Chloe chose a pair of faux-pearl cabochon earrings that suited every occasion, featuring the italic '*P*,' logo in the centre. Together with the gold clutch and black cocktail dress, the total slightly exceeded the budget, but Kim was happy to pay the extra few hundred dollars—since she had just got herself a pay rise.

Chloe de-tagged the garments and kept their price tags for the stock inventory team to take off the system. Again, stock inventory was another area to be very careful of and was painstakingly maintained; come stock take, you could be sure that staff would be held responsible for any missing items.

"Thanks, Chloe... I couldn't have done this without you... I hope we can work together more in the future... You really know your stuff. "

Chloe smiled at her, accepting her olive branch. After all, Chloe would have taken the job too given a chance. She quickly bagged the items and handed them over to Kim so she could get back up to the office with her brand new looks—confident that she had made Kim the most stylish girl the press office had ever seen.

"Yeah—great job *Chloe!* We should have picked out loads of awful things for her... How funny would that have been?" Dom said once she had finally left them.

"I know... I saw that naughty glint in your eye, and I had to stop it!"

"You were probably right to do that... Well done," he said, pleased that she was able to put it all behind her; hoping this was a sign she was returning to her usual self. "I'm not thinking straight today… All I can think about is my third night at The Plaza with Jason."

Chloe was pleased (and inspired) that Dom had a distraction outside of work—she just wished she had one too. Melinda's advice had resonated with her deeply, she had been thinking about it ever since; she also needed something of her own to sink her teeth into. Something that couldn't be taken away from her—especially by Regina. Styling Kim had reminded her just how good she was at her job—but more than that—she *was* a great stylist. She enjoyed styling people, just like she used to on her blog: StacksOfStyle.com or S.O.S for short—and it indeed offered fashion 'S.O.S'. People would comment on her pictures and ask for tips on what to wear, and where to buy runway-worthy looks for less.

It had been months since she had posted last; work was just too demanding, doing all this extra work for free (after having worked all day), had started to lose its allure. Her ambition to succeed at Palazzo had taken over, and evenings getting wasted with Dom in tacky gay bars didn't leave her with all the time in the world to keep it running either. Imagine where she could be now if she hadn't given up? It could have boomed and become an online hit, for all she knew.

Dom spent the day clock-watching, and when the shift finally ended, he quickly changed out of his uniform to rush back home. He was running out of fresh clothes having stayed at The Plaza for two nights (especially clean boxers). Leaving work together, Dom walked with Chloe to the subway, forcing her to catch up with his brisk pace.

"Wow, you're in a hurry… Aren't you going just around the corner anyway?" Chloe said, catching her breath; skipping a step every-now-and-then to keep up.

"I'm in a bit of a rush babe; I need to go home to get some things… I'm running out of socks and briefs, and I need to put these in the washer," he said, referring to the same outfit he had been wearing all weekend.

"You've not had a change of clothes?" Chloe couldn't believe her ears, Dom hated to feel dirty and unwashed clothes were a no-no—but this was an exceptional case.

'This *must* be love!' Chloe thought to herself. The thought of Dom giving up his fashion and hygiene commitments for a man was a sure sign that this could be something special.

"Well, to be fair, I was out of them—more than I was in them. But still, you know how I am... Anyway, I want him to see me in different outfits, turn out some sexy looks and show off my style... I think he'll appreciate that," Dom said with a wink.

His collection of clothes had been carefully selected over the years—working at Palazzo—and now was the time to get their full benefit.

"What are *you* doing this evening?"

"Oh, ya know... Dinner... TV... The usual..."

"Girl, you crazy; you should get out more! You should be putting yourself 'out there' and get some eye candy yourself. Male attention is just what you need right now."

Male attention was far from what she needed right now; work was still on her mind, and more importantly—on her next move. Her motivation at work was depleting even more, and she felt like she needed to take action and responsibility for her career. She was fast approaching the big 'three-O'; the thought of being stuck on the shop floor at Palazzo daunted her more and more each day.

It was as if time was closing in on her—it had now become a race— growing more aware of it than ever before. Forget the female biological body clock—the career clock was notching up at a much faster rate. Not wanting to set herself up for failure once again, she decided to tell Dom of her plans—his reaction would be a good indicator of whether it was a good idea or not.

"Actually, I'm gonna take a look at my blog."

"Your blog—what happened to that?"

"Oh, I just lost interest… I just didn't know what to write about… Or have the time for it, but I think now is the time to take another look at it…"

"You will find things to write about… Come on, look at where we work… There's plenty to write about! I think it's a great idea… Just what you need; a little project outside to keep your mind busy."

"Yes, we all need a *project* outside of work," Chloe said, nudging him with her elbow. She knew exactly what (or more like whom), was Dom's extracurricular project outside of working hours.

*** 

After grabbing his weekend bag and stuffing it with all the essentials, Dom raced back to the hotel to meet Jason. Seeing Jason made sense of his dull day at work; selling handbags and dresses seemed so superficial when he was with him.

'This is what life is all about, *love!*' he thought.

Jason was a romantic, and Dom was a hopeless one, so they made a good match. Jason had arranged for dinner to be served in the hotel suite—very private and romantic. They couldn't take their eyes off each other as they ate pan-fried salmon with asparagus and potatoes. Hoping they would stay in and take the romance level up a notch, Dom was miffed when Jason revealed he had other ideas.

"Right, get your shoes on Mister!" Jason demanded.

"What—where are we going?" Dom said, almost sulking.

"Get your shoes on, and you'll find out…"

Saying no to Jason was tough, but Dom did as he said. He quite liked it when he was assertive and dominant; it drove him wild. Leaving the hotel, not knowing where Jason was taking him, had equally turned him on.

Jason felt like he had got to know so much about Dom, but revealed so little of himself; this was the perfect chance to show him what he was all about. Dom had told Jason about his life in London and showed him his version of New York: the places he would go, the people he would see, and all about his best friend—Chloe. A private date at the art gallery on Fifty-seventh Street—where his work was displayed—was the easiest way to open up to him some more. Presenting his work would tell Dom all he needed to know in an instant; it was a portal into his true self, and he wanted to show that side of himself.

"Okay, wait here," Jason said, leaving him inside the gallery entrance; rushing off into the back of the gallery.

There was no one there; the gallery was silent and still, spotlights buzzed with electricity. It had dawned on Dom that Jason had surprised him with a private preview, just for him. Returning (sans jacket; showing off his body through a tight T-shirt) with a popped bottle of champagne and two plastic flutes, the situation had suddenly turned into the romantic evening he had hoped for.

"What's all this?" Dom said, taking off his jacket in exchange.

"Come…" Jason said, leading him into the first room; skilfully pouring the champagne, handing Dom a glass. "Okay… So these here are mine…"

Dom was taken aback; his attraction to Jason had suddenly leapt ten-fold in his estimation. The room was moodily lit, but in contrast, the walls popped with bursts of colour. Dom slowly stepped closer towards one of the paintings—pending reaction. The main piece stuck out amongst all the others: a portrait of London's most famous supermodel; Kate. Her face had been screen printed on a background with the Union Jack; it was simple yet clever, and it reminded him of his favourite artist—Andy Warhol. Nevertheless, it was a truly striking image—just like how Marilyn had once made an impact on him. Not only was Jason super hot and sexy, but he was also very talented.

"Do you like it?" Although, Jason didn't really need to ask; the expression on Dom's face said it all. He was still staring in awe; his face lit up by a single spotlight as he absorbed the portrait— wholly lost in the moment.

"I love it!" Dom said, answering Jason's question after a while—much to Jason's relief.

"Hopefully it will sell… I have a few buyers interested—a gallery in London seems quite keen," Jason said, eyeing up the paintwork for imperfections. "Hopefully they will want more pieces too… Enough for an entire show."

"Well, you have certainly captured their market by using one of the biggest fashion icons as your subject, not to mention the red, white, and—"

But before he could finish, Jason took him from behind and spun him around—into his arms. Dom could feel the heat of the spotlights beating down on his face like the Sun—or was he blushing? He grabbed Dom's face and kissed him in front of Kate's portrait, which was slightly egotistical (but hot at the same time). Dom's hands clawed at his back, wanting to rip the T-shirt off Jason; it seemed Jason felt the same way (judging by what was prodding into Dom's groin) as he pulled him in for a deeper kiss.

"Let's get outta here…" Jason suggested, kissing him once more with a mouthful of cold and fizzy champagne.

Dom groaned with delight; it was time to leave.

Finally making it back to the hotel (and slightly merry from the champagne), Dom grew impatient to get back to the room; the walk back from the gallery was too long for his liking. Entering the suite, it was a matter of seconds before they both grabbed each other, releasing the tension that had built up between them all evening; their desire for each other was too hard to ignore. Falling onto the bed, Dom felt like he had finally filled the missing part in his life—and it was only just beginning…

Chloe, on the other hand, felt as though her life was stuck on slow-mo, and showed no signs of progressing anytime soon. Sofa surfing, watching TV, Chloe's mind drifted off; wondering what the future could possibly hold for her. She made a mental list of all the failed jobs, plans, and dreams that hadn't worked out in her favour; not getting the promotion had changed her attitude completely. She felt differently towards her job, the company, and most importantly it had changed the way she thought about people in general.

A lengthy stint in retail could easily wear you down and destroy your soul, and that's what was happening to her. All she was sure of, was that Melinda was right; she needed to do something for herself, become self-sufficient, to promote herself and her own talents—instead of depending on Palazzo to hand her a glittering career on a plate. She knew she had to use her time more wisely, time that was slipping through her hands—like a lousy paycheck. But getting motivated after work into using up more energy—on more work—was easier said than done. However, she knew inside that *now* was time to wake up, instead of relaxing on her sofa being idle.

With that shot of reality, Chloe grabbed her laptop and opened up her website. Reluctantly, she typed in the web address for StacksOf-Style.com and entered the administration passcodes for full access to the back-end. The Web page slowly uploaded onto the screen… '*Ouch!*' Chloe winced; it looked much more basic than she had last remembered it, and out-of-date—compared to all of the other fashion blogs that had cropped up since. Every fashionista and style enthusiast had a blog these days, and they were very professional looking too. StacksOf-Style wasn't entirely living up to its name and had lost all recognition of the word style. It definitely needed a revamp and was screaming S.O.S itself!

The graphics were amateur, the articles were dated and no longer relevant—what did she expect—the blog fairies to update it for her? It had been months since she had last checked in, but here it was—her distraction. She began playing around with the layout, trying her best to remember how to use the control panel; it was much more complicated than she had thought.

"Maybe this isn't such a *great* idea after all!" she huffed with frustration.

Fearing she had opened up a can of worms, she glanced at her phone; it was getting late, and having made no significant progress on her blog, decided to crawl into bed. It was calling her; her eyelids felt heavy, and the reality of going to work the next day had started to creep in (a case of the 'school-night' blues, some would say). No matter how much she wanted to make a change in her life, she couldn't resist her tiredness; sleep was precious these days (she always regretted staying up late when she had to get up early for work). For now, her mission to take over the world would have to wait, one more night.

# CHAPTER SIX

Tuesday's at Palazzo was equally as slow as Monday's, and the warm summer weather had made the atmosphere hot and sticky—much like Dominic's sex life. Once again, he was updating Chloe with all the details of the night before; killing time on the shop floor in the process.

"It was so romantic! He took me to this art gallery, where he is showing—he had it closed just for us! He showed me his work which was just amazing; he is so talented, as well as hot! It made me want him even more… I couldn't wait to get back to the hotel and *fu*—"

Chloe clearly wasn't interested, judging by her lacklustre reaction; she looked troubled, and not wanting to brag about his good fortune, Dom changed the subject.

"What did you get up to last night?"

"Oh… The usual… I went home… Had dinner, then watched a movie," she said, lacking enthusiasm; feeling tired from not getting enough sleep (she knew she should have gone to bed earlier).

She felt as though she had only blinked, and then suddenly it was time to get up.

"You're wasting your youth girl! There are men out there to be had!"

"I know… But how can I possibly go out and meet a man when I'm not happy? Besides, I've got to focus… I'm nowhere near where I imagined I would be at my age… It's catching up on me… Don't you see what I mean?"

She knew Dom understood really, but he was in love and hardly saw the world through the same eyes as she did right now. At the same time, she didn't want to bring him down from his high. She could see that he was falling already; he always dived in with his heart when it came to men. She just hoped this wasn't going to go tits-up in the end.

Although California wasn't the other side of the World, Jason did live in another state entirely (a seven-hour flight to the West Coast, to be exact). Chloe thought about the logistics of a long distance relationship but gave up trying to work it out (she had her own problems to solve), and started cleaning a glass counter. Dom could tell she was in a funk about something; watching her furiously clean away (like she was on a caffeine high) told him something else was on her mind.

"So, how was your blog? Did you manage to get much done?" he said, trying to investigate without being blunt about it.

"Don't ask! I'm so out of touch with it all… It's hopeless… I don't know how these people do it! They probably spend thousands on it—which I can't afford—you either have to have money, or know the right people if you want to be successful these days."

"Well, Melinda did say… It's all about who you can network with here," he reminded her.

Just as she was about to open her mouth, Kim walked past and stole the moment. It was like a scene from a shampoo commercial; her hair was perfectly blow-dried into flicks, giving her an '*oomph*' of power as she walked past them. She was wearing her freshly picked uniform: black pants with a cream blouse, teamed with black high-heel pumps, and pearl earrings. She looked great; like the perfect Palazzo employee.

"Morning guys!" she beamed, it was terrific what promotion, and a pay rise could do.

"Wow, Kim… You look amazing! I really did style a great look for you!"

"All thanks to you Chloe!" she said, strutting past with long strides; not stopping to chat for much longer.

Chloe noticed she was carrying a black portfolio, it looked rather important—she clutched it close to her chest with pride. It was a file that Regina and Myra compiled together every season; it had every celebrity, model, and New York socialite's details—ready for them to contact should Myra choose to dress them. A Bible of who's-who in the celebrity and fashion world, although it was nothing more than just pure 'fluff'. The press office never dressed anyone current, or that deserved to be wearing the latest from Palazzo; they treated the press office as a walk-in wardrobe to dress their friends and connections (which were usually a bag of nobodies).

Thanks to Chloe, Myra had already entrusted Kim with the portfolio. She managed to style Kim so well that it shone an entirely different light on her; she wasn't some silly shop girl anymore. Now she had class and an air of importance, making Kim feel (and look) empowered. However, just like Regina, Myra feared competition and would go out of her way to make sure the junior staff never overshadowed her.

Myra was one of those people that looked important as well as acting like it; you could tell she was 'somebody' by the way she stomped around the store. She owned a collection of designer spectacles, and today she wore a pair that pointed up in the corners, in a feline style. Without them, her image was quite bland. Myra was a harsh woman (much like a clone of Regina), and that's precisely why Regina had appointed her as the Head of Press for North America.

Like herself, she knew Myra would never give up her position for anyone; thus keeping her in power, filling a permanent spot in the company that shop floor staff would never have the chance to apply for—but always aspire to. Even if they did manage to get anywhere close, they would surely be stopped from going any further. You see, just when Kim thought she had gotten away from the politics of the shop floor entirely; she had unknowingly gained a new set of rules to learn. Something Kim was going to have to get used to all over again—a new game to learn. The new uniform did Kim wonders (like with most things in Palazzo) it was all about image over substance, but she didn't fool Myra.

She knew Kim had substance; Regina would never have made her promote her otherwise. It took a particular type of person to swallow their pride, hide their personality, and understand the hierarchy of progression; but press office assistant was as good as it was going to get for Kim. Myra didn't really have any charm or personality herself;

she was one of those people that you could easily forget. Although, one quality stood out: she could make you feel inferior within seconds of being in her company; she really thought she was someone quite special. The shop floor staff nicknamed her 'The Troll'. Sylvia, her first assistant, was very close to her; she was her sidekick and relished in the fact she was higher up than a regular sales assistant.

They both nastily used this power, taking great satisfaction in talking down to a weak sales girl, giving her Hell to get something that was out of stock—urgently. When the shit hit the fan, they always managed to pass the blame on to someone else, and usually, it was their fault in the first place. The press archive was badly managed too, loaned clothes never saw the office again, and if they did, they were in desperate need of a good dry clean. Instead of making sure items were returned on time, Myra and Sylvia would much rather hassle sales staff to get new pieces altogether.

This, of course, affected the sales of the department as they ate away at their stock, and you could be sure that they would always need a best seller or a seasonal runway piece that was limited in production. The sales staff believed this was a conspiracy, arranged by Myra and Regina to cut their commission; making it harder for them to achieve the target. Of course, sales staff could never refuse the handing over of an item to press office. If they did, Regina would only overrule them anyway.

Kim had a lot to learn about her new team, but she was kept away by being ordered to manage the portfolio and update it for the season ahead. As this was her first task in her new role (and she was eager to please), Kim had re-arranged the folio in perfect order; she had it colour-coded and sorted in alphabetical order—noting the date when a client had worn Palazzo in the media. She had logged every look loaned, and the event that they had attended wearing it.

In doing so, Kim noticed that most high-profile names in the book very rarely wore a thing from Palazzo these days, and everyone that did so weren't very recognisable. Considering Palazzo was adored and desired by everyone, this discovery shocked her. After all, that was the job of the press office: to make sure the collections were publicised. And more than that, the growth of the brand and its image, were primarily in their hands. Mostly, celebrity press came from Gianni himself; he was well connected (and friends) with many stars: actresses, singers, and famous faces, that he would design one-off pieces for red carpet events. As for promoting the collections—that was Myra's job. Kim's effective organising skills had helped her get the portfolio ready to hand back to Myra pronto, along with a genius idea to shake up their approach—she was sure it would impress Myra on her first day.

*

Sylvia was busy staring into her computer screen, looking as though she were hard at work. As Kim entered, Sylvia quickly minimised her screen window; she could just about make out the web page Sylvia was browsing. Sylvia, on the other hand, had thought she had closed it down in time (she was, in fact, looking at designer shoes on her favourite website), but she was wrong; Kim had honed her hawk nose well from working on the shop floor—she didn't miss a thing.

Myra's office was separated from her assistant's desks with sound-proofed glass walls. It had a great view, one of the best in the entire building. You could watch her yell at staff members in pure silence, which was quite amusing as long as you weren't on the receiving end. Feeling confident and on top of things, Kim sat at her desk; checking her inbox. It felt great to finally have 'Palazzo dot com' after her name.

Nothing awaited her and Sylvia hadn't instructed her with anything else other than to sort the folio—which had been completed already. All she could do was to wait for the perfect opportunity to present the newly reformed portfolio to Myra, along with some ideas of her own. With Fashion Week not too far away, she was eager to leave a good impression in her first week.

"Erm, Sylvia... Is there anything else I can help with at all?" she said.

Sylvia looked up from her screen, annoyed at being disturbed; she had only just resumed shopping for shoes. Sylvia looked half surprised by her question, only half because it was quite hard for her to show any emotion from all the Botox in her face. It was rumoured that she gave her staff discount away to her dentist in exchange for free jabs on her lunch break.

"Shouldn't you be working on the portfolio?"

Sylvia didn't appreciate having a new colleague breathing down her back; she liked things as they were.

"Well, that's the thing... It's kinda finished already, so if there is anything else I can be getting on with..."

Sylvia slowly slinked out of her chair and walked over to Kim's desk. Strutting over, she enjoyed every stride in her new Palazzo fall/winter runway heels (which weren't yet available to buy in-store); no doubt she had 'borrowed' them from the sample library.

"This better be good... Myra will be relying on the folio now we are in new season," she said.

Kim was astonished by her remark. The folio was in bad condition when she had received it from Myra; if she relied on it so much, why wasn't it well kept in the first place? Unknown to Kim, Myra never had a use for the folio; she just gave her that task to keep her busy and off her back, not knowing that she would complete it in one morning.

"When I was sorting through it, I noticed some names we could dress that we haven't for some time, and they would surely get lots of attention and press coverage for us as they are so relevant right now!" Kim said, wanting to please Sylvia and show her she was going to be a good colleague.

Sylvia strained her taught face in an attempt to look even more surprised—it wasn't working.

"Is that so? Well, I'm sure Myra would appreciate your initiative... Actually, you should go into her office now and tell her... She will be finalising the list of people we are going to dress soon, we wouldn't want her to miss anybody important now... Would we?"

Kim paused and stared at her, not knowing whether she was sarcastic or serious.

"Hurry... She is meeting with Regina this afternoon!" Sylvia said, turning away to walk back to her desk, trying her best to stifle a bitchy chuckle.

She knew that it would be a big mistake to tell Myra how to do her job, but it would also entertain her and remind Myra that she was the better assistant. Kim picked up the folio, and with it clutched tightly to her chest, made her way over to the glass case of an office. Myra was on the phone, she seemed to be talking rather loudly with animated hand gestures, although the thick glass walls soaked up any sound. As Kim approached, Myra held up her hand, as if to say: "Wait!"

Kim paused outside the office, just moments away from rapping her fist on the door, but managed to halt just in the nick of time. Myra slammed down the phone and looked at Kim from over her dipped specs, signalling for her to enter. She didn't seem impressed at being disturbed; Kim's confidence turned to nerves in an instant. This was the first time she was addressing her new manager, presenting not only her first completed task but her ideas too.

"Yes?" Myra said sharply.

"Erm... I've finished organising the portfolio," Kim said, handing it over to Myra.

"Oh... Have you now?" Myra said, extending an arm in one sharp movement to snatch it without even looking at her.

She expected to see some half-hearted, rushed job; something that resembled a High School project, but Myra was wrong. Every page was up to date, had a photograph of the client, and all their contact details were correct and current—including their agent or stylist's information. Flicking through the pages and seeing how well presented it was rather annoying. Never had she seen it so... *Professional* looking. Kim was definitely one to watch, and Myra wondered how she had completed it so quickly. Used to lazy bimbo's like Sylvia, she was sure it would have kept her busy for the rest of the week, at least.

"Well, it appears you have successfully completed it already… *Thanks,*" she said sarcastically—now she would have to come up with something else to distract her. She looked up at Kim and gave a half smile. Once again, only half as she too was on the Botox. "Yes, well done… This will be very *useful.*"

Myra waved the folio at her, signalling that it was now time for her to leave, although Kim didn't get the hint. She was delighted with receiving a compliment and saw this as the perfect opportunity to pitch her ideas, just as Sylvia had suggested.

"Actually, I have noticed many popular celebs and personalities haven't worn our designs for some time now… So, at the back is a list of people that we could send out looks to… Especially as we will need to prepare for Fashion Week soon… I'm sure it would help boost sales if we got a few current faces to wear our new collection… The list contains the names of people who are high profile and on the radar at the moment, as well as their agent."

Astonished at her strong pitch, Myra took off her glasses to view Kim with her very own eyes.

'She really is one to watch,' she thought to herself, not used to bold new employees with bright ideas. Myra had to force herself to crack a smile, not wanting to form a new wrinkle.

"*Great!* I'll be sure to take a look… In the meantime, why don't you help the interns hang the new collection in the sample room. Ten boxes just arrived from Milan…"

Helping the interns hang the new collection was more of a punishment than a perk. She had expected to be organising outfits to be sent out to the rich and famous, or liaising with magazines for photo-shoots and articles. Not colour coding and categorising clobber in a sweaty room with a bunch of fashion students on work experience. Leaving the office, Kim walked past Sylvia's desk to make her way to the sample room.

"How did it go?" Sylvia said. She didn't need to ask, of course, already knowing the outcome before it had happened.

"Yep... Good... I'm just going to help the interns hang the new collection... I'll be there if you need me."

Sylvia couldn't help but laugh out loud; she too was one of those girls who loved the power that came with her title and knew exactly how to make sure Kim would remain beneath her. It was all too easy for her and Kim was so willing; she fell for her bitchy prank. After lunch, Myra had ordered Sylvia to make sure Kim was busy for the rest of the week—shredding.

That was Kim's task for the remainder of the week, destroying sensitive documents and correspondence from Palazzo to external contacts, magazines, agents, and partners that were no longer needed. There were boxes and boxes of the stuff, some dating back as far as eight years ago—a never-ending pit of papyrus.

So far, it hadn't exactly lived up to the glamorous job that Kim had imagined it would be; she understood that she would have to start at the bottom rung of the ladder all over again, but this was elementary. Shredding her way into oblivion—zoning out to the monotonous sound of the shredder—Kim started to question her future in fashion entirely, wondering if the press office had been the right move.

**

The shop floor had become a much better place without Kim policing it. Already without a manager, the womenswear team were now a sales associate down as well; Chloe and her colleagues were rushed off their feet. It was always busy during lunchtime, but it seemed more so now that they were even more short staffed. Chloe had been serving a client for the past hour, which had been worthwhile; Kim's departure also meant there was more money to be had from the clients she left behind, which Chloe was happy to snap up and add to her commission.

Just as she was catching her breath, Karen Saunders stepped out of the lift and walked through the womenswear floor. Looking around the department, she saw Chloe and waved. Without a moments rest, Chloe greeted her with an air kiss on either side of her face.

"Hi, honey… Mwah-mwah! How are you? You look busy," Karen said, noticing her slightly pink face as she placed her handbag down on the counter (of course, it was a Palazzo).

"Yeah, it's been hectic today, and one of my colleagues has moved up to the press office—so we are a bit short, to say the least… Anyway, how about you?"

"Oh, work is busy too, so today I'm treating myself to some retail therapy."

"Of course… In fact, I have the perfect dress on hold for you from the new collection… I'll go and get, grab a changing room…"

Chloe left to grab the dress she had parked on her hold rail; she was pro-active when it came to Karen—she was a spender! She loved to serve Karen, she stopped by frequently and never wasted her time. Being a businesswoman, time was crucial to her, and she only came to Palazzo for one thing: to shop! Karen considered Chloe to be her personal stylist; she trusted her opinion when it came to her image, it was vital for her to look good for business, as well as in her private life.

Zipping Karen into a burgundy silk dress from the latest pre-fall collection, Chloe presented a pair of gold shoes that were accented with lace. She knew Karen wouldn't be able to resist them; helping the sale stretch that little bit further. The dress had a draped corset style top and a beautiful skirt with knee length that was very flattering on a slim figure. Standing back from the mirrors, Chloe gave Karen a few moments to take in her reflection.

"Sold! You always manage to suggest a great look every time. You're wasted here you know?"

"Thanks," Chloe said modestly. "I applied for the press office job too, but it didn't work out in my favour…"

"That's because you're too good at your job… I'm sure they can't afford to lose you from the shop floor," Karen said. Even she knew this to be true. "So, what's next for you?" She turned her back, lifting up her hair—prompting Chloe to unzip her.

Pulling down the zip and guiding her back into the changing room, Chloe answered from behind the closed door.

"Oh, I'm not entirely sure… I think I might start to look outside the company for vacancies… It's always good to see what's out there, ya know?"

Karen swung the door open sharply, not quite fully dressed.

"What! If you leave, who will help me? I'll just shop online I guess?"

Karen had flicked a switch in Chloe's head—she was the Queen of the Internet. Finally, Melinda's advice was registering; now she truly understood what she had meant by using clients as contacts, and what a great idea it was. Remembering last night's frustration over her blog, Chloe realised that Karen was the best person to help her. Her online same-day cash loan company had hit the big time; it was estimated in The Financial Magazine's 'Rich List' that she had turned over $50,000,000 in the past year alone. Surely she would know a thing or two about simple blog layouts?

Chloe had built a connection over the years, and although Chloe felt embarrassed, she just had to her ask her for advice; this opportunity was too good to miss. Either way Chloe had nothing to lose and every-thing to gain. Seizing the moment (before the subject changed), Chloe took her chance.

"Actually, I was wondering if you might be able to advise me on something?" Hearing herself say the words, Chloe couldn't believe that she was actually going to ask her for a favour.

This was the first time she had asked a client for something, and it felt wrong; she was the one who provided service, not the other way around. But it was almost as if she had no control over her mouth, which was good—otherwise she might not have plucked up the cour-age. Karen started to dress back into her clothes with the changing room door open ajar so they could talk. She felt comfortable in Chloe's company, plus she was proud of her newly implanted breasts and didn't mind giving other females a glimpse.

"Of course darling, God knows how many favours you have done me over the years, transferring this and holding that… What's the problem?"

"Well, this is the thing… I started a blog a few years ago, but I just got out of touch with it all… You know how busy life gets, what with work and everything else. Recently I thought I'd try writing about fashion again… Last night I looked at my blog, and it's just a mess! I don't know where to start or how to get that professional edge… Do you know what I mean?" Chloe said, trying not to sound too blatant about where she was going with this.

"Of course darling… You have asked the right woman… Why don't I get my web designer to look at it for you?"

"Really? That would be great! Of course, I'd pay you."

Karen's face looked even more aghast than Chloe's at the suggestion of payment.

"Absolutely not! I don't want your money… If it's one thing I do have, it's money, and I'll be delighted to help you out… It will cost me nothing but time to get my team on the case for you. I can see you have talent and you have given me excellent service for the past three years or so… That's priceless to a woman like me. You should be a freelance stylist you know? A website is just the thing you need… Leave it with me."

'A freelance stylist?' Chloe thought to herself. This could be a step in the right direction, but for now, she needed to concentrate on getting StacksOfStyle back on the net. Chloe couldn't believe how easy it had been. Not only had she made a $2,000 sale, but she had also just bagged a free website.

"Well, look… If there is anything else I can do," Chloe offered.

Karen closed in nearer to her, looking around to make sure they were alone.

"Actually, there is something—but say no if you can't do it... I'd totally understand if you didn't want to..."

Chloe grew suspicious of what she was about to ask; wondering why was she speaking so quietly. Now it was Karen's turn to call in a favour.

"I just saw that runway clutch downstairs... You know the one with the gold lace and gorgeous beadwork?"

The Gold Rush clutch bag was a small-sized evening clutch; it was the bag of the season, sought after by many clients due to its limited production. It was luxuriously golden and accented with 18-karat dipped lace and beads. Inside was lined with butter soft gold lambskin leather with a detachable gold chain—so you could wear it both ways; as a shoulder or clutch bag.

"Well, anyway... I refuse to pay $5,000 for it, and I'll doubt it will stay around long enough to go into the sale... So, if you could get some kind of staff discount on it... Then we'll call it even... How about that? I'm sure you guys get a good discount?"

Chloe thought it over in her mind for a second, it was risky, but she didn't want to turn down this great opportunity; would she even would be able to purchase such a high demand item with her staff discount in the first place? Not only that but if she was caught, she could be fired for gross misconduct; staff discount was strictly for personal use, certainly not for personal gain or client favours—and how would she buy it without every nosey colleague noticing?

It was a standard procedure that a member of management authorised staff purchases, and as they hadn't had one for some time, Kim had brought it upon herself to oversee that responsibility. But with her also gone, who else would do that for Chloe without snitching on her? She decided she would worry about the logistics after Karen had left, and grabbed her chance with both hands.

"Okay, sure... But you understand that you can't return it right? I'd get into serious trouble if anyone found out..."

"Oh, of course! Don't worry… You have known me for years. I don't let anyone else serve me here, and you know I never return darling! So, I'll speak to my web developer this afternoon… Just let me know when you're free to drop by my office… You have my number…"

"Great, well… I'm not working this Thursday."

"Well, tomorrow the office is closed for Independence Day, and I've given my staff Thursday morning off… They'll only be late to come in anyway! Come by around lunchtime, and of course, I'll pay you for the bag… Just let me know how much it will be with your discount."

"Excellent—I'll see you on Thursday then."

"I'll look forward to it… I best be getting off… Ring up the dress… Uh!… I'll take the shoes too… Why not? I can wear them with that wonderful gold clutch when it's mine!"

Resurfacing from the changing rooms, as if no secret talks had taken place, Chloe took Karen to the till. She had Dom pack and wrap to save her time, as Karen was in a rush to get back to work. As Chloe put through the payment, her heart sank a little. She couldn't help but feel deceitful; the sense that she was doing wrong had crept in—but she couldn't help feeling optimistic about it at the same time.

As she finalised the bill Dom came out of the packing room carrying Karen's purchase perfectly wrapped, complete with ribbons. Dominic loved it; he was such a label whore and all about the packaging. He handed the bags over to Karen with pride.

"Great to see you once again, thanks for visiting," Chloe rattled off, trying to end their secret deal as professionally and casual as she could.

"Oh… One more thing," Karen said before she rushed off. "Don't mind my asking, but are you single right now?"

"Err, yes… I am," Chloe said, confused by Karen's 'out of nowhere' question.

"Perfect… I'll see you on Thursday."

Dom was waiting for Karen to leave; he could sense that something was going on, Chloe was too formal with a client she knew well—it all seemed rather odd.

"Well done babe... So, she bought the dress in the end after all that time on the hold rail! Mind you, she never disappoints," he said, hoping to start a conversation and find out what was *really* going on.

She didn't answer him; her mind was somewhere else right now, but he knew when she was on another planet—this was one of those moments.

"Err... Hello? Earth to space station Chloe!" he said, popping his head in her face.

Chloe roused from her daze, brushing off Karen's ambush about her being single as well as worrying about the bargain she had just made with her.

"Sorry... I was just thinking about something—"

"Yeah duh! Like I didn't notice... You think I don't know when you're acting all funny? Purrrlease!"

It was Chloe who rolled her eyes this time; Dom never missed a thing. If she thought she could get away with not telling him, then she was mistaken. Now they had cleared the floor of customers, it was a good time to spill. She stepped away from the cash desk to a secluded area on the shop floor; Dom followed her over to the knitwear table, grabbing some already folded sweaters and messed them up—making work for them to appear busy with.

Now they had a disguise should their juicy conversation be interrupted. Dom loved their little work dealings, it made the day go by much faster, and Chloe very much needed his advice.

"Right, okay... So last night—while you were having your wicked way with Jason—I decided to check out StacksOfStyle."

"Yeah, you said... Don't give up on it babe... Just spend some time on it, and you will work it out."

"Well, I might not have to now... When I logged on last night, I realised how much of a job I have on my hands... It looked so *un-stylish!* Anyway, I need to start the site back up because then I could use it to advertise my services as a freelance stylist or something... Ya know, get my name out there... But that's not the news... I was telling Karen about the whole press office thing, and then it dawned on me… She is the Internet Queen! So I thought I'd ask her for a favour…"

"What kind of favour?" Dom said, so far, it was first-class gossip.

"Well, ya know how she has made a fortune online? I thought she must know a thing or two about websites and stuff… So I asked her if she could help me out with mine."

Dom's face lit up as if to say: ``You clever bitch!' He already knew where this was going…

"Of course, she said yes and offered me time with her web developer to help me fix it!" she said, grabbing his arms to shake him with excitement; she couldn't contain it any longer.

"That's amazing! See, all it takes is one little chance meeting to turn things around!" He was impressed with her smart thinking; he knew paying Melinda a visit would prove valuable in the end.

"Yes, but that's not all… in return, she wants me to get her the Gold Rush clutch on staff discount… I mean, what am I going to do?"

"As in the runway bag which has just been delivered?" Dom said, finally seeing the conundrum.

"Yes, exactly… What am I gonna do?" she said, starting to freak out.

Dom mulled it over for a few minutes as they carried on folding in silence; he could see why she was apprehensive, but it wasn't like their colleagues never put through staff purchases on the sly—this was just another one—they just couldn't get caught.

"I'll put it through for you… In fact, I have one on hold for a client—but I don't think she is taking it anymore… No one will check anyway, they only care when we aren't making money!"

"No—we can't do that! I don't wanna get you in trouble…"

She wouldn't have dreamt of asking Dom to do such a thing, he would be putting his neck on the line if anyone found out. He was a true friend and always supported her, but this was a favour too big to ask. Dom, however, saw it as a minor issue, after all, they had no manager and no Kim to spy on them; now was the perfect time to get away with murder.

"Babe, no one will find out… I mean, you did tell her she can't return it… Right?"

"Yeah, of course, I did," Chloe said.

"Right then, that's that… Did you tell her we get fifty percent?"

"No, I wasn't thinking about the particulars!"

"Well, clients don't know how much discount we get… So, tell her we get forty and pocket the ten for yourself."

Dom winked at her; he could always smell the opportunity to make extra money to top up his own shopping money wherever he could. Chloe already felt bad for using her clients to network for her own good, not to mention guilty for misusing her staff discount; to then make money on top made her feel even worse. Dom saw by the unsure look on her face that she was still worrying about it all. If anyone was going to give the game away, it was her!

"Look, it's like Melinda said… We have to be clever and use our contacts to better ourselves to get out of this place… I mean, do you really think that no one else does this? Of course, they do! They just don't shout about it… or let guilt stand in the way."

Feeling a sudden gust of confidence, Chloe couldn't help but agree; she knew Dom was right, it would cost her hundreds, if not thousands of dollars to get a professional even take a look at her website. All Karen wanted, was a little bit of discount, how bad could that be?

"You're right! My lips are sealed, this is our secret… But only if you're sure?"

Dom waved his hand at her; enough with all this second-guessing.

"When do you need to buy it?" he said, encouraging her to forget and just get on with it.

"Well, we scheduled on Thursday, as it's my day off… So I'll need to buy it by tomorrow I guess?"

Dom pursed his lips and cocked his head, talk about giving notice.

"Okay, tomorrow it is then… The morning will probably be best, while it's quiet… I'll get the bag from the stock room; make sure you have your card on you, ready to pay and get it over with quickly… See, things will start to look up from here… Just you wait and see… By the end of the week, you'll have a kick-ass website!" Dom said, folding the last sweater perfectly, placing it on the pile they had worked through; before putting the freshly folded stack back on display.

"So, tell me… What is it you're doing tonight with Jason?" Chloe asked, she wasn't in the mood to listen to him earlier; now she had a stroke of good fortune, she was willing to listen to him gush about Jason—in exchange for the massive he was doing her.

"Last night was romantic and everything, but the week is going so fast! He leaves for L.A on Friday morning, so we are going to spend some quality time together in the hotel room… Last night, we couldn't keep our hands off each other!"

He was pleased she was finally taking an interest and told her everything that happened the previous night—in great detail. Deep down, he knew that his future with Jason was uncertain and figured that by telling Chloe everything as it happened, it would be better than trawling back through it all—should he need a shoulder to cry on. That way, she would know exactly how to deal with the situation, whatever the outcome. Chloe was his best friend, and he would have told her everything eventually; besides, he was too excited to keep it all to himself.

Another influx of customers filled the store, giving them little time to gossip further—which was a good thing. Chloe probably would have felt differently about the arrangement if she had time to overthink it; even though she knew it was wrong, the outcome of going through with it felt so right. Electronic beats pounded through the store as it became bustling again; clients arrived like buses, you would wait around all day for one to come along, and then suddenly—they would all turn up at once!

# CHAPTER SEVEN

**M**rs Ruthenstock was an excellent client (she had been for many years) and was loyal to Chloe's services—she would always bring her a small gift when she came to store. Usually, it was a little box of chocolate truffles or macaroons from the New York patisserie; at Christmas, Chloe would always receive a bottle of champagne from her. Mrs Ruthenstock was in her late fifties, and very well to do; she was always very neatly dressed, well-spoken, and smelt of fresh floral perfume.

Chloe did everything she could do for her, as she could be relied upon for regular expenditure. Clients who made a fuss, argued with staff and were rude, seemed to get everything from the company—from complimentary perfume to refunds—even though the store policy was to only exchange; kind, friendly customers got nothing (except for the excellent service of course, and maybe the odd sale preview discount).

Chloe believed Mrs Ruthenstock deserved the best; she made sure that she was invited to every event, and put pieces aside for her—like she did for Karen. The only difference being that Mrs Ruthenstock would take the expensive pieces made from fur, cashmere, and exotic skins. Having already made a good sale from Karen (and from the rush of clients), Chloe was equally as pleased to see her step out of the elevator. 'Gosh, commission is going to be good this month!' Chloe thought to herself as she went over to greet her.

"Hello, Mrs Ruthenstock… How wonderful to see you!"

"And you Chloe… You look as gorgeous, young, and fresh as ever," Mr Ruthenstock said, walking straight over to the rails to browse through them.

'Gosh, I've been rushing around sweating; I must look like a tramp!' Chloe thought but took the compliment all the same.

"I just thought I'd pop in to see you… Have a look at the new collection."

The fall/winter collection had been delivered in-store already; the fashion calendar ran early to maximise selling time. The summer sale had just finished, they had been ransacked by bargain hunters; there wasn't much left over, and all that was would be packed up and sent to the outlet in New Jersey. The sale period saw a certain kind of customer at Palazzo; it was usually the kind that kicked off, should they not get their own way. They would expect the first-class service, at half the price!

Regular clients would wait until the mayhem of the sale had finished, coming back to shop the new season, and now was that time—when regular clients like Mrs Ruthenstock returned to do some serious shopping. The shop floor was transitioning from summer to autumn; darker colours were being introduced slowly, yellows became oranges, and reds became burgundy—which was the colour of the season. Knitwear in alpaca, pure cashmere, and virgin wools was displayed—instead of ones mixed with silk and cotton for a lighter handle.

A few runway pieces had already been delivered also (the Gold Rush bag that Karen wanted was one of them). Sale shoppers never understood why the fall collection was available while it was still hot outside. They were classed as 'Time Wasters' by the shop floor staff; it was boring having to explain the rules of fashion to someone who *clearly* knew nothing about style in the first place.

They didn't know the behind the scenes logistics, such as designing an entire collection—a whole year ahead—choosing only the best silhouettes, fabrics, and skins. Then, showcasing it at Fashion Week for the press and buyers, before the wholesale team could painstakingly edit runway looks for retail—only then could patterns be sent off to suppliers for production. Samples then got sent to the showrooms for buyers to select for their stores all around the world, and *this* process was why investing in Palazzo was indeed a luxury.

The most loyal shoppers never questioned prices or delivery times; regular clients understood that if they wanted something, that they had to get in early. Pieces were limited and stores sometimes only received one unit in every size—making Palazzo ready-to-wear even more exclusive. This was why customers like Mrs Ruthenstock came right at the start of the season: to make sure they didn't miss out on the very best pieces.

"So, I've had a peek at the catalogue you sent me, and I've marked the items I am interested in," Mrs Ruthenstock said.

Chloe always sent her the lookbook as early as possible, as she was such a big spender.

"Sure, let's take a seat and get comfy… I'll call the butler to fetch us some tea."

Chloe walked her over to a calm and quiet sofa area, next to a gold coffee table which had a beautiful arrangement of fresh flowers on top. Taking Mrs Ruthenstock's jacket, she noticed that it was vintage Palazzo, and very 'in fashion' right now (even though it was from a past collection); it was timeless and chic. Chloe had a sudden brainwave, 'Maybe that's what my first blog article could be about when I relaunch it? Timeless, vintage fashion that you can wear, and wear again?'

Mrs Ruthenstock always had lovely clothes on and kept them in the best condition (her maid dry-cleaned and pressed her wardrobe without her even noticing). She sat down and placed her handbag on the sofa, as Chloe placed her jacket neatly on the backrest of a nearby chair. Chloe was about to call the butler to order tea, but Dom was already on the case (he had caught Chloe's eye from across the floor and gave her a nod to say: 'I got it'). Chloe gave him the thumbs up to say thanks and returned to her client.

"It's so nice to see you… I was wondering when you would visit next, but I didn't want to bother you…"

"Oh, never… I rely on you to get me all the best pieces… Which is why I am here."

The lookbook was a catalogue that featured every exit from the fashion show that had made it past production; from start to finish. Opening it, she leant in closer to show Chloe the wish list she had made.

"So, these are the pieces I would like… First, the coat in look two—it's my favourite so far," she said, pointing to the image.

"Perfect! We have just received it," Chloe confirmed.

"Excellent, so moving on to the dress and the shoes in look three… Does it come in other colours?"

"Just this colour and in black, but I like the burgundy for you—it will set your skin tone off perfectly… Plus it's selling fast."

It was definitely going to be one of the key pieces of the season and looked set to sell-out judging by interest. Of course, Mrs Ruthenstock needed not to worry; Chloe had her size on hold already because her size was very popular. People would assume that the smaller, stick thin sizes were what Palazzo was best known for making—of course, the runway models wore sample sizes, but clients wore *real* sizes. The larger end of the size table was where the money was at; especially with clients like Mrs Ruthenstock, who were in their more 'mature' years so to speak.

"Okay, well that sounds like a 'must'… I'll take both the dress and shoes… Look four is not really me—"

"Oh, I thought that the tweed jacket might go nicely with all the blouses you have, so I set that aside for you too… It's very wearable… Casually on a lunch date, or with a pair of pants to make it a suit… You could even accessorise it with some pearls, or a jewelled pin." Chloe's stylist instincts were kicking in once again.

"All right, well you know best… I'll give it a try." Mrs Ruthenstock always valued Chloe's opinion, she probably knew the contents of her wardrobe better than she did—since she was the one who had sold them to her.

The in-store butler had arrived with refreshments on a gold tray was an elegant teapot, which had the italic 'P,' logo around the base, a small milk jug of the same design, and a matching sugar bowl. Everything in Palazzo had been specially designed, right down to the very last detail; the teacups were stylish and modern—made of white china with an italic '*P*,' moulded as the handle—with painted edges in gold. He poured the tea as Mrs Ruthenstock continued with the list of items she wanted.

Laying down a small selection of chocolates on the coffee table, he caught Chloe's eye and gave her a cheeky wink before leaving. The butlers were notorious for being outrageously flirty with the girls, but their charm didn't work on Chloe—she had seen too many naive girls fall for it all before. Ignoring him, she carried on browsing the catalogue with her client, pointing out designs that were yet to arrive—promising that she would set them aside and call her when they eventually did.

"So… I think that's all for now, but if there is anything else you think I have missed, please show me."

"No, I think you've done pretty well—but I will show you the jacket I mentioned… It's still quite early into the collection anyway, so we have much more to come."

"Fabulous! I know I can rely on you to look after me… I also want some classic blouses, say two white and two black; just to refresh my wardrobe."

"Of course… I'll leave you to enjoy your tea; feel free to browse the rails while I fetch it all for you."

After taking a quick sip of her hot tea, Chloe left Mrs Ruthenstock to gather the items; she was going to need a rail, and some help wouldn't go amiss. As she walked towards the stockroom, Dom followed her.

"So, I take it you need a hand?" he said, having overheard the extensive list of pieces Mrs Ruthenstock had rattled off.

"Please! I have lots to get for her."

The womenswear stockroom was very tidy and sterile, laboratory-like even; it had storage vaults for endless boxes of shoes, and the clothing was hung up on rails—all divided into their garment categories. To an outsider it would look confusing and daunting; everything was so well organised you wouldn't want to touch a thing. The stockroom was just as intimidating as the museum-like displays of the shop floor. Chloe and Dom knew exactly where everything was, and weren't afraid to whizz round collecting the required pieces as fast as possible—and without making a mess too. Years of experience and organising it themselves each season made them stock finding experts.

"Okay, find a rail… I'll get the clothing… Get me the burgundy shoes with the gold heel in size thirty-eight—also the black riding boots with the block heel… And bring those black courts with the short kitten heel."

Chloe flew around the stock room in record timing, as if it were an Olympic event; most of it was safe on her hold rail already—so it wasn't too much trouble. Each team member had a section for themselves to put things on hold for their clients; Chloe and Dom's were the most packed by far. Kim did have a lot on hers too, but now she had left, they had overtaken that space—and called dibs on the stock she had saved also. Grabbing the clothes she had on her rail section in one big swoop, Chloe moved quickly over to the gold roller rail Dom had fetched. It was the quickest way possible to transport it all in one go; Dom helped her to twist and hook the hangers on the rail properly.

"Do you think she is going to take the lot?"

Chloe raised one eyebrow at him—what a stupid question. "Of course she will… Whenever hasn't she? Did you get the shoes?"

"Yep… You bring the rail out—I'll carry the shoes for you."

"Okay—brill… Let's go," Chloe said, not wanting to keep her waiting any longer.

They weren't gone for long—record timing indeed; Mrs Ruthenstock had finished her cup of tea and even ate one of the chocolates from the tray as she waited for them to return. She wasn't disappointed when she saw Chloe emerge with the rail jam-packed full of clothes—with Dom in tow—carrying three shoe boxes of different sizes.

"Hello Dom, how are you?" Mrs Ruthenstock politely asked; he was always on hand to help and often assisted her when Chloe was away.

"Very well thank you, and even better for seeing you Mrs Ruthenstock," Dom said, putting on his poshest, most English sounding voice—which he knew she loved. "Let me know if I can get you anything else, Chloe…"

He placed the boxes down by the sofa before taking his cue to leave, but staying close by should Chloe need him to pack up. Shifting the rail over to the sofa—as close as she could—Mrs Ruthenstock stood up to browse through the rail, flicking through the garments rather quickly. It was obvious she was pleased with what she saw by the look on her face; it was funny what the thrill of shopping did to a woman—no matter what age she was.

"Oh—this is the jacket I suggested… See how beautifully detailed it is? The picture in the lookbook doesn't pick up on the fabric. Since you love the one you're wearing today, I'm sure you will get lots of wear out of this one too…"

"Yes, once again you're right… It's adorable, and *very* useful… I could even wear it over this dress, or with pants… I think I'll take it."

Chloe turned to the shoe boxes Dom had kindly helped her with and lifted the lids on all three, taking out the right foot of each style for her to see.

"I thought I'd show you these too… A classic style, sensible height, and lovely gold lace detailing on the heel—which is one of this season's motifs," Chloe said, presenting a black kitten-heeled court shoe.

Taking hold of the shoe, Mrs Ruthenstock inspected it; once again she was satisfied. Chloe really did understand her style, and this was why she was a loyal customer; she never tried anything on in-store, and very rarely returned things. Chloe knew exactly what size she was; on the odd occasion where an item came up a little bit big or small, Chloe would organise for her driver to bring it back and deliver the correct size (a service that helped Mrs Ruthenstock not waste any of her valuable time).

It was an arrangement they had between each other; a personalised service that she could only get from Chloe. Any other staff member would just be confused and baffled by the idea because it meant putting yourself out there—going the extra mile. Chloe would often make arrangements that made life easier for her clients (even if it meant making hers harder), something that was unrecognised by Regina. All that mattered to her were the end sales figures, and Chloe was undoubtedly pulling them in.

"Okay—very well… I'll take all of these too… If anything's not suitable, I'll call you to let you know… Can you send a driver to deliver to my house today? I'm meeting the Country Club ladies for tea this afternoon, but Sunita will be at home of course."

"Not a problem… I'll have them delivered to your residence within the next hour or so."

Chloe caught Dom's attention from across the floor—a signal for him to help ring up the bill in the packing room. As he did, Chloe picked up Mrs Ruthenstock's jacket to hand it to her. It was a beautiful blend of wool bouclé yarns and silk; mainly pastel blue with white, pink, yellow, and a contrasting heavy black thread running through to make up an intricate tweed pattern. As Chloe helped her to put it on, she noticed how luxurious it felt to touch, and was in excellent condition despite its age.

"This jacket is absolutely lovely on you, and it's perfect for summer," Chloe said.

"Oh, yes—I almost forgot I had this old thing."

Mrs Ruthenstock never needed new clothes; she probably had a wardrobe full of clothes—never worn, still with the tags intact. 'How could she forget she had this jacket? It's glorious!' Chloe thought, sad to hand it over. However, if it were hers, it would be tattered by now—worn to death. But not Mrs Ruthenstock; she had the luxury of rotating clothes, so they never got tatty—and that was just the clothes she owned from Palazzo. How many other boutiques did she shop en masse from, and not worn yet? Still—she kept on shopping.

"If I owned this jacket, I'd have worn it out by now!" Chloe joked, yet telling the truth.

"It is very nice, but sometimes I buy things and don't wear them until years later... In fact, I was going to throw this one out."

Chloe couldn't believe what she was hearing. She would never dream of throwing such a beautiful item away—no matter howled it was. And where exactly would these discarded pieces end up... The garbage? Chloe imagined a charity store somewhere, selling all of Mrs Ruthenstock's cast-offs; a treasure trove full of fashionable gems, unbeknown to the shopkeeper.

"Sometimes, I just give things to my house maid to clear... And she is all too happy to take them off my hands... It really does me a huge favour."

'I bet she does!' Chloe said to herself; it would be an honour to take her old clothes off her hands. She imagined *fucking* Sunita, walking around Brooklyn somewhere; head to toe in designer clobber; not genuinely appreciating their value, or—*gasp*—styling them inappropriately.

Snapping out of her daydream, Chloe led Mrs Ruthenstock to the cash desk. Dom had resurfaced from the packing room with the bill, concealed in a leather folder that was stamped all over with the brand logo. Offering it to Mrs Ruthenstock, she handed him her credit card (a black American Express); not even looking at the total.

"Thank you very much, Dominic... I am arranging a car to deliver the bags this afternoon so I will help you pack in a moment," Chloe said, she wanted to make sure he didn't do all the hard work; that way they could spend time off the shop floor with a purpose.

"A stunning jacket you have there Mrs Ruthenstock," Dom noticed as he took her card.

"Wow! So many compliments from this one jacket... Lucky I rescued it from the garbage pile just yesterday."

"You are serious... You actually throw away your clothes?" Chloe shook her head; she had to double check that she wasn't playing with her.

"Yes, indeed... I edit my wardrobe every now-and-then—make space for the new season—and I end up with a whole heap of things I need to throw out… Sunita and I just went through it all yesterday so I could come shopping today; I can't possibly keep everything… It's a shame we are not the same size… Well—it's not a shame because you have a lovely figure; otherwise, you could have them…"

Chloe felt as though she was about to pass out; her vision and hearing whited out—completely astonished by what she had heard. It was so flippantly said, that she wasn't entirely sure she had heard correctly.

"Sorry—what?" she said, letting her manners slip for a second.

Mrs Ruthenstock laughed.

"You wouldn't want my old threads—"

"I absolutely would! Please don't throw them away; I'd love to see what pieces you have… In fact, I am reviving my fashion blog and looking for new pieces to write about… Your jacket has inspired me to write about vintage fashion; I'm sure I will find inspiration in whatever else you have… Your taste is impeccable!"

"In that case, I'll have them boxed up; my driver will deliver them to your place… Anything you don't like, please send to the church fund for me," she said casually; as if handing over thousands of dollars worth of clothes was no big deal.

Thinking of all the years, the church had been receiving Mrs Ruthenstock's designer donations had stunned Chloe. Surely the church wouldn't appreciate such masterpieces of fashion? They belonged in the Metropolitan Museum—not a rag sale.

"Of course I will!" Chloe said, grabbing the offer with both hands. "Thank you so much—I'll make a donation to them from my own wardrobe to make up for their loss."

"Okay, that's that then… Just write down your address so I can send my driver over…"

Chloe whipped out a business card from her uniform jacket, and scribbled her address and phone number on the back; trying her best to write as clearly as possible—but the excitement was making it quite an effort. Dom had appeared with the signature slip for Mrs Ruthenstock to sign (again, she didn't bother to look at the amount), which she signed—like she had done so many times before; spending had become a habit to her.

"I'm not working on Thursday—if that's not too much trouble?" Chloe's day off looked set to be *very* productive indeed.

"Excellent… I'll have them sent over first thing Thursday morning."

Chloe winced slightly as Mrs Ruthenstock looked at her Williamsburg address on the back of her card (it indeed wasn't the usual Park Lane addresses she was used to). Always a lady, Mrs Ruthenstock promised to keep her word and placed the business card in her purse; she was happy that they were going to a deserving home, and that they would creatively inspire Chloe in some way. Dom handed back her black Amex, along with a small gold envelope containing the store receipt.

"Thank you once again… I will see you all again soon no doubt," Mr.s Ruthenstock said, now ready to leave for her coffee meeting.

"My pleasure… Thank you so much for the clothes too," Chloe said, completely thrilled; waiting for her to leave so she could pinch herself.

Never one to miss a trick, Dom instantly picked up on the fact Chloe was thanking *her* for the clothes, and not the other way around. Chloe walked her over to the lift and pressed the button to call it up to the floor.

"You're very welcome, they will need plenty of altering of course…"

The elevator bell rang and the gold doors parted, Chloe held her arm out to keep the doors open while Mrs Ruthenstock stepped inside.

"Oh that's not a problem I can assure you," Chloe said, reaching inside to press the ground floor button, before quickly stepping away from the closing doors. "Thanks once again… Call me if there is anything else you need." Releasing a deep breath, Chloe couldn't believe what a whirlwind today had been.

"Well done babe—another great sale!" Dom said.

That was the least of her achievements; so far she had negotiated a new website, and now a new wardrobe of clothes! This networking thing was really starting to pay off, and it was becoming more and more natural as she began to seize opportunities that came her way. Why she had never thought of this before, she didn't know; they were right underneath her nose all along. It made coming into work worth so much more—not just to get paid the basic salary—not to mention the commission she would get from achieving her sales target in one day. Realising that she didn't know how much Mrs Ruthenstock had just spent; Chloe quizzed Dom for a breakdown.

Dom gave it a moment's thought.

"There's seven ready-to-wear pieces—three of them were fashion show collection—and three pairs of shoes… Coming to a grand total of $10,000. You will be the top seller again this month at this rate."

Chloe was taken back by how much she had sold; together with Karen's sale, Chloe had made over $12,000. She felt a rush run through her; making money was addictive, and not only had she made the company a profit—but she had come away with an added bonus. Excited and very pleased with herself, she couldn't wait to tell Dom what she had just managed to bag.

"Never mind top seller Dom—I've just scored a *fuck-load* of design-er clothes!"

Chloe was voice was a notch higher with excitement, but she tried her best to keep it low so none of her colleagues would overhear—and snitch—they were already intrigued to find out what she had sold. Chloe led Dom to the packing room, where they could talk more privately; Dom understood that there was gossip to be had, and followed her to discuss it further (and prepare Mrs Ruthenstock's shopping for delivery).

"So, what's happened now?" he asked.

"Well… I had been admiring her jacket since she walked in, and I thought for the relaunch I could do an article about bringing the old into the new…Vintage pieces and stuff…"

"Ooh, how fitting… A bit like your blog—bringing the old into the new…"

"Yes—exactly! Anyway, as you were doing the bill, I told her how wonderful her jacket was; she said she was about to chuck it out! Can you imagine? I bet she has so many clothes, that she doesn't know what to do with them all… So then she tells me that she gives her old stuff to her housemaid," Chloe said, once again in disbelief.

"Eurgh—really? That lucky bitch; *I'd* be her housemaid!"

"I did think that myself, but I'm sure Mrs Ruthenstock wouldn't employ just anyone; I'm sure she has a high standard when it comes to staff…"

"What do you mean—you cheeky cow! I am *very* high standard," Dom said.

"High maintenance more like… She then went on to say that she has lots of old clothes boxed up and ready to be sent to the church charity fund."

"*What?* I just can't even—"

"Don't worry—she has offered to send them over to my place for me to look through before I send them onto the church for her."

"I just can't believe you! How did you manage this?"

"I have no idea—one minute they were going to charity—the next minute they were coming to my place… I guess that's the power of networking with clients."

"We are going to have so much fun going through those boxes!" Dom said, just as excited.

"For sure! I'm having them sent over this Thursday morning before I go to Karen's office… I won't have time to go through them, but at least I'll have something to look forward to when I get back."

"You certainly will… Not only will you be busy with your new website, but now you have something to feature… Hang on… won't they be too big for you? She's like two sizes up?"

"Yeah, but who gives a fuck? Plus, designer sizes are always small anyway; I can always get them altered… I mean, they're not costing me a dime; the least I could do is pay to get them tailored." Nothing could dampen her spirits right now, she was riding a wave and for once had all the answers (rather than Dom for a change).

"I suppose your right there... You could even sell whatever's no good online, and buy something here with discount... Forget giving them to the church! What she doesn't know, won't hurt her," he schemed further.

"That's not a bad idea... But I better not, in case she asks the pastor... I can't rob the Lord himself."

Dom looked at her with one raised eyebrow, as if to say: 'Whatever!'.

"Besides, I'll donate some of my old rags in return." A compromise Chloe would surely keep; she had meant to get round to the task of cleaning out her closet for a long time, and she was a believer in karma. "I'm really getting into this networking thing, aren't I? We should tell Melinda," Chloe said, wanting to share her excitement with her guru.

"Yeah, she would love to hear your good news... Let's pop up to see her before we go home."

Just as they were riding a high, the packing room door swung open with a crash as it hit the wall. Immediately the air turned frosty, and the conversation was squashed in an instant.

"Good afternoon, you two."

Regina had discovered them hiding from the shop floor. Chloe smiled sweetly as usual, while Dom managed to fashion a fake grin (that was fooling no one—certainly not Regina).

"I hope you have been busy this afternoon," she said, peering out the top of her glasses at the vast amount of products on the countertop. She was always suspicious of them when they were together.

"Yes, actually... It's been very busy... Chloe has made $12,000 alone in just two sales."

Chloe wasn't one to brag about her successes, she could always count on Dom to do that for her. Regina, on the other hand, was annoyingly disappointed; naturally, she thought the worst of everyone.

"Is that so? And how much have you sold Mr Fraser... Hmmm?"

Her comment had wiped the smirk off his face; it was true, he hadn't sold much in comparison but couldn't resist snapping back.

"Well, we have to work together—as a team—especially as we are so short staffed these days."

Looking sharply at him, Regina's eyes were trying to work out what his intentions were; was he foolish enough to argue with her? He was so happy outside of work, spending time with Jason, that he really didn't care what she thought of him anymore—the power of love had made him feel invincible.

"Well, you will be pleased to know, that will all change very soon... Arrive an hour earlier tomorrow morning—even if you are on a late shift... I have another announcement to make, and it involves your department... So be here on the shop floor and dressed in uniform for eight a.m. sharp... Don't be late!"

If her arrival alone hadn't already, then this statement definitely killed any excitement they had previously been buzzing from. Satisfied with their surprised expressions, she left them to inform the rest of the team. Waiting for her to be out of sight and earshot, Dom collapsed his upper body onto the worktop and buried his face into his arms.

"Oh God! What now? I wonder what is happening now? This place is like a fucking soap opera! We definitely need to see Melinda now... She will know what's going on."

# CHAPTER EIGHT

Sticking to the plan, Dom and Chloe called the lift; having survived the late shift, it was time to catch up with Melinda before she too went home. Hopefully, she would be able to shed some light on Regina's mysterious meeting. The lift carried them up to personal shopping where the doors pinged open, Sandra was at the desk getting ready to go home.

"Hi, darling! We were hoping to see Melinda," Dom said.

"Go through… She's just getting ready to leave," Sandra said.

She looked tired, and by this point of the day, she really didn't care *who* went through those doors anymore. Walking through to the lounge area, Melinda was by the sofa; putting on her coat and making sure she had all of her belongings. Looking up, she was surprised to see Dom and Chloe again.

"Hello, you two… Can't get enough of this place? Don't you want to go home? I know I do!"

"We thought we would drop by quickly for an update… We don't want to keep you, but we wondered if you knew what was happening in our department?" Dom said, getting straight to the point.

Melinda perched herself on the arm of the sofa, not getting too comfortable; she was desperate to leave, and her husband was probably waiting for her outside as usual.

"You didn't hear this from me okay? You have a new department manager starting next week…"

Chloe's heart sank—yet another promotion that she hadn't been considered for. A sure sign that she was definitely not wanted in the company—but to be fair—she hadn't been checking the staff portal lately (that's if it was even advertised on there in the first place).

"Wow, I can't believe it… Finally, we got a new manager… I hope they're good," she said, sounding flat.

Both Melinda and Dom looked at her like she was stupid; had she forgotten the type of people that Regina employed in such positions?

"Well, one thing you *can* be sure of… He or she will be a messenger for Regina—so approach with caution—one step ahead remember!" Melinda warned.

"Well, Chloe has definitely been doing that… Not only has she done her weekly target in a day, but Karen Saunders has offered to re-design her blog for free—and if that wasn't enough—Mrs Ruthenstock is giving away *all* her unwanted clothes!" Dom said, excitedly spilling Chloe's news yet again.

"Really? Good for you… See what I mean now by being open to possibilities, simply by asking your clients more questions? Just make sure you don't tell anyone else…"

Happy for Chloe (but not in the mood to stay around and chit-chat any longer), Melinda wanted to get the Hell out of this place. Her day had been just as long and draining, having been tied up in meetings preparing events for Fashion Week (as well as her private appointments).

"Anyway… Let's go home shall we?" she said, escorting them to the lift.

Big things were being negotiated in the world of Palazzo and Melinda couldn't afford to say too much. Safe inside the elevator (unless it was bugged—which wouldn't be a surprise), Dom told Melinda how Karen wanted to use Chloe's staff discount and wondered what she thought about it. Her answer was simple:

"Just make sure you do it before your new manager starts next week… And again, *don't* tell anyone! You know as well as I do that you are not the only ones in here doing these things… They're just clever enough not to get caught."

Over the years she had worked at Palazzo, Melinda had seen it all and had an easy solution for almost anything; she simplified everything because, at the end of the day, it was retail—not rocket science. The lift doors pinged open onto the womenswear floor.

"Anyway kids, have a good evening... See you tomorrow," Melinda said.

Saying goodbye, Dom and Chloe headed towards the locker rooms to get changed out of their uniforms, leaving Melinda to ride the lift all the way down to the ground floor.

"What a day! And tomorrow will be another one for the books no doubt... In fact what a week it's been so far," Chloe said, wondering what more could possibly happen.

"Right, so that's it then... Tomorrow I'll put through the discount for you... How are you going to afford to spend two and a half grand?"

"It's a good thing I've been saving all that commission and overtime pay recently... And didn't spend it all getting wasted with you!"

"You have savings? Lucky you... Well, you can always blow it once she repays you, plus making some profit on top... Remember to tell her you can only get her thirty percent!"

'*Thirty?* Earlier it was forty,' Chloe laughed to herself. When being asked for a favour, Dom always made a staff purchase worthwhile by taking a cut of the percentage. It was another way of topping up the bonuses of working at Palazzo, and purchasing the Gold Rush bag for Karen was an investment in her future at the same time. Once Karen repaid her, she'd be back to square one, with an amazing website on top. Having savings made Chloe feel secure; she quite liked the feeling of financial security (she had worked hard for that money), and after receiving Mrs Ruthenstock's hand-me-downs, she wouldn't need to buy clothes for quite a while anyway.

Once again, Dom was looking forward to another night at The Plaza. The week was moving fast, and there were only three more nights to be had before Jason left New York for L.A. Would he ask Dom to go with him? Or even just to visit him? All Dom knew was that the feelings between them were too strong for it to just end here. In his heart, he wished that reality would play out the same way as it did in his head.

Although he knew Jason was attracted to him; he hadn't actually told Dom how he felt beyond the physical side of things—but it was early days for that kind of talk. Dom would gladly declare that he was falling in love with him (but he didn't want to freak him out at the same time) Jason was a 'keeper'. Dom was trying his best to play it cool; but on the inside, he was finding it hard to not let his true feelings spill out.

Only time would tell which way their relationship would go, and he wasn't the only one who was hoping for the best. Chloe hoped that she wouldn't be picking up the pieces after Jason left town (even though she knew that day was coming); she would always be Dom's rock. They were best of friends, and after all the support Dom had given her, it was the least she could do in return.

*

Dom was becoming accustomed to staying at The Plaza; he wondered how on Earth he would get used to living in his apartment ever again after a week of luxury. Dom hoped that he never needed to go back to his old life; he was desperate to get out of retail—love seemed the perfect reason to quit his job. Jason seemed to be the ideal suitor: successful, incredibly handsome, had a great personality, creative, and a little bit older.

Dom laid—spread out on the bed—watching Jason get out of the shower and dry himself, the sight of him was heavenly. For a minute, Dom considered revealing how he really felt about him, but he didn't want to turn him off by being too pushy—or sound desperate. Dom feared the reality, but also didn't want to seem weak for a man he had only just met; he knew he had to make him want him. But what if Jason didn't have feelings him at all, and it was all just a fling?

For now, he preferred not to know and just enjoy the moment while it lasted; he didn't want the fairy-tale to end just yet; he decided to hang on to the dream for one more night at least. He figured that the final night with Jason would be a better occasion to bring up the subject of keeping in touch. Maybe Jason would say something himself by then, or take the lead and invite Dom to L.A? The possibilities were endless, and that's the way Dom preferred it.

Jason seemed to be in good spirits, hugging Dom the minute he walked into the hotel room. 'A sign that he *is* into me,' Dom noted, gathering more evidence to build up his confidence.

"So… I have some good news!" Jason said, walking from the bathroom; towel drying his hair—completely naked.

'What is it with people and announcements lately?' Dom wondered. Could it possibly be that he was about to say that he wanted him to move to L.A so they could be together?

"Today I sold the painting you liked of Kate!" Jason said dropping the towel to lie next to him on the bed.

Although it wasn't exactly what he wanted to hear, it was still good news, and Dom was genuinely pleased for Jason. His visit to New York had been a success in more ways than one.

"Congrats babe!" Dom said, hugging his still wet body, "I would have bought it myself… If I had the money of course. It's amazing!"

"Thank you, Mister."

'Mister?' Dom thought it wasn't exactly what he wanted Jason to call him; something more affectionate would have been more appropriate after he had just called him 'babe'. Dom was growing even more paranoid; was Jason trying to escape from references of love or sweet talk entirely by emasculating it with 'Mister'?

"Actually it's quite ironic… London's South Bank Gallery have purchased it. They said they loved the fact I used such a British icon and just had to have it, and there's more… They want me to loan some more of my work for an exhibition that's opening during London Fashion Week… I mean, it's tight time-wise, but I can get straight on it as soon as I'm back in L.A."

Dom was happy for Jason's achievements, but he couldn't help but feel uneasy about their future when all he wanted to hear was that he too loved him.

"Is everything okay?" Jason asked.

"Yeah of course… I'm pleased for you, really I couldn't be happier. I just had a full-on day at work… that's all."

"Oh, and I'm making you work night shifts too," Jason said, nuzzling into Dom's neck.

"Hmmm, I don't mind… In fact, I don't know what I'm gonna do when you finally go."

There. Dom had said it; he had put it out there, as subtle as it was—but he had finally said it.

"Of course you will," Jason said, sitting up. "You have the rest, of what already looks like a great summer in New York… You will have lots of fun."

'Fun?' thought Dom. 'Maybe that's what all I am to him after all?' Feeling slightly crushed, Dom fought back the sudden urge to cry. The only distraction to ignore the remark was to kiss him. After this week, he may never see him ever again, and all he had to cling onto was the fact that he was with him right now.

Dom decided that he would forget what had just been said (or not said) and go with the flow of the evening. After all, sex with Jason was like nothing he had ever experienced before; the urge to make love to Jason overtook his emotions once more and finally pushed his paranoia to the background of his mind for the time being.

Lying awake in bed, Dom couldn't help but feel shitty and depressed. 'How stupid can I be?' he said to himself. 'Why did I think he would fall in love with someone like me? This was just fun to him. He was in town and just looking for fun. I've been so naive!' Feeling used and sad, he tossed and turned while Jason slept naked next to him—sleeping deeply and untroubled in contrast. His body was warm, and he had a smile on his face as if he had nothing to worry about; another signal that Jason didn't care for him like he did.

Then again, Dominic was no body language expert. All these thoughts and feelings were his own analysis, and it was his own insecurities that had led him to this conclusion. Coming to terms with the fact that he was none the wiser about their future, Dom snuggled closer to Jason and rested his head on his shoulder—placing one arm over his stomach. Jason's fingers slowly fumbled to find Dom's and intertwined into them, grasping his hand as they slept.

**

The alarm went off; it was seven a.m. Dom hadn't slept deeply and woke up straight away, anticipating the bleeping wake-up call and feeling exhausted still. He rolled over and sat up to switch the alarm to snooze. Sensing the weight on the bed shift, Jason yanked him back over to kiss him.

"Is it time to get up?" Jason moaned as they both sank back down into the pillows.

"For me it is… I have to work, but I've booked Friday so I can see you off home."

It was probably the first day off work in his entire history of employment that he wasn't looking forward to.

Waking up—not only tired but down too—Dom knew deep down that his whirlwind romance was one day closer to coming to an end. The inevitable was looming, and he had no inkling of what lay ahead for him; all he knew was that life after Jason (and without him) was going to be a crash back down to reality, and something he didn't want to address before work. A shift at Palazzo on Independence Day; when everyone else had the day off work seemed like a life sentence in jail.

"Come on… What's bothering you? Tell me, man." Jason said, hearing the downbeat tone in his voice.

"Oh, nothing… Just looking forward to finishing work so I can be with you."

Jason accepted his answer and grabbed him, tickling his sides as they playfully wrestled in bed until he was on top. Dom knew he had to snap out of this depression, it wasn't attractive, and he certainly didn't want to turn Jason off him.

He was still here with him, and he needed to savour every last minute; try to make him want him even more. Leaning down and supporting his weight, Jason looked into Dom's eyes. His deep green eyes gave nothing away except lust; all Dom could see was a twinkling soul that he inexplicably connected with. He reached his neck up off the bed to plant a single kiss on Jason's lips, a simple peck that led to a deeper, passionate kiss that he sank into—even though they hadn't brushed their teeth yet.

It was a good job Palazzo was only just down the street otherwise he would be very late indeed. Especially as Jason had intentions of making full use of the bed once more… And then again in the shower. Morning sex was the best, and this was one situation Dom was happy to be late to work for. Finally leaving the hotel room to start the short journey to work, Dom's heart wrenched inside his chest.

He still had time; there were another two nights and a morning to hear the words he wanted to hear so desperately. Inside the elevator down to the lobby, Dom looked in the mirror and laughed at himself. How ridiculous that he was putting so much pressure on their relationship after less than a week. They barely knew each other, but their romance had been so intense that it had felt more like months to him. Dom couldn't explain the feelings he had, he just knew inside that Jason was 'the one'.

*** 

Wednesday morning was a hot and sticky awakening. The Fourth of July was set to be another celebration for Americans everywhere— no matter where in the world. Many businesses closed for the holiday and gave their staff the day off, but not for retail workers. This was another opportunity to cash in on those that didn't have to work and had the day off to treat themselves to some hard-earned luxuries. Of course, for Chloe and Dom, it wasn't a luxury to be at work.

It was ironic that Regina had chosen today of all days to make her anti-independence announcement—well for the womenswear team at least. Since the start of the year, they had been without a department manager; left to fend for themselves—today that would end. Their last manager; Cassie Woods was 'promoted' to another location. She was good at her job, controlling the team with respect and fairness, and that was exactly why she had been moved.

Regina didn't take a liking to her excellent people skills; she held too much authority and made decisions on her own (which she rightly should have), but Regina liked to be feared by all—management included. Cassie wasn't afraid of speaking out in defence of her team or arrange a team bonding night out, and this was a warning sign for Regina. A sign that she had the potential to be far more than just a department manager; so to stop her from going further in the company, Regina moved her to the Palazzo concession inside SAKS as general manager. It was indeed a promotion; but no one wanted the long evening shifts and the long summer and Christmas hours, compared to the luxury of boutique hours and the prestige that came with it.

The womenswear team managed themselves very well without Cassie; Kim had stepped up to act as their department manager, which Regina was grateful for. It meant things would run smoothly without having to spend extra money on finding a new manager right away, and Kim was too happy to score some points—which she had just cashed in on her own promotion. With Kim now gone to the press office, Regina needed a new confidant.

They gathered early on the shop floor as requested; sat awaiting their fate patiently. Sarah was jiggling her legs with her hands between her knees like she was about to pee herself, fretting about what changes were going to be made; while Chloe was calm and collected—thanks to having inside information. Dom was equally as nonchalant about it all, so much so that he hadn't even made it into work yet.

'Where is he?' Chloe wondered, worried he wasn't going to show up at all, scuppering her plans to buy the Gold Rush bag.

Without him, she wouldn't be able to trade the Gold Rush for a new and improved website, which is what she really needed right now to get her out of this Hell-hole. The rest of the team looked on in panic as Regina exited from the lift, walking towards them with strict confidence. She stood in front of them, dressed in her new season uniform (probably stolen from the press archive courtesy of Myra), looking like she was going to enjoy this moment. She rarely had anything to smile about, and when she did, you could be sure she was about to drop a bombshell. That's what excited her the most about being in control: commanding respect and sending ripples of fear through her staff. In return their fear would energise her and make her feel untouchable—always on top.

"Good morning… Thank you for attending slightly earlier than usual, once again," she started.

The sound of footsteps running and slipping on marble interrupted her; she pursed her lips at the annoyance of Dom skidding to the gathering by the sofas, adjusting his tie in an attempt not to appear dishevelled. She had expected Soraya to be late, but even she had arrived on time, making this a perfect opportunity to point it out all the more.

"I'm glad we could *all* make it this morning," Regina said, pierced her eyes into him as her mouth straightened into a thin line. "I won't keep you longer than necessary, that way you can benefit from being here early and get to work with the duties I'm about to give you, but I would like to start by thanking you for working so well over the past six months without a department manager. Your figures were, well, satisfying let's say," she said, glancing briefly at the sales report from the day before.

'Satisfying?' Chloe thought to herself. 'She could at least say well done for *Chloe's* amazing sales in particular. Ungrateful bitch!'

Of course, that was asking for too much. Regina would never congratulate her, especially now she was becoming more and more wary of her intentions. Regina knew that by not congratulating Chloe personally, it would annoy her and that was what she wanted to achieve.

Content that she had successfully pissed her off, Regina continued to dive straight into her news.

"Moving along, I'm very pleased to announce the arrival of your new department manager. Her name is Francesca Manzetti, and she will be starting next Monday; she will be in training with me, and we will tour the store this Friday, and I will introduce her to you all."

Jaws dropped; the news had hit the team like a tornado—all except Chloe and Dom. They were speechless; finally, they would have someone to keep an eye on them—and after getting rid of likeable Cassie—this new manager was sure to be a ball-breaker. Everyone knew that she would be another Regina robot from the start; someone to be careful of. The start of a new era was about to begin, and a game plan was definitely needed, but Dom and Chloe already had theirs, and they couldn't care less about anyone else—this news was *so* yesterday!

"And some more good news… The press team, along with personal shopping and I, have been meeting to discuss this year's Fashion Week events. This year we want something extra special for our clients… The company has exciting things planned, but one thing in particular… I can reveal that Palazzo will be showing for the first time in New York with a special retrospective show to celebrate fifty-five years of Palazzo. So, to coincide we will have an in-store party for select V.I.C's and press contacts, where our talented creative director; Gianni Palazzo will attend. He is very pleased to be in New York for this momentous occasion and is looking forward to meeting everyone at our beautiful store. While you will be required to staff the in-store party, you will not be invited to attend the show—I will be the store's representative along with our press team. I will be meeting with the other departments throughout the day to tell them this amazing news, and more information on the Fashion Week schedule will be revealed soon… in the meantime, we need to get the store ready for his visit. Therefore, I have asked the department managers to give their teams extra tasks to complete in preparation, and you will also have lots to do in preparation for your new manager starting… Is that clear?"

The team all nodded in agreement, not that they had a choice in the matter; she left them with lots to think about, not even allowing questions. As the rest of the team discussed the arrival of both Francesca and Gianni, Dom walked over to Chloe—bored by it already.

"Did you see how she looked at you? Mind you, she gave me a filthy look as well... What happened? Why were you late?" Chloe said.

"Well, ya know... Me and Jason stayed in bed a bit longer... Then the shower and then the bed again..."

Chloe got the hint.

"Well-worth being late for then I take it?"

"*Totally* worth it!" Dom said, raising an eyebrow—their colleagues still talking excitedly about the surprise fashion show and in-store party.

Chloe was also quite excited that Gianni Palazzo himself was coming to their store, although she didn't want to admit it to Dom. Over the years, Chloe had developed a crush on Gianni; he was the sexiest designer in the industry and quite the ladies man—although Dom insisted he was gay. Dom thought every good looking, wealthy, and influential man in fashion was gay; he wasn't wrong most of the time, although he was on this occasion.

In the past, Gianni had publicly dated a string of famous models, Hollywood actresses, and famous socialites—although none of them ever seemed to last for long. When you were as famous and influential as Gianni—with one of the most renowned fashion houses under your name—you could pretty much have whatever and whoever you wanted... And Gianni always got what he wanted! To be fair, he was irresistible, and both gay men and women fawned over his good looks, as much as his coveted designs.

Dom went about the usual routine of checking that the rails on the shop floor had the correct number of items on display; replenishing sold-out pieces, while Chloe dusted the glass tops and shelves. Noticing that their colleagues were still speculating over the news, Dom saw the perfect opportunity to remind Chloe about their pact.

"So, are you going to buy the bag or what?"

"Of course I am," she said, cautiously checking no one else was listening in over her shoulder. "I've been up all night worrying about it!"

"Well, today is the day to do it since next week we will have someone watching our every move no doubt. Call down to the stock room and have them send the bag up to the lift in the stockroom."

"What—right now?"

"Yes, now—it's the time to do it! Everyone is busy gassing about the meeting; they won't suspect a thing and just think we are doing all the work so they can carry on chatting as per... Then, go and collect it and meet me in the packing room... While you're doing that, I'll get the transaction ready on the system... Got your credit card with you?"

"Yep... Bank card is at the ready!" Chloe said, patting the breast pocket of her jacket.

"Okay, then let's go..."

Chloe made a move to call the stock room before remembering one small technicality.

"But wait a minute... How on Earth will I get it up to my locker without anyone noticing I've bought something? They're like vultures in here; they can smell a staff purchase and will want to know I've bought."

"Bitch—lie! If anyone asks, tell them it's a stock transfer, or you're doing something for Kim."

"Sure... I'll call the stock room guys now."

Chloe casually walked over to the small alcove; to the internal computer and phone line, trying to act as normal as possible. Picking up the phone, she dialled the stock room extension—the person on the other end picked up within two rings—answering before the three-ring allowance.

"Stockroom," a male voice answered.

"Hi, morning," she said, poking her head around the corner of the alcove to make sure no one else could overhear her order. She was just as paranoid as the time she and Dom had smoked pot on lunch many years ago.

"It's Chloe from the womenswear floor here… I was wondering if you could send up one Gold Rush bag to our stock room, please? I believe my colleague Dominic Fraser has one on hold," she said, nervously waiting for a response.

"Sure… I'll just check the reservations shelf; please hold."

In the background, Chloe could hear him walk off to find its location, the stock room in the basement was a labyrinth of luxury leather items—but meticulously kept. Chloe waited on the other end patiently; it seemed like forever but in reality was only a minute or two. Picking up the handset, the stock assistant returned to the call.

"Got it… I'll send it up now."

"Thank you," she said quickly, surprised at how easy it had been.

She walked briskly to the stock room—all the way at the other end of the department—she didn't want one of her colleagues to find it in the dumbwaiter before she did and start asking questions. As she walked past the cash desk area, she saw that they were *still* talking about Gianni's visit and the appointment of a new manager—having not yet done any work—let alone bother her about what she was up to.

It was ridiculous how they were still going on about it—but then again—mornings at Palazzo were never usually this exciting; it had provided entertainment that she wouldn't begrudge them of. Dom was shuffling some garments to look busy and saw that she was on her way to collect the bag (a signal for him to make his way into the packing room and get ready to process the transaction speedily).

Chloe punched the security code into the panel on the stock room door to enter, turning the corner where the dumbwaiter was. Sitting there in a dust cover was the elusive Gold Rush bag. The dust-bag was a light beige colour with the 'Palazzo' screen printed in shimmering gold. She quickly picked it up and looked inside; this was the first time she had actually held it in her hand.

Gosh, it was pretty; she could see why it was so expensive and instantly agreed it was worth every cent from just a single glimpse. But she had no time to be hypnotised by a clutch bag right now and made

her way back to the packing room where Dom was waiting for her
to return. Just as she was about to leave the stock room, she found a
used Palazzo shopping bag filled with plastic hangers that had been
discarded by the door—they were also a light beige colour with the
gold italic 'P,' in the centre. The bag was filled with a variety of shirt,
pants, and jacket hangers—the perfect disguise to transport the bag
in—and perfect to take home too. Tomorrow she was expecting Mrs
Ruthenstock's driver to deliver a haul of unwanted clothes, and spare
hangers would undoubtedly be needed.

Passing the gathering—still by the cash desk chatting—Chloe had
succeeded in fooling them to believe she was busy with regular morning chores as she made her way to the packing room; they just assumed
she was doing the jobs they hated to do. Completely unnoticed, Chloe
entered and waved the shopping bag at Dom.

"*Ta-da!* Mission accomplished," she said proudly, taking the dust-
bag out of the carrier full of hangers.

"Excellent, for a moment I thought you were gonna show me a bag
full of hangers… Let me scan it; I've already got your discount profile
up… Gurl you have not bought much have you? I have maxed out my
yearly limit already, and we're only half-way through the year!" he said
as if his nearly diminished discount allowance was the worst thing to
happen to him.

Grabbing the bag, he pulled out the swing tag to scan its barcode.

"Okay, bag that up quickly before someone comes in and sees it."

Chloe did as she was told—quickly placing it back inside the dust-
bag—omitting any kind of gift box, or wrapping it in tissue paper even.
Catching her doing it out the corner of his eye slightly annoyed him;
Dom was a stickler for presentation, but now wasn't the time to get
crafty—the quicker they were done, the better.

"They're all still chatting about the new fucking department manager… I mean get over it… Yes, she is going to be a witch, Regina
employed her," Chloe said.

"Well, you know this place… They just love to gossip, and they don't have the inside knowledge we do remember… We'd be just as shocked I guess. Besides, Gianni Palazzo coming to New York is probably the most exciting thing that's happened to this place in years!"

Chloe was surprised to hear that even the cool 'I don't give a fuck' Dominic Fraser had picked up on how amazing Gianni's Fashion Week visit would be; she was glad that it wasn't just her and could stop feeling pathetic about actually looking forward to it.

"Right, gimme your card bitch—let's finish this!"

Waiting for the authorisation had felt like an eternity, what was wrong with her account? The money was definitely in there, she had transferred funds from her savings into her account the night before. For a brief moment, panic had stirred inside her, but she took a breath of relief when she saw the paper eventually roll out of the card machine, making a bleating sound as it printed.

Spending so much money felt wrong after she had worked so hard to save it in the first place. However, it was to be only this once, and Karen would repay her—and Chloe would have a fabulous website—not to mention all the free clothes from Mrs Ruthenstock to match. Chloe kept reminding herself of her recent good fortune, and this was all for a good reason.

Pushing the guilt to the back of her mind, she signed the bill and swore never to think about it again. Dom handed the receipt over to Chloe, she quickly placed it inside the dust-bag before disguising the whole thing within the shopping bag full of hangers once again.

"Right, thanks for doing that… I'm going to get this bad boy up to my locker before anyone notices we put through the first sale of the day!"

"You're welcome. And remember… Don't give her the receipt! This is our little secret," Dom said, with serious eyes and a sarcastic finger wag; Chloe smiled at him as if to say, 'duh!' and began to leave with the disguised bag.

But just as she went to grab the door handle, Sarah barged her way in, looking for her missing colleagues who hadn't been indulging in the gossip with the rest of them.

"Hello… What are you two doing?"

"Oh nothing," Chloe said, thinking quickly. "Just collecting hangers, I'm sorting through my closet on my day off."

Just as quick as her response, Chloe made a swift exit to escape from further questioning.

'That was close!' She said to herself as she made her way up to the staff changing room; leaving Dom with the fall-out.

Finally making it up to her locker with the bag in tow, she stuffed the awkwardly packed paper bag inside it (which wasn't very spacious, to begin with—what with her day clothes already inside). Having scrunched up the bag in her small locker, she finally managed to close the door shut and locked it—still with a nervous pang in her stomach.

Only when she made it safely out of the building and on her way home could she relax—then would she know that she had gotten away with it entirely. In the back of her mind, she knew that the niggling worry of being found out would fester inside her all day long; she consoled herself with the fact that this was just another regular staff purchase. At the end of the day, she had paid for it.

# CHAPTER NINE

The team dispersed as customers started to trickle in, but Dom hung around the cash desk with Sarah (discussing the arrival of their new department manager and the Fashion Week announcement). Even though he tried to play it cool, Dom was thrilled that Gianni was throwing a party at the store and he would finally get to see him in person—although he would never admit it.

Chloe returned to the shop floor, pulling at the corners of her blazer and flicking her hair away from her shoulders; smartening herself up from rushing back up to her locker before joining them at the till—hoping they had good gossip to take the bag off her mind.

"What do you think Chloe… About the new manager?" Sarah said.

"Nothing really… It was gonna happen sooner or later." She really didn't care less about the new manager; all for they knew, this Francesca woman could actually be quite nice—although it wasn't very likely. With a name like 'Manzetti' she was obviously hired because of her background (so she could talk privately and secretly plot with Regina in Italian).

"I bet she is going to be a right bitch! This place is so dodgy and connected… And why weren't *we* told of the position?" Sarah questioned, not letting the subject go.

She had a point, but Chloe was too busy waiting for the day to end—growing more and more paranoid as time slowly ticked away. She was expecting a security guard to escort her up to the locker room for a spot check any second now. Dom also couldn't wait for the day to be over so he could see Jason; wishing he was still in bed with him—and he probably would have been if it hadn't been for the early meeting call. The week was coming to an agonising end and his time with Jason was closing in. Thinking of Jason, he checked his phone under the counter and saw he had received a message from him.

HEY MAN. MISSED U IN MY BED WHEN U LEFT... I'M
TAKING U OUT 2NITE... SUMWHERE FUN! C U L8R. X

Hearing from Jason had cheered him up in an instant; although he had doubted where his romance with Jason was going, this was a good sign that it was heading where he wanted it to—and there was a kiss at the end. Meanwhile, Sarah reluctantly left to serve a customer, although she would much rather hang out with Dom and Chloe rather than actually do her job.

"So, tell me what's going on with you and Jason?" Chloe said, noticing the massive grin on his face—assuming it must be down to Jason.

Not much else made him smile like this nowadays.

"Well, last night we spent the whole evening in the hotel room," he began, but he wanted to run his fears past Chloe to see if he was going mad. "You know... I'm having a great time, but I'm starting to worry about what will happen when he leaves on Friday."

"What exactly are you worried about?" Although Chloe didn't have to ask; she knew exactly where this conversation was going—she braced herself for what was coming.

"Well, as you know—I really like him... In fact, I think I'm starting to fall in love with him... But I mean, he lives in L.A, and I don't know if I'll ever see him again... I'm worried that I won't be able to get over him... he's just too good to be true. Last night he sensed something was wrong and I didn't know whether to say something about it or not... But I don't want to seem needy, or come on too strong so soon."

"Can't you just tell him that you like him and that you wanna keep in touch? I mean, he can only say yes or no?" Chloe couldn't see what the big deal was.

Of course, she could empathise with the possibility of heartbreak, but at the same time, she didn't see much point in worrying over something that hadn't happened yet—although she was one to talk. Here she was losing her shit over buying the Gold Rush bag and coming up with all kinds of scenarios in her mind; it was ironic how she could see Dom's situation for what it was, but not her own. She figured that nothing terrible had happened and that he had met a hot guy and had a fantastic week, and now he had a new 'friend' in L.A, but Dom wanted more than that.

"Well, you're right… But I guess I don't want to be disappointed. I know I've only just met him, but I just know there is something more between us."

"Everything will be fine… Just be honest and try to tell him how you feel. Maybe he is feeling the same way too… You never know until you tell him."

As always—disturbed by clients—they didn't have much chance to discuss it further; a woman was rifling through the ready-to-wear and making a mess of the rails. At first, Chloe was annoyed with the interruption (she was getting into her heart to heart with Dom), but on closer inspection, she noticed that the woman was striking and well dressed; potentially a big spender; she had great skin with flawless make-up. Chloe quickly broke away from Dom to approach her before anyone else did, there was something about her that drew Chloe to her.

"Good Morning, welcome to Palazzo," she said, fixing the garments on the rails that had been left behind in the customer's path of destruction.

The woman paused from looking at a dress to acknowledge her, giving her a smug look which almost came across as though she were looking down at her.

"If there's anything you need today, please let me—"

"I'm fine for now," she said sharply, whizzing off to the next rail.

Chloe backed off, sensing her service was not wanted—having just cut her off mid-flow. She was obviously just a difficult one—one of those that liked to be rude to show their wealth and power over a sales assistant (they were only slaves to them). Returning to Dom, he carried on telling her about the message he had just received and how he had big plans for the Fourth of July.

"So, where is he taking you?" She asked him, with one eye kept on the woman.

"Well, if I knew that I'd tell you wouldn't I? All he said was that we are going somewhere fun."

"Maybe it's something touristy or tacky—like the Statue Of Liberty… Or going to Times Square," she snorted; she couldn't resist poking fun. "Or maybe you'll take the ferry to Staten Island and back!"

"I guess I'll find out later."

"Just enjoy it, whatever it is."

"Any time spent with Jas—"

*CRASH-KA-LANG!*

Hangers smashed onto the marble floor; expensive dresses fell to a heap, ringing out through the entire department and causing everyone to look over at what was going on. Now Chloe was really pissed at this woman, especially after she had offered to help her in the first place. Now she was interrupting their catch up, but professional as always Chloe pushed her annoyance aside to go help.

"I'm so sorry," the woman said.

"Oh, that's okay… It happens all the time… Some of these clothes are so slippery on the hangers," Chloe said, trying to make her feel at ease, although she didn't seem too embarrassed about it. "The dress you're looking at is proving to be one of this collection's key pieces already."

"Do you have it in size forty-four Italian?"

"Certainly, I'll need to—"

"And this… And this also… Oh, and these pants… Do you have them in more colours?"

"Yes, we have black, burgundy… And the navy of course."

"Great, I'll take all of those in a size forty-four… I'm going to need to check shoes also."

Chloe could see that this woman was definitely not a size forty-four Italian; was she just wasting her time, or did she genuinely not know her size? Sometimes clients would come in and try on incorrect sizes because they weren't familiar with the brand or the European sizing scheme. Others just liked to be difficult and knew full well what size they were, they just wanted to test the assistant and make them run around a bit for their money's worth. Some customers would come in-store just to cause a drama or pretend they were lottery winners but then leave without buying a thing.

Judging by the woman's behaviour so far, Chloe was sure she was a total time-waster. Nevertheless, she still had a job to do and an image to keep; vowing not to let this client get the better of her, she politely nodded and continued with her commitment to deliver excellent customer service. In fact, her rudeness had motivated her to be extra lovely; she wanted to make this woman feel bad about herself by the end of it for giving her hell.

"Certainly Ma'am… I go and check if we have those sizes in stock, please do browse the shoes in the meantime… I will return to assist you further in a moment."

As she walked past the till Dom shrilled '*Time-waster!*' at her. Chloe made a face in agreement, making sure the woman was out of sight but fumed to herself in the stock room as she gathered the items.

"Who does she think she is? I was so polite to her, and this is the thanks I get… I've had enough of this job!" She couldn't take much more; her heart was pumping—things needed to change fast; she needed to get out of here, it was becoming all too much, and her soul was slowly being destroyed.

Sucking up her anger, Chloe went back out onto the shop floor to present the garments to the client. She laid them out on the glass table top in preparation, pulling out all the stops. Looking around for the woman, she found her with an armful of shoes picked off the display. Noticing all the pieces set out on the table, Dom followed Chloe to keep an eye on her should the woman kick off.

'What a bitch,' he thought. 'Making her get all these things from the stockroom when they are clearly too big for her.'

Chloe approached the woman, she was eyeing up shoes with a low block heel—way too conservative for a young woman that was in great shape—she should be buying cute high-heel pumps to show off her legs. She couldn't be any older than thirty-five or so, Chloe assumed.

"Those are wonderful shoes, but I would suggest going for these," she said, picking out a more suitable pair.

Not impressed, the woman handed her the low block-heel style she had in her hand.

"These… In size nine."

Holding her nerve, Chloe looked around; behind her, she saw Dom who had his arms folded—ready to back her up if things got heated.

"Sure," Chloe said through gritted teeth. "Dom, maybe you could fetch these shoes for me while I show *Madam* here the changing rooms?"

Dom sarcastically smiled at the customer and marched off to get the shoes in support of his friend.

"Oh, I don't need to try them… Just wrap them up for me; I'm in a bit of a hurry…"

Chloe couldn't quite believe her luck. This woman was taking thousands of dollars in clothes without trying them on, and not even in her size. The woman would clearly have to traipse all the way back to the store to exchange it all and luckily it would be on Chloe's day off too. But suddenly, her way of thinking suddenly switched. The way she was dressed, her attitude, she knew exactly what she was looking for.

This woman wasn't shopping for herself; she was shopping for her mom or someone older than her. All the pieces were rather conservative (for Palazzo) after all—or maybe she was a personal shopper for a wealthy client? If that was the case, then Chloe needed to bag her as a client; she decided she would try and ask more questions without being too obvious—discretion and privacy was key to building a good relationship with possible high-profile clients.

"Oh, but I would suggest trying them on. I would have chosen a much smaller size for you myself."

Finally, the woman cracked a smile.

"Oh—how polite of you to notice… I *know* I'm not a size forty-four darling! I'm size thirty-six of course… I'm sorry; I should have said these aren't for me…. They are for a client."

Bingo—she was right!

"Oh, I see… No, I'm sorry to have assumed they were for you."

"Not a problem… Sorry for being in such a rush… I'm having a busy week… Photo-shoots, Fashion Week prep, and now one of my biggest clients called me to say she needed some things for her travels last minute… And on Independence Day of course!"

Chloe started to warm to her a little; at least she had apologised— but more than that— with a list of errands like that, she sounded like a top stylist or something and instantly captured Chloe's attention. She walked her over to the glass table where she had the pieces laid out for her to review.

"Well, these are all items in size forty-four that you picked out."

"Excellent… I'll take them all, and the shoes also… What's your name?"

"Chloe, Chloe Ravens," she said, reaching out for a handshake.

From the titbit of information she had given her already, Chloe definitely had the feeling that she just may be worth knowing after all. Taking her hand, the woman shook it lightly and introduced herself.

"I'm Carmen… You've been very helpful… Here—this is my card… Maybe we can keep in touch? I might need lots of Palazzo pieces this season. My client; Lady Darlington has taken a liking to your collection," she said, flicking out a business card with finesse from her classic Chanel handbag.

Taking the card, Chloe quickly glanced at it. It was plain white, beautifully grained—almost like a soft leather—and had her name printed in raised gold lettering.

### Carmen Visconti

*Stylist & Personal Wardrobe Consultant*

Carmen was casually dressed, but stylishly so in black leggings with a shapeless oversized striped shirt that went down to her knees. A chunky necklace hung around her neck which Chloe recognised as a Marni piece; made of acrylic and wooden beads on a leather braided rope. The outfit was completed with a camouflage field jacket and a pair of black military boots. This was a woman who really knew how to look good without having to scream designer logos. Chloe admired her professional looking card before recalling that Carmen had just mentioned the name Lady Darlington.

"Wait… Sorry, did you say these pieces were for Lady Darlington? As in Darlington Cosmetics?"

This was entirely breaking the code of discretion—and maybe this was just a coincidence—but Chloe loved Darlington cosmetics and was a huge fan of their skincare range.

"Yes—exactly. She's a very good client of mine, but when she calls I have to drop everything for her, and I'm just so busy at the moment with other projects."

"I love Darlington Cosmetics, I use their face cream all the time… May I suggest a beautiful jacket for her?"

Lady Darlington was around the same age as Mrs Ruthenstock and was likely to appreciate the tweed jacket that Chloe had picked out for her too. Taking it from the rail, she presented it to Carmen.

"See how beautiful it is? I could see her in this piece."

Taking a closer look, Carmen looked up at Chloe with a brief smile; the jacket was indeed very age appropriate. Noticing she had an eye for style (and a great appearance herself), Carmen decided she would take it to show Lady Darlington. After all, Chloe was right; it was exactly the type of thing Lady Darlington would go for.

"Perfect choice… I'll take it… As I said, she loves your collection this season, so I'm sure she would love this too."

"But, why are you not working with the press office? I'm sure Lady Darlington qualifies for some kind of discount?"

Carmen laughed at her. She was even prettier when she smiled, something that Chloe didn't see in her before—when she was being a cold bitch. Carmen's features were very Mediterranean; she had dark brown hair which was almost elbow-length, glossy and blow-dried to perfection. Her full lips were painted dark red and her golden-brown complexion set off her big green eyes wonderfully. Her voice was slightly accented, and judging by the name on her card, she was probably Italian. Chloe wondered what she had said that was so funny; noticing that Chloe didn't get the joke, Carmen enlightened her.

"You are joking, right? Well, let's just say your press office is so… So difficult to deal with. They never let me borrow stuff and getting things for photo-shoots is near impossible. I have excellent clients too, but they are just not interested… Trust me I've tried! I dress lots of celebrities—without wanting to sound pretentious—and I do a lot of shoots for magazines… Do you know Myra?"

Chloe was stunned to hear that Carmen knew Myra, but not that she was impossible to deal with—that was obvious.

"Of course," Chloe said, intrigued to hear more.

"Well, I've known her for years… We used to work together at Bullet magazine and let's just say we didn't see eye-to-eye. I'm sure because of that she has blacklisted me from having anything to do with this company, but I actually have big budgets to spend… So it's her loss."

"Oh, right… Well, I hope that if you do need anything, you would feel you could ask me instead," Chloe diplomatically said, resisting the urge to bitch about one of her seniors.

She wasn't surprised to hear that Myra had something against her; she had issues with anyone who was more successful than her. Chloe identified with Carmen even more now she had discovered they shared the same frustration about how the press office ran their side of the business, and how Myra did what Myra wanted to do—not what was best for Palazzo.

"Excellent, I will take you up on that… It seems you have a great sense of style, the jacket you picked out is wonderful."

Just as the conversation was starting to get interesting, Dom resurfaced from the stockroom with the shoes.

"Oh great! Thanks, Dom… This is Carmen, she's going to take all of these things here."

Dom rolled his eyes; he knew where this was going. He had been scanning, packing, and wrapping for Chloe all week so far.

Instead of arguing, he nodded and headed off towards the packing room with the items slung over his arm. Chloe was on a roll this week, and he was pleased that the department would reach its target at least, which meant team commission this month would be pretty good.

"Of course… I'll scan the bill through and bring it over," Dom said, leaving them to their conversation.

Chloe was grateful that he was doing all the work while she just did more of what Melinda had suggested. She suddenly felt like Carmen could be a brilliant contact to have and a great source of information, especially for her blog. The all-new StacksOfStyle wasn't even under construction yet, but having just learned the power of networking, there was no time like the present to drop it into the conversation—and Carmen seemed like she knew a thing or two about creating editorial content.

"When you first walked in, I fell in love with your outfit and style," Chloe said, easing in with a compliment. "I knew you must be in the industry in some way… I know this uniform doesn't really show off my personal style, but I have a fashion blog that I run outside of this place."

"Oh, really? That's so cool… I'll have to check it out sometime… Do you have a card?"

Feeling slightly underprepared, Chloe only had her Palazzo business card, but that was better than nothing. She took one out of her jacket pocket and on the back, she wrote the web address for StacksOfStyle.com before handing it over.

"Sorry, I don't have a personal card on me right now, but that's my web address," she said, feeling like an amateur, but maintaining her confidence on the outside.

Dom returned with the bill; Chloe walked Carmen over to the cash desk before showing her the final amount—which she gave a brief glance—it was $7,000. Chloe was racking up the sales like crazy! Carmen took her purse out and presented the second black Amex card of the week.

'I was right; she is a big spender,' Chloe said to herself. She charged her card while Dom fetched and handed over three large Palazzo shopping bags (that were of course beautifully packed, complete with ribbons).

"Thank you so much… If you need to return anything just get in touch. We exchange or give a credit note within fourteen days, but I am sure I can extend that for you if needed."

Of course, Carmen already knew the store policy, she was an experienced stylist after all, but she still appreciated Chloe's kind gesture.

"And thank you once again for all of your help… Sorry, I'm in such a rush, I gotta drop all this off to Lady Darlington, then get over to a party, and then finally I can relax! But I will definitely check out your blog when I get a spare minute."

"Why don't we just get our driver to deliver them straight to Lady Darlington for you?" Chloe offered, trying to make the best first impression possible.

"Really? That would be amazing darling!"

Chloe handed her a customer card and a pen, while Dom took back the shopping bags. Carmen scribbled down the address—it was on Park Avenue—which was close by and super expensive. But then again Darlington Cosmetics was a multi-million dollar company that was at the top of the beauty industry, so Chloe wasn't at all surprised.

"Thank you so much for this. Okay, that's her address… She has an assistant and a housemaid, so just send the bags over as soon as you can."

"Certainly, I'll get the driver to send it over within the next hour."

"Great—now I have time to look my best for the party! Okay, ciao guys," Carmen said, making her way to the elevator to leave.

"Wow, you really are doing well this week Miss. Ravens," Dom said as Carmen raced over to the elevator.

"I know, thanks so much. I owe you one for all the wrapping," Chloe said, waving at Carmen as the lift doors closed.

"That's okay, you can buy me coffee on tea break… So she wasn't a time-waster after all."

"Yeah, I didn't see that coming… Turns out she is a successful stylist. I told her all about my blog… Maybe I could interview her for an article or something? She gave me her card." Chloe said, showing Dom.

"That's awesome… She also gave you the details of one her biggest clients!" Dom pointed out. Carmen had indeed left her with the contact details of Lady Darlington. Chloe sensed another possible opportunity and decided to copy her details into her client book for future reference.

*

It had been another unexpected day; meeting Carmen could prove useful in time, but the day couldn't have come to a more welcoming end. After shedding her drab brown uniform and back into more colourful civilian clothing, Chloe grabbed the bag of hangers (that hid the Gold Rush bag secretly inside). Meeting Carmen made her forget about the guilt and anxiety that had built up from doing this favour; getting the bag out of the building without nosey colleagues finding out what was really beneath the hangers was now her priority. As she approached the staff exit, Chloe showed the security guard her receipt and the inside of her shopping bag—as casually as possible—as if nothing was out of the norm; this was just like any other staff purchase.

Of course, the security guards had no reason to be suspicious of her, staff bought things from the store every day with their discount—it was a just a procedure—and it was just another bag. They weren't the most clued up on the latest fashion trends anyway and let her pass with no questions asked. Chloe, on the other hand, felt a rush, it was almost like she had shoplifted; a rush or euphoria had washed through her body—she had gotten away with it. Dom waited outside for her (having no bags to be checked), waiting to tease her about making a huge deal out of nothing. "There, that wasn't too hard now was it?"

"No—not at all... Thanks so much for doing this for me," Chloe said, leaning in to kiss his cheek. "I'm off home to clear a rail and sort these hangers out for tomorrow... Any more news on what you two are doing tonight?"

"Well, it is Independence Day girlfriend! Hopefully, we're gonna go somewhere to celebrate... I mean, he did say he has something *fun* planned."

Dom was in the mood to party—but not too much of a party—he had to work the next day.

"Okay... Well, I'm gonna give that a miss for once... I remember last year—we got totally hammered... Rather Jason than me this year!"

Struggling with the big shopping bag of hangers that kept slipping off her shoulder, Chloe headed home—while Dom set off down the avenue towards The Plaza hotel. Although he was excited to see Jason again, his party spirit was starting to dampen as he remembered his insecurities about Jason leaving New York without him.

Tonight, however, he would have fun; tonight he wouldn't think of Jason leaving; tonight he would be the Dominic that Jason liked so much when they had first met. And in reality, they had only just met—and it had only been a week since. Dom rationalised all this in his head and told himself to chill-the-fuck-out. Realising that his attraction for Jason was taking over, it was almost bunny boiler behaviour, and he didn't want to appear completely insane. Although, he was clearly mad for Jason.

**

Chloe hadn't heard from Karen since she had visited the store the day before; Chloe knew she was a very busy woman and wondered if she had forgotten all about their arrangement. Of course, she hadn't forgotten at all; Karen had been looking forward to finally getting her hands on the Gold Rush clutch bag all week. Finally home, Chloe sent Karen a text to remind her of their date and started to ponder options for dinner.

Cooking wasn't high on her agenda; she wanted to make a start on preparing for tomorrow instead. A much simpler option was to pick up the phone and order a pizza from the local. With dinner plans sorted, she could make a start on making rail space, sorting through the old clothes that she was getting rid of to make way for the influx of new clothes that was soon to come.

'Where to start?' she thought, not really wanting to throw anything out.

The more she thought about it, the more she just wanted to lay on the sofa and wait for her pizza to arrive; however, she just got stuck into it, overthinking would result in getting nothing done. Chloe yanked hanger after hanger from her closet and chucked it onto her bed, keeping only what was worthy. Old sweaters and shirts—that she didn't even remember owning—made it into a black garbage sack.

She didn't go too mental, who knew what or how much Mrs Ruthenstock was sending over? This was just a quick clear out to make space, and also keep true to her word about donating some items to the church charity. She cleared her silver roller rail, which was used as extra rail space—since her closet was jam-packed—and transferred what was already on there into her closet; clearing it for tomorrow's delivery.

Just as she was getting into it, her phone beeped; Karen had sent a message back. Chloe darted back to the kitchen where she had left her phone to read it. Karen confirmed the time and address of her office—which was over on Madison Avenue. The plan was back on track and Chloe would need to get to bed early if she were to make the most of her day off. Instead of celebrating Independence Day like most Americans, she munched away on her Margherita pizza while watching the fireworks display on TV. Sitting there, her mind drifted off into the future—somewhere into the unknown—the celebrations made her feel sentimental.

"Will I ever achieve the things I want?" she said out loud. "Is this the turning point I am waiting for? Something's gotta give that's for sure…"

In times like this where Dom wasn't around to give her the answer, there was only one person to call: Mom.

"Happy Fourth of July!" Chloe said enthusiastically, as soon as the phone picked up.

"Chloe? I was wondering when you were gonna call… It's so lovely to hear your voice… What are you up to?

"Oh, you know… The usual: work, home, work… Home again."

"Why aren't you out tonight? Usually, you would be celebrating, no?"

"I had to work today, so I'm not really in the mood… Plus, I have a lot to do tomorrow and need to be up early."

"Well, at least you're off tomorrow I guess… What are you up to?"

"Remember my blog? Well, I've decided to give it another go… And a client of mine owns this *really* successful website, and she has agreed to help me redesign it. So I'm going to her offices tomorrow to check it out."

"That's great, let me know once it's up and ready… I'll check it out."

Chloe filled her in on all the latest happenings at Palazzo and her disappointment of not being promoted—it was good to talk about it with someone who had an outside view. The phone call went on for another thirty minutes; Mom was hard to get rid of and always had plenty to say about nothing; the neighbour's dog had died, and the fridge-freezer had packed in. The evening, however, was getting later and after a quick chat with Dad, Chloe said goodbye and hung up to get ready for bed.

After brushing her teeth and applying her Darlington Cosmetics night serum—remembering that she had met her stylist that afternoon—she quickly hung the plastic Palazzo hangers she had brought home from work onto the now empty rail. After taking the top few out of the bag, she uncovered the dust-bag with the Gold Rush safely inside it. She set it on top of her dresser so it would be the first thing she saw in the morning, reminding her not forget to bring it to Karen's office.

Everything was in place and ready; the only thing left to do now was to go to bed. Tucked up in bed, Chloe was far too excited to sleep; she forced her eyes shut and willed herself into a contrived sleep. The merrily drunk people outside her apartment making their way home didn't help either; it would be a long day ahead if she didn't fall to sleep soon. Her mind was alert with excitement and hope, thinking about what tomorrow had in store for her.

***

Dom's evening had been a bit more eventful. Entering the hotel suite, Jason was nowhere to be seen, with no message left either. Dom called his phone but a muffled buzz vibrated on the mattress in the background; he had left his phone on the bed. Assessing that he couldn't have gone far without it, Dom stripped off and stepped in the shower.

Getting fresh before he saw Jason would be a luxury; he had seen Jason straight after work every night, and this was a chance to not smell sweaty for once. Washing under the hot water, Dom slipped into a daze; recalling their first date when they had showered together. The door to the suite slammed, waking him from his lustful thoughts.

"I'm in the shower!" he called out—there was no answer.

Outside, Jason was peeling his sweaty running vest off like a layer of cling film and stepped out of his jogging pants that clung to his hips with a drawstring—kicking them off. Creeping into the bathroom in just his boxers, Jason saw Dom through the steamy glass, before taking them off. He opened the shower door as quietly as he could and gripped Dom's waist from behind, pulling him towards him by surprise; kissing his neck like a vampire.

"*A-ha*—I've gotcha now!"

Dom was shocked but instantly excited—tingling from Jason's touch and imagination—being crept upon in the shower, in some horror movie-like scenario was rather hot!

"Where did you go?" Dom said, turning around to face Jason under the steamy water.

"Just for a jog around the park... I had cabin fever and realised I haven't exercised for days."

His body didn't look like it had missed exercise for days; it was firm and taught, tanned and ripped to perfection. The hot water made his skin redden, and the veins in his muscles pumped out, making him look even more muscular. Dom was turned on even more; he couldn't resist Jason any longer. Going in for a deeper kiss, Dom realised that this was their third shower encounter.

'He must have a thing for shower scenes,' Dom thought.

After they were done in the shower, Jason ordered Dom to get dressed for the evening ahead; all Dom wanted to do was lay in a haze on the bed, but he remembered that he had planned something special.

"So what shall I wear? Why aren't you telling me where we are going?"

"Relax! You always look nice... Just wear whatever... I'm wearing a white shirt, black pants, and my cowboy boots."

Dom was pleased to hear that Jason thought he 'always looked nice' and that not all of his efforts had been wasted. He wondered if Jason had noticed just how taken away by him he was too? It wasn't like Dom had his whole closet with him to choose from; after some deliberation, he picked out a black fitted V-neck silk sweater from his holdall.

The denier was slightly sheer when worn alone, and the neckline plunged down so you could see the crease in his pecs (which were no match for Jason's). He teamed it with a pair of slim black jeans that did justice for his ass, and black leather sneakers that were smart enough to wear to a nightclub—if that was where they were going. Jason was true to his words and wore a white shirt that he had only buttoned halfway—his signature style Dom had noticed—with some jeans and cowboy boots—all he needed now was a Stetson.

"I wish you would tell me where we are going... Is this okay?" Dom said, fussing over his hair.

"Perfect! I like your style... It's so... European," Jason smiled.

"Well, I am from London... You Americans aren't as stylish as us," Dom said, playfully eyeing up his cowboy-inspired look in a questionable manner.

Jason took Dom in a headlock. "Hey, Mister—watch it!" he said.

"Mind my hair!" Dom said, trying his best to sound playful, but he was actually serious about not having his hair messed up after getting it just right. Jason let him go, knowing he would much prefer the consequences anyway; they had a booking to be on time for.

The avenue outside was busy with revellers and the evening was warm; it had been one of the hottest days. Banners and flags were everywhere; shop windows were decked out in red, white, and blue as taxis ferried people to bars and nightspots all over town. By now the streets were grid-locked; all you could hear was the sound of car horns from impatient drivers stuck in traffic.

You could be sure that most were headed for tonight's grand fireworks display that was the highlight event for many. Dom was just happy to be walking along with Jason, enjoying his company and trying to be in the moment; rather than stressing about the future. Pushing Jason for a clue to where they were going, he finally caved in under pressure.

"Well, I thought we would celebrate by having a traditional American burger and fries, so I booked a table at that place you took me to as I loved it so much... Then, I will show you the best Fourth of July you have ever seen!"

Dom's suspicions didn't arouse too much; he equated that to burgers and sex back at the suite, and he wasn't complaining about it. He didn't care much for Independence Day (being from London and all), but he sensed that this year, he may just have a reason to celebrate. He hoped he was about to celebrate a different kind of independence—freed from the mundane world of retail for the sake of true love. After eating, Jason asked the waiter to arrange a taxi (a difficult task on a tight like this), a tip helped somewhat. Dom was confused—wasn't this where they went back to the hotel for the *real* fireworks display?

"Where are you taking me?" Dom said, thrilled yet annoyed at not knowing.

First, the Psycho-style shower ambush; now he was being kidnapped—double hot!

"Okay, eight–four–eight Washington Street please driver," Jason said, slipping him some neatly folded dollar bills.

The address sounded familiar to Dom, but he couldn't place where he recognised it. Swayed by Jason's charms and handsome face, he didn't question it; it was rather exciting not knowing where they were going—and romantic too. Maybe tonight would be the night they declared their love for each other after all? The roads were jam-packed, and their driver was rough, he sure knew the streets and had many drivers swearing and beeping their horns at him for cutting them up. Dom gave up guessing where they were going as they drove deeper into Manhattan and towards the Meatpacking District, but it wasn't until they drove nearer to two towering blocks that he finally worked out where they were going.

"Are we going to—"

"The Standard… There's a huge party tonight that sounded like fun. An artist friend of mine recommended it, so I thought we should check it out," Jason said, smiling at him as he chewed gum.

Stepping out of the car, the driver thanked them—which was a first coming from a New York taxi driver (the tip must have been good). The Standard looked stylish—and busy—from the outside. Dom had been here before, it was a glamorous place and usually required an invitation or guest-list. The eighteenth floor had a rooftop terrace that included a heated tub and pool; it was host to the most fantastic view of the Hudson River and known as 'The Boom-Boom Room'.

It was certainly the party place to be at, with good-looking people everywhere, including a few minor celebrities and drag queens that had made a name for themselves on the nightclub scene. The pool was under-lit with purple neon, above it, a gigantic, glittering mirror ball revolved—flicking shards of light around the place—the DJ played electronic disco beats, setting the party scene. The evening glow made Jason appear even more handsome in his white shirt (if such a thing were possible). Dom noticed people staring at Jason once again, but he was now used to the attention that came with him. A hostess escorted them to a table right by the edge of the rooftop, Jason wasted no time in ordering drinks, handing the hostess his card to set up a tab.

"This is amazing! I can't believe you arranged this; this must be the hottest table in town… Just look at the view… And look at everyone checking you out too!"

"No, they are looking at you, you sexy little fuck!"

Dom was impressed that Jason had pulled this off; this place was rather exclusive and hard to blag. He had been here once before, but only because Stefano was a regular club kid and got him in, often dressing up in a leather harness and making a show with a bunch of transsexuals, he hung around with. This was definitely the way to spend the evening, all of his friends (including Chloe) would be super jealous of him right now.

The hostess returned with an ice bucket and two champagne glasses, setting them down on the table; she quickly poured out two half-full glasses and made her exit, knowing that the fireworks would soon start over the Hudson River (she too didn't want to miss them). Jason picked up his champagne glass and raised it. "A toast… Here's to meeting the most amazing guy, in the most amazing city, and having the most amazing time!"

Dom blushed, but he was happy with what he had just heard. All of his fears about being forgotten beyond this whirlwind of a week were silenced. Indeed, this was the most amazing Fourth of July he had ever experienced. Dom raised and clinked his glass against Jason's as he leant in for a quick kiss… And then bang!

Dom's lips quivered on Jason's mouth from the shock of the first firework unexpectedly going off. They both broke away to look up at a smattering of colour exploding and cascading down the summer night's sky—reflecting in the river below. This was a night that Dom was sure to remember for a very long time.

The vibe on the rooftop was pumping, and the party went on until very late; Dom and Jason had partied well. By now, they were both quite tipsy, and it was getting on towards the early hours of the morning.

"Come on stud… You have work tomorrow, and I haven't quite finished with you yet!" Jason said.

"Why? Do you have another surprise for me?"

Jason nodded and whispered in his ear. "Oh yeah… A very, very, big surprise… And more fireworks!"

Jason's breath against his ear had yet again aroused Dom; he could smell a hint of alcohol on it, which added to the appeal. Although he had enjoyed the night partying at The Standard, Dom couldn't wait to get back to The Plaza for his 'big-bang' finale.

# CHAPTER TEN

Thursday morning meant little sleep and probably a hangover for many across the country. Chloe being one of them—but for different reasons—tossing and turning with excitement throughout the night. Her alarm went off at seven a.m. sharp, the habit to switch it to snooze was automatic, but this was probably the first time that getting up this early on a day off was worthwhile. If this were a typical working day she would feel lethargic and cranky, sleeping in and rushing out the door sans makeup; but this morning was powered by pure motivation and not just caffeine for once.

On a regular day off, she would wake around nine-thirty; maybe do a yoga class, followed by a long brunch—but today she was up super early to get ready. She ate breakfast and showered by eight—just in case Mrs Ruthenstock's driver turned up early—but there had been no messages and no knocks at the door as yet. She leisurely applied her base makeup, which consisted of a light foundation, concealer, and a little bit of rose blush—but still no knock at the door.

Growing impatient, Chloe decided to make full use of the morning and vacuum the flat, it was in need of a spruce, and she didn't want it getting back to Mrs Ruthenstock that her flat was an absolute hole of her place should her driver need to enter. She needn't have worried; still, there had been nothing. It was now getting on towards nine a.m., and she started to wish she had stayed in bed, although the apartment was looking much tidier than before which was satisfying.

Already the need for coffee had kicked in, usually, she would pop to the coffee shop on the corner of her street, but today it had to be instant. She didn't want to miss her delivery, that would be just typical. After making coffee, she grew desperate for the toilet, so skipped to the bathroom, leaving her coffee to cool on the kitchen side. Having just about sat down on the toilet, the door buzzer rang—startling her.

"Typical… I spend all morning waiting, and now he decides to turn up as I'm about to piss!"

Attending to natures call first, she jumped up and out of the bathroom to the intercom—the things she did for fashion. Grabbing the handset off the wall panel, she quickly responded in the hope that he hadn't given up and left already.

"Hi… Chloe Ravens," she said in a rushed breath.

"Good morning—I have two, rather large boxes for you. I will need help, I can't take them upstairs on my own."

Chloe liked the sound of the 'two large boxes', so large that he needed help up the stairs! "I'll be right down."

Chloe had bought Mrs Ruthenstock a 'thank you' card and a small box of her favourite macarons from the patisserie on Fifth Avenue that she was usually gifted to Chloe—now it was her turn. Wedging her apartment door open with a kitchen barstool, she grabbed the gift and her door keys—just in case she stupidly locked herself out.

She ran down the first-floor stairs of the apartment block to open the door to the main entrance in a heartbeat. A grey-haired man dressed in a black suit and chauffeur cap stood outside next to two big storage boxes, already on the doorstep.

"Good morning Miss… Mrs Ruthenstock instructed me to deliver these boxes to this address."

"Yes, that's right. Thank you so much," she said, eyeing up the boxes with delight. "Could you please give this to Mrs Ruthenstock? It's just something small to say thanks."

She passed the driver the card and macarons, wrapped up in a small gift bag (Dom would have been very proud of her gift-wrapping skills).

"Certainly… Now, do you need help bringing these inside?"

"No, thank you, Sir… I will be just fine," she said, too embarrassed to let her client's driver see the inside of her apartment—even if she had just cleaned it.

Besides, her adrenaline would assist her with carrying two heavy boxes up a flight of stairs.

"Okay, well have a great day Miss," he said, lifting his cap slightly.

The driver returned to his car and started to pull out as Chloe bent down to lift the first box. Damn, it was heavy! 'There must be piles of clothes in here,' she estimated. Heaving it inside, she pushed it along with her foot and left it to one side by the mailboxes in the hall. Returning to the other box, she planted her feet shoulder width apart and bent down to put her back into it.

The second box was slightly lighter, although not by much. Lifting it up onto her front—with a helpful nudge of her knee—she decided to carry it straight upstairs, fearing that she might not be able to pick it up again if she put it back down. On the upside, yoga class wasn't needed today—heavy lifting was just as good exercise.

Once outside her door, she dropped the box which made a heavy thud and pushed the box into the entrance of her apartment. Straight away, she headed back down for the other box left in the hall, hoping it hadn't been stolen already (this was Williamsburg). The excitement and eagerness to know what they contained had given her an extra surge of power, so she was able to carry it up the stairs—breaking half-way—before pushing it along the floor with the side of her hip.

Slamming the front door shut, Chloe attempted to rip open one of the boxes; peeling away at the tape; she was too pumped to fetch scissors to do it quickly (and safely). Impatient as ever, and not successful in ripping it open with her bare hands, she looked up and saw a bread knife on the kitchen side. She ran the blade along the sealed box flaps, finally able to rip it open (which would have been much quicker if she had just got a pair of scissors).

Inside, it was packed with layers of scented tissue paper. Her heart started to pump with the thrill of finding out what she had sent over; her heart had found its way to her stomach—but in a good way. Her breathing grew heavier, deep in her abdomen, she couldn't wait any longer. Whipping off the top layer of paper, a flash of gold caught her eye. She lifted it out of the box and stared at it before she could even register what she was looking at.

It was a cropped tweed jacket—woven with gold lurex—from Palazzo, about six collections old. Gasping at its beauty, she held the jacket up to admire; it was in such good condition and hardly worn. Chloe couldn't believe that it was once destined for a charity sale, but happy to now have it safely in her hands—she hugged it with gratitude. After a quick inspection, she placed it to one side remembering that this was only the first piece, and there was more to discover inside the box—not to mention the other box that was left untouched.

Each item was protected by a layer of tissue paper, scented with perfume, adding to the pleasure of unboxing thousands of dollars worth of free clothes even more so. Tossing another sheet behind her, she was pleased to find another jacket; a black Chanel tuxedo blazer. Chloe was in shock and decided that the best course of action from here was to fetch the rail from her bedroom so she could hang the clothes as she unpacked. No one would (or should) chuck a single thread from Chanel on the floor! She carefully hung the jackets onto a plastic Palazzo hanger and placed them on the rail neatly.

Delving further into the box, she could see that there were clothes from all different brands; not just Palazzo. As well as the Chanel and Palazzo jackets, there was also a pair of black three-quarter length pants from Gucci; a geometric printed Prada skirt; a navy Valentino dress, and many more familiar pieces from Palazzo that Chloe had sold her over the years. Glancing at the clock on the oven, she noticed it was ten-thirty already—time had run away with her!

"*Shit*—I need to leave!"

Chloe hot-footed it to the bathroom to refresh her makeup. All that heavy lifting had made her forehead shiny; she blotted and dusted it with powder to restore a matte complexion, before brushing a quick flick of bronzer over her cheekbones. Her hair situation was also a bit scruffy; she quickly pumped some mousse into her hands and scrunched it into her hair, taming stray hairs back into loose waves.

'What should I wear?' she thought—now was not the time to be trying on outfits! She knew she had to live up to the expectation; what did Karen expect her to look like outside of work? After all the fashion advice she had given her, she could hardly turn up looking like a tramp. Worrying about what to wear seemed silly since she just had two large boxes of designer clothes delivered; she couldn't go to Karen's office in only a cami top and jeans, dusty from cardboard boxes and covered in tiny tissue flakes.

Rushing out of the bathroom, her latest arrival caught her eye; the gold Palazzo jacket she had just unpacked looked back at her from the rail where she had left it—answering her fashion conundrum. It would dress up her white cami top and jeans she already had on—without appearing to try-hard—in a casual yet chic way. She dashed into her bedroom and rummaged through her unkempt dresser to find a necklace.

It was only from a cheap chain store, but it finished the look perfectly; mixing and matching with costumes accessories that looked expensive (unless you could afford otherwise), was the secret to dressing up designer pieces. She put the necklace on and opened her closet to find some flat pumps—sensible for running about town in since she was already cutting it fine.

Picking out a light beige pair with a gold buckle that she had purchased tears ago from a Palazzo sample sale, she slipped them on and went back into the living room. In one swoop, she snatched the gold Palazzo jacket off the hanger, then dashed back into the bathroom to check her outfit in the mirror. The jacket looked great! The fit was a little big in the body, but as it was cropped in length; it just seemed like it was meant to be a bit boxy and modern in fit.

Chloe thought she looked perfect for a professional lunch date. Not wanting to be any later than she already was, she grabbed her bag—making sure she had her phone and keys. As she went to leave, she looked at the boxes with a sigh; frustrated to be torn away from the wonders that lay undiscovered. What gems would she find in there?

Determined to be on time, she finally left her apartment, making it onto the sidewalk before pausing. A niggling feeling surfaced—as if someone had tapped her on the shoulder.

"*Shit*...The bag!" she shouted aloud to herself.

Chloe had forgotten the main reason as to why she was going to meet Karen in the first place; probably the first time it hadn't been playing on her mind. She quickly ran back upstairs and grabbed the dust bag from the top of her dresser before emptying the Palazzo bag of hangers onto the floor, and chucking it inside. She also grabbed the garbage bag full of old clothes for the Church Charity, deciding a quick stop off on the way was possible.

She checked her phone on her way back downstairs—it was now past eleven—and only had an hour to get over to Madison Avenue. Taking the subway with a trash bag of clothes was probably not the best option; now was a good time to invest in a cab ride; she didn't want to arrive all flustered and shiny-faced. Hailing a taxi, she skipped over to the car, crouching to speak to the driver through the window.

"Hey—can you take me to Madison Avenue, by Fifty-ninth? Oh... And please stop off at St Bart's on the way."

"Jump in," the driver said, adjusting his meter.

He drove as fast as he could, but inevitably in New York, there was always traffic. Tourists browsed the streets, businessmen rushed to get to lunchtime appointments, and now Chloe was dashing to a 'business meeting' of her own. Relaxing into the backseat of the taxi, she enjoyed the ride knowing that she was about to get the best help possible for her website. Looking out of the taxi window, she smiled to herself—catching her reflection.

She lived in one of the most amazing cities in the world, had great friends and a decent job (even if she did complain about it), and thought she looked rather good in her new jacket. It made her feel like a million dollars—that was the power of high fashion. Of course, she was fed up with the politics at work, but without Palazzo, all the recent opportunities wouldn't have come her way.

Her mind dashed to the boxes sitting back at her flat, thinking about what could be inside them. The few pieces she had unpacked already were real steals—and to think that they were given to her for free! She had assisted Mrs Ruthenstock well over the years, but this was a big re-payment for just doing her job. Chloe's smile grew bigger, things were starting to look up, and life was finally looking good from where she was sitting.

All this daydreaming and staring out of the car window had helped pass the journey in record timing, despite traffic. The cab stopped outside St Bart's Church for Chloe to quickly drop into the homeless shelter with her donations (pathetic in scale and quality to what she had received in exchange).

It was an errand that she could have done without right now, but knew she wouldn't do it otherwise (and the thought of karma biting her back). There was no room for bad luck in her life anymore; having received such good fortune lately, the deed of giving something back made her feel more acceptable and in tune with the universe.

*

The cab pulled up outside a towering office building; it looked very professional from the outside, you could see the security desk and elevators from the revolving glass doors. She paid the driver and added a generous tip—today she felt lucky and wanted to pass some of it on. Madison Avenue was busy with the lunchtime rush, people weaving in and out around her on the sidewalk. Checking Karen's message on her phone, she wanted to make sure the building she stood in front of was the correct one; as she did, Chloe noticed a few heads turn. They were either looking at her amazing vintage Palazzo jacket or because she was standing in their way.

Walking up to the entrance, a young office worker opened the door for her as he left for lunch, giving her a flirtatious smile as he scanned her from head to toe. 'I must be doing *something* right today,' she said to herself. The lobby had the usual marble flooring and pot plant decor with two elevators behind a security desk, to which Chloe made her way to; there was a gate before the elevators which meant she had to get a pass from the security desk.

"Hi, good afternoon… I'm here to meet with Karen Saunders at Dollars4U?" she said.

"Name?" the guard said, wasting no time.

"Chloe… Erm, Ravens."

The security guard checked for her name on his clipboard and handed her a temporary staff pass on a well-used lanyard.

"Take the elevator to the third floor, turn left and you're there."

He motioned towards the gate and pressed the buzzer to let her pass through.

"Thank you, Sir," she said, walking through the glass gates to get to the other side before they shut.

There was a gathering of workers waiting by the elevators and as she joined them, gained a few more looks. Chloe was starting to feel paranoid; had she poorly misjudged her outfit; was her makeup smudged? Whatever it was, she didn't have much time to think about it as the doors pinged open, prompting everyone to shuffle inside.

The elevator car was quite cramped after they had all poured in and pressed their floor buttons with jousting fingertips; personal space was definitely being invaded, but there was just about enough room for Chloe to quickly check her reflection in the mirror. She noticed there were fifteen floors in total, grateful that she only had to go to the third. As the doors closed, Chloe caught the eye of a young man who smiled at her as she primped her hair and blended her under-eye concealer using her clean fingertip (the one she hadn't used to press the button for the third floor).

He had mid length, brown wavy hair and wasn't strikingly handsome to her at first sight; if he hadn't smiled at her, she probably wouldn't have noticed him at all. Feeling awkward at his second-too-long glance, Chloe looked down at her feet; making eye contact with her in such an environment was more intense than what it would be elsewhere; it made her feel even more self-aware.

The elevator stopped on the first and second floors, emptying as it did. Eventually, the doors opened onto the third floor, and Chloe shuffled through the remaining passengers to make her exit. As she did, she brushed arms with her admirer—he too was getting out—still smiling at her; she felt like she had to say something to break the awkwardness.

"Erm… Ys it this way to the offices of Dollars4U?" she said, pointing down the hall to the left.

Still smiling, he answered, "Yeah that's right... You going there too?"

Great… She was stuck with him.

"Err… Yes. I have a meeting with the owner," she said unsure of how much information to give away.

"Cool! I'll buzz you in!"

They walked together down the corridor until they reached the entrance; he opened the door allowing her to pass through first like a gentleman, but she couldn't help but think she was more than capable of getting it herself. Still beaming at her, he overtook to be the first at the front desk.

"Hey Jeanie, this is…" he said, pausing for an introduction.

"Oh… I'm Chloe, Chloe Ravens… Here to see Karen Saunders."

"Oh yes, she is expecting you in her office… I'll take you there in just a moment," Jeanie said, picking up the phone that had been ringing since Chloe had arrived.

"Oh, I can show her," the guy said.

"Good afternoon, Dollars4U," Jeanie answered, before mouthing 'thank you' to him.

"Oh—thanks," Chloe said, not expecting an escort from the random lift creep himself.

His attempt at flirting was way too obvious for her liking, and although she wanted to be polite, there was no way she was trying to tease back. The office layout didn't seem particularly large; she was sure she could have found her own way with a little direction. Past reception was the call centre, banks of desks with workers sat at their computers tapping furiously on their keyboards while talking into headsets to customers.

They walked through the office in silence until they reached the other side which ended with two rooms, boxed off by glass walls; one had a huge conference table surrounded with chairs, the other was Karen's office—it had a silver plaque engraved with her name and title in black lettering.

"Okay, so this is it... I'm Brian by the way," he said, finally introducing himself; holding out his hand.

"Nice to meet you," Chloe said, gingerly shaking his hand—not really wanting to have contact with him.

"Good luck!" Brian said before walking back to his desk, looking back around—twice.

Chloe knocked on Karen's door, after a minute or so the doorknob turned, and the door flung open.

"Hi! You made it... Come on in. Welcome to my office. I always see *you* in your habitat; finally, you get to see *me* in mine," Karen said, air-kissing Chloe on both cheeks.

Chloe stepped inside, looking around; Karen's office was clean white and clutter-free; the glass wall was an incentive to keep it looking perfect at all times.

"Have a seat... Did you have a great time yesterday?" Karen said, perched on top of her desk.

"I had to work, but it was fine," Chloe said, taking a seat in front of the desk; putting her bags down. "How was yours?"

"Well, we were closed for the day, and we have just about made it back to the office today... So, 'great' I'd say! Did you get here okay?"

"Oh yes, fine... I got a taxi—Oh, this is for you..." Chloe said, wasting no time to get to business; she was there for a reason and had kept her side of the bargain.

Chloe handed over the Palazzo bag to her. Karen clapped her hands together and gasped.

"Ah! Thanks so much for this," she squealed. "How much do I owe you?"

"Well, I get fifty percent, so $2,500," Chloe said, deciding that honesty was best; Karen was already doing her a huge favour, she didn't need to milk it.

"Such a bargain!" Karen said, opening the bag excitedly.

'What is it with women and handbags?' Chloe thought to herself, 'If this is her idea of a bargain, then she should see the prices at staff sale!'

"I can't let you keep the bill, unfortunately... If work found out, I will be in serious trouble," Chloe said, making sure she covered her back while Karen was in awe at her newest addition.

Chloe's mind wondered, 'Where *is* the receipt? It must be at home somewhere,' she figured, after emptying the contents of the shopping bag on her bedroom floor in a last minute rush. Karen had whipped the clutch out of its dust-bag in record timing and was looking at it with wide eyes, not bothered in the slightest by what Chloe had just said.

"Of course—no problem... I'm not going to return it anyway... I've wanted it since the day I saw it... I'll transfer the money to your account now," Karen said, carefully putting the bag aside and sitting down at her computer.

Karen swivelled her computer screen around so Chloe could see what she was doing, as she did the office phone rang.

"Yes, Jeanie?"

"Hi Karen, lunch is here. Shall I bring it on through?"

"Thank you, that would be great."

Chloe wondered what it would be like working for Karen. So far she had a good impression, and Karen was always a pleasure to deal with when she shopped at Palazzo. Chloe just knew that Karen must be a great boss to work for; the employees that she had come into contact with so far seemed polite, happy and helpful, and the way Karen spoke to Jeanie was with great warmth and kindness. 'Regina could learn a thing or two from her,' Chloe noted.

"Have you eaten? I ordered us lunch... Do you like Sushi?"

Chloe had forgotten about eating amidst the day's excitement; suddenly her stomach rumbled at the reminder.

"I do...Thank you so much; you really didn't have to."

"My pleasure!"

Jeanie knocked and entered with two lunch bags, putting them down on the desk before leaving to resume her post at the front desk.

"This way we get to hang out a little, and hopefully we will sort out this website of yours! Tell me all about it," Karen said, unpacking the sushi from the bags onto the desk.

Karen listened to Chloe's plans for her blog over lunch, demolishing all of the food that was ordered. Afterwards, Karen saw to the matter of transferring the funds back into Chloe's account, which didn't take long. Karen was a money mastermind and was used to paying out money into people's accounts—that was her business model after all.

"Okay, that's all done," Karen said, getting up from her leather chair—prompting Chloe to do the same. "Come... I'll introduce you to Brian. He is the best at graphics and website layouts and stuff. He is the one responsible for my website."

'Great,' Chloe thought. Would this be the same Brian she had just met? Would she endure his flirting all afternoon long? Karen guided Chloe out of her office and down the hall towards the main office; weaving through the sea of workers, they arrived at Brian's desk which was partitioned off into his own private cubicle.

"Hey, Bri... This is Chloe—my friend from Palazzo I told you about?" Karen said, leaning in to nudge him on the latter. "Chloe, this is my computer genius; Brian."

They both nodded—exchanging awkward looks—not bothering to shake hands all over again.

"Wait… Do you two know each other?" Karen said, feeling like she had missed something.

"We just met in the elevator… Brian was kind enough to show me to your office," Chloe said, keen to squash any thoughts Karen might have had about the two of them 'knowing each other'.

"Oh, right… Well, that's Bri for you… Always helpful. So, Brian… As I said, make her website look a million dollars! God knows you have done that for me a few times… Anyway, I'll leave you *two* to work. Whatever you need, any upgrades or extras, you can put it on our account Bri."

Karen gave them a smirk and a raised eyebrow before leaving, sensing something quite cute and naive between them; like a mother leaving her teenage son to do 'home studies' with his first girlfriend.

"So, let's get started!" Brian said, pulling up a swivel chair for Chloe to sit on.

Chloe took off her jacket and hung it on the back of the chair. It was warm outside, and the office was quite stuffy (along with the added embarrassment which had made her feel flushed).

"Okay, so first things first… Show me what we're working with here," Brian said, pushing his keyboard over to her.

The desk was crammed with magazines and not exactly the executive size, forcing them to sit quite close together. Chloe's arm brushed against his a few times as she punched in her web address on the keyboard, which was somewhat awkward. StacksOfStyle.com had loaded onto the computer monitor and Brian tried his best not to laugh out loud.

"What? What's so funny?" Chloe said, noticing he had dipped his head and covered his grin with his hand.

"Well, it's… No, nothing—nothing we can't fix anyway."

Chloe knew he was laughing at the state she had left it in; it was in a mess from when she had tried to update it herself. Realising that she was sitting with a professional—looking at a shambles of a website— she couldn't do anything but laugh herself. This gave Brian permission to laugh out loud with her, immediately it dissolved the strangeness that brewed between them.

Brian thought Chloe was beautiful and was instantly attracted; from the moment he set eyes on her in the elevator, he knew that this was the girl Karen had told him all about. Although, she was a hundred times better than how Karen had described her. Brian assumed that he would be helping some silly fashion addict air-head—from some stuck-up store—with her pretentious website. Instead, he was introduced to a beautiful, stylish woman with a shit website that made him laugh; not only was she stunning, but she was funny too.

Ignorant of the attraction that Brian had for her, Chloe explained how she wanted S.O.S to look and what she needed it to do.

"Now you understand why I need help huh? I want it to look simple, clean and easy, but most of all—professional. I want to be able to upload pictures and articles easily, and readers to be able to comment on them also… I was thinking, 'StacksOfStyle' at the top with site navigation options…What do you think?"

Brian smiled and opened up a design program.

"Okay, well first things first—let's get you a fantastic looking logo! I've already started work on it actually."

"Oh, yes—right," Chloe said, amazed at the lengths he was going to.

"Your name's Ravens, right?"

By the time she had confirmed, he had already clipped a picture of a raven and was scribbling on the mouse-pad with a stylus. Chloe saw the obvious connection, but was unsure of where this was going—so far it seemed a bit naff. She sat there in silence while he did his thing, trusting and watching him work with such speed.

Watching him do his thing on the computer had made him look different—attractive even—and that very thought unnerved her. In just ten minutes he had a picture of a stylised raven and StacksOfStyle. com in a font that looked like it had been hand-written; all joined up in black. The black raven and the chic black text looked great together;

the raven was strong and gave credibility to the silly name that she had made up one drunken night when registering the domain. Chloe nodded to Brian in a salute that she was happy with it.

"Next, let's upgrade the web-builder you are using. It's old and very limiting; we can just transfer all this over to a straightforward layout, ideal for blogs."

Once again he was clicking around on the computer—downloading this and that from different sites. Chloe couldn't keep up with what was happening on the screen; she had no idea what was going on, but she knew it was all good stuff and was in safe hands. She sat there watching and co-operating with his questions, not wanting to disturb him from working his magic.

"Homepage… When someone logs on, they will see your raven logo and brand name at the top—just like how you want."

'Wow,' thought Chloe, S.O.S was now a brand name! This had put what she was trying to do into context. This was no longer a hobby; it was a stepping-stone to greater, more significant things and she needed to think big if this was going to be a success.

"I'll give you a USB stick with your graphics on so you can use them on other things—like stationary. Next, let's choose a template for the general layout," Brian said, trying not to lose her with technicalities.

Chloe was amazed by Brian's skills; he made, what she struggled with, look so easy, and he was certainly starting to grow on her. They continued to work on the site together for a few more hours. Brian paused every now and then to ask for her opinion, and what she wanted was no hard task; he was a computer wizard, and this was a simple task for him—it was just time-consuming.

They worked hard for the whole afternoon, and by now, the skeleton that Brian had drawn up for the site was starting to get filled up with icons and buttons—and all at Karen's expense. There was no way that Chloe would be able to afford this herself, her site really was going to look a million bucks! Chloe thought she had understood before, but now she really did appreciate the power of networking and having good connections. She had heard the saying lots of times: 'It's not what you know, but who you know'.

It was approaching late afternoon, and Karen had popped over to check on them. "Hey guys," she said, looking at what progress had been made so far. "Wow, that looks so cool! See Chloe… I told you he was a genius—didn't I?"

"Yeah, he is amazing," Chloe said, realising that Brian was smiling at her—obviously pleased that she thought he was 'amazing'.

This time it was Brian that was blushing from all the compliments.

"Oh… It's nothing. I mean… I'll need a few days to complete it, but it's getting there."

"All I need to do now is write some new articles. Brian has archived all my old ones and is going to upload them onto the new site for me. I have a picture gallery and everything now!"

"I love the logo, it looks chic, and the name has a ring to it… I think you could be onto something here… Listen, I have a friend that has an online fashion company, she might be able to advertise your site or something. Maybe if you write about their products, they will advertise your blog in return? Hmmm… Leave it with me!" Karen said, planning Chloe's next move already.

"Wow, really? That would be amazing!" Chloe said, not quite believing Karen could sort her out with an industry contact, helping her even more.

"Brian, give her a working email too so people can contact her direct, and use that logo to create some business cards… She's going to need them!"

"Oh, Karen… Really, I couldn't ask you to do any—"

"No! I won't take no for an answer… You just saved me a small fortune. I'm going to make sure you are fully set up by the time you leave this place. I know all about online businesses, and it's my pleasure to pass on the knowledge. Anyway, I gotta dash to a meeting right now, but you guys carry on. I'll email my friend later and tell her all about you."

Looking at the computer screen for long periods of time was exhausting, and the chair was beginning to get hard and flat against Chloe's ass. 'If *I* need a break, Brian must definitely need one too!' she thought.

"Come on Brian, let's have a break. I'll buy you a coffee, it's the least I can do."

Brian sank back in his chair as he stretched out, flexing his muscles, showing off arms that Chloe didn't see coming; he obviously worked out. Chloe shrugged it off as another attempt to flirt and grabbed her jacket off the back of her chair. She re-glossed her lips in a way that looked as though she was flirting back, but that was far from her intention.

**

The coffee shop was only a few doors down; they managed to find a window seat that looked out onto the busy street. A break was a good idea, even just to get some air and to stretch their legs. Not feeling awkward in Brian's presence anymore, Chloe took the chance to ask Brian about himself. After he had shown her what he could do with her website, the least she could do was show a little interest back.

"So, how long have you been working for Karen?"

"Oh—well, I was working for the company that Karen commissioned to design her website—it had cost her thousands—she almost ran out of budget at one point. Then one day she came to the office, I was so pissed off with work, and she could see that I wasn't happy there. I was the best guy they had—just saying—but still, my boss didn't wanna make me a director. I was so frustrated if you know what I mean…"

"Oh, yeah I sure do—believe me! Working at Palazzo is not all fashion and glamour. My boss is a *fucking* bitch!" Chloe said, sipping her latte.

Her hatred for Regina was so intense that those kinds of words just flew out of her mouth naturally whenever she spoke about her.

Brian shook his head and laughed; that's what he liked about her—she wasn't the stereotypical fashion bimbo. She had guts as well as good looks, and how she had negotiated a new website with Karen showed him she was smart too.

"Right," Brian continued. " So, I was assigned to look after Karen's site—this was like five years ago—she wanted to make a few changes to the site, new buttons and stuff, and I thought to myself… Fuck it, *fuck* this job!"

Now Brian had cursed too, Chloe felt more comfortable in his company; he was also capable of having a potty mouth.

"So what did you do?" Chloe pressed.

"Well, I offered to do the job privately… For much less! And now, I have a great job… Don't get me wrong, it was a lot of hard work at the start as the team was so small, but now we have expanded, and I run the whole art and design team… And you know something else? Karen is an ace boss! She came from nothing and understands that being nice to people and surrounding yourself with the best will eventually pay off in the end."

Hearing his story, Chloe couldn't believe how much they had in common; they had both been rescued by Karen and had been through similar emotions at work—so she told him all about Palazzo.

"Well, I can safely say I know where you're coming from. There was this promotion at work that I was perfect for, but of course, I didn't get it. Only ass-lickers get ahead in that place. Fashion is bitchy, especially retail. Hopefully I will create something that allows me to follow my dream *and* work in fashion at the same time with this blog. Karen offered to help me out—and like you—I offered to do her a 'job' privately in return."

"And what kinda 'job' was that?"

"Basically, I used my staff discount on a handbag."

Brian laughed; it all made sense now as to why she was helping her create a lavish website. Karen was a sucker for fashion—and at a discount.

"So, how much is this handbag? I wanna know how much my expertise is worth," Brian joked.

"Five grand," Chloe said bluntly.

"Whew!"

Brian blew out a breath and raised an eyebrow; he couldn't believe a handbag could cost that much.

"Well, that's the great thing about Karen... She sees potential in people, and yes, you *will* create something for yourself. Karen is probably securing you a deal with her friend as we speak—that's just the person she is."

Impressed with his positive outlook, Chloe was starting to warm up to him. He seemed a bit creepy at first, a sort of stalker that could only be found in elevators waiting for prey—that taught her to judge a book by its cover! Having spent the afternoon with Brian, she had discovered that he was talented and humble with it, which she found very attractive.

She had noted how his hair smelt fresh and clean when he moved his head (he shampooed it every day in the shower), and having watched his manly hands create on the screen in front of her made them seem kind of sexy; when he took off his sweater, she finally saw the athletic frame that hid beneath. Having now had the time to talk and assess her (initially unwanted) admirer accurately, she also realised he was quite handsome underneath his spectacles—putting on a pair of tinted glasses herself to see what was really in front of her. From the moment he first saw Chloe in the elevator until now, he hadn't stopped smiling.

For a moment they sat in silence, but Brian was pleased that she felt comfortable enough to sit there without saying a word and not seem out of place. She was now smiling back at him, and he definitely wanted to see her again. The opportunity was there; a lot of work was still to be done on the website, and there was no way he was going to finish it in one afternoon.

"Listen, thanks for the coffee, but I better get back to the office and pack up for the day."

"Oh—sure no problem… I don't want to keep you," Chloe said, not wanting to be kept either; she was desperate to get back home and sort through the boxes of clothes that sat waiting for her.

"Why don't I carry on working on your site for the rest of the week? Give me your number, I'll call you when it's all done… We can meet for dinner or something, and I'll show you the final result… And your business cards, I'll get those designed and printed right away—so I'll need your number for that too," he said, sliding her a napkin.

'Smooth' Chloe thought to herself. She took out a pen from her bag and jotted down her number.

"Let me know when you're done," she said, passing the folded napkin to him.

Judging by what he had already created, she knew Brian would do an excellent job; giving him more time to work on the site meant that it was going to be even more amazing. That and the fact they had found common ground with how they felt about their professional lives; she was confident Brian would help give her new venture the best chance it could have to succeed.

*** 

Back at the office, most of the Dollars4U staff were getting ready to leave work for the day; desperate to get home after surviving the day with a hangover. Chloe walked back with Brian to his workstation to make sure she hadn't left anything behind and not down a few things she wanted him to include in the new site build.

"Bri, thanks for everything—really!" she said, now on short name terms with him which gave him a giggle. "I've made some points for reference, but just call me if you have any questions—or if there is anything else I can do to help."

"Sure, don't mention it… Leave it with me; StacksOfStyle is in safe hands. It's been a pleasure to meet you."

Not sure whether a kiss on the cheek would be too forward or not, Chloe decided to extend her hand to shake his (much to his disappointment); she had been out of action with men for some time. This time she fully grasped his hand, the warmth was a pleasant sensation she had forgotten about; his man-sized hand was tiny in comparison to hers and cupped it fully.

"Great to meet you too… I'm just gonna say bye to Karen before I go," she said, walking away.

Sweeping one side of her hair behind her ear, she looked back to see Brian still smiling at her. The warm touch of his skin had certainly made an impact on her, and the thrill of possibly finding unexpected romance had given her a surge of energy. Reaching Karen's office, the door was left open which Chloe knocked on before entering.

"Oh, hi—you're still here? I have a dinner tonight… I can't wait to use my new bag! Did Brian sort everything out for you?"

"Yes, thank you so much… He is going to work on it some more, and we'll catch up once he is ready to show me the finished product."

"Oh! You guys are going to meet up? That's a great idea!" (Karen wasn't stupid, she could spot a romance blossoming when she saw one.) "You know, he really is a great guy—a real catch... It's a wonder he hasn't been snapped up already."

Chloe could feel herself blush; she wanted to escape what was clearly a set-up, as well as a helping hand with her website; suddenly realising why Karen had asked if she was single.

"Look, I cannot thank you enough… I'm gonna head off, but seriously, thank you so much!"

"Don't mention it, I'd better be going too… I'll see you soon," Karen said, giving her a hug. "Oh, I nearly forgot… That friend of mine I told you about, the one with the online store? She is sure she can come up with something to help you out and will get back to me with more details."

"What! That would be amazing… I seriously don't know how to thank you," Chloe said, feeling embarrassed once again.

Embarrassment, that seemed to be the theme of the day along with awkwardness and plenty of blushing (and good fortune of course).

"Don't thank me—thank Brian," Karen said, really meaning 'thank me by dating Brian'.

Chloe got the hint loud and clear, it wasn't very subtle after all; she rolled her eyes playfully at Karen, telling her that she knew what she was up to all right.

****

Leaving the offices of Dollars4U, Chloe had a bounce in her walk; she held her head high as she strutted down the avenue, feeling great in her new vintage Palazzo jacket. For once she felt like the city was hers to have, she was finally getting herself out there. Life felt good and dark thoughts of going back to work under Regina's spell didn't seem so daunting anymore; she had something in her life to look forward to... And maybe someone. Walking down Madison and onto Fifth, she stopped to look at the store windows.

Her blog would soon be ready to re-launch, she needed to be prepared to fill it with new and current content. Taking pictures of the window displays with her phone, Chloe decided that she would start by writing a review on the fall/winter collections from some of her favourite designer brands. Then she remembered the boxes waiting for her at home! How could she forget about those? She had been dying to open them all day long. She didn't need to walk the streets of New York for inspiration—it was sitting in her flat waiting for her all along.

# CHAPTER ELEVEN

Chloe's apartment was a mess; sheets of tissue paper were strewn all over the place; two large empty boxes were flattened and taped together, ready to go to the trash. Chloe slumped on her sofa staring in disbelief, staring at a rail packed full of designer clothing—now all belonging to her. The process of unpacking it all had been both exciting and exhausting. She had even run out of plastic hangers to hang them on and had it taken her the most of the evening to unpack (because she was trying things on as she made her way through the of course).

Time was also spent satisfyingly merchandising the clothes on the hangers as if she was opening up a boutique in her apartment (she had indeed received enough to stock a shop). There were over thirty pieces of clothing, five pairs of shoes and three purses. Chloe didn't think that Mrs Ruthenstock would send so much, but she wasn't complaining about it. As well as the Chanel jacket and Gucci pants, there were two Gucci dresses, a Prada pantsuit, and a sexy Dolce & Gabbana dress to name a few—proving just how much Mrs Ruthenstock loved to shop.

The day had been eventful and after a quick bite to eat, Chloe perused through her new collection. Ideas for her blog zoomed through her mind, wishing it was finished already, but she was pleased Brian was taking it seriously and spending time on it—she would have a website to be proud of eventually.

With a flurry of inspiration, Chloe sat at the breakfast bar and opened up her laptop to begin writing about the window displays she had snapped earlier (which were now downloading in the background). The words flew from her brain as her fingers punched at the keys, eager to bang the article out before she forgot what was on her mind; her right hand cramped a little, but she didn't quit.

*As summer transforms to fall, boost your wardrobe with new textures and colours for the coming season. Cropped jackets are a great layer that isn't too heavy when the cold is yet to set in. Summer tones are replaced with burgundies, velvety greens, and burnt oranges; although white sticks around—turning from 'bright' to 'icy' whites—adorned with crystals and pearls for the upcoming party season, as well as mixing with darker tones for a fresh, new winter palette…*

Once she was satisfied with the copy, she started to arrange the pictures around the text, referencing which store they belonged to; getting lost in creating her post with the noise of the TV in the background— hypnotising rather than annoying her. As she typed and clicked away, her cell phone beeped and vibrated harshly on the kitchen side, rousing her from the work-induced coma. Picking it up, she saw a text message from an unknown number had come through; intrigued, she stopped what she was doing to open it.

HI CHLOE… GREAT TO MEET U 2DAY. I HAVE BEEN WORKING SOME MORE ON UR SITE THIS EVENING… HOPE 2B FINISHED SOON… IT'S SIMPLE BUT EF-FECTIVE. R. U. FREE THIS SATURDAY? BRI ; )

Chloe's heart thumped against her chest, she didn't expect to hear from him so soon; it had been a long time since a guy had messaged her to ask her out—even if it was technically a 'business' meeting. However they both disguised it, it was essentially a date. She knew that he liked her, and she was starting to come around to Karen's choice of match, but she was eager to see the finished result more than him. Saving his number into her contacts gave her enough time to think about her reply; she didn't want to come across too enthusiastic and carefully chose her words, saying exactly what she needed to and not much more.

NICE 2 MEET U 2 BRI! SAT IS COOL WITH ME… FINISH WORK @6. MEET 4 DINNER? CHLOE X

Reading back over the message Chloe wondered whether the kiss was too much? It was too late to worry about it now, the message had been sent already, and in a matter of seconds Brian had replied (she pictured him with his phone in his hand waiting for her to message him back).

SOUNDS GR8. I CAN MEET U OUTSIDE WORK... I
KNOW A GREAT PLACE TO EAT NEARBY. BRI X

He too had replied with a kiss, it was all Chloe saw at first and had to read over the message again. She felt a bolt of surprise within her, the kind you only get when a guy messages you to arrange a date, and for once she wouldn't worry about what to wear. In fact, she had already thought about wearing the black Dolce & Gabbana dress that was hanging in front of her—or was that too full-on for the first date? Was this a second date—was this even a date at all? Although she was confused by it all, seeing Brian again meant she would finally get her new website—and that in itself was exciting enough.

After messaging him back to finalise arrangements, Chloe returned to writing—although this time she felt like a *real* writer. Brian had reminded her that she was actually doing this now, not just dreaming about it. Thinking about the future made he look back on how this all started; she remembered how she used to write about how to copy a designer look for less; going back to her roots, she scoured the Internet for affordable pieces to recreate the latest seasonal looks but on a smaller budget.

Looking at her new and luxurious additions, she felt like a kid staring through the window of a toy store at Christmas. The black Dolce & Gabbana dress stood out amongst the rest on the rail, her eye zooming in like a magpie to pick it out. She whipped off her comfy's and pulled the dress off the hanger to try on right away, struggling to do the zipper at the back she just pinched it together as she hot-footed to the bathroom.

Standing in front of the mirror, she went up on tiptoes to mimic heels (saving her from actually digging a pair out from her endless, disorganised collection) and pulled her hair up. It was a rather sexy dress for Mrs Ruthenstock, probably the reason why it was now hers; it was slim-fit and made from slippery black silk, knee length with thin spaghetti straps and detailed stitching around the bust that resembled that of a corset—oozing class as well as sex!

It was perfect—a little too much for a first or even second date—perfect for making an impression as the newest fashionista in town (be it for professional or personal reasons). Chloe skipped back to the rail and flicked through to find a jacket to tone it down with. *Eureka!* She had found exactly what she was looking for and had recalled unpacking this little treasure earlier.

The black Chanel tuxedo jacket would add a touch of class, as well as acting as a modest cover-up. It was cropped in length and slim-fit—making the look very European—and with a simple pair of black pumps, the look would be complete. This mini fashion show gave Chloe enthusiasm to take another look at the rail. There were too many beautiful things to look at properly while unpacking (desperate to finish the task all at once), but she recalled finding an expensive Palazzo evening gown in the selection.

When she had stumbled across it, she couldn't believe her luck and began rifling through to find it, which wasn't hard. The dress was made from beautiful navy silk and embellished heavily with tiny Swarovski crystal beads and sequins of the same colour. It was a long, halter-neck style gown with a revealing keyhole bust; it had a scooped back that fell down low—right down to butt crack territory.

At first glance, there seemed to be a few beads missing, and the hem looked a little tatty (which was probably why it was being thrown out), but to Chloe, it was a diamond in the rough. She had no occasion to wear such couture to, but it looked impressive hanging up on the rail (and eventually in her wardrobe), even in its worn state.

To run alongside her article, Chloe thought it was a good idea to showcase some of the new collection she now proudly owned. Remembering the Palazzo jacket that Mrs Ruthenstock was wearing at the store had inspired her to write about vintage pieces and how to wear them once again. Gold featured heavily in the latest fall/winter Palazzo collection, but it was also a colour that most people already had in their wardrobes—like the gold jacket she now owned.

Chloe took a quick snap of her posing in the mirror with it on and then rushed over to her laptop to find a burgundy dress for under $40 online—mimicking Palazzo's palette of the season—proving that designer looks don't have to cost a fortune. With a little bit of imagination, recycling, and savvy shopping, the latest runway look could be yours to own. This gust of inspiration had transformed an early evening into late night, and Chloe had already written two new entries for her blog—she was on a roll!

It was unusual for Chloe not to message Dom on her day off, but today had been a crazy rush. Likewise, it wasn't like Dom to not send a text at least, but he too was having an eventful day of his own. As she got ready for bed, Chloe wondered what had kept him occupied, and more importantly—how he was feeling. He had been dreading the end of the week since it began, and it was now coming along fast.

*

Hungover and feeling tired from partying the night before didn't help with his lack of energy, willing the hours to pass on the shop floor—not having Chloe on shift with him made the day drag out even more. The womenswear team had numerous tasks to get on with in preparation for the arrival of their new department manager, and Dom had elected himself to tidy the stock room, making sure everything was in clinical order. Being short staffed and busy, the stockroom had suffered lately, and it was starting to look shabby.

Shoeboxes were piled high at pillar ends of corresponding aisles waiting to be put back, and thousands of dollars worth of clothes from a personal shopping appointment had been dumped over a rail and left for days (personal shoppers were notorious for dumping things where they didn't belong after they had no use for them).

The task of tidying and sorting helped to pass a few hours, but he soon got bored of clearing up after everyone else. Dom rather liked working at Palazzo—mainly for the discount and how great it sounded when someone asked him where he worked—but the glamour of it all was starting to slip away for him too. Having spent all week at the five-star Plaza hotel, how could he ever go back to normality?

It was possible that tonight held all the answers to Dom's questions; it was Jason's last evening in New York, and for that reason he was anxious. He knew deep down that any possibility of having a relationship with this guy was a long shot, but he fantasised about moving to L.An and starting a new life with him; somewhere in the back of his mind, it *was* a reality. Although he had been dying to get out of work all day long, when it was finally time to leave, he wished he had more time to think. Think about how to act smooth and try to find the perfect words to say; how would he make Jason see that he had fallen for him without breaking down and embarrassing himself?

Walking down Fifth Avenue towards the hotel slowly in thought, Dom tried his best to prolong the time between now and heartbreak. No matter how hard he tried, each step seemed like two, and before he knew it, he was already in the elevator up to Jason's room. Now outside, he waited for a beat before knocking and leant against the wall. For a moment he thought about not knocking at all and saving the disappointment by ending it all himself, by turning around and going home and never speaking to Jason ever again.

But he wasn't that strong, he cared too much to not know how this would play out and would be plagued by 'what if' for the rest of his life. No one would ever compare to Jason Hart afterwards, he was 'the one', and Dom had to face his fear if he was ever going to get what he wanted. 'This is insane!' he thought and knocked on the door before he could act stupid; there was no point in putting this off any longer. The door opened immediately; Jason stood in the doorway, wet from the shower in just a white towel which put a smile back on Dom's face in an instant.

"You have ten seconds to get in here and on that bed!" Jason said, pulling him in by his shirt, slamming the door shut behind them and pushing him towards the bed as they kissed.

All of Dom's worries faded into the background—but that was the problem—there wasn't an issue with the physical side of things; it was the emotional side that was unclear. Sex was easily mistaken for love, but Dom was no fool to men and knew that sex meant just that; he knew Jason held all the power on this matter. He was older, he was the successful one with a career and could afford to call the shots; he held the key to the future of their relationship.

Dom yearned for this life-changing moment, and he was holding on to the possibility of being happy with Jason in L.A with a tight grip. He had come a long way from London to New York, and now his destiny seemed to be in Los Angeles—or at least in his mind it did. Lying back and enjoying the exhilarating sensation of after sex (much like a good work out at the gym), Dom fully expected another evening in bed with this hunk, but Jason had other ideas.

"Right, get showered and dressed," Jason ordered, jumping up from the bed like a spring.

"Wha—where are we going?"

Couldn't they just lie there and relax? This could have been an excellent opportunity for Dom to bring up the dreaded subject; he was slightly annoyed at having to get dressed to go out again.

"Just for a walk and some dinner… That's all."

Before Dom could contest, Jason had already stepped into the en-suite shower to rinse off the sweat, leaving the main bathroom free for Dom to use. Dom thought about following him in, but then that would just delay things with even more sex. Plus, neither of them had used the small shower next to the bedroom before; they had always used the larger one in the main bathroom which could host an orgy under the rainfall showerhead—he clearly wasn't invited this time.

Instead, Dom did as he was told and quickly washed before picking out what to wear. With not much information to go on, he decided on a tight black T-shirt, jeans and a pair of sneakers, but the simple ensemble needed something else to finish it. He looked up and saw Jason's leather bomber hanging on the back of the chair by the desk—the perfect answer. Or was it a bit cheeky of him he wondered? Dom slipped into it and shrugged it onto his shoulders; it felt a bit big, but Dom liked that, almost like one of Jason's hugs.

Appearing from the bathroom to get dressed, Jason slipped on some boxers and started to get dressed to go out. Dom lay on the bed with his arms resting behind his head, watching him pull on his ripped blue jeans, fastening the buckle of his brown leather belt before throwing on a checked shirt. Feeling like he was being watched, Jason looked up at Dom, buttoning his shirt as he did.

The sight of Dom in his leather jacket made him smile, he thought it was cute of him to wear it (even if it was cheeky of him). Even though he had only just watched him get dressed, Dom wanted to rip Jason's clothes off him for another round, but he resisted. Something told him that Jason wasn't playing this evening—he had a severe glint in his eye which he hadn't seen before.

This authoritative, dominating side made him feel slightly nervous, he didn't want to push his luck too far; he didn't want to get told off. Dom followed him down the hallway, into the elevator and out to the lobby. All the while Jason remained silent, which Dom thought was rather strange, but then he had figured out why. 'He is nervous about bringing up the subject of *us* too,' he thought in a 'Eureka' moment. Outside the hotel, a car awaited them, Jason jogged ahead to get the passenger door.

"Come on, get in… I've got somewhere to take you."

Dom smiled, he knew Jason would have something planned all along, even though he was fooled to believe that there wasn't one. The car took them all the way down to the Financial District until they reached South Street Seaport.

"Pier seventeen please," Jason said.

"What the—where are we going?" Dom was confused as to why in Hell they were here of all places.

"You'll see…"

As they approached the edge of the pier, Dom spotted a boat trip stand advertising tours of New York City by night. It was evident that *this* was where Jason was taking him; Chloe was right, Jason had planned something touristy.

"I've always wanted to see New York City like this and I want you to experience it with me man… I've had the best time ever being here with you, and I thought this would the best way to spend our last evening together," he said as Dom's eyes melted into his.

Dom couldn't believe he had hired a boat just for them; he looked around for other tourists, but no one else was around except for them and the skipper team. This bold statement showed he did care, that he wanted some kind of emotional reminder to remember at least, and that made Dom happy inside. For a moment things were looking good, but as Dom boarded the boat the 'last evening together' speech rang through his head—what did he mean? Was this their *last* evening altogether? Once again the fear and paranoia had settled back in.

He didn't have much time to dwell on it, the boat ride was breath-taking and distracting (although he hated to admit it); he very rarely saw this part of the city, especially by boat along the East River. Alone, they drank champagne as they watched the town go by with the summer breeze on the water drifting through their hair. Dom watched Jason as he tucked it behind his ears, but strands become loose; Jason smiled back at him, full of excitement at the glorious views of New York by riverboat. Dom didn't take his eyes off him as he wondered why Jason would go to all this effort if tonight were indeed their last night together.

The private boat took them to the Downtown helipad where a private helicopter had landed and was once again, obviously waiting for them. Dom looked on in disbelief; was this really happening? Then the reality sank in…

'He expects me to get in that?'

He began to freak out; both scared and amazed at the same time. Dom had never flown in a helicopter before, and this one seemed so fragile and small. Casting a look at him, Jason felt Dom's unease.

"Come on, this is going to be fun!"

Jason had already shaken the pilot's hand and was securing his valuables in the zip compartments of his leather jacket which Dom was wearing. Dom could hardly wimp out now, so without giving it too much thought he did the same (if only he could forget his worries as quickly). Before he could realise what he was doing, Dom was sat in the back of the helicopter gripping Jason's hand—which he squeezed back in comfort. The Pilot's voice came through their headphones as the tour guide waved them off from a safe distance. The blades of the chopper started up, and the pilot flicked switches as the momentum of the rotor blades began to speed up.

"Good evening and welcome to your helicopter tour of New York City. I am your pilot and guide for the journey and will be pointing out various landmarks throughout. So, sit back, relax and enjoy your adventure!"

Lifting off the helipad was a scary and exciting thing for Dom, while Jason's face continued to light up—he hadn't stopped beaming with excitement since they stepped out of the taxi; a contrast to how he was behaving back at the hotel. However, Dom's stomach felt like it flipped as the altitude changed the equilibrium in his body, rising higher and higher in the sky; the feeling was a lot different from that of a plane. A plane felt enclosed, safe and structured compared to this free and daring sensation.

Once accustomed to the way the helicopter glided, Dom began to relax a little; he sat on the edge of his seat, finally being able to focus and take in the sights. After all, the view from up here was quite spectacular; the city lights and traffic were magical—like a scene from a movie. It was almost unbelievable, but the fact he was sat in a helicopter was a reminder that it was indeed real.

Dom pointed out buildings in the blush of the evening sky, in the direction of famous landmarks as the pilot mentioned them through their cans. Dom's fears had quelled once he saw Brooklyn Bridge and the Statue Of Liberty—he had no choice but to be as excited as Jason—it all seemed so small from a bird's-eye view.

"Quick, pass me my phone!" Jason said.

Dom fumbled to retrieve it from the inside zip pocket so Jason could snap away as they skimmed over the Hudson River where the fireworks had illuminated the skies above it the night before and spotted buildings such as the Empire State Building, and where the World Trade Centre Towers once stood. The lights of Times Square shone brightly, as did Jason's eyes.

Seeing how handsome and happy he was in this moment, Dom couldn't help himself and leant in for a quick kiss. Jason accepted with a peck on the lips before pulling him in for a picture. Again, Dom questioned why he would go to all this trouble if he weren't serious about him; in a way, this was proof that he *was* into him. Realising that he should be enjoying the moment rather than worrying about the future, he took a deep breath and came back to the present.

The helicopter started to head back down the Jersey coast to the landing spot just as Dom was starting to enjoy it, but much to his relief at the same time—he had survived the ordeal! Now safely back on the ground, it had taken Dom a while to feel his feet plant back on the tarmac again; his legs felt like jelly with both fear and exhilaration.

"Ready for a close-up?" Jason said, nodding his head in the direction of The Statue Of Liberty.

Dom looked up and then back at Jason to find him jogging ahead, towards another boat that was waiting for them. Dom had already been surprised by the evening's antics, but this was another level. It was clear that Jason was making a statement, a huge one; if Dom wanted confirmation of how he felt, then this was it—it wasn't going to get any more romantic than this! Pushing all doubt out of his mind, Dom decided to run after his dream of love and ran after Jason towards the boat.

It took them along the New York harbour towards the Hudson River which looked fabulous as the evening sky began to turn purple; as the night grew darker. The lights from buildings and traffic had illuminated the city like a fairground and reflected back off the water. The boat finally arrived in front of the Statue Of Liberty where they could take in its glorious sight. Dom hadn't been that impressed by it when he first arrived in New York; it seemed so much smaller than he had imagined, the only previous reference he had was from the movies.

It was a tourist's nightmare, full of queues and pushy people, but it was the city's most famous landmark and something Dom had got used to always being there. However from this viewpoint, Dom changed his mindset; it was easy to take these things for granted on a day to day basis, but this experience made Dom feel grateful for his life and for experiences like this.

"Isn't it amazing?" Jason said, pouring more champagne out for the two of them.

"Yes, it is," was all Dom could manage, still in disbelief with how the evening had turned out; it had been such a whirlwind, Dom felt foolish for having spent most of it second guessing Jason's motives.

"So… When are you coming to visit me in L.A?" Jason said, handing him a full glass.

There, there they were. The words Dom had been waiting to hear, and just like that, his worries disappeared into thin air—as if there was never an issue. He felt stupid that he ever doubted his own charms in the first place; sure, he hadn't asked him to elope with him, but it was a start. It was by far the most logical and realistic offer that Dom could expect, and that satisfied him.

With his personal paranoia now silenced once and for all, Dom took in the wonders around him. For the first time, everything that had happened to him this week had made sense. With the handsome Jason Hart by his side, he felt fortunate that he had met such a beautiful person.

'Dreams really do come true,' he thought to himself and pulled Jason in for a hug as they stared up at the skyline.

"So… You haven't answered my question," Jason said, knowing full well what the answer was.

By the look on Dom's face, it was clear to see that he would be visiting L.A very soon.

**

Jason slept through the night without a stir, his tanned hard body lay heavy into the mattress and was warm like a radiator. Dom, on the other hand, didn't sleep much and frequently woke, turning to look at Jason; taking the opportunity to bring in his tranquil beauty for what felt like could be the last time. The action-packed date had clearly worn him out; he was flying back to L.A in the morning and needed a good night's sleep.

Dom was also tired, but no matter how hard he tried, he couldn't drift off. Not only was this the moment he had been dreading all week, but he was also filled with hope now that Jason had asked him to visit him in L.A There was nothing more he wanted in the world; in fact, he wanted to leave right now and start a new life together right away. Jason could offer Dom security, romance, and fantastic sex. Tossing and turning all night, waiting for dawn—waiting for the final moment when he would say goodbye—eventually made him sleepy.

The alarm clock annoyingly went off at seven a.m., followed by a wake-up call from reception to remind Jason his car was collecting him at nine-thirty sharp. Waking up with a stretch, Jason wrapped his arms around Dom and gave him a kiss on the back of his neck. Without a word, they both pressed their naked bodies together before being interrupted by a knock on the door.

Jason got up to answer; it was the room service lady with breakfast, which Jason wheeled over to the bedside. Dom didn't want to wake up just yet, he would have preferred to lay ignorantly asleep, ignoring the fact that he had only a couple of hours before he had to say goodbye, but he too started to get up. There was no painless way out of this.

"No, wait—stay right there!" Jason said with a cheeky smile. "It's not exactly rock n' roll, but let's get crumbs in the bed—I'm paying for the room, so let's trash it a little."

Dom rubbed his head with a stretch, laughing at Jason's sense of rock n' roll behaviour; considering some of the things they had been up to this week—like partying all night at The Standard and having sex in the shower for most of it. Breakfast in bed was usually a small luxury (like toast and tea while watching daytime programs, hungover from the night before); not poached eggs on thick sliced granary bread, salmon and champagne.

After they ate and drank their one glass of champagne (which seemed to be their choice of drink no matter what time of day it was), they both laid there in each other's arms—covers kicked off to the bottom of the bed. Dom couldn't fully relax, distracted by crumbs annoyingly scratching at him in bed.

"I can't believe you're finally going," Dom said, trying to cover up the sadness in his cracked voice by clearing his throat at the same time.

"I know... I've had the most amazing time, in the most amazing city, with an amazing guy... On top of that, my painting sold and I'm now exhibiting in your hometown!" Jason listed, staring at Dom while caressing his back with his fingertips.

Dom couldn't help but feel weakened, there was only an hour or so left before Jason had to leave for the airport, and he wasn't ready for it.

"You know, I have this room until noon... You should stay and relax after I go."

The thought of being in bed without Jason there—where they had both spent many passionate and romantic nights together—made Dom feel even more upset. He could feel tears starting to well, making his eyes heavy and full; one blink and tears would roll, he knew that he wouldn't be able to stop once they did.

Instead of sobbing into Jason's chest, Dom decided to get up and get showered. He kissed Jason's full lips, closing his eyes as he did and as he got up he dared not to open them again in front of him. Instead, he rolled over to the other side to escape his sight and headed straight to the bathroom.

With his back turned away, Dom opened his eyes, and sure enough, tears ran down his cheeks. He waited until he got inside to wipe them away—he didn't want to show any sign that he was crying. He caught a glimpse of himself in the mirror, but he didn't stop to look—he didn't need to see the pain as well as feel it—stepping straight into the shower.

The whole suite reminded him of Jason, even the shower where they had washed intimately together. Dom turned the tap, and hot water began to rush over his body; water poured down on his face, giving him permission to finally cry into his hands. Sobbing silently at the thought of losing Jason after finding him so randomly, he tried to get a hold of himself.

'This isn't the end,' he wanted to tell himself.

Jason entered the bathroom, and Dom quickly washed his face and wet his hair so he wouldn't see he had been crying. Opening the door, Jason stepped inside, pulling Dom close for one final passionate embrace. Even though this should have been a moment to treasure, Dom couldn't help but wonder if he would ever be able to retake a shower without being reminded of him.

***

Dom sat on the edge of the slept-in, crumb-filled bed watching Jason gather his things.

"Okay, passport—check, ticket—check, room keys—check, bags—check... I think I got everything..."

"Everything but me," Dom said with a sad smile, trying his best not to let himself go again.

So far he had done an excellent job of not crying in front of Jason, but his eyes were like endless wells; it would be a shame to let himself go now at the last hurdle, but it was tough. Jason edged over to him with a lost smile on his face, asking for one last hug without saying a word. Holding Dom's face in his hands, he kissed him gently; he too felt the pain inside, he just didn't show it.

"I haven't forgotten you just yet... Here, write me down your address, email, cell number—everything!"

He tore off a piece of paper from the hotel notepad on the nightstand and handed it over.

"But you have my number already?"

"Yeah I know, but I want to have every possible point of contact on paper in case I lose my phone or something... This way I'll have a back-up, you can't beat old-fashioned pen and paper sometimes."

Hearing this comforted Dom, and he did exactly what he was told in his best possible handwriting so that no characters could be mistaken and it could be clearly read. Name, cell, and email all written down perfectly, Dom passed it back to Jason and watched him fold it neatly, before tucking it safely away into the billfold of his wallet. Dom looked at the alarm clock; it was nearly nine.

'This is it,' he thought. With every minute that passed, he found the difficulty level rise higher and higher, to the point where he felt like he was going to explode like a water bomb landing on pavement from five stories up.

"Come here," Jason said, sensing his emotion.

He wrapped his arms around him as tightly as possible, they stood there in the middle of the room for the next ten minutes just holding each other. Dom could smell his long blonde hair—still wet from the shower—mixed with the distinctive smell of leather from his brown bomber jacket. A tear finally escaped but Dom didn't want to wipe it away, he didn't want to loosen his grip; he wasn't ready to let go just yet. That one tear was all it took for the rest to follow and Dom cried silently into Jason's neck.

"Hey—don't you cry on me!" Jason said, feeling Dom shudder.

Dom remained speechless, the thought of Jason hearing his ugly crying voice—thick from saliva—would embarrass him even more than the sight of his tears had already done.

"I'll call you the moment I reach home… I promise… Stop, you're making me sad—this is hard for me too, man."

Time had finally expired, and Dom felt Jason slowly release, revealing Dom in all his sobbing glory; Jason wiped his tears away.

"Okay… I have to go now, but we will speak in a matter of hours. Everything will be fine, just be happy we found each other… I am."

Dom sniffed a ball of snot back down his throat, not exactly attractive, but it couldn't be helped. Jason opened the door to leave, a hotel porter was waiting to take his bags down already; Jason handed over two brown Louis Vuitton holdalls for him to take down to the car. Instead of following the porter, he turned back around to Dom, removing his jacket.

"This is for you… I know you like it and plus, it has your slobber all over it, so you've marked it as yours now." Jason swooped it over Dom's shoulders, grabbing him by the shoulders to look at his sweet, sad face.

Dom did like it very much, not because it was made from a beautiful leather or how great it looked on him, but because it symbolised Jason in every way. It was the sight of him in it on their first date, the smell of Jason's aftershave and hair mixed in with the leather, knowing the creases in the leather had been made by his body. The jacket wasn't *just* a jacket, it was a part of Jason. His energy had charged it over the years, and now it was all Dom had left to remember him by.

"I can't take your jacket!" Dom said, fighting back more tears at the gesture. 'What a pair of wet knickers I am,' Dom thought. He never thought he would ever cry over a man like this.

"Keep it—not forever though—you can give it back to me when you come to L.A… So you see, if you want me to be reunited with my jacket again, you definitely have to come visit, okay?" Jason cleverly said, before heading to the door for the final time.

"Don't worry I will… And if I don't, then I'll just have to give it back to you at your exhibition in London won't I?"

Dom couldn't believe what he had just said. Hearing the echo of his own words in his ears, he knew he sounded like a complete stalker. Walking out of the hotel room, Jason looked around at Dom one last time—who was waiting for him to leave so he could finally break down and sob into the pillows of where they had once laid.

"And don't lose that sexy London accent either," Jason said, giving a flash of his white-toothed smile one last time.

And then that was it—he was gone.

The final goodbye had happened, and Dom didn't know how to feel, except empty—it was like someone had gutted his insides out. With Jason's leather jacket wrapped around his shoulders, Dom ran over to the bed and collapsed onto Jason's side, desperate to stay close to him. He stayed there for a while, unable to do anything else but smell the bed sheets, wishing he was still there with him. The hotel room had been destroyed of all the wonderful memories of romance and excitement of finding new love, now replaced with loneliness and heartache.

Dom suddenly had the urge to get out of there; an intense sensation of claustrophobia had overtaken, and his emotions were now suffocating him. He needed to remove himself from the scene if he was ever to get on with his life; he needed fresh air. This was it. Jason was gone, but at least Dom had a souvenir to remember him by, and the promise that he would call as soon as he got back to L.A.

Putting the leather bomber jacket on properly, Dom went to the bathroom to splash water on his face, washing his tears away so that he could leave the hotel and walk the streets of New York not looking a complete mess. The last thing he needed was to run into someone he knew and have them question him and ask if he was all right; he didn't even want to speak to Chloe right now. He just wanted to get home and retreat back to his own bed, where he could hide under his duvet for the rest of the day.

# CHAPTER TWELVE

Finally the weekend was on its way, after what seemed like a very long week. Surprisingly Chloe was in a good mood—not because she was happy to work at one of the most luxurious stores on Fifth Avenue—because she was finally moving on with her life. You could say she had that 'Friday feeling' as she made her way to work; she was making things happen and it felt good.

Once dressed in her uniform and on the shop floor, her upbeat attitude soon turned to boredom. She thought of all the things she could be getting on with right now if she weren't at work—like styling looks from her new wardrobe and writing articles for the relaunch of StacksOfStyle. Instead, she had to endure Sarah who was still going on about the arrival of their new department manager.

"Guys, I think I saw her just walk into Regina's office… She looks nice, but I give her a week before she starts calling the shots around here."

All Chloe could think about was how frustrated she was with wasting time, as well as with hearing Sarah's whiny voice; she had that sort of tone that grated on you, like a fork scratching on a plate unexpectedly in public. Unfortunately for her colleagues, Sarah loved the sound of her own voice and was known as the store blabbermouth; she would seek out any gossip she could find, and you could be sure she would pass it on.

Chloe, on the other hand, couldn't give a damn what happened around here anymore. She was finished with Palazzo, and all it was good for was a monthly wage, the discount of course, and the networking potential. Pushing her frustration aside, she distracted herself by tidying some rails and pressing on with the regular duties. To top it off, shifts dragged on, even more, when Dominic wasn't there; remembering her friend, Chloe wondered how he was getting on right now. For all she knew he could be on a plane with Jason to start a new life in Los Angeles, and she wouldn't put it past him either.

The thought of it made her smile, Dom always seemed to land on his feet, and she was sure that he had bagged someone special in Jason—even though she hadn't properly met him. Going over to the corner alcove of the department (where she usually went to check her phone), she quickly thumbed him a message.

HEY GORGEOUS… HOPE EVERYTHING IS OK? AM SURE UR FINE OR ON UR WAY TO L.A ALREADY! HAVE LOTS OF GOSS 4 U! I'M SURE U DO 2! CAN'T WAIT 2 C U… I'LL CALL U ON MY LUNCH BREAK. XXX

Reappearing back onto the shop floor, it seemed that there had been a sudden influx of tourists, forcing Chloe to actually do some work—and the womenswear floor managed to take a good amount of money in the run-up to lunchtime. 'Commission is sure to be good this month,' Chloe figured, having done most of the target herself. She had just rounded up a sale when she surprisingly saw Karen step out of the elevator.

"Hi, Karen… Is everything okay? I didn't expect to see you so soon."

"Oh, I know… But I have some news for you, and while I'm here, I need some new work pumps… The heel on these ones has had it."

Chloe wondered what news she could have. 'If it's about Brian taking a liking to me, then that old news! We are already going on a date,' Chloe joked to herself. She walked Karen over to the shoe department, cut off from the ready-to-wear and ideal for a private chat, away from her nosey colleagues—especially Sarah.

"So my friend that I told you about is interested in giving you a shot… Now, I can't promise anything but if you publicise her site for her on your blog—feature articles on her stock and such—then she will set you up as an affiliate, which means *you* will get a cut of any sales driven by your site… Isn't that amazing?"

"But, my site hasn't even gone back online yet? I don't even know if people will look at it?"

Chloe began to worry that Karen had hyped her up too much, not wanting to appear like an amateur and inexperienced. She also didn't want to let Karen down, as much as not wanting to embarrass herself in the process.

"Look, she knows it's a new site so there is no pressure and she deals with personal stylists and bloggers promoting her site all the time... She is always looking for ways to reach a wider audience and to help trendy fashionistas like you with content... Don't worry! We all have to start somewhere, and of course, people are gonna read it... Bri showed me what he has done so far, and it looks sensational! All you need is some followers and stuff... Get yourself onto Instagram, Twitter and all those social networking sites... I'm sure your friends will join, and then their friends will join, and so forth—isn't that how it works these days?" Karen said without pause for air, making it all sound so simple.

Chloe knew of all these self-marketing tricks, but she hadn't had the time to set up social networks for S.O.S as well as go through her new wardrobe, plan her new website, *and* go to work. However Karen was right, Chloe needed to start promoting her website through social media and made a mental note to start setting it up as soon as she got home.

"Anyway, I'll take a pair of these," Karen said, holding out a black five-inch heeled pump.

She didn't need to tell Chloe her size, she knew all her vital statistics. The shoes were a classic style that was always in stock and another $500 for Chloe to ring through the till. Knowing Karen wouldn't want to try them on, she packed the shoes into a shopping bag out back, ready to finalise the bill upon her return.

"Okay, so before I forget these are her details: email, cell number, and that's her web address... She said to email her when the site is online and she will provide you with all the details to get you all started."

Taking the card, Chloe was surprised yet again; Karen had casually handed her the business card for Veronica Meyer; the CEO and Founder of DivaFeet. DivaFeet was a hugely popular online store; known for affordable fashion accessories that copied the latest designer looks. It had hundreds of thousands of hits a day, it was just typical of Karen to play down the CEO of DivaFeet as 'some friend of hers that happened to own a fashion website'.

Chloe was expecting a celeb stylist, or just some fashion influencer; not the boss of a major e-tailer. This was a great contact to have and one that Chloe would never have made without the help of Karen—proving yet again that networking with clients was where it was at. 'Buying her that bag on staff discount was definitely worth it,' Chloe concluded, putting to rest the last lingering demons of guilt she still had about it.

"I can't thank you enough," Chloe said, shaking her head in disbelief. This partnership was sure to bring a whole bunch of followers, not to mention a second income from the commission she would make from sales.

"Well, like I said yesterday… Just do me a favour and let Brian take you out," Karen said with a smile, handing her credit card over. "He's a fantastic guy; a real catch!"

'Ha! I already am,' Chloe thought, but she wasn't going to tell Karen that—Hell no!

"Well, we'll see… I definitely owe him dinner for all the hard work he has done on the site," she said, trying to sound blasé.

It was embarrassing enough that she could be so predictable, now knowing that Karen had planned to set them up all along; this was the best excuse she could come up with that didn't suggest it *was* a date. Chloe was fooling no one except herself, a date was a date, whichever way you looked at it. Although she was enjoying the attention, she didn't want to lead Brian on; guys were the last on her list of priorities at the moment—she quickly handed back Karen's card to get her off the subject.

"Well, I better get back to the office... Let me know how you get on with Brian and don't forget to call Ronny!"

Karen grabbed her shopping bag from Chloe and gave her a quick air-kiss before hopping into the elevator with finesse—just before it was about to close it's doors on her—waving with her manicured fingertips as if to show them off.

*

Kim's first week in her new job was nearly over. To say that it wasn't exactly what she had imagined was an understatement in the least. All she had been doing so far was menial paperwork and fetching coffees for Myra and Sylvia from Starbucks. Kim had licked-ass and blown Regina's ego for ages to get this position, only to gain a new set of rules to play by. Escaping the backstabbing realms of the shop floor, she had now entered the bitchy domain of the press office (talk about jumping out of the frying pan and into the fire).

The press office was no walk in the park, and her naive approach made her quickly realise, she couldn't afford to let herself slip at such an early stage; Kim was bright enough—and having already mastered the shop floor—she needed to take note of how things ran if she was to win at this game too. Sylvia had already introduced her to just how bitchy things could get; instead of helping her, it seemed she tried her best to make life more difficult. Whenever Kim asked her a question, Sylvia's answer would be to 'Just *Google* it!'. Either she was a bitch, or she actually didn't know herself, but Kim knew the answer and gave up asking her anything work-related.

A week of coffee couriering made Kim see she was once again on the bottom rung of the ladder; soon put in her place after presenting her ideas on the press folio (and as per usual), Myra decided to continue dressing the low profile New York socialites (AKA 'her friends'). Myra believed that by not dressing huge celebrities, it gave Palazzo a higher class to aspire to, which Kim disagreed with entirely.

Every fashion house relied on A-list faces for free advertising, to appeal to their fan-base, and to inspire current pop-culture moments—but not Palazzo. Myra's view was that Gianni knew most of the celebrities personally, he had his team send them clothes all the time—so why should she too? She saw it as a waste of time and money, but that wasn't really working out it seemed.

Fashion advertising was all about celebrity endorsement and desirability, Kim knew that and she had only been doing the job for a week, but she also knew that she had to keep her head down and do what was asked of her until she had earned her rightful place to speak up. The press office was polluted with the classic Palazzo politics, and Kim wasn't going to crack them in just aa lister week.

Myra had kept Kim busy for most of the week going through old emails, documents, contact lists—anything that meant she would be out of her way. Myra and Sylvia were busy booking out new season looks for the very minimal press coverage they had planned (which always appeared to be the same campaign every season), and then there were the plans for the upcoming in-store Fashion Week event. They didn't need a newbie poking her head in with new ideas! Kim had become nothing more than just an office junior, an intern with a paycheck. Kim, being proficient as always, had almost finished with filing and shredding all the backlogged paperwork; she hoped that by doing all this housekeeping she would have finally proved her worth.

Reaching for the last piece of paper, she fed it into the shredder with a breath of satisfaction, watching it sink into the metallic teeth. As she did, the text flow and bullet points jumped out at her—this wasn't an outdated piece of paperwork; she had seen this herself recently; and just like that, she realised the now mangled words were hers—she had written it! Kim's celebrity-dressing list that Myra dismissed was now being destroyed before her very eyes, and if this was meant to be some kind of metaphor, then Kim got the message loud and clear.

"*Kimberly!*" Myra called, noticing that the shredding had come to a halt, meaning that she needed to keep her distracted once more.

She hated being called that, her name was never Kimberly, but Kim for short; her name was simply *just* Kim!

"Can you come here? I have something urgent for you if you are done cleaning."

'Cleaning!' Kim fumed to herself but having learnt the art of killing with kindness she didn't rise to it.

"Of course Myra, what can I do for you?" she said with a bouncy and enthusiastic voice that was far from the truth.

"I need you to pop down to the showroom and supervise the interns… Get the staff sample sale ready as it's only a few days away now…"

"A few days away?" Kim asked.

"Yes, next Wednesday… Oh, didn't I say? I'm quite sure I mentioned it would be one of your responsibilities in your interview?"

Getting the staff sample sale 'ready' didn't just happen out of thin air; you couldn't just 'pop down' to the showroom and get it done in a day. It took week's of planning but this was all beneath Myra, she had been putting it off until her new team member joined so she could pass on the responsibility to her latest arrival to action with gusto.

"Sylvia and I simply can't do everything around here, and since you're *so* organised, you would do a much better job than us—what with all your sales expertise and all… God knows why anyone would want those old rags now, but those shop kids always seem to go crazy for them."

Kim rolled her eyes; 'shop kids?' she questioned. How patronising of her, even if she had dressed it up with a fake compliment. Kim, however, was too happy to get the Hell out of there for a few days, it was a blessing in disguise, and besides, Myra was right; she did have excellent organisational skills, and for the first year ever, this staff sale was going to be the best one yet—thanks to her.

The Palazzo showroom in the Garment District was where all the old season samples were sent to make room for the new collection at Fifth Avenue's office. With the staff sale to be held the following

Wednesday, it left little time for Kim to have everything in order. It felt almost as though Myra was purposely setting her up to fail, but if Kim was ever going to be a part of their crew, she had to prove Myra wrong and pull this event off perfectly.

The day was horribly humid outside, and the city was suffocating with wall-to-wall heat; Kim had been sweating around town all afternoon in her glam new uniform (which was already in desperate need for a dry-clean), but one more trip back to Fifth Avenue was necessary. Leaving the interns to de-box and hang the sale items in the showroom,

Kim made her way back to box up the last of the spring/summer samples that were lurking around, and also give Myra an update on how it was all going. Of course, Myra couldn't care less what was happening, the sight of Kim back in the office had annoyed her; she wanted someone to just get on with what they were told and to do very little else—a bimbo—just like Sylvia.

"Err… Why are you here? There's nothing for you to do *here*… Go back to the showroom and keep an eye on those interns, we don't want them stealing things now do we? We won't have a staff sale at this rate," Myra scoffed with a pompous laugh. "In fact, don't bother coming here next week at all—go straight to the showroom from now on, until it's all over—I'll see you next Thursday... Oh, silly me... Actually, make that the following Monday. I forgot that you'll be needing plenty of time to clear up and send whatever is left over to the outlet in New Jersey. But don't worry, take as much time as necessary."

"But that's a whole week working at the showroom?" Kim defended.

"Yes, my dear… You need to manage the interns during the sale, and I for one am too important to attend a sale for the remnants of *last season!* Gosh, you really are funny Kimberly…"

'Great—just great,' Kim thought. Working the staff sale meant that she would have to work from eight in the morning until very late, to serve staff that would be queuing up outside in the hope of grabbing a bargain handbag from the runway. The staff went crazy for a sample sale—like seagulls swooping down on an old bag of chips.

Not exactly what Kim had envisioned by joining the press team, she was just a glorified sales assistant all over again. Pissed off and rightly so, Kim headed to the staff kitchen for a break. Staff from the fifth-floor office never ate in the staff kitchen with the 'mortals', but Kim longed for a familiar space where she could relax and switch off from the madness.

Down in the staff kitchen, Chloe was sat on her own eating lunch. She always took the first lunch slot, as it was nice and quiet in the staffroom as well as on the shop floor. When she returned an hour later, the store would be buzzing, and she could snap up most of the sales while her colleagues took their break—a clever tactic she had learned over the years and helped her to keep on top of the sales board. Having finished eating, Chloe picked up her phone to call Dom, there was still no news from him, and the suspense was killing her; she needed to know what was going on with him and Jason.

Before she hit the call button, she was surprised to see Kim come in and slump at a table on her own. 'What is she doing here? Shouldn't she be eating upstairs with the rest of her new gang?' Chloe wondered. Now wasn't the time to call Dom, Chloe could sense that Kim was upset about something and probably needed to vent; for the first time ever, she moved her lunch over to Kim's table. Mostly out of curiosity than friendship, but there was a caring streak in Chloe that she just couldn't erase (even for those that hadn't shown consideration for her in the past), it was a weakness but a trait that made Chloe so likeable.

"Mind if I sit here with you?"

Kim looked up and was astonished to see her standing there; she gave Chloe a dimmed smile which Chloe understood as permission to sit down.

"I wasn't expecting to see you in here anymore," Chloe said, breaking the ice.

"Yeah, me too… I'm heading back out to the showroom after lunch, so I just wanted to take a quiet break."

The truth was that Kim felt so lonely up in the press office with her new colleagues that the staff kitchen was the one place where she knew she would find comfort, watching familiar faces pour in and out would help her re-calibrate.

"Oh right… What's going down at the showroom then?"

"Well, I'm working with the interns on the sample sale," Kim offered flippantly, not caring that this was sacred news to staff back on the shop floor.

Chloe's ears pricked up.

Did she hear correctly—staff sample sale? It was the event of the year, a major perk of the job. She wondered why Kim wasn't excited about it and her usual confident, annoying self? Why wasn't she relishing in the fact that she had a secret most of the store would like to know? This was not the Kim she had known and disliked for the past four and a half years. Who was this person and what had she done with the real Kim?

'I need to ask her when this sale is,' Chloe thought, seeing another golden opportunity to benefit herself.

"It's on Wednesday… Showroom one," Kim said, pre-empting the next question without the need for her to ask.

Kim had given up with all the pretence, she was tired, sweaty, and over it already; she too longed for the weekend. 'Wow, that was easy,' Chloe said to herself, wondering why Kim was so deflated. She had just landed the job of her dreams, surely she should be ecstatic at being handed the power trip of organising the staff sale?

'What a waste of a promotion… My promotion!' Chloe thought, but sensed not all was well in paradise—her compassionate side took over.

"Tell me if this is none of my business, but is everything okay?"

Kim paused, slightly suspicious of her kindness, but this was Chloe's olive branch, and she was going to take it. After the week she had, a friend and a good listener were in major need.

"Well, between you and me, I just feel like this job isn't what I was expecting it to be, you know? I thought I'd be working on exciting things—like the upcoming Fashion Week events and stuff—but instead, all I've been doing is shredding years' old paperwork, fetching coffees for those two, and now I have to manage the staff sample sale! On top of that, I have to clear up afterwards and won't be back in the office for another week... That means I won't be involved in any of the planning for Fashion Week and probably end up doing all the bullshit that they forgot to organise."

This was the first time Chloe had heard Kim curse, 'Things must be bad,' she thought and released the ball of resentment that had been building up since she didn't get the job with a deep breath—like a cat hurling up a fur ball—it was no longer an irritation; Myra sounded just as bad as Regina.

'Same shit, different stink,' Chloe figured, it seemed Kim had done her a favour by pipping her to the post. Melinda was right—a promotion didn't guarantee an immediate career or job satisfaction under Regina's rule... and Myra's too apparently.

"Anyway, I better get going... I have lots of samples to box up and take a taxi to the showroom," Kim said, getting up from the table.

"Well, I can help you... If you want?"

"Really—you would do that?" Kim was surprised she would offer to give up her lunch break to help, but Chloe saw a chance to get a sneak preview, as well as doing a good deed.

"Of course I'm sure... Come on, let's get packing! Two sets of hands are better than one," Chloe said, hiding her true excitement to see the leftover pieces in advance of her hawk-like colleagues.

Upstairs, Kim took Chloe to a room which resembled a walk in wardrobe—a mini stock room—the holy grail of Palazzo. It was packed full of clothes on rails in plastic coverings which were doubled up to the ceiling. Most of which was the new collection which had only just arrived, but there was a huge gap where the old season had once been and was waiting for even more new samples to be slotted into.

The remainder of the old collection was easy to spot as they weren't in plastic covers, Chloe noticed that some of the hangers still had the booking notes attached to them, detailing who had once borrowed them. She also saw that some pieces, like footwear, looked worn and battered already. Probably from all the models that had posed in them and ruined them on bizarre photo-shoots in the middle of nowhere, or perhaps from Myra and Sylvia 'borrowing' them on the weekends (which was more likely to be the cause).

"Okay, so I just need help boxing up the ready-to-wear on this rail here. I'll grab a shipper carton, and you can start to take the hangers out, just fold them roughly... They're not going far and plus, I don't really care," Kim said, reflecting her frustration and desire to just get the job done as quickly as possible.

Chloe made a start by picking up a dress, taking out the hanger and folding it in one big swoop like Kim had instructed. She noticed some lovely things and wondered how much they were going to sell for.

'Maybe I should buy some bits with my savings?' she thought, lusting to add more to her ever-growing designer collection.

Luckily, most of what she had seen so far was less desirable, easy for Chloe to fold and move on without getting distracted by them.

As she picked through the rail, she noticed that some of the left-overs were in fact from the runway show—suddenly she remembered an exquisite gown that she just had to find. Rummaging through, Chloe kept her eye out for a white silk gown which was almost see through. The dress was heavily embroidered with beads and embellishments that made a lace-like pattern all over.

The bodice was corseted and would push up a modestly sized cleavage into a worthy bosom, and cinch the smallest of waists into a waif. The skirt was long and floor length with a slight fishtail train that darted out at the back into a sea of pleats. The dress was so expensive, it was never made for the retail collection, and the press team only had the catwalk sample for editorial purposes as it was the talking point of the spring/summer show.

Chloe's heart pumped as she searched through the rail—it wasn't there. 'Oh well,' Chloe thought, knowing it was a long shot. Kim came back into the room with a cumbersome shipper that she could hardly carry empty, let alone once full and heavy with clothes.

"Thanks so much for helping," she said, dropping the box on the floor.

"Don't mention it, I get to see a sneak preview... And you look exhausted, it's the least I can do."

"Yeah, I am... This week has been a roller coaster. Seriously, you don't know how lucky you are! I know we complain about the shop floor, but trust me, it's much more fun than this," Kim said, feeling more and more comfortable with Chloe by her side.

"Well, it could've been me," Chloe said, deciding to open up a little more to her. "Well, not that Regina would have allowed it anyway—like ever!"

"What do you mean?" Kim asked, not following what she was saying.

"Well, I applied for the job too... Obviously, I didn't get it," Chloe said, a little embarrassed to be admitting defeat to her.

"Oh, wow—I had no idea!"

"I didn't want to say anything to anyone in case I didn't get it and make things, you know... Awkward."

Chloe's cheeks were starting to warm, and she could feel herself cringe, she bowed her head and carried on packing clothes.

"I had no idea... Seriously I—"

"Well, you wouldn't... I kept it secret. Anyway, you are perfect for the job."

"Yeah okay," Kim scoffed. "That's what I thought, but it seems Myra hates me already."

Kim bowed her head in suit, also feeling embarrassed that she hadn't met the ideal. It made her think; they were more similar than what they had once thought. Like Chloe, she was no stranger to hard work. During the summer months of her childhood, Kim worked in her father's gift-shop, selling mini Statue Of Liberty mementoes, city maps, and 'I *heart* NY' T-shirts to tourists. He insisted she had the best education, after getting her into the best business school, he was upset to discover she wanted to go into fashion; he couldn't understand why she wanted to work in a shop when he already owned a string of them.

Her appetite for luxury developed at University; all of her friends were obsessed with designer brands, logos, and handbags. Most of the kids were from wealthy families and could afford to splash the cash on expensive clothes; however, Kim was just happy to go along with them for the thrill. Those shopping trips had an impact on her—the sight of the boutique windows on Fifth Avenue had seduced her alone.

They oozed style and luxury, the products looked shiny and expensive behind the brightly lit glass—like mini Broadway productions. Kim loved the way the security guards would open the doors to greet her, the lavish decor inside made her feel like royalty. The handbags on display were like museum artefacts, and the whole experience just made her feel good; it made her feel important, it was like opium to her.

Like most highs, she became addicted; she wanted to be surrounded by beautiful things all of the time, so that was exactly what she did. But she had quickly learnt that to get ahead in fashion, you had to 'lick-ass'. She discovered that managers weren't interested in your ideas or knowledge—just in their own—even if they were wrong (which was most of the time).

"I'm sure it will get better... It's only the first week. Besides, you said it yourself, Myra is just another Regina, and we know how to deal with her now don't we?" Chloe reminded her.

Kim looked up at her and laughed, stirring from her daydream. She was grateful for Chloe's openness as much as for her help.

"Have you seen anything you like?" she said, changing the subject.

"Well, there was one dress I wanted, but I can't see it here," Chloe said, looking around one last time.

"Which one? There's so much more back at the showroom... Maybe I can check for you?"

"Oh, it wouldn't be here... But do you remember that white runway dress with the gold beadwork?"

"Oh, the dress that was so expensive to produce it didn't make the shop floor?"

"Yes, that's the one!"

"Of course I remember it! It was here somewhere..." Kim said rummaging around the rails, digging deep and almost getting lost as she dived down the back of it, "Oh, wait... Here..."

What Chloe was about to witness nearly made her have a mini heart attack. From behind the rail and off the floor, Kim dragged up what looked like the dress in question, only it was grubby and screwed into a ball of madness with threads hanging loose and all sorts. Kim tugged on its hanger—it had got caught on other garments—but continued to yank it up and out from behind the rail. She really didn't give a damn about treating the clothes with care, especially now they were heading straight for the staff sale.

"Please be careful!" Chloe yelped, almost as if Kim were performing an operation.

She didn't want her to rip the dress now she had found it. That would have been Chloe's luck—so near but yet so far. After taking a little more care, Kim held up a sorry looking, grubby, and now greyish fashion show sample in desperate need of attention.

"*Yes!* Oh my God! I have to have it... However, messed up it looks, I don't care! A dry clean will fix it... How much will it be?"

"All runway dresses are gonna be less than a hundred bucks. We need to get rid and make space, and I'm pretty sure this one would just get incinerated anyway."

"Seriously?"

Chloe thought back to the other navy sequin runway gown she had already hanging at home. This one would look amazing next to it, and for $100 or less, it had to be hers.

"Well, I'll put it aside for you if you like? It's so damaged, I'd doubt anyone else would want to buy it," Kim said, not fully understanding how unique this dress was to Chloe. Kim never really understood why staff got so excited about used, haggard samples. She preferred her clothes fresh and new and more importantly, in season. In that respect, she was perfect for the press team.

"You would do that for me?" Chloe said, making sure she wasn't messing around or playing some twisted game with her. 'Bitchy Kim must still be in there somewhere,' she warned herself.

"Of course. Come to the showroom on Wednesday morning to pick it up… Just jump straight to the front of the queue, I'll let you in ahead of everyone so you can make it to work on time. I'll just say you're dropping something off for me or something."

"Thanks, Kim, I owe you one."

"Don't mention it… Just don't say anything to the others!"

The last thing she needed was a rush of employees begging her to put things on hold for them too.

"My lips are sealed," Chloe said, running her thumb and finger across her lips as if to zip it shut.

Kim smiled, she was really enjoying Chloe's company, it was a shame she didn't do so from the very start—maybe they would have been great friends by now.

"Okay, you only have fifteen minutes left on break," Kim said checking her watch. "And I want as much help out of you as I can get. So come on, let's just rip these clothes off the rails and chuck 'em in the box—I'm done with this darn sample sale already."

They quickly got on with the task in hand and chucked everything they could into the carton, which was now as heavy as a breeze-block. They both pushed the box down the hall to the lift with the sides of their hips, it was a good workout on the legs. The security guards at the staff exit checked Kim's authorisation and helped her load it onto a trolley so she could wheel it out onto the avenue with ease.

Kim had cleverly booked a car in advance, one perk of the job was that she now had access to the company car account. Chloe pushed the trolley over to the sidewalk, helping Kim to dump it into the back of the car. Kim thanked Chloe one last time and jumped in, rushing back to the showroom so she could finish what she needed to and get the Hell out of work for the weekend.

Returning sluggishly to the shop floor, Chloe felt the effect of not having much of a break, but it had been worth it, but she remembered something else; she hadn't called Dom to get the latest, she was desperate to know how things had turned out. Hiding in her usual spot (that little alcove with the department computer), she pulled out her phone from her jacket pocket and typed away furiously.

SORRY I DIDN'T CALL… WAS HELPING KIM WIV SAMPLE SALE THINGS. WHY DON'T U COME & STAY @ MINE 2NITE? DINNER & WINE? WE CAN HAVE A GOOD CATCH UP & GO 2 WORK 2GETHER FROM MINE. XXX

Just as she put her phone away, the door that led to the back of house stairs slammed shut, and she heard Regina talking in Italian. Chloe quickly pretended to use the computer, as if she were checking the inventory for an item for a customer. Walking past the alcove, Regina noticed Chloe perched inside, hidden away; she had grown very suspicious of her since the job application and assumed she was up to something, like checking for more internal vacancies on company time.

"Chloe," Regina said, prompting her to turn around and acknowledge her presence.

Regina looked her straight in the eye, trying her best to intimidate and catch her off guard. Another woman stood alongside Regina, she was quite short and petite with dark brown hair that was bobbed and glossy. 'This must be our new department manager,' Chloe instantly thought, who else would she be gossiping with, in Italian?

"This is Francesca, your new department manager," she confirmed with a sly grin.

Finally, Regina now had someone to keep an eye on Chloe at all times and report back with information on what she was up to;

signalling the end of Chloe's free will at work and the beginning of an on-going interrogation. Chloe shook Francesca's hand, determined to appear polite and unaffected by the appointment of a new manager.

"Hello, welcome… I'm Chloe Ravens."

"Nice to finally meet you—I've heard so much about you," Francesca said in an accent tinted with a drop of Italian essence.

'I bet you have,' thought Chloe, and she was right to think so. Francesca smiled back at her, almost sarcastically, she didn't need an introduction; she had heard all about her already from Regina and knew all she needed to on every single team member for that matter.

Regina had spent the whole morning giving Francesca the low-down on the team she would now be in charge of. Especially on Chloe and Dominic, which was mainly the reason why the induction had been called for—to brainwash her against them before she could make up her own mind.

"Those two are very clever… They operate together; they think they're indestructible; they need a close eye on them at all times—not to be trusted! They have been without management for far too long, and they need to fall back into line. Make sure they do and report any suspicious behaviour to me. After all, hiring your own team would be best, and if we can remove these two, everything would be much easier for you in the long run… But first, I need evidence."

Francesca understood that this was one area that would ensure she passed her trial period and secure her respect with Regina—as well as a chance at climbing the golden Palazzo ladder.

"Well, I look forward to seeing you on Monday morning," Francesca smirked.

Regina raised an eyebrow at Chloe as if to say: 'take that you little bitch!'.

But Chloe didn't let it get the better of her; she just smiled sweetly and gave a girly little wave, knowing that would anger them more than some smart remark or a disappointed look. Chloe was finally beginning to understand exactly what it was that made Regina tick and she was enjoying the power it gave her; although she was finding it hard to bite her lip. Inside, Chloe was a volcano waiting to erupt on Mount Regina, with so much she wanted to say to her face—but that was just a fantasy of course. For now, the big '*F-you*' moment would remain a satisfying scenario in her imagination.

**

The day had finally come to an end; staff members made their way to the locker room to get changed in a hurry. Some were chatting about going out that evening, or about what they were getting up tp on the weekend. Chloe was slumped, this week had been action-packed, and her feet buzzed with pain. It was a relief to finally take off her heels. She hadn't even had time to check her phone since texting Dom and wondered if he had taken her up on her offer—three unread messages awaited her.

HEY HUN. NOT SURE… @ HOME IN BED. FEELING SORRY 4 MYSELF… CAN'T BELIEVE HE HAS GONE ALREADY! CHAT LATER. X

PANIC OVER, HE JUST CALLED! WE SPOKE 4 AGES! WHAT TIME SHALL I COME OVER? XXX

NOW I HAVE CABIN FEVER! NEED 2 GET OUT OF THE APARTMENT, HAD A MAD DAY! MEET U OUTSIDE WORK. XXX

Chloe laughed as she read the conversation Dom had with himself via text. That was him all over, a worrier, until things went his way again. Chloe called him back to which he picked up after just one ring.

"Are you outside?" she said.

"Yes, I am… I'm here and waiting for your mother-fucking ass to come out—hurry up!"

Dom sounded like he was in good spirits and Chloe was glad to hear it; she was half expecting him to slit his wrists after Jason had left. Hanging up, she got changed as quickly as possible in a room that was bustling with staff all trying to get out of work at the same time. Finally ready to leave, she fought her way amongst her colleagues to get past the security at the staff exit. Outside on the busy avenue, Chloe looked around for Dom and noticed him standing a few yards down from Palazzo wearing his new leather bomber.

"Hey, you!" Chloe said, greeting him with a hug. "Great jacket! Haven't seen this one before… Where's it from?"

"More like who's it from… It's Jason's, he gave it to me as a memento to remember him by… I have to give it back of course… When I go to L.A!"

"No way! So he asked you to go to L.A?"

"Yeah well, those were his exact words."

"So when? When are you going?"

"I'm not sure right now… I wasn't even sure I'd hear from him again. I was in such a state this morning when he left for the airport, but he called me after he landed and we spoke on the phone for a while."

"Oh-My-God! Should I be buying a new dress?"

"Not just yet… Besides, can you afford it? Forget this old thing, where has *this* jacket come from little Miss. Secret Spender?" Dom said, referring to the gold Palazzo jacket that she had fallen in love with and worn ever since she rescued it from the clutches of the church charity.

"No, no—I didn't buy it. Mrs Ruthenstock gave it to me… It was in the box of clothes she had sent over."

Dom had other things on his mind this week and needed to be reminded of anything that didn't involve a certain Mr Jason Hart.

"*Shit*, I forgot all about that… Lucky you! What else was there?"

"I'll show you when we get home," she said, excited at the opportunity to show off her new haul.

She could hardly wait for a girly Friday night in with her best friend, it had been a long time since they had done so and both had exciting news to share. A night of gossip, wine, fashion, and men was what they both needed, and Dom wasn't the only one with guy-goss these days. Linking his arm with hers, they entered the subway station to catch the train back to Williamsburg and get the night started.

# CHAPTER THIRTEEN

**B**ack at Chloe's apartment, the first thing they did was flick through Mrs Ruthenstock's generous donations. Dom had pretty much filled her in with his situation on the way back, and Chloe spoke briefly of Brian when she could eventually get a word in. Excited by the rail of designer garments, they enthusiastically discussed what pieces were suitable for which occasion and Chloe showed him the articles she had been working on for the site's re-launch.

"I can't believe Mrs R gave you all these clothes!"

"I know, me too! I can't wait to see how my new website is gonna look with all these featured."

"I'm sure it's going to be amazing... So, tell me what happened at Karen's office," Dom said, remembering she briefly mentioned a guy she had met in the elevator. He wasn't ignorant, he was just busy with his own dramas.

"Well, in the morning I received the boxes of clothes, and then I got a cab to the office, I didn't wanna be late… I gave her the clutch, but I didn't charge her the extra ten percent after all—I thought it would too be cheeky of me."

Dom shrugged in agreement, he could see where she was coming from. Karen was helping her out in return, but it was a useful tip to remember for the future should she need to make a quick profit.

"Anyway, in the elevator up to her office there was this guy who kept on looking at me… He made me feel a bit paranoid—like maybe I looked a bit funky or something—as I was excited to wear the gold jacket straight out the box. But when I got to the office, it turned out that *he* was actually Karen's tech guy that she had arranged to help me!"

"And... Was he cute, or was he a creep?"

"At first I was like, 'whatever', totally not bothered—"

"But?" Dom said, sensing there was a big 'but' coming on.

Not answering him, Chloe walked over to the kitchen and looked in the fridge. She hadn't gone food shopping for a while, but there was always an oven pizza in there. Ideal for lazy evenings when she had got home from work and couldn't be bothered to cook, which was quite often on a Friday night. Her figure was perfect for someone of nearly thirty and with such a well 'balanced' diet. The pizza was her favourite topping—double pepperoni on a flatbread base.

"Pizza okay?" she asked, casually changing the subject.

"Pizza is fine, and you know it! Come on, out with it!"

"Fine! Okay, so he was actually quite cute in the end," Chloe said, unwrapping the pizza and preheating the oven.

"And... Is there anything *happening* there?"

"Well, yeah... Kinda. We worked on the site for most of the afternoon—so far it looks great. He's created a logo which is a little raven—he must have done some research beforehand—I was really impressed."

"But were you impressed with him? Were there butterflies? Was there sexual tension? Come on Chloe, it has been ages since you met a guy!"

She didn't need reminding, she knew exactly how long it had been since she had last met a guy. It was at least two years ago, but it didn't bother her too much. In fact, she vowed to stay away from men for a while and concentrate on her career; how can she meet a guy and be happy at the same time, if she wasn't happy with her life?

"Well, yes—I was if you must know... It's funny because at first, I didn't really take any notice, but working closely with him all afternoon I got to see his nice smile and all those things that you only notice when up close with someone for a long time. It was quite sexy watching him do his thing on his computer—he's so intelligent—he whipped up my logo in no time," she said, placing the pizza on the oven shelf.

Chloe opened up the first bottle of wine that they were planning to consume that evening. They had stopped off at the wine store on the way home and picked up three bottles of cheap Pinot Grigio; there was a lot of catching up to be done, and vocal lubrication was required.

"So what bloody happened in the end? Did you snog or what?"

"No! I took him for a coffee to say thanks, we needed a break from the computer screen."

"Is that it—coffee? I was expecting you to say that you woke up at his place or something…"

"Not quite… We got chatting a little and discovered we have a few things in common. Then, he offered to work on my site in his own time, so we are meeting up tomorrow night to go over a few things."

"I knew it—you're finally going on a date!"

Chloe smiled and poured Dom a glass of wine. However much she tried to play down that this wasn't a date, nothing got past Dom. Holding up her wine glass, she proposed a toast. "Here's to my new website, new beginnings, and maybe... A new man!"

They both giggled, clinked glasses and took large mouthfuls of cold crisp wine. Chloe wouldn't say anything else on the matter, not until she knew where she stood with Brian for sure, but it didn't stop them from giggling like schoolgirls about it all night.

*

The pizza had been demolished (and the bottle of wine before it), and they were now sitting on the sofa with bottle number two. Dom had just finished telling her once more in detail about his date around the city via helicopter. Hearing it out aloud sounded as surreal to him as it actually was in reality. Dom couldn't believe it had happened as much as Chloe, which was probably why he had to run through it all over again. He had been so caught up with Jason leaving for L.A that the fantastic content of the night hadn't actually sunken in until now.

"Gosh, you're so lucky… I can't believe he took you on that. Those private trips don't come cheap you know," Chloe said, feeling slightly jealous, but then again the jam-packed rail of clothes reminded her that she hadn't done too poorly herself this week either.

"Well, it was the gallery that had booked it... Today, I web-stalked him a little bit... He's quite a well-known artist in L.A, but I read somewhere that the piece he sold this week went for $50,000!"

"Wow—that much? And he's still alive; just think what it would be worth once he's dead!" Chloe said—now tipsy—gulping down another mouthful of wine; Dom shot her a filthy look at the suggestion of him dying.

Dom drank the last few drops of wine left in his glass, feeling good about his love life for once, having discussed it with Chloe. He started to think that maybe dreams did come true, he had always imagined he would meet a hot guy that could afford to whisk him away and give him a good life—now it seemed like a possibility.

"So anyway... He called you this afternoon—what did he say?"

"Oh, he just wanted to check on me... He knew I was upset when he left. He said that he had been miserable all the way back home too and wished he had taken me with him."

"And obviously, you would have gone with him..."

"Obviously! He mentioned he was going to be busy until the end of the month with work. The South Bank Gallery, who bought his piece, asked him to come up with a few more to feature in an exhibition they are putting together. The deadline is crazy as his name is a last minute addition, but he said I should visit L.A afterwards... Or even better, go to London with him for the opening!"

"You lucky little Devil... You got to hang out with a hot guy in New York and next it will be in L.A, and now London too!"

Chloe made it halfway through the second bottle on her own while Dom had been doing much of the talking. She was happy to be hanging out with him and actually have things to talk about other than bitching about work. Chloe suddenly remembered another nugget of information that she had to tell him. Sitting up from her slumped drunken posture between the sofa edge and the floor, she slammed her glass down on the coffee table so she could animate her hands, almost breaking it off its stem.

"Oh my God—I nearly forgot!"

Dom perked up at her tone of urgency and the prospect of even more fresh gossip, and this sounded important.

"Not only have I got a new rail of clothes; a new website on the way; and a possible date-thing tomorrow night, but Karen has set me up with Veronica Meyer—the owner of DivaFeet… They are friends! She came in today to give me her details, she is willing to promote S.O.S for me on DivaFeet… In return, all I have to do is write about them and include some of their stock in my articles, and I will get a cut of any sales sent through from my website."

Dom couldn't believe that she had made such a high profile contact so soon, the website wasn't even online yet.

"That's amazing! Well done babe, things are really starting to get off the ground already. I wasn't sure if you were serious or not when you told me you were getting your blog back up… I thought it was a rebound thing from not getting the press assistant job, but now it seems it's developing into a proper little business."

Chloe nervously agreed, how was she going to get visitors to her unknown website? How was she even going to keep up with writing fresh, relevant articles and juggle work at the same time? She pushed the sudden panic to the back of her mind, if she carried on this train of thought it would only freak her out more; it was a whole lot easier to just do it, rather than think about doing it, get scared, and then not do it at all. She took another large gulp, her mouth was drying up quickly from all the talking and alcohol that was circulating in her bloodstream; she probably needed a jug of water to cure her thirst, not more wine.

"I know me too! But it has just snowballed… Karen's help came along, and I have all these wonderful clothes to write about, and now I will have this kick-ass—not to mention my first professional partnership… And you've got Jason now, and you're gonna fly off to Hollywood and leave me alone here, but I can come to visit you guys and do some Hollywood styling stuff down there and make it look like I'm International baby, yeah!"

Chloe carried on for a while with her drunken ideas that sounded quite good right there and then, but probably not in the morning when she was sober—at this rate, they would be well and truly hungover by then to even remember it. Dom, however, liked the sound of her plans and wished that they would come true, there was nothing more he wanted than to move to L.A to be with Jason, and to have Chloe visit and hang out in the Californian sun with him.

"I almost forgot… Our new department manager came round the store today with Regina," Chloe dropped into conversation, as she knocked back her glass for the last drop like a true drinker in a bid to quench her thirst.

"What! That's like major news, and you've left it until now to tell me?"

"Yeah well, what's there to say? She's Italian, she's a bitch, and she starts on Monday," Chloe said, pouring the remainder of bottle number two into their glasses.

Dom laughed at how wasted and carefree she was. He hadn't seen her like this for a while and loved it when she was drunk—she turned into a confident minx who didn't mince her words. He likened her behaviour to his in a way, just when sober instead.

**

The alarm clock on her phone jingled and vibrated annoyingly on the coffee table; they had fallen asleep on the sofa after the night ended with some drunken tears and more alcohol—Chloe managed to find a bottle of tequila in the depths of her kitchen cupboards (which seemed like a blessing at the time). Rubbing the sleep away from her eyes, she vaguely remembered sobbing at Dom's situation, which she embarrassingly called a modern-day tragedy.

It was safe to say she was hungover and today was going to be a rough ride—yet again. Chloe got up and went into the kitchen, she flicked the kettle switch down and put some bread in the toaster. Her mouth was dry and stale from not brushing her teeth, and she felt horrid; the last thing she wanted to do was go into work. Pouring the coffee into two mugs, she brought them over to the sofa and placed them down on the table which made a clinking sound that roused Dom.

"Thanks," he groaned, reluctantly sitting up.

"Want some toast? I'm having peanut butter and Jell-O, we need something to last us until lunch."

"Sure, sounds good... Make mine plain—just spread."

Dom took a sip of his hot coffee, not sure if he could stomach anything else. It was just how he liked it, black and strong with just a drop of milk. Munching on their toast, Chloe remembered that she was supposed to be meeting Brian after work—how could she forget? She hadn't performed her nightly skincare regime or even flossed her teeth before crashing out, let alone wash her hair and prepare for a date.

Instead, she had passed out like a drunk on the sofa. She was usually consistent with her bedtime routine which consisted of dental care, applying facial toner with a cotton pad, night-serum and mois-turiser—as well as a separate eye cream—all before wrapping her hair into a twisted plait so it wouldn't get all matted and crazy in the night. All of that had gone out of the window and this morning was to be a crazy hair day.

"*Fucking Hell!* I can't believe it... I am never drinking again—ever!"

Something she kept on telling herself the morning after but hadn't quite managed to adhere to. She had no choice other than to run some mousse through her hair and scrunch it up it, making the most out of the frizz. She hadn't even settled on an outfit, and because she was heading straight out after work to meet Brian, it was something she needed to get together fast.

"What do you think I should wear? Help me, Dom!"

"Just wear some jeans a sweater... It's not like we have to get dressed up for the subway bitch," Dom muttered through a sip of his coffee.

"Erm, hello? I'm meeting Brian this evening... Remember?"

Dom rolled his eyes and reluctantly got up to choose some bits off the rail. Chloe thought that the Dolce & Gabbana dress she had planned to wear was too slutty, too soon. Dom's eye for style was just as sharp as hers, in fact, more so because at least he was still able to pull off an outfit with a hangover. Something she couldn't cope with right now, just the thought of it was making her head spin. 'Whatever she wears from this rail will look great, they're all designer and super chic looking,' he thought to himself.

"Gosh, trust you to leave this until now... Hmmm, I say wear these black pants with the Chanel tux jacket and a simple white blouse from your closet, with some black heels and your black envelope clutch you got in the sale last season—done," Dom said effortlessly, chucking the clothes in Chloe's direction for her to catch.

Happy with his choice (and with no other alternative in mind), Chloe decided to go with his combo. She didn't have time to fuss around, and it looked business-like, classy and feminine—perfect for a first date (that also wasn't a date). Chloe neatly packed it into one of many Palazzo garment bags she had accumulated while working there to help keep creases out.

"Okay, let's shower Mister... We gotta get going."

For a moment she visualised them calling in sick to stay at home to recover—watching daytime movies under the duvet on the sofa—but that would be too obvious to everyone at work that they were pulling a sickie if they were both off. Plus, it would just be their luck that some eagle-eyed colleague had spotted them meeting up outside work the night before.

The journey to work wasn't too bad considering their state. It was a lovely summer morning, bright and fresh, and a Saturday free from weekly commuters. They both wore sunglasses to protect their eyes from the glare of daylight and more importantly, to hide their sins. For a moment, the beautiful weather made them feel like they were heading to the park for a day of chilling. A cruel illusion which was shattered once stood outside Palazzo, moments away from clocking in.

Now changed into their uniforms, the effects of the morning coffee had started to wear off. There was usually a team meeting with the whole store before opening on a Saturday. However today there wasn't one—department managers were holding ones with their own teams instead. Since theirs wasn't due to start until Monday, the womenswear team sat on the sofa, discussing what Monday might mean for them—led by loudmouth Sarah of course.

"She was here yesterday with Regina walking around the store… I'm telling you, they looked like they were the best of friends already. Do you think they already know each other?" she said, stoking the flames a bit more.

'This isn't exactly top-secret knowledge,' Dom thought. Bored, he turned to chat with Chloe, breaking off from the rest of the group.

"So, this Brian guy, where exactly is he taking you?"

"Oh, just a ride around New York in a helicopter… The usual," she giggled. "No, seriously—just some restaurant nearby… I'm not totally sure what to expect. Hopefully, he has completed work on the website, so I owe him dinner at least for all the hard work. I've kinda forgotten what he looks like already… How about Jason? Have you heard anything since yesterday?"

"No, but he's busy creating works of art and settling back into L.A life… I'll shoot him a message later."

The music in the store started to play, a sign that they were about to open. Rather sluggishly, the womenswear team got up from the sofa and started the day with their usual morning rituals. There wasn't much left to do in the department for Francesca's arrival except for the general housekeeping. Dom had cleaned the stockroom to perfection out of boredom during the week, and the team had kept up his standards as none of them wanted to do it all over again.

The morning was going smooth and quick with the flow of tourists and weekend customers pouring in, not their usual top spenders who worked nearby and shopped during the weekdays. Dom and Chloe took an early lunch to grab pancakes, syrup, bacon and eggs from the diner around the block. Their bodies were screaming for them to raise their blood sugars, laying their hangovers to rest once and for all. Plus, they couldn't bear standing on the shop floor with a pounding head and a rumbling stomach that felt like it was eating itself. Trying to serve a customer in this state was torture, and so they made their escape quickly.

Upon their arrival back on the shop floor, Dom spotted Gina and Rob Travers looking around. Gina used to be an exotic dancer and was a walking advert for plastic surgery. You name it, Gina had it; breast implants, Botox, lip and cheek fillers, and a Hollywood nose job to boot. Not content with all that work, she also had paperwhite veneers, a neon tan that could only come from hours of Sun worshipping, and hair extensions that were blow-dried big and high.

She was always dressed head to toe in designer clothes, but they somehow managed to make her look cheaper than she already did— which was quite something. She would wear the logo of any brand with no shame, and many all at once—like cattle stamps. Her husband was just as bad. Rob wasn't attractive and was slightly older than her. It was rumoured he had won the lottery and fell in love with Gina who worked at a Miami strip club, where he had picked her out. He had a boat and a condo there, and they spent the most part of the year topping up their tans on South Beach.

He also had 'work' done, probably to catch up with his wife— which didn't look so good on a man. However, it didn't matter to Gina, she loved him and the lifestyle he gave her. After all, a retired stripper would never be able to hit the big time with a millionaire again, especially in her state; she was Frankenstein's bride. However tacky they looked on the outside, or how common they behaved, they were still nice customers. Dom thought they were entertaining (unlike some stuffy clients Palazzo attracted), and they had taken a shine to Dom—they just loved a fabulous, token gay guy.

Although Dom could be very fussy when it came to style, he also had a tacky side and understood their desire for labels. He could sell them anything that had the '*P,*' logo or 'Palazzo' emblazoned on it; they were an easy target for selling to and Dom gladly obliged to take their money every time.

"Hey, guys!" Dom said, now buzzing from his much needed, sugar-laden lunch.

"Oh, hiya gorgeous! How are you?" Gina said, so loud that everyone in the department could hear her—as well as see her.

"Oh, you know me… I'm fabulous darling; you look great—as always!"

He tried his best to compliment her with undetectable sarcasm as he took in her dreadful outfit, which he was sure was meant to be worn as underwear. '*Fuck* she looks worse every time I see her,' he thought. "And Rob, how are you?" he said, taking his hand to shake.

"I'm good thanks. We are in town to see Gina's parents and do some shopping," he said with a matching paper white smile.

Rob shook Dom's hand that little bit too long, making it slightly awkward. His hands always felt warm and sweaty—Dom would wait until his back was turned to wipe his hand on the back of his trousers. Dom thought Rob secretly liked guys too, he was always overly keen with him and very flamboyant with his clothing choices; but then again, that could just be the effects of new money. Rob always looked him directly in the eye, which unnerved him—there was something behind his eyes that screamed 'murderer!'.

Rob and Gina were in full shopping mode and predictably bypassed all the beautiful products. Crystallised T-shirts, jeans, sneakers, and monogram handbags had all been snapped up in an instant. 'How tragic… All that money and no taste,' Dom thought, but he didn't really care as the bill was over $4,000 already, and that was just in womenswear.

"So what else have you been doing?" Dom asked, trying to work out which bit of surgery was new.

That was like searching for a needle in a haystack, but still a fun game. Gina was only too happy to tell everyone about their fabulous, over-the-top lifestyle and spoke loud enough so that everyone on the shop floor could hear her. She was drawing attention from other shoppers who were mesmerised by her obvious procedures, showing off her new tits in her trashy low-cut top.

'Once a stripper, always a stripper,' Dom said to himself, although he would happily be her given a chance.

"Rob and I have been on this diet thing where you only eat green shit for like a month that has been blended into a smoothie… And then you go get a colonic, which we just had yesterday… Didn't we sweetie?"

Rob nodded proudly in agreement like he had achieved a lot by being on this diet and then having the remnants flushed out of him. His paunchy, middle-aged belly told otherwise—it was no washboard. Seeing these two living the dream, made Dom drift off into imagining what life would be like in Malibu with Jason. He pictured them running along the beach with a big, athletic looking dog—like a Weimaraner or a greyhound—echoing a scene from some kind of homoerotic boy-band video, before crashing back into the conversation.

"Oh yeah, it felt really good… You should try it sometime Dom. You would love it!" Rob said, giving him a wink that creeped him out just that little bit more.

Dom noticed Rob shifting from side to side, looking rather uncomfortable; he could have sworn he heard him let out a fart. 'Yeah and I bet you'd love to see a pipe shoved up my ass,' Dom thought.

"Listen, I'm just gonna use the bathroom before we go… Honey, settle the bill, let's grab some lunch—I'm starving."

Chloe repaid Dom's favour by helping to wrap up while Dom took payment. He then sat on the sofa surrounded by five large shopping bags with Gina, talking about procedures and tans as they waited for Rob to emerge from the bathroom—which was some time. Long enough for Dom to tell her all about meeting Jason.

"Let us know when you're there… We can take you guys out, show you all the amazing places and the West Hollywood gay bars… We go all the time!"

Gina recommended some of her favourite hotspots, but Dom had classier visions for his trip, whenever that would be. After about twenty minutes, Rob finally re-emerged, looking more relieved than before.

"Okay, ready to go?" he said, rubbing his hands together and picking up some of the shopping bags. "Well, it was great to see you, Dom."

Rob looked Dom in the eye once more, almost suggestively, which motivated Dom to get rid of them at once; now they had dropped their money, they had outstayed their welcome.

"Yes, it's been wonderful to see you once again guys... Stay looking fabulous!" Dom said, switching on his novelty campiness which they loved so much.

Chloe and Dom couldn't resist making fun of Rob and Gina the minute they had left.

"Oh my God, she looks like a reject Pussycat Doll!"

"Tell me about it," Dom laughed. "They are harmless, but it's expensive to look that cheap—Good luck to them I say... I mean, don't get me wrong, he is creepy, but you can't blame her for going there—he is loaded!"

"Yep, for some people, that's what makes them happy."

"Did you hear about the colonic diet thing they've been doing? What a madness... And he still looks fat as fuck!"

"Yeah I did, another customer overheard too and looked disgusted," Chloe giggled.

"I'm not surprised he took twenty minutes in that loo!" Dom said.

Chloe laughed out loud at Dom's cattiness, she thought it sounded so much better in his English accent, complete with all the lingo. Working on a Saturday with Dom—with a hangover—wasn't as bad as it first seemed upon waking up. Chloe often thought that the job would eventually turn her to drink, mainly to blot out the boredom, in-store politics, unpleasant customers, and other petty stresses of the retail world.

That and the fact whenever she was still intoxicated at work, she seemed to make much more money than when stone cold sober; she always managed to rack up good sales when she was still under the influence, or deliriously tired from partying the night before. The shop floor had a party vibe itself, everyone was shopping for their weekend outfits to the pumping electronic beats that rang out through the store. Chloe was also looking forward to going out herself, mainly because she was excited to see the finished website, but the more she thought about Brian, the more she grew excited to see him again.

The store had seen plenty of action and had made well over $250,000 in one day. The customer bathroom on the women's floor had also seen some action—it was now out of order, and the plumbing contractor couldn't come out over the weekend to fix it. The shift had finally come to an end, and it was time to get ready to meet Brian.

"Hey, haven't you better get going?" Dom said.

"I sure do… Just gonna take these things back to the stock room, then I'm outta here!" Chloe said, tidying up after her last and final customer of the day.

Typically, last-minute customers always seemed to appear when you were about to end a shift, especially after you had stood around not doing anything for the past hour or so.

"Are you feeling excited?"

"Erm… More intrigued. I don't really know, but I'm excited to see my new website… What are you up to tonight?"

"I'm going home to eat and sleep… I've had a mental week, and I haven't heard from Jason today, so maybe I'll message or give him a call."

"Well, just don't go freaking him out… Give him some space. He is busy remember?"

'What does she know about men?' Dom thought, this was her first date in years, and now she was giving advice on men.

"Get out of here! Have a great time," he urged, pushing her playfully towards the staff stairwell.

# CHAPTER FOURTEEN

This was probably going to be the last time Chloe would get out of work on time for a while before their new manager started on Monday—so she took her chance and headed up to her locker to get changed and freshened up. She had wet-wipes, talcum powder, and deodorant in her locker—handy for times like these. She could feel and smell alcohol seeping from her pores, mixed in with sweat from a hard day's work—a kind of putrid cocktail—and with no time to head home for a shower, this would have to do.

Whipping off her uniform she quickly refreshed herself, making her feel a whole lot better before slipping on her fresh white blouse, and the rest of her evening outfit. The black Gucci pants fit her snugly and were tapered at ankle length—like drain pipes. Slipping on her black Palazzo heels, other staff members began to look on, wondering where she was going all dressed up.

Chloe dashed over to the mirror with a compact and some lip-gloss. She blotted and repaired her current makeup the best she possibly could, taking off the shine from her forehead and cheeks. A red lip made a big difference too, as did the bronzer and eyeliner she applied to turn her day look into night. Darting back to her locker, she pumped hair mousse into her hand, checking her watch as she did; she didn't want to keep Brian waiting, he was probably outside already—but on second thoughts—it was best to be fashionably late and look hot, rather than look a hot mess but on time.

She scrunched her hair with the mousse to give it some bounce, and a fresh smell. Grabbing her black envelope clutch bag, she put all the essentials inside and stashed her daywear inside her locker to take home on Monday. Now ready to leave, she pulled the Chanel dinner jacket off the hanger and draped it over he shoulders, it finished the look perfectly. Taking one last look in the mirror, Chloe thought Dom's styling was just right for the occasion; she really looked the part—a sophisticated young business woman—it made her feel confident. Chloe believed in dressing for the job you wanted and not the job you had, and tonight she was founder and editor of StacksOfStyle.com. One last touch was needed—a spritz of '*Palazzo Gold*' Eau de parfum.

As she walked down the staff stairwell, she attracted attention from curious colleagues. They weren't used to seeing Chloe looking this glam, except for at the staff Christmas ball which was a complete fashion parade (with more faux pas than hits). As she breezed through the staff exit—enjoying the reaction she was getting—she could see Brian standing outside the store with a single red rose. Chloe smiled to herself awkwardly, it was clear that he considered this more than just a handover of her finished website. Brian saw her walking towards him—she was a vision—he had thought she was pretty the day she came to the office, but tonight she was something else entirely.

"Wow, you look... Amazing!"

"Well, thank you... And so do you," Chloe replied, feeling like an idiot already.

Brian was just wearing jeans, a checked shirt with a lightweight jacket, and a pair of simple black shoes. It didn't exactly match what she had on, neither did it scream fashionable (he was no Dominic Fraser in the style department, that was for sure). But he was a fixer-upper, his handsome face was something a man couldn't buy—Rob Travers was proof of that. 'Thank God I didn't wear that sexy black dress,' she thought to herself.

"This is for you," Brian said, holding out the rose.

"Oh... Thank you," she said, not quite knowing what to do with it but to give it a quick sniff—it smelt of nothing. "So... Where are we heading?"

"I thought we would go to the steak grill around the corner... It's nothing special, but the food is good."

Chloe shrugged in agreement, not actually fussed about where they went, she was just eager to see her new website, but Chloe had the sudden feeling that something was amiss. She noticed Brian didn't have his laptop with him, and she definitely didn't bring hers in her tiny clutch. How would he show her the progress he had made on StacksOfStyle?

They walked around the block in silence, occasionally mentioning how each other's day went. Chloe was thankful for the short distance, not only because she was wearing impractical heels for walking in, but also because she felt awkward and rather nervous now knowing that this definitely wasn't just a business dinner. Even though the evening was light and warm, she gave a nervous shrug that ran a shudder up through her entire body—or was she cringing?

The Avenue Grill was exactly how Brian had described it (nothing special), but nice enough for a first date—even though she kept telling herself it wasn't. Walking into the restaurant, she definitely felt over-dressed compared to all the other patrons which consisted mainly of families, tourists, and casually dressed groups of friends. The waiter had seated them at a secluded booth by the window, sensing that this was a date and that they wanted privacy.

'If the waiter thinks this is a date, then it must be,' Chloe said to herself, even though she knew Karen had blindly set her up.

There was no point getting worked up about it now, she was sitting in a green leatherette booth opposite Brian already, and it was a bit too late to start worrying about what level this was on.

Work had given her an appetite again, and she was ready for a glass of wine to help calm her nerves. She didn't expect to feel this way, this was meant to be all about S.O.S; she put the butterflies in her stomach down to the excitement and not first date nerves.

"Can I get a small glass of white wine?" Chloe said, quickly grab-bing the waiter's attention before he left.

"Oh wait, make that a bottle," Brian chipped in.

Chloe winced, she had responsibly planned to limit herself to just two glasses of alcohol—she didn't need a repeat of last night.

"So, what else is new?" Brian said, slicing through any awkwardness that was lingering in the air.

"Oh, nothing really… Work was crazy as usual."

"Nothing? Karen tells me you are going to be a very busy woman these days… The next online sensation she reckons."

Chloe looked at Brian with a blank expression. They had been talking about her at the office, and she didn't know how she felt about that. What else had they discussed, she wondered.

"She gave you a contact right… Some fashion woman?" he said, reading her vacant stare.

"Oh, right yeah," Chloe said, snapping back into the real world. "Well, it turns out her *friend* is a major online retailer."

'*Shit!*'

She had forgotten to email Veronica in favour of getting drunk with Dom, yet again. 'Will I ever learn?' she scolded and made a mental note to email her first thing tomorrow morning. She couldn't screw up this chance to work with such a well-known fashion entrepreneur. Maybe she would adhere to the two-drink limit she set herself after all.

"Well, I was meant to email her and check out her site, but my best friend needed a girls night in. His boyfriend went back to L.A today," Chloe said, sparing him the relationship details of someone he didn't even know.

As it turned out, Brian was pleased to hear all about it as they drank a glass of wine, he agreed—it *was* a modern-day tragedy. They both ordered steak and fries, Chloe hoped she didn't look like a total pig in front of him, but if this date had any kind of chance, then he had to know that she was a girl that could eat more than just a salad. The hunger pangs began to kick in, signalling a full recovery from last night's tequila sesh.

"Anyway, you gotta get on it and email her… Especially now that you have a really cool website."

'Finally, let's get down to business,' Chloe thought, not wanting to bring it up straight away out of politeness.

"Oh yes, of course, I will… So tell me—how is the site looking?" Chloe said, trying her best to ask casually, but wanted him to just get on with it; she was dying to hear details, but she didn't want to appear grabby about it—he had done her a huge favour.

"Well, I said I'd be done with it, and I am… It looks great! We just need to switch it back online and finalise the particulars, which I wanted to talk to you about… How do you want to re-launch it?"

Chloe wasted no time in telling him her plans, how she had written new posts already and that she planned to use her latest wardrobe of designer clobber to write even more. Brian was impressed (after his initial disappointment at not contacting Veronica as yet), but he admired how she had sacrificed a shoulder to cry on for her friend and was able to put self-gain aside. He considered that quality a good sign, definitely his type of girl.

"It sounds like you have everything planned out."

"Yes, I do. I know exactly what I want to do with this site and tomorrow I *will* email Veronica and hopefully get my free advertising sorted… Oh, and I need to set up my social media accounts so I can broaden my audience and socialise with my readers all at the same time. It's all about Instagram and the power of the hashtag these days," she said, reminded by yet another thing she had forgotten to do.

"It certainly is… I'm surprised you're not on there already. I can help you sort all that out and integrate your accounts on the site. Every time you post on-the-go it can automatically feed onto your main page too," he smiled, nodding with a raised eyebrow.

Brian poured out another glass of wine for them. 'This is drink number two,' she mentally counted as he passed her glass—filled way over the measuring line.

"That would be awesome," she said, not fully understanding how that could happen technically, but excited that he did and that once again he would do it for her.

Brian was starting to come across intelligent and attractive again; she remembered why she had taken a liking to him—brains were indeed sexy. Chloe liked his intelligence, as much as his infectious smile that was beginning to make an effect on her, easing her nerves—she was now sort of enjoying herself.

"Oh, I nearly forgot... I made you these... Sounds like you will need them," Brian said, taking out a plastic box from his jacket pocket and passing it over the table.

It was a clear box containing one hundred business cards—exactly what she needed. Taking the lid off, she took one out to admire. It had StacksOfStyle.com in raised black lettering—the same as her website font—with the picture of the raven logo that he had created for her.

### *StacksOfStyle.com*
Chloe Ravens ~ 'The Raven'

"They look fantastic... The Raven?" she said, noticing the added moniker.

"Yeah, I thought it would be a cool name to blog under... See how it has your phone number and email too? I set up a professional email for readers to contact you on... All of which you will have full access and control over."

Brian had his smile on full beam, seeing how happy Chloe was with her new business cards. Chloe liked the idea of writing her blog under an alias, quite clever in fact and she was willing to take his advice on this one since she already had the business card to match. The steaks had arrived, and attention was now drawn to the food in front of them.

It was the perfect meal after such a day, and her hunger made it all the more enjoyable. After the main course, they shared a warm chocolate fondant pudding with vanilla ice cream which was quite intimate for a first date, but they were getting comfortable with each other—thanks to the generous second glass of wine. It had made her relaxed and very talkative.

She told him all about her family in Boston and how she came to New York for her studies but had stayed ever since. Brian was a

New Yorker through and through. As the conversation flowed, Chloe noticed that their bottle of wine was nearly finished and that Brian had ordered another. 'So much for just two glasses,' but she was having such a nice time, it seemed a shame to cut the evening short, so she just went with the flow—she would deal with the aftermath tomorrow.

"So… Going back to your site. When shall we launch it exactly?"

"As soon as possible I guess," she said, slightly tipsy and feeling the effects of alcohol in her system for the second night running. "Tonight!" she shouted.

"Tonight! Don't you wanna build some hype first? Do a countdown until launch?"

"What? No, no, no! It's all ready to go, let's just set this thing free!" Chloe said, throwing her arms in the air. "All that can wait, it just needs to get off my laptop and onto the Net!"

"Cool, let's get this wine to go," Brian suggested.

"Huh?"

"Well, what are we doing here wasting time? Let's get to work on your site… Your place or mine?" he said, giving her a cheeky smile once more.

Brian took care of the bill and ordered the take-out wine from their waiter. 'Is this really happening?' Chloe thought to herself, but she was having too much fun and didn't question it further; she was too excited to re-launch StacksOfStyle once and for all. Grabbing their jackets, they left the restaurant to hail a taxi.

"Wait, let's get a picture of you in front of the restaurant in this out-fit. You're a blogger now remember," Brian said, taking out his phone.

Chloe posed drunkenly outside the restaurant window, draped over the railings, as close to its neon sign as she could—throwing a peace sign last minute.

"Got it! You can do an article about how good the steaks were," Brian teased.

Chloe didn't quite catch the joke and thought it was a good idea to feature local eateries and not just boujie ones. She also knew it was just an excuse to get a picture of her on his phone—a typical guy thing to do.

*

Back at her apartment, she rushed inside ahead of him to clear the kitchen, it was in a bit of a mess—empty wine bottles and a jar of peanut butter had been left out on the kitchen side. Brian laughed at her attempt to tidy up, he didn't really care what state her kitchen was in.

'She should see the state of mine,' he said to himself.

"Erm, come on in… Sit down… Make yourself at home. Can I get you a drink?" she nervously bombarded while fussing around, fluffing up the pillows on the sofa.

Brian waved the bottle of wine at her that they had purchased from the restaurant.

"Oh yeah, right… I'll just get some glasses."

Chloe searched her cupboards for wine glasses, but none were clean, so she quickly rinsed the ones she and Dom had used the night before. Brian looked on in amusement as he took off his jacket and sat down on the sofa, she was hilarious to watch in her merry state. Chloe returned with two wet but clean wine glasses, letting him pour the drink while she put on background music to take the quiet and awkward atmosphere out of the room.

"Okay, so let's get started—where's your laptop?"

It was under the coffee table where she usually kept it, on top of some fashion books. After setting it up in front of them, Brian took over the keyboard to launch the web browser. He typed in her web host address which he had built the framework on—a password bar had popped up to which he tapped in 'gold_jacket'. Chloe laughed, Brian had used what she wore on the day they first met as inspiration; clearly, it had made an impression on him.

Pressing enter, the screen alarmingly went blank before a publisher menu appeared with a range of options. Brian showed her the basic settings of the control panel before clicking 'Site Preview'. Eventually, a whole new website that was completely unrecognisable had filled the screen in front of them. Chloe didn't know where to look first, even though it clearly said StacksOfStyle at the top of the web page, she couldn't believe how professional it had turned out—and that it was all hers.

Sipping her wine, Brian showed her around—it was sensational and nothing like how she had remembered it—now S.O.S looked expensive and very high fashion (despite it being built on an easy template stored on a website server somewhere). "Oh my God! It's *fucking* brilliant! You're a genius!" Chloe said, stamping her feet in excitement.

He showed her how to use the various buttons and pages that he had added. There was the main home page, a photo gallery, a blog page where she could link her social media accounts too, and a contact page that sent emails directly to her new email address. All of this gave her the professional edge she had wanted; she had learnt well from Palazzo, it was all about smoke and mirror and if it worked for them, then it could work for her too.

Brian taught her how to control her new site and how to make changes, which all looked complicated while drunk. He wrote down the various passwords she would need for changing the settings, allowing her to upload and edit things by herself. As Brian continued to show off the new look StacksOfStyle, Chloe felt excited about her future as a fashion blogger. Watching Brian in his computer wizard comfort zone made him look super sexy, or was it the fact she had well surpassed her two drink limit? Either way, he glowed in the light of the computer screen.

"Okay, so as you can see I have integrated the old posts already into the new format, but let's upload a new one so I can show you how easy it is," he said, minimising the window for Chloe to retrieve her files.

Chloe opened the word document about the window displays of Fifth Avenue and vintage fashions. Brian showed her how to copy the text straight into the upload setting which was simple enough, even for her to master while drunk. Clicking 'Submit,' the article began to load onto her blog page.

Any pictures included in an article automatically loaded into her new gallery section, which all seemed fairly straightforward and user-friendly now he had walked her through it; Chloe hoped she would remember all this tomorrow when she was sober. It was now getting quite late into the evening, and they had finished the bottle of wine they brought home from the restaurant. With the tutorial just getting going, Chloe went to find that now half empty bottle of tequila she had made a start on the night before. This time she mixed it with lemonade—having learnt from her mistake of drinking slammers with Dom the night before.

By the time she had come back, Brian had already created the S.O.S official Instagram account for her and synced it to the website, making it easier for her to share the same content across two feeds. He had managed to do so much in such little time, it all seemed simple to him, but to Chloe, it was something she couldn't even imagine possible—recalling how it had looked beforehand. Now it was the chicest looking online destination for fashion and style advice.

"There you go... So whenever you add something on your Instagram, the post will then automatically appear on your main site," he casually said. "All of which you can do from your phone these days... Okay, so are you ready to finally switch it live?"

Seeing it was now midnight, it seemed like the perfect time to give birth to her new baby. Chloe nodded in agreement, excited by it all, knocking back her tequila and lemonade in anticipation. Brian saved the progress he had made and showed her how to access the 'Live/ Invisible' switch in the publisher control panel. "Okay, so now all you have to do is click this button here," he said pushing the laptop over to her side of the coffee table.

Nervous but excitable, Chloe put down her empty glass and took control of the mouse-pad. She clicked the 'Live' button and then typed the web address into a new browser page. After a few minutes, her new site popped up in full glory.

The new homepage looked great, and Chloe wasted no time in taking a snap of it on her phone and posting it straight onto Instagram with fashion related hashtags which Brian had also advised her on. Overcome with joy, she looked at him and gave him an impromptu kiss on the cheek—it came out of nowhere—to which he turned his face and fully locked his lips on hers.

His mouth was soft and warm, nicely opposed by his masculine and rugged stubble around it. The kiss developed naturally as she grabbed his hair at the back of his head to encourage him some more, not that he needed it. Before she knew it, he was trying to move his way on top of her, pushing her back onto the sofa. She didn't want him to stop; it felt good, she leant back without a struggle. She felt his toned arms as he propped himself over her, they were hard and athletic.

Moving her hands on, she wrapped her arms around his broad back. Looks were very deceiving, not the body she had expected from a computer nerd. Chloe slowly stroked one hand down the centre of his back as his mouth moved expertly around hers, tasting the alcohol on both of their breaths. She ran her hand to his firm ass which encouraged him to manoeuvre his leg over hers, positioning himself closer into her.

As the kissing got faster and travelled to her neck, she could feel he was aroused already. She had forgotten just how easily men could get turned on; it had been a long time since she felt a man on top of her and it had taken her by surprise. The wine had made her loose—very loose—and he seemed to know exactly what he was doing. Either that or she was so drunk that anything would do right now. Was this a bad decision that she would regret come morning? Right now she didn't care—she just wanted him to keep doing what he was doing.

This week had been full of surprises, and this was one she definitely did not see coming, but it was unexpectedly welcome. The breeze outside blew through the room and swept over her body, Brian had now magicked her blouse onto the floor beside the sofa; she felt the cool air brush over her clammy skin—it made her tingle. Outside, New York was experiencing a heavy and unexpected summer night's thunderstorm, and so was Chloe—inside her apartment.

# CHAPTER FIFTEEN

Stirring from her sleep, Chloe's head began to pound for the second day running. In the hours of the early morning she felt a chill and tugged on the bed sheets, trying to cover her half exposed body—they felt heavy. Curiously, she began to wake herself with just one bleary eye opened to see what was preventing her from swooping the duvet over her in one. Her head started to spin as she slowly began to focus on the human carcass next to her, only just being able to make out what—and more importantly—who it was.

'*Fuck!*'

Literally—it was all coming back to her. She had slept with Brian, and he was now snoring his head off in her bed (hogging all the damn sheets too).

'How could I sleep with him on the first date?' she asked herself, she didn't even know his surname.

Then she remembered how last night had unfolded and how like usual, she had alcohol to blame for this mess. She didn't even need to screw him, he had already created her new website for free; apparently, there was some kind of attraction between them after all. Chloe propped herself up onto her elbows as the morning light crept through the crack in her curtains which made her squint; it seemed like it was to be another beautiful, sunny day outside but it was too much beauty for a hungover drunk to handle right now.

Looking at Brian, she noticed how still and handsome his face looked. Trying to get out of bed without waking him, she made her way to the kitchen. She didn't need the awkward good morning chit-chat, what she really needed was a jug of water, followed by coffee—and fast! The living room was a mess, empty wine bottles and used glasses were left on the coffee table. Tripping over her blouse as she walked over to collect the glasses, she picked it up and went to throw it towards the bathroom, but remembering she was topless she decided to put it back on—tying the shirt tails around her waist 'Britney' style. Brian's pants were in a heap at the end of the sofa, followed by her bra over the back of a chair—last night was all starting to come back to her.

The sofa cushions were strewn around the floor, and her laptop stared at her blankly, drained of its battery as she forgot to shut it down, distracted by Brian's advances. She rubbed her face and moved towards the kitchen blindly, not fully able to open her eyes and partly not wanting to discover any more reminders of the night before. After gulping lashings of cold water straight from her refrigerator, she flicked the switch on the kettle and reached for a mug and some instant coffee. The sound of clinking china had awakened Brian, and he strolled into the kitchen wearing just his CK boxers that moulded around his hips perfectly.

"Would you like some coffee?" Chloe said, not knowing where to look which was ironic since she already had him.

She couldn't deny it, he didn't look too shabby; he was lean and toned in all the right places, her eyes travelled downwards—Brian flashed a cheeky grin at her—she immediately looked up and continued to heap a spoonful with coffee.

"I think I need one after last night—I wasn't expecting that!"

"Neither was I… Oh *God!*" she laughed, preparing a second cup of coffee.

The kettle seemed like it was taking longer than usual to boil. 'How long is this conversation going to last?" she cringed.

"What's so funny?"

"Oh… It's nothing."

"No… Go on—tell me," he pushed.

"Well, for starters, I don't even know your full name," she began, before the kettle switch finally clicked.

*Hallelujah!* She poured water over the coffee granules waiting to be dissolved in both mugs. Brian had made his way over to her before she could finish stirring and took her from behind. 'Good morning!'

she thought to herself. She could feel him as he pressed against her, something else had been stirred it seemed. Was he going to take her right there and then in the kitchen?

"Matthews—Brian Matthews," he whispered seductively in her ear. "Does that make it all better now?"

He buried his face into her neck, smelling her as he ran his big warm hands down the front of her blouse and onto her naked stomach, and he didn't stop there—he continued downwards, moving towards the inner of her thigh.

'Fuck the coffee,' Chloe thought. 'Fuck *me* instead!'

If she couldn't remember much about last night due to the amount she drank, that didn't matter now—she was about to get a reminder. Chloe suddenly recalled that he was quite adventurous in bed and not at all shy after he requested she kept her knickers on. His geekiness disappeared while busy with ravishing her. Instead, he came across as some kind of sexual beast; Brian knew exactly what he wanted to do with her and he was very confident. 'It's always the quiet ones that surprise you the most,' she said to herself.

"Sex on a Sunday is the best… Especially in the morning," Brian said, and he was damn right about that.

*

Lying in bed, they eventually drank their coffee, which had to be remade as the first round went cold, developing a filmy layer on the surface. They even managed to eat some breakfast, having worked off the alcohol and gained an appetite.

"What have you got planned for today?" he said, with one arm around her.

"Well, I should get ready and put some clothes on for a start… Then I need to post the pics from last night that you took of me, and maybe write a review of the restaurant… And I *really* need contact Veronica—*shit!* I actually have a lot to be doing today," she said, realising that S.O.S was now back online too. Remembering how amazing her website now looked, Chloe felt a sudden burst of excitement to get up and get to work, although she could have quite happily laid there all day in bed with him; in hindsight she felt daft for denying that last night *was* a date—only to take him back to her apartment and have sex.

That wasn't the plan of course, but it was an outcome that didn't seem so bad now that it had happened. Thankfully he too had plans, he was having lunch with his mother (which was just typical), although she didn't mind. This gave her a chance to catch up with Dom and fill him in on her little secret, 'He will die when I tell him,' she thought with a smile on her face, but first, she needed to tackle the growing to-do list.

The moment Brian had left, Chloe fetched the charger to power up her laptop before stepping in the shower for a much-needed wash. Dressed and clean, Chloe turned the laptop on and went to find Veronica's details that Karen had given her, still in the pocket of the jacket she had worn to work that day. Before writing her an email, Chloe looked at DivaFeet.com to do some research first, although she had heard of it before, she had never shopped from it—too spoilt with discount at Palazzo.

She fetched her computer and set it up on the kitchen worktop so she could fetch coffee on tap as she worked. DivaFeet sold ladies footwear, accessories—stocking smaller designer brands as well as their own line. They had a whole assortment ranging from ballet pumps, party platforms, sneakers, and sandals. Browsing the site, Chloe had already noticed a few things that she wouldn't mind having herself, and the prices weren't too crazy either—high-end looking fashion at chain store prices. She also noticed that they had exclusive collaborations with designers, there was also an editorial section featuring content on the latest trends and snippets from press coverage.

If Chloe could somehow impress Veronica and get featured, then S.O.S would gather thousands of new readers in no time at all. This was exactly the opportunity Chloe needed as if everything was falling into place naturally. She opened up her new business email account and drafted an introduction to herself and StacksOfStyle, referring back to Karen as her source of contact.

---

**From:** Chloe Ravens
**To:** Veronica Meyer
**Subject:** StacksOfStyle.com

Dear Veronica,
I apologise for the delay in writing to you, but this email couldn't find you at a better time as StacksOfStyle.com relaunched with an exciting new website!

My passion for styling, giving fashion advice, and writing about current trends and how to recreate runway looks for less led me to start StacksOfStyle. I am sure Karen has told you that I am on the lookout for exciting products and brands to feature. Thus I am very grateful for this opportunity to work with you. Please do check out my site and let me know how to go about working with DivaFeet going forward.

Chloe Ravens
*'The Raven'*

---

Reminded of how fabulous her website now looked, Chloe opened up another browser—the web address was now stored in her favourites tab. She didn't take her eyes off the screen as StacksOfStyle uploaded in front of her. It never looked so good, in fact, she would never tire of seeing this, she was filled with excitement about what the future held.

"This is exactly what I've been waiting for!" she said, almost in disbelief that she had come this far already.

Everything Melinda said about finding joy outside the walls of Palazzo was true, and she was now creating her own career. Looking through the pages of her website, her mind floated to thoughts of

Brian—it had his touch all over it (as had Chloe). Her body was still tingling from their rendezvous, but she dismissed the distraction from her memory.

Brian was just a bit of fun—she needed to stay focused. Browsing the news feed, she could see a couple of random comments had been left on the article she posted late last night. Thanks to the Instagram account Brian had set up, it had flagged the new and re-launched site to people that had searched her hashtags, she was impressed to see that the visitor counter had reached thirty hits already.

Reaching for her phone, she opened up her Instagram and was thrilled to see that she had gained a few followers overnight too. The buzz from discovering people was reading, and liking, what she was doing felt addictive—she wanted more hits, and there was one way to do it—new content. Inspiration wasn't far away; remembering another article she had to write, she checked her phone for the pictures Brian had taken of her in the Chanel dinner jacket outside The Avenue Grill. Most of them weren't at all flattering (she looked quite drunk in most of them), hanging off the railings with one arm in the air and poking her tongue out in another—delete!

After finally finding one which was acceptable to use (with the help of a few filters) she opened up a new word document and began to write. Most importantly, she described what she wore and how it could be easily recreated—already linking product pages back to DivaFeet's website.

*The Avenue Grill, just a short walk away from New York's famous Fifth Avenue, is an excellent hangout for, families, friends, and for that not-too-intimidating first date. A welcoming server will help you find a table for a small or large group or even a window booth for a more private dining experience with a view.*

*The atmosphere is young and relaxed and not far away from other hot-spots. The menu is also relaxed offering well-known classics and mouth-watering steaks served with crispy oregano seasoned fries. For the perfect dinner look, match a classic pair of black pants with a stylish tuxedo jacket, contrasted with a simple Tee underneath for*

*a casual yet smart look (in case you do end up out on the town afterwards). Complete the look with your favourite killer heels, just in case!*
*In need of some new party shoes? Find your perfect soul-mate at DivaFeet.com…*
*'The Raven'*

Slowly figuring out the process for posting articles through trial and error, she prayed she had followed the upload steps correctly (luckily for her, the background working of the new website had been simplified—meaning even drunks could work it out). Not all of the editorial pieces had to be full-on write-ups, smaller bites of daily entries would fill up her feed just as nicely. Next on her list of things to do was to give Dom a call; it was now her turn to dish out some juicy gossip. Dom picked up after just two rings, anticipating her to spill the tea from her date.

"Hey, bitch—what you doing?" Chloe said.

"Hey! Who you calling a bitch, *bitch?* Nothing much… Just showered and cleaned the flat. So… How was last night?"

"Oh gosh, where do I start? So much to tell you… Why don't you come over? We can do something… Looks like it's gonna be a nice day out."

"Yeah… Maybe," he said in a dull tone.

Chloe sensed that missing Jason was the cause for his minimal enthusiasm, but hiding inside his flat all day was not going to help the situation.

"What—get your tight little ass off the couch and get ready. I'm coming over to yours, but before you do anything else—check out the all-new and improved StacksOfStyle! I need to rack up the visitor counter some more…"

"*Shut up!* It's online already? I'm gonna check it out right now!"

Chloe waited for him to open his laptop and after a beat, she could hear him in the background tapping keys frantically.

"*Fuck!* It looks amazing—that guy is brilliant!"

"Yeah, well that's not all he is good at," Chloe said with a sarcastic smile to match; he didn't need to see her facial expression to know what she meant.

"What… Wait… *Ooh!* You slept with him, didn't you?"

Chloe breathed a dry laugh down the line, giving everything away without a single word more.

"You little hussy! Well, you had to pay him back somehow I guess…"

"Look, I'll come over, and we'll grab lunch in the park or some-thing… I'll tell you all about it only when I see you," she said, coaxing him out of his misery, and this was all the motivation he needed to get his ass ready.

"Okay then… Ooh, nice outfit by the way. Is that the cheap little grill near work? Girl… You look drunk!" Dom said, catching up on her post.

"I'll see you later!" Chloe said, ending the call, not wanting to reveal any more details until they met.

Returning to her laptop, there was a reply from Veronica in her inbox already, which Chloe was surprised to see on a Sunday. Veronica was the type of woman who worked seven days a week and always checked her emails on the weekends—you didn't reach her level of success without sheer hard work.

---

**From:** Veronica Meyer
**To:** Chloe Ravens
**Subject:** RE: StacksOfStyle.com

Dear Chloe,
Great to finally hear from you, Karen has told me all about you. I have just checked out your website, and it looks wonderful—con-gratulations on a successful relaunch! I'd definitely like you to feature our stock on your site—in fact, I see that you have already and we are always on the lookout for new influencers to collaborate with.

If you send me over your site logo, I can get an advert set up on our website on our 'Fashion Directory' page. We really want to push the summer shoes we have left in stock, maybe you could do a feature on your blog? I'm happy to send over a pair of shoes to get you started. Just let me know what you think, and we will go from there.

Best,

Veronica,
*V.Meyer@DivaFeet.Com*

---

'Wow, a free pair of shoes!' she instantly noted, and jumped straight online to look through the footwear section, she spotted a few styles that were similar to the runway shoes in the Palazzo collection. Glancing over at her rail of clothes, the navy sequin Palazzo evening gown caught her eye which inspired her to look for a pair of shoes to style it with—and stopped scrolling at a pair of ankle straps that were made from gold mock-croc leather.

Clicking on the shoes for more details, the site suggested a matching clutch bag—it too was made from the same gold material and featured a brass serpent fastening with green stones for eyes. 'Very Cavalli,' she thought. She replied to Veronica's email, thanking her for her help and outlining a rough sketch for a blog entry using the shoes and bag, styled with her vintage Palazzo gown—it was called 'Re-style Your Wardrobe Investments.'

Attaching her new logo to the message, she clicked the 'send' button with a flourish from her fingertips. Feeling inspired and wanting to get dressed up, she turned to the rail for an outfit, perfect for lunch in the park. It needed to be stylish enough to snap and post on Instagram now she was a blogger; she needed to take advantage of every photo opportunity and anyone she could use as a photographer—meaning Dom.

Producing more content would help gain more followers—a daily 'outfit of the day' post would surely help. There were many items on the rail that she hadn't noticed before, having been distracted by the spectacular standout pieces; she picked out a sleeveless leopard print blouse made from silk that tied around the waist like a silk scarf belt. She already owned a pair of beige safari shorts from Palazzo that had cargo style side pockets and a pleated front. She figured that worn together, it would make a great look for an outside summer adventure in the park with Dom.

Changing into her outfit, she accessorised with a thin woven brown leather belt and checked herself out in the mirror. Pleased with how it was looking, she hunted in the mountain of shoes in her bedroom for a pair she knew she had somewhere—tan platform wedges with a gold buckled ankle-strap and a straw basket to finish. A few wooden bangles and a chunky turquoise necklace completed her Central Park safari look. A 'ping' sounded from her laptop in the background—she had received another reply from Veronica. She approved of her idea and product selection and had copied in her assistant who would have the shoes and clutch dispatched to her first thing on Monday morning for her.

"Yes!" Chloe shrilled, things were coming along nicely.

Excited to get out and meet Dom to tell him her even greater news, she quickly chose a pair of sunglasses and grabbed her keys, chucking them into her straw basket. Heading out to leave, she looked around at the cesspit that was her apartment; there were wine bottles, used cups, and plates that she still had to clear up—but it would have to wait. Right now she was dressed to impress, not for cleaning. She didn't think twice about it and left to make her way over to Dom's place.

When he answered the door, to her, he noticed what she was wearing straight away—she had definitely amped up her image for a stroll in the park. He greeted her with a kiss on the cheek before letting her in.

"Great outfit! See what sex can do for you now girl—I haven't seen this look before have I?"

"Thanks, I found the top in the free stuff I got—the rest is mine," she said, posing and twirling like a runway model.

"So, how was last night?" Dom said, with big wide eyes, eager to know more.

"Well, we went for dinner which was nice... We had steak and fries— which I needed after our little night in. Then, he suddenly asked when I would like to re-launch the website, and I said as soon as possible—which he understood as right away! So, we ended up back at mine with some wine and then the next thing I knew, we were making out."

"You go, girl—good for you! It was about time you got some cock."

Dom had had quite the share of it himself lately, which was the problem, (or the lack of it) now Jason had left New York. He was missing him terribly after their intense week together; he knew this would be the case, but he didn't realise just how hard it would be and how strong his feelings for him actually were.

"So, did you hear from Jason?"

"Briefly... We've spoken on the phone, but he doesn't always reply to my messages. I told him I miss him and can't wait to see him, but I feel like I'm not getting the same reaction back."

That conversation with Jason had left him with a sinking feeling in the pit of his stomach. Now Jason was back home and busy with work, it sounded like he would have no time for a guy he met all the way back in New York.

"What makes you say that?" Chloe said.

"Well, now that he's back in L.A, he has a lot of work to do for the London exhibition. The show opens during London Fashion Week, so I understand he is busy but is he that busy that he can't reply or spend some time on the phone?"

"Well, he'll be swamped until after the exhibition—try to give him some space."

"Yeah... I guess. I just hoped to see him much sooner, that's all," Dom said, sounding disheartened.

"Babe—I'm sure he really wants you to visit. It's just the wrong time for him at the moment. Understand that he has an amazing opportunity, and he needs to work hard on it. Anyway, L.A is nice all year round. Come on, let's get outta here and grab some lunch."

They left the confines of Dom's apartment and walked to the subway, riding the train over to Central Park. The day was perfect for lounging in the Sun; stopped at their favourite hot dog stand (the one they could trust) which they hadn't done in quite a while. When the summer came around, they would always spend days off together lazing in the park, topping up their tans and man spotting. There was always plenty of hot guys jogging in the park with their dogs, but this time Dom wasn't interested; there was only one man his mind was stuck on.

They made their towards their usual spot as they ate their hotdogs, it was a getaway from the hustle and bustle of the city around it. The smell of freshly cut grass and trees replaced the fumes of exhaust pipes and the stench of trash on the sidewalk. As they got comfortable on the grass, Chloe went into detail about her unexpected night out, which Dom listened to with full attention.

"So, are you going to see him again?" he asked, interested and slightly jealous at the same time.

"I'm not sure… I'm certainly not going to message him first!"

After a marathon of chatter, Chloe laid back to relax, kicking off her wedges while Dom was strewn topless on the grass—like a starfish so that he didn't get tan lines. They soaked up the warm rays, relaxing from the stresses of city life and Palazzo more so. Tomorrow was set to be another stressful day at work, and they were enjoying what was left of their weekend in peace. Francesca was finally starting her role as their department manager, and everyone had been anticipating how that was going to go down.

It was obvious she would be on Regina's side, but to what extent? Would she be a total bitch straight away, or would she be fair—maybe she would grow to hate Regina too? Either way, they would find out in the coming weeks. Right now, the warm Sunday afternoon was the only thing that mattered—until Chloe's phone beeped. They both looked up to check who's phone broke the silence. Unfortunately for Dom, it wasn't his. Chloe reached into her basket and through squinted eyes from the glare of the Sun, could just about make out the text message.

HOW IS THE RAVEN? LAST NIGHT WAS GREAT FUN... HOPE YOU HAVEN'T CHANGED UR MIND ABOUT ME ALREADY? LET'S DO IT AGAIN SOON—THIS WEEK MAYBE? LET ME KNOW WHEN I CAN SEE U. BRI X

"It's Brian," she said, in a flat tone—like it was almost unwelcome.

"Oh yeah… Saying what?" Dom said, hardly moving from his spot, shielding his eyes from to look in her direction.

"Just that last night was great, and he hopes we can see each other again soon…"

"Well, at least he *wants* to see you again!"

"Stop it… Jason wants to see you again too…"

"Maybe… At least this Brian dude isn't just some hook-up guy."

Chloe tossed her phone back into her basket, she hadn't had a relationship with a man for a while (other than Dom), she decided that keeping it cool would be the best course of action. It had crossed her mind that it was probably a bit too late for playing it cool—considering she had already had slept with him. She wasn't quite sure whether she preferred to have a boyfriend, or just a 'hook-up' as Dom had put it.

Now wasn't such a great time for either, how could she start a relationship and expect it to be good when she wasn't exactly happy with her life as it was right now? She now had an opportunity to change it. Taking her own advice (as she had given to Dom), she knew it was way too premature to worry about whether Brian was just a fuck or a potential boyfriend—she laid back down on the grass, not giving it further thought.

However, Chloe had longed for something exciting to come along for ages, and now it was happening—all at once. She realised how life could change and flip from one day to another, not knowing what awaited you around the corner. She hoped that Dom could see around the corner also, past his current heartache and that Jason also needed time to make his dreams come true.

That was easy for her to say, she was in the same predicament as Jason, did she really have time to date Brian as well as run a website? Being the proud owner of a fashion blog with great prospects meant more to her than having a boyfriend.

"Come on," Dom said out of nowhere. "Let's hit the town for an iced coffee then go home for some dinner… I can tell you're dying to strut the streets in that outfit!"

"Oh, really queen? And I suppose you wore that vest, which fits you like a condom, just to blend in?"

"Honey, I'm as good as a married man remember?"

Laughing at each other's insults, Chloe was glad that he could still laugh and joke, despite being depressed over Jason. They always teased and cursed each other lovingly, and she was pleased that neither Brian or Jason had taken that away. Whatever happened, Chloe knew that she could always count on Dom, and vice-versa. Dom's throw away comment reminded her that she had totally forgotten to take a picture of today's outfit to post onto Instagram.

"Okay, before we leave, take a picture of me in the park with my summer-city safari inspired outfit—today's theme."

Dom rolled his eyes, he thought it sounded naff but co-operated and snapped her a few times with her phone. A few of them didn't meet her approval, not liking this pose and not liking the angle of another. Dom was the perfect and most patient 'Insta-husband,' directing her on how to pose for the camera. Eventually, she settled for one that was worthy of gracing her blog and only once she had run it through a filter.

"Okay, check this out," she said, tilting her phone so he could see. This was the perfect opportunity to try out the mobile upload option

Brian had set up. In a flash, Chloe had posted the photo with the hashtag 'OOTD' amongst others. "Once posted on here, it will be sent to the main site automatically too."

Instantly checking her notifications, she saw a couple of 'likes' and made Dom follow the S.O.S account, so he could 'like' it too—which he did in support. Now it was time to hit the town and feel the buzz of New York on a Sunday afternoon; walking past shop displays, Chloe took more pictures. Dom pointed out some great sights too, like graffiti walls and retro signs, and helped by taking more pictures of her in front of them. Her Instagram was buzzing with today's posts, and her hashtags helped reach new followers.

Walking the sunny streets with a new purpose and feeling proud, she felt wonderfully buoyant. She finally owned something that was her own creation and that no one could take away from her. However, she couldn't help but feel guilty knowing Dom was heartbroken and putting on a brave face, but she was going to pull him out of his funk by keeping him busy—she needed all the help she could get with S.O.S now back online. Determined not to think of anything else but enjoying the rest of the afternoon with her best friend, she strolled the streets of New York feeling like everything was finally starting to fall into place.

**

The womenswear team had been instructed to arrive early on Monday morning; after an exhilarating weekend, Chloe just couldn't find the motivation to get up out of bed. Knowing what was ahead had made her dread this entire coming week, especially when she could be spending it more productively at home.

Francesca's first day meant an end to their free rein at work; the womenswear team had worked well together, mainly because there was no one to tell them what to do and they could just get on with the job. They knew how lucky they had been, but they also knew it would come to an end someday, thanks to Regina's need for complete control and micromanagement. Finally having mustered the energy to get show-ered and dressed, Chloe put on some make-up and made an effort with her hair. First impressions mattered, and she wanted to start off on the right foot with this Francesca. She checked her clothes rail and decided that today she would wear the vintage black Gucci blazer, along with some skinny blue jeans with a simple white T-shirt underneath.

It was a tad dressy for a Monday morning, but she had to make an effort now she was a fashion blogger. Every day now called for a new look and an original image to post online. The jacket was a little bit too big for her, but she pushed up the sleeves and made it work like an oversized blazer. Quickly snapping a selfie in front of the bathroom mirror with her phone, she posed and even gave a pout with her red lips that matched her shoes.

Chloe was starting to look forward to her daily posts now that she had a decent collection of clothes that could cope with demand. She quickly sent the picture via her Instagram to the main site and rushed over to her laptop to make sure it went through. Scrolling through the main feed, she could see the previous articles had been read a few times and some readers had even left comments. The visitor counter had crept up to sixty-five hits in just two days which was a promising start. Checking the time, she grabbed her handbag and headed for the door; she needed to leave pronto if she was to be on time for the early start.

Walking down Fifth Avenue from the subway, Chloe was attracting looks from passersby; men going to work shot her a flirty smile, while women looked on with glares of what could only be described as jealousy. It gave her an extra bounce in her step which was becoming a regular occurrence now she had something she was passionate about outside of work. She was in her own world—so much so that as she ap-proached Palazzo, she didn't even see Regina and Francesca stepping out of a chauffeur-driven company car.

Regina did a double take and tilted down her Palazzo sunglasses (which she had owned since she was a salesgirl and were now highly collectable), and couldn't believe what she was seeing. Chloe, who usually dressed down in sneakers and jeans, was strutting her stuff down the avenue and into the staff entrance looking rather good—too good for a sales girl!

'Tragic… Who does she think she is?' Regina thought, wondering how she still managed to have so much confidence and pride, despite her trying to dampen it.

Regina and Francesca had made their way back to the store, having just visited the offices and showroom in the Garment District as part of her induction. Regina thought it was a good idea to show Francesca first hand what was coming in from the new season; she didn't want her latest member of management to come across as inexperienced to the rather experienced sales team under her—that would only give them the power to disregard her straight away.

Especially as Regina was counting on Francesca to make changes and direct staff that had strayed somewhat. Regina misunderstood talent, personality, and common sense—instead, she saw it as disrespect. Ambition was not welcome in any form—no one was better than her. The main offenders were Chloe and Dom of course and Francesca was now her 'all seeing eye'. Shaking the sight of a glamorous looking Chloe out of her mind, Regina slammed the car door shut and proceeded to walk into the store with her new ally in tow.

The womenswear team had gathered with anticipation by the large sofa on the shop floor. Tristan and Sarah chatted rather enthusiastically for a Monday morning about what was going to happen. Dom rolled his eyes at their pathetic concern, listening to them started to grate on his nerves; they loved to argue and debate about Palazzo dramas.

'So what? We are getting a department manager… Whoopee-do!' he thought, although he too was concerned about his future at Palazzo under a new rule.

Trying to push trivial matters aside, he knew there was life outside the shop; there was nowhere else in the world he would rather be right now other than in L.A. Instead he perched himself down next to Soraya, she wasn't quite ready for work and sat carelessly applying her make-up in a compact mirror as they waited for their impending doom. She wasn't a morning person, the fact that she was on time for another team meeting was a revelation in itself.

And then there was Chloe, who had felt her cell phone buzz in the jacket pocket of her drab brown uniform, and discreetly took it out to read it under the lapel—so she could slip it back inside easily should Regina and Francesca suddenly arrive.

GOOD MORNING RAVEN! U NEVER TEXT ME BACK… LET ME KNOW WHAT TIME UR GOING ON BREAK. I'LL SWING BY & TAKE U4 LUNCH. BRI X

Chloe wasn't sure whether she was ready to see him again just yet and decided to wait before replying, giving her time to come up with a plausible excuse to reject his offer. That and the fact she had to quickly hide her phone as Regina strutted out onto the shop floor, wearing her usual pencil skirt and fitted blazer combo—holding a stack of papers in her hand.

Her heels clacked against the marble floor which had that familiar ring to it, before softening upon entering the carpeted area where they all sat awaiting her. Francesca, the dreaded manager they had all been waiting for, followed closely. Gone was Regina's usual stern expression, replaced by one that was confident with a pursed lip. She was going to enjoy this moment of power, she lived for these moments. Francesca was also decked out in the latest Palazzo collection that she had picked for her uniform: a fitted black velvet blazer with cropped hem trousers, and pointed court shoes that had a gold 'P' buckle on the toe.

Francesca was small and petite, around five-foot-two or so, but the six-inch heels made her feet arch painfully—giving her that extra bit of height she so needed. Her walk was quite a strut, a power walk that was led by her bust which was ample; her posture was that of a dancer—well poised. Her dark brown bobbed hair was down on one side and pushed behind the opposite ear. She wore minimal make-up, but the one thing that stood out was her bright red lipstick.

Chloe recalled a training session they once had on how to wear certain colours to influence your mood. It taught them that when a gentleman was shopping for a new tie, blue represented confidence and trust, while red signified power and leadership. Chloe wondered if lipstick colour had the same significance, and maybe that was the reason why she was feeling extra confident herself—having applied a similar tone to match her shoes.

Chloe thought it was quite the coincidence that both of them were wearing the same hue; clash of the lipsticks, employee Vs manager—round one. Regina and Francesca stood in front of the team enjoying their self-importance as they all sat up and shuffled on the sofa to look more alert.

"Good morning and thank you all for coming in early this morning," Regina said, more jubilantly than ever before.

She glanced over at Chloe with a look that could only be described as disgust; still annoyed by seeing her bounce along the avenue this morning in clothes that suited a career girl; not a has-been shop assistant. After all, Regina had made every effort to squash her enthusiasm and thought that today would have been the equivalent to Doomsday for her, but it appeared to have had the opposite effect.

"Well, I know most of you had met Francesca when we toured the store together last week, but today is her first official day on the shop floor with you—as your manager."

Francesca looked around at her very attentive team members with a beaming smile that seemed genuine and excited to be presented officially. 'Maybe she isn't a bitch?' Chloe reconsidered. 'Maybe she *is* a nice person… Maybe after a few months, she will see that Regina is poison and take our side?' Sometimes Chloe saw the best in people or at least hoped it was in them somewhere, but the cynical side of her conscience told her not to be so stupid and naive.

Of course, she was a bitch, she was employed by Regina; she was on a mission to regiment them like an army. Dom also looked on with suspicion, he too noticed there was something about Francesca that made her seem too confident too quick—like she had one-up on all of them (which of course she did). Chloe's mind had switched off (thinking about what to text back to Brian with), and realised she probably looked zoned out when Regina raised her voice, as if she were directing it towards her:

"*SO I THANK YOU* in advance for your co-operation and kindness in helping Francesca settle in… She has great experience, having worked for many luxury brands, so she has more than the skills necessary to lead a great team. The reason why I have decided to find a department manager for the womenswear floor now, was not only because you were short staffed and that you haven't had a manager for a while, but it was evident to me that some of you need direction. I regret to inform you that the department is down against last year. You failed to sell through on the summer collection and the sale season saw many runway pieces being heavily discounted… Something that has not happened before in this store!"

'Why does management always try and put the blame on us?' Chloe asked herself.

It was hardly their fault the summer collection sucked, they didn't design it; and yes, they *were* short staffed thanks to her strategically promoting Kim. Okay, so they were all capable of selling, but with no manager present it meant they had to take care of everything else: back office emails, stock transfers to other stores, pulling sales reports for Regina, sending out client invitations for events, as well as daily tasks like deliveries, merchandising and actually making money on top of it all! Chloe was fuming inside, her blood was simmering, and she was trying her hardest to suppress it from boiling over.

Speaking out would do her no favours, especially in front of Francesca and anyway, that was Dom's duty. Dom was confident and always opposed Regina in these sort of meetings, pointing out flaws in her plans and delivering clever one-liners; but today he was quite the opposite. Expecting him to say something, Chloe looked over to him, he was sitting there expressionless—like he didn't care at all. 'He definitely isn't with it these days,' she thought. Anyway, this morning Sarah had taken his role and bravely stepped up to the plate.

"But Regina... Everyone knows that the economy isn't doing so well right now—people just aren't spending like they used to!" she said with a slight quiver in her voice which was caused by both nerves and anger.

On this occasion, Chloe had respect for her and was happy to hear her annoyingly squeaky opinion.

"Thank you, Sarah, for your view on the situation, but do you seriously think that I don't know what state of affairs the Western world has faced over the past decade? After all, it *is* the team's job to sell and to deliver a luxury service that is worth paying the price for... Quite frankly, I'm surprised some of you have kept your jobs looking at your personal figures," Regina said with a sarcastic huff, glancing at the sales report in hand.

That had shut Sarah up, knowing it was directed at her. She never was top of the sellers' board; she was too busy spreading gossip amongst her colleagues to do her actual job to the fullest. Chloe's mind had drifted off once again. 'She can't possibly be talking about me,' she thought. She was always on top of her sales, keeping in touch with all her good clients and active in making new ones.

Dom was also an excellent sales associate and worked with Chloe on closing huge sales. They were partners in crime in almost everything, and that was exactly what Regina didn't like about them. Separately, she felt she had more control over them, whereas together they were strong—a unit. They had an unbreakable bond at work, and they were ready to back each other up on almost every matter. Anyway, why would Regina understand their friendship? She was cold hearted with very few friends of her own outside of work; her only friends were members of Palazzo management, and now she had a new friend.

"And that's why Francesca is here... I am confident she will bring this department up to scratch, and I look forward to seeing the results."

Regina looked around at everyone to make sure her point had been made and to make sure no eyes were rolling at her. No one was indispensable and could be sent packing anytime given a good reason, and the disappointing sales figures were a good enough reason for some. However, passive staff like Tristan, Sarah and Soraya were no threat to hear, and thus their jobs were under no real threat either. Sensing a tension forming in the air, Francesca took the lead to step forward and introduce herself, attempting to change the subject and lighten the mood.

"I just want to add that together I know we can make an excellent team and smash all of the targets, and that I am here for all of you—no matter what problems we have," she said in her Italian accent.

You could tell she thought she was something special by the way in which she conducted herself. Regina smiled and listened to Francesca as she dribbled on about how she had heard great things about them all (which Chloe and Dom both knew wasn't true). She was brainwashed to become the ideal Palazzo ambassador, and Chloe and Dom were guaranteed to be number one on her hit list.

Regina had spent most of the morning on the shop floor, keeping an eye on the womenswear team. Making sure they did their duties and that they didn't give Francesca any trouble; she needn't have worried, everyone was on their best behaviour. Sarah was overcompensating with a deep clean of the entire shop floor, scared and threatened that she would lose her job after this morning's ticking off. Even Dom seemed to be getting on with a mini stock inventory, busying himself with checking on the small leather goods drawer.

Chloe observed how everyone had already fallen into line; fear had already settled, and it was amazing how quickly it had infected them. She noticed that even Dom acted differently, submissive and not his usual sassy self—like he had given up on the fight against Regina and the Palazzo machine. Not being with Jason was hitting him hard and it had only been three days since he his departure. Chloe was worried for him but quickly laid her investigation to rest; Regina was clocking her watching everyone else. Feeling her burning stare, Chloe snapped out of it and got on with what she was expected to do—just like everyone else.

# CHAPTER SIXTEEN

Regina had finally left the shop floor for her office, satisfied that her presence and power had successfully scared them into falling in line. She also had a lot of work to be getting on with, what with Fashion Week looming. Melinda and Myra were busy putting together the in-store event that Gianni Palazzo was hosting at Fifth Avenue, and Regina was, of course, overseeing every detail. Over in Milan, Gianni and his team were also busy with producing not just one collection for Milan Fashion Week, but with preparing the retrospective fashion show and raiding the house's archive to wow the world with at New York Fashion Week—celebrating their fifty-five years heritage.

Meanwhile, Francesca was busy making her own mark on Palazzo by organising the team lunch rota. They usually just took it upon themselves to take lunch whenever they liked, as long as the floor was sufficiently covered. Chloe had managed to keep her usual slot of noon and decided to reply to Brian's message. Going for lunch with him suddenly seemed like the perfect antidote to escape from the politics and gave her something to look forward to at least. Being the serial 'texter' that he was, he replied within seconds saying he would be waiting outside the store for her.

Making her way down the stairs to the staff exit, Chloe was relieved to be seeing him after the depressing start to the day, but as she saw him waiting there, wearing a big cheesy grin, she suddenly felt embarrassed. The last time she saw him, she was naked in bed doing things that she didn't envision doing; now they were having a civilised lunch. She was aware that this was their second date, which had her asking—are they 'together' now? It was all a bit confusing, but she just needed some form of escapism, and if that was in the shape of Brian—then so be it.

"Hey Raven!" he said, kissing her cheek.

She looked around, she didn't want any of her nosey colleagues seeing them and spreading rumours around work already; being the subject of gossip was not what she needed right now. But she was pleased that Brian took the lead, dispelling any awkwardness left between them after their encounter.

"Love the uniform babe! We may have to make use of that…"

Chloe forgot he was a kinky bastard and blushed a little—not because of his suggestion—because she was horrified to be seeing him in her drab work clothes. They headed to a nearby diner and ordered sandwiches and coffee, a quick and easy lunch.

"So, how's your Monday been so far?" Brian said as they waited for their food to arrive.

"Don't ask! So now we have this new manager, and already you can see the change in people… Everyone is sucking up to her—even Dominic… That's why I'm glad to have my website and goals outside of that place," Chloe said, getting ready to take a bite of the grilled cheese sandwich the waiter had just put down in front of her.

Brian didn't really get why working in a shop was so stressful, but then again, no one would unless they had done so for themselves.

"Jeez, who knew working in a store would be so… Political. I could never work like that, but I'm glad you like the new website."

Chloe couldn't resist his smile, showing all of his white teeth through his lovely thick lips.

"Thanks again for helping me," warming up to him all over again.

Brian leant in to kiss her on the lips, making a smacking sound that annoyed the woman eating next to them (clearly single and bitter about it). Brian was good at taking Chloe's mind off work, in fact too much as she had to run back to work ten minutes late. She slipped back onto the shop floor, hoping that no one had noticed. The speed of the afternoon had unfortunately been set from the morning: boring, and contrived.

Francesca was playing it cool by not interfering too much, mainly just observing how her new team worked together. Regina had also popped down to check up on how things were going—so far Francesca was living up to expectation as everyone seemed to look alert. Call it paranoia, but Chloe could feel Regina watching her the most. Thankfully Carmen had popped back in to save the day from being a total waste of time. She wanted to check if more new pieces from the fall/winter collection had arrived yet, hoping to catch some things she was desperately in need of. Chloe had spotted her the moment she stepped out of the elevator, she was too glam to miss and made quite an entrance with her style and confident attitude.

Chloe launched herself quickly to greet her before her colleagues could steal her away. Chloe wasn't sure if Carmen would remember her, but she needn't have worried as she walked straight up to her and kissed her on both cheeks—happy that she had finally found a reliable person to help her at Palazzo.

"Ciao, how are you my darling? Lady Darlington loved the pieces I picked up for her the other day, especially the jacket you suggested… Here, this is for you."

She handed her a small Darlington Cosmetics gift bag, much to Chloe's surprise and delight. Peeking inside, she recognised the packaging of expensive anti-ageing face creams and serums that she loved.

"Oh, wow—thank you so much! You really didn't have to; I knew she would love that jacket."

"Don't mention it… I'm shopping for another client of mine; I'm looking for one of the gowns from the fashion show, do you have them in yet?"

"Which one?" Chloe said, handing her the look-book.

Flicking straight to the back pages to the evening section, Carmen pointed at one of the red carpet dresses.

"Ah, yes… We don't have that dress right now, but I believe we are going to receive two pieces," Chloe said, instantly recognising the dress from the order book.

It was one of the most desired dresses from the season and probably hard to find, as personal shopping had a list of their wealthiest clients booked in to try them in advance.

"*Damn!* Do you think you can try and get me one by next week—Thursday?"

"I'll check on the system, but I can't promise… Usually, we receive these pieces later on in the season. It's still quite early, and personal shopping has a waiting list for them too; usually, we receive the show gowns around late October."

"Hmmm, and we both know Myra won't be any help," Carmen laughed making sure it was just the two of them in earshot.

But Francesca was trying to listen in on them from afar, trying to decipher Chloe. She was impressed with her extensive knowledge on the collection, threatened by it even, and for some reason, she appeared different compared to the other team members. Carmen couldn't quite put her finger on it either, but something about Chloe *was* different. Many sales assistants had been too intimidated by Carmen in the past to actually be of any real help to her. For this reason, Carmen could see that she had potential; she wasn't some bumbling sales idiot that she came across all too often.

Francesca now understood why Regina had told her to keep an eye on her; having kept watch on her for most of the day already, she could see that Chloe had a certain way with clients, had excellent customer service skills, along with the experience of how things worked in this company. Something Francesca would have to learn for herself to keep up with the competition—and her job.

Chloe appeared to be quite savvy, and Francesca wondered why she hadn't been considered for the manager role herself, immediately she realised that Regina's warning against her wasn't a lie. Chloe *was* too good for her own good, and if she wanted to keep on Regina's side, then she would have to play her game also and look out for this Chloe Ravens she had heard so much about.

"Okay, look don't worry… I'm in a bit of a rush looking for an evening gown for a *huge* client of mine—I can't say who of course—she has a major event coming up, but call me if anything comes in before Thursday."

Carmen gave the shop floor a quick scan before she left in case she missed something. Chloe recalled her first meeting with Carmen—she had written down her website details on the back of a business card (which she had most likely lost by now). Now Chloe had professional looking business cards for StacksOfStyle and pulled one out of her jacket pocket (which she now kept on her for moments like this); Melinda's advice rang through her mind.

"Before you go… Last time I didn't have one on me to give you—but this is my card in case you ever need anything. This is my website I told you about, look me up," Chloe said, handing her a crisp new card face up so she could see her logo and web address.

"Oh yes, you have a blog right?"

"I sure do… Fashion and lifestyle, that sort of thing. I upload new pics every day of my outfits, and I'm working with DivaFeet, presenting some style ideas for summer."

"Cool, sounds amazing… I'll check it out… Okay, gotta run but I'll see you soon. Ciao!" Carmen placed the card in her purse and left just as quickly as she had appeared—the woman was clearly on a mission.

The customer toilets on the womenswear floor had been out of order since Saturday afternoon, and it was no wonder; the plumber had discovered a soiled pair of men's boxer briefs stuffed down the U-bend. Upon hearing this information (from no other than in-house reporter Sarah), Chloe went to find Dom straight away.

Stifling giggles as she searched the floor, trying to keep composure in the form of customers, she rushed to find him; he needed cheering up, and this was the perfect antidote. She found him hiding in the alcove of course.

"Dom—Dom! Have you heard about the customer toilet? Rob Travers must have shit himself after that colonic and stuffed his boxers down the toilet!"

"What? Shut the *fuck* up!" he bellowed through a hearty laugh.

Francesca immediately appeared from out of nowhere and shot them both a look of distaste. Chloe was also in no fit state, bent over and howling with laughter. 'These two *do* need direction,' she thought to herself and left, having made her point. They both straightened up a little with apologetic faces, enough to make her move, no doubt to take notes on the matter for Regina.

"You just can't make shit this up," Dom said, this time in a hushed tone. "Just in time for Francesca—a shitty pair of boxers—the perfect welcome gift I say!"

Chloe was right, it did cheer him up. They both had huge smiles on their faces for the rest of the day and couldn't help but laugh every time they saw Francesca. She, on the other hand, didn't find it quite so funny and wasn't enjoying her staff laughing at her misfortune to deal with such a thing on her first day. Now being the one in charge, the plumber presented her with a plastic baggy containing the evidence. Not quite the glamorous first day at Palazzo she had been expecting.

*

Veronica had stuck to her word. Tuesday morning, after getting dressed and posting another outfit onto S.O.S, a package arrived at the door—it was the shoes and clutch she had requested. Chloe ripped open the box in sheer excitement to look at her freebies but had no time to try them on, she was already running late for work having spent ages deliberating today's look.

The journey to work was becoming rather enjoyable, strutting her stuff down the streets of New York knowing that she was turning heads; it was wonderful what a little bit of effort could do. If only she had done this before, she might not have been single for so long. Chloe had her love for fashion back again, something Regina couldn't kill forever. Even though she was late for work yet again and had a new boss to impress, she didn't care—she felt great. Her primary objective was to get through the day so she could go home and start writing her article for DivaFeet.

Work was becoming even stiffer and unbearable; the womenswear team were already under Francesca's spell, and Chloe noticed she too was being overly friendly to everyone—fake even. Chloe was growing even more suspicious of her, but Sarah was weak and had fallen for her bullshit.

"She's not so bad after all… I really like her."

'What an idiot,' Chloe said to herself, it wasn't that long ago she was talking about how much of a bitch she was going to be. Sarah was easily influenced, and Chloe wasn't going to waste her time explaining that Francesca was just lying low to observe them in their natural habitat before she shook things up. It would be a waste of time trying to explain the rules of the game to her. All that mattered was that she knew them for herself and kept one step ahead. Chloe also noticed that Dom was keeping his head down for the second day running, she hadn't had much opportunity to catch up with him the day before, other than laughing about 'shit-gate'.

Chloe planned to take lunch with him and lend an ear, but Francesca squashed that idea; no two members of staff were allowed to go on break together from now on, she didn't want the floor left short on staff. Instead of a peaceful lunch break on her own, Brian had surprised her by showing up outside again. At first, Chloe was annoyed that he presumed she would want to go for lunch with him two days in a row, but Brian seemed to break the day up nicely and took her mind away from the daft world of Palazzo, and made her feel quite special, wanted even.

They headed to the diner again which was becoming their regular spot. Chloe spoke of her excitement at receiving the stock for her article and how she couldn't wait to get home to work on it. An hour seemed to whizz by in no time at all in his company, but it wasn't enough for him, he wanted to see her on her own—in private.

"So, let's meet on Saturday… I have the whole weekend free—we can do anything you want," he said, hinting at the possibility of staying over once more with a raised eyebrow.

"Erm… Okay—can I get back to you on that?" She said with hesitation in her voice.

"Sure… Lunch tomorrow, same time?"

"Tomorrow is our staff sample sale," she quickly remembered, it was the perfect excuse not to see him for the third day running and elevate his expectations too soon. "I'm going before work, so I might need to make up my hour at lunch."

"Perfect, so let's do breakfast in the morning instead," he suggested, not giving up.

"Erm… Let's just meet at the weekend."

The more time Chloe spent with him, the more she began to like him, but the fact he was wanted to see her every day was a little bit of a turn off for her; she was busy with S.O.S now and didn't need some clingy guy taking up all of her time. When she thought about it, she didn't think of him at all when she was alone; she was too consumed with making her dream happen and getting her new site out there for the world to see, and when she wasn't doing that she was at work—which was a complete waste of time.

She didn't want to waste any more time outside of work when she could be pushing forward with her goal; the longer she procrastinated, the longer she would be staying at Palazzo. Even though she starting to admit she was attracted to him, she was also adamant he wasn't going to distract her from her goals; he would remain just another hobby of hers until further notice. There was no harm in having fun she figured, but Brian was fully committed and serious.

Chloe was late back from lunch again after finally getting rid of Brian who was desperate to keep her for as long as he could. After fixing her make-up, she made her way back to the floor and tried her best to blend in—like she had been there all along. No one seemed to notice or say anything, so she figured she must have gotten away with it. Chloe knew that she had to be careful and was sure that Francesca would be keeping note of every wrong foot placed.

Tomorrow she would make an extra effort to be early for work and back on time from lunch. Not seeing Brian would help, he was the main cause of her taking extra time on break. Even though he was too keen for her liking, she found it hard to peel herself away from him, relaxed in his company unlike when at work—which was beginning to grind her down each day. That afternoon, Regina had been sniffing around on the shop floor with Francesca. Deep in conversation with folded arms, speaking in Italian no doubt about the staff. Chloe wished she could understand what they were saying but could guess that Francesca was probably filling her in on her observations so far; she didn't need to speak the language to tell that they were bitching about them—or her more like.

Maybe it was Chloe's paranoia from her lateness, but she couldn't ignore the stares flickering in her direction every now and then. Posters for tomorrow's sample sale had also been put up in the back of house areas, and everyone was excited about it—especially Sarah. Chloe was excited about it too and almost forgot about the dress Kim had kindly put aside for her, that meant she definitely had to wake up early. Not just to be at work on time, but to give her enough time to get down to the showroom and get to work before her shift started; being late because of the sample sale was not an option and would definitely make her look like enemy number one. Besides, waking up for the sample sale wasn't going to be a problem; it was ironic how she could get up early to shop, but not for a shift.

Dom kept his distance for the rest of the day, hardly talking to Chloe—or anyone else for that matter. He was occupied with feeling sorry for himself and needed someone to pull him out of his funk, just like how he did with Chloe after not getting the press office job. However, Chloe was busy with the website and now Brian, and didn't need a lovesick puppy to look after on top of things; she also didn't understand why he was so self-destructive about it all.

Jason just needed time to get his work done, and in some ways, she could empathise with him; she wouldn't be surprised if he was getting annoyed with Dom and his constant phone calls and messaging, she had her own annoyance that she could relate to. Being disturbed by Brian's constant messaging and demands to spend time together was a little overwhelming, she had not long just had lunch with him, and he was already bombarding her with messages; arranging breakfast before work tomorrow even though she had made it clear she was going to the staff sale before work.

Chloe started to wonder if seeing Brian was a good thing, after all, it only seemed a good idea when she was with him. Outside of his presence, she couldn't really care less; he certainly wasn't going to be the love of her life. If he were, she would be slightly disappointed, she always envisioned someone would whisk her off her feet and take care of her—financially as well as physically. But now she was learning that standing on your own two feet and looking after yourself was much more satisfying than depending on a man to bring you happiness—she just wished Dom could see that too. She knew that she needed to make more of an effort with Dom, he was her best friend, and she didn't want him to get hurt, but at the same time he needed to calm down; he was acting like someone had died.

Maybe she could take his mind off Jason somehow, just like how Brian managed to make Chloe forget about work. Work was boring her to tears, and she was counting down the hours until home time, which had seemed to prolong the afternoon even more. The seconds turned into minutes, and minutes turned into hours. There was only one thing on her mind, and it wasn't Brian—starting the article for DivaFeet and finally getting her hands on the shoes and bag that awaited her back home. She was eager to get the ball rolling and get her working relationship with Veronica off the ground on a good note.

When she was finally free to go, Chloe ran up to the locker room to get changed out of her uniform and onto the subway as fast as she could, not even saying goodbye to Dom who had hoped she would go for a drink with him after work. Instead, he decided to take the long walk home, walking past The Plaza—but not going inside this time. The subway was packed as usual with human traffic and gave plenty of time for Chloe to think about her article. She decided that she would snap a picture of herself wearing the navy vintage Palazzo sequin gown with the shoes and bag, then photograph the two items separately, outlining the product details and a link to buy directly from DivaFeet's website. The article itself would be about styling an old wardrobe favourite with inexpensive accessories for an updated look, something that S.O.S would be known for.

The minute she got through her apartment door, Chloe whipped off her outerwear and changed into her usual pair of shorts and cami top to get comfortable. Excitedly, she settled down to the task of de-boxing the parcel from DivaFeet; taking out the shoebox, she placed it on the kitchen counter. Ignoring her hunger pangs, she lifted the lid of the box; this was way more important than eating right now, she carefully delved through the tissue paper to take out one of the shoes—holding it up in the kitchen light for inspection. Her initial response was that they were very good quality and was pleasantly surprised to see that they were at an affordable price of just $100.

The heel of the gold sandal was six-inches high, including the small one-centimetre platform, giving maximum height. The main upper was made up of thins straps that intertwined around the foot, the closure was a thin ankle strap with a small gold buckle. Going back to the parcel, she took out the clutch which was wrapped in more tissue paper inside a DivaFeet dust-bag. Unwrapping it, she revealed the clutch bag which was covered in the same golden leather, featuring a brass snake fastening at the top.

Its green rhinestone eyes made it look more expensive than its recommended retail price, but still—it wasn't anywhere near the same craftsmanship and quality that she was accustomed to at Palazzo. She docked her iPod into the stereo and played some eighties electronic beats, setting the mood for getting dressed up—it was time for a mini photo-shoot.

She skipped to the bathroom to completely re-do her make-up with a new base of foundation and concealer highlight. She then continued with a smokey eyeshadow, a dark burgundy lipstick, and added bronzer with a harder colour of blush on top of it before tackling her mane of messy blonde waves. She scraped it back and pinned the front section halfway, leaving her hair to cascade down her neck and away from her face. She gave the back a boost with some hairspray and brushed it big and full on the ends.

Hopping out of the bathroom, she headed into the living room where the rail of clothes had now taken residence. She stripped off her lounge clothes (not even checking to see if the blinds were drawn) and peeled the navy vintage Palazzo gown of its hanger. Stepping into the dress, she pulled it up over her body and struggled slightly with the fastening. It was a little too big for her as the scoop back almost showed some butt crack; she nearly tripped over the hemline as she sat down to put the shoes on. After she had fastened the sandals around her ankles, she hitched the dress up and grabbed the clutch off the kitchen side so she could excitedly check herself out in the bathroom.

Looking back at her reflection had made her want to go out and party, she was all dressed up with nowhere to go. 'Maybe I should call Dom and go out after all?' The thought didn't last long, she reminded herself that this was work, and also it was only Tuesday night. Plus, tomorrow was the staff sample sale, and she needed to be up early if she was going to have any hope of scoring some bargains. She spent the next fifteen minutes admiring herself and visualising situations where she could turn up dressed like this, imagining the dropped jaws from onlookers as she entered the room. She even pretended to give an interview on the red carpet and for a moment, completely lost herself in her own hype.

"Oh, this old thing? Its vintage Palazzo—no longer available from the fashion house but given to me for this special occasion."

After allowing her mind to wander for some time, she grabbed her phone to start her solo photo-shoot. Annoyingly, there was another message from Brian awaiting her, but she didn't have time for him right now; she was busy, and he should have known better as she told him all about it at lunch. It took a few attempts to get the lighting and angle right, but she got there in the end. She pretended that paparazzi were calling for her photo, helping her to adopt a confident model-like pose. She even went out onto her balcony to catch the orange sunset in the sky for a series of pouty selfies. This was as close to stepping out she was going to get for tonight.

After posing and prancing around her apartment to the music, she didn't want to take the dress off, but she also didn't want to spoil it. It was delicate and a masterpiece not to be ruined, already having lost some of its beads from its previous owner. She reluctantly took it off and got dressed back into her lounge clothes, carefully hanging it back on the rail. She cleared her coffee table and merchandised the sandals and clutch bag with the DivaFeet tags on show, along with the shoe box and packaging that came with them for her product shots. The gold leather shone in the pictures and looked much more expensive in photos than it did in reality.

Chloe's stomach rumbled in the background, there was no getting away from the fact she was starving, so she fetched the obligatory cheese macaroni meal for one and slammed it in the microwave. She multi-tasked eating with constructing the article on her laptop using DivaFeet's logo and links to the website. Chloe was quite happy with the novice pictures she had taken for her first attempt, the dress looked amazing and equally so did she wearing it.

Adding the best picture of herself posing on her balcony, into the article, it served as the main photo with the smaller product pictures and details surrounding. Chloe pushed it through the upload wizard straight away, and while that was publishing, she ran her favourite picture through a filter on Instagram to post. After which, she could see that the article had successfully uploaded and double checked her website online to make sure it looked great and had no typo's—she really should have checked that first.

There it was, her first article with DivaFeet, she excitedly sent Veronica an email to let her know that it was live. For a moment she had worried that she should have sent it to her first for her approval, but it didn't matter as Veronica emailed back congratulating her. She loved it so much, she told Chloe she could keep the pieces as a 'thank you' gift. 'Result,' Chloe thought, she could get used to this.

She had heard of stylists, and fashion folk receiving freebies and wondered how they managed it—now she knew. This was her first freebie to come out of blogging, and she was hopeful that there would be many more to come. That's if you didn't include all the free clothes and the website upgrade she had received for no cost already (that's if you didn't count serving Mrs Ruthenstock at Palazzo for years and giving Brian sex of course).

Most of the evening was spent looking at her new website and promoting it across her social media accounts, answering to the few comments that had been left. Happy that things were starting to fall into place, she browsed the clothes rail and picked out an outfit for tomorrow; she had to get up early for the sample sale and picking her outfit now would save time in the morning. With her look pre-planned, she took off her make-up and gave herself a facial using the cream and serum Carmen had gifted her.

Finally climbing into bed, she felt satisfied and fulfilled; ending the day with something productive made the rest of the day seem worthwhile. She was so excited about the future and the potential of StacksOfStyle that she was too stimulated to sleep now—ideas whizzed through her mind, and she contemplated getting up now to start writing them. But knowing she needed to get to sleep for the early start ahead, she tossed and turned with her eyes clamped shut, willing herself to drift off…

**

Chloe wasn't not impressed by the five-thirty a.m. wake up call she had set the alarm for; she slept through the night very lightly, and her eyes stung upon opening them, but today was the sample sale, and it was well worth getting up for. The first task—after showering and a quick cup of green tea—was to upload her outfit of the day post. She was thankful that she had chosen it before bed and snapped a flat-lay of it rather than getting dolled up for a shoot. Getting glam for Instagram this early in the morning was not the thing to do, and she would have plenty of opportunities to take a pic of her wearing it later; she could use the well lit fitting rooms at Palazzo for a more sophisticated setting.

The outfit consisted of a red and black checked shirt with a pair of distressed, black denim shorts, black tights, heavy military boots and a denim jacket. Topped off with her messy wavy hair, a pair of blacked-out Ray-Ban Wayfarers and a leather Palazzo hobo she had purchased at a previous staff sale. She posted a picture of it all laid out perfectly with a few emoji's and the caption: 'Bargain hunter realness'. She had just enough time to check the reaction of the DivaFeet article she had posted before leaving the apartment, it had already attracted a few comments from readers saying how great the DivaFeet pieces looked. Some said they were going to snap them up, and one reader even enquired about the dress—but that wasn't for sale.

This was great publicity, not only for her but also for DivaFeet, and Chloe hoped she had made a good first impression. Checking the visitor counter, she was amazed to see that the number had almost doubled overnight. Everything was going to plan very smoothly, almost too well. Chloe couldn't believe her luck and wondered when things were going to go wrong like they usually did; shrugging off the negative vibes and determined to ride the waves of her success, Chloe quickly got dressed and left to embark on her journey to the Garment District.

Leaving the apartment this early in the morning seemed wrong, she wasn't in her usual rush to get to work and had plenty of time to make the journey. The strut in her walk which was beginning to come by default carried her all the way to the subway station even with no passers-by to boost her ego (except the garbage guys). On the train, early morning riders stared at her choice of clothes, it was the sort of outfit that a pop star would wear on her day off to get papped in, not the office where they were most likely heading. Maybe they thought she was indeed a pop star undercover—she exuded that sort of confidence and glamour beneath her blacked-out shades.

The Garment District was where most of the fashion brands had set up office and Palazzo had their very own building. The office housed many departments such as the buying team, payroll, merchandising, as well as the wholesale showrooms for the Americas. The queue outside the headquarters was vast and almost ran around the block. There were tonnes of employees that had arrived early in the hope of grabbing last season's unwanted leftovers at a heavily discounted price. Chloe had no idea that Palazzo employed so many staff in one city—it seemed to grow each year—and certainly hadn't recognised anyone's face. It appeared that many were of Chinese or Japanese origin, hard-core fashionistas who couldn't resist a sale or a bargain for a family member back home.

It was now half-past seven and Chloe was bang on time, but she didn't need to worry about lining up with the rest of them. In return for helping her out, Kim told her to walk straight in to collect the dress she was holding for her—that way she wouldn't be late for work too. There was no point in Kim doing all the hard work, setting up the sale for Myra if she couldn't do favours for *her* friends, and she now considered Chloe as one.

However Chloe was embarrassed to walk past the queue, all of whom had probably been waiting for hours already; they eyeballed her, wondering who this girl thought she was pushing her way in. Walking up the steps to the entrance, she rang the showroom buzzer. There were two security guards at the reception desk inside getting ready for the many visitors to rush them. They watched and listened as Chloe spoke into the entrance intercom.

"Sale starts at eight sharp... In fact, they are running late, so hold your horses," one of the security guards barked down the microphone.

"Yeah—sure, but I'm Chloe Ravens from the Fifth Avenue store... I'm here for Kim Wei from press," she said, hoping that she would indeed be let in as Kim had promised.

The buzzer cut off sharply. Chloe waited for a few moments, surrounded by unhappy staff.

"She can't just stroll to the front!" she heard one say.

"I've been here since four a.m.!" another protested, but no one was brave enough to confront her directly.

Chloe could feel the daggers in her back and looked around, awkwardly smiling at the many angry faces now staring at her; she too would be pissed off if she had been waiting in line that long, but she had earned this privilege.

"Oh, I'm just here to drop something off for the press office," she lied, hoping that would calm them down.

Thankfully, Kim came down from the showroom to let her in, she looked fresh and wide awake which Chloe thought was quite the achievement since she must have started very early indeed. One of the security guards came to unlock the door and helped her squeeze through the tiniest of gaps, without opening the glass door fully and quickly closing it shut as the crowd tried to surge forward to enter.

Chloe was relieved, not only to have avoided the embarrassment of being turned away but that she also didn't need to wait outside with the rest of them, they were like vultures. Instead, she could make her way up to the first floor in peace and quiet, which was a luxury at a sample sale. The head office staff always had the first pick of the sample sale goods the day before, so Chloe was fortunate to get this preview herself, being just a sales assistant.

"Thanks so much, Kim... I couldn't have waited outside with that lot."

"No problem... Anyway, come on up. We are running a bit late, so you have some time on your own to shop. I have your dress behind the checkout so come over when you're done, but be quick. I want you gone before we officially open—I don't want a riot when they see you shopping and not working."

Opening the door to showroom one, Kim revealed an Aladdin's cave of couture that had been forgotten about. Some of it looked sad, hanging there by a thread, all battered and used—but somewhere mixed in with that lot were hidden gems. The selection also included stock that hadn't sold in the previous sales. Some were from independent retailers that had returned past season collections for a credit note towards their new season order—meaning many pieces were brand new with tags and in perfect condition at a fraction of their original price (which was why it was so popular with the staff).

Looking around, Chloe was almost speechless. The clothes hung on the rails jam packed like sardines in a can, but to her, they shone like jewels. Her eye for fashion was very well trained to enable her to single out pieces and recall the exact collection they were from, eliminating the rubbish almost instantly. Her plans to keep her savings after being paid back from Karen seemed to go out of the window as she noticed a dress from about three seasons ago.

It was a long jersey dress that was attached to a gold choker—very slim-fitting with a slit up the front that was almost thigh high—and was super sexy. Chloe had always loved this dress but could never afford it; she quickly checked the size label, luckily it was ex-stock and not a sample size which was just perfect.

'I'll have that thank you!' Chloe happily said to herself.

But there was a problem.

Hanging on the rail next to it was another one she had wanted badly, a black silk gown with gold 'P,' engraved buttons down the side attaching the front section to the back of the dress—very revealing but an iconic piece—but deciding to be sensible, she put it back and just kept hold of the red dress. Mindful of her time limit, she sped along to rifle through the jumble and tat—she would leave that to the desperados waiting outside.

Moving along, there was a table of accessories. A black medium-sized python handbag was sitting there amongst the standard leather goods, wallets and key-rings, helping it to stand out even more. Chloe almost gasped when she saw it and grabbed it with both hands, having flung the red dress over her arm.

"It's fab isn't it?" Kim said, walking over to her. "There were only two—obviously I took one."

"How much is it?"

"That's the best bit... $300! They have a bad paint job on the edging, but you can hardly notice it—you should totally get it."

Chloe didn't need encouragement and handed Kim the red dress and bag to pack without saying a word.

"I'll just put these with the gold dress then... I'll have it all packed ready for you," Kim said with a laugh. "You have five minutes before we open, and then I have to chuck you out, okay?"

Chloe understood and nodded her head, she gave Kim her bank card and quickly did another scan to make sure she didn't leave anything behind. In desperation she picked out a pair of classic leather court shoes, an impulse buy, but they were so cheap it was an offence not to. She would only regret it later that day if she didn't get them and would need to rush back on her lunch break in the hope that they hadn't already sold, which they would have of course.

"Okay, so two dresses at $80 each, the python bag and these shoes... That makes the total $560 please."

"Wait!" Chloe said, rushing back on a whim to grab the black dress before she could regret it.

An intern packed her items quickly into a white non-branded paper bag as Chloe finalised her payment with Kim. She felt guilty at overspending but was equally pleased with what she had got for that price, which was worth thousands at retail value.

"Thanks so much for doing this for me, Kim... I owe you one." Chloe said, she never thought she would see the day where she would owe Kim anything, but this was a massive favour she was grateful for.

"Don't mention it... You were a friend when I needed one the most, you deserve it. Okay, now get out of here!" Kim said, handing her the shopping bag full of bargains with her receipt and bank card.

Chloe left the showroom to make her way to Fifth Avenue, she was already tired and the prospect of standing up all day was not appealing. The security guard let her out before finally opening the doors to the frenzied crowd outside. Excited by her frivolous morning, she messaged Brian to see if he was around for a quick coffee since he offered to meet her for breakfast anyway. She had caught him just in time, he was on his way to the office and rather surprised to see her message but pleased by it.

They arranged to meet at the diner, and when she arrived, she found him sitting at the window bench drinking filter coffee. Brian watched her struggling with her massive shopping bag, trying not to hit other patrons with it during the busy morning breakfast rush.

"What the Hell did you buy so early in the morning?" he said, in what sounded like a scolding tone.

Chloe felt like she was being told off, like a husband that was furious at his wife for spending their life savings. Noticing her arrival, a waitress came over and took Chloe's order for a filter coffee, which she served straight away out of a cafetière.

"Duh! Today is the staff sale I told you about... Remember? My friend Kim who works in the press office put some things aside for me to collect."

Hearing herself call Kim a friend sounded weird but she was more bothered by Brian's tone of voice, it was her money, and she would spend it however she liked. They sat there for a while and drank their coffee in an awkward silence.

"I didn't expect to see you until Saturday, so this is a nice surprise," he said, trying to change the subject.

"Well, you wanted to meet for breakfast, so here I am... I knew you would be heading into work right about now, so I thought I'd take you up on your offer."

"Oh, you did now? Only yesterday you didn't seem so enthusiastic."

It hadn't even been a full week since they had got together and already he was acting like the kind of loved-up boyfriend that made you want to vomit. Chloe did like him, but she was beginning to wonder if he wanted more from her than what she was prepared to give. Did he think he was her serious boyfriend? Realising that the time was coming up to nine already, she downed her coffee and got up to say goodbye.

"Okay, I gotta shoot."

"Already?"

"I have to run down Fifth with this bag in tow, and I can't be late, our new manager is clocking me," she reminded him.

"Oh, yes... How's that all going?"

"Same old... She is holding back for now, but I'm sure she is secretly plotting to make life a misery for me... Anyway, I'm gone!"

Chloe picked up her shopping bag and gave Brian a kiss on the cheek. She was starting to feel sorry about her stern attitude towards him this morning; she didn't mean to be a bitch, he was a nice guy—a bit too full on but a really nice guy. She couldn't help but feel that she had led him on by sleeping with him on their first date, making him believe she was open to a full-time relationship.

To not break his heart, she needed to make a decision to date or ditch him. The brisk walk down Fifth Avenue had turned into a sprint which left Chloe breathless. She wasn't late, but she wasn't exactly early either. She stuffed the shopping bag into her locker which was a workout in itself, before getting changed and heading down to her department. The womenswear team were all gathered around a glass counter, analysing the new rota.

"What's going on?" Chloe said.

"She's changed the *fucking* shifts!" Sarah said. "I needed that day off as well!"

"Calm down, I'm sure I can swap with you," Chloe said, feeling generous from her early morning spend.

Sarah rolled her eyes at her. "Look! You and Dom are now on different shifts too."

Chloe snatched the rota out of her hand. It was true, Francesca had changed the shift patterns around so that she and Dom were no longer working the same shift together. Chloe remained on mornings while Dom was moved to the evening shift, and then they would swap around the following week. Dom was going through a hard time as it was and the shop floor was their chance to catch up on a daily basis. Realising that working late shifts could also impact on her upload schedule for S.O.S, Chloe felt her blood begin to boil—this was the start of things to come.

Francesca had not only changed the rota, but she had also changed around the stock room which meant they all had to take it in turns doing laborious tasks for no good reason to shift it around to her new layout, making no big difference to its productivity. The stockroom was immaculate as it was, Dom had made sure it was perfect in anticipation of her arrival.

She also decided that they would all come in early on Monday mornings for staff training sessions, meaning that they had to arrive earlier and not get paid for it—even the late shifters. Who in their right mind wanted to be at work early on a Monday morning for free? Chloe knew that now was the time to get out of Palazzo for good, but to go where? She couldn't bear the thought of going to another store, and the retail world was the same no matter where you went. Same shit, different stink. What she really needed to do was get out of retail entirely, which would prove to be hard since she wanted a career in fashion.

'I'm too old for this,' she thought. She needed a head office job, behind a desk and free from all this customer service bullshit, but there was no way Regina would let her move to the head office of Palazzo now. Now more than ever, Chloe needed to make StacksOfStyle a success, but it was early days, and she couldn't live off a free pair of shoes every now and then. She needed to find a way to monetise S.O.S, by doing what she loved—but that seemed like a long way off. Feeling trapped, all she could do was to suck it up and keep playing the game and keep on working on S.O.S. There was no getting away from it, hard work and more stress was what her life would entail for the foreseeable future.

# CHAPTER SEVENTEEN

It had been a long and stressful week, and the end of it was very welcome. The shift change wasn't as bad as first expected and with just a two-hour difference, Chloe managed to talk to Dom at work still. His mood was on a decline and Chloe was grateful to spend two hours less a day around him in fact, it was beginning to wear thin. Francesca had made several observations in her first week, and the friendship between Dom and Chloe was one of them. She could see how close they were as Chloe consoled him over his depression—Jason wasn't returning his calls or messages.

Chloe's lateness back from lunch breaks also hadn't gone amiss. Personally, this week was a winner for Chloe but not so good for her day job. None of her good clients come in to rack up huge bills meaning her sales had taken a dramatic dip compared to the week before. To Francesca, it seemed she did little else other than socialise, take extra time on breaks and use the fitting rooms to take selfies in her well-put-together looks that she came dressed to work in every day.

She kept Chloe on the early shift in the hope that she would carry on being late, having noticed that early mornings weren't quite her thing either. That should be enough ammunition to make a complaint against her and impress Regina in a short period of time. Making an example of Chloe would make her look good and serve as a warning to the rest of the team—in case they had notions of becoming complacent too. Regina was hungry to hear negative feedback about Chloe, especially on facts like timekeeping and behaviour which she could very easily pull her up on, and enjoy doing so.

Saturday was a chance to rest from the week and enjoy a full weekend to herself for once. Chloe hadn't posted any new articles other than the usual daily snaps of her outfits and accessories, which she was now committed to; waking up early to log on and catch up with her followers would be a morning well spent. Heading to the kitchen (sans hangover for once), she stretched her arms to wake herself up—her phoned beeped rousing her even more. It was a message from Brian of course.

MORNING RAVEN... LOOKING FORWARD TO OUR DATE TO-
NIGHT... HOW ABOUT A MOVIE & DINNER? U PICK THE
FILM. BRI X

Brian had been pestering her with texts all week (mainly because she stopped messaging him back), but she was determined to use the weekend to make progress with the website. She felt bad for ignoring him, he was a nice guy, and he had helped her with her, but male attention was an unwanted distraction—especially now that leaving Palazzo for good was a priority. But she did long for some avenue of fun to let out pent-up stress now that Dom was a hermit.

'Why can't I have my cake and eat it?' she asked herself, she was only a mere fashion blogger; it wasn't like she was an in-demand stylist with no time to spare at all. The fear of being a failure and not in the career she wanted at her age had piled on the pressure, not Brian—she needed to relax!

It seemed unfair she was taking it out on him—and there was her answer: date Brian. He would certainly take the edge of things and help her forget the worries of work life. 'Hmmm... A classic movie date,' she thought, tonight she would focus on having fun and not all about work for once.

The clothes rail hadn't moved from her living room for the second weekend, it was starting to buckle from the weight of the luxury fabrics, proving too much for a mass-produced piece from Swedish furniture store. In fact, there was hardly any room on there now she had added the three dresses she had purchased from the sample sale.

After she downed a coffee to feel more alert, she made herself breakfast—a sliced banana in a bowl of bran flakes covered with soya milk. Healthy eating started and stopped in the mornings, but the intention was there. As she ate, she mustered the energy to reply to Brian.

GR8 THE MOVIES! HAVEN'T BEEN 4 AGES, I'LL CHECK WHAT'S ON… DINNER AFTER SOUNDS GR8. STAY AT MINE? RAVEN X

By suggesting he stayed over, she knew full well it would end up with sex. That would definitely keep him satisfied, and there was no point in seeing him if he wasn't going to please her. 'I might as well use this to my advantage,' she decided; having her cake and eating it was an option after all. Not quite ready to get washed and dressed, Chloe opened up her laptop to check her emails.

There was a lot of admin emails triggered from the S.O.S website notifying her of activity since she had last logged in. Being such a busy week, Chloe had only been checking Instagram on her phone, not fully appreciating all the 'likes' and comments she had received on the articles she had posted. Her visitor counter had now soared and was above five hundred hits. 'The extra advertising from DivaFeet must be working,' she thought. Impressed by the number of readers, she scrolled through the main feed, going through every post she had uploaded with a fine tooth comb—and she was amazed at what she saw.

'Wow, nice jacket! Totes Chanel all the way, loving all your outfits!'

'What a cool style you have. Love the gold shoes! Can't believe they are from DivaFeet and a hundred bucks, will buy them for sure!'

'Super cool dress, Palazzo rocks! Lovely shoes and bag—goes to show chain store and designer *can* work together!'

Reading these comments, Chloe was excited by all the positive feedback and astounded that people were actually reading StacksOfStyle! More importantly, they were interested in her style and opinion on fashion. This is what she lived for, inspiring people to dress, and to dress for less too; but she hadn't managed to write anything new, or even photograph her new additions from the staff sale for the website.

She was too shattered from the added psychical and emotional stress of having a new manager at work that she granted herself a few nights off doing anything at all—ensuring she would be on time for work instead of burning the candle. The thought of coming home to more work (no matter how productive it might be for her future) didn't interest her, but at least she had time for grocery shopping which she had neglected recently in favour of quick and easy microwave meals.

Catching up on what she had missed inspired her to write new articles, she had to get her sample sale haul up there for everyone to see. They were her new babies, and she was desperate to showcase them, especially now she had more eyes watching her, and she was sure her bargains would get even more comments. Gaining more followers on Instagram had become somewhat of an obsession, and new content was the only thing that drove them to her website. These new posts would help her appear like an established stylist, even if she wasn't quite that just yet.

Fashion was all about image, and that was the one lesson Palazzo had successfully taught her. Chloe couldn't believe the rate that her site was growing, she knew she could do more if only she put the effort in and she had to strike fast while there was momentum. This was why StacksOfStyle hadn't been successful the first time around, and there was no way she was going to fail yet again.

Chloe reminded herself of how far she had come in such little time; StacksOfStyle was a complete can of worms not so long ago. Assessing her achievement, she knew Brian deserved more respect than what she was giving him. The temptation to watch daytime television rather than planning editorial for the site called her, but there was no time for procrastination, so she dragged her lazy ass to the shower instead.

Her hair was in need of a good wash and tonight's date called for it; taking last week's date into account, sex was probably on the cards. 'No, not probably—definitely!' she told herself. Chloe had gained quite an appetite now she had broken her dry spell, and Brian was good for something other than fixing her website. Taking note that Brian had a bit of underwear fetish from last time he had stayed over, she picked out some lingerie: a black see-through lace bra and matching thong. She even considered getting out the stockings and suspenders belt from a Halloween outfit she had in her closet (which didn't get much of an airing). Talk about encouragement, but she figured it was a sure way to make up for her lack of enthusiasm lately.

*

'How To Get Laid, In Seven Days' was a romantic comedy that quite frankly Chloe could have written, directed, and starred in—because it was exactly what she had achieved for herself recently. The movie definitely caught Brian's imagination, he seemed to squirm in his seat when the female lead finally seduced her man by wearing a sexy corset in the bedroom. Chloe was certain that the activities she had planned for later that evening would go down very well, and she expected Brian to go down very well too—on her—once he saw what she had lined up for 'evening-wear'.

Deciding to bypass dining out in favour of a pizza slice, they headed straight back to Chloe's apartment. Brian couldn't keep his hands off her in the cab back to hers, and the minute they got inside, he took off his denim jacket and flung it across the room—possessed with lust.

"Someone enjoyed the film," Chloe said playfully as he pulled her close.

"Well, I think we could have done a bit better if I'm honest."

"Oh yeah? You gonna show me how to laid in seven days?" she unusually flirted back; matching his level of kinkiness.

"I think I already did," he laughed as he kissed her. "Just fuck your web programmer."

Chloe slapped his chest in jest as she snorted out laughter. This was exactly why she was she liked him; he was *funny* and sexy. Waking up satisfied on Sunday (and not only from a good night's sleep), Chloe felt at ease lying next to Brian—unlike the last time. Today was set to be another stress-free day before the week ahead was about to start. She had planned to spend the morning with Brian, maybe even do brunch, before she got rid of him to get working on taking pictures of her new dresses and writing new articles.

Juggling work, Dom, Brian and S.O.S all seemed possible now she had stopped worrying herself about it and was just doing it. She started to get up out of bed to go make coffee, and as she did, she checked her phone on the bedside table. She hadn't bothered checking her cellphone, pre-occupied with Brian and forgot to put it on charge overnight; it was on its last bar of battery but enough to see she had a message from Dom waiting for her.

HEY… WHAT UR UP 2 2DAY? WAS GONNA POP ROUND. DON'T WANNA SPEND THE DAY IN MY FLAT ALONE & WE HAVEN'T SEEN EACH OTHER MUCH. X

Chloe felt for him, here she was in bed with Brian when her best friend was lonely and heartbroken at not being in bed with his hunk. Just a few weeks ago, it was him who was consoling her about not getting promoted; she felt slightly guilty at not spending as much time as she would like to, but she felt terrible cancelling brunch with Brian at the same time. Relationships were much trickier than what she had remembered and dividing time between friends, work, and boyfriends were something she had little experience in.

Determined to succeed at managing everything and everyone in her life, Chloe messaged him back to say that he could come over later that evening after she had written her latest piece for S.O.S, he could help with the photography at least. That way they had something to take his mind of Jason and away from talking about relationships altogether. She couldn't bear the thought of having this conversation with him all over again; she would probably end up snapping at him and saying something she would regret, but that he needed to hear all the same. Sticking to her plan, she arranged to take Brian out for brunch. Spending time with him was becoming much more bearable, but she was also aware that she was acting rather like his girlfriend; in the back of her mind she second-guessed her actions. She never imagined she would date such a 'safe' guy, which is why none of her past relationships worked out.

It was early days, but already he seemed besotted with her—Chloe wasn't quite there yet. Walking back to her place hand in hand, she couldn't help but feel she was leading him on, but it felt like the thing to do, so went with it. Even though living in the 'here and now' felt right, she couldn't ignore the doubts that gnawed away on her mind.

**

One thing she couldn't argue with was that time flew by when she was with Brian; she had failed to get rid of him after brunch, which meant she was now behind on her writing schedule. The evening had come around sooner than what she would have liked, and the 'back to school' feeling started to creep in once the Sun had set, but at least she had Dom to keep her busy for the rest of the evening.

"Right, time to go," she bravely said in a light but stern voice. "Dom's coming over soon, and I need to get some work done for the site."

"Sounds like you don't want me to meet him," Brian said in jest, but secretly he was serious.

"Whatever—move," she said rolling her eyes sarcastically back at him, but also meaning it.

She didn't particularly want them to meet at this stage, it would only be awkward, and she didn't want to push her love life down Dom's throat at such a sensitive time. But unknowing to her, he was eager to leave his place all day and had arrived at Chloe's slightly earlier than expected.

"*Shit!*" Chloe said at the sound of her buzzer. "That must be Dom already," she said, not releasing the entrance door for Dom straight away.

"Gosh, calm down… What's the worst that could happen?" Brian said, putting on his worn-in running sneakers that were probably the only pair he owned and used for both gym and casual wear.

'Well, yeah,' Chloe thought to herself, holding his jacket for him to take; already holding the door open for him and buzzing Dom in.

"Okay, I'm outta here," he said, kissing her goodbye, purposely taking his time by teasing his lips.

At this point his attempt at being seductive wasn't working, she just wanted to kiss him and get rid; but it was inevitable that they would pass each other on the staircase anyway, she may as well introduce them now.

Dom had raced up the stairs—taking two steps at a time—and caught Brian pushing his luck with Chloe. 'This is slightly awkward,' he thought. He was walking in on his best friend kissing a guy he had never met, but knew everything about; he decided to hold back on the final step on the landing. Sensing another presence, Chloe opened her eyes mid-kiss and saw Dom standing there, grimacing almost. She too felt awkward, she hadn't planned on rubbing it in his face, and they certainly didn't need to cross each other's path.

"Dom!" she said, parting from Brian abruptly. "This is Dom… Dom—Brian."

"Hi… Nice to finally meet you," Brian said, extending his hand out for a manly handshake. "I've heard so much about you…"
"Likewise," Dom said, taking his hand while giving him a subtle scan from head to toe. 'Handsome face—bad shoes,' he noted.

"Anyway… I best be off—have a great night guys… It was nice to meet you, Dom."

"Hopefully we can all spend time together soon?" Dom suggested, but Chloe shot him a look as if to say: 'Stop it!'.

With Brian now scampering down the stairs to leave, they went inside; Dom waited for her to shut the door before giving his verdict.

"He is sexy, you lucky bitch!"

"Yeah, he's not bad I suppose."

Not bad and sexy were two different things, Dom had good taste in men, and he knew what he was talking about—even if he did wear awful shoes. He hadn't pictured Chloe with a wholesome looking guy such as Brian but figured that was a good thing for her.

"Anyway, I finally went food shopping so I thought we could cook dinner," she said, changing the subject. "But first, let me show you what I got from the sample sale!"

Dom could instantly identify the new pieces hanging on the rail, he too had a well-trained eye for fashion, and the runway dress stood out from the rest.

"*What!* I should have gone too!" Dom said, slightly jealous that he was feeling too sorry for himself to get out of bed early that day.

"Oh, forget it… There wasn't much menswear there anyway—You know how it is."

"How the Hell did you get these pieces?" Dom said, noticing the python bag that was sitting under the rail, merchandised like a shop display—as well as the black dress with gold buttons down the side which he held up with a questionable expression.

"I know—I know… But I couldn't resist it—it's a iconic piece," Chloe said, which Dom couldn't argue with. "Anyway, a week ago I saw Kim at work—she was really stressed out about organising the sale on her own. Myra and Sylvia were working on the Fashion Week event so lumbered her with all the sale prep. I felt sorry for her and said I'd help her out."

"You… Felt sorry for *her?*"

"Yes, but that's not the story… When I went to help with boxing the stock up, we came across this dress, and she offered to put it on hold for me… All this other stuff I just bagged on the day—she got me early access."

"And you didn't invite me?" Dom said, slightly put out that she hadn't invited him along too.

Chloe said sorry with a shrug and a grin through gritted teeth, not knowing how to explain herself. Dom dismissed the opportunity for an argument, marvelling at the bargain of the year that was the black python bag instead; precisely the sort of thing he would have bought himself to re-sell online. Despite being pissed off with her for not taking him to the sample sale, he seemed to be in good spirits, and Chloe wondered whether she should ask what was going on with him and Jason—maybe he had heard from him, and things had changed. Not wanting to bring him down, but wanting to lend an ear at the same time, she cautiously broached the subject.

"I spoke to him on Thursday. He apologised for not being in touch, but he has been busy working on his exhibition pieces."

"See… I told you he was just getting on with his work. You need to respect that and try not to bother him too much with messages and phone calls… He is an artist, they need their space."

"Yeah I suppose so, I just feel like he is trying to get rid of me now he is back in L.A."

Dom felt like he had served the purpose of a New York tour guide and business trip gigolo, and now Jason was done him. 'How could he after all those dates and romantic nights in the hotel?' Dom asked himself.

"Anyway he has switched his phone off now, so I can't get hold of him at all… And yes, I have tried calling him. I just had to—last night, I couldn't stop myself. I needed to hear his voice and now I know I can't reach him, I feel even worse! I sent him a text—I know I shouldn't have—but you know how it is."

"Maybe he just ran out of battery or something?" Chloe said trying to soothe him and escape a meltdown when all she wanted to do was talk about herself for once.

"Well, if he did, wouldn't he reply by now?" Dom said, getting angry that she couldn't see his point.

Chloe was equally annoyed, he wasn't listening, and without thinking through what she was about to say, she snapped. "You need to chill the *fuck* out dude… Even if he did want to see you again, you are not making yourself look attractive by stalking him down—nobody wants a bunny boiler!"

'She has a point,' he thought. Chloe was usually sympathetic, but sometimes the truth needed to be said and if anyone could be blunt with him, it was her. Noticing that he was getting back to his depressive ways, she decided to change the topic.

"Come on… Everything will work out in the end, isn't that what you always tell me? And look… So far it has worked out for me—like it will for you too." She gave him a hug, breaking the moment with a smack on his ass. "Right, bitch—let's get to work!"

Chloe fetched her make-up box from the bathroom and set up a mirror in the living room. Dom sat on the sofa with her and went through the various compacts and colours she had collected over the years that she couldn't bring herself to throw out, but probably should have; some were new, and some were so old they looked like they would give you some kind of skin infection.

They decided to style the white and gold dress first as that was her favourite, and by far the biggest bargain. It was a one-of-a-kind showstopper that would be sure to attract more followers and online attention. They chose nude tones and basic colours that would go well with the dress, enabling them to build up the intensity on top of it for the other two dresses which required something more dramatic. Chloe prepared her base foundation, and Dom directed the tone and style for the eye make-up.

She styled her hair into a simple up-do and Dom helped her to step into the gown. 'It could do with a dry clean,' he noted, that was the trouble with these sample sale items. Nevertheless, it looked stunning on her, and it wouldn't show up in pictures. Once again she used the shoes and bag that Veronica had sent her as an extra push for her products and could tag DiveFeet in the article once again.

The accessories highlighted the gold details perfectly and styled with another Palazzo dress, you would never guess they weren't designer pieces also. The living room was cluttered with make-up on the coffee table, clothes all over the place, and other stuff lying around from having not done much cleaning this weekend—not a great backdrop for such a stunning look.

"No worries, let's just take pictures outside in the hallway and on the street," Dom said.

The landing of her apartment building looked like a New York hotel corridor and would be a more appropriate setting than a messy apartment—although that could have been quite in Vogue too. Dom positioned Chloe leaning against the white wall with the other apartment doors in the background fading down the hall behind her. Using her phone, he snapped her in several poses, telling her what to do and where to look and how. Once they were happy with a few shots, they went back inside to prepare for the next look.

Next up to be styled was the red dress with the gold choker halter neck. Chloe added blood red lipstick and a harsher blush higher on the cheekbone to suit. Dom recommended more eyeliner and to add more of a smokey effect around her eyes which worked well with the sexy style and colour of the dress for an evening look. The gold shoes also went very well with the red dress, but she decided to drop the bag as she didn't want it to look like it was the only bag she owned (which couldn't be further from the truth).

Again, Dom photographed and directed her, this time venturing outside onto the sidewalk below her apartment window. He snapped her walking down the street and turning around; the dusky summer's evening light looked great on camera, giving a cosmetic finish to the pictures without processing them through a filter. The last dress to capture was the revealing black gown with gold buttons, but Chloe didn't think she had the body to pull that off right now, so she swapped it with a simple black evening number that Mrs R had included in her haul. It went nicely with the pair of shoes she had picked up, also on a whim. They were black leather, pointy stilettos that were stamped with the italic '*P*,' monogram all over with a gold metal spike heel.

Chloe wiped off the red lipstick and replaced it with a gothic dark purple tone and added a shimmery silver eyeshadow above her cheek to highlight; Dom messed and teased her hair with a comb to go for a sexy high-fashion zombie look. She grabbed the python bag and headed out to take more pictures in the hall and on the street. By now, it was getting darker outside, and it matched the slightly macabre look they had aimed for. Chloe was starting to relax into posing for the camera and proving to be quite the model, playing up to Dom and nailing the shots in just a few clicks—ignoring quizzical looks from passers-by who asked themselves who the Hell she thought she was.

When they had finished the photo-shoot, Chloe washed off her makeup and made a start on preparing dinner; they had been working for a few hours which was rather tiring and gave them an appetite. At least Chloe had successfully taken Dom's mind away from Jason for one evening and was enjoying his visit. As dinner cooked, Dom helped her eliminate some of the pieces on the rail, consolidating it to evening, runway, and expensive pieces that required an occasion, all of the wearable items like blouses and pants were now stored in her closet which had space since she had given away some of her old clothes to charity.

Chloe didn't usually cook, but tonight was an exception as she had a guest and Dom was quite a fussy eater; she grilled chicken breasts and made roast potatoes and vegetables, but Dom soon took over and showed her how to turn it into an English style Sunday roast—although grilled chicken was slightly healthier. However, Dom whisked up a batter to make Yorkshire puddings which weren't so healthy, but he had made them for Chloe before, and she loved them. This weekend was all about indulgence, and she was pleased to see him have an appetite, having guessed he hadn't been eating much recently.

The usual gym-toned and ripped Dom was starting to look a little bit on the thin side, and she was beginning to worry about him taking care of himself. She dared not saying anything to him about it (he hated it when people said he looked as though he had lost weight after spending so many hours in the gym trying to gain it), but it was true, he hadn't been taking care, and his regular gym routine had gone out of the window since Jason had left. She knew he didn't need reminding, so she kept her mouth shut.

After eating, which had satisfied their hunger, complete with peanut butter ice cream for dessert, they got around to uploading the pictures onto her laptop to arrange them into an article—mentioning where they were from and from what season. The pictures looked so much better taken by someone else and on 'location' compared to her just holding up her phone in the bathroom mirror or in the fittings rooms at work.

Dom showed her how to manipulate the contrast and colours on her laptop which added a professional touch and an editorial edge, which she hadn't even considered doing before. Chloe posted the best ones on her Instagram and showed Dom the attention that some of her older posts had received. He was impressed with how the site was progressing and as excited about it as she was.

Now she was done posting the new pictures and writing her article, she left her laptop open for it to upload onto StacksOfStyle in the background while they chilled in front of the TV and enjoyed the last few moments of the weekend. During a commercial break of 'Keeping Up With Kelly Kaslon' Chloe eagerly checked the website to make sure the article was visible on her homepage—she clicked refresh and was amazed at what she found.

"Dom, look!"

He sat up, excited by her reaction to look at the computer screen and was also amazed at how many comments had been left already—the new article had only just posted online which he had forgotten entirely about, engrossed by Karly Kaslon's superficial life problems. Now that Chloe had linked her site to her social feeds, it was easy for readers to see when new posts were online. Chloe could feel happiness building up inside her heart as they read the various comments from a growing army of followers, it was a feeling that was growing every day doing what she loved. Chloe jumped up out of her seat unexpectedly, startled by her phone. She waited for a beat before picking it up, not recognising the number.

"Who the Hell could this be now?"

"I dunno… Answer it and find out," Dom shrugged.

It was probably a wrong number or one of those annoying tele-sales people trying to sell you something you didn't want or need on a Sunday night.

"Hello?"

"Chloe?" a female voice answered back.

"Yes—speaking…"

"Hi, sorry to call you on a Sunday evening… It's Carmen… From Palazzo—the stylist?"

Chloe's heart nearly stopped beating. 'It's Car-men,' she mouthed to Dom, who relaxed back on the sofa as Karly K came back on, turning on the subtitles so he didn't miss any action.

"Oh, hi… No problem—how are you?"

'What does she want? Probably my staff discount or something,' she thought.

"I'm fine thanks, darling… Anyway, I was calling you because I checked out your site the other day—it looks fantastic! I'm actually following you on Instagram now, and I was just sat here scrolling, and I saw your new dresses."

'*Fuck!* She's following StacksOfStyle,' she said to herself, her heart had now resumed a fast pace, eager to know what she wanted—sensing something great was about to come her way.

"I love your pictures, you look so cool! I hope you get to wear those dresses out and about somewhere glam?"

"Oh, no I just shot them for the site; I don't really go out anywhere these days."

It was true, she had nowhere to go in all those glamorous and expensive looking dresses except for the cinema with Brian, although she could have dressed up for him back at the apartment. Just owning such fabulous pieces was satisfying to her, but it a shame that they were just wasting away on her rail, not seeing the light of day. If they stayed in her apartment forever, then the moths would surely get to dine on some fine quality threads sooner or later.

"Where did you get all those amazing pieces?"

"Oh, you know, collected them over the years working at Palazzo… Here and there," Chloe said, being vague about exactly how she had come to own runway and vintage fashions.

Carmen wouldn't have minded that they were from sample sales and cast-offs handed down from clients; this was a woman who worked as a stylist freelance. Stylists relied on discounts, freebies, and connections to survive and make money. Very rarely would a stylist actually buy things for photo-shoots and would just borrow them from stores and press offices (something that wasn't possible at Palazzo with Myra Parks guarding the distribution). If Carmen knew the truth of how she had acquired all these items, then she would have applauded Chloe for her nerve and negotiation skills.

The website alone was enough for Carmen to be impressed with her, websites were expensive, time-consuming to run, and Chloe's looked very sophisticated. Sure, Carmen also had a website, but it was just a page outlining her portfolio of clients and how to contact her for her services. Chloe had been on the phone to Carmen for quite a while, by now Karly K had finished, and Dom flicked the channel over to a reality-singing contest.

He couldn't make much out from the conversation, just lots of 'yeah's' and 'ah-ha's'. When Chloe did finally end the call, she jumped up on the sofa cushions and screamed, causing Dom to flinch and shoot her a look as if to say: 'Really bitch?'

"What the fu—" he started.

"Sorry, but this is so *fucking* cool!" Chloe said, grabbing the remote and Turing the TV off, so he had no other option but to listen to her news. "Get this… She said she wants to meet me for a coffee tomorrow lunchtime… She has some projects that she thinks I could help her with!"

"What kind of projects?" Dom said, not fully understanding why she was so excited by some stylist from work calling her up on a Sunday night.

"Don't you see? She likes what I'm doing, and she is very well connected… Working with Carmen will get me some great experience, she has celebrity clients and magazine contacts."

"Pah! She probably just wants your discount," Dom said, cynical about it all.

He had experienced first-hand that when life gave you an exciting chance, it would no doubt come to a disappointing end—he didn't want her to get her hopes up too soon so quick only to be used like he had been. However Chloe knew this was something more than that, magical things had been happening to her recently, just by following her heart and doing her own thing; she was certain this was no different to all these other opportunities that seemed like they were meant to be. Carmen's vagueness made her proposition sound all the more exciting, Chloe's imagination was all over the place.

She told herself that it was probably nothing major but somewhere in the back of her mind, Chloe had the feeling that something great was about to happen. She felt a sensation building up inside of her, the kind that only stirred within you when dreams started to mysteriously creep into reality from out of the blue. And just like that, the Sunday night blues vanished, and for once, she couldn't wait for Monday to begin.

# CHAPTER EIGHTEEN

Mondays weren't usually this welcome, but this one was different, it had intrigue and excitement written all over it. Chloe had hardly slept after Carmen's phone call the night before, they had had to meet for lunch to discuss a project she was working on and wanted to speak about it face to face rather than on the phone, which sounded mysterious. Chloe didn't know exactly how she could help but she was interested to find out.

Carmen had come to the shop floor to meet her, which of course didn't go unnoticed by Francesca but Chloe didn't care what she thought. This was now the second time this woman had visited Chloe on the shop floor, and they seemed too friendly for her liking. Having friends visit the store during working hours was not allowed, even though Carmen was first and foremost a client, either way, it was noted.

"Ciao Chloe… Ready for lunch?" she said giving her an air kiss on both cheeks in true fashion etiquette.

"Sure, would you give me a moment?" she said, sensing Francesca snooping on them in her peripheral vision.

"Of course, I'll wait outside," Carmen said following Chloe's subtle side-eye over to Francesca, who pretended to be busy by rifling through a rail.

Carmen took the stairs, sauntering past Francesca, "Ciao," she said, with a sarcastic little wave, clocking that she was Chloe's boss.

"I'm just going on lunch, is that okay?" Chloe asked her, it was pathetic that she had to even ask.

"Of course it is, just don't be late," Francesca said, checking her wristwatch so she could clock her in and out to the second.

Chloe left by the staff exit to meet Carmen who was outside looking at the window display.

"*Urgh!* Sorry about that—that's my new boss," Chloe explained, unbuttoning her blouse so she could feel fresh air on her skin, now she was free from the stuffy shop floor.

"She seems like a barrel of laughs, darling! Come, let's grab food—I know how this works—you only have an hour before you have to be back."

Walking to a nearby sandwich shop, Chloe could feel her phone vibrate in her jacket pocket. She reached inside and took it half out so she could see the screen—it was Brian. She didn't have time to speak to him now, and she definitely couldn't meet him for lunch, he would have to wait until later. The waitress loved Carmen's look and noticed Chloe's Palazzo uniform which looked chic compared to her overalls—she sat them down by the window on display like mannequins in the hope of giving the establishment a trendy appearance to passing trade.

"Thanks for meeting me on your lunch break… Sorry if I made things awkward for you back there," Carmen started.

"Oh, that's fine… Now we have this new manager we are all on our best behaviour—well trying to be at least. Anyway, I'm pleased you like my website, and for your call."

"I love your website, who developed it for you?"

"Oh, well my boyfriend… *Friend*, he's an expert," Chloe said, stumbling on the boyfriend part, not quite used to or comfortable with the term just yet. 'What *is* Brian?' she asked herself at that moment; she really had to make a decision.

Could she call Brian her boyfriend? Even though she wasn't keen on the title, she supposed he was her boyfriend in more ways than one; she made a note to call him back when she could, feeling bad for not taking his call. Carmen looked at her with a raised eyebrow, 'clever girl,' she thought. Chloe ordered a turkey-light sub and a diet coke, while Carmen just ordered a black coffee. She watched Chloe devour her sub, impressed not only by her blog but also by her appetite and slender figure.

"The pieces you have in your collection are amazing," Carmen said.

"Oh, thanks… Most of them are new, so I'm having fun writing about them and stuff."

"Oh really? How come they are new? Some of those dresses are vintage."

The tone in her voice was very speculative, and Chloe picked up that she probably wanted to know how she had obtained them, especially the Palazzo gown and the runway pieces.

"Well, some I bought from sales and stuff—perks of the job—and a lot of them were given to me by a very good client of mine."

"A *very* good client I'd say!"

Carmen was beyond impressed, this girl certainly knew how to get what she wanted from people; she was also just as clever and a successful stylist in her own right, but it was mainly thanks to her sexy European looks that had gotten her so far.

"Well, I have to say well done… Even in my time on the shop floor I never managed to bag designer clothes from clients," she said, taking a sip of her coffee.

"Oh, you worked in a store too?"

Chloe had just assumed that she was some glamazon that had been recognised for her great style from birth, not acknowledging her possible past experience in the fashion industry.

"Oh, yes… I worked on Fifth Avenue too, just like you—I *hated* it, but we all have to start somewhere… I always wanted more, so I started to attend parties, and parties became private appointments, and soon enough those turned into invitations to Fashion Week."

"Fashion Week—as in New York Fashion Week?"

"No, Mars Fashion Week," she laughed. "Yes, my dear… What else do you think I'm talking about? I was tired of working in a shop, and I felt I was worth so much more… Do you know what I mean?"

"Oh yeah, *totally!* I've tried moving to the press office, but that didn't work out for me."

"Let me guess, Regina Hall stopped you from getting there right?"

'How did she know?' Chloe wondered. Carmen could see by the puzzled look in Chloe's eyes that her brain was ticking over, trying to work out why she knew so much about how Palazzo worked on the inside.

"I know all about Myra and Regina, honey... I've come across them many times at Fashion Week. In fact, all of the stylists in town know what those two are like... Remember the first time we met? I told you about Myra and how difficult she is to deal with, didn't I?"

It was slowly coming back to her, she didn't realise at the time that it would be so significant and had discarded this information. It was times like this that made her understand just how small New York could be, and the fashion world for that matter—it was all so connected. You had to be careful in this industry, it seemed everyone knew everyone and a good reputation was paramount to being successful in a city like New York. Carmen took another sip of coffee.

"No matter how hard I tried to be nice to them, to never ask for a single dime in commission, they treated me like trash! Refusing to give my client's appointments or loan pieces to me. Of course, I still have to shop at Palazzo because some of my clients are fans of the brand, but I don't get any commission or recognition for it—and believe me—I have clients who can spend! Never in my years of working freelance has Regina or Myra given me a discount or a measly invite to a collection launch—*nothing!* Not even for my celebrity clients. In the end, I stopped shopping at your store, I prefer the department stores just to avoid seeing them on the off-chance. The only way a celebrity gets to wear a Palazzo dress is if they buy it themselves or get it direct from Milan—from Gianni himself... I mean this is New York for fuck's sake! Anything is possible here, but not with Palazzo; it's so frustrating and very boring, so I gave up trying in the end."

Chloe was amazed by what she was hearing, Regina was something else. Her calculating ways went further than what Chloe could imagine, but what did she have to do with it? How could she possibly help?

'This was the part where she asks for staff discount,' Chloe presumed.

"Anyway, do you see where I'm going here?"

"Erm… You want to use my staff discount right?"

"*Ha!* Not exactly, but if you are offering… Listen, darling—you have potential… You're networking skills are proof, and clearly, you know how to *work* people with a wardrobe like yours."

Chloe's face was still blank. Carmen rolled her eyes at her; maybe she wasn't that clever after all.

"Do I have to spell it out? Become a stylist! You already have lots of runway pieces from Palazzo, and you could get more with your discount darling—make some profit as well as a standard wage… Then, when the time is right, you leave and so styling full-time."

Chloe searched her mind, where had she heard that before? Then she remembered what Dom had said about making money off Karen's favour, but she was also sidetracked by Carmen's career advice.

"A stylist—do you really think so? I mean that's what I want, but do you think I actually could?"

"Honey, look around you… Everyone is a *fucking* stylist in this city, and most of them don't have the talent that you do, or the ability to grab freebies like you have… Besides you already are a stylist. Your website is being followed by many already, and most stylists I know don't even have a website—let alone a partnership with an online retailer!"

Carmen was right, hearing all her achievements strung together in one sentence like that made her realise just what she had amassed in such a short space of time. It wasn't until someone else pointed out what you had, that you realised how far you had come.

"But how do I start?" Chloe said, not seeing a clear way to make the transition. Working at Palazzo and on her website was gruelling enough as it was, adding another string to her bow wasn't what she had in mind.

"That's where I can help… You have the fashions, and I have the clients… Remember last week, I was looking for a dress? Well, thanks to you I've found it… I want to buy that navy sequin Palazzo gown… I'm dressing Gabriela Gracia next week for her movie premiere, and it is just perfect for her! I will give you $3,000 for it."

'Three–thousand–dollars!' Chloe counted in her mind, but at the same time she didn't really want to part with it; not yet, not before she had the chance to wear it. But who was she kidding, she had nowhere to go to in that dress and $3,000 sounded far more attractive than a dress she had gotten for free sitting in her apartment waiting for the moths to come—and it would look so much better on Gabriela Gracia than her anyway.

Gabriela was a Latin-American pop star that was well known for her curves and stunning figure as much as her talent. She regularly topped the world's most beautiful woman polls and was as famous as celebrities come. Her boyfriend, Guy-X, was a multi-millionaire, award-winning rapper and she was known for her fashion sense and flawless style. She had to wear everything before anyone else did, or pieces that were hard to find and one-of-a-kind. That's why the navy gown was perfect, it was a vintage piece that you could be sure no one else on the red carpet would be wearing—they would be wearing current collections which was so predictable, and Gabriela was anything but that.

"Think about it, but I must know by the end of today… The premiere is this Thursday, and I don't have a backup plan right now," Carmen said with a hint of panic as she downed the last drop of coffee like a true Italian.

Chloe didn't need to think too hard, the money alone was too good to turn down, and this could potentially open up other possibilities.

"But the gown is missing beads and sequins, it needs cleaning and—"

"Don't worry—bring the dress to me and I'll have my seamstress fix it. Plus, she is tiny so we can get extra fabric from the inches of hemline that we'll need to chop off," Carmen said, sensing that Chloe was coming around to the idea. "Look, I want to help you—help you get out of that store… Help me dress Gabriela, and I can help you do just that… I can't afford to lose her as a client, and you could do with her as one. She could probably call Gianni Palazzo himself and get that dress for free, but that is why she pays me, and I can't fail her! I'll even try and get you on the crew list so you can come and dress her with me, get some hands-on experience and then come to the after party with me… You'll get to meet some very influential people in New York, and with your drive, soon enough you won't even need me."

Chloe was sold, this was what she had been hoping for since day one when she had met Carmen, now it was finally happening, she had to grasp it with both hands—and that's exactly what she did. Her lunch break was coming to an end but not wanting to leave just yet, Chloe accepted and arranged to meet the very next day to hand over the dress.

Inevitably, returning back late from her meeting, Chloe tried to integrate herself back onto the shop floor and not as successfully as before (not that she had gone totally unnoticed the last time). Monitoring her tardiness, Francesca had noted at least three occasions where Chloe had been late for work or back from lunch, and she was starting to get fed up with it; she took it rather personally, it showed a lack of respect for her as her new manager. The lunch date with Carmen had inspired Chloe so much that she didn't really care what she thought of her anyway. Carmen had given her a glimpse of what life could be outside this place and was excited at the prospect of meeting Gabriela Gracia and mixing in celebrity circles, but for now, she did need her day job to pay the bills.

Much to Francesca's annoyance, Chloe didn't bother to even apologise or do much else other than talking to Dom about how amazing things were starting to turn out (a little insensitive of her considering Dom had helped her all weekend and she didn't bother asking him about how he was feeling). She decided not to tell him who the dress was for, sworn to secrecy by Carmen, and she didn't want to brag. His depression was coming back in waves; happy/sad/happy/sad, while Chloe was just riding one big tidal wave of opportunities and good fortune.

*

After work, Chloe rushed home as quickly as possible (on public transport) to get the dress and run back out to a specialist dry cleaner, who wanted $90 for an express clean on a luxury garment. Initially, she thought it was a bit steep, but she had no choice if she wanted to appear professional, so she just paid the expense foreseeing that it would be worth it in the end.

She was about to make a $3,000 profit on a dress she didn't even pay for in the first place, so spending ninety bucks on the cleaning bill was a small price to pay. That meant that she would have to collect the dress and then dash back to meet Carmen during her lunch break the next day—and then be back to work herself (and on time if possible). Running around town after work meant a late dinner and late to bed, after she had checked in on the progress of S.O.S and her Instagram page.

There just wasn't enough time in the day, and inevitably, Chloe woke up late for work the following morning. She simply couldn't fall into a deep sleep from the sheer excitement that she was dressing one of the world's biggest stars. The thought of making some extra cash also pleased her, and it meant that she could replenish her savings after spending a good chunk of it at the sample sale. As for Brian, she forgot all about returning his call.

Chloe also had to pull together a quick outfit for her daily post now she had a responsibility to her followers to be consistent and keep them engaged—it was easy to lose followers but hard to gain them. Turning up to work every day looking glam also sparked her colleagues to talk about her.

"Where are you going?"

"Why are you dressing up for work?"

"How can you afford all these designer clothes?" were all questions Chloe batted off on a daily; she told them it must have something to do with having a new boyfriend which wasn't a complete lie, she couldn't let Brian see her looking a mess.

Talking of which, it was only Tuesday, but as usual, Brian had sent her a barrage of texts, which she was obviously ignoring. She had no time for all that now she was dressing a Hollywood star. As planned, Chloe kept her word and met Carmen again on her lunch-break. Taking her lunch later than usual to collect the dress, she dashed to catch the subway a few stops to the cleaners; getting a taxi would be an extra expense that wasn't necessary, and the traffic would be awful at this time, but the trains were just as bad.

The dry cleaners serviced the dress overnight and had it ready to go zipped up in a garment bag for her, which had already taken thirty minutes out of her break. Running out of time, Chloe rushed back onto the subway with the dress over her arm. Running around on a hot day, dressed in a synthetic uniform and wearing heels was not the glamorous job of a stylist that she had imagined, but it was part of the reality.

Just as she was taking the steps down to the subway, her phone rang. Thinking it was Carmen calling to find out where she was, she took her phone out to answer the call but saw it was Brian yet again and rejected it before heading underground. The train back to Fifth Avenue was even busier, making the trip longer than it needed to be and the heaviness of the garment bag made her arms ache.

Finally dashing out of the station, and with not much time left at all, she made her way to meet Carmen at the sandwich shop near work again. Meanwhile, Carmen sat waiting—checking her watch. She too was short for time, and Chloe was certainly taking hers. Gabriela had given her a specific time slot for the fitting, which was only half an hour long before she took a press interview for her new film. Worried,

Carmen rang her several times, but it failed to connect with her being en-route on the subway. Just as Carmen had got up to leave, thinking she had changed her mind, Chloe barged through the door, red-faced and gasping for life.

"You made it! I thought you weren't gonna turn up… I was shitting myself, darling!" Carmen said, taking the dress off her.

"I'm—so—sorry," Chloe said taking breaths between her words

"Okay, I have to run—I'll be in touch." Carmen kissed Chloe's cheeks and left, just as quick as Chloe had made her entrance, with the dress now safely in hand.

All that running around gave Chloe no time to grab lunch, and where was this money she had been offered? What she didn't know was that stylists were always the last people in line to get paid and she would have to wait a while before that eventually dripped down to her. Chloe had just ten minutes left on lunch and managed to grab a ready-made baguette before heading back to work with it. She almost ate it in three bites, and as she did, she couldn't help but feel stupid that she had just handed over a vintage runway gown to a woman she virtually didn't know.

Chloe hoped that she hadn't made a colossal mistake and that Carmen was legit. Back in the locker room, Chloe blotted her make-up with a paper napkin that came with her baguette, sweat was dripping off her brow, and she tried her best to look a bit more presentable. Her feet were killing and had started to swell after the trek across town she had just made; just the thought of having to complete the rest of her shift in these shoes made her feel exhausted—now she actually had to endure the pain.

Down on the shop floor, and just moments away from being late yet again, Francesca looked at her with disgust—she was sweating like a pig. 'This girl is strange… Where has she been? Jogging around the park?' she thought to herself.

"Chloe," she called to her as she approached. "You are as red as a tomato and dripping like a faucet! Please go and make yourself look presentable for clients!" Francesca snapped in her Italian hinted accent, which made her sound even more authoritative.

At first, Chloe was rather annoyed at the suggestion she wasn't fit to work, but on second thoughts she saw the upside of gaining a few extra minutes to get herself together. 'What a bitch!' She thought, if Francesca wanted her to look impeccable then she would have to wait for it to happen. Chloe went back upstairs to grab a bag of chips from the vending machine, then took her sweet ass time to blot her face and cool down a bit. Sitting on a bench by her locker, she took her phone out of her jacket pocket and saw Brian had tried to call her five times; she didn't even have time for a proper lunch herself let alone speak to him.

Chloe sat there with her face in her hands, she was a mess. In some ways her current appearance was a reflection of her life; she felt as though she was spinning too many plates and at any moment now, one of them would crash to the floor, but which one that would be, she didn't know. Once she had gathered herself and resurfaced, she grabbed Dom and pulled him over to the glass table where they could catch up and still be visible should a customer walk in and need assistance.

"Can you believe that bitch sent me away to fix myself up? I look ten times better than her—and that's without the effort!"

"Well, you did look a hot mess," Dom said, growing tired of her selfish bullshit.

She was so self-absorbed it was unreal, but there was a hint of jealousy in his voice; he wished he could have something to not only be motivated about but also keep his mind busy with something else other than Jason. He too needed a new direction, but all he had to cling to was Jason and Chloe—and she was moving on with her life much like Jason was with his. Dom was beginning to feel like all he had was Palazzo, and that was a depressing thought—even his friendship with Chloe seemed fake.

"Well, so would you be if you were rushing around town for Gabriela Gracia!" Chloe retaliated, dodging the dagger he had just thrown at her with his comment.

"Wait—*what*?"

Dom was confused, what did Gabriela Gracia, one of his pop idols have to do with her looking like a complete whack job? He loved Gabriela and knew every word and dance move to her hit song 'Gabi From The Ghetto'. Did he hear her correctly?

"Yup… That's right. Carmen is dressing Gabriela for her premiere this week and saw the navy gown on S.O.S—that's why she called me the other night. She is buying it from me, but not only that, I get to dress her too!"

"Wow, that's incredible," Dom said, flat and with no emotion; not the reaction Chloe thought she would get at sharing this exciting (and secret) news with him.

Somewhere deep down, Dom was happy for her; normally he would be shrieking the shop down at news like this, but nothing excited him anymore. His heart was too broken and not even 'Gabi From The Ghetto' could pull him out of his misery. Finally seeing how down he was, Chloe started to feel bad for bragging about her success while he was going through heartache. She made a mental note not to show off all the time, which would be very hard for her with so much going on right now. She was like a kid on Christmas morning, and she wanted to be able to tell her best friend all about it, but she also didn't want to be a total douche bag either.

Going home was all she could think about for the rest of the afternoon and her feet expanded with pain the minute she took her uniform shoes off. The thought of putting back on her own heels to head home added to the pain, and a taxi was too much of a luxury to excuse; she would have to block out her throbbing feet and power on home.

And once she was home, there was plenty more for to be done, even though it was work she actually wanted to do, the day seemed endless and had robbed her of valuable energy to do what she actually wanted to do with her life. Still, the first thing she did when she got in (aside from kicking off her shoes in relief and leaving them at the door) was to switch on her laptop. She had received an email from Veronica which she opened first, asking if she would like to pick more stock as she had noticed a spike in sales of the gold shoes and bag coming from StacksOfStyle. Chloe was thrilled to get more freebies, and from the news that she would now be earning commission from sales through her web links—a second income was what she needed if she was ever going to leave Palazzo.

Even though it wasn't much now, she was sure she could grow it and browsed DivaFeet immediately for inspiration on what to select next, before she had even considered what to eat for dinner—right now fashion was her diet. While scanning the glossy web pages, her ringing phone interrupted her flow. 'Brian,' she thought without even checking, but the phone kept on ringing which forced her to look. Seeing it was, in fact, Carmen, she couldn't help but feel relieved.

"Ciao, darling… I just wanted to call you to say thank you for sorting out the dress. Sorry I had to rush off like that… Listen, the dress looks amazing on her, she wants to wear it. I've got you on her entourage list as my assistant, so I'll send you the location of where she is staying on Thursday, okay?"

Chloe couldn't believe that this was actually happening and that Carmen was for real—she was actually going to dress Gabriela Gracia! All she needed to do now was to come up with an excuse so Francesca would let her leave early. 'Being extra early for work and staying on for the late shift tomorrow should buy me some time,' she figured. It would be gruelling, but worth it and a sacrifice Chloe was willing to make.

**

Thursday had come around, and Chloe had kept herself busy in her own time by ordering more pieces from DivaFeet to feature on her website, as well as planning what to write about them; staying up until Midnight, absorbed in her work. Needless to say, she didn't make it into work early to clock up some time owed. Instead, she fabricated an emergency doctors appointment, which Francesca couldn't refuse.

"I'm so sorry, but as you've noticed I haven't been my usual self... I've had a high temperature and fever all week—you saw I was so flushed the other day—I must be coming down with something. I called my doctor, and he said to come in for a check-up as soon as I can, there's this *thing* going around... I'd hate to make the team sick," she said coughing, putting on her best flu-ridden voice.

Chloe was excused in just enough time to rush home to get showered before heading back out to meet Carmen. She wanted to look the part and ooze style, she was about to meet one of the most stylish women in the world. Chloe decided to finally wear the sexy Dolce & Gabbana dress that she had been waiting to wear, and this indeed was the occasion to rock it. Her outfit was completed with the shoes and gold clutch from DivaFeet she had been plugging on S.O.S—she had to be seen to be taking her own advice after all.

Carmen messaged her with the secret location of where Gabriela was staying, although her whereabouts was never a secret as she was followed by paparazzi twenty-four-seven. The Waldorf Towers on Park Avenue was too close to work for her liking; Chloe hoped she didn't bump into anyone she knew, that would have ruined her alibi and Regina would just love that. To avoid that possibility, Chloe splashed out on a taxi to take her safely to the hotel incognito. Sat in the back seat of the car she took her phone out of her bag and began typing a message to Brian.

HI... I AM SO SORRY FOR NOT BEING ABLE TO SPEAK
THIS WEE...

But it was no good, it would only strike up endless texting and questioning about when he could see her next, and in reality, she didn't know if that would be possible; she quickly backspaced and put her phone back inside her clutch. The Waldorf Towers was pure luxury and exactly the kind of place a superstar would stay at. Carmen had notified the concierge to direct Chloe up to the penthouse where there was a team of make-up artists and hairdressers fussing around one woman; Gabriela was such a high profile that her entourage helped her to get ready wherever she went.

Tonight was the night of her debut film premiere in which she starred as the lead role of a Hispanic dancer growing up in Brooklyn, hitting the big time on Broadway against all the odds with no formal training—just raw talent and determination to succeed. The penthouse floor was flanked by security all the way down the corridor. After a quick body and bag search, one of Gabriela's personal security guards took her to the most expensive suite in the entire hotel: The Royal Suite. Now outside the room, the guard spoke in code into his radio mic before Gabriela's assistant finally opened the door.

"Yes?" she said, peering out from the partially opened door.

"Miss Gracia has a visitor," the guard said.

"Hi… I'm Chloe Ravens," she clarified, in case her assistant thought she was a fan that had blagged her way up.

"Wait here," she said, closing the door.

Chloe was left standing outside for about ten minutes, wondering if she should just turn around and go, saving herself from the embarrassment of being escorted out of the building by Gabi's burly security guard—but Carmen eventually appeared at the door to greet her.

"Hi, its fine—she's with me," Carmen said, pulling Chloe into the suite by her arm. "You look fab! Glad you could make it."

"Is this okay?" Chloe said, seeing Carmen dressed in just jeans and an oversized man's shirt; she felt extremely overdressed.

"Gabi is already dressed, and now the team are putting the finishing touches on her hair and make-up… Come, I'll introduce you."

Chloe followed her into the dressing room, which was a circus of people all bustling around; she could see Gabriela sat at a vanity table, surrounded by a team of people brushing and dabbing at her face—suddenly she threw her hands up into the air.

"Okay, everyone out of the room… Except for my hair and make-up team!"

All her mignons quickly grabbed whatever they needed from the room and left as soon as they could; feeling uncomfortable, Chloe began to edge back out with them.

"Not you!" Carmen laughed. "You *are* part of the team."

Chloe awkwardly smiled back at Carmen, intimidated by Gabriela's behaviour. She came across like some typical actress who thought she was untouchable and could order people to do whatever she wanted.

"Gabi… This is Chloe… She helped me source the dress you're wearing tonight."

She didn't react straight away; instead, she inspected her freshly applied make-up in the mirror. With a swish of the dress's tail, she finally stood up to face them, looking like a Goddess. Chloe couldn't believe that *The* Gabriela Gracia was stood in front of her—wearing her dress! From the back, the dress cowed down showing off the crease of her spine and was fitted to her curves with perfection. It looked like an entirely different dress compared to the one Chloe had once worn in her humble apartment. Her hair and makeup were flawless, she looked just like the pictures you saw in magazines—photo-shopped.

"Hi, I'm Gabi… So nice to meet you," she smiled sweetly, offering her dainty and perfectly manicured hand. "It's so hard these days to find something so unique, and tonight is an important night in my career, so I thank you so much for helping me with my dress. When Carmen sent me your picture, I knew I just had to have it!"

In a flash, Chloe's perception had changed, not everyone with power was a complete bitch after all.

"Sorry about all that just now, I just needed some space… It was getting way too hot in here, and I don't want to arrive all sweaty with makeup melt. My assistant will arrange the payment for the dress by tomorrow if that's okay Carmen?"

"That's good for us, and good luck for tonight!" Carmen said, giving her a distant hug, so she didn't crease her dress or smudge her face.

"It's been such a pleasure to meet you, Miss Gracia… Good luck for tonight, I'm sure you will be just perfect," Chloe said, wincing at hearing her speak like some fan-girl.

"Oh… Please—call me Gabi," she said, her eyes falling on Chloe's golden clutch. "Oh wow, I love your bag! Where is that from?"

"Chloe here has a blog… She gets things sent in for her to feature on her site," Carmen said, stepping in before Chloe had the chance to answer back.

"Is that so? I'll have to check it out… May I see it?"

"Sure," Chloe said, unable to refuse a megastar. "It's actually just a 'cheapy' from DivaFeet," apologising for it not being a designer brand.

"I love a bargain! It goes perfectly with this dress actually," Gabi said, posing with it in front of the vanity table mirror.

"Oh, it's yours… Keep it."

Carmen smiled at Chloe, she was learning fast. Tomorrow morning Gabriela Gracia would be front-page news, along with that dress and *that* bag, and Veronica would be pleased about it too. Chloe quickly took out her make-up and keys, transferring them into Carmen's shoulder bag which now weighed like a brick.

"This is my card… That's my website, StacksOfStyle."

"Well, that you certainly do have… Sorry, I couldn't invite you to the premiere, but I'll see you guys later at the after-party, right?"

There was a knock at the door, Gabi's entourage had come to whisk her away to Times Square where the premiere was being held, leaving fashionably late for her arrival.

"Misss Gracia, the car is ready for you now."

"Great, I'm coming… Gotta go, but I'll you later girls!"

As Gabi walked out of the room, Chloe got a preview of how amazing the dress looked and moved as it should, and the gold bag looked rather expensive with it. Proof that it didn't matter where your fashions came from, but rather who wore it.

***

While the premiere was in full swing, Carmen slipped into something more appropriate for the party, and together with Chloe's corset dress, they lived up to the persona of a celebrity stylist. The after party was located downtown in an unused warehouse that was transformed for the evening with silk drapes, carpets, atmospheric lighting and extremely hot waiters—Guy-X was on the DJ decks, Walking through the room, Carmen pointed out the whos-who of New York amongst the obvious celebrity faces. "There's Roy Mendez, oh and look—that's Lisa Lennard over there with Sacha Delal."

Chloe was used to seeing the odd A-lister in Palazzo, but with this many in the same room at once, she couldn't help but feel star struck. There had made their way over to the main bar, which was serving free champagne all night long, to celebrate their first styling success together.

"Here's to your first time working as a professional stylist," Carmen said, holding up a glass of champagne to toast.

Chloe clinked her glass with Carmen's and took a gulp, 'I could get used to this,' she thought.

"I reckon we make a great duo you and me," Carmen said over the pumping music, smiling at her as she guzzled down her fizz. Watching Chloe drink, Carmen knew she was right to take a chance on her; she was her type of party girl. "I mean, look at us… Successful young women who are just as stylish and sexy as the stars we dress."

"Hey girls!" Gabi greeted from behind. "Hope you're having a fabulous time… I was so nervous when I stepped out of the car onto the carpet, but this dress… Oh my, it gave me such confidence and just carried me like a pair of wings!"

"Where's my beautiful superstar out here tonight?" Guy-X called out on the mic.

"Ooh—that's me," Gabi said, hitching up her dress and holding up her glass to make her way through the crowd to the DJ booth.

Chloe laughed, she was obviously enjoying the free bar as much as they were. The party was in full swing and as just successful as the movie had been with the critics it seemed. Looking around, Chloe could hardly believe she was mingling with the stars and enjoying her own popularity. Looking like famous stars themselves, Chloe and Carmen had managed to get photographed on several occasions by the press that was covering the event, ensuring it would end up in every magazine and tabloid around the globe. Chloe felt great when they asked who she was and what she did; finally she could say she was a stylist and a fashion influencer.

"I'm Chloe Ravens—The Raven of StacksOfStyle.com," she confidently said as she swished her hair away from her face.

'Thank God for champagne,' she thought to herself, she had lost count how what glass number this was. The bubbles had given her extra-added confidence, something that she wouldn't be thankful for come morning when she had to wake up for work. 'Fuck work,' she decided, and carried on partying with Carmen, who as a freelance stylist could afford to be up all hours—unlike her.

# CHAPTER NINETEEN

C hloe woke up sharp to the sound of her phone alarm ringing; she had stayed out at the star-studded bash until the very early hours, allowing herself just three hours of sleep. She reached for her phone to mute it without even looking, causing it to crash to the floor as she rolled back over to sleep some more…

It only seemed like fifteen minutes had passed, but finally, she roused to look for her phone and check the time—it wasn't on the bedside table like usual. She sat up, fuzzy headed, looking around for it in her bed sheets, before finally finding it on the floor. She reached over the side of her bed and touched the screen to light it up so she could see how long she had to get ready for work. 'Gah—work!' she thought, now tasting how dry her mouth was, struggling to open her stinging, tired eyes.

"Oh, no it can't be!" she panicked, the time on the screen finally registering in her head.

It was eight fifty-two a.m. already.

Not only was she mad at herself for making such a junior error on a work night, but she felt awful; she still had the outfit (and makeup) on from last night, along with some super big bed hair—she was also super late for work. At least she wouldn't be going in with a hangover, she hadn't had enough hours to sleep off the effects of the copious amounts of free champagne she had consumed. There was no time for a shower now, she didn't even have time to change clothes, so she brushed her teeth and quickly washed her face before whacking on some concealer in an attempt to look fresh and wide awake—the rest of the face could wait until later.

Hopping around the apartment in a drunken panic, she put her heels back on (not the most practical choice for running late), she couldn't exactly wear Converse with her Dolce & Gabbana cocktail dress. She grabbed her brown messenger bag that totally didn't go with the look and left her apartment to make a run for the subway, tripping up in her heels as she did. This was the first morning she hadn't posted an outfit on S.O.S, but she had so many pictures on her phone from last night to post that would be far more appropriate—hooker-chic was not one of the trends this season.

Chloe had made it to work twenty minutes late (which was record timing considering what state she was in) and slipped straight into cleaning the glass tops as if she had always been there, but she had failed.

"Oh—My—God! You look a total wreck!" Dom said, laughing at her sans-makeup face and crazy hair that was tied back with a band into a loose ponytail.

"Shhh! It's not funny!"

"Why didn't you just call in sick you idiot?"

Chloe didn't appreciate his observations, or obvious solution to her troubles right now, and carried on cleaning fast and furious—the energy drink she had downed on the subway was starting to kick in.

"You're still hammered! I take it last night was a roaring success then?" Dom said rather jealous, gone were the days where they would turn up to work drunk together and got each other through the day.

"Oh, Dom it was amazing! Gabriela looked amazing, and she was so lovely too," Chloe shrieked, perking up at having someone to talk to about her amazing experience rubbing shoulders with the stars.

Hearing her voice, Francesca looked over to confirm if Chloe had indeed made it to work, she had been recording her lateness, and this was another strike. Furthermore, this was the second time she had turned up for work in an unfit state. Plus, she was meant to be sick—not hungover, which she apparently was; watching her talking animatedly was a huge giveaway, there was nothing wrong with this girl. Everything was adding up, all the lateness's from the previous week and now this; Chloe Ravens turning up to work late, smelling of booze and smoke, and looking like she worked the checkout at the dollar store rather than a luxury designer store on Fifth Avenue. 'Surely this is enough to report back to Regina with already?' Francesca thought to herself.

Francesca was starting to dislike this girl herself, it was all too easy to stick to her word and keep an eye on her, she wasn't exactly a hard nut to crack; she was setting up her fall all by herself. Blinded by her success outside of work, and the fact that she just didn't care about Palazzo anymore, Chloe was demotivated to work the shop floor and had lost respect for the job—which meant she had lost respect for Regina and she certainly wasn't showing any for Francesca.

Lunchtime couldn't come around quick enough, and Chloe took the earliest hour possible, she was hanging badly. All that champagne had made her feel rough and sickly, and working on an empty stomach wasn't helping either. Not to mention her pounding head which was now starting to throb under the spotlights, she had already taken the maximum amount of painkillers for it. Chloe walked briskly to the diner for a hearty takeaway brunch, she couldn't face sitting in a busy restaurant and quickly raced back to work to consume her calorific hangover cure of pancakes, syrup, and bacon.

This way she wouldn't have to worry about rushing back to work too. The journey there and back to the staff kitchen was again in record timing, it was amazing what a severe hangover could make you do to survive. Wolfing down her much-needed lunch, her colleagues looked on and watched her tucking into it as if she were competing in a pan-cake-eating contest.

Having finished her breakfast-cum-lunch, she sat back in her chair and took out her phone. She hadn't had time to check it since she woke up to see she was dreadfully late; there were several missed calls and texts, mostly from Brian which was becoming a daily issue. He was desperate to know what he had done to deserve being ignored as well as wanting to see her, which was the problem.

Chloe didn't have time to see him, and when she thought about it, she wasn't particularly interested to see him—he too was holding her back—StacksOfStyle was her main focus now. Flicking past and pretending his messages didn't exist, she excitedly moved on to Carmen's text. She had sent a picture of the NY Times front page featuring Gabi, posing with *that* bag.

Chloe was amazed, that whole entire look that had made front page news was all her doing—right down to the accessories. Basking in that wonderful thought, finally believing in her talent herself, the phone rang, almost vibrating out of her hand. An unknown number flashed up on the screen, she quickly accepted it without question, wondering who this could be.

"Hello?" Chloe said, sounding like a drag queen with an alcohol ravaged voice.

"Oh my, I just had to call you straight away... I've just seen the press coverage this morning—Gabriela Gracia is holding our bag! Our customer care phone lines are slammed with calls about it; we've had to prioritise the re-order! Then I noticed she was wearing the gown from your article, and I thought to myself, I bet Chloe has something to do with this... Am I right?"

"Yes, yes you are," Chloe said, amazed at what she was hearing.

"How on Earth did you manage to style the one and only Gabriela Gracia? Karen was right about you—you're going to be big kiddo! Listen, feel free to request anything you want for clients, articles and whatever else... We will send it over to you A.S.A.P if this is what you can do."

Without purposely doing so, Chloe now had Veronica wrapped around her little finger. Press coverage this good was hard to get, and Chloe had got it without even trying—or paying. Thanks to her accidental PR stunt, Chloe had cemented her relationship with DivaFeet and could be sure to count on Veronica to supply her with much more free stuff. Veronica's call had seemed to banish Chloe's hangover altogether, receiving this good news was better than popping an aspirin. Chloe was inspired her to post the pictures taken from last night's party on Instagram, getting 'likes' in seconds having tagged Gabriela in her posts, instantly accessing her vast fan base of over a million followers.

Meanwhile, with Chloe out of sight, Francesca took the chance to skip up to Regina's office, proud to have some solid evidence to report back with already and to prove her worth in such a short time. Regina was delighted to hear the list of wrongdoings; pretending to be sick, turning up late for work, and not meeting the high grooming standards of Palazzo. It was clear that Chloe had become complacent, even with a new manager, Regina didn't want to give her any more chances. This was all she needed to discuss Chloe's future a Palazzo with Victoria, but it needed to be done legally and professionally; Regina made sure she played by Palazzo's rule book.

"Well, thank you for letting me know... I warned the team last week of the position they are all in, and you have already spoken Miss Ravens about her appearance and attitude yourself. I will investigate this further, for now, keep on watching your team—you are doing a fantastic job."

"Should I raise it again with her so she can make changes?" Francesca said, thinking she should have spoken to Chloe privately first.

As much as she wanted to succeed at Palazzo, there had an ounce of humanity left in her that felt slightly bad for reporting Chloe; she didn't really want to make enemies in her first week as manager. But then again, Chloe was no enemy compared to Regina and Francesca had been around the block in retail to know that sometimes you had to give head to get ahead. Sucking up to Regina was definitely worth more than it was trying to be nice to Chloe and point out her mistakes; she had her own career to think about.

"No, this shouldn't be any more concern for you... Just focus on the rest of your team, you are doing very well indeed, and it's only your first week. Who knows where you will be in three months time?"

Regina knew exactly how to make people respect her, especially ones that wanted to be 'something' at Palazzo. She thought everyone in fashion wanted to be just like her: powerful, and more importantly, surrounded by glamour and prestige every day.

"You know Melinda our V.I.C client manager is retiring after this season? I am currently seeking for someone to take over," Regina said.

Francesca's heart started to pump, 'Could she mean me?' she asked herself. She had struck up a professional relationship with Regina with no misunderstanding or emotion getting in the way (just how Regina liked it), and speaking Italian was an advantage, but maybe she could see something more in her already? There was only one way to find out, and that was to give Regina what she wanted: Chloe's head on a silver platter; besides, what could Chloe Ravens, a silly shop girl offer her compared to Regina Hall, store director?

*

It was a relief to finally get home after what seemed to be a very long day, the heels came off the minute she got through the building door so she could run up the stairs to her apartment. Stripping off the cocktail dress that now stuck to her like a second skin (having worn it for almost twenty-four hours) and finally having a shower was also high on her agenda, but she couldn't wait to tell Carmen her exciting news and dialled her number as she got undressed.

"Carmen, you are not going to guess what happened today!" she said, without even saying hello first.

"Hmmm, let me guess… You had a horrible hangover—because I sure as Hell did—then you were late for work, right?"

"Well, yes—but that's not why I'm calling you! Veronica saw the press coverage of Gabi from last night carrying her clutch, and she knew it was down to me because of my feature on S.O.S wearing the exact same dress."

"Honey, even I knew that was a clever move… I bet she is over the Moon!"

"She said I can have whatever I want from DivaFeet to feature on the website… I know it's not exactly high-end, but it's a great connection to have."

"Of course it is—I told you, you have achieved so much that other stylists are all gagging for! This is amazing, you need to believe in yourself more... Look, I have to go but why don't we catch up tomorrow? I should have payment cleared from Gabi for the dress."

Amidst all the fantastic news, Chloe had forgotten that on top of it all, she was $3,000 richer too.

"Amazing, I actually have it off... That dumb new manager of mine tried to twist the rota to screw us all over but didn't see she gave me two weekends off in a row!"

"Well, I just hope she doesn't make you pay for it later," Carmen said, knowing the retail game all too well for herself. "Okay, let's meet at Buvette, West Village—say eleven?"

"Great! See you there," Chloe said, knowing that Carmen would know the best spots to have brunch in town.

After ending the call, Chloe logged onto to S.O.S to check in and see how things were looking. The visitor counter was well past a thousand now, and her Instagram feed had received numerous 'likes' and new followers thanks to her celebrity endorsement from Gabriela who had seen Chloe's tag and followed her back. Noticing that Gabi's official Instagram account, the one with the little blue tick, was now following her—a nobody—gave her a boost.

"*Yes!*" She shrieked with excitement, clutching her fists and punching the air.

With this sudden surge of confidence in herself, the desire to create new content ignited within her, she now had Gabriela Gracia watching her as well as her army of fans all wanting to copy her style. Remembering Veronica's promise, she jumped straight onto DivaFeet.com to look for more bags and shoes to order. Selecting an array of shoes and handbags for her 'Summer Sole-stice' edit, she sent in her wishlist to Veronica's team, who she now had direct contact with.

Like always, the evening had flown by, it was ironic that the day lingered at work, but the minute she was engrossed in her own work at home, it sped past in rapid timing. Her eyes were now burning from tiredness and from straining to look at her laptop screen, eager to submit her samples request to receive her goodies fast, bed was calling her; she wanted to wake up refreshed and have time to dress nicely for her brunch date with Carmen, so she succumbed.

It was the only thing she could think about all day long, and now it was finally time to catch up on the sleep she had missed the night before. Laying in bed, her feet buzzed with both pain and relief from not being constricted in ridiculous shoes anymore, and she was equally buzzing from having made such an impact on the celebrity styling scene so soon—all thanks to Carmen. Without her, none of this would be happening, and Chloe couldn't wait to surround herself in her company once again; when she was with her, she felt like she could achieve her dreams.

**

She had to Google Buvette (having never been before) and after a quick search saw that it was a little bistro serving small plates of French-inspired cuisine; a relaxed yet trendy place it seemed. After yesterday's torture wearing heels all day, Chloe opted for a pair of comfy sneakers with an oversized striped shirt and a pair of summer shorts. On her way over to meet Carmen, she couldn't help but ask herself why she was so keen on helping *her* become a stylist.

'There must be another reason why she wants to help a complete stranger,' she told herself, sensing she was too good to be true and made a mental note to find out over brunch.

Carmen always sat at a small table for two near the bar. Waiting for Chloe to arrive, she sipped on her Americano, still wearing her blacked-out shades; the day was bright outside, and her eyes hadn't adjusted to indoor lighting just yet, having strolled from her place to Buvette, which was her local.

"Over here," she called, spotting Chloe walk in and look around for her.

"Hey, morning—how are you?" Chloe said, as Carmen took off her sunglasses and got up to greet her with a kiss.

"Just fantastic, darling but I'm starving… Let's order."

Carmen waived down the waiter and ordered a selection of her favourites without even asking Chloe what she wanted; she knew what was best on the menu, and Chloe had trusted her thus far.

"So, how have you been since the party?" Chloe asked.

"Busy darling, more clients in town and more events to dress them for—it *never* stops. Maybe you can help…"

"Actually, that's what I wanted to ask you," Chloe said, wondering how to bring the subject up without sounding like she was feeling sketchy about her; the last thing she wanted to do was to offend her after everything she had done so far. "You've been *so* good to me, and I was just thinking—"

"Why?" Carmen interjected, pre-empting where she was going. "Well, I kinda see myself in you… *You* are driven to succeed! I wish I had a website and clients chucking clothes at me when I first started out—it would have made everything so much easier…"

"And how did you start out?"

"Like I said, I worked in a store just like you—at Maison Marais… Although it was a great place to work, it just wasn't enough for me. After a while, the clients I made there started to ask me for advice on other designers and collections, having built up their trust in my opinion… Of course, I was delighted to help them so I would arrange my lunch breaks so I could visit other stores and choose outfits for them… Sometimes they would give me a tip, but at the time, I did it mostly because I loved to do it—I wasn't thinking about the money—I was young… Then, that grew into coffees, lunches, and dinner dates with them and their friends. They too would ask me to find outfits for them, wedding dresses, whole new wardrobes for their holidays in the Hamptons—that sort of thing… Before I knew it, I had no time to work full-time in a store anymore—so I took a risk and left! Styling became my job, and I was starting to earn more money doing that than standing in a store all day, waiting for customers to come along. Now, I go to them, and the best bit is, I'm free to do whatever I want in the city I love! I discovered that I could work for myself, not making money to line someone else's pocket. As my client book grew, so did my relationships with the stores, they saw I was coming in regularly with good clients and spending huge amounts of money. That's how I got offered discounts from stores, which helped to make an extra profit… But not Palazzo! No, Myra thinks I am not good enough for them."

"So, you used to work with her right? What happened to make her hate you so much?" Chloe said, by now her cappuccino had arrived, just in time for the gossip.

It all seemed very petty to Chloe, but she knew that the world of fashion was shallow, one big drama and the slightest little thing could be taken out of context, resulting in your reputation being marred forever; nevertheless, she needed to know.

"I already told you…" Carmen said, getting annoyed at trawling through her history again.

It was frustrating to re-live the past now she was so far away from it, but she knew it was essential information if she was going to success-fully take Chloe under her wing and help her not make the mistakes she had once done. She took a deep breath and another sip of coffee before continuing her tale, one of bittersweet revenge that was sure to prick Chloe's ears.

"I used to work with her at Bullet magazine, one of my first editorial jobs… We were holding this party for some launch—Anyway—I was beginning to make a name for myself; At the time, I just had started working with Gabriela, a case of being in the right place at the right time—which you will come to know."

Chloe nodded in agreement, she already knew exactly what she meant; meeting Carmen seemed to be one of those fateful events that were just meant to be.

"So, back to the party… I saw Regina, and I knew who she was, I knew she was the one to get through to at Palazzo, so I went up to introduce myself. At first, we seemed to be getting along nicely—she even told me about this press office position she was trying to fill—which sounded interesting, but not me... Myra, always jealous, saw us talking and hijacked the conversation, found out about this job and well... The rest is history. But that's not all, as soon as Myra left Bullet magazine and started at Palazzo, I contacted her to loan some dresses. I was bringing in lots of clients but got no discount. Myra told me that they didn't need re-sellers—me—a re-seller? Honey, I have some of the biggest client's in this town, I don't need eBay, thank you very much... So I went over her head and called Regina, but she said the same thing, I can only assume Myra poisoned her against me... Chloe, I can see that you don't want to be stuck there all your life; you want to get out of the retail game too. If you didn't, you wouldn't have your own website... You are just like me... You just need to break free and take the risk I took."

Listening to Carmen, it all made sense; she had a vendetta against Myra and Regina and wanted to use Chloe as some kind of pawn in a game of fashion-wars. Either way, Chloe knew what side she preferred to be on—Carmen was her very own 'check-mate'.

"Come, mangia!" Carmen ordered her as the waiter placed down several plates of food.

After brunch Carmen took Chloe to Fifth Avenue, she wanted to show her where she started and to inspire her some more. Maison Marais was a Parisian house, famed for their luggage and leather goods bearing the 'MM' monogram, synonymous with fashion lovers and label addicts world-wide; Palazzo's competitor on and off the runway. The minute they stepped through the grand glass doors, it was as if a famous person had entered the store.

Carmen was very well known and respected by the staff—a stark contrast to how she was treated at Palazzo. Looking around the store, Chloe noticed the classic style, it's decor wasn't flashy or glitzy like Palazzo. The interior design was somewhat dated yet chic; light wood panelled walls with simple glass vitrines showcasing their leather goods.

"Carmen?" a voice said from behind.

"Ciao, Dionne… How are you, my love? Chloe, this is Dionne Blanc, the store director," Carmen said.

Dionne was a tall, thin woman with a crystal clear complexion. She was probably a lot older than she looked, given her position, but she was polished—like a supermodel. She was wearing a light grey, wool-boucle suit with a matching pencil skirt and a set of pearls.

"Enchanté, very nice to meet you, Chloe," Dionne said with a slight French tone in her voice.

"We just dropped by to see the new collection… Chloe here has been working with me, she is a stylist as well, and a very good one too."

Chloe was embarrassed but thankful for the compliment and fumbled around in her messenger bag for a business card. Taking one out, the raven logo flashed before her eyes, reminding her of Brian and how she had tossed him to the side recently after he had given so much of his time to help her; she handed Dionne her card to get the thought of him out of her head.

"Is that so? I will check it out," Dionne said taking her card and offering hers in polite exchange.

"In fact, Chloe helped me with Gabriela's premiere dress."

"Such a high profile client already… Maybe next time you will choose one of ours?"

"Of course, that's why we are here… Now Chloe is working with me, maybe you could add her to my discount account?"

"If Carmen speaks so highly of you, then you should be on our database under your own account," Dionne said as if it giving out discounts was no trouble at all. "I'll get my team to that set up for you… Ladies, lovely to see you both but I have to be at a very important meeting… I'll look forward to seeing you again soon Chloe," Dionne said kissing them both on the cheek before leaving.

They made their way up to the womenswear floor to browse the rails, discussing some of the new arrivals but nothing impressed them; Maison Marais had a slow summer season and if this collection was anything to go by, so would their winter. Seeing all there was to see, they said goodbye to the shop-floor staff that Carmen knew. Outside on the avenue, and away from the store's entrance, Carmen grabbed Chloe by the arm.

"*You* are the luckiest girl in this city, I swear it!"

"Why—what's happened?"

"Wake up! You now get discount at Maison Marais! *Hello?* That means you now get twenty percent off everything, which is fabulous, but not for your bank account of course."

It hadn't sunk in with Chloe yet, but it was true, a twenty percent discount was indeed very fabulous and a dream come true for most women. Riding this wave of luck, they stopped off at a few more boutiques so Carmen could introduce her to the most important contacts she had there. Carmen began explaining how freelance styling worked, with many stores allowing you to take stock on loan without paying upfront so you could visit a client in their private surroundings. Then, they could try the pieces on before they purchased, and from many brands all at once without having to visit a single store. Perfect for clients with hectic schedules, or just ones that had so much money to spend, they loved the novelty of having a personal shopper to brag to their friends about—having a personal shopper was a status symbol.

Securing a discount with Maison Marais was a real coup, but with Carmen's help, she presented Chloe to her contacts up and down Fifth Avenue for the rest of the afternoon. Many other stores had agreed to give Chloe stylist discount on the basis that Carmen didn't need to recommend anyone, especially not a competitor; her opinion was highly valued, and if Chloe spent like Carmen did in their stores, then they would be the real winners. Meeting Carmen's black-book of designer brands, and repeating herself over and over, had drained both Chloe's energy levels and her stash of business cards.

The afternoon was now getting on, and Chloe wanted to get home as DivaFeet were express delivering her newly requested items, and she didn't want to miss the driver.

"Today has been really fun, thanks so much for your help. I feel confident and ready to make this career change work."

"Oh, please... Don't mention it, you deserve it... Anyway, here's the cheque for the dress."

Carmen handed over a brand new crisp cheque, straight from the bank of Gracia—from an endless pit of money being the multi-million selling artist that she was—it was like handing over small change for her. A rush ran through Chloe's body as she saw the zero's, not expecting the payment so soon. 'This is what I earn in two months working at Palazzo!' she thought, believing that this career change could indeed work out.

"One more thing... That black Palazzo evening gown you have, the one you posted on S.O.S last Sunday? Well, I may have another client interested... Are you ready to do it all over again?"

That was a stupid question, the money and the glamorous parties that came with it had seduced her, of course, she was interested. After all, it was a free dress Mrs R had given her which she wasn't overly attached to. Agreeing to sell the dress and saying goodbye to Carmen, Chloe rushed to the bank to drop the cheque into the self-service machine, she wanted to put the money straight into her account for safe-keeping.

Having savings squirrelled away was essential if she was going to become a freelance stylist; she would never know when she might need it to buy things for clients, or for herself now she was mixing in high profile circles as the latest stylist in New York—she had to look the part. But she didn't need to worry too much about dwindling her cash away on designer dresses now Carmen had set her up with a list of contacts at some of the most elite designer brands. Stylists had worked years to achieve what Chloe had in one afternoon, and it was all thanks to Carmen's reputation.

Back at her apartment, several boxes had arrived as promised. Once again Chloe had picked the most expensive looking pieces from pages of mass-made fashions that could easily be fashion fails. But

Chloe had the knack of seeing the potential in a bargain and knew how to style and make them appeal to women that were into high-fashion without the high prices. Unboxing her new stock, she took pictures with her phone, so she had an inventory to remind her of what she had to write about.

Now she had a clear sense of direction of where her life was going, inspiration seemed to overfill her brain and ideas for articles were no longer hard to come by. The first was going to be her 'Summer Sole-stice' edit of the hottest summer shoes that she had promised Veronica she would write, but inspired by Karen's love for the Gold Rush clutch, Chloe had also ordered a selection of bags that didn't need to break the bank.

One of them was a black quilted leatherette baguette style bag with an oxidised silver chain shoulder strap, the clasp was a giant pearl that was set inside a gold case, making it look superior. She wanted to post all of it onto Instagram right away, but instead, she came up with a writing schedule and upload strategy for the coming week, not wanting to use up all of her new content in one go.

*** 

Sunday had gone by in a flash, as usual, but it wasn't wasted. The 'Ravens Guide To Summer Sole-stice' had been written and uploaded, complete with product shots, links and picture of Chloe's feet modelling the styles—which she had taken bent over double to get the shot. Now Dom wasn't speaking to her outside of work, she no longer had a photographer on tap.

The rest of the evening was spent resting as the week ahead was set to be as exciting and stressful as the last, what with dressing an elite New York socialite; Aurielle Huntington wanted everything, and she wanted it right now! Chloe had expected the megastar, Gabriela Gracia, to be demanding, not some unknown rich girl who needed a slap. Although she didn't mind, all she could think about was the money; $1,500, which she agreed to split with Carmen, they were sticking together and so far made a great team.

For most of the week, Chloe had a few more days hungover at work, hating her life on the shop floor but loving her new life on the scene. Carmen had taken her out to the parties that were starting to crop up in the city; New York Fashion Week was looming, and the buzz was circling around town. Fashion houses were preparing their events and stores were becoming busy again as industry insiders and fashionistas clambered to get their looks together in preparation.

The same vibe had taken over Palazzo, but Chloe was to busy networking, partying, and schmoozing with her new fashion friends to notice the panic that was setting in. Melinda had been working hard with Regina and Myra on the V.I.C event where the man himself, company owner and creative director, Gianni Palazzo was to host. For the first time in New York, Palazzo was going to show at New York Fashion Week—although it wasn't the main runway show for the collection.

It was certainly going to create fantastic press coverage in the run-up to the showing of their next spring/summer show at Milan Fashion Week, that was eagerly anticipated just as much as this special event. The buzz of the retrospective show, celebrating Palazzo's fifty-five years in fashion, made it the highlight of Fashion Week; Palazzo was about to hit the headlines in a big way doing what Gianni did best—creating desirability and hype around the brand.

It also hadn't escaped Myra's attention that Palazzo was starting to have much more media coverage than usual and with hard to find vintage pieces too. First, it was Gabi at her premiere wearing *that* dress, then Aurielle Huntington at The Whitney Gallery charity gala. It got the fashion journalists all talking about Gianni coming to New York with his 'greatest hits' and unknown to Myra, Chloe was the reason behind it all.

Chloe was also learning that hangovers were a thing to expect when going out with Carmen. Not wanting to be late for her shifts, and instead of traipsing all the way back to Williamsburg after a party in the early hours, Chloe stayed over at Carmen's place, which was much closer to work in Chelsea. She had also become entertainment for her colleagues, each morning they loved to see what outfit she had worn the night before—watching her turn up to work looking like a hooker who had stayed out. Made even funnier because she was usually the quiet girl who loved her job and arrived at work on time, and in flat shoes and jeans.

Now she had blossomed into a Queen of the Night, a crown she had stolen from Dominic. It was he who was the frequent dirty stop out, it was as if they had bumped heads and exchanged places. Now Dominic was the one that turned up to work in sneakers and jeans and on time; whereas before, every day was a fashion show to him. Jason's departure had changed him, not that Chloe had time for it, she was over his self-pity and refused to feed it. Word had also got out about Chloe's blog and her colleagues, especially Sarah, were gossiping about her:

"How did she dress Gabriela Gracia?"

"How did she afford her website?"

"How much money is she making?"

"I heard she's leaving now she dresses celebrities!"

With Dom and Chloe now on different shifts, thanks to Francesca's new rota, he had to have someone to chat with, to whisk the hours of the shop floor away—and Sarah was good for gossip. She knew everything, and if she didn't, she'd still have a theory or opinion on it. These juicy rumours hadn't escaped Francesca's attention either, and she made a mental note of it in her bank of evidence against Chloe—she was sure that outside activities such as this were a conflict of interest and a breach of her contract.

Out of work hobbies that were affecting work performance was a serious matter, and after checking StacksOfStyle for herself, she saw with her own eyes that the rumours were true. She too was somewhat suspicious of how Chloe had gained vintage Palazzo dresses, but something, in particular, had struck her like lightning. Francesca took out the work diary and flicked back to the day Chloe had left early to go home sick. Her face dropped, she couldn't believe what she had just discovered, but now wasn't the time to get her fired. She needed her for the in-store event and couldn't afford to be short on staff with Gianni visiting—her reputation and character was also on the line.

As the following days went by, Chloe spent more time with Carmen than she had with her best friend Dom, and had practically ignored every message Brian had sent her for the last two weeks. She was having too much fun out furthering her career, and Dom needed space to get over Jason anyway. When he was ready to join her, Chloe intended to pick him up and take him out on the town again—providing she wasn't busy with Carmen, StacksOfStyle, and styling celebrity clients.

Dom didn't quite see it that way, he was rather upset that his best friend had forgotten him when he needed her the most. After everything they had been through, all the support he had given her, all the advice and deeply personal conversations they had shared, suddenly meant nothing. It had been almost two weeks since he had heard from Jason and life itself seemed worthless without him. To make matters worse, the only person he could confide in was busy parading around town with some woman she had barely known for five minutes, while he spent his evenings alone and miserable.

He had told her everything about Jason, and she was the only one that could possibly understand him. Chloe's perspective was quite different, her thoughts were that Dom had an exciting week in a five-star hotel with a sex God (which was more than what most experienced) and that he should just get over it already and be grateful for what it was—just a bit of fun. Dom, on the other hand, had witnessed Chloe blossom into a career-driven selfish bitch, who only cared about her own personal gain and was willing to stamp out her friendship with him at the drop of a hat.

What he needed was a change of his own, and that was exactly what he had in mind. A phone call to his mother back home in London had reminded him of what he missed the most—his mom and his hometown. Right now, he was searching for something that would make him feel comfortable and safe, and there was no one else that could do that except for his mother. Especially now, he had nothing left in New York except for a flashy apartment and a job he was indifferent about.

Dom wasn't the only man in Chloe's life that her party behaviour had affected; Brian hadn't heard from her at all, despite his best efforts and he had enough of her bullshit ways, returning none of his texts and rejecting all of his calls. Like she had always said before: 'Career before relationships', and she was sticking to that promise she had made to herself. Brian had even turned up at her flat to try and catch her, but of course, she wasn't at home, she was out frolicking with Carmen at a party, rubbing shoulders with the elite set of New York. 'Is she over me already?' he wondered, getting the hint.

The truth was, she had forgotten about him entirely, she had utterly wiped him off her radar. Quite funny considering that a fortnight ago she was screwing him on their first date. 'Did she just sleep with me for a new website, and now it's successful, I'm no longer needed?' Brian wondered, just as upset and heartbroken as Dom—together they would have made a good couple.

Brian liked Chloe a lot, and at first, he thought she wasn't like most girls in fashion, but she had proved him wrong; she was just the same as all the others. She was living up to the stereotype of the typical girl who was addicted to fashion and was prepared to do anything to get what she wanted… And that, she was.

# CHAPTER TWENTY

Gianni was getting ready to make his trip over to New York from Milan. He was busy putting the finishing touches to the spring/summer collection, he usually wouldn't leave the atelier at such a crucial time, but this trip was vital for the brand. The weeks leading up to Milan Fashion Week were some of the most manic in the calendar for the design studio as they rushed to complete runway samples for the show and edit looks for final approval.

Palazzo always had the eyes of the industry and media on them, and this year they had to produce something special, something different from all the other houses, something that would boost their profile even higher and Gianni had that up his sleeve in more ways than one. Flying to New York was an important business trip he had to take, and not just for the retrospective show. Making the most of his time in the States, he locked in several meetings with the board of investors, which he was very excited about. If all went well, Palazzo was guaranteed to be the talk of Fashion Week even without the retrospective.

Gianni and his team had put together a show of the house's most iconic pieces from the past fifty-five years to remind the world just how important they were, but this was only the start—a new era of Palazzo was about to be born. Gianni had his assistant make a profile of the recent press coverage for him to go through, making use of the nine hours flight onboard his private jet. Naturally it included Gabriela Gracia, which he was delighted to see, it was a great example of what was to come at the retrospective show he had curated from the archive.

'Regina and Myra really know what they are doing,' he said to himself. Dressing people in vintage pieces ahead of the show was a genius idea which Gianni put down to the fact that Regina was always one step ahead, even past him.

For weeks the staff at Fifth Avenue had been preparing the store for Gianni's arrival. The stock rooms were in complete laboratory order, cleaners and carpenters had surveyed the store to repair and professionally clean the furnishings back to their original glory. Carpets were changed, door handles were renewed, and staff were given brand new uniforms in readiness. Anyone that turned up for work on the day unpresentable would be sent home with no pay and a written warning.

Carmen had also landed a Fashion Week job, styling the show for Hilary Van Furstein; a very high profile New York designer, and it would be the perfect opportunity for Chloe to get first-hand experience from behind the scenes. She needed Chloe to start work on it with her immediately, as there was little time to finalise details, but Carmen was known for producing excellent job on a tight deadline. She could pull anything off in a short period of time and knew Chloe was up to her speed (and standard), and someone she could rely on, as well as help her in the process, so called her straight away with another offer.

"*What?* You want me to help *you* with Hilary's show?" Chloe said, again in disbelief but knowing she was for real; she just couldn't believe how fast things were moving.

"Sure—I mean you have to experience Fashion Week as a stylist and not just a spectator... Plus, you will get to hand out all of those business cards you have and make some serious connections, darling."

Chloe didn't need to be enticed and agreed to help her on the spot. Life was about to get crazy, what with the event at work, her writing schedule for S.O.S, and now as an assistant on the Hilary Van Furstein show! Listing all these things in her mind, Chloe began to drift off on the other end of the line.

"Hellooo... Are you still there?"

"Still here... It's just that, I'm not sure if I can do it. Next week will be very busy at work with Gianni coming to town, and we have this event at work and—"

"Who gives a *fuck?* Listen to me! They don't care about you, honey; it's Fashion Week for fuck's sake! A freelance stylist doesn't turn down

Fashion Week, okay? This is the most important date in our diaries…
Do you know how many people would beg me for this job?" Carmen
said, trying her best to make Chloe see what an excellent opportunity
this was, and that it was hers to take.

This was turning out to be Chloe's moment to change her life, she
had always feared not achieving her career goals by the age of thirty,
and here she was deliberating whether to take it, now it was within
her reach. Sometimes, people let the fear get the better of them and
stopped themselves from progressing, not quite ready for an immediate
life-changing opportunity, but Chloe was definitely prepared. Carmen
was right, this was essential for her and Palazzo didn't care about
her—they could replace her within a week.

*

Chloe's responsibilities and opportunities weren't the only things
she was struggling to juggle; Brian had managed to ambush her after
weeks of not having contact. She was just in the middle of serving a
customer at the small leather goods counter when Brian had walked
straight up to her—desperate for an explanation.

"Are you ignoring me?" He said, not caring about the customer.

"Oh hi… No—not at all… I've just been so busy… Erm, just
excuse me a moment."

The customer was taking her time to select a wallet, so she left
her comparing two styles while she took Brian away to a corner for a
discreet chat.

"Brian, I'm so sorry, but the website has become this monster
that's getting bigger and bigger… A stylist has noticed my posts and
introduced me to Gabriela Gracia and ever since then I've just been
so busy… Not to mention all the events we are having here that I will
have to stay late for, and now I'm preparing for a major Fashion show."

"Wow… So you have your own collection already," Brian sarcastically quipped.

Chloe gave him a look, she wasn't impressed; she couldn't be dealing with his petty sarcasm (no matter how called for it was). Yes, she had been shitty about contacting him, but he could at least be understanding and supportive. She thought he would, especially after he had helped her with the website for this exact purpose. Surely he knew she wasn't just doing this 'fashion thing' for fun? She wanted to make a career out of it, and she was determined this time; no one, no man, no friend—no matter who they were—was going to get in her way of success, and that included both Dom and Brian.

"Well, when you can fit me into your hectic schedule let me know," Brian said before walking away with a huff.

'Why is he like this?' she asked herself, failing to see his point of view, after all, she never said they were serious. They were just seeing each other, exclusively of course, but casually at the same time—in her mind at least. It was now clear to her that Brian thought otherwise.

"Brian—Brian!" she called after him, not wanting to make a scene on the shop floor but also not wanting to leave things like this. "Look… I just need some space, I need to do my work—I need to make a *real* go of this. I'm sorry if you were expecting more from me, but I never said I was willing to give up everything—and I'm sorry if I wasn't clear on that—but I just can't give you any more than what I have already… Including my time."

She had only been seeing him for a month, and she was already breaking up with him; she couldn't believe she had the guts to say it, but it was the truth, and she was adamant in her decision, it was her way or the highway.

"Well, you coulda told me you were just using me from the start, Chloe… Jeez!"

A few customers had heard him raise his voice as he said it, they turned to catch the action—Francesca included who tried her best to distract them from the public fracas.

"Can I show you anything Madam?" she asked a prying customer while shooting Chloe an angry look.

Brian was gobsmacked by her answer. 'How could she do this?' he thought, not expecting her to be so blunt about it. He knew she wasn't some fluffy pushover, but he still didn't expect her to be so direct about it either. He had reconstructed her website for her as a favour to his boss, she didn't need to sleep with him and lead him on. The fact that she had done so had sent the wrong signal and made him think that she genuinely had feelings for him like he did for her. Chloe did like Brian, more than what she would care to admit, but typically everything had turned up at once like buses, and it was typical that now her dream career was taking off that a man would appear also.

Aware he was making a scene, and with not much more to be said, he walked away—and she wasn't going to stop him. Besides, if she did go after him, she would only have to let him down again, and this was the easiest way to rip the Band-Aid off. Instead, she took a deep breath to regain composure and returned to her client—who was still deliberating over the same two wallets she had left her with.

It was a strange day for staff at Palazzo, most were on edge due to Gianni's impending visit, and some were just on edge—period. Dom was one of them, Chloe had hardly seen him all day on the shop floor and heard from Sarah that he had been to see Regina, which she dismissed as pure lies—he would never! Finally, she saw him emerge from the staff stairwell, he had indeed been off the shop floor, but where and waht he had been up to wasn't important right now.

"Oh my God, Dom, there you are," she said, trying to instigate the usual chatter. "Where have you been?"

"Oh, I just had to arrange some time off—that's all" he brushed off.

"You will never guess what just happened! Brian had the cheek to come here and question me, in front of everyone, about our relationship—I mean what the *fuck* dude!"

Dom wasn't impressed, in fact, he was surprised she hadn't asked him why he was taking time off and if everything was all right? It was as if she hadn't heard him at all, she wasn't bothered by what he had to say. This was another blow to their friendship and proof that Chloe really didn't care about anyone else, but Chloe.

"I could see Francesca spying on me, just loving that I was causing a stir so she could go and snitch on me to Regina," she continued.

"Whatever Chloe," he said, before walking over to a customer.

He didn't particularly want to serve a client right now, but he had to get away from her before he too confronted her about her self-absorption and caused another argument—not that she would listen or get the message anyway.

Chloe let him flounce off, if he was going to be like that, then she didn't want to speak to him; quite frankly she thought he was childish and it had been week's since Jason had left town—it was time to get over it. She thought he would at least be sympathetic to her situation, having gone through a break up himself.

Then again she wasn't that bothered and wasn't heartbroken like he was; she was too busy to care, and it was a relief to finally have Brian out of her hair. A break from Dom was also necessary, and she decided that from now, she wouldn't bother speaking to him until he had fixed himself up. 'When the time is right, he will come to me,' she thought, there was no use trying to force him back into the real world.

After work, Chloe met up with Carmen to view possible locations for the show and planned what the goody bags would include for the front row guests. All these fine details that went into a show had her thinking about StacksOfStyle and how busy she would be over Fashion Week. Even with Brian now out of the equation, she couldn't help but worry if she could keep up with it all.

Not wanting to risk her partnership with DivaFeet, Chloe emailed Veronica to let her know she was going to be busy. Veronica didn't really care, she was just happy she had a savvy new stylist on her books that was now connected with one of New York's most famous designers—and working on her show. She knew Chloe was exceptional and her glowing portfolio of clients had not gone unnoticed. Veronica was also set to be busy during Fashion Week and suggested they meet up between shows so they could finally meet one another. Fashion Week was perfect for networking and meeting with people in the industry and Veronica, ever the businesswoman on the lookout for an opportunity had a very clever idea that she wanted to run past Chloe.

**

Working with Carmen on the Hilary Van Furstein show had made time fly by. Doing night shifts with her after a day's work at Palazzo had been full on and was taking its toll on her already. Francesca was also cracking the whip in preparation for the in-store event. The womenswear department was immaculate, and a successful store visit from Gianni would undoubtedly seal her contract past probation. The only other thing she could do to help herself was to give Regina a reason to fire Chloe Ravens, which wasn't proving to be difficult.

As if she didn't have enough ammunition already, the long list of wrongdoings was growing by the day. Chloe's standards were seriously slipping (if they could any further) and after discovering her extracurricular activities, involving what could be possibly old Palazzo stock, Francesca now understood why. Not to mention the debacle on the shop floor with a lover—that was the icing on the cake—she couldn't have given her much more to complain about if she tried.

Although she was burning the candle at both ends, Chloe knew she had to be on her best behaviour at the Palazzo event, and with tons of things to work on for Fashion Week outside of work (not to mention her writing and upload schedule), she knew she had to take a step back. Chloe swapped nights out with Carmen for early evenings in bed that involved lots of emails and posting on Instagram. Getting to bed early and back on her regular skin care regime also meant she was on time for work for once. She just needed to get this crazy-ass week over with and then she could look forward to Hilary's fashion show.

The eve of New York Fashion Week was the day Palazzo, Fifth Avenue had been waiting for (with every other fashion victim)—an unofficial Fashion Week opening celebration. The most luxurious and expensive catering had been laid on, canapés and champagne were ready to be handed out by handsome waiters that had been hired from a top modelling agency, and VIP clients were due to attend by invitation only.

A production company had turned the shop floor into a party venue overnight, complete with a celebrity DJ playing trendy electro beats sure to fool anyone into thinking they were a model themselves strutting the runway, and urge them to spend thousands in a heartbeat. Only clients who had spent a hefty sum that year had been invited to the in-store event, hosted by the man himself—they didn't want him meeting any old riff-raff; you could be sure that Rob and Gina Travers wouldn't be there.

Thankfully for Myra, the Milan press office had invited all the A-listers they wanted present at Gianni's request; mostly consisting of his friends from the fashion, film and music scene along with the most important magazine editors, photographers and fashion royalty of New York that would be sure to say only positive things. Tabloid paparazzi and journalists had gathered outside behind a red rope that was cordoned off and flanked by security guards, waiting for the arrival of Gianni—a space had been reserved for his town car to pull into which the security had trouble keeping clear from taxi's and Uber's dropping off attendees.

He was to appear on the red carpet that led to the main entrance of the store, the doors of which were also guarded by his own security guards complete with earpieces and black sunglasses, even though it was evening. They would control the door and make sure only guests with invitations were allowed inside and turn away anyone that dared enter without one (how shameful), but there would surely be a few that would embarrass themselves by trying.

It didn't matter how tired she was, Chloe was excited that she would finally get to see Gianni in the flesh. Her experience from these sorts of events was that it appeared fun and exciting to those on the outside, but a nuisance to the staff. The past few weeks had been stressful and working late at a party was the last thing she needed, however glamorous it sounded, but she couldn't deny that this was a moment she had been waiting for her whole career. She had plenty of things to be getting on with for the fashion show but the thought of seeing him, maybe even meeting him, made it one not to miss. On the upside, at least she would get to spend the evening with Dom, she knew she owed him an apology as he had stayed clear of her since their spat.

He was in a good mood for once, pumped from all the excitement and glitz of a Fashion Week event—almost as if he were the one host-ing it. Chloe also noticed that he seemed a lot happier than what he had been lately—she was glad to see that he was finally getting over Jason and understanding that life offered much more than just men. Secretly, it was because he had finally come to a decision about his future and after speaking with his mother on the phone, he knew he was making the right choice. A choice that would change his life and help him forget all about his heartache in New York.

The store had closed much earlier than usual for the final prepa-rations, and HR had laid on food for the staff in the kitchen which consisted of fresh fruits, salads, cold meats, Italian artisan bread and plates of pasta. This was one of the perks when working a Palazzo event, and a smart way to make sure staff didn't need to leave the prem-ises, ensuring all staff members would be in the same place at—ready for show time.

Francesca had called a staff meeting just before the doors opened to ensure everyone was presentable and up to her high standard of grooming. Their uniform had to be immaculate, she made them polish their shoes, tidy their hair and retouch their makeup (Dom included), ready for her inspection.

"Okay everyone—looking good... Just so we know what we are all doing this evening, I have a few things to run through. Soraya—you are on the leather goods counter while Sarah is covering shoes. Tristan—you will stand at the top of the stairs and greet people when they come up. As the top sellers, Chloe and Dominic will be serving the ready-to-wear area," she said, wishing she had other staff to nominate with this task, but she knew they were the top team members to talk about the collection—so she had no other option. "Have a great night everyone and may I just remind you to always be your best and exude the Palazzo core values… And certainly *no* drinking alcohol! The drink provided is strictly for guests only and anyone caught disobeying this rule will be dealt with accordingly."

With the staff now groomed, fed and back on the shop floor in their places, bang on seven p.m., the doors could finally open. Guests started to enter dressed in their finest Palazzo garments, showing off pieces they had bought from the brand over their years of loyal custom. Hardcore fashionistas wore entirely new collection ensembles in a bid to impress the creative director himself; some of them looked tragic and over the top—like a Palazzo clone with no personality of their own—all emblazoned in the italic '*P*,' logo. It turned out that Rob and Gina would have been right at home. Editors of fashion magazines air kissed one another, you could tell by the frosty air between them that they didn't like each other but still continued on with the charade.

With guests pouring in and paparazzi outside snapping away, the event was well and truly underway. An hour had barely passed, and a whole crate of champagne had been guzzled already. Attendees scoffed the canapés like they had missed dinner, others just dismissed them and looked like they didn't eat at all, never mind a tiny morsel touch their lips.

The womenswear floor was pumping and full to capacity, it really *was* like a party—an exclusive nightclub even—surrounded by fashion and fashionable people alike. The music was much louder than usual, and everyone was in high spirits, including Dominic who was strutting around the department taking to guests like it was his house party. He had managed to sneak two glasses of champagne from a chiselled waiter he had taken a fancy to and hid them in the little alcove.

"Oi… Chloe," he beckoned, making sure no one else heard or saw. "Come, let's have a drink…"

Chloe followed him to the stock inventory corner and giggled at the sight of the two champagne flutes. He was so naughty sometimes, but she was glad the mischievous Dom was back—even if it was just for one night.

"Didn't you hear Francesca?" she playfully warned with a cheeky grin, knowing full well he had.

"Oh, *fuck* her! Do you seriously expect me to work late and not drink a drop of alcohol, while we watch these bunch of *cunts* drink themselves into oblivion? Bottoms up I say—a toast," he said, holding up his glass.

Chloe stopped laughing, this was a poignant moment. No matter how long they hadn't spoken for, whatever they had been through together, they were still good friends.

"To friendship!" she said, cutting in before he could.

Dom, smiled, almost looking tearful at her gesture. They stood looking at each other, expecting someone to say something or be the one to apologise first. He knew he had to tell her about his plans, but he just couldn't bring himself to—there wasn't enough time to explain his reasoning—so he clinked her glass and took a sip cautiously, not wanting to get caught. The champagne tasted better than usual: fun and dangerous, like forbidden fruits.

"Look, Dom… I know I haven't—"

"—Before you say anything, I…" Dom began, finally plucking up the gall to just come out and say it, only to be interrupted by the sound of high heels click-clacking on the wood floor.

"*Francesca!*" Dom whispered, taking her champagne glass and hiding them both behind some folders on the top shelf.

Chloe made her way out onto the shop floor to stall Francesca, as if she were just looking for an item for a client on the system—but it was only Sarah.

"What are you guys up to?"

Sarah was stupid but not that stupid; she knew exactly what they were up to and Dom knew exactly what she wanted.

"It's in there, on the top shelf—don't drink it all… And don't tell anyone!" he said, rolling his eyes over to the alcove.

Allowing her to share the champagne brought her in on the fun, and it was better than her bitching to their colleagues about drinking behind Francesca's back. A blacked-out limo had pulled up outside the store—Gianni had arrived! As he stepped out of the car, a blitz of camera flashes sprayed in succession.

"Mr Palazzo, what can you tell us about the upcoming show in New York?" One journalist said, hi-jacking him from across the red rope.

"What made you choose New York for this homage to the family business?" Another quizzed, extending his arm out that little bit too close to Gianni, causing his security to push the mic away.

"New York is the heart of fashion and style—it's an honour to be here," he said, expertly batting them off with a seductive smile and giving nothing away.

He posed for the waiting photographers outside and waved to fans that had queued up outside to take pictures on their phones, before being escorted inside by his bodyguards. Regina was standing in the foyer, ready to greet him along with Melinda and Myra—this was the moment she had been working hard towards for months. When he had finally made his way inside, with by Joli by his side, Regina made an instant beeline—making sure she was the very first to greet him.

"Welcome to your Fifth Avenue store, Mr Palazzo."

Regina's eyes seemed to light up like no one had ever seen before; it was funny what a handsome man could do, even to someone as cold-hearted as her—he made her look like an ordinary woman for once. No matter how powerful or strong-minded she was, she was still like every other human being with a weakness for good looks.

"Thank you, Regina, so lovely to see you again… I am very pleased to be here," he said, greeting her with a kiss before turning to greet Myra and Melinda.

Regina signalled with her hand for a waiter to bring them champagne at once.

"Well, it looks like you have done a great job with this event, and I am particularly impressed with the press coverage we have had lately in America… It all ties in nicely with the retrospective show, don't you think?"

Regina and Myra had seen the pictures of Gabriela and Aurielle in the magazines, but it had nothing to do with them. They were in the dark about it as much as he was; it indeed wasn't Myra's doing, in fact, she had thought it was something he must have arranged. The press office had been busy rounding up the media in preparation for the event and Fashion Week itself to even think about dressing celebrities. Besides, Myra always thought that people like Gabriela Gracia could afford Palazzo and shouldn't be begging to borrow it from her instead.

"Of course, Mr Palazzo… We are all committed to the future success of the brand," Regina said, diverting the conversation away from the possible questions that she didn't have an answer for.

"And how's Mrs Rogers? I have heard that you will take retirement after this year?" he said.

Melinda was happy about retiring, now it was her chance to enjoy life. Although she had enjoyed some parts of working for Palazzo, she was also pleased to see the back of it all, including Regina. "Yes, it's true… I am leaving. I have had many happy years here working for your family, but it's time to cash my chips in I'm afraid."

"Melinda will, of course, be working with us to make sure the transition to the next client manager will run smoothly," Regina said, stepping in to own the conversation once again. "Who is yet to be appointed… We are currently in search with HR for an appropriate successor."

Gianni really didn't care that much, his job was to make sure the designs and collections were irresistible, to make customers flock to the stores to snap up every season; employing staff was what he paid Regina for and far beneath his role. Designing the clothes and being the creative director was stressful enough. He had investors to answer to and big plans for the brand that he wanted backing on, so company profits were his top priority. Some luxury brands had seen profits fall, reflecting the troubles of the economy. Even though the summer season hadn't exactly flown off the shelves, Palazzo showed no signs of slowing down concerning desire; although Gianni saw it necessary to make some cuts if he was going to pull off his next move.

Already the current fall/winter collection was rushing off the rails as fast as it was being delivered, but that was due to the reduction in the number of pieces that had actually been produced. Volume had been slashed, which made the collection appear popular, even if it meant that the company would make a bit less this season; to the customer, it would make the collection seem to be a sell-out, and customers always wanted what they couldn't have—restoring desire and interest in the brand. Less was more and the less there was of it, the more exclusive Palazzo would be; this clever tactic was just a glimpse into his entre-preneurial skills.

Gianni entertained and charmed the official reporters and press representatives that were allowed inside; he was handsome and rugged all at the same time, everyone was fawning over him. His suit was well cut to fit, made by Palazzo, of course, he never wore clothing from other fashion houses; he was the figurehead of the brand an exuded the dream lifestyle it sold. Gianni was good looking, and he knew it, with his dark brown hair—almost black—and the most dazzling blue eyes you could ever imagine.

His designer stubble was neatly trimmed and perfect, not a bald patch or nick in sight, growing downwards in one perfect direction. His skin was clear and robust looking with very few lines, the kind of tracks that made a man sexy. When he entered a room, he commanded it well with a presence that was both powerful and sexual. It was a wonder he was still single, there were rumours that he was gay—something that Dom had hoped was true—why else would an attractive man be single when he could have anyone he wanted? The truth was that he was far too busy to settle down—he enjoyed the jet set lifestyle too much—sleeping with different models in different cities whenever he chose and had none of the exhausting ties that came with a traditional relationship.

Regina and Myra spent the night introducing him to the very best clients the store looked after and touring the floors with him so he could inspect the refurbishment and standards. He was impressed with what he saw, but like Regina, he was always one step ahead. "We are fitting a new concept in our Omotesando store in Japan… If all goes to plan, we could be looking at a possible re-fit for Fifth Avenue also, but that's something we'll discuss this week at our meeting Regina."

The scheduled meeting took up a whole day with the board of directors all present. A meeting that had Regina salivating at the potential to boost her career at Palazzo further, along with her reputation within the fashion industry altogether. The accessories floor was buzzing with guests, and after mingling with most of them, they moved up to the menswear floor. As well as meeting the team, Gianni met some of the richest men in the city that wore his clothes. Meanwhile, upstairs in womenswear, Dom was serving an Arabic client of his that was shopping for her many daughters.

Chloe had been enlisted to model dresses for her, which Chloe was too happy to oblige. She was too nervous to meet Gianni face to face and was sure to make an idiot of herself if she were lucky enough to speak to him. Instead, she would be busy modelling and didn't care if it ended up being a complete waste of time; it got her off the shop floor and away from the spotlight.

By the time Chloe had tried on the first dress and was back in the changing room to try on another, Regina had led Gianni onto the womenswear floor with their entourage. She introduced him to Francesca as the new department manager—her new shining star—and the three of them stood there speaking in Italian, trying to woo him with the Italian connection.

Many of the female guests were waiting close by to greet him, waiting for them to finish chatting, pandering over how handsome he looked and taking in his aura, clearly intoxicated by his good looks. He could see that he had adoring fans waiting, so cut Francesca's blabber short, much to her disappointment.

"You are a genius!" one woman gushed.

"Your clothes are masterpieces," said another.

"I only wear Palazzo," a client said, twirling for his approval.

Politely accepting all of the cliché lines he was used to being thrown at him, Gianni took in his surroundings. He was quite impressed with the department, all of heir hard work had paid off; the merchandising was impeccable, the floor was perfect, and he could see how staff interacted with clients thanks to Dom putting on his best performance over at the fitting rooms. As the entourage passed the changing room area, Gianni stopped to watch Dom in action with his client.

"This is Dominic Fraser, one of our most successful and reputable sales associates," Regina said, pursing her lips with a slight annoyance.

Normally she wouldn't have taken the time to compliment him but since asking to meet her earlier that week to hand in his resignation, he was tolerable for now—he was no longer an issue. The next floor to see was personal shopping, the end of Gianni's in-store appearance, where they would hold a dinner with the directors of the board and ease their way into talks about Palazzo's future.

With Chloe out of sight and nowhere to be seen, Regina was eager for them to move on and gestured towards the elevators. But just as they were about to turn around to leave, Chloe stepped out of the fitting room in a floor length gown that was corseted—pushing up her cleavage into a provocative bosom. None the wiser about what she had just walked into, she pulled her long blonde wavy hair to one side and over her shoulder.

Her makeup looked flawless under the changing room lights that made you appear air-brushed in the mirrors. Slowly, Chloe could feel the many eyes staring at her as she walked towards Dom's client to take a turn. As she stepped around and swished the long skirt of the dress, she locked eyes with Gianni. '*Shit!*' she yelped inside, in total disbelief that this was happening.

It couldn't have been more perfectly timed!

Her first instinct was to run back into the fitting room, but she had to remain professional; she was stood in front of the whole party—her managers and the owner and visionary himself. She had connected with his electric blue eyes, they seemed to attract like magnets, and for a moment she forgot about what she was doing. A strange but inviting feeling rushed through her body, quickening her heartbeat. She couldn't explain the feeling other than the fact that she too wasn't immune to Gianni Palazzo's good looks and powerful aura.

It seemed like minutes had passed, but in reality, it was only seconded, as if the moment had played out in slow motion. It was evident to everyone that Gianni found Chloe very striking and beautiful, but especially dressed in one of his creations. The last time he saw this dress on a woman was at the collection's fashion show earlier in the year. He remembered the skinny model that wore it, of course, she looked impeccable, but the curves of Chloe's body seemed to make it look sexier than he had ever imagined it would. The dress suddenly became real and not one of his illusions anymore; Chloe was a real woman, and she was breathing new life into his art, which excited him very much.

Regina was gobsmacked, but more so by Gianni's reaction, he had practically unzipped and undressed her with his eyes on the spot. Jealous and angered by her stealing the limelight, Regina made sure it wasn't for much longer and pressed the tour onwards.

"*A-hem...* Now, shall we go to the V.I.C floor for the private dinner with our business partners, Mr Palazzo?"

As she led him away, she shot Chloe a look, a look that said: 'Get out of that dress at once, you wench!' Regina couldn't hate her more if she tried, but it had escalated to a new height now she had obviously attracted the lustful desire of their creative director, the man who made it all happen.

The truth was, it wasn't just Chloe that she hated, she hated any woman that owned such youthful qualities to attract a man. It reminded her of the stupid whore that run off with her husband many years ago. Yes, that's right, Regina was at one point in her life capable of loving another human being, but her love of the job had got in the way. Being a workaholic was essential in becoming successful, especially after stealing it from under Melinda's feet. Turning her back on her husband, she put all her energy into work, work, and work! Keeping her power in Palazzo had possessed her, and it wasn't until many years later that she discovered her husband was seeing one of her employees.

Rita was a pretty, young girl who was confident, talented—much like Chloe Ravens in that respect. She even championed Rita for a promotion to an assistant store manager, impressed by her motivated attitude towards work. To Regina, Chloe was in the same category: the ambitious shop girl who had stabbed her in the back and stole her husband. But Regina was far too intelligent to let a stupid slut get the better of her; like how she had taken her position, you had to know the rules of the game to be able to cheat them.

Regina had found out about their affair after going back to work late one Friday night, having forgotten reports he needed to go over on the weekend. It was certainly a shock to see Rita and her husband having sex in one of the stock rooms on CCTV. Instead of marching down to catch them, she went about her business, as if nothing had happened, while she plotted her revenge against both of them.

Eventually, a store manager position had popped up at the outlet in New Jersey, and Regina promoted Rita without a second thought, forcing her to relocate. Rita had no choice on the matter, especially after Regina played back the footage of her and her husband at it like rabbits. As for her husband… Regina had all the evidence she needed to divorce him on her terms, exercising her power over her marriage like she did at work—refusing to accept any responsibility in neglecting their relationship. She had lost the only person in her life that had ever loved her, and she had traded that all in for Palazzo.

Palazzo provided her with much comfort and distraction during her divorce, she had no time for heartache or emotional signs of weakness. She was now officially married to her job, it was all she had left and refused to be defeated by covering up her pain with work pride. She hated the paranoia of her staff gossiping behind her back, shamed by a shop girl who had spread rumours all over town in spite of her dismissal.

Rita had taken away her power, and that made Regina determined never to lose it again, but it was something that Chloe managed to do without even realising it. Every time Regina saw Chloe's face, she saw the bitch that had humiliated her and wrecked her marriage. Watching Chloe flirt with Gianni, looking amazing in one of his dresses, had made Regina remember the seedy, grainy footage—discovering two people she had once trusted betraying her. Some might say that karma was now coming back to bite her, but Chloe Ravens had to go, and it was simply just a matter of time.

# CHAPTER TWENTY-ONE

Fashion week had arrived. New York had been blessed with an excellent summer and the fashion season was about to kick off around the world; New York, London, Milan and Paris. Carmen was manic finalising preparations for the Hilary Van Furstein show, and with the Palazzo event out of the way, Chloe was excited to work on her first ever fashion show. Hilary's collections were feminine and bold, featuring recognisable prints on chic wrap dresses which had become her signature style.

Hilary always showed at Pier 57 Hudson River Park, which was usually booked up by other designers during Fashion Week, but they always reserved the space for New York's homegrown designer who had hit the fashion main stage; one of the largest exports of American luxury fashion. The turnaround would have to be quick and completed overnight, then the place would need stripping again for another show the very next day.

But what Hilary wanted, Hilary got, and it was now down to Carmen to pull it all off. Chloe had booked two days holiday in advance, so she didn't have to worry about lying to Francesca again, but she was glad to get rid of her while Gianni was in town—as was Regina. The last thing she needed was for her to make an embarrassment of herself in front of him, which she had already done in Regina's eyes. For Chloe, working at Fashion Week was exciting and an experience to remember, but it wasn't all glamour and hijinks.

Hilary had cast her models for the show with Carmen both assisting and putting the looks together for her. With the show just a day away, Chloe was drafted in to help Hilary's production team with pinning and adjusting the garments on the models, but as she worked away, she couldn't help but think of Gianni and that look in his eyes that had lingered on her mind ever since. All sorts of questions rattled through her brain—he had dazzled her with his blue eyes—and even though she knew it meant nothing (and never would), she let her imagination run wild.

Did he know who she was? Had he asked Regina who she was? Will she ever see him again? Even out of work, she was thinking about being at work, and for the first time in ages, she actually wished she was there. Maybe if she were working, he would come back to see her? All for she knew, he could on the shop floor right now while she was a seamstresses' slave.

Now she understood how Dom felt when he met Jason on out of the blue, and why he had fallen so hard for him. Back on speaking terms with him, she told him about how Gianni had flirted with her, but he played down the whole scenario—having learnt that such magical experiences of sudden attraction weren't all as they seemed.

"He was just staring at your tits babe—don't go falling in love! Trust me, you don't need that right now… Besides, he's probably banging some hooker as we speak back at his penthouse."

Speaking of Dom, he too had booked a day off so he could see to his plans, in fact, Regina had been very accommodating to his departure and was thrilled at his departure; with him gone, it left Chloe vulnerable—exactly the position she wanted her in. In the past, Fashion Week was an excuse for Chloe and Dom to party, they always got dressed up to the hilt and blagged their way into rooftop parties and fashion shows and often succeeded—looking the part of a fashion insider and knowing how to wrangle their way through any guest list.

This year they wouldn't need to try as Chloe was not only working on a show, but Carmen had all the contacts they needed to get into almost any party they could want. Dom had no intentions of partying his last weeks in New York away, he had lots of last-minute arrangements and packing to get on with. He had hoped to break the news to Chloe, and Fashion Week wasn't ideal either as he knew she was busy and would have a meltdown on top of what would be complete madness already. She would only try to talk him out of leaving anyway, and his mind was made up already—this was happening. Not saying a word was a blessing, it meant he could get on with what he needed to in peace, and she could focus on what was important to her—networking—although he knew he had to tell her soon.

On a short break, Chloe messaged Dom to fill him in with the latest backstage news and that any party they desired was at their fingertips. She wanted to see him and make up for lost time, but she didn't get the response she was quite expecting, in fact, there wasn't one, which had her wondering—maybe their friendship wasn't taking off where they had left it?

Quickly getting back to sewing hems, her mind skipped back to that moment she had shared with Gianni and how she wished she had said something—anything—even just hello, but at the time she was dumbstruck. In retrospect, she played out all the smart one-liners she could have given and kicked herself at the lost opportunity. To get herself back on track with the job in hand, she told herself that Dom was probably right about him just being blinded by her cleavage in that dress.

Then again, she did get checked out by the most desirable man in fashion, and that would make any woman dream about being with him—which is exactly what she did. She couldn't help herself, especially now she had a taste of sex and men wanting her. Every now and then, graphic images of herself having hot steamy sex with Gianni popped into her head.

She knew he would be good in bed, you could tell a handsome man like that knew exactly what he was doing in the bedroom department; either that or he would typically have a tiny and useless dick. Chloe enjoyed her brief fantasy, her imagination was probably the closest she would get to having sex with him after all, and she enjoyed thinking just about it for a moment.

"Chloe—*Chloe?* Where is this girl—I need that dress now!" Carmen yelled from somewhere between a rail and a steamer.

Chloe snapped out of her daze and appeared with the finished dress in hand. "Coming!"

Sadly not literally, like how she had just been imagining…

*

The grand tent for the Palazzo retrospective had been erected in Central Park, and the stage was being built for the show, which was on everyone's lips—even those that had no clue about fashion. It was going to be the highlight of the entire week, and the closing show, receiving an invite would be like winning the lottery to a fashion addict.

To be there, you simply had to be one of the elite set of New York's fashion scene or a darling of the Industry. You could guarantee that the front row would consist of editors, critics, famous actresses, pop-stars and their latest squeezes; no doubt Regina and Myra would worm their way in too, keeping up the pretence that they were important enough to be there.

But before all that could happen, there was something Gianni had been anticipating for months that was now becoming a reality; the retrospective show was just the icing on the cake—a showstopper. Everyone on the board of Palazzo had gathered at the company's head office in the Garment District. Regina, Myra and Melinda were also present as it involved future plans for the Fifth Avenue store.

"Thank you all for coming," Gianni started. "Firstly, I would like to say a big thank you to Regina, Myra and Melinda for organising such an amazing event last night at our gorgeous Fifth Avenue store."

Everyone clapped as Regina and Myra looked pleased with themselves; getting his seal of approval was a great achievement for them and especially for Regina—it was another gold star next to her name. Melinda, however, couldn't care less, getting the crème de la crème of New York together for a soiree was hardly rocket science, and after this season, she wouldn't have to deal with this shit anymore. Fake smiles, backstabbing and a whole lot of fuss over 'fashion' would not be missed.

"Today I am honoured to reveal what I have been working on with our directors for the past six months... An agreement which will see Palazzo not only become one of the biggest luxury brands for many more generations to come but also as a luxury fashion group that will make a mark on our industry and welcome other brands into our house—sharing our heritage and craftsmanship know-how to create a new home for fashion designers. It is my pleasure to announce that we have been approved to acquire one of the most iconic houses in the history of fashion: Maison Marais!"

Everyone around the table clapped, especially Regina who was once again on the prowl for a higher position of power in this newly formed company.

"The take over will be effective as soon as we confirm our bid. In front of you are the plans and financial cost—and profit forecast—of buying Maison Marais, which will create 'The Palazzo Group'. I wish to confirm our offer to buy imminently and will set forward our plan, which includes a refurbishment of their Fifth Avenue store to relaunch the house next year—as well as a new store concept for Palazzo Fifth Avenue the following year. Rejuvenating and reinventing our brands will secure our future not only as the most luxurious brand in the world but also as a creator and conservator of fashion for the future."

The room erupted in applause once more, signalling that approval was guaranteed.

**

The day of Hilary's show had arrived, the stage had been built, and the production and sound teams had moved in to set up. Carmen had a town car booked at the expense of H.V.F and collected Chloe from her apartment at four a.m; the show wasn't until lunchtime that afternoon, but there were many things to be getting on with and time would slip away in what would seem like only minutes as they rushed to piece it all together.

Building the set overnight meant that an early rehearsal was called so that everyone knew where they had to be and the models didn't make any mistakes during the actual show. Chloe was instructed to wear a comfortable outfit to work in—blue fitted jeans and a simple white T-shirt with '*H.V.F*' embroidered on the chest—which Carmen had given her. "You must only wear Hilary... Well, for the show and after-party at least," Carmen had warned her.

Designers could be sensitive about guests wearing their peer's clothes at their very own show, it was your duty to pay homage to the mastermind behind the brand by wearing only their designs. It looked bad if the stylist and her assistant were wearing another label, or even worse—no label. Chloe didn't get what the fuss was about, it wasn't like she was sat in the front row; she was backstage with Carmen and the models, but she understood and most importantly, wanted to fit in. This was her first 'Fashion Week freebie', and free clothes were happily accepted on any terms.

When they arrived at Pier 57, models were lounging around playing on their phones while others had their hair in curlers already, and some were having extensions fitted; backstage was already heating up with a thick atmosphere of steam and hairspray. This hotbed of tension and excitement would be Chloe's office for the day; her first assignment was to arrange all of the looks onto the rails with the model's name and exit number. All of the models had two or three looks, which meant Chloe had to help them quickly get changed, while the hair and make-up artists attended to them.

'What if I don't get a model out on time?' she panicked.

She hadn't done anything like this before, and for a designer of such great importance. Looking at Carmen and seeing how busy and stressed she was had calmed Chloe's nerves; she was under much more pressure to deliver a romping show, and Chloe's task was a walk in the park in comparison. Not only had Carmen helped to choreograph the show, but she had also assisted Hilary with piecing together every look, showcasing the collection in its most stylish light possible. Yes, Hilary had designed the collection, but Carmen had some responsibility for how the show visually and how it would be received by the critics. She had helped Hilary come to some important decisions over the past two weeks, deciding which pieces to cut, what to keep, and which models to use.

"Good morning, everyone!"

The entire room looked to see that the star designer herself had arrived. Hilary walked in the room with her silvery blonde perfectly hair blow-dried, wearing one of her latest creations, tossing her pink leather biker jacket and handbag over a director's chair bearing her name on the back.

"Okay… Are we all set for the run-through?" Hilary asked.

"Yes, let's start," Carmen said, clapping her hands so everyone would listen up.

"Everyone, listen up," Hilary called out from her chair, taking her Starbuck's coffee cup that her assistant had timed perfectly so it would be still steaming hot.

Models, make-up, and hair all gathered round to listen to the genius behind the collection they were representing—Chloe included.

"I design clothes for real women; mothers, daughters, wives, girlfriends, mistresses, and even those that can't afford my clothes but want to copy my style. When you walk out on that runway, I want you to be all of those in one; sexy, confident, shy, powerful, submissive, and sweet… Okay, enough jabber… Let's see this all together—hair and make-up—no need for you to prep the girls yet, I just want to see the looks and the walk… Let's go please—*now!*" Hilary snapped, the pressure was starting to get to her.

Chloe rushed over to the rail to pick out 'look one' and matched the name to the snapshot of the model it belonged to—Ivana. The trouble was, they all looked like Ivana's. Hilary walked out to the front of the runway to view the show from the spectator's perspective, and from the front of house, she called out again—to which Chloe panicked.

"Okay, let's go I said… We haven't got all day, and we need to get this *perfect!*"

This was not a time for Chloe to lose her shit now.

"Chloe, get all the girls into their first look and send them to me by the exit," Carmen ordered her.

From somewhere that she didn't know existed, Chloe managed to pull out a voice of authority to whip the models into line, grabbing her clipboard that had the run of show schedule.

"Okay ladies… Ivana, Martha, Desiree, Talulah, Clara, Maisie, Nomi and Georgia—you are the first section of walkers—followed by Tumi, Kiki, Lulu, Jourdan, Zizi, Whitney and Minnie… Once you come off you, come back to your rail, strip, and get dressed for your second look—which I will help you with—and so forth… Carmen will make sure you are perfect before you walk out and direct you."

The models all flocked to their stations to quickly get dressed; Chloe was amazed to see them—like a flock of sheep—all doing what she had told them to. The run through went on for much longer than expected with Hilary stopping the show to give her two cents.

"No, not like that… You are *sexy*, you are *powerful!* I don't want to see hunched over shoulders—chin up for goodness sakes!"

Carmen rushed out onto the runway to align the model just how Hilary had directed, pulling her shoulders back and arranging her hand on her hip, with the other swinging low with a clutch bag scrunched in her hand. Time was now ticking over, so much so, that they had to rush through some of the final looks, so they had enough time to go through it once again perfectly.

Backstage, Chloe was a dripping mess, her T-shirt was almost see-through, and her makeup was near non-existent having wiped her brow several times. Her mass of curls, heavy with sweat was now bungled up into some kind of messy top-knot—not a great look, but it was necessary. Plus, the more dishevelled you looked, the more of a professional stylist you appeared to be; but not in Carmen's case, she was always polished and pristine—she could have stepped out onto the runway herself should a model twist her ankle Chloe had thought. It was amazing how the early start had transformed into mid-morning already; a mix of work, adrenaline, and nerves had powered Chloe through the rehearsal, and she was relying on more of it to power her through the actual show—along with caffeine.

The run-through gave Chloe confidence in what she was doing, realising how quickly the models had to get changed in between their exits (which was barely a couple of minutes) and as one girl went on, another came off and got into their next look. The models weren't helpful getting in and out of clothes either; Chloe was amazed at the attitude on some of them.

"Ouch, that hurt!" one yelped as Chloe zipped her into a dress.

They were divas—and that was without the hair and makeup. She brushed it off, she had no time for attitude as she rushed to get the clothes (which were strewn all over the place) back onto the rails in order of exit once again before the show started for real. This was certainly not a glamorous job and not entirely what she had expected, but it was a learning curve that she was grateful for at the same time. Having backstage access to a major designer show, as well as being able to put it on her resume, was a 'money-can't-buy' experience.

It was now approaching showtime, and Pier 57 had received an influx of industry darlings fresh from one of the morning shows. Outside in the reception area, large floral displays were set-up in front of a wall emblazoned with H.V.F all over it. Photographers had arranged themselves in front, ready to capture the attendees in all their glory—no doubt prepared to snap the fashion fails and quickly have them emailed over to the tabloids—ready for ripping to shreds by some fashion critic who wasn't important enough to attend herself.

Waiters were serving Cristal champagne to guests that had turned up on time while the prominent editors and fashion writers raced around town in their private cars to get from one show to another. A show never started without the important people present and usually always started late despite the mad rush to be on time. The front row was always the last to be filled and was treated to an exclusive goody bag which Chloe had put together the day before.

The goody bag itself was not just any party bag; it was a silver calf leather H.V.F shopping tote—a limited edition colour that wouldn't be produced for retail. Inside was the latest touchscreen phone with a limited edition H.V.F signature patterned case with their initials on the back, a spa weekend at a top luxury five-star hotel, tons of makeup, H.V.F perfumes and a gift voucher to use at any of her boutiques around the world. All in all, this exclusive gift was worth over $4,000. 'Wow! Now that's a freebie,' Chloe thought, taking note to try and snag one later herself if she could.

The catwalk was still covered in the clear plastic sheeting, protecting the shiny white lacquer from premature scuff marks from the crew—waiting to be peeled off just before the show started. It was now nearing the deadline for showtime; the models wore white robes as they had their hair and makeup done. Some had already been seen to and were fanning themselves to keep cool and matte in the heat that filled backstage. Not only was it a hot day, but all the heat from lighting and electrical equipment such as blow dryers and straighteners (not to mention the fuss of backstage shenanigans) had created an overwhelming humidity in the atmosphere. Two giant industrial fans circled, pumping warm air back out, not exactly helping the situation.

"Chloe, start helping the girls get into their first looks—now!" Carmen yelled from across the room.

She was busy directing the backstage production team, using her hands to gesture as she explained what she wanted. Hilary was busy assisting seamstresses finalising last-minute alterations—the whole room was in panic mode—but she seemed calm and collected; unlike earlier. If you were thinking of becoming a designer, then the sight of this would either turn you on or turn you off. Chloe always knew that this all went on backstage at a fashion show, but she could never have imagined the intense pressure and tension that circulated through her—she tried to imagine how she would feel if it was her show.

The seats along the runway were now starting to get filled, and Chloe had helped most of the girls into their first outfit. Music was pumping out of the sound system in the main-stage area, sounding slightly muffled and unrecognisable from backstage, while Carmen shifted garments on models to sit on their hips correctly. A photographer had shoved a lens in her face as she was trying to tell a model how to swish her bag as she walked—'Click—Flash'.

"Carmen, Carmen, look this way," the cameraman said. "I'm *fucking* working!" she screamed back. "Can't you see?"

"Okay everyone, gather round," Hilary called through the hustle and bustle. "We are about to start, and I just want to thank you all for all your hard work, and I just want to say… Have *fun!*"

Even though the entire crew applauded her with gusto and excitement, she seemed nervous. Taking in a deep breath, she looked over to the stage manager to signal she was ready to start. The stage manager was a short, stocky woman with tits down to her stomach; she had a harsh butch manner which gave the impression she meant business. She wore a headset that was linked to the front of house manager, sound desk and lighting controller. After a few moments of listening intently into her cans, she signalled to Hilary with her hand to say: 'five minutes'.

The front row was now finally full, even Vogue's editor had arrived; sitting there waiting was the most important of fashion royalty, and they expected another spectacular show. The covering that sheathed the runway was finally pulled back, revealing a glossy walkway that looked slippery and wet under the lights. Chloe was nervous for the models, the collection featured high platform shoes, that were undoubtedly unwearable for 'real people' with 'real lives' like Hilary had described—which was a sign of the world she lived in. The stage manager marched over to Hilary with her clipboard, she was still arranging the models and checking they were in exit order with Carmen.

"Okay, Ms Van Furstein—all is ready when you are," she said, to which Hilary nodded with a deep breath and a smile.

The front of house lights dipped to blackout, and the background music faded down, hundreds of conversations that were a muffled mess from backstage were stunned to silence as the lights came back up. The first model stepped out onto the runway to a light and fun sixties song that had been remixed, and in what only seemed like seconds, she had turned off the runway and over to Chloe—ready to change into her next look. All of the models followed this pattern, and Chloe was over-whelmed with how fast it was all happening, compared to the rehearsal.

In the middle section, there was a small break where the lights and music transitioned for the evening wear looks, giving Chloe a small window to catch up on dressing the models; they would then re-join the exit line where Carmen would re-jig their outfits, suitable for step-ping out onto the catwalk. Hair and make-up fussed over the models which made it even harder to get them changed in time, and Chloe noticed how they weren't complaining in the presence of the designer herself (unlike during the run-through), and she was even surprised to see them actually having fun on the job—model life began to look attractive after all.

The whole show felt like it was just ten minutes long, but was, in fact, triple and Chloe was exhausted. Hilary took her bow on the runway to the sound of applause, from backstage, it sounded like the collection was a success—but you could never be sure. Within minutes of the show ending, the critics (who had just applauded) would be ready to either cut the show to shreds or give a glowing review. It was amazing how people in fashion could be so fickle and two-faced, but at the end of the day, it was the editorial and sales that truly mattered.

"Well done Chloe—you did a fantastic job... I can't believe we did it!" Carmen said, taking her by her shoulders and looking pleased now that the madness was over.

Hilary had returned backstage to be greeted by the models, all kissing and congratulating her. She hugged Carmen and thanked her with a massive bouquet of flowers she had been given on the runway before being whisked off by her assistant to give interviews and attend to photo calls. For Chloe, the real hard work was only just beginning, she had the task of boxing the collection up and having it all sent back to Hilary's studio.

The hair and make-up team were packing up their tools and carpenters, and technicians already began to strip the runway the minute guests had left their seats. Models tried their best to take their clothes with them, but it was Chloe's duty to make sure everything was accounted for and that nothing was stolen. It wasn't true about models getting free clothes, well not during Fashion Week anyway.

All of the looks had to be sent back to the studio, where they would serve as samples in the showroom during buying season, and then for editorial requests. It was crucial that none went missing, the design team would freak out and worry that counterfeit copies could hit the stores before the actual collection did, although you could expect the chain stores would do their best to reproduce it from online images almost overnight anyway.

Chloe was hungry, tired, aching and overall spent after shoving the clothes into clear garment bags and back onto the rails, ready for the vans to whisk them away. The thought of her bed was a comforting one, but she could forget that; Carmen had other ideas.

"Okay, you shoot off… Get some rest and take a shower, after you load the rails onto the van of course. I will come and get you from your apartment… Say, seven?"

"What—what for?" Chloe said, thinking that the day was over.

"The dinner… Didn't I tell you? Hilary is having a dinner party at Cipriani… You have to be there!"

Stepping out later that evening after she had gotten home from a hectic day wasn't what she had in mind, but dinner with one of the most celebrated designers was not something you turned down—especially after regretting not properly meeting Gianni—suddenly she found the energy.

"Okay—sure… But what do I wear?" she said, remembering that she should only wear H.V.F.

"Here—take this," Carmen said, handing her a gift bag. "Go to a boutique and grab something quick... I gotta get ready myself—catch you later!"

Chloe was pleased to not only to get an invite to the dinner party but to also get her hands on a limited edition silver H.V.F tote. Inside it was all the goodies she had packed herself for the front row guests, including a gift voucher worth $500. This gave Chloe a second wind; she always had the energy for a shopping trip—especially a free one. Having bagged her second free gift of the day, Chloe left Pier 57 for the subway to take her towards Hilary's store on Mercer Street.

The sales assistant was extremely helpful, noticing that Chloe had a coveted silver H.V.F tote on her arm and that she must have been a guest at the show (and therefore must be very important) helped. The assistant handpicked a selection of dresses for her to try on, from which she chose a simple wrap-dress printed with a banana leaf pattern in pistachio green. She had already pictured wearing it together with the new shoes and bag she had received from DivaFeet—mixing designer fashion with the affordable was her signature style now.

Leaving the store with her shopping bag swinging from her arm, Chloe didn't have enough time for a nap, but her adrenaline was seeing her through the late afternoon just fine; the second she got in, she stripped and showered before doing her make-up all over again with green and gold eyeshadow to complement the dress. Carmen had stuck to her word; a black town car honked its horn outside at seven p.m. on the dot, while Chloe was applying the finishing touches to her face with some shimmery bronzer.

She quickly loaded her clutch, strapped on her high-heel sandals and threw her treasured gold vintage Palazzo jacket over her shoulders to head downstairs. She felt lucky to be dining with a celebrity designer and her fabulous circle of friends, and the new dress filled her with a heady rush of glamour and sex appeal, knowing she looked the business. Carmen sat in the backseat, looking as fresh and fabulous as ever like she had just woken up and stepped out for the first time that day.

"Wow, you look great! You should wear Hilary more often… It really suits you," she said, happy to have her party partner back in arm.

"Well, I would if I could afford it!"

"Oh, you will… I'm sure of it."

*\*\*\**

Even though the day had been gruelling, it all seemed worthwhile sat next to Carmen in one of the most elite restaurants in town, and sat just a short distance away from Hilary herself, who had noted her sense of style—wearing one of her designs did, in fact, do the trick. The rich, famous and well connected all dined here and Chloe was thrilled to be one of Hilary's guests; mixing with those calibres of people herself at the table—another perk of the job.

Chloe could see the allure of it all now, the early mornings, the stress and hard work, it all resulted in expensive treats that most couldn't afford but to them was everyday life. 'This is probably how Carmen survives working freelance,' she thought, lapping up the fine cuisine; the last time she had eaten out was with Brian at the Avenue Grill.

After dinner, Carmen and Chloe got up to go to the bathroom together, taking the opportunity to take a selfie in a grand hallway mirror on the way, which Chloe uploaded onto Instagram so that her followers would see her having a great time at a plush restaurant. When they had returned, the guests at the table had switched seats to talk to one another, and Carmen took the chance to introduce Chloe to Hilary personally.

"Hilary, this is Chloe Ravens, my friend that I told you about."

"Oh, yes—nice to meet you. So, you are the Raven behind StacksOfStyle?"

'Hilary Van Furstein has heard of my website?' Chloe shrieked inside, just speaking to Hilary Van Furstein in person was an achievement in itself.

"I told Hilary about your site when I proposed that you helped me with the show," Carmen said.

"Yes, I like to make sure all of my assistants know what they are doing when working on one of my shows, and I have to say, I was very impressed... I love the way you mix designer, with the affordable... It's very urban, very innocent—much like your outfit tonight. Don't lose that," she said, referring to the way Chloe had mixed and matched her very own dress this evening.

'Wow,' Chloe thought. 'Hilary Van Furstein has just complimented *me* on *my* style!'

"I love this dress on you too... The colour on you is fantastic and the way you have accessorised it with gold... I hope to see this ensemble on your website, in fact, this is my card—that's my assistant's number right there. She'll arrange any pieces you want to borrow from our press office from the next collection... Seems only fair since you have helped us with the show—call it a favour returned."

Chloe took her card in disbelief, Fashion Week was indeed living up to its expectation, and it was only day one. Here she was, wearing a free designer dress worth $500, at a free dinner party at Cipriani, and gaining Hilary Van Furstein's press office as a contact; talk about a case of being in the right place at the right time—just like Carmen had once told her. Still on good form (thanks to a Methuselah of champagne), the party continued at Soho House, at which point Hilary had called it a day.

Enchanted by the super stylish surroundings of the rooftop pool area, there was one thing that was missing—Dom. She sat down on a sun lounger, breathing in the fresh air of the summer evening, and tried her best to type him a message. Somehow, getting some fresh air wasn't such a good idea, she struggled to compose a typo-free text and realised how drunk she actually was as she struggled with the simple task.

I CUN'T BELIEVE IT! WE JUSF HAD DINMER WIF HIL-
VERY! WISH U WERE ERE, LET'S DO SUM FARTIES THIS
  WEK WIV KERMIT OK? U AVE 2 MEEEET HER!!! XXX

Squinting her bleary eyes at the bright glare of her screen in the night, the mistakes started to come into focus. 'He'll get what I mean,' she figured, stashing her phone back in her clutch before she could drunkenly leave it on the sun lounger.

"Hey, here you are," Carmen said, walking over to her. "Listen I've had enough, wanna share a cab?"

Tired and drunk, they sensibly called time on the celebrations; the rest of the week wasn't going to be spent in bed recovering. Carmen had arranged for them to take in the best of Fashion Week once more, this time as a spectator. Only one thing stood in Chloe's way—work—but she wasn't going to let that stop her from seizing the moment. It wasn't like she called in sick often, and she didn't really care about Palazzo right now at this moment; taking full advantage of Carmen's contacts, and experience was far more important, and it was working well so far.

'What harm could a single sick day do?' she thought, her attendance had been immaculate for the past five years—she was due a sick day… Or two.

# CHAPTER TWENTY-TWO

The Palazzo store was having a hectic week, and it showed no signs of slowing down; an influx of customers and fashion folk had flocked to the store thanks to Fashion Week. Some were just students or tourists looking around the store as if it were a museum, taking anything that was free—from perfume samples to catalogues. Probably to cut up for their college projects, which the staff found rather annoying as there were never any around when you needed them for an actual paying customer.

The restaurant on the third floor was also packed with every fashionista in town that wanted to be seen, for the ones who couldn't get into any fashion shows, this was the next best thing. The womenswear floor was just as frenzied as they were *two* staff members down, with Chloe calling in sick and Dom taking time off for his move, the womenswear team was missing their key staff members. The floor was so hectic, they had to borrow someone to cover from the accessories department for the day.

Dom hadn't said a word about going on vacation to his colleagues; usually, he bragged and rubbed everyone's nose in the exotic locations he would be visiting thanks to the 'Bank of Daddy'. This time, he gave no clues as to how he would be spending his time away from work; not even Chloe knew what he had planned, something that had been playing on Dom's mind—he just didn't know when or how to break it to her.

Meanwhile, Chloe was at home eating a fried breakfast, she needed the carbs and calories to soak up the champagne from the night before. It was the only thing that would cure her hunger and hangover all at once, accompanied with lashings of coffee. Having the morning free allowed Chloe time to do some work on S.O.S, adding new posts and emailing Veronica who had wanted to meet up at some point during

Fashion Week. As she clicked the send button the email, her phone rang.

"Hi, *aheeerm*—Carmen," she answered, clearing her throat.

"*Eurgh*—I don't know about you, but I feel rough as *fuck!*"

"Me too *girl!*"

"Well, anyway, ready to go see a show? I have two tickets to see Lisa Lennard at five."

"Hell yeah!" Chloe said, excited and shocked to be invited to another major fashion show, although all she really wanted to do was relax at home.

"*Perfect*, I'll send over the address for the show… Meet me there. Ciao for now…"

Lisa was an iconic nineties girl group member—The Vibe Girls—turned fashion designer, whose collections were now hot property and this was hard to turn down. Hanging up the call, Chloe's hangover had suddenly dissolved into a burst of happiness, and she was equally as surprised to see that Veronica had already emailed her back.

---

**From:** Veronica Meyer
**To:** Chloe Ravens
**Subject:** Commission Outline Proposal

Hi Chloe,
Your ears must have been burning; I was just writing this email when I received yours!

I am delighted with the current sales figures on products that you have featured on S.O.S. Attached is a contract agreement for a commission scheme I would like to offer you, where you will earn ten percent (paid monthly) from sales of goods that have featured on your site that lead customers to purchase from DivaFeet from your links.

Please print and sign the attached contract and send it back to me ASAP.

Looking forward to catching up, what's your schedule like for this week?

Regards,
Veronica
V.Meyer@DivaFeet.Com

---

Not only had StacksOfStlye now doubled its number of followers and readers, but Chloe was starting to make a name for herself. '*Yes!*' she rejoiced, finally she would make some money from her website, only a small amount mind, but it was a start. Chloe immediately typed a reply, suggesting they meet that afternoon as she was wanted to make the day off work as productive as possible. Since she was already going to be out and about in town at a friend's fashion show, Veronica invited her to a liquid aprés lunch and sent her the location of the after show party to meet her at.

The thought of consuming more alcohol churned Chloe's stomach, but a Cosmo was probably what she needed to set her straight. With a full day ahead of her planned out, she got herself in the shower, her headache had completed washed away down the bathtub drain (as well as mirky water from her makeup she had slept in yet again). Standing in the shower, feeling as though the water was rejuvenating her, Chloe was beginning to think that taking the day off work was working in her favour after all—and not just an excuse to feel sorry for herself.

*

Polina from accessories was lost and completely out of her comfort zone, eaten alive by the womenswear clients. They sighed and tutted at her for taking far too long fetching stock and for being cagey when asked questions that she simply didn't have the knowledge to answer. It wasn't until an experienced employee wasn't there that the rest of the team appreciated their input. Chloe was an asset to the womenswear department, her product knowledge and customer service were second to none—maybe to Dominic—but his absence had doubled the effect on the department's performance.

Poor Polina, she was the sweetest girl in the store, but she couldn't stand her ground and deal with complaints well. Overpowering customers would regularly exercise their rights and walk all over her to get what they wanted, she was an easy target. Because of her sweet nature, she had the knack of attracting total assholes of clients who knew they could bully her into getting a discount, a refund instead of the regular seven days 'exchange only' policy, or even free stuff—depending on how escalated the complaint was.

To make matters worse, Karen Saunders marched out of the lift onto the busy shop floor, clearly in a huff. She was due to attend a party herself and having to come in-store was a real inconvenience. Quickly, she paced the department looking for Chloe; unable to find her (or Dom, who she knew she could also trust), she typically approached Polina—the worst person she could have asked to help.

"Hi, I'm looking for Chloe Ravens?" she asked bluntly, still looking around for her in case she was mistaken.

Finally, a customer with a question that Polina actually knew the answer to.

"Oh, she's not here today… Is there anything I can help you with Ma'am?" she asked politely, albeit nervous about what the next question could possibly be.

"Well, I'd prefer to see Chloe, I need to get my bag fixed ASAP!" Karen said, rather annoyed at the extra obstacle—a dithering sales girl.

"Unfortunately she is not well today and called in sick, maybe I can help you?"

"Fine—Look at this!" Karen said, shoving a Palazzo dust-bag in her face.

Polina reached inside and took out the Gold Rush bag, and as she did, links of gold chain fell to the floor—some scattered under the leather goods counter—never to be seen again until the store would get a refit no doubt.

"Oh, this is not good," Polina said, scrambling together some sort of apology. "What happened?"

"*What happened?* I'll tell you what happened... A very expensive, and brand new bag might I add, broke on me and caused embarrassment at a very high profile party last night—that's what happened! It's bad quality, and you have the cheek to charge me two grand!"

"Five thousand," Polina corrected. "I believe this bag is $5,000, it's new season, from the runway—"

"I don't care if it's from Timbuktu! A piece of trash is what it is! What are you going to do about it?"

"Oh... Erm... I will get my m-m-manager to see you right away," Polina said, stumbling over her words. Enraged clients and faulty returns was another aspect of customer service that she was unable to deal with confidently.

Karen rolled her eyes, she didn't have time for this, she wanted this dealt with immediately; she was hoping to wear it to a fashion show that afternoon. The fact that another member of staff was serving her was frustrating enough, aside from the embarrassment it had caused her. Polina ran to fetch Francesca from the small office where she was busy with emails and reporting. It was funny how managers always found important admin to do when the floor was both short on staff and busy.

Francesca sulked as Polina pathetically explained the situation to her, interrupting and forcing her to deal with a customer. Tearing herself away from the office, Francesca strutted out onto the shop floor with an air of self-importance: tits first—head held high—complete with loud heel clacks.

"Hello, good afternoon *Madam*," she said pretentiously, which had irked Karen right away.

'Who does this woman thinks she is?' Karen asked herself, sensing that Francesca was looking down her nose at her, which she was (it was a natural reaction).

"Well, I usually deal with Chloe… I'm a very good client," Karen fought back, but she didn't have time to go through her lavish spend history.

Determined not to be defeated and sensing that Karen was starting to get fresh with her, Francesca stood her ground; she still had the enthusiasm that only a recently appointed retail manager could have: slightly arrogant and very proud of her position.

"Is that so? I'm the manager here, Francesca Manzetti," she introduced with a cock of her head and a raised brow.

"Well, you're just the person I need to see then… Look, my bag has broken! I was going to wear it tonight and I can't now… I've only used it once—it wasn't exactly cheap either," Karen barked, annoyed even more by Francesca's attitude than the broken bag itself.

"Oh… I'm sorry to hear that… Do you have your receipt?"

Chloe would never ask her for such a boring thing, she was a regular client not a thief; Chloe would never treat her like this, so why should she put up with it from some woman she had only just met?

"Look—I shop here all the time, can't you look it up or something?"

Francesca was enjoying the opportunity to exude her power over a customer, it made her feel managerial and important, which is what she loved most about the job.

"Well, Ms…?" she prompted, looking up at her like she was a nobody—a chancer who had come to return a counterfeit bag in exchange for a real one.

"Saunders, Karen Saunders."

"Well, Ms Saunders, I'm pleased to tell you that as a good client, I am sure Chloe would have created a profile on our database—therefore this transaction will be stored in our computer system."

Feeling quite pleased with herself, Francesca hoped deep down that there would be no trace of her sale, assuming this limited edition piece was a fake—the real reason to why it had broken into a thousand pieces. Searching the database, she found Karen's account, the last bill she could see was for a new season dress and a pair of black heels—no sign of a Gold Rush bag. Upon further investigation, it was true that she was a good customer; her profile totalled sales worth over $200,000. Francesca was forced to come to terms that Karen *was* a serious client after all.

But how did she buy this bag? Where did she buy it from? If she is such a good customer, why didn't Chloe put it through under her profile? All these questions ran through Francesca's head, it had sparked the professional do-gooder inside her, as both curiosity and suspicion settled in. She sensed something wasn't quite right here, and as the department manager, it was her duty to get to the bottom of it.

"Hmmm, there doesn't seem to be this item purchased on your account which is strange," Francesca said, slightly warming to her now she knew she was a big spender.

"Well, that's just *absurd!* Look I have the damn bag in my hand haven't I?"

"And you bought it yourself you say—from our store?" Francesca said, squeezing more details from her; hoping she would slip up and reveal the truth about how she had obtained this bag.

This got Karen thinking... She hadn't given it much thought before, but Karen suddenly remembered that Chloe had bought it for her using her staff discount.

'*Shit!* Maybe I should have gone to a different store. I would hate to get Chloe into trouble, and this new manager seems like a real *bitch!*' Karen thought.

But there was no need to back down now, feeling like she had successfully stood her ground and made her importance known, Francesca practised her excellent customer service skills by proceeding to live the Palazzo core value of exceeding the client's expectations. The Gold Rush bag was extremely limited, and V.I.C customers had mostly snapped them up.

It was so limited that only stores in major cities had received it, and only a thousand units had been produced worldwide; each bag had been uniquely numbered inside, proving its exclusivity. She checked the inner pocket of the clutch where a leather tab stamped '*PALAZZO Made In Italy* #0150' was sewn into the gold lambskin lining. Francesca excused herself to call down to the stockroom manager who confirmed that their store had received '#0148' to '#0152,' proving that the bag had in fact been purchased from their store.

Francesca was a true ambassador of Palazzo (or so she thought) and was delighted with her detective skills so far. This was her time to shine and could possibly steal one of Chloe's best clients from her; she was willing to go the extra mile to make herself look good. Returning to the shop floor, Francesca had some good news for Karen.

"Miss Saunders, I can see that you *are* a very loyal customer and yes, you *do* have what seems to be a faulty bag... This is one of our runway bags, handcrafted by the best artisans in Italy; therefore we have a very limited number available... We do happen to have one left in stock—so I shall proceed to exchange it for you out of goodwill—and I will make sure the new one is added to your client profile for future reference."

Karen was defeated, it pained her to say thank you, but she succumbed to Francesca's generous offer. After all, she had got the result she wanted and without coming clean about Chloe buying it for her, so why wouldn't she accept? After sending Polina to collect the new piece from the ground floor display, Francesca proceeded to exchange the faulty bag. Karen was relieved that she hadn't ratted Chloe out and that she could now go to the ball, after all, leaving Palazzo with a new best friend—Francesca.

With Karen out of the equation, the real investigation was about to begin; someone had to be blamed for this. Looking up its product number on the system, Francesca found the Gold Rush bag on the inventory, it was showing one unit in-store—the faulty one she had just returned—clicking on the bag's details, she brought up the sales history onto the screen. There were only four clients that had purchased the bag overall, but one name stood out from the rest, one that interested her very much: Chloe Ravens.

There it was on the screen in front of her, Chloe's staff purchase bill for one Gold Rush bag—but that wasn't enough for her. Rummaging to the bottom of the dust-bag, she found a crumpled up piece of paper. Unravelling it, she was surprised to find that it was, in fact, a store receipt matching the transaction on Chloe's account. Not only was it hard proof confirming Chloe's purchase, but it also revealed that Dom had put the sale through for her; she finally had what she needed to bring both of them down in a scandalous way.

After checking her facts in the staff handbook, which was now her bible, Francesca was both delighted and shocked by what she had just uncovered; she was officially on course to become Regina's number one. Instead of waiting for Chloe's return to give her a chance to own up to any offence, Francesca practically flew up the staff stairwell to the office. This was her ticket to instant promotion and the demise of Chloe Ravens, which Regina had become so enthralled with, was about to begin thanks to her.

Francesca walked down the fifth-floor corridor towards Regina's office, once more tits first and head held high with pride, through the office's glass walls she could see that Regina was on the phone, so she lightly tapped on the door to get her attention. Regina looked up and finished her call, which was in Italian, probably to the head office back in Milan.

"Francesca, what is it?" she said quick and short, apparently busy with Gianni being in town and organising the retrospective show.

"Well, I have discovered something that I feel will be of interest to you."

"Is that so?" Regina said, looking up and taking off her glasses, rubbing her tired eyes.

Francesca didn't know where to start, but she was going to take her time and enjoy every bit—this was her defining moment in proving her worth.

"I was just wondering if you could clear a few things up for me... It is forbidden for staff to purchase new collection stock on staff discount for the first three months, isn't it? Especially something limited—let's say—a Gold Rush bag?"

"Well, yes… That's all in our contract and guidelines which you can read about in the staff handbook Francesca—"

"—And it is considered misconduct for staff to make a purchase without a managers approval first?"

"Yes, of course!" Regina snapped.

"Oh, and just one more thing—are staff allowed to buy stock with their discount for clients?"

"Well, yes, of course, it is Francesca. Is that all? I have lots to be getting on with."

"Well, no, it isn't actually… Just now, a client came in to return a broken Gold Rush bag purchased from our store, and I have linked it back to a staff account."

Now she had captured Regina's attention. No one had ever dared answer Regina back unless they had a good enough reason to, and Regina sensed that Francesca had something worthy to reveal.

"The bag was faulty, and the client had no proof of purchase, also I couldn't trace it back to the client's profile on our system at first."

"*So…* Which staff member has broken the rules?" Regina shrilled, frustrated at being teased with titbits of information and wanting to know who had dared disrespect her authority by disregarding company policy.

Standing there, arms folded, confident and strong, Francesca finally gave it to her.

"So, I traced it back to Chloe Ravens, that's what! And what's more, the staff receipt was left inside the dust-bag," Francesca said, finally dropping the microphone and the broken bag with all its bits and pieces onto her desk, along with the incriminating receipt. "But there is more… It has come to my attention that Chloe's erratic behaviour at work recently is due to outside influences."

This was becoming very interesting; indeed, Regina looked at Francesca with a golden ray of light; she was her secret weapon and favourite member of staff right now. "Go on," she begged, excited by how much further this could go. She didn't need anything else, she could sack Chloe on the spot, but the thought of there being something deeper whetted her appetite for more salacious discoveries.

"It has come to my attention, from staff discussion, that Chloe runs a fashion blog, which seems to be true... I can show you now," Francesca said approaching Regina's side of the desk.

Regina wheeled her leather office chair back and angled her screen and keyboard towards her. Francesca tapped in StackOfStyle.com and stood back while she waited for Regina to explore Chloe's little venture.

"Have you noticed that there is quite a lot of Palazzo pieces featured in her articles? Even the dress worn by Gabriela Gracia... And today she called in sick, you can clearly see she has been enjoying Fashion Week instead of being unwell in bed, but that's not all... On the day of Gabriela Gracia's premiere, Chloe told me she needed to leave work to see a doctor."

Francesca scrolled to find Chloe's posting of her that night at the premieres' after party with Carmen and Gabi dripping off Chloe's arms.

"See here, this post proves that she was at the premiere and not sick like she had told me... And in an earlier post, she is wearing this same dress... Possibly a second client she has been using her discount for, or just a coincidence? Now, I haven't had a chance to investigate further as I wanted to let you know immediately, but it seems Chloe and Dom could be running a little scam on the side... If you take a look at the receipt, you can see Dom put the sale through for her. I'd say it's definitely worth checking to see if he has been helping her buy all these pieces too."

Francesca's words were like sweet music to Regina's ears, as if she had sung them even. Regina had been waiting for what had seemed like an eternity for a reason to force Chloe out of the company and finally get rid of this *silly* girl who infuriated her immensely. But not only that, Regina was delighted Francesca had caught Dom assisting her in gross misconduct; Regina had waited patiently for something like this to crop up, and thanks to Francesca's detective work, here it finally was.

"Well, I wouldn't worry about Dominic Fraser, he has handed in his resignation to me—which I was going to tell you about—he isn't coming back to work... But this evidence certainly puts him in the frame, and I will be making sure this is marked on his employee record so he can never seek employment with Palazzo ever again."

But there were so many more questions circulating around Regina's head: the website, the vintage Palazzo pieces, *that* Palazzo dress Gabriela Gracia had so famously worn... Could this all be down to Chloe Ravens? Regina knew she was clever, but it seems she had underestimated her. It was time to put a stop to this once and for all, especially now Gianni was in town, he clearly had a soft spot for Chloe after undressing her with his eyes at the store party.

'Could you imagine if he found out that Chloe was the one responsible for dressing Gabriela Gracia in vintage Palazzo? He would just love her even more and probably promote her even.' All these thoughts made Regina both anxious and determined; none of this could get out, it would only make her look as though she had no clue about what was going on in her own store.

"This is, of course, an HR matter now, so none of this is to be discussed other than with me... Is that clear? I wouldn't want a silly comment said on a whim to ruin your progression here at Palazzo, not after you have earned it with all this hard work and diligence," Regina threatened with a sense of hope all in one.

Regina marched Francesca back down to the shop floor to view Chloe's illegal staff purchase on the system, eagle-eyed Sarah knew something huge was about to erupt and had already begun gossiping about it; within moments the rest of the team working that day knew of a suspicious sale that was being investigated by Regina. Staff grew paranoid in case they were the ones being caught out; almost every employee had an eBay account on the side to make extra money. Seeing all the evidence she needed for herself, made this day one of significance for Regina, and one she would remember for a very long time.

Regina wore a huge grin all day long, satisfied that she had an offence worthy of HR's attention and raised it with Victoria for investigation—there was no way she was going to let these two ruin her track record of keeping tight control over the store. Both Chloe and Dom had committed gross misconduct and with all the other fodder, such as her sickness record, turning up to work reeking of alcohol, coming back late from lunch breaks—not to mention her website and extracurricular activities.

Regina was positive she had a good enough argument to finally finish her. This was the nail in the coffin for Chloe, her days were numbered, and without Dom by her side, she was as good as gone already.

**

Unaware of what was going on at work, Chloe was rather enjoying her day off, she had successfully nursed herself back to normal, replied to all her emails and even posted new material on S.O.S for her growing army of fashion followers. It was now approaching lunchtime, and Chloe started to select an outfit for the evening ahead from her closet, choosing a simple black dress with the Chanel dinner jacket over it, completed with black heels and one of the new clutch bags from DivaFeet—perfect for a fashion party and for meeting Veronica.

She stocked up her clutch with lip-gloss, her door keys, and business cards—just in case. Chloe pumped out nineties dance music from her computer as she got herself ready to get her in the mood while doing her makeup. She was excited about finally meeting Veronica, the woman who was helping her make StacksOfStyle an online style destination. She scrunched her hair with mousse and applied striking dark makeup that was enough to transition her from afternoon into the evening—and possibly the night knowing Carmen.

The back of Fifth Avenue, along Central Park, was lined with tents that were holding shows and events for Fashion Week, including the show space next to the Metropolitan Museum of Art where the Palazzo show was to be held. Chloe arrived at the tent holding an after-show drinks reception for an up and coming New York avant-garde designer which DivaFeet had sponsored—their logo was everywhere.

Thankfully Veronica had remembered to put Chloe's name down on the guest list at the door, avoiding her from being turned away (not that she would in the outfit she was wearing). Once inside, Chloe began the task of finding a woman she didn't know, or what she looked like for that matter. Luckily Veronica had noticed her, having seen her selfies plastered on S.O.S daily.

"Hi, Chloe… Or should I say The Raven?" laughed a short woman wearing a printed wrap dress and black blazer combo.

Veronica was five foot nothing (and that was in towering heels) and looked about fifty or so—although the Botox and fillers had muddled Chloe's evaluation somewhat. She had a business-like air about her, but warm at the same time—like the cool aunt that you got drunk with over the Christmas holidays—except this was the middle of the afternoon and judging by the cocktail in her hand, she had already made a start.

"Yes, and you must be Veronica," Chloe said, shaking her hand. "I love your dress."

"Well, I saw your post wearing a Hilary Van Furstein dress and thought I'd get one myself… She should be paying you commission too!"

'Now, that's not a bad idea,' Chloe thought.

"I just love your website… Everyone is talking about it in the office, sales figures on the items you feature rocket as soon as you post! And to have Gabriela Gracia carry our bag was just genius," Veronica said, beckoning to a waiter for more cocktails to be brought over as she guided Chloe to a table to sit down and talk business. "So, what do you think about the commission scheme I sent over?"

"It sounds great, as you know making a profit from what you love to do is the best way to make money, and I'm grateful for your offer."

"Good… Well, there was one more thing that I was thinking about that you might be interested in. As you can see from the sponsorship of this show, I am always on the lookout for new talent, and I love to invest in young people who have potential, and I think you could be one of them… How would you feel about designing a unique and exclusive collaboration with DivaFeet?"

Chloe's face dropped— did she hear correctly?

"Now, I know we don't have much time, but as you have an eye for style and that you are gathering quite a following, I think it you could make it work… Just a small line of accessories that you would wear if you had the chance to make your own pieces. What do you think?" Veronica clasped her hands together and rested her chin on them, watching the surprise in Chloe's face, knowing that she was about to change her life; philanthropy was something Veronica enjoyed very much if it was something she could support and give the right advice to.

Chloe didn't have to think for very long, this was a once in a lifetime opportunity and something she had often wished for in the future, she just didn't expect it to come so soon.

"Well, I think that would be just amazing!" she said with a laugh, was this really happening?

"Karen told me you have great style, and she does always look good herself, thanks to you it seems… Plus, it says so in your brand name—StacksOfStyle!"

Veronica could spot an opportunity from a mile off, and Chloe was a no-brainer for her, especially with her links to a high profile celebrity. Chloe had personality, drive, and ambition, and that was very marketable; Veronica knew just how to make Chloe a style icon overnight that could make money for her also while helping Chloe with her career at the same time.

Nothing in life was ever completely for free, but this was an excellent opportunity for Chloe, and she didn't mind Veronica using her name to make money, she could do with being exploited to make her name known to a broader audience. Chloe was amazed at what she was hearing but wondered how this collaboration would work exactly.

"We could simply design a range of shoes and accessories together and endorse them with your name… I was thinking about calling the range: 'Raven, by Chloe Ravens'. Simple yet aspirational—it would be a mix of lux and accessible fashion for the discount fashion lover—just like you," Veronica said, presenting her brainwave in an already well-packaged brand.

Chloe was delighted, this was turning out to be the best business meeting ever, she couldn't believe how everything was falling into place so quickly; she was sure to make a load of cash from such a deal, as well as introducing her designing and styling skills to the masses.

"Think about it, honey… You are beautiful, young and trendy, we could have you modelling in the campaign, billboards, buses, and mag-azines… And your website would rocket through the roof!" Veronica added.

'It's already rocketing through the roof thanks to you,' Chloe thought, thinking about the impact DivaFeet had on her website already and what a collaboration would also do. Suddenly Brian flashed across her mind, without him none of this would be happening right now; it was thanks to his computer skills, time and affection for Chloe that she was now raking in the benefits. Chloe realised that she hadn't exactly treated him with respect. 'After all the madness of Fashion Week, I am going to get back in touch with him,' she noted mentally, but only to apologise, she didn't want to be getting mixed up in a relationship right now with such possibilities on the horizon.

For the first time in her life, things felt like they were in favour of her developing a career she could be proud of, something she thought she had failed on as she was approaching the end of her twenties, and there was no way she was going to give that up for anyone. She was determined to make this her destiny, it was now only a matter of time before she left Palazzo for better things.

Over several drinks, they discussed the endless possibilities of working together on a capsule collection and had agreed on meeting the following week again, after Fashion Week was out of the way, to get the ball rolling. They would have to work hard and fast if they wanted to get the collection out before the holiday season, but luckily Veronica knew manufacturers that would be able to mass produce a small scale collection quite quickly—and more importantly—cheaply! Chloe felt her vibrate in her clutch, it was Carmen calling to see if she was on track to meet her and had sent her the location of Lisa Lennard's show.

"Okay Veronica, let's do this… I'll be in touch next week, but right now I better run—I'm attending the Lisa Lennard show," she said, getting up to kiss Veronica on both sides of the cheek—like one did at these kinds of events.

"*The* Lisa Lennard?" Veronica said, impressed with the name drop. "Well, you are making the most of the scene, aren't you? I'm just glad you're carrying one of our bags! Try and get her to pose with it like you did with Gabriela for me."

"Don't you worry about that," Chloe reassured. "Let's take a pic to celebrate our new partnership," Chloe suggested, taking out her phone to take a picture of them both for her Instagram. No doubt this moment would provide great content for when it was time to announce her collection.

"Oh yes, of course… I guess this *is* the start of many more posts with DivaFeet," Veronica said, excited with her new show pony, she was confident she was backing the right horse.

"Well, it was fabulous finally meeting you Veronica, I can't thank you enough for the opportunities you have given me so far, and I am excited about our little collaboration."

"You are so welcome, for now, keep this under wraps until we iron out the legal particulars… Speak soon, and remember what I said about Lisa Lennard!"

Chloe hadn't thought about the contractual side of things, but right now she didn't need to; the cocktails had loosened her up, and the successful meeting had made her feel confident. As she strutted out of the tent in her tight-fitting dress, she could feel eyes on her, surveying her outfit. Onlookers surely noticed her Chanel jacket, courtesy of Mrs Ruthenstock (if only she knew the breath of new life Chloe was giving her old cast-offs). Chloe felt like she had already finally made it, here she was strutting around Fashion Week having just secured her very own collection. Outside, Chloe was finally able to answer her phone that had been ringing non-stop.

"Where are you? I've been trying to get hold of you—did you get my messages?"

"Hi, Carmen… Yes, I'm on my way!" she confirmed, hurrying to get out of Central Park and back to the roadside to catch a cab.

The show's location was a secret, only revealed to guests an hour before it was due to start in the Meatpacking District. '*Fuck!*' Chloe thought, she had less than forty minutes to reach the other side of the city in rush hour madness. Everyone at Fashion Week travelled by private car (which Chloe had already started to become accustomed to when out with Carmen), but she had no choice but to ride the subway, which was so not glam in her designer outfit.

\*\*\*

Carmen waited impatiently outside the venue for her, which was a disused warehouse. She was slightly pissed with Chloe for being late, but then again fashion shows always started late anyway. When Chloe did finally arrive it was hard for Carmen to be mad at her, she had her partner in crime back on her arm—and she looked fantastic.

"I'm *so* sorry I'm late, but you are not going to believe what's just happened!" Chloe said, grabbing Carmen's arms in a quick embrace.

"Tell me all about it after the show darling, come… We have to take our seats."

A gathering of paparazzi waiting to capture celebrities as they entered surrounded the entrance, Lisa knew everyone in the entertainment circles of New York, and they all turned up to support her; the moment Chloe and Carmen stepped onto the red carpet, cameras started to flash. Dressed up to the hilt, they both looked chic and glamorous, and to the cameramen, they could be some famous socialites worth photographing, just in case.

The show was exactly what people expected from a pop star-turned-designer—more of the same thing she had been churning out for the past five seasons, just in different colours and fabrics, but it didn't stop them from lapping it up. Chloe enjoyed the show too, but all she could think about was what she would design for her line with DivaFeet; she couldn't wait for the end so she could share the exciting news with Carmen, who she knew would be happy for her, and hoped would help her design it. Chloe needed someone with experience to guide her and Carmen had been a great mentor so far, she would be able to help her make it a success and get the most out of it as possible.

The lights came up on the runway, and everyone clapped as the stick-thin Lisa Lennard came out to take her bow. It wasn't just a 'head dip' like most designers did, feigning modesty—no—Lisa did a full strut down the runway to stoke a pose at the end of it. You could take the girl out of the girl-group, but you couldn't take away the want and desperation for fame and attention.

"Let's get some champagne!" Carmen said, wasting no time to enjoy the free bar once more.

Chloe didn't need to be enticed, her excitement had made her want to celebrate, and champagne was the perfect way to tell Carmen the good news.

"So, where were you this afternoon? I've been trying to reach you all day."

"You are never gonna guess—Veronica asked me to meet her for lunch. I'm now on a commission scheme with them to earn money from the products I sell for them."

"That's fantastic! I told you could make money from being a stylist, didn't I? So, what was she like?"

"She was so lovely in person, but wait, that's not all... We got chatting, and she came up with this idea of making a capsule collection together!"

"Shut the *fuck* up!" Carmen screamed, loud enough for other guests to stop their conversations and look around to see what kind of woman had sworn like that at the Lisa Lennard after party.

"She's calling it 'Raven, by Chloe Ravens'. Can you believe that?"

"Are you serious? I don't know how you do it, I'm jealous! Do you know how hard I have been trying to get something like that all my career? And then you just show up and walk right into it!" Carmen said, with sarcasm and love. "But, I am proud of you kid... Just remember me when you're famous!"

"Well, that's the thing... I'm gonna need you *bitch!* You gotta help with me with this, I have no clue what I'm doing!"

Carmen smiled, they truly were partners in crime. Carmen started to tear up, she couldn't believe what a friend she had made in Chloe and raised her glass to accept her proposal. After clinking glasses, Chloe took a huge gulp, knowing that Carmen was on board made her feel she was in safe hands. As she tilted her head back for another intake of fizz, she spotted Karen from across the room.

"Oh my—Karen's here!" Chloe said, happy to see her, she had much to thank her for and couldn't wait to tell her how well things had gone with Veronica; she owed Karen as much as she did Carmen.

Chloe excused herself and made her way over to. Carmen didn't mind as she seemed to know everyone there as usual and took the time to catch up with acquaintances; this was a networking event for her as much as it was for Chloe, and she had a lot of catching up to do now Chloe was fast making her own progress.

"Karen," Chloe said, approaching from behind.

Karen turned around, recognising the voice but not knowing whom it belonged to. She was both surprised and excited when she saw who it was.

"Chloe—*arghhh!* What are you doing here?" Karen shrieked, hugging her before kissing both sides of her face, careful not to smudge either hers or Chloe's makeup. "Well, not *what* are you doing here, oh… You know what I mean!"

"Where do I start? Thanks to you, everything is kicking off… The website is amazing, and now I have a deal with Veronica for a future project! Everything is going well," Chloe briefed, too excited to go into details, and the music was too loud to hold a full-blown conversation that her good news was worthy of—that could wait.

"Well, thank Brian, not me!" Karen said, which got Chloe thinking about Brian for the second time today.

'Gosh, I've been a total bitch to him,' she thought before she zoomed in on what Karen was holding in her hand—the infamous Gold Rush bag.

"You're finally using your clutch I see."

"Oh, don't get me started," Karen said, reminding herself of her earlier trip to Palazzo. "I wore it last night, but it broke on me… I was mortified! I was at a party and the chain snapped—the bag crashed to the floor, and this thing is so darn heavy it made quite a scene! There were chain links everywhere, and everyone was looking at me like I had a fake or something… Anyway, it's cool, today I popped into your store to exchange it and *voila!*"

Chloe's heart sank instantly, 'She did what?' The feeling that she was about to collapse into a ball of mess had quelled inside her; her face must have dropped and turned green because Karen was very quick to reassure her.

"Oh, honey, don't worry… I didn't say anything about you getting it with your discount for me… So don't worry! At first, your new manager was a right bitch, but then I explained that I was such a good client of yours, she looked me up on the database and simply exchanged it. She wasn't so bad in the end, once she saw how much I spend with you no doubt."

All this information started to swirl inside Chloe's head. 'Looking you up on database... Bag... My staff purchase... *Fuck!*' she thought. Chloe's eyes were vacant, it must have been a minute or so that she had been wearing a lost and alarmed expression.

"Chloe? Are you okay?" Karen said, noticing her face had turned white even with makeup on.

"Yeah... Erm, I'm fine," she said, which of course she wasn't but after everything Karen had done for her, she could hardly say: 'No you *fucking bitch*, you just got me fired, but thank you very much!'.

"I need the bathroom, " Chloe excused, wanting to get out of this place as soon as possible. "Erm, let's meet for lunch or something..."

"Sure... Call me," Karen said, slightly worried but letting her go.

Chloe needed fresh air, and fast. The commotion around her, the loud music, and the fear of being fired from her job had overwhelmed her—she *was* going to pass out! The giddiness from both Karen's confession and the free champagne she had drowned herself with made her feel sick. Chloe pushed past the crowd, making her way outside onto the smoker's patio, asking a random guy for a cigarette. She didn't smoke—only socially, but now was a good time to start up again she figured.

Sitting outside alone on a bench, she grabbed two full glasses of champagne from a passing waiter, hoping the alcohol and nicotine would numb the shock. Then she had a sudden flash—Dom! She had put him in just as much trouble and needed to warn him, although he might already know and been questioned about it—she had to speak with him in case he had more news on the matter. Chloe made several attempts to reach him, but her calls kept on going to voicemail—leaving a message was better than nothing.

"Dom, we're in *trouble!* The bag broke, Karen returned it, and Francesca exchanged it for her... We are basically *fuuucked!* Call me back as soon as you get this message!"

Chloe hung up and sat there for the next half an hour, thinking about how delighted Francesca would have been to snitch on her and tried to figure out what could have happened with minimal facts. But she didn't need to, she could picture exactly what would have happened in her head, just like a movie. 'What's gonna happen at work tomorrow?' she wondered, would she be marched into Regina's office immediately or would they let her sweat? It was amazing how life could suddenly change, one moment she was celebrating a bright future and the next worrying about keeping a job she hated, but paid the rent and depended on at the same time.

Carmen poked her head outside after searching endlessly for Chloe inside. The smoking area was the only place left to look and didn't expect to find her in, she was surprised to find her sitting down on her own, looking like she was suffering a breakdown; she looked like she was going to puke, which wouldn't be cool at such an event. She was already causing a scene just by looking depressed at Lisa Lennard's party where everyone was on cloud nine just by being there.

"What's up—is everything okay?"

Silence, Chloe was stunned still.

"What's happened?" Carmen said, worried at the sight of her and from the lack of response.

"I just got fired from Palazzo."

"What do you mean?"

'How could she lose her job at Lisa Lennard's party?' Carmen thought to herself, she had never seen her like this before. She handed her another glass of champagne, but Chloe pushed it away—this wasn't the girl she knew and had to get to the bottom of it, now very concerned.

"When I went to speak with Karen, she told me she had returned the bag I bought for her on discount—you know, the one I got her in exchange for help with my site?" Chloe filled in, knowing Carmen would get what she meant without going into all the details.

"Oh, honey… Look everything is going to be just fine… Plus, you don't really need that job anymore… Look at you, you're flying!" Carmen said, trying to ease her mind.

"Yes, but that's not paying my rent right now! I can't… I gotta go."

"No, Don't go like this… Let's grab a coffee and talk."

"No—no thank you, I want to go home."

"Okay, fine… Let me get you a car at least," Carmen offered, she couldn't let her go home like this all the way back to Williamsburg on the train, but Chloe got up and stormed off.

Carmen let her flee, there was nothing she could say or do to make this better and figured that the sooner Chloe got Palazzo out of her system, the better. Outside, Chloe hailed a taxi, she didn't think it was a good look to be seen crying on the subway wearing Chanel either.

Sitting in the back seat of the car, the thought of Dominic's involvement in all of this mess returned to her. She needed to speak with him pronto (for all she knew, he could have been fired already), she had to warn him and try to come up with some kind of plan or story that would cover his back, although she didn't know how to get past Regina on this one. Chloe couldn't think straight, let alone come up with a master plan that had a perfect explanation for all this. She could handle the prospect of her losing her job, but being the cause of Dom losing his was something she couldn't bear to think about; it wasn't fair if he went down for her silly scam too.

# CHAPTER TWENTY-THREE

Chloe had made it back to her apartment without breaking down, but the moment she closed the front door behind her, she was a blubbering wreck. She had managed to get undressed—flinging her Chanel jacket on the bedroom floor without a care—and changed into her comfy PJ's. She took off her makeup with a single face wipe—not really caring if she had got all the foundation off. Still, in a panic, she tried to call Dom several times, leaving voicemails and text messages, but it was no good—he was still unreachable.

For the first time, he wasn't there for her; you could say she was getting a dose of her own medicine. There was nothing she could do except curl up on the sofa feeling sorry for herself with her phone in hand, hoping Dom would eventually call back. At least tomorrow was Saturday, but that didn't help matters—she was scheduled to work which she just couldn't face.

*

Waking up on the sofa, the room was illuminated soft yellow from the morning light, having not closed the curtains. Pondering whether to go to work or not, she sat up and stared into space, like she was still dreaming (or having a nightmare). Either way, she had to speak to Dom. She tried his phone again; he hadn't replied to her previous voicemails or messages, and she *had* to tell him what was going on before they both got to work.

Hopefully, he would have some kind of cunning plan to make it all better like he usually did, but his phone kept on ringing. Although, it was still quite early; he was probably still in bed, or in the shower getting ready for work but after a few more attempts, Dom finally picked up.

"I've really *fucked* things up," Chloe blurted out, not even saying hello first.

He thought it was quite ironic really, it should have been him calling her with the news. 'How did she find out?' He had meant to tell her, but it was never the right time, they kept getting interrupted at work, or she was too busy with Carmen to care about him, and now she had managed to find out somehow about his plans, but how? He hadn't told anyone other than Regina, but it was amazing how things managed to leak out and circulate around the gossip mongers at Palazzo.

"Chloe, I'm *so* sorry... I tried to tell you..."

"*What*... You mean you knew?" Chloe said, shocked that he hadn't been in touch to warn her; was their friendship that damaged, that he too would sabotage her—or even worse—did he snitch on her to save himself?

Dom was the only other person who knew about it after all. 'No, he wouldn't have... Would he?' But Dom was just as confused as she was, she had no right to be mad at him; she hadn't exactly been there for him after Jason left, and now he had made a decision to move on with his life—she couldn't be mad at him for that.

"Well, of course... I've known for some time that this is the right decision... Look, just because everything is going great for you, it doesn't mean to say it is for me okay?" Dom said, stern and sarcastic.

"Oh, so you're in on this too then? How could you stab me in the back like this?" Chloe argued, surprised at his betrayal.

"Look, I'm moving on with my life... What's wrong with that? I tried to tell you I was leaving, but it just was never the right time... I'm sorry you found out like this, but it wasn't the way I intended it—how *did* you find out?"

There was silence down the phone, Chloe was confused more than ever before; did he really just say what she thought she heard? It just didn't connect with her story, it was clear he was talking about something else entirely and once again she was only worrying about herself.

"Chloe—are you there? Look… I know this sounds bad, but I really tried to tell you the other night at the store event, but Sarah interrupted us… I handed in my notice at work… I'm gone—I've left Palazzo."

Dom couldn't believe the words had actually come out of his mouth, hearing them aloud sounded very strange, like it was definite— no turning back. Yes, he had resigned, but there was still a possibility he could stay in New York and just find another job elsewhere. It sounded just as strange to Chloe, her heart sank into her stomach at the prospect of him leaving Palazzo, she began to feel sick once more—now she had really lost everything. It was selfish of her, but all she could think of was how she was going to get through this alone?

And with that thought, she started to cry. Dom could hear her sobbing down the phone, and the silence was far too long since anyone had said a word, he had to break it.

"Chloe—are you there?"

"I—I didn't know about you leaving… I wasn't calling you about that," Chloe said quietly down the phone, still in shock.

"Oh, *shit!* Right… I see… So, what are you calling about?" Dom asked, realising that they had got their conversations crossed and he had just dropped a massive bombshell on her in such a blasé way—but at least she now knew.

"I'm talking about my ass being fired from Palazzo, that's what!"

"How—why?" she had surprised him just as much as he had surprised her.

"Karen returned the bag I got for her on discount and Francesca exchanged it for her—I called in sick yesterday, so I wasn't there to sort it out—don't you see? Francesca has obviously told Regina, and now I'm screwed!"

Dom instantly understood her dilemma and couldn't quite believe it either, they both had massive news to tell each other.

"*Fuck!* That's crazy; I thought you told her she couldn't return it?"

"Duh—I did!"

"So, wait a minute... How did you find out about it if you weren't at work? Tell me exactly what's happened, from the beginning."

After explaining how she had bumped into Karen at the Lisa Lennard party, she half expected him to come out with some big plan, but she also understood that he had checked out of Palazzo already and had other things on his mind other than dodging Regina's bullets. It was time Chloe was more responsible for actions and stop waiting for other people to mop up her mess.

"What am I going to do?" she asked.

"Well, since I've left, I could always take the rap for you? Just say it was all my idea," he suggested, not caring about that place anymore.

"No, that's not gonna work... You know Regina will be out for my blood, especially now you've quit!" Chloe pointed out.

"Well, there is only one thing to do then I suppose."

Whatever it was, it had to be good; she was hoping for a witty one-liner to use against Regina—if there was one good enough this time.

"Resign," Dom said, short and sweet.

"*Resign!*" she shouted down the phone, this wasn't what she wanted to hear.

"Well, let's face it... Your heart's not really 'in it' anymore, you're too busy with StacksOfStyle and Carmen, and making contacts and shit... I'm sure something will come of that. If you resigned, it would technically mean that you left and wasn't fired, which of course is what Regina will make sure will happen anyway... So, stay one step ahead remember? Resigning before she can sack you will mean you can still use Palazzo as a reference... You could walk into any store and get some part-time job while you focus on styling and stuff, without having to explain why you were dismissed—think about it."

He had a good point, but it wasn't going to solve everything. The shame and embarrassment of being caught doing such a thing at work ashamed her, and it was sure to be the talking point once it had got out, but it was time Chloe put her pride aside and dealt with things.

"I suppose I don't have a choice," she said, giving in to the reality of the situation.

Dom was right yet again, resigning was better than getting fired. Suddenly, Chloe began to realise that working in Palazzo wasn't so bad after all, the job she hated so much wasn't actually that bad. It was true that you didn't miss what you had until it was gone and Chloe's safety net wasn't there to catch her anymore; she was now going it alone, if she liked it or not.

"So, what are *you* going to do? Have you found some amazing new job or something?" Chloe asked, realising that it wasn't always about her for once and intrigued as to why he was leaving.

"Not exactly… I'm going back to London," he finally revealed.

"*What*—no!" Chloe screamed, so loud, Dom had to hold the phone away from his ear.

"Yeah, I went to see Regina to hand in my notice this week—she was thrilled! You should have seen her face—eurgh—it killed me, but at the same time I don't care… She told me how much of a loss I will be to the store, blah, blah, blah—not meaning a word of it of course. I knew she would be pleased to see the back of me, so I took the opportunity to ask to take time owed so I could prepare for the move, and she was like—sure. So, you see. I've taken all my holiday time so I can pack things up for London."

"What are you saying? That's it—you've left already?"

"Honey—Regina practically rolled out the red carpet for me to go—but like I said, I'm cool with that."

"Aren't you going to have a leaving drink or something?" Chloe said, still not believing he was leaving for London and further to that, he had left Palazzo already.

She reached for a box of tissues, this was too much to take in.

"No… I mean, *we* can—and will—of course, but as for the rest of them, I don't really care if I never see them again, to be honest."

Not only had she lost her job, but she had lost her best friend to another country entirely, and all along she was worried that she would be no longer seeing him at work on a daily basis. Now she wouldn't see him at all. Tears started to fill her eyes, she couldn't bear the thought of losing everything, friends included. Tissues were strewn around her as she wiped and snotted her way through them.

"Look, it's just for the rest of the year then I'm coming back," he said, trying to soften the blow, but he knew that anything he said would sound bad right now.

"When did you decide all this—and how could you without me?"

Dom didn't see it coming himself if anything, he thought he would be leaving to spend the rest of his life with Jason in L.A. Since Jason had gone and Chloe was so busy with her own life, Dom had been spending more time on the phone with his mother back in London. They were always close, and she visited him every December near to Christmas, and he hadn't been back to London in quite a while, it was where he was born and spent his childhood; he wanted to go home.

Dom's father looked after him all right—financially speaking—but he too was busy with his own life, and Dom was old enough to be independent. Returning to London sounded like the perfect answer to all of his problems. It wasn't men, or friends, or work—it was New York that was the problem. City life was getting too much for him, and yes, he was technically going to another city that could eat you up in an instant, but the difference was that was where his mom was—and that was precisely who Dom needed right now.

Rather than making a grand exit, Dom decided he would leave Palazzo quietly and slink off without all the attention and emotions that came with it. And of course, Regina was happy to get rid of him. She knew without him that Chloe would be vulnerable; however, she never dreamt that it would ever be this easy to get rid of her too. Explaining this all to Chloe had calmed her down, she could see his point of view, and her only reasons she had for him staying was for herself (yet again).

"So, when are you going to London?"

"I have to check flights, but as soon as possible... Maybe next week..." Dom said, wincing, knowing that this was another blow.

"What the—"

"Don't be upset… You can visit me in London, and I'll be back in the New Year—I'm just going to spend some time with my mum," Dom said, trying to reassure her again that this wasn't a permanent thing.

"But what if you decide to stay?" Chloe sniffed, by now she had already gone through an entire box of tissues.

"Well, then you will come and visit me in London! It would be great, especially for your website articles… Look—I'm sorry—all of this must be a massive shock for you, but seriously, you'll be fine. Carmen will find you work… You already have some money saved that you can survive on for a while."

"I feel like we have grown apart so quickly… How did this all happen?" Chloe asked, both angry and sad that she had let her friendship with Dom slip away so frivolously.

The simple truth was that Jason had damaged him. His heart wasn't 'in it' either, and not just with work, with life in general—like all purpose had been sucked out of him. Not only had he met and lost the love of his life, but he felt he had lost his best friend too. He loved Chloe, but he was hurt by her; she hadn't been there for him when he really needed her friendship the most—ditched for opportunities that would benefit her career instead.

It was true, he never asked her to comfort him, but it would have been nice not to have needed to ask her at the same time; someone to notice his pain and to make him feel that he wasn't alone, to tell him that everything was going to be okay. He thought that his best friend was the one to do just that. He had imagined she would turn up at his apartment out of the blue with a film and cookie dough ice cream to cheer him up, or maybe she would cook him dinner while he spoke endlessly of Jason, cried on her shoulder, and drank copious amounts of wine together like the old days. Instead, she was busy furthering herself and her career, galavanting around town with her new best friend.

He wasn't jealous, he just felt like he was a liability and was stopping her from doing what she wanted; he knew she was on a mission to succeed and seeing her do that also made him want the same for himself. It was true, she hadn't been there for him after all that he had done for her, he had put his neck on the line for her, and here she was again, demanding that he came up with some big plan to save her. It was all about her, her, *her!* Chloe realised she had been selfish and it made her feel awful, knowing that she was capable of ditching her best friend—not to mention Brian at the same time.

"I'm so sorry… You're always so strong when it comes to guys, I just thought that this one was taking a bit longer to get over… And yes, I have been focusing on myself lately, but I have to… You made me realise that if anything," she said, owning her mistakes for the first time.

"I know, and I didn't want to spoil things for you… You have opportunities that need to be taken, I'm not mad at you for that. I also have a chance, a choice, and I've taken it… I just hope you can see that."

"I can't believe what a bitch I've been!"

"Don't *worry*, we will always be friends—I promise!"

"So, I guess this means I'll never see you again?" she said, feeling as though she was splitting up from a boyfriend, it was the same kind of pain she was experiencing—more than what she had felt for Brian anyway.

"Now you're just being dramatic! Like I said, I'll be back… I mean, I have my apartment here and all my stuff… I just need to get away for a while."

They had spent over an hour on the phone and Chloe needed to get a move on if she was going to get to work, although she really didn't want to. She hadn't even managed to tell him about all the exciting stuff, although it didn't seem so appealing right now. So much had been revealed in such a short time, she was emotionally drained and too tired to even think about showing her sorry face at Palazzo.

Forcing herself to work the weekend, knowing her head was on the chopping block, would be pure Hell—having to bat off gossip and interrogation from her colleagues no doubt on top of it all. It was all too much to take in, but she had no choice but to accept that it was happening. Her future—Dom's future—was all about to change and there was only one lesson to learn out of this: to carry on going forward; life wasn't going to stop, she just had to get through this moment. The question was, whether to make an appearance at work or not?

"I'm meant to be at work today, but I don't think I can face it," she said, unsure of what to do with herself.

"Well, if you're gonna leave, you may as well just call in sick until Monday… It's not like HR will drag you into the office on the weekend. Just rest and do nothing, but get your resignation letter sorted ready for Monday… I mean, Regina will take her best shot to fire you the minute you walk through the door—she will drag you through that entire store to make a point to everyone like some trophy killing—be one step ahead of her remember. Resign before they fire you—don't let her win Chloe."

Dom was right, her only option was to quit, that way Regina wouldn't get total satisfaction. After hanging up the phone, instead of crying herself into oblivion, she opened up her laptop and started to write a brief and direct resignation letter. Even though she was the loser in this situation, she was a winner in other areas of her life. She had lots more going on for her, she was just too bound to Palazzo to make a real go of them; now was the time to break free and really go for her dreams.

Even calling the store to say she wouldn't be returning to work until Monday made her stomach flip, luckily Soraya had picked up the phone to take the message, but it hadn't escaped her that something was going on. "What did you do? Everyone is saying you've been stealing things for your blog," she said.

Chloe could hear her salivating down the line; hoping for an exclusive. She couldn't believe the rumours had already started to spread—and false ones at that. All she could do was hang up on her to cry once more, where she would fester in her slept-in PJ's for most of the day, not even bothering to shower or eat.

**

The weekend seemed long, not like usual, when they would disappear as quickly as they began. Chloe spent most of it locked away in her apartment, not answering calls or messages from anyone. Carmen was one of those trying to get in touch, but Chloe didn't want to hear what she had to say and she definitely didn't want to go out partying. Speaking to Dom had made her see that *she* was the one that had to get herself out of this predicament, and the thought of showing her face at some Fashion Week party amidst all this drama made her feel sick. She wanted to be as far away as possible from fashion altogether and forget her life—for just for one moment.

The anticipation of going to work had kept her awake all Sunday night, after one of the worst weekends ever, it was now time to face Regina. She hadn't slept well knowing that today was *the* day she had been dreading, and woke up early. It had been a while that she was up early on a Monday morning for work, not sleeping in and rushing to get ready. The morning was cool and crisp—soon to be burnt away once the Sun had fully come up—and as she sat up in bed she shuddered with nerves, rather than from the cold air. The reality of what lay ahead dawned, and she started to feel nervously sick about going into work, but there was no getting away from it; the sooner she dealt with it, the better.

'I'm taking control of my life and my actions,' she reminded herself, and with that, she took a deep breath and swung her legs out of bed.

The moment her feet hit the floor, she knew what she had to do to prepare herself, but first—coffee. As she walked into the kitchen, she caught sight of the crisp white envelope on the counter that contained her resignation letter, which she printed before going to bed. After weighing up her options, she knew Dom was right (like he always was) and in the end, he did have a good plan for her. Even though she had blown him out, he still was full of good advice. Chloe couldn't believe how she had treated him, and now she was losing him for good.

Today was set to be one of *those* days from the very start, but as she took a shower, her mind started to play out imaginary scenarios of what was going to go down—conversing with herself and pre-empting what Regina was going to hit her with. She envisioned how the whole thing was going to unfold, it consumed her mind as her body robotically took over with washing and shampooing her hair, while she focused on witty comebacks and points of argument in her defence. Chloe was mentally preparing herself for a fight, riling herself up to be in the mood for a showdown; at one pointed she slapped her hand against the bathroom tiles as if it was Regina's face.

She could feel the poison, like an acid, brewing in the pit of her stomach. 'This is exactly what Regina wants, she wants me to be angry,' she thought, and immediately stopped her mind from roller coasting out of control. She turned the water off and grabbed the towel off the rail to get out, she had spent long enough under the shower, allowing her mind to spiral. Plus, she needed extra time to do her hair and makeup, if she was going into battle with Regina then she wanted to look good—a flawless face of makeup was today's form of war paint— she wasn't going to allow them to see her looking shabby and beaten.

After going through all the times she had worked extra hard at Palazzo, been mistreated or taken advantage of, Chloe realised that she *was* indeed the victor, and no one would take advantage of her ever again. Yes, the thought of leaving and going it alone was scary, but she was about to be free from a toxic environment; a place that was holding her back creatively, emotionally, and in her career.

She thought about how much she had earned from freelancing with Carmen (and that was without even trying) and imagined how much more that could be if she really put some effort into it. The fact that she would be her own boss, and enjoy her work for once, gave her the extra strength to pick out a killer outfit; purposely choosing to wear all vintage Palazzo pieces to rub her colleague's noses in it, showing off what Mrs Ruthenstock had given her without feeling guilty. The journey to work seemed foreign, even though she was taking the same old route that she had done for so many years. She felt numb—like she was walking into the lion's den—in fact, everything about the day felt different; even the train was unusually on time.

Having pushed her way onto a jam-packed train, she looked around and started to notice every little detail: the way the train smelt, the herd of commuters, all the things she had taken for granted before—almost as if she too was leaving New York. It was true her life was about to change, but whether it was for good or bad was something that she would just have to wait to find out; only time would tell.

Walking into Palazzo also felt weird, as if the building itself had turned against her like she was already an outsider. Walking past the staff kitchen and into the locker room, she could hear her colleagues buzz about the upcoming fashion show (all of which seemed so trivial to her right now); they immediately swapped their loud and excitable chatter for whispers the moment they saw her pass. She didn't need to hear their words to know that they were gossiping about her, but if it were someone else, she would be doing the same no doubt. Feeling like a stranger in the place where she had spent so many years, it suddenly dawned on her that she would, in fact, miss it all; as much as it held her back and filled her with frustration, she also had things to be grateful for.

All the funny mishaps and dramas of the shop floor (of which she was now the hot topic), the fun memories of working with Dom, her stylish designer closet thanks to sample sales and staff discount—even for her website. If she hadn't met Karen, she would never have met Brian and got herself sorted with StacksOfStyle. Recognising her selfish behaviour lately had made her think about how she had chucked him to the curb, like a used cigarette butt, which she felt terrible about; if Dom was upset with her, then Brian was sure to be crushed.

While getting changed into her uniform, something else had crossed her mind. She was so sure that today was to be her 'finale‘, but Regina didn't know, that she knew, that they had discovered her incriminating staff purchase. 'Wow, how confusing,' she thought, but it was somewhat of an upper hand, she was more prepared than they thought. Working at Palazzo was a joke at times, but this was turning out to be a farce! Dressed in her brown suit—possibly for the last time— Chloe headed down to her department with her resignation letter at the ready in her blazer pocket; she hated this damn uniform, at least it was one thing she wasn't going to miss about the job.

On the shop floor, she tried her best to carry on as usual, despite wanting to walk straight up to the office and slam her resignation down on Regina's desk. She walked through it in her mind—trying to decide on the best action to take—all the while Sarah chewed off her ear, trying to get details from her and divulging in what she had heard (or made up in her head more like). Realising she wasn't going to get a word out of her, she changed the subject.

"And how handsome is Gianni in real life? I swear he was giving me the eye at the party the other night—I mean—I totally would!"

Chloe wanted to tell her to shut the *fuck* up, if he was flirting with anyone, it was her! However, more enemies weren't what she needed right now; she had to keep calm, if she snapped then Sarah would only coax her into telling all—that was not an option. Telling Sarah the truth was as good as announcing her resignation over the store tannoy.

"Chloe—you're here!" Soraya called as she walked out onto the shop floor, followed by Tristan. "We didn't think we'd see you again… Have you heard about Dom leaving?”"

'Gosh, nothing is a secret in this place," Chloe thought, rolling her eyes; it was amazing how much got out so soon.

Now Soraya had asked, it wasn't long before Sarah went on to tell her about how Regina and Francesca had found a suspicious staff purchase on the system and that they were now investigating—which they all knew was her doing.

Hearing this made Chloe's hair stand on end.

'What's been said? How much do people know?' she asked herself, her mind started to crumble from confident to a nervous wreck.

It was typical that the rumours had already begun circulating, this was classic Palazzo gossip fodder, the daily drama was what people turned up to work for after all— besides the commission and discount of course.

"Okay, look… I basically bought a client—" Chloe started, but was interrupted just in the nick of time.

"Morning everyone, gather around the sofas… I have the weekly figures, and I have some news to share with you all," Francesca said, walking out onto the shop floor, having just collected the sales figures and targets from the office.

Chloe noticed the huge smile on her face, especially as she set eyes on her. 'This woman has been here for five minutes, and already she's acting like she owns the joint,' she thought, feeling anger brewing up inside her again. The team sat on the sofa, excited by this 'news' she had to share, knowing that something scandalous was finally about to be uncovered any moment now.

"So before we begin a new week, as you know, Dominic hasn't been at work the past few days… He has sadly decided to leave and last week was his last at Palazzo; thus he will not be returning to work. This was his wish to leave quietly, he didn't want any fanfare or a leaving drink, but I am sure we all wish him well and thank him for all the hard work and years he has devoted to this company… Please give Dom a round of applause in his absence."

The all clapped weakly—this was hardly breaking news.

"Moving on, last week was a great week for us," Francesca continued as Chloe zoned out, figures and targets were no longer her concern.

All through the morning meeting Chloe felt uncomfortable, she couldn't help but think: 'Bitch, you know what I've done! Come and get me—I'm ready for you!'

After the meeting had ended, Chloe lingered for a moment while her colleagues got up to start the daily chores, expecting Francesca to confront her. Instead, she just gave her a look, a vacant stare, as if she was expecting Chloe to confess everything to her on the spot. As Chloe stared into her eyes, a conversation without words was exchanged; today was the day that they were going to drag her into the office—it was just a question of when.

But nothing happened all morning in fact, no clients, no phone calls, no sign of Regina, and no meeting with HR—it all seemed odd. One thing that Chloe did notice was Francesca's absence, probably speaking with Regina and Victoria, planning their action against her. Left without a manager, the team huddled around a glass table to resume where they had left off.

"So, Chloe, did you know Dom was leaving?" Sarah asked, eager to hear the full gory story first hand.

"I only found out this weekend," she replied quick and short, not wanting to discuss his business or hers for that matter.

"Where have *you* been more to the point," Soraya added. "Were you *really* sick? Everyone knows you have a website now and have been hanging around celebs at Fashion Week girl—"

"—Never mind that, what were you going to say before Francesca came?" Sarah added.

"Nothing... I needed some time off, that's all... And my website really isn't any of your business!"

"Guys, leave her alone.... She's right—it's none of our business," Tristan said, putting his arm around her.

Chloe appreciated him not stoking the fire further, but she knew that telling them the truth was better than having some amped up version of events flying around about her.

"Okay, guys... You win—I purchased a Gold Rush bag for my client with my discount."

Finally squeezing some information out of her, Sarah and Soraya's faces lit up, looking at each other with raised eyebrows as they chewed their cheeks with excitement.

"Don't act like you all don't to it either!" Chloe chipped in. "And then, of course, she returned it, and Francesca and Regina discovered what I have done—*ta-da!* Satisfied now?"

Having told them what they wanted to hear, Chloe separated herself for the rest of the morning, but she could hear from afar that they were talking about how Dom must have been fired because of her. Chloe couldn't stand hearing them gossip about him like that, she didn't want his reputation to be ruined after all he had done for the company. But it was no use giving out any more information, they only heard what they wanted to hear—and the truth was far more boring than what they wanted it to be—so she let them have their fun. After today, they would mean nothing to her anyway.

***

Lunchtime finally came around, and Chloe couldn't wait to escape the shop floor, which now felt like a prison cell. Sat in the staff room picking at her sandwich, her appetite had completely vanished. Although she had escaped questioning on the shop floor from her colleagues, she had traded them for side looks and glances from other staff members who had all heard (and passed on) Chinese whispers about her.

Looking at her phone for the first time that day, Chloe began to read a whole stream of messages from Carmen asking her how she was and what was happening at work. The truth was, she didn't actually know yet and decided to call her, it was easier than trying to explain over text, and it was an excuse to leave the awkwardness of the staff kitchen; she headed outside onto the avenue where she could talk more freely.

"So, what's going on?" Carmen eagerly asked.

"Well, nothing... I'm a sitting duck! I'm just waiting for them to question me."

"Girl, grow some *fucking* cahonna's and get yourself out of there! Just tell them you are leaving as of today and enjoy it! You are *never* going back there... It's done! Give that Regina a piece of your mind and come join me. I'm going to a show, and it will be far more productive than standing on the shop floor waiting for them to behead you—trust me! We have a capsule collection to design remember?"

Carmen was right, Chloe needed to get her fight back on and deal with this situation to the best of her advantage. This wasn't going to be pretty, either way, so she might as well own it; plus, it was true, she did have a capsule collection to design, and there was no time for procrastination. Once again, Regina and the grip Palazzo had over her made Chloe forget about all the good things that were happening in her life. This was it—this was the moment she had been waiting for. Her appetite suddenly came back, and Chloe munched the remainder of her sandwich like a fighter, ready to confront Francesca and Regina with a full stomach. She was going to get *them* by surprise, instead of the other way around.

# CHAPTER TWENTY-FOUR

Chloe re-applied her makeup, spritzed on some perfume, and primed her hair before bounding back down the staff stairwell. Her posture was different, akin to Francesca's head high, tits first stance—it was a walk of power not shame. This was what power felt like, and she was going to enjoy it, even though inside she was shitting herself. Throwing open the door that led from the back of house onto the shop floor with a hearty swing, causing it to thud against the wall behind it, Chloe walked straight up to Francesca in what felt like an out-of-body experience.

"Francesca… We need to talk," she started.

"Oh, right… Okay, Shall we go out back?" Francesca answered, surprised and unsure of what to do; she was the one who was meant to drag her ass up to Regina.

"No, you know what this is about… I want to see you and Regina—right now," Chloe demanded.

"I see… I'll call up to the office and see if now is a good time," Francesca said before marching off to call Victoria for advice—suddenly she was out of her depth.

Chloe's public request on the shop floor to see Regina created another round of speculation from her colleagues. 'Let the gossip commence,' Chloe thought as Sarah immediately approached her.

"What's going on?" she asked, tailing her voice up higher at the end.

"Oh… You'll find out."

Following Francesca up to the office in silence, she tried her best to stamp her heels against the stairs to appear confident, but Chloe couldfeel tears well up in her eyes—she dabbed them away quickly before Francesca could turn around and see.

'No!' she told herself. 'They are not going to get to me, I am going to go in there and do myself justice.'

Arriving on the fifth floor, they made their way to the offices; Francesca knocked on Victoria's door, which she opened wearing her usual corporate, jacket and skirt outfit.

"Come on in," she said with an awkward smile.

Victoria seemed calm and indifferent, much to Chloe's surprise. She expected her to be pumped full of self-importance, having the chance to fire a member of staff, laying down the law and actually getting to do some serious work for once. Instead, she seemed compassionate and almost sorry for her, but Chloe reminded herself that Palazzo HR was useless at their job and Victoria was just another Regina-bot.

Stepping into her office further, Chloe saw Regina sat behind the desk, waiting for her like a lamb to slaughter; she was thumbing through what looked like Chloe's record of employment. This was the moment Regina had been waiting for, the fall of Chloe Ravens was about to begin. Approaching the desk, Chloe saw that Regina was looking at some screenshots from CCTV footage of Chloe and Dom on the day of the sale in question. The staff receipt she had foolishly left in the dust-bag, along with the bag itself, was all present too—staring back at her on the desk—taunting her almost.

"Please take a seat," Regina offered dryly, knowing what was about to come was a very satisfying power to hold, and she had longed for it for some time.

Victoria closed the door and took her seat next to Regina, as did Francesca; all three were lined up in front of Chloe's face, she was outnumbered. Victoria looked at Regina for permission to begin the meeting, moving and wiggling awkwardly in her seat. She seemed more nervous than Chloe was, probably forced by Regina into doing her dirty work for her; like a puppet with Regina's hand up her backside, metaphorically speaking anyway.

"Thank you for coming to see us, Chloe… We have been alerted by your department manager about an issue involving you and a client of yours. We have investigated the CCTV and our database records to try to understand the situation, and of course, out of fairness we wish to talk to you about it before we come to a conclusion."

'Fairness,' Chloe thought, nothing in Palazzo was fair, and three against one was already pretty unfair; it was clear they were taking this seriously, but what could she say? She couldn't exactly lie when all the evidence was laid bare in front of her. She knew that the only thing to do was, to be honest, own up, take the flak, and deal with the consequences. It was time she acted like an adult and not like some selfish child, rules were rules, and she had broken them at the end of the day.

"Well, there isn't much I can say… Hindsight is a wonderful thing, and now I see I have acted wrongly—I can only apologise," Chloe said, trying to disguise the quiver in her shaky voice—reminding herself that she was powerful and confident.

There was a short silence, Regina looked at Victoria surprised as if she expected some argumentative excuse in return—not an admission. Chloe was rather satisfied, seeing the brief look of disappointment on their faces, but she knew she had given them what they wanted. Victoria understood that it was her cue to lead with more jabber on staff compliance and store policy—and more importantly—to just get rid of her.

"Well, thank you for your honesty… However, we have to remind you that staff discount is for employees and their family members—not for friends—and especially not for clients. This puts us in a very uncomfortable situation with Ms Saunders, and we hope not to lose her as a valuable client because of this… I'm sure you can understand how much we rely on the relationships we have with our clients, and our professionalism in doing so—you also put your colleague at risk. Luckily for Dominic, he has already resigned. Otherwise, you would have put him in a very vulnerable position. Therefore we are left with no other option than to take immediate action against you and terminate your contract with Palazzo… Do you have anything else to add?"

This was now Chloe's chance to say what was on her mind, to get it all out of her system before she walked away; anything she said now didn't matter anyway. There was a moment of defeat, a moment where she could have easily just taken action against her, but one look at Regina's smug face changed all that. There was no way she was going down without one last fight, one last thing to make them remember Chloe Ravens forever. She turned her gaze towards Regina directly, this was her first and only chance to put Regina in her place, and she was sure as Hell going to take it.

"Actually, yes, there is… I want to add that I only acted out of frustration—frustrated that I wasn't recognised by my managers for all the hard work I have put in over the years of my employment here. You fail to see positive qualities in your staff and to reward them appropriately, instead, you take advantage of them! Drain them of all hope and enthusiasm… Especially when they take an interest in the company, enough to apply for a promotion!" Chloe snapped, now back in her groove; she had her mojo back, but so had Regina—fully knowing where she was going with this.

"We fairly interviewed you for the press office position Chloe, but you just simply wasn't right for it… And in fact, your record of attendance recently has proven that we were right not to promote you. It has also come to my attention that you have lied to Francesca so you can take days off 'sick' so you can attend Fashion Week parties. I have seen your social media proving that and actually, Chloe, may I remind you that taking employment outside of Palazzo without my approval is also a breach of contract. Your website alone is enough for me to dismiss you. Now, I'm sorry you have taken this personally, but you have done wrong here on multiple levels, and you have even dragged your friend into all of this, forcing him to resign… Do you know how much of a burden you have put on him?" Regina argued back, hoping this stab would knock her.

"Well, firstly, if you are referring to Dominic leaving then you are wrong—and I find it unprofessional for you to bring up other members of staff who are not present to speak for themselves! Secondly, as far as the next level in my career is concerned, it has nothing to do with this company—thankfully—and it never would because you stand in the way of talent! You like puppets—like this one here," Chloe said, flicking her hand towards Francesca. "And yes, I do take this personally… What I have done? So kill me, I took a few days off sick after working extremely hard, giving my all to this company for years! And yes, I admit to using my staff discount for a client, but guess what—everyone does it! What are you going to do? Fire the whole store?" Chloe sarcastically quipped, but Regina wasn't going to let her have the final word on the matter.

"Well, it's your duty to tell us if anyone is misusing their discount. It is an abuse of company benefits and the rules are in place for everyone."

"Is that so? Then let's start with you," Chloe snapped.

Regina was stunned by her braveness. 'How dare you,' she thought. If there was any chance of her keeping her job, then she had certainly blown it now, but to Hell with it, Chloe was on a roll. All this stress for a shop job was just not worth it, and she was now happy to be pushed—this felt good. She could feel the poison leaving her body, replaced by golden honey, repairing any damage that this place had ever done to her.

Now was the time to get out for good and there was no point sitting here getting upset, begging for their forgiveness. Unleashing years of pent-up frustration on Regina felt terrific, something she had only fantasised about before but was now actually doing it. She had even surprised herself with her confidence, but she was going for the home run.

"You use your discount for all your *friends*, who come in during work hours and we have to serve them like normal customers… At least I did it behind your back and not in front of your face like you do to us… And you're a director! *Ha*—that's a joke! Ever heard of learning from the best? All this hypocrisy comes from the top Regina—meaning you… It's your negative attitude that leads to this toxic environment you've created, and for good people like me to misuse benefits… So what should I do now? Take a grievance out against you? Don't worry—I wouldn't put myself through the unnecessary stress—I quit!" Chloe said, whipping out her letter, slamming it down on the table with a slap of her palm before getting up to make her exit.

Regina was shocked, stunned, and silenced all at once—as was Francesca and Victoria. In all her years Regina had never experienced such a dressing down, and Chloe Ravens was the one to finally give it to her. There were no words to describe how angry she felt, but she couldn't argue back; besides, she had gotten her way and pushed Chloe over the edge and out of Palazzo. Feeling as though she had exorcised some demons, Chloe stormed out with a smirk on her face, making sure the office door shut with a heavy slam behind her, so heavy and loud that it rattled the glass windows.

Running down the stairs, she ignored everyone on the way, desperate to leave the building altogether. Emerging on the shop floor had made her colleagues head's turn, they had been speculating about what was being said in Regina's office; this was as exciting as the shop floor got and they were desperate to know the full story—so far, they only had titbits of information and Sarah's take on the situation. Sarah, being the staff spokesperson that she was, galloped up to Chloe in sheer excitement, tugging her arm and forcing her to halt.

"Hey, Chloe… Where have you been? Won't you tell us what's happened? We do care you know…"

Chloe smiled at her, you had to give it to her, she was persistent. This was her chance to set the record straight in her own voice, not from Francesca's point of view—and certainly not from Regina. Soraya and Tristan also saw that Chloe was back and ran over to hear the latest news from the horse's mouth.

"As I said, I used my staff discount for a client, and I'm not gonna stay here any longer for them to have such a hold over me… And just know that Dom has left to go back to London—he didn't have a part in *any* of this. So, guys, I'm outta here! If you want my advice, don't let these *bitches* get you down… And by 'bitches', I mean Regina and Francesca!"

"So what are you going to do now?" Soraya asked.

"Watch me…" Chloe said as she continued marching towards the staff exit, taking off her jacket and starting to unbutton her blouse as she left the floor—flicking her head to make her hair swish like she was starring in a tampon commercial.

'Wow!' she thought, she didn't expect such a rush to overcome her—it felt so good. Her colleagues all stood there, ignoring waiting customers as they watched her depart in disbelief. Sarah smiled as Chloe walked out with her head held high and her name intact—something she could only dream of having the strength to do herself. Chloe was a trailblazer, a Palazzo pioneer, a martyr for the staff and for that, Sarah would make it her mission to spread the real story of what had happened in her honour.

"That's my girl!" Sarah said proudly.

*

Walking out on her job seemed like a good idea in the heat of the moment, but arriving back home, Chloe wondered what in the Hell she had just done. Until she remembered the look on Regina's face, like she had slapped her hard with her bare hand. Chloe called Dom on her way home to fill him in on the action and invited him round to her place. She had so much to tell him, along with the more positive news of her upcoming collection with DivaFeet; it didn't take long for him to come over (he too had news for her) and Chloe was glad to have his company after being so neglectful, a sign of how genuinely loyal he was to her.

"I'm telling you, Dom, you should have seen her face! It was so satisfying—she even tried to bring you into it—but I sure shut her up! And as I walked out, I made sure the team knew you had left on your own accord and that I was the one who screwed up."

Dom smiled, he respected her efforts to clear his name, although he wasn't bothered in the slightest by what they thought of him. Although it was only afternoon, they cracked open the bottle of champagne Dom had brought with him to celebrate their new beginnings together—what was this new era going to deliver for them? Sure, Chloe had savings, but not more than three months rent at the most. That very thought had started to freak her out, and Dom could see she was beginning to lose grip, coming to terms with reality now she had time to digest it all.

"Look, I know it must seem weird right now, but you said it yourself—you're so busy with other projects and commitments at the moment," Dom said, trying to bring her back into the right state of mind.

"Yeah, but that's not gonna pay the rent, is it?" Chloe argued back, thinking about her plan of action, which was so far was none existent.

It was true, she would still need to work in the meantime, but the question of 'doing what' was hanging over her head; styling had brought in some money but nothing concrete, and yes, she had an upcoming collaboration with DivaFeet—but that wasn't set in stone either and could be dropped if Veronica wished.

"I also have to tell you something—but don't freak out okay?" Dom said, learning from his previous mistake of holding back from her.

"Go on…" Chloe said nervously, not sure she could take any more surprises but thought that maybe, just maybe, he had changed his mind about leaving New York.

"I've booked a flight back to London for this Friday," he winced.

"*What!* So soon? But what about your flat, what about all your stuff, what about…"

Chloe stopped herself, she was about to say: 'What about me?' but had learned the hard way about being selfish.

"I know, I know… My dad wants me to pack all my things into storage so he can rent out the apartment while I'm away… I've been de-cluttering all day and packing things up that I'm not taking with me."

Then, a sudden brainwave flashed across his mind: 'She should move into my place,' he cleverly thought.

It was the perfect solution; it was better than letting a stranger live there, and most of his belongings could remain too—and he could return whenever he liked. Dom made a mental note to call his dad first before telling her, just in case, but he was sure that his father would be happy that he had found a trustworthy tenant for him. Chloe's phone rang, interrupting both hers and Dom's train of thoughts—it was Carmen. She had been thinking about Chloe all day long, and like everyone else, she wanted to know what had happened.

"Hi, Carmen… Sorry, I haven't got back to you—I've had a mental day as you can imagine."

"*So?* What happened?"

"Well, I quit basically… If I didn't leave, then they would have fired me anyway—I mean they practically did… So let's just say, I gave it to Regina and left with a bang!" Chloe said, making light of the situation, it was all she could do to save herself from crumbling.

"No way! What exactly did you say?"

Chloe filled Carmen in on the in's and out's of the meeting, elaborating on some parts, proud of her performance. It was the only way she knew how to deal with it all. By not acknowledging the fact she was now jobless, it made the reality more manageable—and losing the plot was not an option right now.

"That's brilliant! You wanna know something else that's great?" Carmen said, with a hint of suspense in her voice, like she was about to reveal something that was of perfect timing. "Well, you know there is this big event next week to close Fashion Week?"

"Eurgh, how could I forget; I'm trying to forget that place exists!" Chloe said; even having just quit, she still couldn't get away from Palazzo.

"Well, anyway—Gabriela has just called me to ask if we can find her another dress for it—she has been looking at your website and is very interested in the gold embroidered gown you have… You know,

that showpiece from last season? And not only have I negotiated another budget of $3,000—which you could do with right now—but I have
bagged invites on Gabi's list to the show and after party!"

Chloe jumped up onto the sofa and screamed down the phone—
did she just hear correctly?

'What the fuck's going on?' Dom mouthed to Chloe, just as shocked
but her sudden reaction.

Carmen wasn't only well connected, but quite clever too, and like
Dom, she always had a good move up her sleeve.

"Oh—but wait! That dress is an old press sample—it's a mess—
there's rips, missing beads, it badly needs a clean; a lot of work will be
needed on it," Chloe said, remembering the state it was in when Kim
had rescued it from the depths of the press office cupboard.

"Let me worry about all that… What Gabi wants, Gabi gets—anyway—she is a midget remember? We will end up cutting most of the
length off again so we will have plenty of spare beads and fabric to play
with, I'll get seamstresses on it right away… Just get me that dress first
thing tomorrow, and you're on the list—okay?"

"Deal! If it means we get to go to the Palazzo show, then it's yours!
Oh, can Dominic come too?" Chloe added in before Carmen could
hang up.

Dom's ears pricked up, he too wondered if he had heard correctly
and was now perched up next to Chloe, waiting for her to get off the
phone.

"It would be great if we were there after we have both left Palazzo
on such scandalous terms! Could you imagine if Regina saw us there?"
Chloe laughed, imaging the magical moment in her head.

"What? Dom's left too—you didn't get him sacked as well did you?"
Carmen said.

"No—no… This bitch has decided to leave for London and didn't
tell me… Anyway, he can tell you himself when you two finally meet."

"Well, I'll see what I can do… But you are right—Regina would
just hate that. Especially as you will be with *me* too!" Carmen sniggered,

it was just as beneficial to her as it was to them to bump into Regina with them on either arm at the Palazzo retrospective show—the jewel in the crown of New York Fashion Week.

The look on Regina's face would be priceless, and she certainly wouldn't be expecting to see them at the most prestigious show of New York Fashion Week, especially after she had managed to get rid of them; it would make them look like they were already onto bigger and better things—which they were. Hanging up the phone, Chloe sighed a breath of relief and turned to Dom. Sometimes things happened for a reason and when at rock bottom, the only way was up, and that's exactly where Chloe was now heading.

"Babe, you better re-arrange your flight; we're going to the Palazzo show!" she revealed triumphantly and with a look of sweet revenge on her face.

**

*His hands skimmed her waist, the feeling was magnetic—it made her stomach quiver which she could feel deep down—it was borderline foreplay, his touch was that powerful. Staring into his steely blue eyes, she ran her hands through his thick, dark long hair and gave it a tug as she pulled him forward for a deeper kiss. She could feel him pressed up against her, as was her mouth, hard against his...*

Chloe woke up sharp and alert. The night was sticky with no air, and she was hot and flustered; she got up to open the window to allow a breeze in. It was two a.m., and she was disgruntled about being woken up after an emotionally draining day, but it wasn't like she had work in the morning. Suddenly her erotic dream hit her, she had been dreaming about Gianni, and with the retrospective show in just a day's time, the possibility of seeing him all over again excited her, and she hoped she would get even closer this time.

# CHAPTER TWENTY-FIVE

Chloe imagined that losing her job would mean moping around her apartment feeling sorry for herself, but she couldn't have been more wrong—there wasn't to be a single moment more to think about it. Today's priority was to get the dress over to Carmen before anything else, she carefully packed it in some tissue and a garment bag, ready for a car to whizz it over to her. Carmen had booked in a fitting with Gabi that same afternoon, eager to start the alteration process as they were pressed for time. Seamstresses would have to work through the night to repair the damage, cutting off most of the hem once again to patch up missing panels of fabric to breath new life into it and get it red-carpet ready.

With that out of the way and with no day job to rush to, Chloe made the most of it and went to a yoga class before coming back home to avocado on toast and a protein shake brunch. She loved working out (something else she had been neglecting) and was reminded of how good exercise made her feel; she needed to feel toned and slender at the ultimate event in the fashion calendar. Just the thought of attending the most exclusive event of Fashion Week had sweetened the blow of losing her job, and that Dom was soon to leave for London. On top of all that, she was dressing the celebrity of the moment again and was slowly building a reputation of being able to source unique vintage pieces.

The added possibility of seeing Gianni face to face once again made it even more exciting if such a thing were possible. Although she knew that the amount of security that followed him everywhere meant that she probably wouldn't even get a sniff of his aftershave. Having all this to look forward to had made Chloe feel like a star, she had butterflies in her stomach just thinking about it.

She had a feeling, a feeling that brewed in the pit of her stomach, this time it was a good feeling—her life was taking the desperate turn she yearned for, and she had to look smoking hot for it. Being seen by Regina made her both nervous and happy, she had already wiped the smile off her face but this was a chance to show her just how resilient she was, and that Palazzo wasn't the end of her career—it was just the beginning.

Dom wasn't able to rearrange his flight back to London, but he wasn't going to miss this for anything—being hungover on the plane the morning after was a price worth paying. He had also spoken to his father about finding the perfect person to move in and look after the apartment while he was gone. Dom's father was enjoying the summer in Hawaii with his wife too much to even care, which was to Chloe's advantage.

"So, you won't mind my friend Chloe staying at my apartment until I get back then?" Dom asked, even though it was more of a demand than a request.

"Well, do I have a say in the matter?"

"Not really," Dom confirmed.

"Well, she's still gonna have to pay me rent—right?" He could hear Dom puffing a sigh down the line. "Do you know just how much I could get for your place?"

"Yes, dad, but Chloe is reliable—think about all the money you will save from putting my stuff into storage? I'll tell her that you will charge her a subsidised rent, seeing as she's safeguarding both the property and my belongings… Enjoy the rest of your holiday! Oh—say hi to Sheena for me," Dom said, trying to butter up his father by being kind to Sheena for once.

Meanwhile, Chloe was searching for something to wear for the show, and she had learnt from working on the Hilary Van Furstein show that she had to wear no other than Palazzo (which was typical now she no longer had staff discount at her fingertips). It was more important than finding another job, and this *was* kind of work-related.

Of course, there was only one dress she had that would fit the occasion—the white and gold corset dress that she had purchased from the sample sale at a bargain price. Unfortunately, that was the only dress Gabriela was interested in wearing herself, and she was right too, once fixed it would be fit for a superstar like her. Selling it was a double-edged sword, it was the dress of her dreams but at the same time having three grand in her back pocket seemed more alluring to her with no steady income.

The money wasn't the only incentive to sell, as well as dressing a celebrity, it also granted tickets to the Palazzo retrospective show which money couldn't buy. After trying on blazers, tops and skirts, Chloe came across two other dresses purchased at the Palazzo sample sale which hadn't had an outing. The options were the black silk dress or the red jersey dress with the gold halter neck bangle, eventually deciding the latter was the best option for a glittering bash. She had dismissed it before, but on second glance, it was sexy enough without being too 'try-hard' like the black dress which was attached only by buttons down the side, plus, she had only just gotten herself back in the gym and could imagine her pale body bulging through the buttons like soft dough—she had to look her best.

The red dress was sexy enough with its thigh-high slit and halter neck style, it showed just the right amount of skin. Holding the dress up against herself in the mirror, her imagination started to run wild. She envisioned herself wearing it on the red carpet against her loosely curled blonde hair and was sure she would stand out for all the right reasons—and that's exactly what she aimed to do. She wanted to make people ask 'who's that girl?' and to grab the attention of everyone around her—Gianni included. And hopefully she would bump into Regina—accidentally of course—who would no doubt still be stuck in her boring blazer and pencil skirt, even at the fashion event of the year.

With her outfit trauma now out of the way, Chloe headed over to Dom's apartment. He had been very busy packing for London and throwing out all the unnecessary crap he had collected over the years.

It was only fair that Chloe helped him, it was the least she could do now she was back on board with being his best friend.

"I want to make as much space as possible," Dom said as he went around the apartment with a black sack.

"Surely you can leave some things here, you're only going to London for six months—or so you said!" Chloe reminded him with a suspiciously raised eyebrow.

"I can't take *everything* with me!" Dom said, holding up a Barbie doll he once bought from a vintage fair, asking for her opinion on whether to keep or trash—Chloe whipped it out of hand and stashed it in her handbag. "Besides, I've found someone to live here and pay the bills, look after the place until I get back… I'm just taking the essentials to London—everything else can go… Anyway, I will want to buy more stuff there, obviously!"

And he wasn't lying about that, Dom was a shopaholic and especially when in London where his mom loved to spoil him in Knightsbridge. Dom preferred designer clothes of course and luckily for him, so did she.

"So who's gonna move in here?" Chloe said, upset at losing her Manhattan crash-pad where she had stayed over after wild nights out.

"You," Dom said casually, not even looking up from chucking stuff into the black bin liner.

"*What?*" Chloe gasped, confused by his answer.

"Yes, *you!* I mean, I need someone here, and you need a cheap place to rent… We own the place so just pay the bills and keep the place clean while I'm gone, then when I return we can review the situation."

He had the whole thing worked out, another example of how she could always rely on him no matter what; she couldn't believe just how lucky she was, even after what their friendship had been through lately. Walking out of her job, not knowing where she would end up had suddenly all turned out to be okay. Not knowing what to say, Chloe threw herself at him for a big hug, feeling tears of joy and relief in her eyes.

"You're such an amazing friend… Thank you!"

She was going to miss him very much, but by living in his apartment, it felt like a definite way of keeping their friendship intact, even with him gone. This would also allow her to breathe a little about her future before diving into a dead-end job out of desperation just to pay the rent. She got on the phone to her landlord right away to let him know she would be leaving as soon as possible, she had neither time or money to waste.

After helping him pack and clean up, a break was much needed, so they left the apartment for fresh air and to make their way to back to Chloe's for a take-out dinner. Checking her phone en route, she saw she had a long email from Veronica called 'Project Raven' which intrigued her, but there was also a text from Carmen about the fitting which she read straight away.

CIAO CHLOE, SUCCESS! GABI LOVES THE DRESS, AND IT FITS LIKE A GLOVE… YOU'VE DONE IT AGAIN. OH & BOTH U & DOM R ON THE LIST FOR THE SHOW AND PARTY :) XXX

Chloe was thrilled that everything was going well and that their invites were sealed, as was Dom. Forget the standard Palazzo leaving party in the bar around the block from Fifth Avenue—this was the leaving party he really wanted! Back at her apartment, she checked her inbox immediately to read Veronica's email. It seemed she wasn't too drunk to remember what they had discussed during their meeting.

---

**From:** Veronica Meyer
**To:** Chloe Ravens
**Subject:** Project Raven

Chloe,
It was so lovely to finally meet you and catch up, Karen said she bumped

into you at the Lisa Lennard party... Anyway, I have attached some of my ideas for the 'Raven by Chloe Ravens' for DivaFeet collaboration. I spoke to my team, and we want it to retail over the Holiday period—since that's our busiest time of year—and it will maximise exposure for a new designer such as yourself.

That leaves us with just a month to design it and get it ready for production with our manufacturers. Think glitz, glam, and luxurious—send me your ideas, and I will arrange a meeting with our design team right away. I would like around ten different items: five shoes/five bags for example, but I'll leave that to your imagination.

Just concentrate on the designs for now and the overall look of the collection. I will consult with my team and then we can all meet to share our ideas!

Ciao for now,

Veronica
V.Meyer@DivaFeet.Com

---

"*Fuck!*" Chloe shouted at the top of her voice so her neighbours could hear; this was really happening.

"What now?" Dom said, going through the top kitchen drawer to find the take-out menu for the Thai restaurant he loved in her neighbourhood.

"It's Veronica, she's emailed me the details about the collection—she wants a line of ten pieces!"

Chloe was eager to start researching ideas for the collection straight away, but she had all the inspiration she needed coming to her. Vintage pieces were all the rage, and with the Palazzo retrospective show set to be the talk of the fashion world, she could simply take inspiration from the show and Palazzo's past collections. Of course, she would have to change the logo and patterns, make them better with her own Raven logo even. 'Raven by Chloe Ravens' was going to be a huge success, she thought she could see it happening before, but now she could feel it.

"I know you're excited and all that jazz, but you also need to start going through your stuff…" Dom said, looking around her apartment which was cluttered with clothes.

"Oh, wait… I haven't shown you what I'm wearing to the show yet!" Chloe dashed out of the room to grab her outfit which was hanging up on the back of her bedroom door. "What do ya think?" she said, holding it up against her.

Dom nodded in agreement, but it got him thinking before he finished packing he would need to find an outfit to wear too. 'Maybe this is a bad idea,' he thought, looking at the menu in his hand.

"Anyway, I'll have plenty of time to pack when you leave… Won't I?" Chloe said sarcastically as she reached in her handbag, pulled out the Barbie she rescued from the trash bag and set her up next to the key dish by the door.

But he had a point, she did a lot of junk that needed throwing out that would take time to sift through; she just couldn't be bothered right now, what with everything else going on right now. Old clothes she no longer wore (but still clung onto) could go to the church charity fund— karma was important to her now she had a turn of good luck—which seemed the right thing to do since Mrs Ruthenstock had supplied her with an entire new designer wardrobe. After ordering some food, they attempted to tidy and sort through her life's belongings while Chloe took this chance to pick Dom's brain about what she should design, while she still had his genius mind on tap.

"This show is going to be the most talked about fashion event and those things you can't buy anymore… So I was thinking, I could fill that gap with my own version… I do have the inside knowledge after all," she beamed, proud of her artistic direction.

"Sounds like a great idea—just make sure you don't completely rip them off—you don't want a lawsuit as well as P45," he joked, meaning it at the same time.

Chloe wasn't just making this collection for the money, it was about revenge; finally, she would be doing something she loved and was in control of. The amount of exposure it would garner was also priceless, and she was sure it would open more doors for her—even though she didn't dream of becoming the next big fashion designer—this could turn out to be a commercial money-making machine, and one that she desperately needed. That was another point, she had never asked how much she would earn from all this? Chloe made a note to go through all the particulars with Carmen, she would know what to do and charge for such a partnership.

By now, they had given up trying to choose what to keep and what to trash from her never-ending closet—she would have to see to that herself when she had the time, and the delivery guy was now outside. Sitting on the sofa with their Thai spread laid out on the coffee table, Chloe opened up her laptop so they could research Palazzo's past collections while they ate.

"Maybe my brand logo should be my Raven logo too? Tie the website and the label together," Chloe said through mouthfuls of noodles.

She got up to grab a card from her purse to show him, the raven emblem was now her signature, but it reminded her of Brian every fucking time she saw it. She couldn't keep on feeling like this forever, karma was a bitch, and there was no way it was coming back to haunt her this time—not now—she already had learnt her lesson. Chloe tried to think about a way to apologise to Brian but her constantly ringing phone made it impossible. Noticing it was Carmen, she picked up.

"Chloe, darling—I need your help!"

"Sure, what is it?"

"I need something to wear for the show, do you have anything I can borrow?"

Chloe could hear the panic in her voice.

"Wait a minute—you need me to dress you too?" Chloe said, laughing down the phone. 'Isn't she the professional stylist who is meant to be advising *me* on what to wear?' she thought.

"*Ha!* Very funny... I have lots of things I can wear, but I don't have anything from Palazzo, and as I have taught you—one only wears clothes by the designer who's night it is. You must have something decent for me to wear after years of staff discount—no?"

Carmen had a point, Chloe had her own little archive going on from all the purchases her wages went on over the past four and a half years.

"Hmmm... Let me think," Chloe said dashing over to the rail. To find something appropriate. "How about a black Chanel tux jacket and pants?"

"No darling—*listen* to me," Carmen said strongly; Chloe could hear that she was using her hands to gesture like a true Italian—she didn't need to see her to know that was exactly what she was doing right now. "It has to be *Palazzo!*"

It seemed she still had much to more to teach her.

"Of course—I wasn't thinking."

Chloe went back to the drawing board and clapped eyes on the red dress she had her heart set on wearing, which meant there was only one other option left. "Okay... I think I've found it!" she said, holding up the sexy black silk dress for Dom's approval—he made an 'OK' sign with a wink.

"Wonderful darling—send me a pic, I want to see it."

Chloe put her on hold while she sent over a snap of the dress.

"Okay, now you really are after my gig aren't you?" Carmen joked, loving what she saw.

If anyone was going to pull off such an iconic and striking dress, showing body with no option but to go bra-less, then it was Carmen; her lithe figure and petite breasts would do the dress justice. For a minute, Chloe worried that Carmen would steal the limelight away from Gianni, should she be lucky to see him again—she shook her head and told herself she was being silly. This was the least she could do for Carmen and selfishness had got her nowhere so far.

"Can you meet me first thing tomorrow?"

"Where?"

She didn't even know the plan for dressing Gabi yet, let alone Carmen. This styling lark was always a last minute thing when it came down to details, which Chloe was now becoming accustomed to; being a hot sweaty mess rushing around town before a major event was the norm.

"Meet me at nine for breakfast in town, Sadelle's in SoHo—we need to go over a few things before the show… But night-night for now, speak tomorrow!" Carmen said, hanging up the phone now she had crossed that task off her list.

"What was that all about?" Dom asked.

"Carmen needs to borrow a dress for tomorrow night," Chloe said, realising that the day had finally come.

And just like that, another bomb dropped—tomorrow they were finally going to the Palazzo retrospective fashion show. Chloe suddenly dropped the fork, she needed to prep, get some beauty sleep and apply a quick fake tan if she was going to look her best.

*

Thursday had sprung like a panther in the wild. Waking up a brown mess, sticking to the bedsheets, Chloe got up and rinsed off the fake tan she had Dom help her apply evenly to her back before he headed home, revealing a light colour that was sure to look horrible in the daylight but good enough for the evening. She quickly got ready and stuffed Carmen's dress into a paper palazzo bag (her kitchen cupboard was full of them) and left her apartment for the trip into town.

Even though she had quit her nine-to-five, she was still doing the early morning commute. It was crazy to think that the final day of New York Fashion Week was now here, and so much had happened in between. Riding the Hell train to meet Carmen, Chloe thought about everything that had happened to her; she had indeed experienced the best and worst of it— what a crazy ride it had been from fashion shows, parties, and being jobless—all in one week. It was even crazier to think that she was now attending the hottest event of the week, despite everything. Her endless thoughts had helped her will the journey away, finally arriving at Sadelle's.

"Thank you so much for this," Carmen said, immediately unzipping the garment bag to inspect Chloe's choice of dress; it was sexy and daring, just like her character, but most importantly it was Palazzo. "This will do perfectly. Okay, so Gabi is staying on Park Avenue—I'll send you the exact details later—but meet me there at five... Bring everything you need to get ready there."

"Sounds good," Chloe said, counting how many hours that left her with to prepare. "So how did the fitting go? That dress was battered, I hope it wasn't too much work... The alteration will probably cost just as much as the dress!"

"It's still being worked on as we speak, but honey, Gabi doesn't care. That dress was a catwalk only piece that no one else has worn—the fucking show itself won't even have it on the runway. When she turns up in that dress people will gag, and that's all she cares about," Carmen said, draining her coffee cup empty. "Okay, I gotta be off now, so much to do and so little time... See you later darling, and *don't* be late!" she said, getting up to kiss Chloe goodbye.

After paying the breakfast bill Carmen had left her with, Chloe left Sadelle's to walk off her bagel. Eating out was a luxury, and with no job she told herself to calm down on the unnecessary expenses, having ordered a takeaway the night before too. Since she was in town and it was early enough for the boutiques to not be busy yet, she headed to Maison Marais on Fifth where she now had a discount—avoiding Palazzo on the way by crossing the sidewalk and back over again.

"Good Morning Ma'am," a security guard said as he opened the door for her to enter, she was probably the first customer of the day.

She made her way to the menswear department, which was quite small compared to the first floor of Palazzo which was dedicated to men's fashion; Chloe had forgotten how impressive Palazzo was, having been blinded and immune to it all for years. Classic tailoring, simple white shirts, silk ties and classic casual wear was the signature Maison Marais style. It was perfect for the gentlemen who loved luxury and not labels—someone just like Brian.

"Good morning, Can I help you with anything?"

Chloe clocked the perky assistant's uniform straight away—a dull, ill-fitted suit with low block-heel pumps, and a silk necktie which she could just make out was printed with the 'MM' monogram all over. Having to wear a staff uniform was something Chloe wasn't going to miss.

"I'm just looking for a gift for a friend of mine," Chloe said, although she was far from being friends with Brian at this point.

The assistant quickly presented her with some of the finest cashmere sweaters that money could buy, but Chloe didn't have a huge budget (especially for someone she wasn't hoping to impress), this was just a small gesture.

"These are beautiful, but I was thinking of something a bit more…"

"Certainly Ma'am," the assistant said, instantly getting the hint; no one would get up this early to drop a small fortune.

After some time, the assistant returned with a simple black merino wool sweater, which was very basic but it would do the job; along with her discount, it would be affordable and substantial. Brian would hate anything too jazzy anyway, and she didn't want to spend too much on something that was probably destined for the bin anyway once he saw who it was from.

"Perfect, I'll take a size large please," Chloe said with a smile. "Oh, could you gift wrap it too?"

'How original,' the assistant thought as she rolled her eyes. Recognising that look of frustration, Chloe smiled and remembered what it was like to have a customer bust your balls first thing in the morning for something that wouldn't scratch the surface on your daily target. Now she was one of *those* customers that felt like an eternity to serve, only for them to choose the cheapest item on offer.

"Oh, and I get discount too… I have a stylist's account here," Chloe said, trying her best to not sound like even more of a cheapskate.

"Certainly Ma'am," the assistant smirked, searching the system but unable to find a client profile for her, let alone a discount.

"Dionne added me to the discount list just last week," Chloe explained, name-dropping the most senior person in-store.

"Certainly… I'll be back in a moment; I'm sure it's just a technical error," the assistant said, sensing this was going to be a complete waste of time.

After about fifteen minutes of waiting for the assistant to return, Chloe felt even more like a time-waster than before and hoped she wasn't going to be embarrassed by being rejected for a discount on a low priced item.

"Chloe, hi," Dionne said, coming out of her office to see her. "I'm so sorry I haven't managed to add you to the system yet… Anna, would you kindly set Chloe up with our stylist discount? Thanks."

"Of course," Anna said, clearly disappointed that Chloe was legit and walked off with the sweater to follow instructions from her boss.

"So sorry about that, it's been very busy with Fashion Week and with Gianni Palazzo in town," Dionne apologised.

One thing struck Chloe more than any feelings of embarrassment, she thought it strange that Dionne said it was extra busy with Gianni in town. 'Why would she be involved with him?' she asked herself. Maison Marais was a completely independent company and had no ties with Palazzo—a competitor even. Dionne continued to talk, making Chloe forget what she had just said, passing it off as general Fashion Week chit-chat.

"How is Carmen? Busy too no doubt… Every Fashion Week she is busy, one of the best in the business."

"Yes, she worked on the Hilary Van Furstein show last week, I helped her out with it, it was an amazing experience."

"Excellent, are you working on anything else together?"

"Yes, we are dressing Gabriela Gracia once again for the Palazzo show this evening," Chloe revealed, wondering if she should have let that slip.

"That's excellent! Will you be there too?"

"Yes, we'll be there—I'm so excited—I can't wait!" Chloe said as Anna returned with one very chic, professionally wrapped boutique bag that even Dom would have approved of.

"Perfect—I'll see you later!" Dionne said, before rushing back to her office.

Chloe was once again confused but passed it off as her misunderstanding. 'Why would she be at the Palazzo show? She must mean in general rather than literally,' she assumed. With that thought, she paid for the sweater with her discount now set up, and left the store, taking extra care to cross the avenue and back over again, so she didn't walk past Palazzo of course. The offices of Dollars4U were just a few blocks away, so she decided to drop it off right away in case she had second thoughts later. Entering the office building, she walked straight up to the security desk, this time knowing where to go.

"Hi, could I leave this here for Brian Matthews? He works in the offices for Dollars4U," Chloe said.

"Sure lady, no problem," The security guard answered back.

She quickly scribbled a note on one of her business cards and poked it inside the bag.

*Bri, sorry for everything and thank you… I owe you everything!*
*Please accept this gift. I feel terrible. Hopefully, you will forgive me in time…*
*Chloe*

Chloe left the building as quickly as she could, the last thing she wanted was to bump into Brian or even worse—Karen! It would be awkward seeing her after their conversation at the party last week, and she was sure that Francesca would have made every effort to let Karen know she had left Palazzo in a bid to dirty her name and steal her client.

Unknown to Chloe, the Palazzo shop floor was now rife with gossip thanks to Sarah. She had spread the true word of Chloe's exit and even elaborating on how she had stormed up to the office and told Regina to go *fuck* herself before walking out. It wasn't entirely false, but Sarah thought Chloe deserved a dramatic departure to be remembered by. But all of that was in the past now, Chloe had plenty to be getting on with and had no time to waste; she had to get ready for the fashion show, and she had to look fabulous for it. The day was flying by, and it was already approaching lunchtime, leaving her famished by all the rushing about town.

Meanwhile, Dom was stressing over his outfit too, he was just as bad as the girls when it came to his clothes and had been up early for a fresh haircut and a sun-bed session. Chloe had made it back to Williamsburg (having grabbed a salad on the way instead of a burger), and as she walked up to her apartment, she was amazed to find a surprise visitor at her doorstep.

"Melinda?" Chloe called out.

Melinda turned around in a jump, frightened by Chloe's silent stealth attack from behind. "Oh! Chloe, sorry—I wasn't expecting you to creep up on me like that," she said, catching her breath from the shock.

"Sorry, I didn't mean to scare you… What are you doing here?" Chloe asked, wondering what the occasion was, but pleased to see her all the same.

"Well, you and Dom left Palazzo with no goodbye or leaving party or anything, and I just wanted to come and see you… Dom told me about what has been happening… I know you two haven't been close recently, but I hope you're still friends?"

She had a point, Chloe did just walk out on her job without warning and on very suspicious terms. Melinda deserved a goodbye at least, especially after all the advice she had given her.

'Great,' Chloe thought. 'Another person I've forgotten all about after they've helped me out'. This was a common theme with her lately, and the extent of her selfishness was revealing itself in every crevice of her life.

"I'm so sorry… Come inside, I'll make us tea," Chloe said, opening the front door.

Once inside the apartment, Melinda sat at the breakfast bar as Chloe boiled the kettle and set up the only china cup she had for her, along with her favourite mug for herself.

"So, how come you're not at work?"

"Oh, well I said I was meeting a client—which I was… I'm just taking a detour on my way back," Melinda said with a wink.

"Well, thank you for dropping by… It's nice to see you, and I'm sorry for not telling you… Things have been mad lately. My life has been turned upside down—great things have happened—but at the sacrifice of others."

She didn't need to explain herself, Melinda was a woman of experience, and by now she had seen it all in her time at Palazzo. Chloe poured out the tea along with two slices of fruit cake, which she would just pick at (she had a dress to fit into). Taking a bar stool, Chloe sat opposite Melinda, she had probably come with wise words, and she was happy to hear them after the whirlwind that had stirred up and destroyed the norm. Talking to Melinda was like talking to mother who knew best, and Melinda really did know best.

"So, I take it you heard what happened?" Chloe started.

"Honey, you know as much as I do that those walls talk! Listen, you are not the first person—and certainly won't be the last—that Regina will be jealous of and try to destroy… She did you another favour if you ask me," Melinda said, blowing into her tea.

The thought of everyone finding out and talking about her made Chloe cringe. How could she ever face her ex-colleagues again? She certainly couldn't go into the store ever again after all this.

"Look—don't worry about all that… At least you left with a bang! Much more interesting than just leaving to go and work across Avenue in another store like most… You will be cemented in the Palazzo hall of fame for many years to come," Melinda giggled as she took a sip of her cooling tea.

Already Chloe felt comforted and laughed at the situation for the first time. It was true, at least people were talking about her, which was better than being forgotten about and not spoken of ever again—and all the better for winding Regina up even more. Sure, Chloe was gone, but her name would still haunt her; there was no getting shot of her that easily, she was now a store legend.

"How are you going to cope with Dom going to London?"

"Oh, you know about that too?"

"Of course—I couldn't tell you—that was up to him."

"Oh Melinda, I have been such a bad friend… I was so wrapped up in my life that everything else just went out of the window," Chloe said, resting her face in her hands in shame.

She knew there was no need to explain and that Dom would have already filled her in regarding the goings on of her life, and how lucky she had been of late. Luckily for her, Melinda wasn't the kind of woman to judge, she knew all about young girls in fashion who were ambitious and hopeful of a career; she was sympathetic having suffered at Regina's hand in the past herself. However, she knew that Chloe was also not a malicious person and what had happened to her this summer was just fate turning its hand.

"Oh, don't be silly Chloe… You had good opportunities come your way, and you simply took them… I can't help but feel that I am to blame for all this in the first place."

"You? This isn't your fault," Chloe laughed.

"Well, it was me who encouraged you… It was me that told you to take opportunities, seek connections. I also encouraged you to use your staff discount I guess, but I didn't mean for you to lose your job because of it," Melinda said apologetically.

Embarrassment was a feeling that seemed to dominate Chloe at present. After following her head for so long and getting nowhere, the only other option was to follow her heart, but at what expense? Her friendships, her self-image being tarnished, gaining a step up in her career? It was her heart that had led her to this point, taking Karen up on her offer of a free website, dating Brian, reviving her website. Equally, it was her heart that had told her to be selfish and neglect both Brian and Dom at the same time. This is what embarrassed her the most, how she had become a person of no heart towards two people that loved and supported her.

Suddenly, like a bolt out of the blue, Chloe had an epiphany. Right there and then she empathised with Regina. If you asked her to do so just an hour ago, she would have thought it impossible, but right now it was a different story. She could suddenly see why Regina was so ambitious, so rigid in her ways, and how she had always got what she wanted; it was exactly the life Chloe had been living—driven and determined—but cut-throat and selfish.

Without realising it, she had progressed herself to the top by using people like stepping stones to a place where she had once only imagined. Having a successful website, successful friends in the industry, powerful connections wanting to work with you, and invitations to the most fabulous parties in New York—and at what price? Chloe was just like Regina, a total bitch. The thought of having similarities to that witch made her spine curl.

"You have nothing to be sorry for Melinda… I'm responsible for my own actions, I am an adult, and it's time I acted like one. I am so grateful to have worked at Palazzo with you guys… Without it, I wouldn't be where I am today. I'm just sorry for letting this all get in-between me and Dom… A lesson I have well and truly now learnt."

Melinda's presence was never a simple one, she had a reason behind her visit and talking to Chloe over tea and cake confirmed that she was the right person to be in charge of what she had worked on for most of her career.

"Well, you have a good opportunity of your own now, and there is no shame in that… We all take chances in life, the difference with you, is that you acknowledge your mistakes and that is where so many others go wrong my dear—now it is time to learn and move on... I want to give you this, a leaving gift if you like," Melinda said, reaching for her handbag.

Out of her vintage Palazzo tote, she presented what looked like a journal, a considerably thick one at that. As Melinda handed it over to her, Chloe recognised it from the Palazzo stationary collection.

"Wow, Melinda, thank you... There was no need," Chloe said, taking the italic '*P*,' embossed lavender leather journal from her.

"Open it," Melinda said, draining her teacup as she watched with a grin.

Chloe opened the journal and turned the pages. It was full of names and addresses, all in alphabetical order but Chloe was puzzled as to what these all meant.

"I made you a copy... It's every client, every person I have known and is worth knowing in this city—in this industry even. I can't bear to leave it to anyone else... I hear Regina is planning to move Francesca to my position when I leave—the thought of that imbecile inheriting my contacts repulses me. If anyone deserves it, it's you! If you're going to go it alone, you will be needing this."

This wasn't just a journal of names and numbers, this was a compendium of New York's rich list, the big spenders, the movers and shakers that personal shoppers and huge companies dreamed of having their hands on.

"Melinda, I can't—I don't know what to say..."

"Oh honey—don't act shy in front of me! I can see how you interact with people," Melinda laughed. "You have the gift of the gab... All of this didn't happen to you just by chance... I'm confident you will know who to contact and when the time is right."

"Thank you," Chloe said, not quite believing that Melinda would do such a kind thing for her.

"Don't thank me... Plus, I'm not retiring entirely... You don't just give it *all* up, do you? And at my age, you can do with some extra cash on the side," she winked cheekily. "I'm sure we will work together again at some point… I suppose I better be off—back to work I go," Melinda said, getting up and grabbing her things.

Chloe walked her down to the street and gave her a warm hug, the kind your mom gave when you left her to go it alone in the big bad city.

"Will you see Dom to the airport?" Melinda said.

"Yep, first thing tomorrow morning—but God knows what state he'll be in, or me for that matter."

"Oh, are you guys going out to celebrate?"

And for once, there was something that Dom hadn't managed to tell her about.

"Well, I had a plus one for this evening," Chloe said, sounding vague so she could revel in Melinda's delight when she revealed that they were attending the Palazzo show.

"For what?" Melinda said, wondering what was worth going out the night before an early morning flight.

"Well, the Palazzo show of course," Chloe said, curling her lips up into a juicy smile, waiting for Melinda's reaction.

"My girl! How on earth did you manage that?" Melinda shrieked, grabbing Chloe by her elbows with excitement, almost pulling her arms off with the strength of an orangutan.

"Well, I've been dressing Gabriela Gracia with Carmen, and I'm down on her guest list… Carmen introduced me to her when we dressed Gabi for her movie premiere."

"*What?*" Melinda gasped, suddenly all the dominoes had fallen in her mind. "It's *you* that's been dressing her in Palazzo? *Whoa-ha!* You are a very clever girl! Myra and Regina have been taking the credit for it, and all this time… It was you!"

Melinda knew Chloe had her head screwed on her shoulders, but this was next level ingenuity.

"Will you be there too?" Chloe said, thinking how wonderful it would be if the three of them were there altogether.

"Yes, of course… It's my last professional engagement for Palazzo… But I can't wait to see Regina's face when she sees you two there—and when it finally comes out that you have been the one dressing Gabriela Gracia all along," Melinda said shaking her head in disbelief.

Chloe shrugged and laughed with Melinda as they said their goodbyes, well, it was more of a 'see you later'. Standing there on her doorstep, feeling the warmth of the summer's day on her face, Chloe finally felt free from Palazzo, and tonight was the closing chapter. Being forced to leave was the worst thing she had ever faced, but somehow it was also the best.

Life wasn't all that bad when she thought about it, she had managed to save some money doing her styling gigs, and she was about to get paid for dressing Gabriela again. Then there was her deal with DivaFeet, which was sure to earn her a pretty sum. On top of all that, she now had the most extensive client book she could ever wish for.

All in all, things were going great, except for discovering the similarity between her and Regina but that would soon to be corrected. Chloe and Dom were going to have the last laugh, and it was going to be epic. The Palazzo retrospective fashion show was going to be a milestone she wasn't going forget for a very long time… And neither would Regina.

# CHAPTER TWENTY-SIX

Chloe made her way over to Dom's apartment, her soon to be new home, as soon as Melinda left. It was easier to get to Gabi's hotel from his place, and they had lots to catch up on after Melinda's impromptu visit. The show was to start at around eight p.m., and there was much preparation to be done. Chloe and Dom vowed to hit the gym on his block in the last bid attempt to look their best for the evening, then afterwards she would get herself ready to meet Carmen.

The gym was excruciating but needed. Dom had pumped up his chest and arms enthusiastically and caught the eye of a few male admirers. 'This place is a total cruising ground... No wonder he works out so often and has such a great bod... The guys here are *freakin'* hot!' Chloe thought. After they had done their own separate workouts, they met by the mats for a stretch and some much-needed core exercises, but Chloe took a moment to give Dom the low-down rather than work on her abs.

"So after I returned from meeting Carmen, I came home to find Melinda on my doorstep."

"Melinda? Why was she in your neck of the woods?" he asked between crunches.

"I know! It was so nice to see her, but there was a reason... She had come by to drop off a leaving gift."

"Oh, did she get you a Palazzo diary too?" Dom said (she had given him the same gift in black).

"But does yours have every contact for every client she has ever had?"

"What?" Dom said, now giving up on his sit-ups to chat instead. "She gave *you* her entire client book?"

"I know, and what's more, I told her we'll be seeing her later on at the show... She was thrilled!"

"Talking of which, we better go… I'm going for a sauna and steam—see you outside in twenty."

"Sure… No jiggy-jiggy!" Chloe laughed, hitting him with her gym towel as he got up.

Back at the apartment they quickly ate a healthy grilled chicken and a rocket leaf salad, which Dom had prepped earlier, washed down with a protein shake. Now that Chloe was to stay at his place, Dom had tried his best to make space earlier that day by throwing even more stuff out and storing the belongings he wanted to keep into an unused walk-in closet. The kind of room where you kept dumbbells and keep-fit paraphernalia that hadn't seen the light of day since they were purchased. As he cleared stuff into the closet, Dom came across the leather jacket that Jason had given to him to remember him by.

Reminded of Jason yet again, Dom couldn't bring himself to leave the jacket behind and set it aside to bring with him to London. Chloe noticed the jacket hanging on the back of a chair in the kitchen, she felt bad that he still hankered after him, even though he was making a fresh start in London to leave all that nonsense behind. But none of that mattered right now, the day had flown by thanks to the sheer excitement of the evening ahead of them, and neither of them knew what to expect, but that was what was exciting.

The same could be said over at the tent in Central Park which was to hold the most famous fashion show in New York to date. Lighting technicians, stage managers, caterers and waiters all worked around the clock to prepare for it. Outside, photographers, journalists and news broadcasters had all been arriving since the night before to set up their spot to capture the very best of the red carpet.

The Palazzo team had also arrived from Milan with the archive collection that was being shown and was busy steaming out creases and assigning them to the models that had been hand-picked by Gianni. Most of the models were already in town working on other shows, but Gianni had pulled in fashion's big-guns to help publicise the show to the max. Naomi, Kate, Linda, Cindy and Claudia had all agreed to walk the runway for this fantastic event that would cement Palazzo into fashion history; if it hadn't been already.

No one did big budget glamorous shows like this anymore; Gianni wanted a show that took the glamour of collections past and the decadence of the nineties to make it extra special. He had a lot riding on this show, but he was a visionary, an artist, and a magician; he knew exactly what worked and what didn't when it came to fashion and most importantly, publicity. He had invested a lot of money into revamping Palazzo (much like his father did when he had handed down the empire to him). It was now Gianni's duty to secure Palazzo for the future once again as well as making a legacy to match. And after this week, he was confident that he was going to do just that—what with buying Maison Marais and forming The Palazzo Group.

*

Chloe left Dom's apartment at precisely four p.m to meet Carmen, giving him plenty of time and space to ready himself (Chloe knew he would take longer than her to get ready). The hotel on Park Avenue had paparazzi hanging around outside it, but none bothered Chloe when she entered—they were all waiting for Gabriela to emerge. Once inside she checked in at the reception, and the concierge summoned a bell boy to take her up to Gabriela's room; this time her name was down on the door as Gabriela's stylist, and she was taken straight up to her suite with no hesitation.

Things seemed much calmer this time, and even the security had cleared her to enter fuss-free. Gabi's personal assistant opened the door to greet her, vaguely remembering her from the last time and guided her through to the dressing room. Gabriela hadn't yet arrived it seemed, but Carmen and the makeup artist were discussing ideas and colour palettes in the dressing room.

"Chloe," Carmen said, noticing her enter. "This is Zoe, Gabi's makeup artist."

"Hi, nice to meet you," Chloe said politely as Carmen took her luggage and stored them in an airing cupboard out of the way.

"Great to meet you too," Zoe said. "As this dress is all down to you, what colours do you think we should use?"

Chloe had imagined many times how she would wear the dress herself, fantasising about turning up somewhere looking like a million dollars. A fantasy which was not far away—just not in *that* dress.

"Well, the obvious is to go for gold, metallic eyeshadows, glittering bronzers, a touch of highlight on the cheekbones… But I think the lips should have a splash of colour—like red. And her hair scraped back into a ponytail away from her face."

"Wow, are you after my job too?" Zoe joked, shooting a look at Carmen.

"Hi bitches!" A camp voice said, out of nowhere; right on cue, Gabi's hairdresser had arrived

"Gray… Darling, you're here," Zoe greeted with a kiss.

Gray was tall and thin, flamboyant, and obviously gay man (who had very little hair himself which was ironic).

"We're just discussing Gabi's look," Carmen said, also giving him a kiss on both sides of his bearded face.

"Well, last night I was here straightening her hair into the early hours, on her insistence," he said, throwing his designer leather tote down onto the chaise.

"Chloe suggested a pony, scraped off the face," Zoe said, turning to her as a way of introduction, stirring the pot at the same time.

"Is that so?" Gray said, looking at Chloe who he thought was just an extra in the room and not part of the actual crew.

Despite already coming across her on the eve of the premiere, he didn't recognise her face; Gabi kept very close company when it came down to who dressed and styled her for public appearances, and this was a newcomer to him. Turning to Chloe with narrowed eyes, he pondered for a while, picturing how her idea would look in his head. The room went silent, you could hear the electricity buzz in the room it was that quiet; Chloe was sure she was about to be put in her place, who was she to tell him how to do his job? Gray had been doing Gabi's hair for nearly a decade.

"Hmm, I think that could be quite chic… A dramatic difference to her usual full and bodied style," he finally said, giving Chloe a camp wink and a pat on her head.

Chloe smiled. A smile that found a warm place inside her, somewhere that made her feel she belonged in a room full of top professionals at the top of their game; not disregarded like she had been at Palazzo. The suite was now getting busier and busier; more and more people were coming and going, getting the room ready for Gabi's arrival with fresh flowers, a trolley of fruits and room temperature water. Chloe could sense that something was just waiting to happen and that something turned out to be a someone.

A door opened, from what appeared to be the bedroom next door, and in walked a barefooted Gabi wearing a navy blue silk dressing gown with the initial 'G' embroidered onto the chest pocket. Her hair was poker straight, just like how Gray had described, and sans makeup. Chloe was pleased to see that she too had dark circles around her eyes, proof that the power of celebrity was all smoke and mirror, or in Gabriela's case, an entourage of assistants. The only thing that was perfect was her finger and toenails with a French manicure freshly applied.

"Hi ladies… So good to see you all again," Gabi said, as she went around the room kissing everyone. "You too Gray! You're one of the ladies too," she jested, pinching his nipple.

It was like someone had suddenly turned her personality switch on as she worked the room. Chloe thought she had just witnessed her warm-up for the waiting public, but moments later a cameraman followed her in. Gabi was being filmed for her new reality TV show: 'Just Gabi from the Ghetto,' covering her daily life, the glitz and glamour, and also the mundane that would fool viewers into thinking she was just like them too.

"Chloe Ravens," she said, taking her by her shoulders. "Thank you once again for getting me this amazing dress. When I saw it on your website, I said to Carmen: 'Get me that dress!' Didn't I?" to which Carmen nodded in agreement, proud of her apprentice.

Chloe couldn't believe that one of the many viewers on the visitor counter of StacksOfStyle had been none other than Gabriela Gracia! She also couldn't believe that Gabi was advertising her website on her reality TV show, that's if the footage didn't end up on the cutting room floor first. Gabi sat in her chair in front of a huge mirror as Zoe and Gray ran their ideas by Gabi, of which she agreed to—although Gray did have to talk her into letting him try an up-do rather than how she had originally wanted it.

In what seemed like a nanosecond from her giving approval, Zoe was already brushing foundation onto her skin with a flat brush—like she was painting onto a blank canvas. Gray made sure he had all his equipment ready for when Zoe had finished applying the base layer and was brushing through some hair extensions he whipped out from his case, always ready to go.

"*You,*" Gray said sharply. "Since this style is your idea, you can be my assistant."

A task that he didn't trust just anyone with and Chloe could sense it. The pressure to perform was building inside her, she gulped so loudly, she was sure it would be picked up on camera; she didn't even do her own hair, let alone a megastar's (scrunched up curls with a pump of mousse was as good as it got).

"Okay, so here's all the grips... Keep the hairspray close by, brushes, and comb," he listed as he handed them all to her at once. "Hold the blow dryer for me and point it downwards... Down and flat! Stay close, but don't get in my way!" he warned, sealed with another wink to calm her.

Carmen couldn't help but laugh (she had once been in her shoes), Chloe looked like a deer caught in headlights. By now, Zoe had applied the foundation and concealer; Gabi's skin was now looking clear and blemish free—the rest she would finish after Gray had worked his magic. Gray stepped into his position promptly, knowing the routine like a dance, and started to play with Gabi's hair. Gathering the length and pulling it up and away from her face, he looked in the mirror with squinted eyes, trying to see the final vision before he began.

"Brush," he ordered with his hand out for Chloe to react. "Hairspray and grips... *Now* please!"

"He means you," Zoe said, not even looking up from cleaning her makeup brush.

Chloe was startled, she had set all the equipment down on the vanity table to free her hands; she grabbed the brush and grips quickly with shaking hands and gave them to him before going back for the large can of Elnett.

"Blow!" he shouted, louder and sharper the longer she took.

After a few minutes of being told off, she soon got the hang of it. She didn't want to be yelled at in front of Gabriela, 'how embarrassing,' she thought, and that was her main motivation to keep up with him. That and the fact the footage could end up on TV, which it certainly would if she made a mess of things.

Gray had taken an hour or so to finish the style which saw them into the beginning of the evening. They didn't have long to go before she would have to leave, but then again, she didn't have very far to go. Gabriela's hair was sleek, shiny, and now scraped back into a long flat ponytail aided by extensions—just how Chloe had imagined.

"Well, done honey," Gray said, pulling Chloe in for a side hug.

Zoe hadn't moved from her spot and was ready to step back at the moment Gray got out of the way. Chloe noticed that Carmen had now laid out the dress, shoes and handbag—all of which were vintage Palazzo.

"Wow, it looks amazing... Where did you get the shoes and bag from?" Chloe said, it definitely wasn't from Myra's press office, that was for sure.

"They are from Gabi's own collection… I dug them out of her wardrobe earlier today."

They looked hardly used, but then again, Gabi probably had so many free clothes given to her that it was impossible to wear anything twice. Checking back in on the action, Zoe had now completed Gabi's makeup in no time at all; her face was radiant and contoured. Her skin had a glowing sheen across her cheek and brow bones, which made her look Amazonian and bronzed. Her eyes were smokey and accented with gold eyeshadow that was so sharp, it looked like it had been airbrushed on—not a mistake or a fleck out of place. Gabi didn't like the idea of red lip colour, so Zoe opted for a nude tone that made her look like she was ready to pound the runway herself.

It was now time for her to get dressed, and for the camera's to leave the room for once. Carmen and Chloe helped Gabi step into the gown, she wore nothing but a flesh coloured thong (there was no need for a bra), her body was toned and tight (no need for Spanx either). Rather childishly, Chloe couldn't help but think: 'I've just seen Gabriela Gracia's boobs,' as Carmen placed silicone fillets under Gabi's breasts with tit-tape. They then helped each other pull the dress up over her hips and up to her armpits.

"Hold the corset together while I zip her up," Carmen said.

Unlike hairstyling, this was something Chloe knew how to do and held the power mesh corset together while Carmen gently fastened the zip—careful not to bust it at the last hurdle. Gabi arranged her breasts into the cups of the bustier, lifting them up and together to make a cleavage that wasn't too tacky for a high-fashion event. Once Carmen was satisfied that the dress was correctly fitted, she gave Chloe the go-ahead to finish with closing the hook and eye fastening at the back. It looked very different from how Chloe had remembered it last, hanging on her rail at home.

It had gone from a grubby discount frock to a fitted and sparkling piece of couture fit for a star. Carmen and Chloe helped Gabi step into her white Palazzo sandals and each fastened either side of the ankle straps for her. Gray zoomed back in with hairspray and a brush once more to perfect the flat ponytail as soon as they had finished dressing her. Chloe took a step back to admire the look in its entirety; she looked amazing, as good off the screen, as on. The gown fitted her body like it was made just for her and her hair and make-up were straight out of a fashion spread, which Chloe felt proud at having a hand in—after all the dress, the face, the hair was all her idea.

Gabi was now ready to go, just in time to work the red carpet over at Central Park. Her entourage was summoned to escort her down to the foyer of the hotel, where paparazzi eagerly awaited for her to appear. As she stepped into a blacked-out S.U.V, the camera's flashed and clicked like crazy as they tried to get the best shot of her before anyone else—immediately selling it to the press within minutes. Gabi ignored their calls to pose for them, and her security guard shut the car door to whisk her away to the venue. A few photographers quickly mounted their motorbikes and zoomed off after her, sticking their lens' as close against the window as possible.

Once she was gone, everyone back at the hotel suite breathed a sigh of relief, but not for long. Not only did they have to pack up, but they also had to get ready themselves. The real pandemonium was about to break out between Zoe and Gray, who both ran into the bathroom at the same time. Chloe looked on, not quite knowing what to do herself.

"Don't worry," Carmen said. "We'll get ready in the other room now Gabi has gone, then Zoe and Gray will do our hair and makeup. The show won't start until at least half past, maybe nine even… Everyone knows they never run on time and plus, the early entry is for the stars to parade the red carpet… It takes at least an hour to get them all in and seated."

Chloe grew even more excited, the thought of Zoe and Gray making her over to perfection just like Gabi reassured her that she too would look red carpet worthy in case she did see Regina, and more importantly Gianni. Although they would have to be quick, there wasn't much time left before they had to leave if they were going to make it through the circus that was bound to be surrounding Central Park by now. Even though she had already showered at the gym, this afternoon's activity had made Chloe sweat with excitement and nervousness, so she had a quick rinse to freshen up, careful not to get her hair too wet. Gray's receding hairline meant he didn't need to worry about his own hair, he was busy applying bronzer in the mirror, sucking in his cheeks as he swept it over his face with large flourishes.

"Hurry up bitches! If you *all* want your hair done…" he called out, not deferring from his own reflection in the mirror.

Carmen had already changed into her black dress and was ready to be the first to sit in the chair for him. 'Wow,' Chloe thought, Carmen looked smoking hot. The svelte black dress with cut-out sides, pinned together with gold buttons made her look sensational; for a moment Chloe wondered if she had made the wrong choice and should have worn it herself.

The room was filled with the sound of hairdryers and action, but no one spoke a word. Chloe whipped her dress out of its garment bag and onto her body in a matter of seconds. Red, it was fabulously red, and the gold shiny bangle halter neck had inspired Zoe straight away.

"Hmm, gold accents and red lipstick would be perfect for *this* dress… Come," she said, inspired by Chloe's original idea.

Chloe shut her eyes as Zoe worked on her, she could feel the cool liquid foundation spread across her face and Zoe's fingers smudging concealer around her eyes, followed by dustings of powder; she was a true professional who knew exactly how to apply makeup in record timing. Using the same gold eyeshadow she had used on Gabi, she lightly brushed it on Chloe's brow bone and blended in a darker tone around to give a similar smokey effect. She bronzed her cheeks and finished it all off with vamp-red lipstick which was very seductive, glossed over to provide a wet look.

"Next!" Gray yelled.

Chloe and Carmen swapped places, Carmen's hair was perfectly straight, and centre parted. She always had great looking hair, but

Gray had somehow made it look glossier than ever before, as if she had just stepped out of a shampoo ad.

"Now, what shall we do with… *This*," Gray said sarcastically, looking at Chloe's vast amount of blonde, curly hair—slightly damp from her shower.

He didn't think it over too long and went straight in with a cylinder brush and blow dryer, then a curling tong, picking out sections of hair. He scraped back the front and sprayed it before gripping it down with hairpins. The final result was much neater—loose curls that cascaded down her back and away from her face—allowing her to fully show off her newly applied face.

As she looked in the mirror, she wondered if this was how she would look all the time if she were rich and famous? She couldn't believe it was her reflection staring back at her. Time was disappearing fast as Gray worked on Zoe's hair, while Chloe and Carmen finished with shoes and accessories before stuffing away their belongings into their overnight bags.

"Hey, guys," Gabi's assistant said entering the suite. "Your car's waiting downstairs and is getting moved on by traffic cops—so you better hurry up."

This news made everyone flap around the room like chickens, finalising their outfits and stashing their belongings into bags, making sure they didn't leave anything behind.

"Don't worry guys! I'll take your bags down to reception for you to collect tomorrow morning, just make sure your name's on them," Gabi's assistant offered, causing them to dump their luggage at her feet so they could all dash downstairs.

**

As the elevator doors opened onto the hotel's lobby, guests and staff all looked at them in awe as they stepped out dressed to kill. Outside waiting for them was a black town car, but by now the photographers had already left to follow Gabi to the venue and snap other stars. Sitting in the back of the car, Chloe couldn't help but feel elated and nervous, but something was missing... Then she remembered.

"*Shit*, Dom!"

"Who's Dom?" Gray said.

"Chloe's friend," Carmen said quickly, this was not story time. She was rather anxious herself which Chloe had never seen in her before.

"Ooh... Is he hot?"

Chloe checked her phone to see a stream of panicked messages which she had missed while getting ready.

HEY HUN. I'M ERE, WHERE R U GUYS?

OK GABI HAS ARRIVED, SHE LOOKS SENSATIONAL!
WHERE U @ X

Dom had been waiting around for them for over an hour already and was starting to panic that they had forgotten all about him. In the back of the car, Chloe replied to let him know they were on their way and were definitely not standing him up. The traffic was backed up with limo's and town cars, and it was now past eight p.m with, only half an hour left before the show was due to start.

"Driver, let us out here please," Carmen commanded.

"We're not there yet!" Gray snapped.

"Darling, if we sit here any longer we will miss the show... If we get out here, we can make a run for it."

"Run?" he said with a scoff.

"Yes, *run!* We are only a block or two away... If us girls can run in heels, you can run in your flat shoes, Miss Gray!"

The car pulled up, Carmen had her hand on the door latch ready to leap out.

'How glam,' Chloe thought to herself, but it was all part of the fun, and she was not going to miss the show if her life depended on it. She stuffed her phone back into her clutch and got ready for the mini-marathon through the busy streets to Central Park. Seventy-ninth St Transverse, beside the Metropolitan, was closed off and gridlocked with cars dropping off attendees. The entire place was impossible to navigate with crowds of tourists all vying to see what was going on; it was buzzing with reporters and photographers—some had passes to get past the security, others were just trying their luck.

The Palazzo tent was huge and lit up with the brand logo on the sides, the ground leading up to it from the roadside was carpeted (you could easily forget that you were in Central Park), while the italic '$P$,' logo shone all over the carpet by laser light. Step and repeat walls featuring 'Celebrating 55 Years of Fashion in Association with N.Y.F.W' lined the backdrop of the red carpet entrance, which was where most of the action was taking place.

Chloe fumbled for her phone to call Dom while they dashed through security, flashing their passes and getting their bags checked, but priorities first—she stopped as the other walked briskly on to take a selfie—only after did she call him.

"Hi babe, where are you at?" Chloe said as she caught up with the others.

"Tell him to meet us at the side entrance, they won't let us go through the main one," Carmen shouted, looking back to see she had finally caught up.

After directing him, Chloe followed her mini entourage, who seemed to know exactly where they were going, which Chloe was glad of as she had no idea; After all, they were seasoned fashion week-ers, schmoozing their way into events and parties every season. As they approached the entrance, Chloe caught sight of Dom keeping a look out for them, he looked relieved when he spotted Chloe strutting in her heels towards him.

"Chloe, you look amazing!" he said.

"Oh, and what am $I$? The dog's dinner?" Carmen said in jest.

"Oh, Dom… This is Carmen—Carmen—Dom," Chloe quickly reeled off.

Dom was wearing a slim-fitted black velvet jacket and plain black pants with black suede Cuban heeled boots and a crisp white shirt that was slightly open at the neck. A sexy, masculine aftershave wafted through the evening breeze; his efforts were not wasted on Gray, who was giving him the once-over with a flirtatious eye. They didn't have much time to exchange pleasantries and began approaching the entrance which was flanked by two security guards and a woman who looked like a model herself. She was checking passes and crossing names off a list—she was the one to get past.

"Hi, good evening… We are the Gabriela Gracia party of five guests," Carmen said with confidence.

The woman gave a dry smile and seemed to take her time checking the list. Chloe had a sinking feeling that maybe they weren't on the list at all, but was soon put at ease when she looked up and smiled, before reeling off a long and well-rehearsed speech.

"Welcome to the Palazzo show… There is no re-admittance once you leave this area. There is strictly no smoking, photography, or recording allowed inside. You can sit anywhere on the left side of the runway except for the first five rows… Enjoy the show!"

The security guard made them pass through a metal detector before allowing them inside, checking the contents of their purses once more—including Gray's leather pouch. Afterwards, they were greeted by a fabulous bar area where guests mingled, enjoying the flow of free champagne. There were no famous faces in the bar, they were on the other side in the VIP zone being interviewed by various fashion reporters and news anchors from around the globe. The tent must have been at least half the size of a football field Chloe had estimated, despite having never been to a football game in her life.

They had arrived in just enough time to guzzle a quick glass of champagne, free booze and schmoozing was what these events were all about, and Chloe took the opportunity to post her selfie on Instagram.

The bar was still full, and no one seemed in a rush to get seated. Typically, Carmen had spotted someone she knew, it was only a matter of time before Carmen was off greeting acquaintances from the fashion industry and she wasn't the only one.

"Chloe! Dom! Oh my gosh, you guys look amazing!" Kim said, opening her arms for an embrace. "I never thought I'd see you guys again, let alone *here!* What are you doing here?" she said, curious as to how they had blagged an invite.

"We're here to see the show of course... My client, I styled for tonight invited us," Chloe said, skimming over whom her client really was.

"Yeah, she dressed Gabriela Gracia!" Dom blurted out, making sure Kim knew exactly who.

"You styled... Of course, she is wearing that dress I put on hold for you at the sample sale!"

Chloe nodded rather embarrassingly but shrugged it off. Not only had she been sacked for misusing her discount, but she had dressed a celebrity courtesy of the staff sample sale (busted), but that didn't matter now.

"So, how about you? What are you doing here?" Chloe asked, changing the subject.

"Working of course... So, hold on... Does that mean you've been dressing Gabriela Gracia this whole summer too?" Kim said, putting two and two together about where she was getting her vintage palazzo gowns from.

"Yes, okay... It was all me!" Chloe said, giving up on any further pretence; she was fired already so letting Kim know couldn't hurt.

"That's so funny! Myra and Regina have been taking the credit, wondering how she had got the dresses... And all along it was you! I heard what happened by the way, with your discount and stuff."

Of course she had, Sarah was all over that story, but naturally the rest of the staff were just as curious about the mystery behind Chloe and Dom's departure; many versions of had been circulated, proof that Chloe was well and truly cemented into the Palazzo hall of fame for generations of staff members to come.

"Apparently you told Regina to go '*F*,' herself?" Kim laughed. Well, it wasn't exactly the words Chloe had used verbatim, but the intention wasn't far off. "Speaking of Regina, she will *freak* when she sees you two!"

"Yeah, and we can't *fucking* wait…" Dom added.

As they stood talking, Dionne approached from behind; Dom and Kim stopped the conversation to look at her, wondering who it was that was coming over—Chloe turned to see what they were looking at.

"Chloe… I thought it was you," Dionne greeted with a kiss. "Oh my gosh, you look stunning!" she said, which was the reaction Chloe had been getting all night and wanted to get. It filled her with confidence and a feeling that only a star could hold from enamoured fans.

"Thank you, Dionne… You look beautiful as always," Chloe said, rather surprised to see her, even though she said she would be attending. "These are my friends, Dom and Kim,"

"Pleased to meet you both."

"Kim works in the press department for Palazzo and has helped set all this up," Chloe said, still trying to figure out why the director of Maison Marais would be present at a competitor show; not knowing the story behind Palazzo buying them.

Introducing Kim to the store director of Maison Marais seemed like an excellent contact for her to have, even though she and Dom had given her grief over the years. But seeing how much life there was outside of palazzo had made her want the same for Kim too. Also, it would be great if staff suddenly dropped like flies after their departure, causing a mass exodus—that would only look bad on Regina.

"Is that so? Amazing… Congratulations, I'm sure your boss is very pleased with you… I know I would be."

Interrupting their conversation, Chloe's phone beeped. It was a text from Carmen telling them to meet her by the entrance of the auditorium.

"Oh, sorry guys, but we have to go… Maybe we'll see you later?" Chloe said, grabbing Dom's arm.

"Sure, the show will be starting soon… The after-party is just next door in the museum… See you there," Kim said.

Chloe and Dom left Kim and Dionne in conversation to weave through the guests to find Carmen and the guys. Having seen an old colleague from her Bullet magazine days, Carmen had secured them better seats than where they were initially allocated to sit—in the forbidden section of the first five rows.

Bob Carter was now the editor at Bullet magazine and had spotted Carmen in her jaw-dropping dress and invited her to sit with him (probably hoping to impress and secure a date with her). Even though he continued to speak to her breasts, Carmen didn't care if it meant they were closer to the runway and in the presence of the most important people in fashion.

\*\*\*

Entering the auditorium, Chloe and Dom looked at each other in glee. Bleachers were full of benches cascaded up along the sides and a large clear plexiglass runway, which was lit from the inside making it appear golden, dominated in the centre. A large, gold italic 'P,' hung above the runway and two large screens displaying the iconic Palazzo print were situated either side of the stage.

It was like a movie set with cameras set up to film the show and replay it back onto the screens, and live on the Internet. The scale of production matched that of a stadium concert, not a one-night-only fashion show—a large sum of money had clearly been spent. Photographers were poised at the very end of the runway in their own pit, ready to capture the most iconic moments of the night.

Carmen led them to where they were sitting which was precisely on the fifth row and in good view of the A-list guests sitting below. Chloe could instantly point out Gabi in the front row, she was sitting next to another pop singer. Rachel Rodriguez was a pop sensation since she was just sixteen years old and always in the media (for the right and wrong reasons); she was sat with her current boyfriend, a famous dancer she had started dating while on her latest world tour and would probably dump after this event.

Getting accustomed to her surroundings, Chloe noticed that it wasn't as large as she had once thought, blinded by the initial opulence of it all; there were only another ten rows or so behind them. It dawned on Chloe just how lucky she was to be sitting there, these really were the most coveted seats in town right now. Looking around, she could name people she had recognised from magazines, TV shows, music and fashion.

By now the auditorium was filling up rather quickly, a sign that the show was about to start; it was now approaching nine thirty, a whole hour after it was scheduled to begin, Carmen was right. Tilly Cooper took her seat in her usual spot, just seats away from Vogue's editor on the front row—who was still nowhere to be seen. Tilly was about a hundred years old and a New York fashion icon; she always wore crazy outfits and famously said that fashion would be the death of her, and the front row would be her deathbed.

Just behind her in the next row, Chloe could make out Myra, Melinda and Regina—all making people get up so they could usher down into their seats. Chloe and Dom giggled, judging their mundane outfits—having come straight from work no doubt—Melinda looked fabulous of course in a gold brocade pencil skirt and matching blazer (she usually saved it for the staff Christmas party).

With the editor of Vogue now sat down, the house lights dipped causing the audience to hush as the auditorium sat in blackout for a split second, before coming up bright and golden to a loud burst of sound, transforming into pumping house music remixed by DJ of the moment, Mark Hanson. It was so loud, the bass went through Chloe's stomach which made her even more excited as she sat on the edge of her seat, waiting for the first model to emerge from the cloud of dry-ice that flooded the stage. It was all happening so quickly, but Chloe remembered that it was from this iconic show that she would draw inspiration for her upcoming DivaFeet collection. She tried as hard as possible to concentrate on the details, even though she could just look back on the coverage afterwards, there was sure to be enough of it splashed everywhere.

The first model appeared in a swimsuit, which was made out of a famous tropical print, wearing huge sunglasses with a straw basket and sporting heels way too high for the beach or pool. Model after model, the looks were instantly recognisable as the best Palazzo pieces from the past. The audience gasped as the first famous model, Naomi, appeared in a floor-length purple maxi dress from the '97 spring/ summer collection—one of the best selling Palazzo collections to date. She looked amazing as always, and Dom nudged Chloe with his elbow as she walked down the runway, passing them by.

This was an experience that he would remember forever and all the better for sharing it with Chloe. He always knew she would pay him back for being a shitty friend and this was the perfect way to do it before he went back to London. Kate appeared next on the runway and passed Naomi in a metallic silver metal-mesh mini dress, recreating a scene that fashion had not seen for many years. This was a definite crowd pleaser, and photographers flashes were going like crazy to capture this moment—almost acting like a strobe. This image was sure to make the front page news around the world.

Chloe stopped watching the show for a moment and focused on Regina, she seemed happy and for once had a smile on her face. The show was as crucial to her as it was to Chloe and Dom; it signified all the years she had worked at Palazzo, watching it pass her by like a movie of her memory. She had seen many, if not all, of these collections first-hand in-store and it was a retrospective of her career too.

Chloe's empathy for Regina deepened, and the bitter feeling she held for her felt like it was disappearing as she connected the significance. Something she once thought impossible, but it was proof that sometimes the impossible was achievable—just in case she needed more evidence of that truth. Chloe snapped out of her daydream and brought her eyes back onto the runway.

The music mixed into an electronic beat as the show romped on from one famous look to another. Linda and Claudia made their walk down the runway with the other models of today (that didn't have quite the same gravitas in the modelling world as the 'Supers' did). The models all appeared to be having fun with beaming smiles on their faces, not the usual 'schmize' they had perfected; this was a celebration!

The finale saw Naomi, Kate, Linda, Cindy and Claudia all walk down the Runway together in evening dresses from the current fall/winter runway collection, an excellent advertisement for the pieces that were hitting the stores in the coming months. As they walked to the end of the catwalk, they paused to be photographed by the many cameras all pointing and strobing at them, not throwing them off in the slightest. The entire audience defied the 'no photography' rule as they captured this iconic moment on their phones. It felt as though fashion history was being made before their eyes.

Chloe immediately posted her snap onto Instagram, using hashtags copied from her previous post that evening to make sure everyone knew the founder of StacksOfStyle was important enough to be at the show. The show ended with the whole cast of models walking back down the catwalk and off stage—one would exit right, the next left and so on—until no more was left except the supermodels who encouraged the audience to clap for Gianni to come out and take a bow.

Eventually, he did come out onto the runway, buttoning up his jacket and running his fingers through his tousled hair like he was taken casually by surprise. Naomi and Kate grabbed him by either side and walked him down the runway to pose for the cameras and the adoring spectators who had all stood up to applaud him. Gianni could feel the many eyes burning into him from all around, and as he looked in Chloe's direction, she got that feeling again.

That sensation deep inside her, the same sense as when he very first noticed her at the store event on Fifth Avenue. 'Can he see me?' she wondered, even past all the flashing lights and into the darkness? Gianni looked around and took at the moment before running off the stage with Naomi and Kate in tow. The house lights turned back up to full beam, and people had already started to leave to fill the bars outside to fuel up on free champagne before they went to the official after-party next door.

"Wow, wasn't that amazing?" Carmen said, looking down the row at Chloe and Dom.

"It sure was," Bob Carter said, still eyeing up Carmen in her sexy dress. "So, shall we move on to the party and have some drinks?"

"Of course, darling… We'll see you in there," she said, trying her best to get rid of him at the earliest possible moment.

Carmen quickly gathered her gang and edged them outside, leading them back down the carpet and onto the roadside by Fifth Avenue.

"But it's quicker to go this way to the Metropolitan," Chloe said, pointing in the opposite direction.

"Darling, that party is for the masses… We are going to the *real* after-party!" Carmen said, trying to hail a taxi.

It was vital that they arrived promptly after the show, twenty minutes later and it didn't matter who they were—once the party reached capacity, there was no letting anyone pass. Chloe and Dom looked at each other in surprise, she had thought that there could be no more surprises to the evening (it was already as fabulous as it could possibly be), but it seemed that the night was only just beginning.

# CHAPTER TWENTY-SEVEN

They had arrived by taxi at the New York Public Library, much to Chloe's surprise. Forty-second Street was just as much of a commotion as Central Park was, with tabloid photographers already lined up behind iron rails, completely blocking the road. As they got out of the car, Carmen headed straight for the side entrance steps which was manned by security, the others followed close by not wanting to get left behind.

After showing her show pass and dropping Gabi's name, the guards checked the list and allowed Carmen to pass through, having made sure they acknowledged the rest of her party first. Gabi's assistant had ensured the entire entourage was down on the list, saving an awkward moment in front of the crowds of paparazzi. Many a fashion tantrum had been caught on camera and made viral online, it was part of the fun of Fashion Week.

Inside, a gold carpet lined the hall with candle-lit lanterns all the way up to the Celeste Bartos Forum, where the evening's lavish celebration was to be held. Chloe nudged Dom with joy and a goofy sense of excitement as they made their way through the hall, this was some leaving bash for him. Carmen zoomed on ahead with confidence and walked through the grand glass doors which were held open and flanked by two large vases of flowers that must have cost at least $1,000 each at least. Past these doors, was a reception room where the official press covering the event awaited in front of press boards emblazoned with Palazzo's monogram to photograph celebrities and other A-listers against.

Chloe thought that they could just breeze straight past this section, not being anybody of significance, but she was amazed to watch Carmen saunter straight up and pose for the clicking cameras as they lapped her up—and in that dress, it was hard for them not to. She was a seasoned fashion veteran and knew exactly what to do with her hands and where to place her feet, she even tilted her head and swished her hair; she certainly lived up to the expectation of a celebrity stylist.

Looking on, Chloe started to panic, she didn't know what to do with herself; was she really going to try and pretend to be someone famous? Could she pull this off successfully without making a complete fool of herself? She hadn't even practised posing in the mirror (something she now wished she'd thought of). Gray grabbed Dom's arm and whisked him off inside to the main party, completely dismissing the whole parade to grab a drink in hopes of getting him drunk and chatting him up, Zoe followed leaving Chloe looking like a lost lamb.

She stalled from making an idiot of herself by taking out her compact to check her makeup (it was perfect and hadn't budged an inch). If she had applied it herself, then it would have been a hot mess, but Zoe knew how to make a face last all night long, and there was nothing else left to do other than to suck it up: either walk on through to the party or take her chance and strike a pose.

Chloe shook, her head, she was making a mountain out of nothing and opted to casually walk past and follow Carmen on into the main party, before she lost everyone for the rest of the evening. Flicking her hair off her shoulders, trying to look unaffected by it all, she made her way to the forum's entrance but was startled when a woman with a clipboard stopped her from passing.

"Ma'am… Your picture," she said, guiding her to the step and repeat wall.

'*Fuck*,' she thought, there was no escaping embarrassment now.

As she made her way onto the 'X' marked with tape she was stunned to see the camera's already clicking and flashing at her.

'Do they really want a picture of *me?*' she asked herself, amazed that they were fooled by her.

The red dress on the gold carpet was a fabulous contrast, set off by its gold bangle halter-neck which shone under the lights; unbeknown to her, she looked sensational. Photographers called out for her to look their way—probably mistaking her for a socialite she presumed (she certainly looked like one). At first, she didn't quite know what to do, hands on hip or down by her side? Eventually, she got the hang of it like she had seen many celebrities do in magazines: angled to the side, one hand on hip, left leg crossed over with a slight pop of the knee and a pouty smile.

She turned for the cameras, now settling into her stride she was actually starting to enjoy herself. Chloe could see why famous people became addicted to attention, she felt alive! When she had satisfied them, she began to walk towards thew awaiting reporters in the media section—this she could definitely skip. The thrill of having her picture taken unexpectedly was enough to make her feel like a star and wasn't going to be offended by being escorted straight past them. After all, she wasn't famous, no one would want to bother questioning her.

However, back at the show in Central Park, one of the official reporters (who had whisked off as soon as the show started to take her position at the party) asked Gabi who had dressed her, to which she was only too happy to name drop.

"My dress is Palazzo, from StacksOfStyle.com."

Thanks to modern-day technology, this scoop-seeking reporter quickly searched the Internet on her phone and found a picture of Chloe wearing the exact same dress. As Chloe walked past the row of journalists, the reporter called out to her.

"Miss Ravens—Chloe Ravens!"

Chloe looked over her shoulder, 'Did someone just say my name—surely they didn't mean her? 'Who would know my name here?' Everyone she knew present was already inside the party.

"Chloe Ravens, Su Ming for StyleAsia TV," encouraging her to pause for an interview.

Chloe could hardly believe it, how did she know who she was? 'The Chinese and Japanese *are* crazy for fashion,' Chloe thought. Maybe she was an online success overseas without even knowing it?

"Hi, How are you?" she answered, not knowing how to react other than to be polite.

"StyleAsia TV wants to know, where *did* you find Gabriela Gracia's couture gown for this evening?" she said, pointing her microphone in Chloe's face.

Hearing that Chloe was Gabriela Gracia's stylist, other reporters followed suit and stuck out their microphones in a bid to not miss a thing.

"Erm... Well, it was hanging on my rail in my apartment for a while, Gabi saw a picture of it on my website—which I had posted—and the rest is history I guess..."

Chloe left out the details of how she had acquired the dress, she could hardly say she had bought it from a Palazzo staff sample sale, where she no longer works due to abusing her staff discount, could she?

"So it was from your own private collection? You must have a great wardrobe," Su said. "Who's your favourite designer?"

"Well, it has to be Gianni Palazzo, of course," she quickly reeled off, thanking herself for thinking swiftly; it was the Palazzo retrospective after-party, she couldn't exactly say Karl Lagerfeld—that would have been awkward.

Inside the party, Carmen grabbed two glasses of champagne off a passing waiter's tray, only to look back and see that Chloe was nowhere to be seen.

"Dom... Where's Chloe?" she shouted into his hear over the loud music.

"We left her with you, no?"

Carmen placed the champagne back down and headed back out to the entrance to see where she had gotten to but was amazed to find Chloe glowing in the attention from the reporters. Carmen couldn't help but smile, this was her girl; she was remarkably impressed with her audacity. Not wanting to stand around looking like her groupie, she ran back in to grab Dom so he too could see their girl in action—ready to reunite with her after she was done having her moment.

Outside on the street, the photographer's rushed over to a black saloon car—their camera flashes setting off in furious succession as they called out—someone significant had obviously just arrived. The car doors opened swiftly and out walked Gianni Palazzo himself, led by his personal bodyguards. He waved to the crowd as he buttoned up his jacket, before being taken inside where he walked up the gold carpeted hall and straight into the press room. Instantly noticing the commotion around him as he entered the room, Chloe was frozen on the spot—everything else faded into the background.

"Can you tell us about StacksOfStyle and how you started it?" Su pressed, calm and in control; she wasn't flustered by a designer entering a room, this was the norm for her.

Chloe was in a trance, everything had completely zoned out around her, and once again, she didn't know what to do herself. But the expensive production, the press boards featuring the Palazzo logo, the reporters that lined up waiting for him, none of it bothered Gianni. As he took his position on the carpet, it was the vision of a beautiful woman in a sexy red dress that caught his attention—it was recognisably one of his designs.

The way the fabric clung to her body, the thigh-high slit, the way her hair fell down her back and the shape of her svelte legs in high-heeled sandals all made her shine. Scanning her once more from feet up, his eyes finally met hers and was hit with a jolt. He had met her once before, but from where he didn't know. It was like his mind had been woken up from a coma, suddenly awakened to remember a beautiful woman he had once known; Gianni was a man who had whatever and whoever he wanted, and this time he would make sure she didn't escape him.

As his piercing blue eyes burned into hers through the flashing cameras, the feeling of excitement and butterflies returned to Chloe's stomach. He gave her a seductive smile which seemed to linger, which made Chloe's heart skip with excitement, but he looked away to resume posing for the press—taking his eyes back to her every now and then.

"My blog is… Sorry–where was I? Oh, you can visit my website at StacksOfStyle.com—all one word," Chloe said, just getting the plug in.

Needing to know more about this beauty before she got away again, Gianni thanked the photographers and excused himself so he could move onto the reporters. He was eager to get closer to her, a master of seduction and knew how to make a move in an elegant and classy way that wasn't too obvious. As he approached the journalists to answer their questions, they all extended their arms over the velvet rope, shoving recording devices in front of him—Su included.

"Mr Palazzo, congratulations on another amazing show… Tonight we saw Palazzo's greatest hits, but what will next season's collection bring to the world of fashion?" one journalist asked.

"Thank you, you will just have to wait until next week for that," he said coolly, glancing over at Chloe who looked slightly awkward as she slinked off quietly into the party now that Su was done with her—but Gianni wasn't going to let her go that easily.

"Sorry, can I just… Ma'am… May I say how wonderful you look in that dress—*my* dress."

Chloe stopped in her tracks, her shoulders hitched up at the sound of him addressing her. She turned around slowly, just in case it was someone else he was referring to; if she had got this wrong, then it would make her want to just die! As she turned to face him, it was clear that he was talking to her—his mouth curled up into a smile showing his beautiful white teeth.

The electric sensation she had felt when he had very first set eyes on her back at that night on Fifth Avenue returned; she was starstruck, glued to the spot and unable to move, fearful that her legs would give way and she would take a tumble in front of everyone. It was as though his stare had taken control of her, captivating her with his gaze like Medusa.

'I better say something,' she thought, sensing that she had paused for far too long; aware she had an audience. "Thank you." She dipped her head shyly, it was all she could manage.

His blue eyes were extremely seducing, and his dark hair made them come alive; just the sight of him alone had made Chloe want him. Sex with Brian was fantastic and had aroused her appetite for men again, but she was sure it would be a hundred times better with Gianni. He was a very attractive man, never mind powerful, rich and famous. Maybe that had something to do with it, she had to admit that power did, in fact, turn her on. Gianni took a step closer, Chloe couldn't believe what was happening—even if she had fantasised about it many times over as she lay awake in bed at night.

Now closer to her than ever before, Chloe could make out his cute dimples hidden in his rugged but neatly trimmed stubble. She went to push a strand of hair behind her ear as a default reaction, but forgot that there was no hair to push away—it was already swept back off her face.

"A picture of you both please, Mr Palazzo!"

It was Mario, the most famous photographer on the planet who was officially documenting the evening for Palazzo's press archive. '*Fuck!*' Chloe thought, realising who it was. Not only was she standing there with Gianni Palazzo, but she was about to be photographed by the world's most famous fashion photographer. As Mario poised himself to take the picture, so did the others resulting in a blinding wall of constant flashing. Without hesitation, Gianni wrapped his hand around her waist, pulling her in even more closer to him.

There it was, that touch—the same touch from her dream but it felt so much better in reality. She could feel his body warmth against her, and all she wanted to do was to melt into him, but she had to keep it together. She had the world's media attention on her, yet his cologne was intoxicating, making her tingle deep down. It was a feeling she couldn't explain.

'Is it possible to reach climax through the sense of smell alone?' she quickly thought, now starting to lose her shit; like a swan, she was serene on the outside but flapping inside. Even the touch of his hand around her waist was enough to set her off; she could only imagine what it would feel like to be touched all over by him, but the press carpet wasn't the place for sexual fantasies.

"Where do I recognise you from?" Gianni whispered to her.

The feeling of his breath hitting her ear made the tiny hairs on her skin stand on end.

"Err… I was at the event in your Fifth Avenue store the other week," she said discreetly, unsure whether he would remember.

"Ah… Yes, of course," he said still looking down the camera lens'.

Remembering that she was posing for them, she resumed her newly learnt position: hand on hip, left leg crossed over, slight pop in the hip and a pouty smile. They turned right, left and to the centre, pleasing all that had clambered to capture this moment. Chloe wondered if she should take a picture herself (even if it was cheesy for her to do so), this moment may never come again, and the guys might not believe her that this had happened if she didn't have evidence.

Seizing the chance to snap a quick pic, Chloe took out her phone to take a 'selfie' of them both, but her hand was too shaky. Noticing the image was blurry, Gianni grabbed her phone and positioned it up above them (he knew his angles) and took the picture for her, playing up to it with a 'peace' sign. 'This will be my 'most liked' post on Instagram,' she thought as he handed it back with a smile.

Now they were done posing, Chloe assumed this was the part where she finally left him to take the reporters seriously, but she was amazed to feel Gianni reach for her hand instead. The feeling of his warm raw skin on hers made her quiver with shock; his masculine hand cupped hers, tiny in comparison. He thanked the crowd and began to pull her away with him towards the entrance of the forum.

"Let's go inside shall we?" he said smoothly in her ear. His breath was a heady mix of soft mint and liquor—it turned her on even more.

As his security cleared the way for them, Chloe felt as though she was going to collapse onto the floor right there and then but Gianni took the lead, forcing her to follow. As they approached the entrance, a gathering of officials awaited him, and to Chloe's utter amazement she was face-to-face with none other than Myra, Melinda and Regina-*fucking*-Hall!

Regina's jaw dropped, she couldn't hide her astonishment either. Not only was this silly girl (that she thought she had gotten rid of) at the most prestigious party in New York, but she had turned up with the main man himself. '*Shit!*' was Chloe's initial thought, but she caught sight of Melinda standing behind Regina with her hand clapped over her mouth, holding in laughter—clearly impressed and elated for her.

This was the 'bitch slap' that Chloe had been waiting to give Regina all these years—and on behalf of all her ex-colleagues at Palazzo too. Chloe wasn't going to waste this moment, gone were the nerves and awkwardness; she stood upright and confident to face her nemesis. She wasn't going to say hello or even acknowledge that they knew each—Regina was now just another stranger to her—instead, she just smiled back knowingly, before turning to Gianni.

"Thank you for your escort Mr Palazzo," she said flirtatiously, enjoying every second.

"You're very welcome… May I ask your name?"

Offering Gianni her hand to kiss, she looked at Regina.

"The Raven—Chloe Ravens," she said, making it crystal clear that she was indeed here and present. "I'll see you later… I hope, " she said, batting her eyes once, slowly.

Chloe brushed past Regina, totally ignoring Myra to give Melinda a brief kiss before making her way into the party, where she saw Carmen and Dom waiting for her at the entrance—who were equally just as astonished at her arrival.

"Erm… Good evening Mr Palazzo," Regina struggled to spit out.

Gianni couldn't take his eyes off Chloe's hips as she snaked them on purpose, taking every step in her stride. Working her high heels and skin-tight dress as she walked over to Carmen—who had watched the whole affair with Dom by her side, and gave Myra a sarcastic little wave with her fingers the second she clapped eyes on her.

Chloe desperately wanted to whoop and cheer but managed to keep it together until they were safely away from the circus—looking up to the Gods to say: 'thank you' once her back was turned. She confidently strutted away with Carmen (who pivoted on her toes with a flourish, as if to say to Myra: 'Bye bitch') into the forum to find the rest of the gang. Regina's hateful stare followed Chloe and that annoying stylist who had once begged her for a discount, and even worse—Dominic Fraser!

Regina was enveloped in a mixture of emotions: anger, surprise, shame and shock all at the same time. New York was a small city, especially in fashion circles, and that was something that had come back to bite her for the very first time. It was apparent that Chloe Ravens wasn't so easy to erase after all, and had successfully shown her who *was* the boss. Chloe was younger, more attractive than her, enough to steal the show and seduce Gianni in front of everyone—there was no denying it had happened—Mario had caught it all on camera as did Chloe.

Something Regina would never be able to do, no matter how hard she worked; she didn't desire him, but the thought that Chloe was able to mesmerise him just by being herself irritated her. She didn't even think Chloe looked that special compared to all the other women there, and out of all of them, 'Why her?' she asked herself.

*

"What the *fuck* just happened?" Carmen screamed, trying her hardest not to make a scene.

"She-just-killed-it!" Dom confirmed equally as thrilled. "That's what just happened…"

"Come, let's find a table… If we want to eat we need to get seated," Carmen said, leading the way past the bar and towards the main hall.

The Celeste Bartos Forum was stunning, exactly where you would expect such a glamorous event to be held. The grand thirty foot-high glass domed ceiling made it feel like you were outside at a garden party, displaying the evening sky in full glory. The hall underneath the glass saucer dome was turned into a dance floor, with round gala tables around the edge where a five-course meal was being served.

Carmen found a table with a few empty seats, others occupied by stragglers who were instantly intimidated and got up to make way the moment Carmen approached, wearing a look on her face which said: 'Move bitches!'. Chloe, Dom, Grey and Zoe took over the table, and within seconds waiters were pouring champagne and placing down cutlery and plates.

"Okay, so come on—spill…" Carmen said, pulling Chloe in and kissing her head in pure delight at what she had had just managed to pull off.

Dom scooted his chair closer so he could join the conversation, naturally wanting to know everything.

"I—I can't explain… One minute I was talking to some reporter, the next I was standing with him being photographed. Then, I was face to face with Regina!"

"Tonight, we are going to party!" Carmen shrieked.

"Dom, he remembered me from the event!" Chloe said, grabbing his knee and giving his leg an excitable shake.

She couldn't describe how she felt, all she could do was take a large gulp of champagne and sit back in her chair, relishing in what had just happened to her.

"What did he say…" Dom said, also taking a swig of champagne.

"He asked me where he had seen me before… I said, at the event last week."

Carmen listened, looking blank, having no understanding that there was a history.

"So, wait a minute… you met him before?"

"Yes, sort of," Chloe said quickly, unable to speak still.

She couldn't keep her mind off Gianni's stare—trying to figure out what all of this meant. Her hand still tingled from where he had kissed it; she could still feel where his lips had been. Noticing that she was too shook, Dom filled in for her.

"Basically we had an in-store event—before she was fired of course—and—"

"Guys... You made it!" Gabi said, interrupting Dom's story, not knowing that they desperately needed to run through the evening's drama to make sense of it all.

Gabi was with none other than Rachel Rodriguez and her boyfriend Hunter—trying to find a table to sit. The catering staff immediately noticed who she was and instantly made space, bringing more chairs for them to sit down. Dom's jaw dropped, not only had his idol just greeted them, now she was sitting just an arm's reach away from him—with Rachel Rodriguez who was also a gay man's icon.

"*We* made it? No—Chloe has made it!" Carmen said. "I swear, this is the luckiest bitch I have ever met!"

"Why, what's happened?" Gabi said, what could be more amazing than this party right now?

"Well, not only did Chloe get 'papped' on the way in here, but she got pictured with Gianni, *aaand* he was clearly flirting with her!"

"No way!" Gabi leant back in her chair and slapped her leg as she laughed.

"No, I mean—like he was practically fucking her on the carpet!" Carmen finished off sensationally.

"You watch out for that one lady... If I know Gianni—oh, to Hell with it... He *is* very handsome, isn't he?" Gabi said, waving her hand in dismissal at what she was going to say.

All Chloe could do was nod in agreement, she had no clue what was going on anymore; here she was surrounded by stars, discussing her business—and it felt amazing. She looked around, hoping to find Gianni staring at her again after having stalked the place down for her, but the crowd around her was too thick—there was no way she would spot him from here. Her heart sank a little, was that all there was to be on the matter?

"Champagne... Waiter... More champagne please," Gabi shouted, getting back into the party mode; she was now officially off-duty and needed a drink.

So far the evening had been like a scene from a movie, hanging out with Gabi and Rachel as well as her friends, and finally getting a chance to stick her two fingers up at Regina in the most fabulous way. Everywhere Chloe looked, top names in the industry had draped themselves around the place, this was the most amazing night she had experienced by far. Her eyes came back to the table as she looked at Dom, she was happy to be sharing this moment with him.

"If you told me a month ago that I would be sitting here with you at the Palazzo Retrospective party, I would have said that you were crazy!" Chloe said, pulling him to one side.

"I know—me too! I guess this is just another example of never giving up in life... No matter how hard things get," Dom said rather profoundly. "This just shows that sometimes you have to take that leap of faith... We would never be here if we were both stuck working on the shop floor... On that note, I'm going to find Melinda."

**

Gianni was growing tired and bored with the many introductions Regina and Myra had lined up for him—not to mention the boring table of guests (mainly investors and directors) he was due to sit with—his whole week had been filled with tedious meetings with them tying up the Maison Marais deal. What he really wanted to do was to find this Chloe Ravens and loosen up a little, this was a party after all.

'I need a freaking cocktail,' he said to himself as he walked around with Regina and Myra, like two dogs on a leash.

"Do you know anything of this Chloe Ravens?" he asked, grabbing a Martini from a waiter while looking out towards the dance floor as if he was trying to pinpoint someone.

"No—nothing! Never seen her in my life," Regina said sharply, ending any possibility of entertaining this conversation.

What she really wanted to say was: 'She's a fucking lying, thieving little tramp who stole from your company you blind asshole!' But that wouldn't go down very well, restraint was one of her many talents.

"Just some fashion blogger I think," Myra quickly added; Regina shot her a look: 'shut up, you fool,' she said without needing to say a single word.

"Mr Palazzo, may I just take this chance to let you know that I am fully behind the decision to acquire Maison Marais and welcome them to the Palazzo family," Regina started, but Gianni's mind was elsewhere.

His eyes scanned the room, moving quickly around the party (almost like he was swiping left on a dating App) until he finally found who he was looking for. Chloe wasn't hard to spot with her cascading hair, dressed in a vibrant red dress—she stood out from the rest of the crowd. The fact she was surrounded by some of the most famous stars in the world didn't exactly make her a wallflower either. Regina's eyes followed his to see who he was craning his neck to get a look at; the night couldn't have gone any worse for Regina, Chloe was taunting her.

'Look at her sitting there, sipping champagne like a *whore* in that cheap dress from a year ago,' she cursed inside.

"Okay ladies, this is where we say goodnight… Thank you for everything—stay and enjoy the party won't you?" Gianni said, making an escape from a night filled with work chatter.

"Oh, you are leaving already?" Regina said, unsatisfied at not being able to give the whole speech about why she should be director of the newly formed Palazzo Group.

"Nope… Just going to enjoy the night with some old faces I haven't seen in a while… Excuse me, ladies."

As he stepped onto the dance floor, people tried to stop him for kisses and photos, trying to get his attention which he batted off politely and professionally. He was used to this scale of attention on a daily basis and knew how to handle it like a gentleman. He zoned in on Chloe's table like a hawk, ensuring he could follow her should she get up and dart, until he finally made it to her table.

"Hello, Gabi… It's been forever!" he said, as she stood up to kiss him. "You look out of this world by the way."

"Thank you my darling… It's one of yours ya know…"

"Of course… In fact, I don't think we ended up producing this one for the collection, how on Earth did you get it?"

"All thanks to my stylists… This is Carmen and Chloe," Gabi introduced with the palm of her hand.

"Oh, you again… I see you know my friend here… So, how come we haven't met before, seeing as you're Gabi's fashion fairy?" he asked; he had blocked everyone else out of the conversation and spoke only to Chloe.

There it was again, that sexual energy, the pent-up tension she felt for him. It was as though she was building towards a climax, just from the excitement and attention she was getting from such a sexy, handsome and powerful man.

"—Chloe found the dress for me," Gabi interrupted, trying to win his attention back.

"Is that so? Well, you must have very good contacts because if I recall rightly, this was just a runway sample?"

Chloe could feel her cheeks begin to flush. 'Has Regina told him the truth?' she fretted.

"Yes, she's amazing… She found my premiere dress too," Gabi added. "She is the new kid on the block when it comes to style… You should check out her website."

Bingo—Gianni had wondered who was behind the cunning tactics of dressing Gabi in vintage Palazzo ahead of the retrospective show. It was as though she and Gianni shared the same creative vision, maybe this explained the chemistry between them? Gianni knew deep down that Myra wasn't original enough to have come up with such an idea, there must have been another brain behind the expert timing and

PR—it would take someone as creative and daring as himself to come up with that.

*Was* she as daring as he was?

'Maybe she is the one…' he asked himself, looking through half cut sultry eyes; trying to figure her out.

The brand was about to go through a major new phase in its history; Palazzo was about to become stronger, more important, even more, iconic and he needed the best-of-the-best on his side. All the while, his gaze started to make Chloe giddy—she had to break away—she looked down at the floor.

"Well, Miss Ravens… Congratulations and thank you for doing such a wonderful job dressing Gabi in my creations… Sorry, you didn't say where you got them from?"

'Good question,' Chloe thought as she looked back up, worrying about how she was going to explain the runway sample Gabi was wearing. 'Should I tell him the truth?'.

"Well, it wasn't from your store! Us stylist's get no discount from you and your press department! They are so *stupid*, they never let us borrow anything, and we are dressing Gabriela!" Carmen said with sarcastic confidence that helped her get away with such fiery comments. If she weren't as stunning as she was, she probably wouldn't, but she also didn't have anything to lose.

"Well, I will have to change that… I'll make sure that you are added to our official press contact list worldwide Miss Ravens, and Miss…?"

"Carmen Visconti, but call me Carmen."

"Well, I'd better do the rounds… Enjoy the evening… I'll see you around?" he said to Chloe, brushing her arm with his fingertips, sending another electric shock through her body. "I'll be sure to check out your website."

Fumbling around in her purse, her heart began to sink. How could she forget her *fucking* business cards? Gianni kissed her cheek and gave her a seductive wink before heading back to the room of guests. Again, he was mobbed on his way back through and just like that, he disappeared—deep into the crowd. Chloe was dazzled, it took a few moments for her to regain composure. Gabi and Carmen stared at her, it was clear that Gianni was smitten; he hadn't kissed anyone else goodbye.

"*What?*" Chloe snapped as she reapplied her lipstick, knowing full well what they were thinking.

Missing out on what had just happened, Dom returned to the table with Melinda in arm. Since this was her last work gig, she too wanted to have some fun and accepted Dom's offer to join them at their star-studded table, knowing that this was going to piss Regina off even more. After all these years, it was now Melinda's turn to have a dig at Regina too, and there was no better occasion. Melinda didn't give a damn anymore, she was leaving Palazzo and the Regina regime behind for good. Reunited, the infamous trio raised a glass of champagne.

"Here's to the future kiddos," Melinda toasted. "Didn't I tell you there was a life outside Palazzo?"

# CHAPTER TWENTY-EIGHT

Partying until four in the morning seemed like a good idea at the time, but not when the alarm was waking her up at six-thirty, that same morning. Nonetheless, it was the perfect night to celebrate starting life as a freelance stylist—like Carmen had said—she had been fortunate so far. Staying over at Dom's place made sense as she was going to see him off back to London from JFK airport, but the early morning wake up call wasn't so welcome; hungover and extremely tired, they both dragged themselves out of bed. Dom quickly took a shower to freshen up for the flight, but Chloe made do with one of his jersey tracksuits and a pair of shades and baseball cap to hide her sins.

Hearing the taxi beep its horn outside, they each took one of his suitcases full of clothes down to load the car up. Carrying his suitcase out to the cab felt like torture to Chloe, not only was she heaving a tonne early in the morning feeling (and looking) like total crap, but she was also losing her friend; for Dom it was a different story, it was the first time in a long while that he was returning to London.

The excitement of seeing his mother cancelled out the tiredness for now (he could catch up on sleep once on the plane), but he was sad to be leaving both New York and Chloe. Especially after they had a ball at the party and rekindled their friendship, just like old times. They sat in the back of the cab en-route to the airport in silence, which was good (because Chloe was a walking zombie), and it was early enough that not even the driver tried to initiate chatter. But there was nothing Chloe could say to fill the void—she was about to say goodbye to her best friend. Plus, she was still dumbfounded by the events of the night before.

She dared not speak of it just in case Dom said she was crazy and it had, in fact, all been nothing but a drunken dream—it seemed that insane just thinking about it. Her Instagram account, however, confirmed the reality, she had never received so many 'likes' and new followers overnight—it had skyrocketed into the thousands. The 'selfie' of her and Gianni had sent her account into orbit; Gabi had also tagged Chloe in her posts, which made her army of loyal fans follow back.

With the end of Fashion Week, traffic filled the city with fashion folk all leaving town, now moving on to the next stop—London. On the way to JFK, Dom had plenty of time to take in the streets of New York one last time. It wasn't too late to change his mind and stay, but he didn't want to; he was ready for an adventure in London.

The party was a great reminder of how life could be in the city and a great excuse to come back to it in the future (not that he needed one). Chloe was a major reason to come back for, he was sure she was on to greater things, and now that their friendship had healed, he hoped to be a part of her success one day. Right now, he needed to create his own and London seemed the right place to do that. Breaking the silence, Dom recalled the events of his wild last night in New York.

"*Biiitch*... Last night was crazy... I wonder if Gianni will call you?"

Chloe was asking herself the same question; he was a busy man, and she hadn't exactly made things easy for him in that respect. Foolishly forgetting to bring her business cards was an epic fail and Dom's reminder made her cringe at her elementary error.

"Well, the only hope I have is if Gabi gives him my number—which she would have to get from Carmen first... In that case, Carmen would tell me... Or, if he emails me through the website, but he is busy with Milan Fashion Week now... I doubt he will have time for internet stalking," Chloe said.

She desperately wanted him to contact her somehow; it was as if a fairytale was about to spring into her life, just like how she had dreamt but thought would never happen. Could one of the world's most desired men really be into her? Thinking back on last night, Chloe couldn't deny there was an air of chemistry between them. Even Gabi and Carmen had noticed it, it couldn't have been all in her head.

Reaching the airport, they had miraculously managed to leave the apartment in just enough time with only half an hour before the check-in desk was to close. This was it, the moment Chloe thought would never come had arrived. There were so many words to be said, but neither of them matched what she felt inside (along with the fact she couldn't string a sentence together right now). Instead, they just hugged each other.

"I miss you already," Chloe said, holding back tears.

Thank goodness for the sunglasses, but Dom could hear the crack in her voice and knew it wasn't because of last night's antics.

"Don't… You'll start me off," he said, not wanting to sob in public. "Oh—wait… I almost forgot!"

Dom reached into his jacket pocket, and after some fiddling about, he took out a set of keys which he dangled in front of her.

"*You'll* be needing these… Now, I don't wanna come home to a shit hole! *No* parties and definitely *no* sex in my bed… If you do, you better burn that mattress before I get back!"

Chloe laughed, snapping out of sadness for a brief second at his witty attempt of distracting her from saying an emotional goodbye— but deep down she knew that the thought of heterosexuals at it on his memory foam mattress freaked him out.

"Dom… I can't thank you enough," she said, taking her sunglasses off to rest them on the brim of her baseball cap so he could see just how grateful she was through eye contact alone; she was too choked to say anything more.

She reached out to him once again, she was surely going to miss his sassy comments. It was nearly time for him to leave and go through to customs; they had dragged out every last minute, and now he had to go.

"I'll be back before you know it," he said, trying to comfort her. "We can video call and email, you need to let me know as soon as you hear from Gianni remember… *Don't* forget!"

Chloe wiped her eyes, Dom could see tears brewing; she was about to blow, they were red and puffy, but that could have been due to the amount of alcohol she consumed only a few hours ago.

"Yeah sure, I know… I mean it's not like you're about to die! Well, not unless the plane crashes," she said, realising her joke was ill-timed.

"Oh, well thank you very much; talk about jinxing my flight bitch!"

"Sorry… You'll be fine, and you will get to London safely!" Chloe said, with a voice which was about to flood into a sob any second now.

"Anyway, you're gonna be super busy with designing your collection," Dom said, trying to evade crying himself by reminding her that this was a good thing for her too. "You need space to knuckle down and work—make sure you fill me in on everything… Well, this is it… I guess I'd better go."

Chloe grabbed Dom close once more and kissed his cheek, burying her face into his neck for a deep hug. She had tried her best for as long as she could, but her shoulders shuddered, and tears rolled out silently. As she sank her face into his jacket, trying to mop up her tears, it had dawned on her that he wouldn't be around through such a life-changing moment—she wasn't sure if she could face it without him. Dom slowly pulled away and wiped her cheeks before taking the sunglasses off her cap and back onto her face to cover up her eyes.

"Here… Nobody wants to see this hot mess… I'm not dying remember… Call me, email me—it will be like I've never gone away."

*"This is a call for all British Airways passengers flying to London on flight BA 1594 to please go the to gate for boarding—all passengers for flight BA 1594, please start boarding, thank you."*

"*Shit*, that's you—you better go!"

Dom looked up at the departures board to see 'boarding' flashing next to his flight number.

"Yup, that's me—I gotta run," he said, giving her one final hug.

"*Run!*" Chloe said, letting go of him.

Taking the chance to leave her, he ran towards the customs gate; he still had to go through to the departures lounge, which meant no time for Duty-Free shopping. He dared not to look back around, but as he joined the line for security to check his passport and hand luggage, he turned for a final wave.

'Do not cry—do not cry!' was the mantra Chloe chanted in her head, but it wasn't working. She watched him until she could no longer see his head in the crowd of travellers—now completely out of sight. She stood still for a moment unsure of what to do next until she started to feel sick as her dry mouth made her head spin—along with her emotions.

She hadn't even had a coffee yet, let alone breakfast but there was no way she could eat now; all she could do was take a seat on a nearby metal bench and put her head between her legs. 'Maybe he'll come running back out to say he's changed his mind?' she hoped. But after about fifteen minutes of sitting there looking at the floor, she realised it wasn't so and headed over to a kiosk to get a bottle of water, which she downed almost in one, and a strong coffee. All she wanted to do now was to get back to Williamsburg and start moving her stuff into Dom's apartment.

She didn't want to be alone in her place; she wanted to be as close to Dom as possible and moving in as soon as she could was the next best thing. Now she understood how he felt when Jason had left him, and with that realisation, she fully comprehended his reasoning for wanting to leave New York altogether. After waiting in line for thirty minutes at the taxi rank, Chloe finally got into a car.

It smelt like pine air freshener, and the seats were covered in a cheap black plastic sheet—easy to clean vomit off no doubt which could be hers if he didn't drive carefully. As the cab drove off, Chloe pulled the hood of her zip-up track top over her baseball cap and hid behind her shades. If she was going to cry, she didn't want the driver to see and then try to start a conversation what was the matter.

Driving back through the city, Chloe remembered all of the great times she had spent with Dom as she stared out of the car window. She began to laugh at how ironic the situation was, she had thought Dom was dramatic by leaving, but it was her that was being the drama queen now; 'You're My Best Friend' had strangely come on the radio. 'How fitting, Queen for a queen,' she said to herself and managed to smile at her own joke. 'Life is going to be okay,' she reassured herself as she stared at the passing streets.

The sound of her phone ringing woke her from her daydream, it was Carmen. 'Surely it's too early, even for her?' Chloe thought, Carmen had partied just as hard as her.

"He-hello?" Chloe croaked out, from her alcohol ravaged voice. Hearing it had made her remember the pack of Marlboro's she smoked out of drunkenness.

"Oh. My. God!" Carmen screeched down the phone. Chloe held it away from her ear, it was too early for this much enthusiasm. "Have you seen the front page of the New York News?"

'No, I haven't seen the *fucking* front page of the New York *fucking* News!' Chloe wanted to say; she had barely seen the light of day through squinted, teary eyes filtered through sunglasses, let alone read an actual newspaper.

"I have literally crawled out of my bed to take Dom to the airport, and that's about it. Why… Should I have?"

"Well, yes… Because you're on it… With Gianni!"

"*Shut up!*" Chloe screamed back, sounding more like a bark. "Is this some kind of cruel joke? If it is, ha-ha, hilarious…"

"No—seriously, you look fantastic! I suggest you go get yourself a copy, *pronto!*"

And that's exactly what she did. The moment she saw a newsstand, she made the driver pull over. She could see the front page headline covering the Palazzo party as soon as she opened the door and purchased two copies from the vendor before running back to the car. She stared at the front page in total disbelief as the driver continued the journey; on the left-hand side, the length of the entire page was the picture of her and Gianni taken on the gold carpet.

She was relieved that her attempt at posing had translated well and his hand looked rather comfortable around her waist, resting on her hip like they were an item. Seeing it in print in front of her made her feel his touch all over again, only to be disturbed by the accompanying headline and teaser to the full article inside; suddenly she was awake and able to focus her vision.

### GIANNI PALAZZO'S LADY IN RED

*Palazzo's creative director pictured with his new beau, Chloe Ravens; stylist and founder of StacksOfStyle.com. Stylist to the stars, Ravens, dressed Gabriela Gracia for the retrospective fashion event in Central Park who dazzled in a couture gown from Palazzo. Miss Ravens also made an impression on the arm of the designer at the after-party, held later that evening at NYPL. As well as his provocative designs, Gianni Palazzo is also known for his multitude of relations with women from the big screen, music and fashion. Leaving everyone wondering: How long will Ravens last?*

Chloe put the paper down on her lap in shock at what had been written about her; she called Carmen back right away—was this really happening or was she still asleep and dreaming?

"Okay, first of all, this writer is *so* wrong… I am *not* his latest conquest, and I am definitely *not* his new beau!"

"Yet!" Carmen said. "What's your plans for the rest of the day anyway?"

"Right now, I'm on my way back home… I need a shower, big time!"

"Well, call me as soon as you are ready and fixed up… We have to make a plan!"

"For what?" Chloe said, designing the capsule collection was the last thing on her mind.

"You're famous now girl! We need to plan how we are going to make the most of this attention," Carmen said, pointing out that Chloe had now been thrust into the centre of the world's media.

Chloe had heard about people's lives changing overnight, but it was insane to think that hers was changing just as quickly—this was the moment she had been waiting for, and it almost seemed as though it was happening too fast—but it was too late to take a step back now. Chloe *was* hot property now, thanks to this salacious news story. A flood of anxious thoughts filled her body as she thought about who else would have seen the article—her mother included. On the other hand, she smiled at the thought of her ex-colleagues reading it at work this morning in the staff kitchen, this was bound to start another round of rumours.

'Will Gianni see this?' she questioned, she wouldn't want him to think of her as some attention seeking wannabe. 'And what about Regina? She is gonna freak!' she thought, which slowly turned into a grin, acknowledging the upside to this sudden burst of fame (if that's what she could call it).

Regina didn't usually read the papers but today was different, Palazzo was bound to be splashed across the pages, and she wanted to catch up on the press coverage. The Palazzo retrospective was branded as 'a catalogue of fashion icons' and 'decades of style and glamour in one, definitive show'. It had been a romping success, and the images of Kate, Naomi, Cindy and Linda with Gianni on the catwalk featured on TV networks all around the world.

But as she made her way down to the local tabloids, she was stunned to see Chloe's picture with Gianni plastered on the front page of several publications. Even though these weren't the most respected concerning journalism, they were the most read by New Yorkers—and she *did* freak… For the second time this week!

Seeing Chloe looking as good as any celebrity in the news, was a kick in the teeth—especially after all her endeavours to diminish her. And reading the article was even worse, Regina knew this was a story that wasn't going to go away easily—like how she had hoped Chloe would fade away (which was so far impossible).

*

With just a week left, Gianni was also leaving New York for Milan so he could finalise the runway exits in time for Fashion Week. But before his departure, he called one last meeting with the senior management. A brunch was being held on the personal shopping floor of the Fifth Avenue store, where they had all gathered to hear Gianni give a parting speech, concluding his New York trip.

As they waited for him to arrive, Regina and Myra separated themselves so they could discuss Chloe's impromptu appearance in private, and to vent their disgust and embarrassment of her being behind the latest Palazzo PR stunt of dressing Gabriela. The fact that she had made the headlines with Gianni took this situation to another level altogether. They appeared to be so familiar with each other. 'How did she meet him?' Myra wondered, but of course, Regina could trace back to the very moment, remembering the brief moment they had at the in-store event. It was stored in the memory banks of her brain. Somewhere, there was an archive of hate especially for ex-staff members like Chloe Ravens, but she too was dumbfounded as to how she had managed to make an entrance with him.

How was Regina going to solve a problem like Chloe? She just wasn't going away, and now Chloe had a new fan in Gianni, Regina feared she would never get rid of her; the war wasn't over, it was just starting. The sound of mixed conversations in the room was silenced as Gianni entered, to which Regina paused her plotting to start a round of applause for everyone to take heed. Gianni waved to the room and took his place in front of everyone.

"Ladies and Gentlemen, thank you all for being here… Well, firstly I will start by saying what a splendid trip I have had. It's amazing how hard you have all worked to make this store one of our most luxurious in the world! The past week has been a moment in the company's history, and I hope for you, that it will be something you will never forget. Without you, I couldn't have done what I set out to achieve. I send many thanks to everyone involved with the show, but also to every employee that makes this brand the best... I have already heard from our fellow colleagues in Europe, and they have all said what an amazing job we have done here, but more importantly, how excited they are for the future... A future I can promise will be bright, thanks to the support you have all given me, with our next venture... This week we showed the world our glorious past, but soon we will unveil it's most innovative future... I am very excited to announce that we have now officially acquired Maison Marais, thus creating The Palazzo Group!"

The room erupted into applause, and Regina's eyes widened with the hope of promotion once more, completely forgetting about Chloe altogether; once she was the group director, she would have complete control—an even more formidable power in the company than what she was now. Her mastermind was paused once again as Gianni continued his speech.

"The merger will commence with effect from the next financial year while we set out our five-year plan... Ahead of this, I am also delighted to announce that I have appointed Jean-Paul Baptiste as the new creative director for the house, which in turn, means that we hope to acquire his signature line in the near future—expanding our portfolio of luxury fashion brands under The Palazzo Group. The official press release will be issued from Milan later today, which I am sure will be breaking news for us, along with last night's events."

It was true, Palazzo was going to be huge for the foreseeable future. And what was to come would be highly reported and watched by the entire fashion industry as they eagerly awaited for the new direction of the iconic French fashion house to be unveiled. Appointing a new creative director was also going to be big news.

Jean-Paul Baptiste had already made a significant name with his own line being snapped up every season since he left college; his first collection was famously purchased in its entirety by an editor, who was now his muse.

"I would also like to thank Regina and her team for all her hard work, which without, we wouldn't enjoy the success we do already—and *will* have in the future as a group," Gianni said, as he shook Regina's hand and kissed either side of her face.

She looked smug as everyone present applauded her, a huge grin spread across her face. She had understood this to mean she was in line to be appointed as director for the newly formed group and that she was already in line for the job without the need to beg. Gianni, however, was just as smart as she was and said exactly what she wanted to hear to make her keep working hard, yes, he too was a 'Licker'.

After all, he would never find another human willing to give up their life for Palazzo like she had; Regina did the work of three managers for the price of one. Her desire to be recognised, successful and influential had made her a hate figure—but to her, it was a small price to pay.

"One more thing," he continued. "I am also very proud to announce that our fabulous retrospective show will be touring the world in our very own Palazzo exhibition... Starting here in New York, next spring at The Metropolitan Museum Of Art."

Gianni was a true showman, a natural born entertainer and everyone was left excited by his departing news. But before he left for his flight back to Milan, he had requested a private meeting with Myra and Regina (this was where Regina would be appointed as group director, she had assumed). The three of them sat around a huge glass table in the boardroom on the fifth floor.

"Well, ladies... I have to say thank you for your outstanding work... I couldn't have done this without you. Before I go, I want to ask for your help on one more thing... I have discovered a talent that could help us in our growth as a luxury group... A raw talent that is so striking, it is like she is reading our minds... I want you to find this Chloe Ravens and offer her a job with The Palazzo Group," he revealed.

Regina's heart nearly stopped (a rare sign that reminded her she still had one); her smug face from all his earlier compliments had vanished and was replaced with a look of sheer horror. For a split second, she could hardly believe what she was hearing, expecting him to say he was only joking, but he wasn't; he was looking at Regina directly in the eye with a look that was as serious as could be. Before replying, she turned to Myra who was also just as surprised.

"But... I don't think she will—" Regina stammered before being abruptly halted.

"—Oh I think she will be great! The way she styled Gabriela Gracia in our vintage dresses was pure genius," Gianni said with a smile, tilting his head at Myra in a way that said he was on to her complacent ways.

Even though he wasn't one to tell people off in a mean manner, he still wasn't a man that allowed himself to be walked over. Regina couldn't believe it; things just seemed to go from bad to worse, and just as she thought she had this all under control, he wanted her to employ her again! 'If only he *really* knew the truth about her,' Regina scorned. But then again, Gianni was a man who always got what he wanted, and if she wanted a promotion, she would need to comply.

The fact that Chloe had worked for Palazzo before would only intrigue him even more. Instead, she would deal with this situation herself by agreeing to his request, only to squash it later down the line. With him out of the picture, she could manipulate Chloe's future, like she had done for the past five years—she would make sure of that. Regina stopped her mind from pre-planning the 'how' and 'when' she would end all this nonsense and dropped back into the conversation— Gianni was still rambling on about how amazing this 'unknown' talent was.

"I mean, she would be a huge coup... I want you to find her."

"—Oh, but Mr Palazzo... I have just hired a new assistant," Myra said.

"Oh no," he laughed. "I was thinking more senior level than an assistant... She could be head of styling, work with our entire portfolio, dress even more celebrities—maximise the full use of our new brands. She can work with you on styling more and more VIP's, come up with co-branded events—that sort of thing… Whatever, at first, I want to give her free rein… See what she comes up with on her own…"

"Of course Mr Palazzo, we will contact her on your behalf," Regina stepped in, eager to end this conversation so he could just leave her to squash it.

"Excellent, well I will have the HR team back in Milan draw up a proposal for her."

"Very well Mr Palazzo… I will let you know what she says about it, pleased I'm sure… In fact, I will get in touch today to see if she is available to come in for a meeting… Just to see if she is as wonderful as you say," Regina added, with a fake smile that hurt her face.

"Oh, she is amazing! Check out her website… I'm surprised you haven't heard of her already."

'Oh, I've heard of her all right,' Regina thought.

**

Chloe had arrived back at her apartment, and it was a relief—heading straight into the shower. She felt yucky and dirty from the antics of the previous night out, and from taking Dom to the airport without washing. Chloe always believed that there was nothing better than a hot shower at your own place. She hadn't been home for more than half an hour, but when she got out of the shower, the apartment buzzer rang. Wrapping herself in a bathrobe, she dashed over to the intercom.

"Hey, it's me… Let me in!" Carmen answered.

Excited by the front page news, she had turned up with coffee and Chloe's overnight bag which she had collected from the hotel reception on her way over. Chloe buzzed Carmen into the building and dashed to her bedroom to throw on some shorts and a tank top. As she did, her phone caught her eye—it was flashing like crazy. She had missed dozens of calls from her mother and could see a barrage of text messages all queuing up for her to read.

It appeared that everyone had caught up with the press coverage and Chloe had a lot of explaining to do. Not to mention the influx of notifications she had from her Instagram—she didn't have time to check it all now. There was a light rap on the door and standing on the other side was Carmen with a copy of the New York News featuring Chloe's picture covering her face.

"Oh hi… I'm Chloe Ravens the hottest girl on the planet right now! Who? Gianni Palazzo? Oh yeah, he is as talented in the bedroom as he is a designer!" Carmen mocked as Chloe opened the door, barging her way in; laughing at her own joke.

Chloe was just glad to see an extra cup of coffee in her hand which she took without hesitation or invitation.

"Did Dom get his plane okay?" Carmen said.

"Yeah, all fine… I was a bit emotional, but your call certainly got me out of that funk."

"I'm surprised you hadn't seen it already… Have you heard from him yet?" Carmen said.

"I've had like two hours sleep, and I just saw my best friend off to another country with a monster hangover, the last thing I was thinking was to check the newspapers in case I made front page… And no, I haven't heard from him. I'm sure he is a very busy man this morning, and the last thing on his mind is me!"

"Ouch—hangover still pounding?" Carmen said, picking up on a slight short temper. "Well, you never know… Stranger things have been happening recently. Anyway, enjoy the free publicity darling… People pay thousands for that in this city. Plus, it's great for your website—not to mention your collection," Carmen reminded her.

Right on cue, Chloe's phone rang—this time it wasn't her mother. "Oh—look," Chloe said, showing Carmen the caller ID.

"Well, answer it then!" she prompted.

"Hi, Veronica," Chloe said, trying her best to sound chirpy.

"Hi, honey! I have just seen your picture on the front page of my paper this morning! You look fab-u-lous, what a great stunt you have pulled… How on Earth did you manage that?" Veronica said.

'Yes, it was a great stunt,' Chloe thought to herself, but how she had managed, it was a mystery to her too. Chloe switched the call to speakerphone so Carmen could listen in on the conversation, saving her to relay it all to her after.

"So listen… Me and the designers want to see you as soon as! We want to get this collection off the ground, ride the coattails of your publicity. Don't worry about sketches and stuff like that… Instead, come down and see us straight away. Our designers will do all the work, you just tell them how it should look. We don't have time to mess around here, right now you could be hot property, and it's all about timing in this business… We are gonna make you a style icon baby! Already people are wondering who is this new girl on Gianni Palazzo's arm, but now they will find out… So come down around four-ish, I'll email you the office address."

But before Chloe could confirm, Veronica had hung up—saying no to her was not an option.

"Wow, sounds like things are *really* about to happen," Carmen said. "Anyway, how much is she *actually* paying you for this?"

Chloe stared at Carmen with a blank expression. Not just due to a fuzzy head, but because they had never talked about money.

"You are clever, but you still have a lot to learn… Money makes the world go round—including yours—especially yours! I'm coming with you… I'll have your money sorted out in no time, and then, and only then will we talk with her designers."

Carmen was a fighter, and she never let anyone walk over her, she knew how people in this industry worked and sometimes people took advantage of you. Doing you a 'favour' by propelling you into the public eye without sharing a cut of the profit for your genius ideas was just one of their well-known tactics. Carmen wasn't going to let this happen to Chloe; she felt responsible for her, she had helped her this far it would be criminal to leave her at the last hurdle. It was also in her interests that she looked after Chloe and kept her close by, this could be just as profitable for her too.

Chloe was just glad to have Carmen as a friend and a mentor by her side to help her through all this now she didn't have Dom. During a well deserved, albeit light lunch, Chloe filled Carmen in on her idea of making a collection that was 'vintage Palazzo' inspired, which Carmen found very funny and ironic, but clever at the same time.

"Okay, so we are going to go in there, and you're gonna leave the money talk to me... I will get you an advance. Has she not offered you any kind of ball-park figure?"

Chloe thought it over, she couldn't remember there ever being any talk of payment whatsoever. So much had gone on these past two weeks, she barely remembered what she had for breakfast (except today, of course, that was easy—nothing). Carmen took the long pause as a fact that she had no idea how much she was could earn from this collaboration project.

"Don't worry... I will get you forty percent at least," Carmen said confidently.

With very little time left, they rapidly got their act together. Chloe gathered the few Palazzo accessories she owned to show the designers the type of look and feel to the collection she was going for, which was rather ambitious for a budget brand to recreate. The shoes she had bought from the sample sale were an excellent template for the designers to copy—not too complicated but an example of elegance and quality.

True to her word, Veronica had emailed DivaFeet's office address, getting lost and flustered wouldn't help them maintain their cool when they really needed it the most. Confidence and calm was the key to making this meeting a successful one.

***

DivaFeet's headquarters were a lot different compared to the no expense spared head offices of Palazzo but still furnished nicely as you would expect from a fashion brand. Everyone from digital marketing, photography, customer care, buying and merchandising—and an in-house design team—were all housed under one roof, with a separate warehouse in New Jersey from where orders were shipped from.

Carmen and Chloe were greeted enthusiastically at the reception by a young girl, who seemed very proud to work there, her dress sense was youthful and over accessorised (she definitely took advantage of her staff discount). She offered Chloe and Carmen a seat while she called through to Veronica's office.

"Hi, Veronica... Yes, I have Chloe Ravens here for you... Uh-huh, sure, will do... She's on her way," the receptionist said.

Within seconds, Veronica met them in the small reception area and filled it with her large personality just as quickly.

"So glad you could make it at such short notice!" she said in her brash, loud voice, going in for a kiss on the cheek.

Chloe could see her clocking Carmen, wondering who she was, and why she was with her.

"This is my business partner; Carmen Visconti," Chloe said. "We work together on styling projects and more recently with Gabi; Carmen deals with the financial side of things too," she said, dropping in the subject of payment as soon as she could.

"Oh, I didn't realise there were two of you behind all of this," Veronica said, sensing she was about to cut a hard deal. "Nice to meet you, Carmen... Shall we go through to my office? I have some of our best designers just dying to meet you."

Veronica led the way to the boardroom, it had a long glass table and six leather chairs dotted around it. Sitting there waiting were two girls from her design team. They looked like they were fresh out of fashion college and probably paid poorly; probably just doing it to put the experience on their resume's, Chloe assumed, ready to trade in for grander things later.

"This is Chloe and Carmen—this is Sam and Lily—my designers."

Veronica was a woman who had a sound business mind, but what she didn't know was that Carmen was a very determined character when she needed to be, and also savvy.

"Thanks for coming down… So as you know, Chloe and I discussed this project just this week… Alongside our multi-brand offering, we also produce our own range, and I thought it would be great to collaborate on a designer capsule with the hottest new thing in fashion—you! But, I am sure you are anxious about what kind of contract we will be offering. Firstly, don't worry, I have all of that sorted out…"

"Well, that's the thing," Carmen interrupted. "We aren't worried as much, after all, it is you parting with your money here," she said with a smile, breaking the ice for what she was about to drop. "To be direct, we want forty percent profit from the collection, and an advance of $10,000 for our ideas and vision of the collection—excluding profits."

Veronica screwed up her face, she wasn't used to being told what to do, and how to do it—this was *her* company.

"Well, I have to say… I appreciate you wanting to make the maximum profit but without my business, marketing, design team and experience—you wouldn't have a collaboration at all… Don't you agree?" Veronica said, standing her ground.

Chloe started to feel sorry about the situation, she didn't want to piss Veronica off and lose this deal entirely. What was Carmen doing? Chloe couldn't afford to lose this contract, even though she had lost her job, she didn't really care about the money; it was more about getting a foot in the door for future prospects more than anything. Chloe sat there, unable to look Veronica in the eye, hoping Carmen knew what she was doing.

"I agree… But I think Chloe has proven herself to be a brand all on her own, and we have received other offers in light of her current popularity… However as she has loyalty to you, we are committed to doing business with you, but you need to match the offers on the table from other retailers if we are going to work together," Carmen said.

Veronica was starting to get slightly annoyed. You could see it in her face, it had gone red and rigid like stone, clenching her jaw. Veronica was trying her best to bite her lip, but she knew Carmen had a good point. Before she could get a word in, Carmen continued her case.

"Also, I'd like to add that Chloe has managed to sell many of your products through her website reaching out to a new audience, which you have kindly arranged the commission for, but there has been extra publicity that is unrecognised in the form of celebrity styling. Gabriela Gracia famously carried your clutch to her film premiere; also Chloe has raised her own profile, today's press illustrates that—not to mention her social media platforms have garnered thousands of followers in very little time. So, in effect, you have expanded your market just through being associated with StacksOfStyle... Thousands of visitors are onsite as we speak thanks to her connection with Gianni Palazzo... Now, how exciting would it be to work with Chloe Ravens exclusively before anyone else? You can be the one to say you started her career... Why risk such a great business relationship over a small request, considering how much money you will make from all this?"

Veronica seemed to calm down, as did Chloe. Listening to Carmen's pitch had made Chloe realise just how much she was worth. Carmen was right, she *was* worth every cent and could probably go to another retailer and secure a deal all on her own. Veronica thought it over in her head and scribbled some figures down on a piece of paper in front of her. Carmen looked at Chloe and smiled, she was confident that she had achieved her goal.

Sam and Lily smiled at them both sarcastically, almost staring them out as if to be ready to back their boss at any moment, but they didn't have to, Veronica came to a rapid decision.

"Okay... A forty percent royalty on the profit it is, but with a $6,000 advance," she offered sternly, at least she would still be the principal shareholder in the project.

"Sounds great to me!" Chloe said, happy to be sealing the deal on Veronica's terms, and not giving Carmen a chance to counter the offer.

"Done!" Veronica said, offering her hand to shake on it.

Chloe stood up and shook her hand.

Veronica then turned to Carmen to shake hers, with extra added grip. If it weren't for her, she would be getting Chloe for much less—free even—but that was business at the end of the day, and something in her gut told her that Chloe *was* a good investment.

"I will have the contract arranged with my solicitor this afternoon… Is that all?" Veronica said, wrapping up the meeting, knowing they wouldn't reveal any ideas until a contract was signed.

Chloe felt Veronica's annoyance, so to sweeten her up, she showed her and the designers a few ideas, an insight into what she would be getting for her money. Chloe and Carmen began to present clearly and with passion. Still buzzing from the Palazzo show the night before, they shared their stories of famous faces and free champagne with Sam and Lily who were lapping up the glamour that was their lives.

"So you see, we want to produce a collection with the same appeal of a luxury fashion house, something aspirational yet affordable—style for everyone!" Chloe said, painting the picture for her 'Raven by Chloe Ravens' line.

Sam and Lily were impressed with what they heard and furiously started to sketch line drawings of the Palazzo shoes Chloe had brought to the meeting. They seemed rather excited to be working on a project that appeared to have style and a sense of luxury about it; they too felt like they were benefitting from this collaboration, if it were a success, it would be another score on their resume's.

"Well, I think this meeting has been a success," Veronica said, rubbing her hands together. "So, you shall receive the contract and then we will meet again to get this all down and designed for production. Let's say, first thing Monday Morning? We need to get cracking if we want to meet our deadline of the Holiday season."

Leaving the meeting with a feeling of achievement, Carmen and Chloe couldn't wait to get outside the building to jump with excitement.

"Oh my gosh—that was such a buzz! For a moment I thought, '*Fuck!*' I hope she knows where she is going with this?" Chloe said, pushing her hair back, resting her hands on her forehead in relief.

"I know, I could tell…Both of your faces were very entertaining to watch… She is a lovely lady, but this is business, and you never mix friendship with business! Better to clear the air before any mess can happen… And now you are $6,000 richer—and some once the collection sells!" Carmen said.

Chloe was filled with joy. She didn't need to worry about money for a few months at least, who knew where this would lead to? Even if Gianni never contacted her, or saw her ever again, there was the possibility that he would see her designs and own brand blossom—especially if it propelled her into the mainstream. Chloe couldn't help her mind from jumping from one idea to the next, the possibilities seemed endless.

"Oh, by the way," Carmen said, digging around in her handbag. "When I went to collect our bags from the hotel this morning, Gabi's assistant left this envelope at the desk for you."

"What is it?" Chloe said, ripping it open straight away.

It was a cheque for $3,000; the money for the Palazzo gown she had promised her. Chloe felt embarrassed, how could she accept this money after Carmen had just brokered a deal for her? Not to mention everything else that she had done for her lately, she had taken Chloe under her wing.

"It's yours," Chloe said, closing the envelope and handing it back to Carmen.

"*What?* Don't be silly… You earned that… Besides, you did me a favour remember."

"And what you did back there was more than what I could ever do for you… It's only fair."

"No—I can't…" Carmen said, starting to walk on ahead, ignoring the offer. "Let's grab lunch… I'll let you pay for that at least."

Chloe stood still in her tracks, she was deadly serious.

"No, I mean it... This is just $3,000, but you just got me six in advance, plus forty percent on profits... Take the damn cheque!"

Carmen looked at Chloe, realising she had made the right choice in backing her. Just like how Veronica had invested in Chloe, Carmen did the same with her time and friendship, getting paid wasn't her motivation in exchange for her knowledge. But then again, Chloe did have a point—she had just made her a hefty sum—if this were a consultancy job, she would have charged more for her expertise.

"Okay... Fine... But I only take cash."

Surprised at her demand, Chloe gave Carmen a raised eyebrow as if to say: 'Really?'.

"Okay... Cash it is... Whatever, just take the money."

"The cheque is in *your* name bitch! It's no good to me... But your money is," Carmen said with a chuckle.

Chloe laughed at her own stupidity, of course, Carmen wasn't being a diva, she was being clever. Chloe was so giddy with excitement and with being able to give something back, she had forgotten the obvious.

"Lunch is still on you though... You can afford Cipriani now," Carmen said, linking arms with her.

****

Regina had a plan, a plan to get rid of Chloe Ravens once and for all. It was something she had become obsessed with (and something she hadn't been very successful at so far), but this time would be different. Regina had researched and stalked Chloe online all day long on her office computer. The sight of her successful *little* website made her want to vomit her guts up into the trash can beside her desk.

To see her doing well outside of Palazzo was another blow, she couldn't believe that this girl could make something of herself without her help. She just couldn't stand that Chloe had proved her wrong, but this was where her success would end. There was no way Chloe was to come back into Palazzo with a title, and even worse, have a fling with Gianni under her nose. There were things to be said and rules that needed to be laid down if this town was going to be big enough for the both of them to thrive in fashion.

# CHAPTER TWENTY-NINE

After finding her home address on the internal system, Regina made her way over to pay an impromptu visit; hoping to catch Chloe unexpectedly and intimidate her like how she knew best. Just because she wasn't her manager anymore, it didn't mean she shouldn't fear her. Tonight, instead of analysing sales reports and catching up on emails, Regina's homework was making sure Chloe understood she wasn't welcome back at Palazzo under any circumstances.

Taking a private taxi with blacked-out windows through Williamsburg was a new experience, she wouldn't want to be seen dead in such a part town. 'Up and coming' equated to 'run down' in her opinion, she couldn't help but turn her nose up at the sight of graffiti that graced exposed brick walls (not recognising it as 'street art,' but an eyesore).

"Just pull up a few doors away from the address please driver," Regina said, in case Chloe happened to look out her window and see her or even worse, catch her at the doorstep.

As the taxi pulled to the curb, Regina was calm and collected, but on the inside, she was pumped for a fight.

"Wait here for me," she said, waving an extra $50 bill between her fingertips at the driver.

Standing outside Chloe's apartment block, Regina checked the address to make sure she definitely had the correct place. 'This is her place all right, it looks cheap enough,' she thought. She rang the buzzer, annoyed that it was an intercom entry system, Chloe wasn't exactly going to invite her in for tea and biscuits. Either way, Regina was going to speak to her, even if she had to bust down her door herself; her career and reputation depended on it.

Chloe had just finished brushing her teeth and had changed into her usual shorts and tank top to lounge in. It had been a very emotional, exciting and tiring day and lunch with Carmen had turned into dinner, and naturally, it had included a few bottles of wine—she was now ready for bed. She had plenty to do (StacksOfStyle had been neglected somewhat recently) and she still had to post her review and pictures from the Palazzo show and after-party. Especially now she had a platform and media eyes on her, and the website's visitor counter was soaring with everyone wanting to know more about Gianni's new interest.

Before getting to bed Chloe checked her emails, hoping there was an email from Gianni. She hadn't made her mind up about his intentions or what the impact of the what happened would mean, but the unexpected made it even more exciting. Upon login, she was shocked to see an inbox inundated with messages. From what she could see, it was mainly journalists doing their research, contacting her with interview questions for their gossip columns.

Being photographed with one of the world's most prolific fashion designers (and bachelors) certainly had projected her into the public eye, whether she liked it or not. There was one very interesting email address that stood out from all of the rest, but before she could read it, the door buzzer sounded. 'Who would be calling at this time?' she thought. Maybe it was someone pressing the buzzer by accident? In-trigued by who it could be, Chloe left her laptop to answer it.

"Yup?" She said, with her finger on the speakerphone button.

No one answered back, she concluded that it was probably just kids messing about.

She sat back down to finally read that email that had caught her eye. To her surprise, Vogue had requested to feature her in the Decem-ber issue, and was enquiring whether she would be available for an interview. But just as she was about to read the email once over again, to make sure she wasn't misunderstood—still half-drunk—there was a loud thud at the door; a hard and heavy rap from a fist.

It startled her and made her heart leap into her throat, she tried to grasp control of her breath. The banging on the door continued, she was sure whoever it was would kick the door down if she didn't open it first. Living alone made things like this even scarier, maybe it was a burglar coming to ransack the place, knowing a single woman lived here on her own, having scoped out the place for week's and noticing that she was hardly home at night.

Or could it be some crazy person who had seen her in the paper and found out where she lived and wanted to be best friends? It was a bit early for stalkers but all kinds of thoughts ran through her head, she ran to the kitchen and grabbed a carving knife from the top drawer. Holding it close by her side, she made sure the latch was on the door before daring to open it.

"Who is it?" she called through the door, then she remembered what happened in horror films. The intruder wasn't exactly going to say: 'crazy murderer here, coming to kill you!'.

Turning the lock slowly, so it didn't make a sound (which was near impossible), Chloe opened the door ajar and peeked through the slither of a gap. To her utter amazement, Regina was standing in her hallway. 'What the Hell is she doing here?'.

"Not going to invite me in?" Regina said, wedging her foot in the doorway so she couldn't slam it shut on her; she glanced down at the knife in her hand. "Planning on stabbing me, are you? I bet you would just love that, wouldn't you?"

Chloe was stunned still. Having Regina visit was worse than an intruder, just as bad as a serial killer in Chloe's opinion—in fact, she would have preferred that—at least she would stand a chance with a weapon in hand. It was true, she would love to stab the bitch after all she had put her through, but it was her wits that had to be razor sharp.

"So, are you going to let me in or just make me stand here all night?" she said with a smirk from catching Chloe by surprise. Even though this wasn't her territory, the intrusive act of surprise gave her all the power she needed to feel in charge.

Chloe released the latch and began to open the door, and Regina barged her way in. She stopped in her tracks to size up the place, it was nothing in comparison to her luxuriously furnished home that she once shared with her husband. She threw her handbag down on the breakfast bar, making a thud like it were a bag of bricks. Reams of paperwork that she carried home every night had the same effect in weight.

"I suppose you're wondering what I'm doing here?"

Indeed she was, Chloe couldn't believe that Regina was actually here, in her apartment. She didn't know what to do with herself, but feeling silly with a knife in her hand—she put it back in the drawer.

"I know why you're here," Chloe said, turning to face her with folded arms to hide her shaking hands, trying her best to assume a firm stance and take the lead.

"It looks like you have created quite a stir…"

Chloe remained silent, she wanted to hear what Regina had to say. She wasn't her boss anymore, and technically she could report her for stealing personal information from the database, but she knew Regina would just deny it and Victoria from HR would back her up in any situation; Chloe had to fight fire with an extinguisher and settle this feud once and for all.

"*Such* a stir… You even managed to catch the eye of Mr Palazzo himself… Not exactly five-star is it?" Regina said, walking around her flat, evaluating her living space further. "You and your little website have attracted much attention I see… God knows why it granted you an invite to the show… You and your 'fashion friends' were very lucky to be there—and with Dominic Fraser too… Good to see that you were able to forgive him after his betrayal."

"For your information, what I do or where I go is none of your damn business! Dom has never betrayed me, he is a loyal friend! Something you wouldn't know about," Chloe said, no longer able to stand there silent.

"Oh, yes… So loyal… So loyal he handed his notice into me after I requested a meeting with him… Of course, I confronted him about your little staff discount arrangement you two had going on… He'd rather leave and see you pay than take responsibility."

By spinning a web of lies and making Chloe doubt what had really happened, she now had Chloe where she wanted—thrown off-guard and confused.

"That's not what happened, and you know it!" Chloe fought back, refusing to believe Dom had thrown her to the wolves. "Dom is a friend—a real friend—something you wouldn't understand."

"The point is, no matter how good you think you are, you will always screw it up in the end... Believe me, I admire you for wanting to succeed, but it will never happen... Do you think I got to where I am today by being friends with everybody? Swanning around town in slutty dresses, trying to make men fall for me that are way out of my league? You can't just go around being *nice* to people... No—they take you for granted, it's a sign of weakness! You can't be friends with everyone... *Oh look at me, everybody loves me*," Regina mocked, with an evil laugh.

Chloe was confused, she had never seen Regina like this before; she was wild and crazy, possessed even. For a moment she considered getting the knife back out of the drawer and chasing her out of the apartment, but Regina didn't give her the chance to react.

"Well, you have succeeded to get one person to like you it seems... And a very important person too. That is *quite* an achievement, but not for a cheap *whore!* Yes, I saw you... Flirting with him shamelessly in front of the cameras! He can have any woman he wants, you know? Why would he be interested in you—*hmmm?* A normal, *fat* girl like you... I mean look at you—you are nothing!" she scoffed, flicking her hand to gesture at her simple loungewear instead of designer lingerie.

"If you've come round here for insults Regina, then I will gladly trade," Chloe said, she wasn't going to stand there in her own home and be insulted by someone who had no business being there.

"My point is this, you like him more than he likes you... The person he likes, isn't real is it? That version doesn't *really* exist... The real you is a thief who stole from his company, made trysts with his clients behind my back, and was difficult to work with—even trying to turn your colleagues against me... If only he knew... Would he still like you then do you think?"

"So what... Go on and tell him everything; I couldn't care less... I don't even know him! We just met last night—that's it! Everything else is just in your twisted head," Chloe said, knowing full well that she wanted to see him again somehow.

"Of course," Regina said, laughing off her attempt at playing it cool. "He is the most successful designer in the world... Of course you 'just happened' to stumble across him conveniently at the after-party... You've wanted to climb the ladder ever since you started working at Palazzo, and I ensured that you never did! Now, I don't know how you managed it, but it seems that you have risen from the ashes... You have another chance, but I am here to make sure you don't take that chance."

Chloe wasn't following, Regina's crazy talk had lost her completely. 'What does she mean, second chance?' Chloe wondered. Regina could see she was baffled expression, so continued with her power monologue.

"He has asked me to find you... To ask you to work for him in fact. Of course, I am going to tell him you declined, tell him you're too busy whoring yourself out to the whole of New York, with that social slut you've been hanging around with."

There was a pause. Chloe couldn't believe what she was hearing. Regina had sunk to a new low, a level she would never have stooped to at Palazzo but now she wasn't her boss, she could be her hateful, authentic self and speak how she wanted. But more than Regina's behaviour, her words had shocked her. Gianni wanted her to work for him, he had personally requested her to join Palazzo again, not knowing that she had only just quit. Chloe mulled it over for a moment, but Regina's last words were left ringing in her ears.

"Slut? That *slut* is one of the most successful stylists in town! It was *us* that have been styling Gabriela Gracia, *us* that put Palazzo in the papers before Fashion Week! That's more than what you and your crony Myra have ever done put together!"

"Oh, I know all about your pathetic attempts—you don't need to tell me. Now, Gianni will pursue you, of course, he won't be satisfied when I tell him you said no to his generous offer... I suppose you could try to develop some kind of relationship with him, date him even? Although I shouldn't think he will be that desperate once he has used you, you will be just another one of his has-been's! But that's not the point—you could accept, but I will still be your manager, and I will make it impossible for you all over again... Do you really want to re-live the past? I can drag you through the mud slowly and pick you apart with your history, *girl!* You see, they will never get rid of me, I am irreplaceable Chloe; they will never find someone like me that can do all the things I can do... I have been with this company for half of my lifetime, I know it better than anyone else does... And with the company set to grow bigger than ever, I will become even more powerful in this industry than your tiny little brain could ever imagine possible... You, on the other hand, are like any other silly wannabe... You could tell him how much of a bad a person I am, you could try to get me fired, but the fact is, you won't! You will never get rid of me because this is where it stops! I *swear,* I will make it my mission to destroy your career if you accept this offer, and you know how determined I can be... Or, you could just ignore his advances and forget about me, just like how I will forget you... A much simpler way to go about your sad life, don't you think? You will have your little Internet career, and I will have mine."

Chloe raged with anger. 'How dare she come here and dictate what I can, and can't do'.

"You're right... You *are* irreplaceable Regina... Amazing Regina Hall who knows best—how would they find someone just as vile as you? You are a disgusting and heartless *bitch!* It must be a sad life you lead, to know that no one truly likes you for the person you really are... The fact you have to come round here and threaten pathetic little *me*—as you put it—to protect your career, is just pathetic! Your sad existence revolves around work, and when you take that away, you are the one who is nothing—*nothing!* Now, I suggest you get the *fuck* out of my apartment before I call the cops and make a complaint about you to Gianni myself!" Chloe said, opening the front door for Regina to leave.

There was so much more Chloe wanted to say, but she was too angry and shook up to think clearly; telling her where to stick it was the next best thing to actually stabbing her. Regina picked up her handbag and looked Chloe in the eye one last time.

"Is *this* what Gianni has to look forward to? *Pah!*" Regina said through a bitchy laugh.

"Well, it's more than what you could offer… You might be irreplaceable to him in the workplace—and maybe I can't compete with that—but you will never match me in the bedroom you rank old bitter bitch! I can *fuck* up your career just by *fucking* Gianni… Don't you forget that!"

Regina wanted to slap her, but she was right; if she gained Gianni's trust (and she had certainly caught his eye thus far), then she could potentially poison him against her if they were ever to become more than just a fling. Defeated, she headed to the door, holding her power by not taking her eyes off Chloe as she did.

"Thank you so much for visiting," Chloe finished sarcastically, slamming the door shut and forcing Regina out with a nudge from the door.

Chloe was left shaken and angered. She wanted to yell out at the top of her voice and expel the leftover aggression; she even considered chasing after her to continue the argument, having now come up with more points to fire at her. It was amazing how after the moment you could suddenly come up with loads of material to use, but she resisted acting out of anger. She couldn't be responsible for her actions in such a state, and besides, Regina was gone. It was done. Instead, she called Carmen who instantly got in a cab to make her way over—this was major!

\*

"This is the ultimate compliment!" Carmen said, but Chloe looked at her as if she were mad. "Of course it is… Finally, you are a real threat to her, and she knows it… Don't you see? It's *you* that holds power now… I wouldn't worry, Gianni will be in touch to find out why you turned down such a great opportunity, and you can tell him everything."

Carmen took a swig of wine that she had bought over, Chloe had already backed a full glass to steady her nerves; the rush of adrenaline had sobered her up, despite having had quite enough earlier.

"I can't do that… I'll just look like some whiny child. Plus, the Sun shines out of Regina's ass… Like she said, she's irreplaceable. He's not gonna take my side over hers," Chloe said, pacing the room still angered while Carmen lounged on the sofa, entertained by the juicy gossip.

"If I know men when they are blinded by the female charm, then I'm sure he will listen to what you have to say," Carmen said, picking up Chloe's laptop, distracted by the message on the screen.

"Maybe she's right… I mean, all of this is just a fantasy… Too good to be true," Chloe said.

"Uh-huh," Carmen said, zoning out from the conversation while reading the open email. "Erm—what's this?"

"What's what?" Chloe said, now pouring out another glass of wine for herself.

"Girl, you are like a cat—nine lives or what!"

'What now?' Chloe wondered, her life was a roller-coaster, and she wanted to get off; her head was spinning from all of it—she put down the wine.

"Vogue an interview for the December issue, that's what!" Carmen said, turning the laptop around so Chloe could see.

Regina's rude interruption had made her forget all about the email from Vogue. Suddenly, Chloe was reminded that it was indeed too good, but all true. There was no time for puking now; it was time for revenge. Carmen was right yet again—she *was* a threat—seeing her in the pages of Vogue would remind Regina just how popular she had become, and she couldn't stop her with her petty threats. Chloe had learnt about getting revenge from the best bitch she knew.

**

Jason had been busy all summer working on pieces commissioned by the South Bank Gallery that was to be put on display in their 'London Calling' Exhibition, they also wanted pieces from his archive that tied in with London Fashion Week. Jason's picture of the famous English supermodel, Kate, had attracted lots of attention in the UK press and even from Kate herself, who wanted her own piece to display in her home.

All through the summer, he had worked hard on getting his collection together and shipped to London in time for a once in a lifetime opportunity. He was determined not to let Dominic's constant messaging and phone calls distract him by ignoring them, but it didn't mean that he wasn't thinking of him—quite the opposite. Dom was his muse, his motivation to produce new work on demand. Jason was scheduled to fly out to London for the installation, but he wanted one particular person to be there with him.

He had an idea and called Dom's phone straight away, but it was no good—there was no answer. He tried again and again for an answer, but it was as if his phone had been turned off. Jason's heart sank as his calls kept going to voicemail. Jason grabbed his wallet from his jacket and rifled through it frantically, he knew it was in here somewhere. He had kept it for safekeeping since the day he left New York… And there it was, folded up in one of the card slots—the piece of paper that Dom had carefully written down all his details on.

***

The press release stating that Palazzo had acquired Maison Marais hit the news globally, and even though it was a Saturday, Regina made herself busy with work. Pressing matters occupied her mind, she had to dispel Gianni's interest in Chloe, fast.

---

**From:** Regina Hall
**To:** Gianni Palazzo
<u>**Subject:** Miss Chloe Ravens</u>

Dear Mr Palazzo,
I am writing to inform you that I have personally contacted tried Miss Ravens to deliver your offer. Upon meeting with her yesterday, I explained your interest in her employment at Palazzo. Unfortunately, after consideration, she declined due to other work commitments that she is currently engaged with. She did, however, ask me to thank you and wishes Palazzo all the best for the future.

All the best for the show next week, do let me know if I can be of further assistance.

Kind regards,

Regina Hall
Store Director
**Palazzo S.P.A**
**Fifth Avenue, New York.**

---

Gianni was also working over the weekend, casting and fitting models for the upcoming spring/summer show in Milan. A hundred models must have walked for him and his assistants already. Human beings that looked as though they belonged on another planet with pretty faces, slender frames and long limbs. However, his mind was elsewhere. With the press release of the newly formed Palazzo Group now the talk of the fashion industry.

He had pre-recorded an official announcement, but the press wanted more; they wanted him for everything, from photo shoots to interviews, but he needed to focus on making the next collection a hit. With still no word from New York either, his mind just couldn't settle; ever since he had left, he just couldn't stop thinking about her. He had thought about reaching out through her website, he had looked at it enough times just to see her face, but that was too predictable and not his style.

Everything he did had to have style, including flirting with women. Why do the dirty work when you could get someone else to do it for you? That was what having staff was for. Refreshing his inbox on his phone, the email from Regina had come through. He quickly skimmed through the email, which wasn't to his liking, but it didn't bother him all the same. 'She's just playing the game,' he thought.

Usually, women jumped to sleep with him on the first night, and then pestered him non-stop for the rest of the year to see him again. His assistant Joli was his part-time 'fixer' and dealt with all the enquiries from unwanted attention seekers that were no longer in fashion. He rather liked the chase Chloe was giving him, even though he knew he would eventually get his own way.

"Okay, I think we should take a break and then come back to look over the selections… Joli—Joli," he called out, she was never too far away.

Joli had been his assistant for many years and had put up with some shit over the years, but she knew exactly how to handle him. She was professional and mature enough to just get the job done with minimal fuss and maximum results. She had built up quite the 'black-book' of contacts from being his assistant that helped her accomplish anything he threw at her. She came to his side with her journal and pen in hand, ready for his instruction: more coffee and maybe a pack of Vogue cigarettes. Gianni only smoked when he was stressed with a show, or when the company was in the spotlight for the wrong reasons.

"Joli, I want you to find the address of Chloe Ravens in New York… She's the stylist that runs that website I told you about… Remember? That girl I was photographed within New York—her."

Of course, Joli knew who he was talking about. She had fielded many enquiries from journalists and gossip columns asking for an official comment about their connection. By now, Joli had become a matchmaking queen and accomplished at cyberstalking. Every detail of personal information could be found on social network sites, even search engines did the trick nowadays. But deciding that contacting Chloe through her website was the first port of call, Joli had devised a plan within minutes.

"Gianni, I have a contact for Miss Ravens. What would you like me to do from here?" she said, never one to let him down.

"I want you to book the best hotel in Milan, first-class flights and arrange an invite to our show—front row seat… I want it express delivered to her immediately… Whatever you need to do—just do it!"

Joli rolled her eyes and walked off to start her mission as Gianni called an end to the break. He was confident he was going to get his way and could now focus on getting back to work. What woman would turn down an all expenses paid trip to Italy to see a fashion show? Certain that Chloe would succumb to this offer, he carried on with the casting, seeming lighter and less stressed than before.

Unaware of the history behind Chloe's legacy at Palazzo, Joli called the New York press office. She hoped she could simply pass most of the admin onto them; she had more important jobs to finish (Fashion Week was the most hectic week in her schedule), she didn't need anything extra on her plate. Fortunately, unlike Regina, Myra had taken the weekend off—exhausted from the previous week—and had made her newest assistant cover the weekend.

Kim had to be in the office all weekend, in case there were any urgent enquiries following New York Fashion Week and the breaking news of The Palazzo Group deal; not to mention the announcement that the retrospective show was going to be the next exhibition fashion lovers would flock to. However, most of the correspondence was being handled from the Milan office, making the already empty office extremely quiet.

With not much to do and growing bored and restless by the minute, Kim filled the hours by trying on the new collection. Something she wouldn't get to do with Myra and Sylvia bossing her around when they returned to work on Monday. Annoyingly, just as she was about to slip on a runway gown, the phone suddenly rang. Sometimes, Myra liked to check up on her, making sure she answered the phone within three rings. Kim counted them and proceeded to answer on cue, trying her best not to stumble and rip the half-zipped chiffon dress.

"Good afternoon Palazzo New York press office," she said in one long breath.

"Hi, it's Joli… Gianni's assistant."

"Oh, hi there—I'm Kim, Myra's assistant… How can I help?" she said, having only seen Joli's name on Myra's emails before, but knew exactly who she was.

"I need your help with a request from Mr Palazzo himself, which I hope you can assist with. As you can imagine it's busy here in Milan with the show and I can't fulfil the requirements from here."

"Of course, Myra's not here right now, but I will make sure I get the message over to her right away."

"Perfect… Gianni would like Miss Chloe Ravens to attend the show in a week's time as his personal guest. Would you be able to contact her and arrange first class flights that suit her schedule? We can cover all costs on our end."

Kim couldn't believe what she was hearing. Rumours had been rife about Chloe dating Gianni, all because of their picture in the New York News. Everyone wondered why she had left so quickly and mysteriously, only to suddenly turn up on the bosses arm at the event of the year. Sarah had told everyone that they had fallen in love and she was moving to Milan to be with him, it now seemed that this was more of a prediction than a rumour!

Joli continued with her instructions on the other end of the line. "I'll book the hotel and email you the booking reference, which you can then pass on... What I need you to do, is deliver an invite to her for the show along with first-class flight tickets. You must make sure she gets it this afternoon, Gianni wants them delivered by hand; not by post, not by courier, not even a singing telegram... Got that? Now, I have located a contact email through her website—"

"Oh, that's perfectly fine... In fact, I know her quite well; we used to work together many moons ago, and we are due for a catch up anyway. You can be assured that I will deal with this myself as a matter of priority," Kim said, excited to be delivering this news to Chloe in person.

Kim knew she had to be the one to deliver this information to Chloe; if she handed it over to Myra, she would only tell Regina, and together they would put a stop to it all. She wasn't going to give them the satisfaction. For once, Joli had managed to contact someone from the New York press office that seemed to know what they were doing! Joli made a note in her notebook to remember Kim's name for the next time she had a dilemma concerning Chloe Ravens that needed sorting efficiently (which she knew was bound to happen with Gianni smitten by her).

But Kim was only too happy to help, she also had become frustrated with the store politics and Myra's management style—or lack of. Of course, she would be in deep shit when Myra and Regina heard about this, and if they found out she had a hand in it all, but she didn't care. It would only be a personal attack, she had approval from way above their heads, and Kim had received a backup offer of her own that she was now considering.

Thanks to Chloe introducing her to Dionne at the fashion show, she had been asked to work at Maison Marais as her personal assistant. Dionne had been looking for someone to manage her day-to-day work life, accompany her to events and other tasks that required someone with a brain. Especially as Dionne knew that the take over was imminent and having someone who knew the inside workings of Palazzo was an advantage.

It was definitely a step-up from doing Myra's banal daily errands, and this phone call had helped her come to a decision. She didn't want to be stuck at Palazzo forever either, the take-over of Maison Marais seemed like an excellent opportunity to jump ship and start a new exciting era in both her own career and in Maison Marais' history. Ending the call with Joli, Kim was happy to finally have something to do that was worth coming in on the weekend for—and it was a fun task that made her heart skip with the romanticism of it all. Mischievously, she worked away on the request with precision, sporting a huge grin as she did, sending emails back and forth to Joli confirm all the arrangements were in place from her side.

There was only one thing left to do, and that was to deliver the invite herself, ensuring it wouldn't be intercepted by Myra and Regina upon their return to work. Like Regina, she found Chloe's address on the system (this time for good use) and jumped in a cab immediately. It was also a chance for Kim to share her good news too, and to say thanks for her new job. Chloe had really helped her out lately, and to think that at first, they didn't see eye-to-eye. Now they were allies, and Kim was about to deliver some very exciting news that would once again stoke the flames of gossip at Palazzo.

# CHAPTER THIRTY

Since losing her job, life had been a whirlwind but the weekend was no excuse to stop now. Regina's visit had motivated her to move out and into Dom's apartment as soon as she could. Boxing up her belongings was a good way to distract her brain from all the craziness that filled it. As she zoomed around packing, she ran through the night before in her head, over and over. Coming up with various quips she wished she had thought of at the time.

Her heart pumped with venom as she frantically packed her life away into a city of cardboard that now filled her living room. She felt like she was having a heart attack, her body and mind both doing overtime all at once. She stopped herself from what she was doing and sat on a stool in the kitchen, staring at the mess she had made, she tried to process what was happening. Was this really what she wanted? Chasing powerful men, gossip in newspapers being printed about her, enemies that she thought she had escaped turning up at her door with new ultimatums?

Even the upcoming collaboration with DivaFeet seemed daunting, she could feel the pressure and expectation on her brewing within— but this is what she wanted (or thought she did at least). One thing that she couldn't argue with was that she had definitely changed her life before she hit the age of thirty. What she needed was a break away somewhere, but she had a project in the pipeline and an interview with Vogue to give, she couldn't disappear and go off grid now. Chloe was tired, exhausted of all this running around and schmoozing with people to make a name for herself. Why couldn't people just want her for her talent and hard work?

Regina wanted to ruin her (still), Karen wanted her for the discount, Brian wanted a trophy girlfriend, and Veronica wanted a protégée to make money out of. And to top it all off, Gianni Palazzo had offered her a job back at Palazzo—the golden Heaven that was really Hell disguised in luxury. Chloe questioned his intentions, but she would only be lying to herself by saying she didn't want him too, she lusted after him and couldn't deny her feelings or her ambitions for that matter. Gianni was all anyone wanted to talk to her about, Veronica, Carmen, Regina and now Vogue. If they all saw something was there between Gianni and her, then she wasn't the only crazy one. With that realisation, she knew she had to keep on going; she had to stay one step ahead.

Having calmed herself down, she returned to packing. Looking around at the Kitchen, she couldn't bear to pack up all the plates and utensils, except for her favourite 'cat' mug, of course. Clothing was the most important thing to pack if she was going to start living at Dom's, she needed her closet and luxuries at least; everything else could wait until her lease was up.

The wardrobe situation had grown over the past few months, designer clothes were a 'keeper', and anything else was for the trash or charity. Organising them into neatly folded 'keep' and 'trash' piles, her apartment buzzer rang. She stood up straight, and her heart started to quicken again, this time out of fear. The last time it rang, she had answered it to a psycho.

It buzzed again.

Chloe gingerly pressed the answer button on the intercom, waiting a few seconds to see if the other person spoke first, which they didn't. She paused for a beat more before finally feeling stupid for being a prisoner in her own home.

"Who is it?" she said, almost threatening.

"Chloe, it's Kim… From Palazzo."

'What the fu—,' she said to herself, stunned yet again that another ex-colleague had turned up uninvited on her doorstep. 'What the Hell does she want?' Chloe wondered. There was only one way to find out.

"Oh… Hi… What a surprise… Are you alone?" Chloe said, hoping there wasn't another surprise visitor with her.

"Err, yeah... I'm alone... Let me in, I need to tell you something!"

It appeared everyone had news for her these days, but she was intrigued to hear what she had to say.

"Okay, come on up."

Kim ran up the stairs as fast as she could, powered by her excitement; she couldn't wait to see Chloe's face when she finally broke the news to her. Chloe could hear Kim's heels pounding up the stairs as she opened the door, before seeing her on the landing.

"Oh my God, Chloe!" Kim said, out of breath and flinging her arms around her, like best friends reunited.

"Come in," Chloe said, opening the door for her. "Can I get you a drink or something?"

"Coffee, please... If you have," Kim said, not wanting to put her out.

"Me—not have coffee? Have we met?" Chloe said with a laugh as she flicked the kettle switch and got two mugs, that she was planning on leaving behind, out of the cupboard.

"Are you moving out?" she said, noticing the boxes and mess strewn around the place. "Sorry if I'm disturbing you."

"Oh don't worry... I needed a break anyway," Chloe said, not wanting to give out too much information about her new address. It was home visits like this she was trying to avoid. "Anyway... What are you doing here—not that I don't want you here," Chloe said, trying not to come off rudely.

"Well, I got a phone call at work, and I nearly freaked out—I just had to speak to you!"

"It's Saturday! Why are you at work—milk and sugar?"

"A splash of milk, no sugar, please... Myra took the weekend off, and I have to be in the office because of the merger deal, and in case anything comes in off the back of the press from last week."

"Typical Myra," Chloe huffed with a raised look on her face, knowing all too well how Palazzo operated. "Taking the weekend off and making her staff work."

"Anyway… Listen to me!" Kim said, eager to get on and tell her the exciting news. "Joli called the office and asked me to deliver this to you in person," she said, rifling through her purse.

"Deliver what?" Chloe said, passing her a cup of hot coffee, just the way she had ordered it. "And who the *fuck* is Joli?"

Kim giggled at hearing Chloe swear, but she found it even more hilarious that she didn't know who Joli was, but had managed to become quite familiar with Gianni.

"Joli… Gianni's assistant… *That* Joli."

Chloe still hadn't heard of her.

"Oh, right," she said, wishing Kim would just get on with it, especially now she knew Gianni had something to do with her house call.

"Anyway, she was adamant that I hand deliver this to you," Kim said, passing her a '*P*,' embossed on the front of the envelope.

"What's this?" Chloe said, puzzled as to what was so crucial in this thin envelope, that she had to come by to give it to her in person.

"Just open it!" Kim said.

Chloe put her coffee down, she hadn't taken a sip yet and began to open it a she looked at Kim suspiciously.

"Sorry, but what's this?" Chloe said, unfolding a print out for what seemed to be a flight booking with her name on.

"It's for you, you're going to Milan Fashion Week… Gianni has asked you to be there as his guest!" Kim said, finally explaining the cause for her visit, and why it was so important. Chloe looked up at her.

Did she hear correctly? 'Did she just say what I thought she said?' she asked herself. She was expecting an email, or a phone call at the very least—not first class tickets to Milan! Here it was, a message from Gianni that said loud and clear that he was very much interested in her. Kim could see her trying to make sense of it all in her head.

"Yes, you heard me… I have reserved flights—I need your passport details by the way—Joli's booking the hotel, and one VIP ticket for a front row seat at the Palazzo show in Milan awaits you there… All expenses paid!" Kim said with animated hands, taking a sip of coffee now she had said everything she needed to get out.

Kim was expecting her to jump with joy, but instead, Chloe put the envelope down and took a seat. This was big news, huge in fact, too big to take it all in. Somewhere, deep down, she knew it was great news, but a part of her couldn't believe what was happening. Kim was disappointed by her reaction, she was expecting her to scream and whoop, not this lacklustre response—like she had delivered her a lousy credit card bill. Then again, she could sympathise with Chloe at the same time, this would have shocked her too if she were in her shoes.

"Look… I know you must be questioning all this, but Joli made it very clear he wants you to be there… Gianni Palazzo wants *you* at his fashion show! Now, if I were you, I'd get my shit together and get on that plane!"

Hearing Kim curse woke Chloe out of her daze, making her laugh and bringing her back into the real world.

"Can you imagine Regina's face when she discovers you were at the Milan show too? *She* doesn't even get to go to Milan! You are like… Above her now!"

That was the trouble, Chloe could imagine her face—she had already seen it.

"You know, when she finds out you went to all this trouble to give this to me, you will be in trouble too… And she will find out!" Chloe said, making sure she wasn't risking her job just for her, just like how Dom did.

"To Hell with Palazzo… I'm leaving anyway," Kim said, waving off Chloe's concern with a flick of her wrist.

"*What*—you're leaving? But I thought you were a Palazzo girl?" Chloe said, miffed and even more shocked at this statement, more than the news of her going to Milan—that was at least believable.

'What is going on here?' Chloe questioned. The world had suddenly gone mad; nothing seemed normal anymore. Some crazy things had happened this summer, but it was now getting out of hand.

"Well, thanks to you, I have a new job… Dionne has offered me a job as her personal assistant… I take it you have heard all about Palazzo buying Maison Marais?"

"*What!* No, I haven't had a moments peace!" Chloe said, utterly astounded.

That's what Regina meant when she said Palazzo was set to become more prominent than ever; the world had indeed gone crazy!

"Where have you been? It's major news… Palazzo is now The Palazzo Group. The merger comes into effect starting next year, and Dionne needs someone who knows how Palazzo works, and Regina too for that matter… So, I've decided to leave Palazzo and join Maison Marais before there's an internal process to apply and all that crap. It's going to be a fresh start, and I'm excited to be part of something from the very beginning… Maybe then I can get my foot in the door and get noticed."

"I can't believe it! Congratulations, Dionne is lovely… Such a difference to Regina and Myra. I'm sure you will be very happy working with her," Chloe said, taking it all in.

"I *am* very happy… And I want you to be happy too, so go to Milan!"

Chloe smiled at her, in her head, she had already made the decision to go. Her primary motivation was to see Gianni again, but of course, sitting front row at one of the most famous fashion shows would be just as thrilling. It had once been her dream to go to Milan Fashion Week—now it was her reality—and with confirmation that she would see Gianni again, it seemed even more like a movie than real life.

'Dreams do come true,' Chloe thought to herself, even though it did sound rather corny. She still couldn't comprehend where all this was leading to, but if she genuinely wanted to know, then there was only one way to find out.

\*

Life had certainly been full of surprises, and that was only taking the past forty-eight hours into consideration. To feel normality again, Chloe booked a van to drive her and her life in boxes over to Dom's apartment. So much in her life had changed rapidly, it was only right her living space evolved with her—and the sooner, the better. It was a haven, not even Carmen would know where she was. Dom's place smelt like him, but it felt different, something was missing—him. She began to look around, switching on the lights, almost expecting him to jump out on her so she could tell him all about what had happened, but she knew she was just kidding herself.

"Oh well Dom, you're missing out on some serious goss girl," she said, throwing the keys in the dish on the coffee table.

Outside, a dozen hefty boxes of clothes, make-up and toiletries awaited her. Opening all of the windows, a light breeze swept through the apartment which seemed to clear her head with it. She looked out of the window at her new surroundings—Greenwich Village. As she looked at the street below the window sill, her mind began to drift off, staring at nothing in particular as questions resurfaced.

She shook her head to dissolve them—this was meant to be an escape. A cup of green tea was in order. Chloe made her way into the kitchen to fill up the kettle, she stood in front of it, staring—not thinking a single thought. As it reached a boiling point, the doorbell rang.

"Typical," she said. "Not a moments peace!"

For a moment, she considered whether she should answer it, but it felt silly not to; it was her place now, and she would have to open the door to someone sooner or later. Plus it couldn't be anyone she knew calling for her, not even Carmen, so she deemed it safe to answer.

Opening the door, Chloe was surprised to find a tall and handsome man at the door.

"Hi, do you need a hand with these boxes?"

Chloe's initial thought was: 'Phwoar!' and he certainly looked like he could handle the boxes with ease, with his broad and muscular build.

She wasn't going to turn down free labour from a hot guy.

"Would you? That's so kind... I'm only just moving in," she said as he lifted a box like it was a feather. "Are you my neighbour?"

She hoped this dish was indeed living next door, although she knew his face from somewhere.

"Err, not quite." He placed the box down in the apartment hallway. "Is Dominic here?" he said, looking slightly confused at finding her instead.

"Erm, no he's not actually, but I'm a friend of his. Can I take a message?" she said, still unable to fathom who he was.

"No, I'd rather speak to him if possible... Do you know where I can find him? I tried his number, and there was no answer, and I went to his workplace, and they said he had left?"

"Yeah, that's right... Sorry, I'm Chloe," she said, extending her hand to shake his.

"Oh, you're Chloe—I'm Jason... Jason Hart."

Suddenly, it clicked. Chloe did know this guy! Furthermore, she wondered what he was doing here. She was just as confused as Dom probably would be right now if he were here.

"You better come in," she said, there was some explaining to be done.

Jason helped with the rest of the boxes before entering, she was going to make him work for information.

"So... Jason—nice to meet you by the way—but why exactly are you looking for Dom after you ignored all his calls and messages, and blew him out?" Chloe said, folding her arms.

Dom would hate her for doing this, but he didn't exactly have a choice, and he would thank her for it later. Jason looked like a deer caught in headlights, but just as he was about to open his mouth, Chloe jumped in first.

"No—don't tell me; it's him you need to say all this to... All I'm saying is that you really fucked him up, dude... He liked you so much, but when you left, you took a piece of my friend too... And yes, I haven't exactly been a good friend to him either, but that's not the point. You shouldn't have behaved like that... He doesn't deserve to be shit on like that!" Chloe said, feeling a bit hypocritical. "So anyway, why are you here *now?*" Jason took a deep breath before answering, he knew what she said was right, but it wasn't how he had intended it.

"Well, the reason why I haven't been in contact is because I've been working on my exhibition... It means a lot to me, and I just needed time... I tried to explain this to him, but I guess he didn't believe me? And yes, you're right, Dom doesn't deserve to be mistreated, but look at it from my perspective... I meet a nice guy who lives in another city—who I hardly knew—and then I get an opportunity to take my career in a new direction... What would you have done?"

Chloe could see where he was coming from. She too had taken choices at the expense of others so she could elevate her career. She felt stupid for laying into him, she knew exactly which option she would choose if she were in his shoes—she *had* made it herself. She was just as guilty for shitting on Dom as he was at the end of the day.

"Look, he's not here... He's gone back to London," Chloe said, hanging her head; she felt sadness for Jason, but more Dom's sake.

"Great!" Jason said, perking up with wide eyes. "So where can I find him?"

It took a while for Chloe to realise what was so great about this situation, but she got there in the end. 'Oh yes,' she understood; it *was* great. Dom was in London, and Jason was showing his exhibition there. Surely this was proof that sometimes things really did happen for a reason? The same way things were aligning so she could see Gianni again.

"Yes, of course... So when are you going to London?" Chloe said.

"Tonight—right away... I have a car waiting downstairs taking me to the airport... I wanted him to come with me, so I came all this way to find him—can you help? What do I do?" he said.

Chloe could hear the panic in his voice; she rolled her eyes at him, romance was well and truly still alive it seemed. 'What is it with men

wanting to surprise their lovers with trips to Europe all of a sudden?'
she asked herself.

"Okay, look… I'm guessing I have the same details as you do… Cell
phone and email address… Message him straight away! He's probably
just turned his phone off while he adjusts to UK time… I'm sure he
will answer eventually. In the meantime, I will try and get hold of him
for you. He said we would be online, he promised me in fact! That's the
best I can offer I'm afraid," Chloe said, much to Jason's relief at having
her help to track him down.

Jason's face beamed with a hopeful smile. In fact this was the
perfect outcome, they would both be in London at the same time and
hopefully reunited.

"Yes! Thank you, Chloe… I'll email him on the way to the airport!"

Jason hugged her hard. It was clear to her how much Dom meant
to him, she just hoped Dom was checking his emails and willing to
meet him once more after telling himself he was over him.

"Good luck! Maybe you can bring the boy back for me?" Chloe
said with a laugh, which she truly meant.

"I'll do my best!"

"Just don't *fuck* it up again, okay?"

Armed with information, and desperate to get to London, Jason
left to catch his flight. He had a mission to accomplish, not only putting
on a good art show but also to find Dom. Chloe shook her head as she
watched him leave in a flash. 'Life is crazy for the both of us,' she said
to herself, happy that Dom was about to get a pleasant surprise too.
She just hoped it was a welcome one after he had intentionally run
away to London from it.

Chloe finally poured herself that cup of green tea and slumped
on the plush sofa in the living room. All these twists and unexpected
visitors bearing news had exhausted her for one day. As she sank into
the cushions and took a sip, she took a deep breath, finally feeling like
things were working out for the best.

'Life is full of chances and choices,' she thought.

As the afternoon dipped into dusk, the orange glow from the Sun made the place feel warm, like home. Suddenly a rational thought popped into her head: 'I guess some paths lead one way, and some lead to another... The key is not to regret which one you take, but to have faith that the road you do take will be the right one for you in the end'.

This was probably the most grown-up thing she had acknowledged in her whole entire life, but it was a lesson learnt well—finally. With that thought ingrained in her mind, Chloe looked forward to what her latest decision would bring, with the attitude of whatever happens, happens! Of course, she knew exactly what she wanted to happen, but she would have to wait until she got to Milan to see what the future had in store for her. Chloe knew life was about to change yet again, and excitingly so, but she had no idea just how much...

COMING SOON!

Another Farce On Fifth Avenue:

# *The Raven Returns*

Lightning Source UK Ltd.
Milton Keynes UK
UKHW020738121218
333871UK00001B/56/P